'Dazzling, seductive and pointed.'

'All brilliant light and scorching heat . . . Grimwood has successfully mingled fantasy with reality to make an unusual, believable, and absorbing mystery.'
Sunday Telegraph

'Set to cement his position in both critical and public opinion. With four previous books behind him, Grimwood started well and has steadily improved, honed and entertained . . . the pacing of this book is near perfect.'
Murder One

'Blends alternative SF and hard-boiled mystery . . . Grimwood artfully unveils the changed world that has developed in the many decades since WWI ended differently. Ashraf, a lifelong underdog and pawn, emerges as a resourceful and deadly foe, adapting quickly to survive in a game where the rules and the playing field shift repeatedly. SF and mystery fans will be pleased.'
Publishers Weekly

'A good example of cross-genre fertilization – in this case, setting a cleverly constructed whodunit within the larger context of a vivid, thoroughly imagined alternate history. The result is substantial entertainment that is alternately violent and touching, exotic and strangely familiar. Grimwood's El Iskandryia is a place worth visiting. The next two instalments, *Effendi* and *Felaheen*, can't appear too soon.'
Washington Post

'Utterly compelling. Ashraf is mysterious without being remote, and his quest to solve the dual mysteries of the book makes for fascinating reading. Grimwood has built a solid alternate history, completely plausible in every detail and peopled by characters as unique as El Iskandryia itself.'
Romantic Times

'A mature balance between sensibility and action in what's essentially a rite of passage story allied with a detective thriller – deftly told and laced with neat ideas.'
Time Out

'A convincing portrait of a man shaking off the demons of his past and becoming, finally, the person he was meant to be . . . a well-crafted and absorbing novel.'
SFSite

'Reading *Pashazade*, a vibrant and living city is evoked . . . this rich exotic setting provides a background for Grimwood's story in which excitement and adventure are inevitable . . . when it comes to winding up the tension [Grimwood] is certainly no slouch.'
SFRevu

Effendi

'If you're not reading Jon Courtenay Grimwood then you don't know how subtle and daring fiction can be.'   Michael Marshall Smith

'An intriguing cross-genre premise that allows for a lot of fun.' *Observer*

'JCG has emerged over the last few years as one of the more interesting newer British novelists . . . No one else is doing anything like it – or even trying to. Grimwood actually seems to have *been* in the places he makes up.'   *Locus*

'A head-trip of a mystery novel . . . *Effendi* is the second of JCG's examinations of the relationship between the West and Islam through an outsider's eyes. Unsteadying, fast-paced and furious.'   *Big Issue*

'One of the finest novels I've read in some time . . . such a treat.'
SFSite

'*Pashazade* and now *Effendi* reeled me in within the first few pages . . . fast, furious, fun and elegant, the Arabesk trilogy is one of the best things to hit bookstores in a while.'   *SFRevu*

'By turns affectionate, engrossing and bewildering, so that great anticipation is created . . . these books go straight into the tiny to-be-read-again-as-soon-as-possible pile.'   *Interzone*

'If *Pashazade* was a success, *Effendi* is a triumph. JCG has taken the direction he embarked upon with the first book, mirrored and echoed the narrative structure therein and pushed his writing to another level.'
The Third Alternative

'It's specific and detailed and immersive as hell . . . Essential reading for anyone who read *Pashazade*. And if you haven't, go and buy it, then buy this.'   *SFX Magazine*

'The dazzling *Pashazade* was always going to be a hard act to follow, but it comes as little surprise that the prodigally-talented Grimwood has pulled off the trick. His way with a sentence has a baroque finesse that makes these unclassifiable novels as elegantly written as they are rich in imaginative energy.'   *Publishing News*

'Grimwood's alternate history setting of the city of El Iskandryia (reminiscent of the exotic location, politics and intrigues of Lawrence Durrell's Alexandria Quartet) is wonderfully realised, as are the characters . . .'   *Vector*

'*Pashazade* was, quite simply, the best SF novel I read last year, and *Effendi* is a worthy successor . . . All of Grimwood's trademarks are present here in spades: edgy, streetwise prose, a fiendishly and rewardingly complex plot, plenty of black humour and his usual immaculate pace.'   *Outland*

'Details are what JCG's books are all about. A wealth of them, building up to a world that sucks you in . . . It's a suitably gripping setup and Grimwood doesn't waste it.'   *Starburst*

Felaheen

'A major landmark in JCG's career . . . the only real heavyweight work of orientalist post-cyberpunk fiction ever written and I am green with envy . . . if you have time to read just one trilogy a year, get the Arabesk books. Otherwise you're missing out.'   Charlie Stross

'[Grimwood] once again delivers his trademark mixture of vividly realized characters and evocation of place. By turns a political thriller, a murder mystery and a search for identity, *Felaheen* is SF at its most inventive. Grimwood's spare, hard-working prose evokes a richly-textured world, which we sense extending beyond the edges of the page. The truth remains elusive until the very end, and even then we won't be sure of everything. But the journey will be well worth travelling, and the scenery is spectacular.'   *Guardian*

'With the Arabesk books Grimwood, quite unfairly, pulls off five genres: SF, fantasy, crime, literary and noir.'   *Big Issue*

'An action thriller that has the unusual distinction of appealing to fans of several fiction genres . . . This could well be the year of Jon Courtenay Grimwood.'   *Bookseller*

'Literary SF is a field full of writers who can handle big plotlines. Few though have Grimwood's way with a sly observation or careful metaphor . . . Closer to greatness with every single novel.'   *SFX Magazine*

'Rounded characters, Byzantine plotlines and deft, streetwise prose mark JCG as one of the finest writers in the genre today . . . Well worth the wait.'   *Ottakars Online*

'The back alleys and courts of North Africa come alive in JCG's *Felaheen* . . . Food, violence and the exercise of intelligence.' *Time Out*

'As always, Grimwood has created a rich, vivid tapestry of plot and character, from the apparently mundane death of a chef to Raf's macabre and brilliantly depicted trek across the salt fields. Highly recommended.'

Starburst

'*Effendi* was one of the best novels of 2002, *Felaheen* equals it and perhaps even surpasses . . . More, please!'

Dreamwatch

'Delve into the mysterious world of *Felaheen* . . . An inventive hybrid, mixing the best elements of thriller, romance and SF.'

Company Magazine

Arabesk

PASHAZADE • EFFENDI • FELAHEEN

The Ashraf Bey Mysteries

JON COURTENAY GRIMWOOD

GOLLANCZ

LONDON

This volume © JonCG 2007
Pashazade © JonCG 2001
Effendi © JonCG 2002
Felaheen © JonCG 2003

The right of Jon Courtenay Grimwood to be identified as the
author of this work has been asserted by him in accordance
with the Copyright, Designs and Patents Act 1988.

Pashazade first published in Great Britain in 2001 by Simon & Schuster
Effendi first published in Great Britain in 2002 by Simon & Schuster
Felaheen first published in Great Britain in 2003 by Simon & Schuster

An imprint of the Orion Publishing Group
Orion House, 5 Upper St Martin's Lane, London WC2H 9EA
An Hachette Livre UK company

A CIP catalogue record for this book is
available from the British Library

ISBN 978 0 57508 132 1

1 3 5 7 9 10 8 6 4 2

Typeset at The Spartan Press Ltd,
Lymington, Hants

Printed in Great Britain at
Mackays of Chatham, plc, Chatham, Kent

The Orion Publishing Group's policy is to use papers
that are natural, renewable and recyclable products and
made from wood grown in sustainable forests. The logging
and manufacturing processes are expected to conform to
the environmental regulations of the country of origin.

www.orionbooks.co.uk

PASHAZADE

For the girl with red hair
Standing under the bridge at Waterloo
And for the ex-lead guitarist of the Sepuku Chihuahuas.
Same as it ever was . . .

However many ways there may be of being alive, it is certain
That there are vastly more ways of being dead . . .
— Professor Richard Dawkins, *The Blind Watchmaker*

CHAPTER 1

6th July

The sound of fountains came in stereo. A deep splash from the court-yard below and a lighter trickle from the next room, where open arches cut in a wall overlooking the courtyard had marble balustrades stretched between matching pillars.

It was that kind of house.

Old, historic, near-derelict in places.

'Ambient temp eighty-one Fahrenheit, humidity sixty-two per cent . . .' The American spoke clearly, reading the data from the face of his watch, then glanced through a smashed window to what little he could see of the sky outside.

'Passing cloud, no direct sunlight.'

Dropping clumsily onto one knee, Felix Abrinsky touched the marble floor with nicotine-stained fingers, confirming to himself that this statement was correct. The tiles were warm but not hot. No latent heat had been stored up from that morning's sunshine to radiate back into the afternoon air.

Bizarrely, it took Felix less effort to stand than it had done to kneel, though he needed to pause to catch his breath all the same. And the silver-ringed hand that came up to wipe sweat from his forehead only succeeded in smearing grease across his scalp and down his thinning ponytail.

Police regulations demanded he wear a face mask, surgical gloves and – in his case – a sweatband to stop himself from accidentally polluting biological evidence. But Felix was Chief of Detectives and so far as he was concerned that meant he could approach the crime scene how he liked, which was loose, casual and lateral. Not to mention semi-drunk. All the virtues that first got him thrown out of the police in Los Angeles.

Besides, if you wanted to talk about *should have been*, then he *should*

7

have been on holiday. And he would have managed it too, if this particular buck hadn't been bumped up the line so fast it practically hit the wall parking itself right outside his office door.

The body in the chair was fresh, still warm to his touch. Stiffness had set in to the arms – but then, rigor happened fast when a victim was borderline anorexic. And even without the woman's thinness there was North Africa's heat to add into the equation. Heat always upped the rate at which rigor gripped a corpse.

On his arrival Felix had considered obtaining an immediate body temperature. But habit made him do the crime-scene grabs first, then work a grid through the victim's office, tweezering up clues. And technically, since she was obviously dead, he'd already broken his own regulations by checking under her jaw for a carotid pulse.

'Covering the body prior to site shots.'

Some cities used electronic observers, 360-degree fish-eye vids, wired for movement and sound. El Iskandryia used the human kind, when it bothered to use observers at all. The silksuit Felix had selected stood in the doorway, doing exactly what he'd been told, which was shut up and stay out of the way.

From a foil packet Felix extracted a sheet of tissue-thin gauze designed to protect the woman's modesty in death, as surely as a scarf round her head would have hidden her hair on the streets in life. Except there was no scarf, because the woman had been stabbed in her own house, at her own desk, in her own office . . .

'Starting location shots,' said the fat man and lifted an old Speed Graphic. The camera was linked to his even more ancient LAPD-issue chronograph, which would back up each shot as it was taken, just as the camera would automatically stamp *time, date* and *orientation* across the bottom edge of each new shot.

15.30:
July 6:
SouthSouthWest.

All the same, Felix dictated a description of what he was doing, working fast to photograph the little office from every angle. Only when this was done could he start work on the body.

'Exposure five. Al-Mansur madersa. Upstairs. Interior. West wall and corner of office taken from door. Speed Graphic Digilux. Fifty-millimetre lens. K400-equivalence.'

The dictation did no more than tell the court what camera had been used, what the shot showed and what the light was like: something the camera readouts told them anyway. But he'd learned his craft back when Speed Graphics still took acetate and defence attorneys jumped on any

8

conflict of technical information, no matter how small. And besides, Felix spoke not really to his camera or watch but to himself.

These days defence attorneys weren't an issue. If the Chief of Detectives said someone had committed a crime that was usually good enough for a judge. The suspect went down. Unfortunately it had taken Felix a few months to realize this and there were three cases from his early days in El Iskandryia which still gave him sleepless nights – four cases, if he was being unusually hard on himself.

'Exposure eleven. Al-Mansur madersa. Upstairs. Interior. Open door to office, taken from broken mashrabiya window in south wall adjacent to Rue Sherif . . .'

Mashrabiyas were, originally, shaded balconies where water jugs could be left to cool. But the term had long since come to signify both the balcony and the ornately carved screen that hid those in the balcony from the street below. Marble was commonplace for the screen, as was gilded or painted wood.

The smashed mashrabiya at the al-Mansur madersa had been carved two hundred years before from a single slab of alabaster and now lay in shards on the floor, apparently kicked in from outside. That the balcony was fifteen feet above a traffic-laden street only made the break-in more unlikely. Unless one factored in the *Thiergarten* who apparently could move unseen, kill silently and climb walls like flies . . .

Felix sighed. Whatever else Berlin had to buy for its agents abroad, their deadly reputation came free.

Officially, of course, Berlin was El Iskandryia's ally. Merely an equal partner in a bigger, three-way alliance with Stambul and Paris. Unofficially, French influence kept itself to Morocco, while Berlin's advisers flooded the rest of the littoral and Stambul banked its taking from the Suez Canal and did pretty much what it was told.

Politics – now there was one subject Felix spent a lot of time trying to avoid.

Grunting crossly, the fat man wiped fresh sweat from his face and grabbed two shots of a ridiculous rag dog, quite out of keeping with the cold elegance of the Khedivian desk on which it sat.

And then, having put off what came next for long enough, Felix turned his camera on the corpse.

'Exposure thirteen. Al-Mansur madersa. Upstairs. Interior. The body, taken from front of desk . . .' Felix whipped off the modesty cloth and took his second look at the dead woman's wounds. They were no more pleasant than the first time round.

Once started, he worked swiftly on the crime grabs, moving in to get specific shots of the ripped-open blouse, the nails broken on one

9

hand, the trickle of blood dried to a stark black ribbon down her side.

The woman was in her early forties. Middle height. Brown eyes staring blankly at the ceiling. Short, expensively cut black hair – elegant, obviously. The very fact her eyes were clear and the cornea unclouded told Felix that she was less than six hours dead, but he knew that anyway and put her death at two hours ago at the most.

One of her elbows was flopped across the arm of her chair and her head had tipped right back, the muscle relaxation that precedes rigor having smoothed her face until it looked more serene in death than it ever did in life: infinitely more serene than it did glaring out from that afternoon's *Iskandryian* open on the desk in front of her.

'Berlin furious as society widow slams RenSchmiss.'

And those in El Iskandryia's German community who believed in the legal right to slash open each other's face for the sake of highly prized duelling scars had slammed right back, from the look of things . . . Punching a button on the side of his Speed Graphic, Felix reduced the depth of field until it showed only what he wanted the judge to see. The injuries in sharp focus.

To him the victim was no longer human: that was where he differed both from his boss and underlings – and from Madame Mila, the coroner, who would already be on her way. To them, what slumped in that chair was still a woman. Deserving all the respect and modesty that the law allowed.

Which was why Felix had put the rest of his day on hold to make it to the scene of the crime first. Back in the City of Angels, where Felix had trained, he'd have grabbed a few more corpse shots, lifted dabs, collected up handleable bio like hair and stashed it in evidence bags and then vacuumed the victim's clothes, one garment at a time, again putting the dust into separate sachets.

And then, with the victim's original position recorded beyond all possible doubt, he'd have had a medical technician take the body some place near but non-critical and remove the clothes so Felix could photograph the naked corpse, wound by wound and bruise by bruise.

But that wasn't the way crime against women was handled in El Iskandryia. At least not officially, and this, regrettably, was unquestionably a very official crime. The victim had once been married to an important man, there were rumours that she was badly in debt – to whom, nobody seemed to know – and she'd been outspoken enough to upset the young khedive's German advisers.

This was the kind of crime that required press conferences, photo opportunities and fancy political footwork, all of which would get in the way of actually solving the murder.

Reaching into his pocket, Felix palmed a silver hip flask and opened it by flipping back its spring-loaded top with a single flick of the thumb. Like most things in his life, practice was all it took.

CHAPTER 2

Three days before Chief Felix found his holiday plans suddenly ruined, the silent observer from the doorway of the al-Mansur madersa had been sitting at a café table, thinking. Of course, back then the observer hadn't yet met Felix and still mostly thought of himself as ZeeZee.

This, however, was in the process of changing. As for what he would become, he hadn't yet decided. And he had no good reason to be sat in the sun anyway.

Which took care of *who, what* and *why* . . .

Where? was simpler. According to the fox, looking down from space revealed a green wedge of delta driven into yellow sand. Nature fighting the elements. Or rather, nature fighting itself . . .

The fox was big on *who, what, why* and *where*. That had long been one of its more irritating functions. The fox lived inside ZeeZee's head. Most of the time it stayed there.

It used to ask him those kind of questions all the time when he was a child. But foxes live faster than humans and it was old now, tired. Mostly, though, he could still sense it lurking behind his eyes, and occasionally it took over. ZeeZee was fine with the fox. He had been ever since he'd realised it was meant to be there. And sometimes, back in the early days when they used to talk a lot, what the fox had told him was even interesting.

. . . looking down from space revealed a green wedge of delta driven into yellow sand. Stretching a hundred miles from south to north, over 125 miles at its topmost point and far longer than that if measured along the inlets and lakes of its almost fractal coastline, the delta fought back against a parched wasteland that dropped 2,000 feet into the desolate Qattara Depression only a day's drive away.

Far to the delta's southwest was the Great Sand Sea, an area so blasted in places by heat that the silica of some dunes had melted to chunks of clear, green-yellow glass. More than 1400 tonnes of the purest natural glass in the world lay strewn across the surface of the Sand Sea like fist-sized jewels. With a melting point 500 degrees higher than most natural glass, the sand-sea variety was so tough that a standard geological party trick was to heat a lump of the stuff until it was red-hot and then drop it into cold water. The interest was in what the glass *didn't* do . . . which was splinter.

Scientific argument raged about whether the glass had been formed when an ancient meteorite had hit the desert full on or whether a meteorite had cut through Earth's atmosphere at a shallow angle to skim the surface of the Sand Sea like a stone skipping across water, creating glass from the friction of its contact.

What was known was that a piece of the glass had been taken from the desert and carved into the shape of a sacred scarab, set into gold and given to a king. The scarab had been found by Wilhelm Dorpfeld in the tomb of Tutankhamen and was now in the Khedival Museum at Umm el-Dunya.

The green of the delta spread in a silt-rich patchwork of rice fields, date palms, villages and towns opening out like a fan from just north of Umm el-Dunya until it hit the southern edge of the Mediterranean where, in winter, waves crashed along barren, deserted beaches.

Three main roads cut through the delta, supports for the giant fan. And though one route led direct from the capital to El Iskandryia, few of those who used this road journeyed its full distance. People either flew over the delta or took the faster desert highway – a long strip of blacktop, where convict road-gangs engaged in a ceaseless war with the wind-shifted gravel that tried to eat the road at its edges.

The free city faced north, at the westernmost edge of the delta, limited on its northern side by the Mediterranean and to the south by a lake as long as the city itself. Necessity had made the inhabitants build and then build again on their narrow strip of land, until Iskandryia stretched over twenty miles from one side to the other but was never more than five miles deep at any point.

Looked at from any one of the spy satellites that hourly passed over-head, Isk appeared as a long grey rectangle bounded top and bottom by blue, with verdant green on the right and arid grit-grey to the left.

Increasing the magnification produced recognizable districts, from El Anfushi's narrow side streets (built on what had once been an ancient causeway jutting between Western and Eastern harbour) to the ornate Victorian offices of Place Manshiya and the stuccoed villas and Moorish follies lining the Corniche: that elegant coastal strip which ran east and featured houses so exclusive their owners could afford to keep them

13

staffed all year but use them for only six weeks in high summer when the capital became unbearably hot.

There were two gaps in the grand buildings lining the Corniche. One gap formed Place Orabi, which stretched from the shore back to a statue of Khedive Mohammed, the point where Place Orabi intersected with Place Manshiya, a different square that ran west to east along Orabi's southern end.

To the east of Orabi was the second gap, which intersected with nothing at all. Place Zaghloul was named after the nationalist leader who in early 1916 had personally negotiated the Berlin Accord with Kaiser Wilhelm.

The political descendants of the Zaghloul party stressed that their man's actions had led to Iskandryia's status as a free city and Egypt's return to enlightened Islamic government as an autonomous, khedival province of the Ottoman Empire. Opponents pointed out that – well over a century later – the Kaiser's supposedly temporary German advisers were with them still.

The French were a newer addition to the North African cabal. Their place in the alliance cemented fifty years back by judicious marriages between Bonaparte princelings and both the Hohenzollerns and descendants of Mehmed V Rashid, Sublime Porte at the time of the original treaty.

South from Place Zaghloul ran Rue Missala, a thoroughfare lined with restaurants. And right on the corner, with entrances on both Zaghloul Square and the rue, sat Le Trianon, Iskandryia's most famous Art Nouveau café. On its walls were equally famous paintings, a series of seven increasingly unlikely tableaux depicting full-breasted dancers, naked save open shirts and jewelled slippers.

The fox didn't like the paintings. But then, the fox was a purist and had problems with Orientalist kitsch. And the fact that the fox was invisible to everyone but ZeeZee didn't make it any less real. Though it wasn't real, of course, not in the way the yellow cabs lurching along Rue Missala were real. ZeeZee had come up with a number of explanations for its existence. The fox's favourite was that it was an autonomous construct of unprocessed dark memory.

In other times it might have been regarded as a ghost . . .

Sitting outside Le Trianon in an area roped off from pedestrians, the thin blond man with the flowing beard and tangled dreadlocks washed down his second croissant with the dregs of his third cappuccino, and wished that what passed for breakfast at the madersa where he was staying would feed more than a stray mouse.

14

Ashraf al-Mansur – known as ZeeZee to the police, his therapist, and a Chinese Triad boss who was undoubtedly even now searching the world to have him killed – had hated the interior of Le Trianon on sight. But since he'd needed to find somewhere to spend his mornings, this café was where he'd taken to eating. Now he just found the interior irritating.

'Another capuccino, Your Excellency?'

Adjusting his Versace shades and brushing pastry flakes from the sleeve of his black silk suit, the young man nodded. 'Why not,' he said slowly. It wasn't like he had anything else to do.

'Very good, Your Excellency.' The Italian waiter bustled away, totally ignoring two English tourists who'd been waiting ten minutes for him to take their order. It was Saturday morning, four days after he'd arrived in the city, two days after he'd first met the industrialist Hamzah Quitrimala and one day after he'd finally agreed to marry the man's 'difficult' daughter. And every day, bar the the day he'd actually arrived, he'd visited the café.

So now he was being treated as a regular. Which made sense because, by treating him as such, the patron hoped that was what he would become. Besides, once the patron had discovered that the excellency with the matted beard and odd hair would be working upstairs, it became inevitable that ZeeZee should take his place in a magic group who got tables when they wanted, exactly where they wanted them.

Situated directly over the café were the offices of the Third Circle of Irrigation, famous as the department where Iskandryia's greatest poet, Constantine Cavafy, once worked. What the Third Circle actually did Zee-Zee had no idea, despite having arrived on time at the offices every morning for the last three days. He was beginning to think they did nothing.

Certainly his assistant had looked deeply shocked that first morning when ZeeZee suggested he be told how the office operated. Politely, speaking English with an immaculate accent, the older man had made a firm but smiling counter-suggestion. His excellency might like to try Le Trianon, which was where many of the other directors spent their mornings – and their afternoons, too, come to that.

ZeeZee's office occupied a corner site and his excellency had done enough corporate shit in the US to know the prestige *that* carried. What was more, it overlooked Zaghloul and Missala, making it prime real estate. And everyone in the office was polite, way too polite, which meant Hamzah Quitrimala had a big mouth. Albeit no bigger than ZeeZee's own, because his had been the throwaway comment that started a rumour-become-certain-fact that he was a traumatized survivor from one of the greatest fundamentalist atrocities in living history.

15

'Your Excellency . . .' It was the patron himself, rather than the waiter who'd taken the original order. Putting the cappuccino carefully on the table, the patron picked up a crumb-strewn plate and hesitated.

'Did Your Excellency enjoy breakfast?'

ZeeZee nodded, adding, '*Mumken lehsab,*' as he instinctively scrawled an imaginary pen across an imaginary payment slip in the universal demand for the bill.

'Of course . . . Although perhaps His Excellency would like to keep a tab?'

'Perhaps he would.'

Make like a chameleon. Acclimatize, was what the fox said. If you had time, that was, and ZeeZee was making time. Whether his position with the Third Circle made the difference or the fact that he ranked as a bey, life in El Iskandryia was proving easier than he'd ever dreamed possible when he stepped off the plane. But then, after prison, almost anything was going to be an improvement.

He just wished he could remember at what point the fox had disappeared. He was pretty sure it had been there right up to the point they hit Immigration. And ZeeZee always hated it when the fox went invisible on him. It was like suddenly not being able to see in the dark.

CHAPTER 3

Tiri had definitely been there when ZeeZee first landed in Iskandryia, twisting itself in and out of people's legs, sometimes so thinned by distance that ZeeZee lost track of everything but the fox's silver tail and hacking cough.

Too many cigarettes, a biology master had told him years before, when ZeeZee had asked why a cub stood choking in a distant field, shoulders hunched as it tried to throw up a splinter of bone. The other men present had laughed and one had rumpled the small boy's blond hair.

My own little wild animal, the visitor called him. That was just before ZeeZee decided to fail all his exams . . .

'Read this.' An immigration officer in khaki thrust a green embarkation card into ZeeZee's hand and waved him towards the end of a queue. There were several queues, all moving inexorably towards a row of desks where simple polygraphs stood waiting, their guts exposed to the air. A golem-featured man from the line alongside glanced over and ZeeZee thought for a moment he was going to nod or say something. But he just stared at ZeeZee's matted hair and then looked away.

It was one of those evenings.

On the card was a list of statements to be read aloud, in a choice of French, Arabic, German or English . . .

He wasn't a drug addict.

He wasn't infectious.

He didn't plan to overthrow the khedive . . .

So far so good. ZeeZee skimmed his eyes down the next three prohibitions against entering El Iskandryia.

He wasn't planning to purchase for export any classical or Pharaonic artefacts.

He didn't belong to a proscribed fundamentalist group.

17

He'd never been charged with murder. *Except he had . . .*

It might have been the last prohibition that made ZeeZee sweat, or it could have been the lack of air-conditioning. Whatever, he was still sweating when he reached the head of his queue to find himself facing a middle-aged man who wore a fez, an oiled moustache, a gold lapel pin shaped in the name of God and a rectangular tag that announced he was Sergeant Aziz.

'Where did your journey begin?' demanded the sergeant.

'America,' said ZeeZee and Aziz nodded. Given the bleached dread-locks, hobo beard and beige elephants stampeding across an ill-fitting sports shirt, it was unlikely the thin man came from anywhere else.

'Make your declaration,' the sergeant said. So ZeeZee put his hand on the plate and let Aziz click shut a wrist band. Then he swore his beliefs away, only stumbling when he reached the final prohibition.

'Again,' demanded the sergeant.

'I have never murdered anybody,' said ZeeZee flatly and every diode on the cheap Matsui lie detector stayed green. On the far side of the desk the fox grinned like the fox he was and, without thinking, ZeeZee grinned back.

Drugged or drunk, Aziz decided, his eyes flicking from the passenger's darkened armpits to his bead-slicked forehead. Either way, he was suspect.

'ID card?' Irritation made the sergeant snap his fingers.

'I've got this,' ZeeZee said apologetically. The document he proffered was unmistakable, its cover pure white and hand-stitched from Moroccan leather softer than velvet.

'*Excellency* . . .' In place of a sneering NCO stood a man in shock, career options cashing themselves in right in front of his own eyes. The diplomatic pass he now held was registered to a *pashazade*, the son of a pasha, senior grade. Basic survival instinct made Sergeant Aziz forget everything except his need to make the sweating tourist someone else's problem.

Not even bothering to stamp the *carte blanche*, the sergeant clicked his fingers for a jellaba-clad orderly and ordered the underling to escort the pasha to the fast-track desk and quickly.

Eyes like a maniac, beard like a dervish and a pair of combats that were way too long in the leg . . . plus the man kept looking round for something he obviously couldn't see. Captain Yousef was worried. He had an apartment in a block off Rue Maamoun that needed repairs to its balcony, he'd only just made Captain and – God be praised – his wife was pregnant for the third time. He couldn't afford to make a mistake.

But which would be the mistake? To hold a notable with a *carte blanche* for questioning or to let through someone who couldn't look less like a real bey? The call was impossible to make and the implications of getting it wrong were horrific – for himself and his wife, for his children, his home . . .

'Sir . . .' Captain Yousef's accent was elegantly Cairene. His words those of someone born not in El Iskandryia but in the capital. All the same, his voice shook as he asked his question. 'Do you have some secondary form of identity?'

The notable in the elephant shirt and shades said nothing and did nothing except shrug. It was obvious that his answer was no.

Looking from slumped man to the elegant Ottoman diplomatic passport, Captain Yousef had real trouble reconciling the dishevelled mess in front of him with the photograph encrypted on the *carte*'s chip that gave his family as al-Mansur and his place of birth as Tunis.

The passport was five years old, almost expired. The encrypted picture showed someone clean-shaven, neatly dressed, who stared hawk-eyed at the camera. While this man looked like the worst kind of American, the poor kind.

And yet.

And yet . . .

'Ashraf Al-Mansur?'

The man began to shrug, caught himself and smiled for the first time since he'd entered the room. It was a rueful, what-the-fuck-am-I-doing-here smile. Not the kind that the Captain had ever seen from a real bey.

Casually Captain Yousef adjusted his red fez with one hand, while touching a discreet buzzer on the underside of his desk. Trying to enter El Iskandryia on a fake passport was a serious crime. Pretending to be a notable was even worse. And when that passport was a diplomatic one, then . . . The Captain didn't waste time worrying about it further. No point. His decision was a good one, and besides, it was no longer his business. Orders specifically said to pass this kind of problem straight to the top.

CHAPTER 4

'Merde, merde, merde . . .'

The dark-haired girl hit a key and switched search engines, looking for one that worked. So far she'd spent twenty highly illegal minutes learning precisely nothing about her future husband, who was probably even now at the al-Mansur madersa, delivered there from the airport in some smoke-windowed Daimler stretch.

al-Mansur

Nothing.

Ashraf Bey.

Nothing.

Pashazade Ashraf.

Nothing.

It was enough to set off another litany of swear words. Zara bint-Hamzah spoke Arabic but swore in perfect Cairene French for the simple reason, established in childhood, that neither of her parents understood it.

She also spoke English, as did her father, though she spoke hers with a New York twang. Two years studying at Columbia did that to you. Only that bit of her life was dead now and she was back home. And didn't she know it.

Ashraf Bey might as well not exist for all the record he'd left of his life to date. *'Putain de merde . . .'* Without thinking, Zara gulped the last of her slimmers' biscuit – rolled oats, rolled wholewheat, glycerol, sorbitol and xenical – total calories fifty-seven – and ruined any calorific benefits by pouring herself another coffee and mixing the liquid with a large teaspoon of what looked like dirty diamonds but was really raw sugar.

Just looking at the ragged crystals made Zara long for a few good old-fashioned pop rocks of freebase, something to heighten her courage or

20

stupefy her nerves. Misusing the Library's LuxorEon3 terminal didn't come easily – not to her, anyway. Only these days she was clean, had been since she was fifteen, and all she had for courage was a Sony earbead. So she upped the volume on DJ Avatar and went back to her flat panel.

The fact that Ashraf couldn't be found on the empire-wide voting list held at the Library of Iskandryia Zara put down to his rank as a bey. Sons of emirs were probably too rarefied to be recorded on an openly accessible database. More puzzling was his complete absence from the Library's proscribed database and from the web itself. Out there Ottoman law meant nothing. So, on the web at least, there should have been some ghost of a record.

This was a man who'd spent seven years in America. That was the point her father had used to sell the marriage: how much they'd have in common. (By which he meant they'd both been corrupted by the same culture.)

But according to every credit agency she'd accessed, the bey's rating wasn't so much bad as simply non-existent. No charge cards, no bank account, no mortgage had ever been issued in his name. More bizarrely still, he'd never posted to any internet newsgroup, never chatted, never had an e-address – at least, not under his own name. The man to whom she was days away from becoming very publicly engaged had left no trace of his life to date, no shadow. Not out there in what Zara now thought of as the real world, and not in the Ottoman world, either.

It wasn't a good feeling.

Her own entry in the city register was brief, short and depressing. Though flesh would be added to its bleak bones at the end of the week when data was updated to take account of her father's new rank.

Zara had no illusions about how he'd attained the rank *effendi*. A bey could not be expected to marry the granddaughter of a *falah*. So her elderly, half-blind grandfather was to be moved from his mud-brick home in Siwa to a new house on the outskirts of Isk. With the new house were promised orange trees he couldn't see, irrigated lawns he'd consider a criminal waste of precious water and the honorific *effendi*. The fact that *his* father was now effendi made her father effendi, which made her respectable enough to marry.

Zara was the price and her dowry was the prize. Love didn't enter into it and nor, for once, did complicated family alliances. The only alliance that interested the bey's aunt was with her father's money. The deal stank and was morally wrong; but as her mother had angrily explained, this was how things were done. And the very fact that – for once – her mother managed to keep her hands to herself told Zara just how worried the woman was that her daughter might do something stupid, like refuse.

Mind you, first off, they'd been worried that if they let her go to Columbia she wouldn't return when her two years in New York were over. Then they'd been worried she might *disgrace* herself while over there. Now . . .

Merde indeed.

A mouthful of now-cold coffee warned Zara that she'd overrun her own safety margin. It was time for her to log off and go pack up her little cubbyhole before Zara's boss realized what she'd been doing with her last day in the department: breaking every regulation she could find, starting with unauthorized use of a LuxorEon3.

There was only one computer matrix in the city: IOL. Available through subterranean snakes of optic that crawled in conduits beneath the sidewalks to feed everything from cheap edge-of-network devices in local schools to the complex hierarchy of information appliances used in the Library itself.

The network was wired with optic rather than relying on radio because cable withstood EMP and those inconvenient, mujahadeen-inspired charged-particle things that scrambled radio signals elsewhere in North Africa. The wiring of the city had been done in record time, with roads ruthlessly ripped up, rivers drained and inconvenient buildings bulldozed. What Ove Arup had insisted would take twelve months minimum had been finished in six and even then General Koenig Pasha, the city's governor, hadn't been happy: he'd wanted it done in three.

And though the city streets were an open and fluid mass of architectural styles, crammed with all races and religions, the network running beneath those streets was anything but . . . It was utterly hermetic, completely sealed. Only the room where Zara sat, a cupboard-like alcove of the Library, acted as a node for those with permission to swim in the wider, wilder waters where information apparently wanted to be free but mostly seemed to expect you to buy it.

Zara clicked her way out of a credit-check site that kept demanding an account number for a charge card she no longer owned and shut down the connection.

If she was traced then Zara could undoubtedly count for help on the fact she had no previous record. Besides, the new marble floor of the triangular foyer below came directly out of her father's pocket. Disgrace her, and the director definitely wouldn't get his new roof.

Money was power. Zara was about to add *Even dirty money*, then amended it in her head to *Especially dirty money*. Dirty money carried with it the threat of unpredictability. Of course, *dirty money* eventually turned into *new money*, with all the scrabble for respectability that the term suggested. And *new money* lay on its back and opened its legs, *or did it by proxy*.

Zara shuddered.

Somewhere out of sight, beyond the sweep of the Eastern Harbour and beyond where the peninsula of the old Turko-Arabic quarter jutted into the sea to separate the Eastern Harbour's elegance from the warehouses and squalor of the West, somewhere out there flames lit the approaching evening like dancing devils, signature of the Midas Refinery.

A $1.8 billion complex that processed 100,000 barrels a day.

Out there on the edge of the desert, low-value heavy oil got an upgrade to petroleum gas, naphtha, aviation fuel and diesel for export to Europe. Though the public face of Midas was a minor Napoleonic princeling, her father owned 27.3 per cent through a holding company. It was more than enough.

Reaching into her bag, Zara pulled out a page torn from an American student magazine and began to read it for the fifth time. This was how she had to erase her traces from the network to become a ghost. There was much talk of command lines, Linux and Mozilla which she ignored, skimming down the page until she got to a paragraph for users prepared just to do what they were told.

Zara did exactly what it said. If the article was right she was now in the clear. If not, well, too bad . . . Did they want a new roof or didn't they?

When she returned to her job – if her new husband ever allowed her back – it would be to a different department of the Library. None of her male bosses would talk to her, except to give orders or collect information. Most of them would not even look in her direction in case their glance was seen and misinterpreted.

She'd made plenty of mistakes in her nineteen years, but the biggest by far was ever turning up at the airport in New York. Her parents had been right to be worried, whereas she was just naive for not wondering why they wanted her home for the summer. Leaving Columbia for Isk because she was touched they'd been missing her was about as stupid as anyone could get.

Now she was stuck with an arranged marriage and Zara could just imagine to what . . . Some spoilt, prissy little cokehead dressed in PaulSmith International. She'd watched enough episodes of *Rich & Famous* to know what to expect.

CHAPTER 5

First isolated as a pure chemical in 1820, but sourced from shrubs long before that and spread across the littoral a thousand years earlier by the armies of Islam, caffeine was the North African drug of choice and something of a local vice. Which was fine with ZeeZee. He'd spent time at both Scottish and Swiss boarding schools and could think of worse ones . . .

Lifting the airport cup to his lips, ZeeZee winced as the scalding black mud burnt his lips. The taste was of sweetened silt and *arabica* beans that hadn't been gently roasted so much as charred to death in their very own *auto-da-fé*.

'Best let it cool,' announced an elderly, whipcord-thin man who was sat opposite facing him over a low table.

'Yeah,' said ZeeZee. 'Thanks for warning me.'

General Saeed Koenig Pasha smiled and sipped from his own cup. Until thirty minutes ago the General had been bored. And then serendipity had seen him arrive at the airport just as all the fools on the scene started to panic about having breached diplomatic protocol.

Now he had the object of their worries in front of him, and the General had to admit he could see their problem. Not that he would ever, under any circumstances admit that to any of them. All the same, in his long and detailed experience as Governor of El Iskandryia, beys came in three types.

Old ones who lived in rambling palaces and wrote to him complaining about the laxity of the young.

Middle-aged ones who were too worried about their expanding bellies and nagging wives to have time to trouble him.

And young ones who drove too fast, lived hard and had acquired bad habits in foreign countries, without acquiring the necessary wisdom to realize that was where their bad habits should have been left – at least, when it came to displaying them in public.

24

This last type was what he had half been expecting to meet. Someone elegant and urbane, if somewhat louche. Instead the young man opposite looked, sounded and smelled like an American hobo. He had ill-fitting clothes, his hair was twisted into ugly locks and his face was hidden by a long, matted beard. Luckily the General had visited West-Coast America enough to know that this was a look often adopted by the children of the very rich.

He hadn't introduced himself to the al-Mansur boy and didn't intend to do so. All the same, it *would* have been his signature that bounced the boy out of the country, had him sent to jail or even killed; if he'd followed the first instinct of a certain Colonel Gasparin, instead of doing what the idiot Colonel should have done right at the start. Place a call to Lady Nafisa at her madersa.

Besides, if his staff really believed it was coincidence that saw the General arrive at the airport at exactly that point, then they really were fools and he'd be replacing the lot of them. He had his own reasons for being interested in the family of Lady Jalila al-Mansur.

'You could formally complain,' said the General. 'You have that right.' He didn't say anything more, just cocked his head to one side and waited to see which way the boy would play it.

'Not worth it,' said ZeeZee, standing up. He was in a hastily cleared VIP lounge at Iskandryia airport where Gasparin had escorted him as soon as the Colonel had been told ZeeZee's passport was genuine. 'The man was just playing his part . . . That's all any of us can do.'

He smiled at the older man's sudden sideways glance.

The area around them was done out in ersatz Rococo Islamic, all mirrored arches, peacock-blue tiles, white marble slabs and a splashy alabaster fountain that sounded like a woman pissing. ZeeZee got the feeling that the General couldn't wait to get away either.

Too close, thought ZeeZee as he headed for the exit. Way, way too close. He slipped the *carte blanche* into the breast pocket of his pug-ugly sports shirt and headed for a gap in the barriers.

Near the front of the barrier stood a chauffeur wearing peaked cap and polished boots, with a printed board that read *Ashraf al-Mansur* resting in the crook of his elbow. ZeeZee walked past the man without even breaking his stride.

First things first, and that meant hitting the local shops.

ZeeZee's other clothes were on their way to Zanzibar in an overhead locker, courtesy of Ottoman Airways. At least he sincerely hoped they were. He'd left his briefcase behind at Cairo aboard the Seattle/Zanzibar flight for exactly that purpose.

Everything he stood up in had been bought duty-free on the plane, paid for with a platinum HKS that had arrived along with his passport. And yellow shirts with beige elephants weren't his first or even second choice of clothing. The garment was what the Boeing's on-board boutique had had in his size.

Cairo was where he'd switched planes, to a Lufthansa local flight. There'd been one moment in a steel-and-glass corridor between Cairo arrivals and local departures when he'd been tempted to keep walking and lose himself in the chaos of the capital.

Quite why he hadn't was a question ZeeZee would ask himself later, when he finally stopped moving long enough to think. But first he needed new clothes and then he had to find the al-Mansur madersa, whatever that was . . .

CHAPTER 6

29th June

'Now the graveyard was haunted by Ifrits who were of the Only True Faith,' announced Hani. Her new uncle was late. Her aunt was furious about something, as always. So the small child was busy amusing herself.

'And in that night, as Hassan lay sleeping with his head leaning against his father's grave, came an Ifritah who marvelled at Hassan's loveliness and cried, "Glory to the True God. This is a creature from paradise." Then the Ifritah spiralled high into the dark firmament as was her custom and there met a Djinn on the wing who saluted her and she asked, "Where hast thou come from?"

' "From old Cairo," he replied.

' "Wilt thou come and look at the loveliness of the boy who sleeps in yonder graveyard? For thou wilt see no boy more beautiful."

'And the Djinn nodded and said, "I will . . ." And together they descended through the chill night sky to where Hassan . . .'

'Stop talking to yourself,' demanded Lady Nafisa, as she swept through the door of the haramlek's nursery and frowned at the sight of a puppy set in the middle of a spreading puddle. If there was anything she hated worse than Hani wasting her time on computer games it was that animal.

'I'm not talking to myself, I'm writing a story for Ali-Din.'

The child's tone was scrupulously polite. But her dark eyes were defiant and she looked at her puppy with pride.

'And I've already warned you,' said Lady Nafisa firmly, 'not to bring that thing up to the nursery.'

'But it's my nursery and I always mop up after him.' At nine Hani already considered herself too old to beg, so she kept her voice steady, as if she really couldn't see why there should be a problem. This was an old argument. One that had got her slapped at least twice and sent up to her room more times than she could remember.

'Ali-Din belongs in the courtyard and besides . . .'

'Yes, I know,' Hani said heavily, 'Ali-Din is a boy dog.'

Nothing male was allowed on the third floor of the al-Mansur madersa, Aunt Nafisa's house on Rue Sherif. In the five hundred years it had been standing no man had entered the haremlek. Now there was no one but Hani or her aunt to use the echoing rooms, where dust gathered in a dry fountain and geckos died and desiccated, unnoticed and unmourned.

'Disobey me again and I have him destroyed.'

'What if I change his name?' Hani demanded, not even prepared to acknowledge her aunt's threat. 'Then can he be female?'

'No,' Lady Nafisa hissed in irritation, resisting the urge to re-check her watch. A Cartier case with Swiss mechanical movement, it was elegant, tiny and unfailingly accurate. Which hadn't stopped her checking it every five minutes for the last hour, ever since the driver she'd hired at unnecessary expense had called in to report that her nephew was not on the plane.

And when she told him firmly that Ashraf was very definitely on that flight because she'd had a call from the General himself, the driver had replied tartly that, in that case, perhaps the bey didn't want to be collected and had put the phone down on her. No doubt he'd want paying, too, even if he'd failed in the job he was hired to do.

'Why can't Ali-Din be female?'

'Because I say so,' Lady Nafisa snapped. 'Now take Ali-Din down to the courtyard.' And she left before the child had a chance to defy her openly.

CHAPTER 7

Between Iskandryia airport and Place Orabi ran a Carey bus. It made stops on the way at Shallalat Gardens, Masr Station and the Attarine Mosque, but Place Orabi was the terminus and that was where all the remaining passengers but ZeeZee clambered off.

At least three conflicting varieties of Rai drifted in through the open doorway of the bus, blasting from cafés in the square. But ZeeZee couldn't even recognize the instruments, never mind the styles. He was tired, cross and hot. He hadn't slept since he'd snorted his last line of crystalMeth two days before and was trying very hard not to think about the approaching comedown, and that was making him more edgy still.

All he knew was that he needed to look his best.

A new identity needed a new look, because personality was a performance put on by the self for the self, or some such shit. ZeeZee felt much too wasted to remember the fox's actual line.

In fact, ZeeZee would happily have stayed on board the bus and shuttled his way back to the airport. Only that didn't seem to be an option. A recording in three languages was telling him it was time to leave. When that didn't work, the driver took to turning the inside lights on and off to signal they'd arrived.

'Yeah, yeah,' said ZeeZee and levered himself out of a plastic seat, leaving sweat marks where his back and buttocks had been. 'Where can I buy some decent clothes?'

The driver looked up from punching digits into a logbook but said nothing.

Wearily, ZeeZee peeled a $5 note from the roll in his back pocket. 'Clothes?'

'Rue Faransa,' the man said, lifting the note from between ZeeZee's fingers and making it disappear as if by magic. 'Have a nice evening.'

*

'You shouldn't be here,' ZeeZee told the man with the knife. In Iskandryia tourists had more chance of being run over by a taxi than being mugged. It said so in a travel short on ZeeZee's internal flight. Though maybe that wasn't such a comforting statistic, given that taxi accidents seemed to be a regular occurrence. And the golem-faced man from the airport certainly seemed to be real enough.

'Just give me your wallet.'

Golem features nodded down to a glass blade he was holding at his side. A deep groove ran along both sides, put there to help blood flow freely.

'I don't have a wallet,' said ZeeZee, which was the truth. He had an iris-specific platinum HKS card in one back pocket of his combats and his *carte blanche* in the other. Other than that, nothing. No rings, not even a watch. Well, only the Omega he'd bought duty-free on the plane and the G-Shock in his pocket, and he wasn't about to give up either of those. For the average mugger, ZeeZee was a big disappointment. Actually, as a mugger's target he was bad news, full stop.

ZeeZee kept his voice soft, unthreatening. For good measure he tried a small half-smile. But darkness visible already drew an unseen circle around them both and inside his head the fox was smiling as it memorized the layout of a tiny alley, a street at the back of Rue Faransa, so narrow and insignificant it appeared on no maps and the panniers of long-dead donkeys had managed to scratch grooves into both walls at once.

'Wallet,' repeated golem features. There was a dogged determination to his voice but his small eyes were clean. Whatever need he was feeding it wasn't chemical. *'Now.'* He raised the knife slightly to show he was serious.

'And I've already told you,' someone said, using ZeeZee's voice, 'he doesn't have one.' Most people would have stepped back, away from the sharp blade. ZeeZee stepped in close, until he could see tiny broken veins on the man's nose and smell stale garlic on his breath. It was definitely the man from the neighbouring queue at the airport, and he was still staring at ZeeZee's hair.

'No wallet. No cash. And besides . . .' ZeeZee smiled. 'If you need a knife, you're batting in the wrong league . . .'

The man opened his mouth.

'No,' ZeeZee said firmly.

Golem features shrugged. 'Too bad,' he said. And then his blade whipped up, aimed at a point behind ZeeZee's diaphragm – except that ZeeZee was already some place else. Pain blossoming across his side as he pivoted sideways to let the knife scrape across his ribs. *Ugly but not*

30

life-threatening. The status report concerned his wound, ZeeZee realized, not his opponent.

Dodging the next blow was easier. All ZeeZee had to do was pivot to take the putative knee to the groin on his hip.

'You're going to die,' said the attacker flatly, seeing ZeeZee's gaze flick round the deserted and darkened alley.

ZeeZee laughed.

'I died years ago,' he said and unravelled in one fluid sweep, a sideways twist creating exactly the right amount of space to let him bring his palm up under the man's chin, snapping back his skull so hard the sound of teeth breaking echoed off both alley walls. Without further hesitation, ZeeZee buried his forearm in a suddenly exposed throat and crushed the golem's larynx.

The follow-through, where ZeeZee's elbow swept back to crack the skull and drop the man to the dirt was unnecessary, but he did it anyway. The old Rasta he'd learnt from had been very strict about always completing each sequence.

In all, it took less than two seconds. And had there been anyone else in that alley to watch, which there wasn't, they'd have been presented with moves so fluid, so controlled that they could have passed for some deadly ballet.

'Shit,' said ZeeZee, blinking hard. Two courses of primal therapy, a complete twelve-point plan and three years of anger management straight down the drain. Personally, he blamed the fox.

Under a blue blazer golem features carried a new ceramic Colt in a flashy leather shoulder holster, the fancy saddle-stitched kind with a chrome buckle just guaranteed to show up under a full body scan. So maybe he wasn't such a professional after all.

Apart from that, the idiot was clean, right down to labels cut out of his clothes and no keys of any description in any of his pockets. The only other thing of interest was a Polaroid in a crumpled manila envelope. ZeeZee knew exactly what the shot would show even before he examined it. But he was wrong.

He wasn't the man in the photo staring out at the world through hooded eyes, because he'd never worn a goatee beard like that or had elegant hair swept back behind his ears. And he'd definitely never worn a drop pearl earring. But the man in the picture *was* him. The high cheekbones were his, the heavy nose, the whole shape of the face was the same, right down to his mouth.

And in the background of the picture, just out of focus behind the man, was a soaring minaret outlined against a shockingly blue sky. The mosque to which the minaret was attached was impressive, heart-breakingly beautiful and undoubtedly famous, but ZeeZee could honestly say he didn't recognize it.

Pocketing the Polaroid, ZeeZee rolled the body against a wall and left it there.

'Head south towards the equestrian statue of Khedive Mohammed Ali, turn right at Place Manshiya and walk briskly on. The road directly ahead is Rue Faransa . . .'

ZeeZee thanked the map without thinking, not noticing the glance he got from other tourists waiting their turn. Talking to machinery was a prison quirk. Even in soft habitats like Huntsville it could be the closest anyone got to a day's decent conversation.

Walking briskly was out, what with the gash over his ribs taped shut with instant skin from a chemist behind the bus station, but he managed a slow stroll through the square towards the waiting statue.

From the Khedive's bronze turban and fierce beard, to his gut bound round with a vast cummerbund, and the ornate horse pistol hanging from his saddle, Mohammed Ali was impossible to miss; though his mount looked unnaturally square at the corners, as if the sculptor had used up all the roundness available to replicate the Khedive's impressive bulk.

ZeeZee stopped rubber-necking Mohammed the moment he realized he was the only person on Place Mohammed paying Khedive the slightest attention. He didn't want to look the tourist, even when that was so obviously what he was.

The first three shops in Rue Faransa sold bric-a-brac masquerading as antiques. A Bakelite radio in one window caught ZeeZee's eye but when he went inside to examine it he discovered that someone had replaced the original valves with a cheap Somali chipset. So he put the radio back in the window and retreated under the shopkeeper's watchful eye.

Two clothes boutiques followed, both in the process of closing for the night and both featuring short dresses in washed-out silk by designers ZeeZee had never heard of, though given the prices displayed in pounds Iskandryian, US dollars and Reichsmarks, everyone else obviously had.

The next shop looked much more promising. It sold menswear, was still open and, even better than that, had an industrial-strength air-conditioning unit sticking straight out into the street. ZeeZee couldn't tell how expensive the suits in the window were from their price tags because there weren't any such tags – which probably made the garments concerned seriously upscale. But since it wasn't really his charge card he could live with that.

Something tastefully restrained was playing on the sound system as he entered. Gorecki probably. One wall was matte black, the rest sand-blasted brick. All of which left ZeeZee as singularly unimpressed as he was by the intimidating elegance of the boutique's French manager, the simplicity of her stark granite desk, and her three obsidian-topped work tables.

ZeeZee might heal unnaturally fast but he was still in too much pain from his ribs and far too strung out to take note of the shop's expensively understated detail. All he noticed was a framed page from *Esquire*, showing a man wearing a black tee under a loose lightweight black coat with matching trousers. The shoes the model wore had Cuban heels and sloped to a point at the toes. The outfit looked elegant, sophisticated and just slightly threatening. But most of all it looked cool. Not fashion-victim cool, just as if the model wasn't overheating.

'That,' said ZeeZee, nodding at the cover and putting his card on the counter. 'I want that.'

The glance the woman gave his card was so fleeting ZeeZee almost missed it. 'Good choice,' she said. 'Good choice.' Pushing herself up off a silver chair, the manager stepped quickly behind ZeeZee and ran one slim hand across his shoulders and then down his spine from his neck to the small of his back. And even as ZeeZee tensed, the manager was across the other side of the boutique, standing next to a rack of jackets, muttering measurements under her breath.

'Smart silk,' she told ZeeZee, returning with a coat. 'Double-stitched, jet buttons, silk half-lining. Ideal for this weather.' She slung the garment across ZeeZee's back, not bothering to get her only customer of the evening to thread his arms through the sleeves. 'If it hangs okay like this then the fit is good. I'll check sleeve length later, but it will be fine.'

She stepped towards ZeeZee and hesitated as he stepped swiftly back. 'I need to check your waist,' she said. 'If that's a problem I have a tape . . .'

'No problem.' ZeeZee stood as the woman touched her fingers together over his spine and deftly smoothed the tips around his waist until they met slightly below his navel. If she noticed the heavy cross-hatches of tape coming down from his damaged ribs she didn't mention it.

'Thirty, maybe thirty-one. We'll try both. Okay, now the length.' She skimmed one hand up ZeeZee's inside leg and nodded. 'Thirty-three . . .' A pair of silk trousers joined the jacket, leaving only a black cotton tee that the woman selected from a pile on the obsidian-topped table. Shoes came last.

'The changing room's through there.'

33

There was a black curtain screening off a tiny corner of the boutique, a CCT camera bolted baldly to the bare brick wall.

'How about shades?' ZeeZee asked when he emerged, his duty-free clothes and shoes crumpled into a bundle in his hands.

She shrugged, the merest hint of an apology. 'I'm afraid not, but Versace's across the street . . .'

ZeeZee initialled the slip she handed him without checking the amount, dropped his old clothes in a bin and took a small silver-and-red business card the woman was offering. It was only when he felt its weight that he realized the card really was silver, the hallmarked kind.

'We make hotel calls,' said the manager. 'If your itinerary is too crowded to allow for a revisit. Our number is in enamel.'

CHAPTER 8

'I don't usually . . .'

The boy with the cats-eye contacts nodded like he understood and Zara took a good look and realized that he did. Which was just as well, because someone had to understand that she had her reasons for not wanting to be back.

'Where are we going . . . ?'

She knew the answer to that because he'd already told her, but asking again was easier than trying to remember, particularly as remembering might bring back something best forgotten.

'My place,' said the boy.

Her answering smile was wry, almost ironic. There were a dozen reasons why this was an extremely bad idea.

'Okay,' said Zara and climbed onto the waiting tram.

Where?

The elderly woman who'd stumbled into ZeeZee from behind when he suddenly stopped dead took one look at the foreigner's scowling face and decided to keep walking, in another direction. Not that ZeeZee even noticed: he was too busy stripping down his memory, deleting taste, smell and extraneous movement to find a simple primary colour.

There.

It took ZeeZee a split second to reassure himself that the people on the tram weren't staring at him because he was dripping blood (he'd already sealed the knife cut with surgical glue from his complimentary Pan American medical kit before taping his ribs with skin from the all-night pharmacist). And it wasn't his suit that worried the people on the green tram, even though most of the other men wore flowing jellabas. It was his beard and dreadlocks. Or maybe it was the shades.

Too bad.

35

And yes, once they'd been a trademark of his, but that had been by accident – and besides, it had been in another country. He wore shades from necessity because without them his eyes swallowed too much light. Just one of the little childhood modifications for which he had his mother's friends to thank.

Lately he'd taken to wearing polarized contacts but his supply was back at Huntsville along with his stash of crystalMeth and the rest of his life. Except it wasn't just life he'd been doing at Hunstville, it had been all day *and* all night, life with no option of parole. Which was still a pretty good result, given the district attorney had been going for throwing the big red switch.

'Excuse me.' ZeeZee stepped carefully across some market trader's outstretched boots and slid between two thick-set construction workers in concrete-splashed jellabas.

His brain was headed for what the fox would call a five-car crash and he needed that seat. Besides, that was where the girl sat, the girl he'd seen hesitate, then get on a green tram. The one whose sadness was flash-frozen to the inside of his eyes like lightning.

Though maybe that was just the meth.

ZeeZee knew immediately why his seat had been left free when the tram braked suddenly and the girl shot forward, straight into him. No amount of cologne could hide the reek of alcohol.

'I'm sorry,' said the boy beside her. He half stood, then sank back into his seat and turned away with the embarrassment of the still-young. Fourteen, thought ZeeZee, fifteen at the most. Silver hair, gold tear, laser tattoo. Not as hard as he wanted to be.

Politely, ZeeZee put one hand on each of the girl's shoulders and pushed her back into her seat. The slightest of nods was all he got by way of acknowledgement. And it was obvious that she didn't trust herself to speak. As if sitting very still could hide the fact that she was too drunk to stand. A birthday or leaving do, ZeeZee decided, noting the card clutched loosely in her fingers and the bunch of orchids wilting on her lap.

Birthday parties gave good access. He'd used them back in Seattle. People's guards came down, making it easy to get close. Much closer than they mostly wanted: but then that was ZeeZee's speciality, getting close to targets who spent time and money keeping people like him at arm's length.

Style was a key factor and ZeeZee could do style. Looking right got you through doors that remained closed to others. Neatness, youth and an ability to blend. There'd been few places he couldn't enter if needs must . . . There was even a name for it. Negative capability . . .

ZeeZee smiled.

He was still smiling when the girl hunched forward and dribbled vomit from her mouth onto the tram floor between his shoes. She didn't do anything as vulgar as actually throw up, she just let the alcohol make its own return trip.

'Sorry.' That was the boy again.

ZeeZee shrugged. 'It happens.'

At Rue Sherif, ZeeZee pushed himself up off his seat and paused. He needed to know who she was, but he also needed to get off at this stop. Most of all, he wanted to tell the boy not to worry. But anything he said would have drawn attention to the girl's plight, so ZeeZee just nodded and kept going. He'd been those people, both of them. Just not for a long time.

CHAPTER 9

29th June

Lodging House & Eating Shop read the old sign at the corner of Abu Dadrda and Rue Cif, though the building in question showed nothing but empty spaces where windows and door should have been. At ground level even the floorboards were missing, long wooden joists stretching out over darkness that dropped to a cellar below.

A plank had been nailed crudely across the open doorway as vague warning of the dangers that hid inside. And over by the far wall in the darkness something glittered that might have been glass reflected in the headlights of a car but proved to be a fox when ZeeZee removed his shades to take a proper look.

'Later,' said ZeeZee and the fox grinned toothily, saying nothing.

ZeeZee didn't believe in omens and of his many childhood demons only the arctic fox remained untamed. And Tiriganaq was more afraid of him than ZeeZee was of the fox. Because, if necessary, ZeeZee could stop answering and then it wouldn't matter if the fox called itself *Tiriganaq, Smoke* or *Earl Grey Malkin*, it would be alone.

Still, they'd always faced trouble together before, so ZeeZee couldn't imagine how he might have thought the fox would lie low this time.

Above them both, three-storey walls gave way to a thin night sky, softened and faded by a sodium glare that didn't stretch far enough down to reach the sidewalk, had there been one.

East of El-Gomruk and south of Manshiya, but way too far north to be Karmus or Moharrem Bey, ZeeZee wasn't sure what this district was called. It had been blank of any name on the map at the tram station, its streets cross-hatched to tell cash-rich tourists that here was where they could find Iskandryia's famous souks.

ZeeZee could see the map clearly in his head, right down to the pink cross-hatching, but that meant nothing. There was very little from his life that he couldn't see in his head once he'd remembered where it was filed.

38

The entrance ZeeZee wanted turned out to be a narrow arch between two shops, one of which sold beaten brassware, the other old computers in shades of pastel. Between them was a door without a knocker. At head height was a peeling sign that read *On ne visite pas*.

Straightening his shoulders, ZeeZee rapped hard on the ancient door and then regretted it as noise crashed like thunder down both sides of the street. He knocked again, more gently this time.

'What do you want?'

At least, ZeeZee imagined that was what the man on the other side of the door said, though he didn't recognize the language.

'I'm looking for Lady Nafisa,' said ZeeZee.

Nafisa. The voice turned the word over as if tasting it.

'Yes,' said ZeeZee. 'My aunt.'

'Why didn't you say so?' In the space where the door had been stood an old man, the stub of a cheroot gripped between his right thumb and skeletal first finger. Dark eyes examined ZeeZee's face and then the man stepped to one side. 'Our house is your house.' This time round he spoke in French, with a voice raw from a lifetime of cheap cigars.

There were five bolts on that door and the old man secured them all, including one that fixed straight up into the top of the arch and another that drove into the worn surface of a stained flagstone.

'This way.'

An arch in the side of the entrance room led left, followed by an immediate right turn through a second arch, which was when ZeeZee realized the shabby corridor he was in was really the start of a small, very simple maze leading to an ugly, obsessively-neat garden immediately beyond.

On either side of the garden stood open-fronted rooms, little more than flat roofs supported by sandstone pillars over a cracked terracotta floor. And at the far end of the garden was an ornate marble arch set in a simple brick wall. Once the formal garden had been naked to the sky but someone, years back, had roofed it over with steel and glass, panes of which were now cracked and dirty.

The glass roof was obviously old. The frame supporting it was riveted to crossbeams that were held in place by cast-iron pillars, and a century's worth of paint had crusted round the rivets and smoothed the Doric decoration on the plinths to a bland ripple.

'This way.' The old man vanished through the marble arch into a cavernous, empty room where water didn't so much fall from a fountain as run bubbling down a freestanding slab of marble.

'*Shazarwan*,' announced the man and ZeeZee guessed he was naming the strange object.

Open arches on the far side of the room led into an open courtyard, smaller than the garden and tiled with white stone. In the centre stood a fountain carved from a single block of horsehair marble. But what ZeeZee noticed was the impossibly ornate four-storey house that rose at the far end of the courtyard.

Soft uplights pulled detail from a carved balustrade and threw its huge arches into shadow. If the al-Mansur madersa was meant to impress, then it succeeded.

Jerking his chin towards stairs that started up the outside of the madersa, then turned in under an arch to continue inside, the thin man stood back.

'Nafisa . . .' He said simply.

ZeeZee went.

'You're late,' said a voice that ZeeZee tracked to a small woman angrily pacing near the top of the stairs. Backlit by wall lights, Lady Nafisa looked thin and birdlike, a neat faceless shadow but an angry one.

'Am I?' ZeeZee's first reaction was to apologize, then insist his flight was late, even though she'd know from her driver that this was untrue. But he didn't let himself do either. Instead, he shrugged and kept climbing, as if not caring if he walked straight through her.

'Shit happens,' he said as he reached the top and stared round at a huge room, open to the night through its arches on one side. Since heights and he didn't agree with each other, he didn't go look at the view. 'And besides, someone wanted a word.'

Lady Nafisa stopped suddenly. 'You saw somebody you knew?'

'Other way round,' said ZeeZee. 'He thought he knew me.'

They spoke French because that was the language Lady Nafisa had first used. Yet when it came, her switch to English was so fluent ZeeZee wasn't even certain she was aware of making it.

'I sent a car for you. A stretch Daimler-Benz.' She was doing her best to smile but there was real anger in her eyes. Which was fine with ZeeZee because he was pretty sure that, behind the expensive anonymity of the Versace shades she'd unwittingly bought for him there was real anger in his too.

Families had that effect on him and no family more strongly than his own. If she really was family, which remained to be proved.

'I make my own way,' said ZeeZee.

The woman stared at him. And behind the fashion-plate suit she saw ghosts of her husband backed up like reflections in a mirror. 'Later,' she said hastily. 'We can deal with this later . . .'

As if on cue, the skeletal porter from the rear entrance strode in clutching a brass tray that he placed on a three-legged wooden contraption which seemed to be waiting for it.

'This is Khartoum,' said Lady Nafisa, as if talking about a dog. 'He's from the Sudan so *you* can say anything you like in front of him.'

Meaning he didn't speak English, presumably.

'Unless, of course,' said ZeeZee, 'I say it in French, Arabic or whatever that other language was.'

Nafisa sighed. 'German,' she said heavily. 'I can see you're going to be like your father.'

Father? ZeeZee stared at her.

'Precise to the point of irritation.'

ZeeZee hadn't meant to be precise, merely glib. And since he'd never met his father and the last time he'd seen her, his mother still regarded the truth as something so fluid that identical sentences could mean opposite things on different days, he had no idea if Lady Nafisa even knew who his father was. Somehow he doubted it. Some undiscovered theory of chaos seemed to be the only thing that made sense of his family life to date.

Aim to please, shoot to kill. That had been one of Wild Boy's phrases back before Huntsville, when he and Wild were still not quite enemies. 'We aim to please,' said ZeeZee.

'We?'

Yeah, we . . . ZeeZee clicked his heels and bowed slightly, almost as if he meant it. *Me and the fox.*

'Stupid that is,' the sudden voice behind ZeeZee was cutting in its contempt. 'Clicking your heels. No one really behaves like that in Iskandryia. I knew you'd be stupid.'

'*Hana.*'

'Hani,' corrected the girl.

Lady Nafisa sighed.

'Anyway, *Hani* what?' the child asked angrily, walking into the light. She had oil smeared across the palms of both her hands and bare ankles from where she'd slid down an elevator cable.

'You've got the floodlights on,' she said to Lady Nafisa and stalked over to a balustrade to examine the courtyard below. '*And* the fountain . . .' The small girl turned her head to stare at ZeeZee. 'You're honoured.' Her voice was bitter. 'She doesn't turn the lights on for anyone. She wouldn't even turn them on for my birthday party.'

'They were broken,' Lady Nafisa said fiercely.

'And now they're mended.' It didn't look like she believed her aunt for a minute.

'I'm Raf,' said ZeeZee.

41

'Ashraf,' corrected the child, scornfully. 'Don't I know it. She's talked of nothing else for days . . .'

'Hani.' Lady Nafisa's voice was hard.

'Yes, I know. Hani, be good. Hani, disappear . . .' The small girl turned round and stamped back towards the lift. 'You don't look like you're worth all the fuss,' she said cuttingly and slammed the grille, leaving ZeeZee with the impression of a small, furious animal glaring through the bars of a cage.

CHAPTER 10

Dawn came in low, the sky clear and turquoise blue. And Hamzah Quitrimala knew exactly how it would look out on the water. The breaking light would catch one wave after another, until a ribbon of sun stretched from the horizon to the glass-sided cockpit of his 15,000bhp VSV. Fifty feet long, maybe ten at its widest, the boat was ex-police issue, chisel-prowed but flared at the stern. Stealth-sheeted and proof against infrared sensors.

It ran every month, midweek, without fail.

Diamonds carried to a pick-up point south of Iraklion/medical supplies brought back – Hamzah had captained the run himself when he was younger. Of course, in his day the boats had been nothing like as fast, but they had still done the job and been back before the second daybreak – which was more than Hamzah could say for his current crew.

He was going to have to find himself a new captain. But first he had a bey to see . . .

'Ashraf al-Mansur,' repeated ZeeZee. 'Known to his friends as Raf.'

ZeeZee emptied his mind and let the name roll over him. When he opened his eyes five minutes later the change was made and he was someone else, though boiling fog still filled the *hamman*, making it impossible for whoever he was to see the door.

In fact, so thick was the steam that Raf could hardly see his own feet, which might also have had something to do with the slick of sweat running down his forehead to drip into his eyes.

He stank, though not as much as when he woke first thing the previous morning, in a pool of perspiration that smelled sweet as blood and sour as dysentery. That was twenty-four hours ago, when his piss had been black. Now the colour was nearing normal as his body began to adjust to its lack of crystalMeth. It was his mind that was still addicted.

43

Raf was naked. In a domed room filled with naked women. Except the women were on the walls – pictures only, depicting a dozen dancers, their breasts full and bare, each plump *mons* hidden behind a wisp of fabric fashioned from tiny tesserae, marble fragments glued into place more than a century before by some artist keen to preserve a slight air of decency.

In Huntsville, in the days before Dr Millbank, recalcitrant convicts were broken by being locked in a hot-box and broiled. In El Iskandryia, even first thing in the morning, people had to book for the privilege.

Raf wasn't sure he understood why his aunt considered a Turkish bath the ideal place for him to meet Dr Hamzah Quitrimala Effendi. But here he was, still waiting for the man to show.

Sweat beads almost bubbled from his stomach and chest, and already he felt dehydrated.

'Your Excellency?'

Raf opened his eyes to see a man whose shoulders would make those of most sumo wrestlers look puny. A blue suit hung tent-like from his frame, its fabric already gone limp in the steam. In one ear was a gold Sony earbead, the kind you were meant to notice.

'Your Excellency?'

That was him, Raf realized. He nodded.

'The boss will be with you in a minute. He apologizes for being late.' Job done, the huge Russian took up position against the opposite wall, apparently impervious to the heat that soon had sweat rolling down his pink face.

'You Ashraf?' A thickset man strode in, hand already outstretched, gut protruding. 'Good to meet you.' He too was unashamedly naked, his uncovered genitals at eye height to where Raf sat on a marble bench.

Raf stood.

'Dr Hamzah Effendi?'

A lightning grin flashed across the man's face, then vanished, leaving only a wry, almost self-mocking smile. Lady Nafisa had insisted that Raf should remember to add the honorific to Hamzah's name. It was a neat touch.

The newcomer had the kind of handshake Raf expected. Strong but slightly clumsy, and brief as if he'd finally learned not to grab the hand of every contact and wring it heartily. Heavy gold links circled one wrist and on his middle finger was a huge ring set with a cabouchon ruby. Both screamed money but neither said anything about restraint.

Reading people was one of Raf's skills, like eidetic memory and night sight: he knew that and accepted it. It came from living in institutions . . . Swiss boarding school from the age of five, a Scottish school

44

after that, three years working for Hu San in Seattle and then Huntsville. He'd been inside institutions all his life and only one of them had been a prison – the others just felt like it. They also felt safe. Raf wasn't stupid enough to deny that.

'Nasty scar,' said Hamzah.

'Yeah.'

'Recent.' Hamzah added. It wasn't a question. He examined the cut along Raf's ribs with a practised eye, taking in the double strip of plastic skin.

'Slipped and cut myself,' said Raf. Which was possible. Not true, admittedly, but no less unlikely than being mugged by a golem with a photograph of him that wasn't. 'My own fault,' Raf added. 'Should have been more careful.'

'And that?'

Raf's shoulder looked, at first glance, like a map of some capital city of damaged flesh, lines radiating out from a densely scarred centre. 'Long story,' said Raf. 'Maybe some other time.'

If the steam room was hot, the plunge pool outside was so cold that Raf thought his heart would stop and his lungs never unfreeze.

'Lovely isn't it?' Hamzah said happily as they both bobbed to the surface. Raf scowled, but only because he had no breath left to speak.

'Strange,' said Hamzah as he kicked his way towards marble steps. 'I would have thought your father had a dozen Turkish baths . . .' He let his words trickle into a silence that stretched ever longer – until Raf finally realized the man wasn't just making conversation, he expected an answer.

Which was fair enough. Hamzah undoubtedly wanted to know what he was getting for his money. Raf's big problem was that he didn't have an easy reply.

'I lived with my mother,' Raf said, then stopped, because that wasn't strictly true either . . . For a start she wasn't really his mother and he hadn't really lived with her. Or maybe she was. Her opinion on that changed with the wind. And maybe he had . . .

'I boarded at various schools. England, Scotland, Switzerland.'

'Your ma was American?'

'English, living in New York.'

Hamzah shrugged as if it was all the same. Which it probably was to him. 'I'm told her name is well known . . .'

'Not unless you're a fan of the National Geographic channel,' said Raf. 'She campaigned for animal equality and worked on documentaries. Remember that film about meerkats?' Hamzah looked blank until Raf put his hands up like paws and swung his head from side to side, as if watching for danger.

Hamzah nodded.

'She did the camera work,' said Raf, clambering out of the water ahead of Hamzah. 'Syndicated in six continents. You can still get the screen saver. She took a flat fee of $1,500 and used it to fly down to Brazil to film vampire bats. Remember the baby panda trying to eat bamboo . . . ? The young fox playing in the snow? The white tiger cub with the empty Coke bottle? Well, she did camera on those, too.'

Animal porn, just a different kind. Cuddly images for a cold planet, used to fund the stuff that really interested her, like filming predators. Not that he was bitter or anything. 'She did a lot of the work for love,' said Raf, forcing himself to be fair. It had to be for love, because, God knew, there'd been little enough money in it. And it probably wasn't her fault that the only way she could cope with a damaged world was by examining it through a lens or the bottom of a vodka bottle. But then, nor was her life his fault either, whatever she might have said . . .

'Let's go back to the steam room.'

Hamzah smiled. 'Getting a taste for it, eh?'

Sitting side by side and naked in the boiling mist, both men knew the real interview was beginning. But Lady Nafisa hadn't made clear to Raf who had final approval. All she'd said was that he shouldn't commit to any fact that could be checked, that he should keep answers vague and always return a question with a question.

She might know that Raf had spent years locked in a Seattle jail but there was no reason why Hamzah had to know too.

'You've been in America?' The industrialist's voice was studiedly relaxed, almost urbane. He hardly glanced at an ugly slash of scar tissue above Raf's right hip and when he did it was fleeting. Raf could have told him about the operation he'd had at five on a kidney but that story was as boring as the month he'd spent wired to machines.

'Were you working over there?'

'Something like that.' Raf stood and stretched, twisting his head to one side like a man with a bad crick in his neck. It fooled neither of them.

'Lady Nafisa mentioned that you were an honorary attaché.'

Did she? Reluctant to lie outright, Raf retreated into something close to the truth. 'To be honest,' he said, 'most of my time was spent on a doctorate.'

Behind bars, with limited web access and no on-campus visits.

'Finance?' Hamzah asked, looking suddenly interested.

'No,' said Raf. 'Alternative timelines. They've very big in the US right

46

now.' That, at least, was true. 'It's a way of understanding what happened by looking at what didn't but quite easily might have done . . . You know, say America had actually joined the Third Balkan War . . .'

'They stayed neutral. So did we.'

'Not the 1966–75 conflict,' said Raf, 'The *Third* Balkan, 1914–15. Say Woodrow Wilson hadn't cut a deal between Berlin and London but had sent in troops on Britain's side. London might have been victorious. The Kaiser might have been fatally weakened . . .'

'The Kaiser was always going to win,' Hamzah said flatly. 'History is what God writes.'

Raf sighed. 'Just imagine,' he said. 'The Prussian empire breaks up in 1923, just as the Austro-Hungarians almost did. Might the Ottomans have fallen? What would have happened to Egypt's Khedive?'

'*The Khedive* . . .' Hamzah knew better than to accuse a bey of treason. Especially not one who was about to marry his daughter. And no doubt, all this *what if* was merely some sophisticated game played by people without real jobs. But it sounded like treason to him.

Besides, Hamzah knew what *had* happened. Every schoolboy across North Africa knew that Islam had trampled colonialism into the ground. On Suvla plain, the English king's own servants from Sandringham had been killed to the last man. The slaughter at Gallipoli broke the warmongers' spirit.

Fatally weakened, the British were driven from Egypt by General Saad Zaghloul. Having stolen Libya in 1911, Italy was forced to give it back six years later, and the French relinquished Tunis.

Fifteen years of smouldering unrest followed. Nationalists, fundamentalists, Bolsheviks . . . but money from the Arabian oilfields bought them all off in the end. Mosques were built, hospitals erected and schools set up to educate the children of the poor. His grandfather had been one of them. The child of a *felah* who sharecropped a single strip of Nile mud far to the south of Iskandryia and resented bitterly the interference of *effendi* who demanded his child attend class when there was *bersim* to gather and irrigation channels to be kept open with a broad-bladed hoe.

From *felah* to *effendi* in three generations. That was worth something. And Hamzah's doctorate was in engineering. Which was worth something too. The industrialist nodded to his bodyguard and stood up to go. He had bribes to pay, building contracts to negotiate, a new captain to find for the Iraklion run.

Olga, his PA, would be waiting at the office with a long list of people to see and calls he should make. Most of which he would ignore.

'Where were you an attaché?' The final question was asked from politeness alone. Beys were obviously different and Hamzah made no pretence of seeing any value in the theories expounded by his future son-in-law.

'Seattle,' said Raf.

Hamzah sat down again. This time when his gaze flicked to the slash across Raf's ribs they stayed there. And when he looked back again there was something in his eyes that looked very like guilt.

One heavy hand came up to rest briefly on Raf's shoulder. 'I had no idea. No one told me.'

Raf said nothing because that was what someone who'd worked unofficially at the Seattle consulate would have said.

'That's confidential, obviously,' Raf muttered finally. 'So please don't mention it to anyone.'

'But I have to tell . . .'

'No,' said Raf, looking Hamzah straight in the eyes. 'What I did was insignificant. An *honorary* attaché is just someone's unpaid assistant.'

'And the person you worked for is dead.' It wasn't a question. Hamzah had watched the official broadcasts. And even if he hadn't, the bombing of the consulate in Seattle by Sword of God fundamentalists had filled the world's newsfeeds, swamped the radio stations and briefly turned even pirate TV into rolling 24-hour news channels.

Image after image had been bounced round the planet. Bodies being pulled from the wreckage of a concrete building with heavy balconies. Viewers only knew the consulate once had balconies because CNN researchers had found 'before' shots to emphasize the horror of what came after.

One car bomb alone would have caused structural damage. But the consulate had main streets on three of its sides and the delivery trucks had been perfectly synchronized, their drivers in constant communication. The police deduced that the suicide bombers had been in regular radio contact from several charred fragments of circuit-board and the say-so of a thirteen-year-old band scanner, who'd been irritated to find crypted static where he was expecting juicy neighbourhood gossip.

CHAPTER 11

The free city was not just built on the rubble of its own history, it used that rubble in the rebuilding. Greek columns reshaped by Roman artisans now formed part of mosque doorways, having been ripped from an earlier Byzantine church. So, too, the cultures had mixed. Until the rich mix became its own culture.

Berlin thought El Iskandryia barbarous, the White House feared it, and Baghdad dismissed the metropolis as decadent and forgotten by God. But *realpolitik* demanded a Mediterranean free port where oil, cotton and particularly information could be traded. And El Isk got the job.

Roman, Byzantine, Coptic, Muslim . . . If ancient Babylon was the whore, then El Iskandryia had long been the courtesan: though for Islam's conquering army she was a sister to be brought back into the family. Napoleon called the city five shacks built over a dung heap. Nelson, being British, couldn't even get the sex right and dismissed the city as a crippled dog. But the insults meant nothing to Isk . . .

For Isk was hermaphrodite, ageless. A vampire of a city. Venerable and elegant, with a taste for fresh blood – a taste that it kept hidden behind stately boulevards and impeccable manners, in daylight at least. Night-time found the city stretching itself and yawning to reveal ancient fangs. Though the half-smile never left its face and the dark glint never left its eye.

And to assume Isk had a single identity was to misunderstand the Gordian complexity of its personality. The vampire existed parallel to the blonde innocent-eyed victim, the virgin inside the whore. There never had been only one city at any time in El Iskandryia's history. And for all its ancient glory, there were days when Isk was afraid of its own shadow, of the tarnished side of the mirror it held up to the world.

Days like now, when all that showed inside on Le Trianon's bar

49

screen was a rerun of that morning's executions in Riyadh. A Saudi paedophile and a Sudanese found guilty of sorcery, both losing their heads in the flash of a sword blade, then losing them again in slow motion.

Family.

Ashraf al-Mansur, who was doing his best not to think of himself as ZeeZee, rolled the word round his mouth and spat it out. He'd never had one and wasn't sure why he'd want to start now. As a child, in Zurich, he'd known boys at the Academy with families. Seen the strange effect it had on them. They cried from homesickness at the start of term and then no longer felt at home when they went back for the holidays. Their parents were worse. The kind of people who talked about roots and forgot those were what kept vegetables in the ground.

Besides, Raf didn't need roots. He came with a 8000-line guarantee that promised his *genetic heritability* would always outweigh *social calibration.* Whatever the fuck that meant.

At first, given the number of zeros after the first number in the price, Raf thought that his mother must really love him . . . But later, when he looked at her accounts for the year of his birth, he found that ninety-five per cent of the cost of the genetic manipulation had been met by Bayer-Rochelle and the rest she'd written off over five years against tax.

Oh, and the pharmaceutical company had totally funded her next three expeditions and made a sizeable one-off donation to a pressure group for which she was official photographer. It was around that time she'd stopped campaigning against non-transparent genome research.

On the evening he arrived Lady Nafisa had made clear the payment she intended to collect for digging him out of Huntsville. Though what she talked about was the need for family members to help each other, to accept their responsibilities.

'I don't have a family,' Raf had said. 'I *had* a mother. And when I wanted to talk to her I'd call her agent.'

Lady Nafisa had looked at him. 'Your father is my brother-in-law. That makes us family.'

Her brother-in-law . . . 'My father was a backpacker,' said Raf. 'From Goteborg. My mother didn't even get his name.' The man had apparently been hired for a week to drive his mother across the Sahel when she was filming the Libyan striped weasel, probably because she was too wasted to steer the vehicle herself.

'No.' Lady Nafisa shook her head. 'You must listen to me. The Emir of Tunis is your father.'

'Yeah, right,' said Raf. 'That well-known Swede.'

'Blue eyes, white hair, high cheekbones. You're Berber,' Lady Nafisa told him crossly. 'Look it up . . . And while you're at it, take a good look at this.' Only Raf didn't need to take a good look because he'd seen the picture before – the palm trees, the minaret, the man with the drop-pearl earring.

'Your father,' said Lady Nafisa.

Raf wanted to say that she was talking to the wrong man: but then suddenly realised he was the one who'd got it wrong. It wasn't his responsibilities they were discussing – or not just his – it was her responsibilities to him. An odd and uncomfortable thought.

'I knew he had a brat by an American,' Lady Nafisa said. 'And that he paid your mother a small allowance, but he does that for all his bastards, he can afford it. But he also told me you were illegitimate. And he lied.'

She handed Raf a letter.

Beneath the words *Isaac and Sons. Commissioners of Oaths*, a rush of Arabic flowed right to left across expensive paper like tiny waves. Raf could no more read it than fly. 'What does it say?' Raf asked, handing it back.

'On 30 April . . . Pashazade Zari al-Mansur, only son of the Emir of Tunis, married Sally Welham at a private ceremony in an annex of the Great al-Zaytuna Mosque,' Lady Nafisa recited from memory. 'She was his third wife. He divorced her five days later.'

'My mother was already married.'

Lady Nafisa made no pretence of scanning the paper. 'My informant says not . . . Your real name is Ashraf al-Mansur. Under Ottoman law you hold the rank of *bey*, which entitles you to a senior post in the Public Service.' She glanced up. 'We'll talk about that later. You have *carte blanche* anywhere in Ottoman North Africa from Tunis to Stambul and you have diplomatic immunity everywhere else in the world, for any crime except murder . . .'

Raf pushed his empty coffee cup aside and prepared to stand, but the moment he began to ease back his chair a waiter materialized at his side and shifted it for him. Seconds later the *patron* himself appeared.

'Will we be seeing Your Excellency soon?'

'Monday morning, I would imagine,' said Raf and the small man smiled.

'I'll reserve your table.' He glanced at the English-language newspaper Ashraf had downloaded from a stall. 'And I'll have a copy of *The Alexandrian* waiting . . .'

A sluggish breeze rolling lazily off the sea faded as Raf headed inland. Away from the Corniche the hot midday air was muggy, with humidity high enough to merit a warning on the local newsfeed. Common sense said grab the nearest air-conditioned taxi, but Raf ignored the sweat beginning to build under his thick beard and headed south on foot towards Lady Nafisa's house.

Between Le Trianon and Rue Abu Dadrda, Raf found one *boulevard*, four *rues* and a quiet tree-lined *place* named al-Mansur, historical detritus of the family to which he now belonged.

And Raf was more than halfway across the *place* before he finally realized why Nafisa's roofed-over garden inspired in him such hatred.

CHAPTER 12

Seattle

Out at Huntsville the rain did more than merely drum on glass: it fell like buckshot. But before there could be Huntsville, the city of Seattle had to exist – and the fox blamed that on a man called Asa Mercer.

On 16 January 1866, Mercer left New York with thirty-four unmarried girls bound for a new settlement at Puget Sound on the Pacific coast. He'd hoped to bring more than 700 but, it was still an improvement on his first expedition to collect marriageable women. Then he had persuaded only eleven to make the dangerous trip. Maybe it had been the rumours of rain that put them off, maybe it had been the distance, or the fact that the war was only recently over . . . Whatever, that had been then and this was later.

It still rained though, because in Seattle this was what the weather did – even ZeeZee knew that. And the rain drummed off city sidewalks, or beat on sun canopies raised in hope over empty tables outside cafés.

But out at Huntsville the rain did more than merely drum, its buckshot fell on the glass roof of the jail, twenty-four/seven. At least, that was what it felt like to ZeeZee those first few months he was there. Until the snow came and with it silence.

A masterpiece of nineteenth-century iron and glass, built twenty-five years after Paxton first led the way by using prefabricated sections for London's famous Crystal Palace, Huntsville Penitentiary was a monument to man's ingenuity – and stupidity.

Not the stupidity of the convicts who ended up there but of the architects, philanthropists and politicians of Washington State. Men who wanted their names immortalized in a correctional glass cathedral that turned out, in practice, to function as little more than an ice house.

Two riots in three winters went some way towards convincing the governor that the design was not as humane as he'd been led to believe. Since five identical penitentiaries had already been built in other states to the same plan, and all had been unsuccessful, this didn't come as a surprise to his critics.

By 1930, nearly sixty years later, all were ruins except Huntsville. In 1979 Huntsville was finally decommissioned. And then, in the final year of the twentieth century, Californian therapist Dr Anthony Millbank published his revolutionary work on lux therapy.

Crime, said Dr Millbank, wasn't merely a matter of incorrect socialization, food allergy or genetic malfunction, which in animals was called bad blood. Therefore social therapy, healthy meals and carefully selected drugs were not the complete answer.

Most crime was urban. What most urban dwellers lacked was natural light. It was therefore obvious that light-deprivation was a contributory factor in crime. Since most of middle America believed that original sin rather than genetics, allergies or lack of breastfeeding led to crime, they paid little attention to the latest addition to the list of contributory causes. Though a teenage serial killer who drained, labelled and later drank the chilled blood of his victims mixed with Stolichnaya gained brief notoriety by claiming his murderous tendencies were caused by an aversion to food, shopping malls and daylight.

But Dr Millbank persisted, helped both by appearances on Oprah and data showing that the gene cFos (a marker for the human internal clock) peaked only once under artificial light, at dawn, but expressed at dawn and dusk in natural light.

There was, in Dr Millbank's opinion, a distinct and irrefutable correlation between artificial light and crime.

The gradual shifts in light-intensity and wavelength that caused humans to adjust peacefully to the transition between night and day were missing in urban society. And basic research showed that under the artificial conditions imposed by electric light, even lab rats and gerbils became restless and unsettled.

How much better, then, for naturally unsettled people – like prisoners – to benefit from lux therapy rather than live under a regime governed by harmful artificial light . . .

No state in the US would fund a new penitentiary based on the ideas of Dr Millbank, so he applied for a private licence and founded his own prison, buying Huntsville cheap from the city of Seattle – which was delighted to offload its responsibility for a decaying Victorian masterpiece.

Dr Millbank's price was that five miles afforest and scrub around Huntsville should officially be declared a dark-sky preserve, with light-pollution strictly controlled within this perimeter. Heating was installed, lifts, carpets . . . a gym, a weights room, an Olympic-size swimming pool.

Huntsville wasn't just unique in being run according to the theories of

Dr Anthony Millbank. It was the only penitentiary in the US allowed to charge its inmates hotel fees. To be incarcerated at Huntsville cost money: about the same as sending a child to a good Ivy League university. Everyone loved the place, except the police. The state saved money on prisoners, those incarcerated mixed with a better class of criminal and there was none of the gang violence endemic in most other American prisons. The kind of people who belonged in gangs couldn't afford the fees.

It wasn't that the inmates were all white, all Anglo-Saxon or all Protestant. From the very start, right from the turn of the century, there was a rich mix of embezzlers, capi di capi and drug barons of every ethnic origin. The only thing they had in common was that they were all very definitely not poor.

Justifying the existence of Huntsville, however, proved a politician's nightmare. Democrats hated the prison's elitist credentials, Republicans loathed the softness of its regime: but when a senator from one party was caught bribing a congressman from another, Huntsville was where both elected to serve their sentences.

Statistics put inmate violence at almost zero and for once they were accurate. Violence happened, but not often, and violence between prisoners and staff was literally unknown. Which was why ZeeZee Welham's unprovoked attack on the elderly, white-haired Dr Millbank sent shock waves through every elegant Huntsville walkway.

Merely punching any member of staff would have been horrifying enough. But to grip Dr Millbank himself by his scraggy throat and drag him across his own desk to plant a blow that split his lip as if it had been a ripe plum was beyond belief. So far beyond belief that Dr Millbank announced on the spot that what ZeeZee needed was not punishment but psychiatric help. His words left a fine spray of blood across his attacker's tangled beard and broad chest, but even then he handed ZeeZee a Kleenex from a box by his desk.

It made ZeeZee want to punch him all over again.

All of which explained how ZeeZee found himself in the passenger seat of a Lincoln Continental coming off the 522 onto Interstate 5, with Lake Washington on one side and Puget Sound on the other, on his way to psychiatric assessment at a hospital in Tacoma.

The man driving him to Mount Olive Hospital was Clem Burke, a bull from a downstate prison who was undergoing compulsory rehabilitation at Huntsville after taking a nightstick to the skull of an inmate at his old jail. Making Clem Burke work as a warder at Huntsville was probably constitutionally illegal: he certainly regarded it as cruel and unusual.

'You know what I'd do with you?'

ZeeZee looked across as Clem swung the heavy Lincoln out into the fast lane and overtook an old Beetle, nudging so close that the VW got almost buffeted off the freeway.

'Let me guess . . .'

'Nah,' said Clem. 'Don't bother. You couldn't begin to imagine. 'He shifted down a gear and slid past a truck on its nearside, angrily flicking it the finger when the Mack hit its brakes and flashed its lights.

'This Shitville do-gooding crap. It's bullshit. You don't just hit the Governor and get away with it.' The Lincoln lurched forward, closing up a gap before anyone could pull into it.

'Rehabilitation not working, then?' ZeeZee asked innocently.

He enjoyed watching the veins stand out on Clem's fat neck and his face turn an even deeper shade of purple.

'Solitary,' snarled Clem. 'That's what you need. Stripped naked in a sweatbox; till you as pink and pretty as a baby. Then I'd give your ass to some Boss Nigra . . . That's what. That's the way any real prison would do it.'

A real prison probably would, too. But then, someone was paying ZeeZee's fees precisely to ensure stuff like that didn't happen. And ZeeZee had a pretty good idea where that money came from. A Chinese woman who knew who really put a .22 through the back of Micky O'Brian's head and watched him crumple as the sub-sonic slug ricocheted around the inside of his skull, scrambling what was left of Micky's brains after a $15,000-a-month crack habit had magimixed its share. And Hu San wasn't someone ZeeZee wanted to upset. Not now, not ever . . .

Mentioning her name in public would have been a quicker way of committing suicide than standing up in court to claim he'd killed Micky, he'd meant to kill Micky and, given half a chance, he'd kill Micky again. And which way should he go for the electric chair?

All of which would have been a lie.

ZeeZee kept his eyes on the interstate, watching the approach signs for SeaTac Airport and the other cars. Which was more than Clem Burke did.

'What do you think of that, then?' Clem asked. He was chewing the inside of his lip at the thought of ZeeZee pegged out in some sweatbox or on his knees tossing salad for a war daddy.

'Well?' Clem demanded.

'It's not going to happen,' said ZeeZee. At least, not now. He'd spent a lot of time in the remand centre worrying about what came next. Wondering what the rippers inside might have in mind for a polite blond boy with a nice English accent.

So he did his own attitude adjustment, before anyone else got the chance. Within a month his prissy accent was gone – still obviously English, but flatter and harder. He took up exercise in his cell. And then, when his shoulders had developed and his arms had grown stronger, he braved the gym. In the weeks that followed he let his hair grow, gave up shaving and stopped washing until his skin finally found its balance.

His life was a Xerox, a copy. And the original wasn't his. Never had been. He was a mirror, in which people saw what they wanted to see; and in him they soon saw a J-Cat, ready for the Ding Wing, walking the very edge of psychosis.

He took up tai chi – minus the sword, obviously. Volunteered to act as kick bag to a hard-ass elderly rasta with a thing for Capoeira. He learned ginga, rabo de arraia and queixada as well as esquiva and a few other basic defensive moves, but mostly he learned blade technique, though to the badges and white-shirts it just looked like dance. But then that was the whole point of a martial art which had survived by disguising itself as something else.

'Do your own time,' warned the rasta and ZeeZee did. He kept himself to himself, didn't pry, didn't boast, lost the fights he couldn't win or absolutely couldn't avoid, until one week he won, then won again, earning himself space. And when the rasta nicknamed him after some hick redneck band, ZeeZee took it as a compliment and waxed his own matted hair into embryo dreadlocks.

But as age nineteen slid into twenty and a date still wasn't set for his trial, ZeeZee kept on fretting, right up to the morning a suited lawyer turned up in his holding cell at Remand3 and put the basis of a cast-iron insanity plea in front of him.

It was elegant, it was sweet and all ZeeZee had to do was agree: but it was only when the lawyer mentioned 'ville that ZeeZee nodded and reached for a pen.

'I didn't kill anyone,' he told Clem suddenly.

'Yeah,' Clem hawked out his window, just missing the windscreen of a passing saloon. 'That's something else I'd kick out of you cons at Shitville. All that "Poor me, I'm innocent" shit. If you weren't guilty you wouldn't be there. How fucking simple do you want it?'

ZeeZee silently shook his head. In his case guilty didn't come into it. He was either innocent or mad, not that Dr Millbank used such words. Hysterically amnesiac was what had made it onto ZeeZee's files. He knew: the doctor had powered up a screen just to show him.

The insanity plea on offer was simple. ZeeZee couldn't be convicted of murdering Micky O'Brian because he didn't know he'd done it. His fingerprints might be on the Wilson Combat thrown down by Micky's body, they might also be on a couple of .22LR in its magazine and all over the conversion unit that had replaced the Wilson's usual .45 barrel, but ZeeZee genuinely didn't know he'd fired the shot.

Even though the police had found him in O'Brian's house overlooking Puget Sound, standing in the hallway with Micky dead in the gallery at the top of the stairs.

Every lie-detector test ZeeZee took came up clean, and he'd taken five, three of them in sterile-lab conditions. He'd had CT and MRI and, according to the expert witness lined up for his trial, the scans revealed fear and anxiety but absolutely no guilt. At the demand of the police, he'd undergone full hypnotic memory-recall. He recalled nothing.

The defence was simple.

ZeeZee believed he was not guilty, except all the evidence said he was. Ergo, to use his lawyer's phrase, he was innocent through insanity. Except that ZeeZee knew the lawyer realized that wasn't how it went. ZeeZee might not be guilty but he wasn't insane. Insanity would involve naming Hu San.

'Hey!' ZeeZee nodded at a black pick-up only inches from the front of Clem's Lincoln. 'What gives?'

'Asshole won't pull over.'

'Look,' said ZeeZee, drawing his knees up into the brace position. 'We're in the slow lane, Chief. Where's he going to move?'

'That's not my problem,' Clem announced, but he edged back slightly. And just as ZeeZee was about to sigh with relief, Clem hit the gas again, lurching the Lincoln straight into the back of the pick-up. Metal shrieked and locked, and then the Lincoln twisted sideways, did half a revolution and came to a halt on the hard shoulder fifty yards later. Fifty yards in which ZeeZee sat in the passenger seat aware he was going down the interstate, backwards . . .

Very sensibly, the pick-up truck kept going, dragging the ripped-off remains of a Lincoln's bumper behind it in a flashy display of sparks.

'Jesus,' said ZeeZee when he could say anything at all. 'You trying to kill me?'

'No,' said Clem. 'Nothing that simple.' He fished in the car's glove compartment and came out with a matt black Para Ordnance .45 – the 15-round, police-issue model.

ZeeZee didn't register the make, finish or calibre. He was too busy looking at the void of its muzzle, which pointed straight at his head.

'This is where you escape,' announced Clem. 'And over there's where you run, towards that nice big sign saying Flight Departures.'

'And just about here's where you shoot me in the back,' said ZeeZee, nodding to a spot ten paces from the car.

'No,' Clem shook his head as he leaned across and shoved open ZeeZee's door. 'I'm retiring and you're my pension plan.' Reaching under his seat, Clem yanked out a briefcase. 'The combination's your DOB.' He grinned sourly. 'I don't want to know what's in here. Just make sure you open it well away from my car . . .'

'Who's paying you?'

Clem didn't know, but he had no intention of admitting that to ZeeZee.

'Tell me,' ZeeZee insisted. What with remand, taking the plea and developing his designer mad-fuck persona, he'd put a lot of effort into staying alive.

Clem pulled back the slide on the Para Ordnance.

Stay and get shot, run and ditto. It had been a day full of shit choices. But what really scared ZeeZee was that the whole wired-out scenario had Wild Boy stamped all over it and ZeeZee didn't trust Hu San's deputy. The Boss – now, she'd have done it differently, smoothly.

'I'm not going unless you tell me,' ZeeZee said, slamming shut his door. No one tried to escape from Huntsville because no one could afford to. A bond was posted prior to arrival. Any attempt to escape automatically forfeited the bond, which was a multiple of the number of years in the sentence times a sliding scale according to the severity of the crime and the perp's previous . . . Killing a police informant – ZeeZee didn't even want to think what his bond would have been set at.

Unless it really was Hu San organizing this, busting out of Huntsville was just a quick way to commit suicide. Marginally less dramatic than standing up in court to name the woman. But only marginally . . .

'Your choice,' said Clem, raising the automatic. He was smiling.

The briefcase was retro Alessi, with a numerical lock and little purple LCDs that glowed through black glass: Fooler loops were built into its sides and the handle housed a semi-AI whose sole job was to inform airport scanners that the contents were covered by diplomatic protocol.

Holding his breath, ZeeZee started counting to ten in his head and lifted the lid. He reached seventeen before he realized he could stop now. His initial haul from the case was a plane ticket, a white passport and a strip of photos from one of those Kodak booths found at stations. The smiling girl in the shots was young, dark-skinned, middle Eastern. Four different poses, but each frame showed the same wide-eyed teenager.

ZeeZee flicked open the ticket and scanned the details. All the real data was encoded in a strip running along the outer edge of the front cover: the printout inside was just a reminder. It was made out to Ashraf al-Mansur, OA-273 flight to Cairo, with a connecting flight to El Iskandryia, taking off—

In about fifteen minutes, according to ZeeZee's watch. He checked the passport and blinked as his own face stared up at him, only shaved and without the dreadlocks, surrounded by a sea of unreadable foreign type.

That the photograph had him wearing a suit and tie he'd never seen before was weird, but what really weirded him out was the simple English phrase across the top of each page.

Everyone had heard of diplomatic immunity.

In a small pocket in the lining of the lid was a platinum HKS, with a holo of his face on the reverse, stamped over with a mesh of laser thread. Finding the card was enough to make ZeeZee ransack every slot, pocket and zipped compartment in the case but he discovered nothing else, except a crumpled Mexican quality-control slip and a torn sachet of silica gel.

The check-in desk for the flight had already closed but ZeeZee stared round in such obvious distress that a girl two desks down trotted off to get an Ottoman Airways official.

'I'm on flight OA-273.'

'I'm sorry, sir, your gate's closed.'

'But I have . . .'

'It shut twenty minutes ago.'

Mutely, ZeeZee thrust his ticket at the American woman who took it with a frown, as if actually touching the thing might commit her to something. She flicked back the cover to glance at the counterfoil, then looked at ZeeZee: taking in the blond biker beard and beeswaxed dreadlocks, the pale blue Huntsville jumpsuit and tatty trainers.

'Something wrong?' ZeeZee had trouble keeping the anxiety out of his voice.

Yes, there was, but not in the way he meant. Counterfoils were discreetly colour-coded for priority, to avoid bouncing the wrong people off over-booked flights. The scale ran green up though red. ZeeZee's ticket was coded gold.

'Can I see your passport, please, sir?' Her face was white with hostility.

She didn't even bother to take the small booklet ZeeZee tried to hand over. Instead, she made sure her fingers didn't touch his as she handed ZeeZee back his ticket.

'I'll see what we can do about stopping the plane.'

He was waved through Security, which was probably just as well. And then a black kid with three gold nose rings hurled ZeeZee through the crowds filling Departures, horn beeping as ZeeZee gripped tight to a rail that ran around the back seat of the little electric buggy.

'Man, I love that,' announced the kid as he slammed to a halt.

'Some ride,' agreed ZeeZee, clambering off.

'Yeah.' The driver did as near to a skid turn as he could manage with an electric cart on the carpeted floor of an embarkation tunnel. 'A rock god in a hurry. It's the only thing makes my life worth living.'

Once aboard the *Alle Volante*, ZeeZee was shown to his cabin. A tiny cubicle with a shower stall, chair and the kind of double bed that might just fit two people if both were fashionably thin and intended to spend most of the flight on top of each other. For one person it was ideal.

The catalogue of duty-free goods was the same as it ever was – full of overpriced and ugly items that probably seemed a good idea at the time. ZeeZee skimmed through a dozen screens, adding to his basket a shirt, combats, new shoes, a silver Omega, a black G-Shock and hair clippers, along with a choice of complimentary medical kit that came free because he'd racked up more than $2500. He chose number three, which claimed it was essential for tropical emergencies and came with malaria patches, surgical glue, unbreakable condoms and a generalized snake-venom antidote.

When the screen asked for payment ZeeZee fed it the number on his new card and in reply got a smiling cartoon valet who assured him all the goods would be delivered within five minutes.

Halfway across the Atlantic, ZeeZee turned up the screen again and found a local Seattle newsfeed. Any reference to his own escape had been relegated to non-news by the murder in Kabul of the mujahadeen general Sheikh el-Halana.

ZeeZee knew all about Sheikh el-Halana: the whole world knew. Two weeks back, fundamentalists had bombed the Ottoman consulate in Seattle, killing thirty-five and destroying the consulate, its computers, its listening centre and most of its records. The FBI had spent twelve days saying nothing, then announced there was little likelihood of getting enough evidence to convict. And now, two days after that announcement, the man widely suspected of being behind the bombing was dead.

Somewhere on the outer edges of ZeeZee's tired brain a plan began to gel. Reaching for the complimentary in-flight notebook, he scrawled seven words on the first page, crossed one word out, added another two and circled them all individually before joining them together with a rapid flurry of lines. His next identity now had a little flesh on its bones.

CHAPTER 13

When Ali-Din was bored he peed on the tiles. Hani didn't have that option. She wasn't even allowed to visit the lavatory when Aunt Nafisa had company. She wasn't allowed books and she certainly wasn't allowed her Nintendo gamepad.

'Wiping up Ali-Din's puddle with her shawl, Hani screwed the sodden cloth into a bundle and stuffed it under her chair for Khartoum to find. Hani was bored, too, and lunch hadn't even started. To make things worse, it looked as if lunch might not start for ages. Ashraf was late and everyone was pretending they didn't mind.

Well, she *did* mind, she minded a lot . . . Aunt Nafisa had forced her into a dress and kept at the knots in her hair until Hani's scalp hurt.

The woman Ashraf was going to marry didn't look that happy, either. She was prettier than Hani had expected – dark, though, with black hair cut so short it probably didn't need to be brushed at all. She wasn't wearing a proper dress, either . . . just a long scarlet coat with baggy trousers underneath. There were three holes in one of her ears but no earrings in any of the holes.

Zara caught Hani staring and forced a smile. Instantly the child snatched away her glance, then looked back. When Hani married it was going to be to a pasha, rich and handsome, Aunt Nafisa had promised. Ashraf was a bey, which was almost as good, but he looked weird. Aunt Nafisa said that was because he'd been doing secret work for the government. And no, Hani wasn't allowed to ask him about it.

Everyone in the *qaa* was sitting on silver chairs, except for the big man leaning against a pillar. Probably he was worried he might break his if he sat on it. The chairs were classically French, made a hundred and fifty years earlier when Third Empire was what families like theirs had wanted, so Aunt Nafisa had told her.

But instead of the cabinet maker covering each chair-back with walnut

62

veneer, he'd finished the entire frame – legs, back and sides – with a tissue-like sheet of beaten silver. And the matching chest of drawers, divan and semi-circular occasional tables had their own share of similar ornamentation. All of the madersa furniture on display in the public rooms was *haute* Third Empire, refracted through Ottoman eyes. It looked ugly to Hani but she'd learnt to keep that opinion to herself; although she suspected her aunt agreed.

'Sorry . . .' Steps rang on the marble stairs leading up to the *qaa* and Hani forgot furniture at the same moment as she stopped being bored.

'Ashraf!' Lady Nafisa's voice hovered between fury and thinly disguised relief that he'd shown at all. Smoke had been twisting up from the kitchens for at least an hour. And while Nafisa's cook Donna might have been spit-roasting a goat over an open fire of juniper twigs, Hani's money was on something in an oven beginning to burn.

'I'm sorry,' said Raf, looking round the *qaa*. 'I was at my office.'

'On a *Saturday*?' Hani snorted, not bothering to disguise the disbelief in her voice. Even she could lie better than that.

'He went to his office.' She hooked Ali-Din up onto her lap and rubbed her nose in his fur, ignoring her aunt's scowl. It said something about how determined Aunt Nafisa was that things should go smoothly that she didn't immediately order Hani to take the puppy outside.

'Yes,' said Raf. 'And then I walked home.'

'Doesn't look far on a map,' growled a voice Raf knew. 'Rather different against the crowds.' Hamzah Effendi left his place at the balustrade, wrung Raf's hand heartily and retreated back to his pillar.

'Lady N doesn't like it,' he said, waving a fat cigar. 'Nor does my wife. Don't blame you going to the office. Probably the only place you can get some peace. Still,' he said, 'you're here now and that's what counts.' Dropping his cigar to the floor, Hamzah ground the butt under heel.

Lady Nafisa tried not to wince.

'My nephew, Pashazade al-Mansur, Ashraf Bey,' she said to a short thickset woman loaded down with more gold than the federal reserve. 'His father is the Emir of Tunis.' Lady Nafisa sounded as if she was selling a horse at auction.

'Ashraf, this is Madame Rahina . . .' It was obvious from the shock on the fat woman's face that her husband hadn't warned her about Raf's beard or dreadlocks.

'. . . And you know Dr Hamzah Quitrimala Effendi, who owns HZ Oil . . .'

'Bloody hard work,' said Hamzah, tapping a fresh cigar from a leather case that looked like it should contain shotgun shells. 'Pity you took that job at the Third Circle. Could have done with a good man on board. God knows, Kamil's never going to be up to—'

Both Lady Nafisa and Hamzah's wife suddenly found something else to talk about, so Raf never heard who Kamil was or what he wasn't up to. But from the frown on the face of Federal Reserve and the quarrelsome expression of Hamzah Effendi himself, Raf guessed that, whoever he was, they argued about him a lot.

'And this is my daughter,' said Madame Rahina hastily. 'She has a very good job at the New Alexandrian Library.'

'We've met,' said Raf.

Madame Rahina looked at him in shock.

'Four days ago,' said Raf, talking to the girl. 'On a green tram. Going south, heading for Rue Derida. You were carrying flowers.'

'It can't have been Zara,' Madame Rahina said firmly. 'She stayed over with a friend in Abukir. They both caught the most terrible food poisoning.'

'Then I must be wrong.' Raf peeled off his glasses and dropped them in his pocket. 'Still . . .' he shrugged, 'I'm surprised there are two such attractive girls in El Iskandryia.'

Zara shot him a look that mixed relief with outrage and her mother smirked. But it was Hamzah Effendi who spoke. 'Nasty stuff, food poisoning,' he said, looking at Zara.

'It's disgraceful,' said Lady Nafisa firmly from her end of the table. 'Completely disgraceful that we let immigrants mutilate each other in the name of *RenSchmiss*. I've written to General Saeed himself and asked him to complain to the Khedive . . .'

She glanced to her right, as if daring Hamzah to argue. There was no fear the person sat to her left would disagree. So far, Madame Rahina had nodded fiercely every time Lady Nafisa opened her mouth.

The big man just shrugged, though from his position at the other end of the table Raf couldn't tell if this was because Hamzah couldn't be bothered to argue or because he genuinely didn't concern himself with Germans.

'What's *RenSchmiss*?' Hani asked.

The table went very still.

'I'll tell you later,' Lady Nafisa said, in a voice that meant she wouldn't.

'I want to know *now*,' Hani demanded. She dipped sticky fingers into a bowl of warm water and rose petals, shook them dry and sat back. Everything about her said she wasn't going to rest easy until someone had answered.

'*Hani*,' said her aunt.

'Well?' The small girl tugged Raf's sleeve and when he shrugged she turned to Zara. Hani could put up with Ali-Din being banished while they ate but didn't see why she had to put up with not understanding what everybody else was talking about as well.

'You tell me.'

Zara smiled as she dipped her own fingers in a rose bowl and shook them. 'Have you seen those gashes German boys have on their cheeks?'

Hani shook her head.

'We think it looks ugly but it's tradition for them,' said Zara. '*Renommer schmiss*, the scars prove their bravery. When boys like that get to about fifteen, they go to a gymnasium, put on special jackets, helmets and metal goggles. And then they stand absolutely still, while an opponent slashes open their face . . .'

'Zara wrote a paper on it at Columbia,' Madame Rahina said hastily.

'Not to be encouraged,' Lady Nafisa said. She might have been talking about *RenSchmiss* but her comment could equally apply to letting girls go abroad to college. 'Cousin Jalila and I have also sent a letter to *El Iskandryia* demanding the practice be banned.'

'We also have our traditions,' Zara said quietly, 'ones which they could call—'

Lady Nafisa set her mouth into a straight line. 'No,' she said. 'There is a difference between barbarism and the medical demands for a healthy life.'

Hani giggled. The mention of healthy living had brought a smirk on her face. 'You know where my Aunt Jalila goes?' she whispered to Raf when he bent to listen.

He shook his head.

It involved hoses and bottoms.

Lunch was in the *qaa*, at an oval table cast from marble dust and inlaid along the top with swirling Persian-blue tesserae arranged as a peacock displaying its tail. Matching benches curved down both sides of the table. Only Lady Nafisa had a chair.

The main part of the meal was goat, split open and spit-roasted until the flesh was so tender no knife was necessary and hot mouthfuls could be pinched off between finger and thumb. Two French waiters from a local café carried the dishes from the kitchens, Lady Nafisa having promised to pay what they demanded, provided they wore their uniforms from the café and the uniforms were clean.

Food as politics and food as blackmail: both theories had been regurgitated more times than anyone could remember. But food as an elaborate dance, somewhere between etiquette and preening display, that was new to Raf. Though not to Isk, where the conspicuous consumption – not of rich or rare ingredients, though both were there – but of time itself was as ancient as the elaborate laws governing hospitality.

Time given was what was on display.

In Isk, just as in Tunis, Marrakesh or Fez, ceremonial food required preparation: the more preparation, the greater the respect being offered to guests. Tradition also demanded that ingredients be divided into small portions, wrapped in filo or hidden beneath pastry in pies, rolled in crushed nuts or stuffed into vegetables that had been lovingly hollowed out or cored. Food bought at a stall or fast-food joint was different. No one expected Burger King to be anything other than cheap, swift and anodyne. But in the home, it was almost an insult to offer guests food that looked as if preparing it took anything less than total commitment.

Served with the roast kid was a silver-edged clay bowl of saffron rice, plus a dish of red couscous, a chicken tajine where the juices had been sweetened with honey and reduced to a sticky syrup, fried red mullet with marjoram, and fresh matlou bread, which Lady Nafisa asked Raf to break and portion out in order of precedence. Hani got her chunk last, being both female and a child.

All the recipes chosen were classically Tunisian: which was to say that they were really from Andalusia, carried to North Africa when the defeated Moors finally retreated from Spain in the fifteenth century. Except that Andalusian cookery had originated in North Africa in the first place, having been taken to Spain several centuries earlier by the armies of Islam. Its complexity of flavour a response by Islamic cooks to the new ingredients they suddenly found surrounding them.

Lady Nafisa had decreed the cuisine be Megrib to remind everyone of Ashraf's heritage. And every dish relentlessly reinforced the fact. Even the fried *brieks*, small paper-thin pastries stuffed with vegetables, eggs or chicken, were a Tunisian staple. Raf's aunt was making sure Hamzah appreciated exactly what he was getting. A genuine Berber princeling, a real bey.

If Hamzah hadn't decided to talk up his own end of the bargain, then disaster wouldn't have struck; but he did and so it began, with a compliment from the girl's father.

'She's a good kid,' Hamzah said firmly.

'Dad.'

'She doesn't make a fuss. Doesn't cry over stupid things.' He paused. 'Actually, she doesn't cry at all. Gets wound up occasionally, like girls do. Usually over animals or children. Stuff that can't be changed . . .'

Zara snorted.

'You don't agree?' Raf asked. 'That things can't be changed?' He only meant to make conversation but it was obvious from Madame Rahina's sudden silence that she didn't think he'd like Zara's answer.

'What's to agree?' said Zara. Her slate-grey eyes came up to meet his and for the first time that afternoon she didn't blink or look away. 'And what does it matter if I believe things can be changed or not? In Iskandryia, daughters don't have opinions . . . Or rights.'

'Zara.' Her father sounded more concerned than angry.

'No rights?' Raf's voice was gentle. 'Why not?'

'Tradition,' said Zara bitterly. She stood up from the table. 'You see Dad's case over there?' The briefcase was Calvin Klein, black crocodile skin. 'That contains ten per cent of my dowry. You get a further fifty per cent when we marry, minus whatever your aunt's already had for expenses. The remainder you don't get for twelve months.'

From the surprise on Raf's face it was obvious he hadn't known money was involved at all.

'Twelve months . . . ?'

'Apparently that's meant to stop you beating me.' Zara stepped away from the bench. 'Well, for the first year, at least . . .' She turned to her father. 'I'm sorry. I need to get some air.'

'*Go after her*,' Raf's aunt hissed as Raf stood watching Zara go.

'And say what?'

'Anything you like.' Lady Nafisa was almost shaking with fury. 'All girls get nervous before their wedding. Make something up. Tell her whatever she wants to hear.'

Raf nodded. 'Okay,' he said. So he did.

As soon as Raf saw Monday morning's newsfeeds, he tried to ring Zara. But she wouldn't take his calls. Raf knew she was at Villa Hamzah because the butler who answered made no pretence of her being anywhere else. The girl just didn't want to talk to him.

He kept calling and by that evening the butler could recognize Raf's voice without him having to give his name. But she still wasn't taking his calls.

'No luck,' said Raf and tapped his watch strap, breaking the connection. He was in the *qaa*, his back to a wall. And it was obvious from the anger twisting Lady Nafisa's face that she'd dearly have loved to have him lifted bodily, carried to the edge and tossed to the flagstones below. Hani had been slapped and sent to the haremlek for nothing more than being there when Lady Nafisa finally and completely lost her temper. So

67

far, Lady Nafisa had tried ordering and begging, now she was trying moral blackmail.

'You've ruined her. You know that, don't you?' Fury and three arguments had worn Nafisa's voice to an ugly rasp. The first had begun as Madame Rahina stormed out, dragging Zara behind her. The second took place the following day, when Raf angrily told his aunt there were no circumstances under which he would marry the girl. And finally there had been today's, the third and worst.

Raf skimmed the evening paper she'd just handed him. The compulsory box-out on page two featured General Koenig Pasha's new crackdown on smuggling, with separate pix showing the young Khedive, the General and sunrise over Western Harbour. General Koenig Pasha's was the biggest picture by far. The rest of the paper was filled with what interested Lady Nafisa.

'Oil heiress jilted . . .' The story wasn't going to go away. That morning's Zaghloulist tabloid had been more upfront, less pleasant. *Dumped dumpy* read the kindest comment. Above it an unflattering and outdated grab showed Zara in a voluminous swimming costume, aged about fifteen, all expanding chest and puppy fat. The fact she no longer looked anything like that was nowhere mentioned.

'Do you realize what you've done?' Lady Nafisa asked furiously.

Raf sighed. Her question was entirely rhetorical. He'd tried several times to explain himself but Lady Nafisa wouldn't even let him reach the end of a sentence.

'She's disgraced,' said his aunt. 'Unmarriable. You think anyone in El Iskandryia wants your cast-offs?'

'She's hardly a cast-off,' Raf said angrily. 'Besides, her father's worth millions.'

'Billions,' Lady Nafisa corrected him without even thinking about it. 'That's not the point. No one who matters will marry her now.'

'Maybe she doesn't want to marry *someone who matters* . . .' Raf said between gritted teeth. He put as much scorn into the words as possible. 'Maybe she doesn't want to get married at all.'

'That's not how life works,' said Lady Nafisa. 'You know nothing about it.'

'No.' Raf tossed the paper onto the marble floor. 'You're right, I don't. But I don't like what I've seen so far.'

'And I suppose you prefer prison?'

'To this?' said Raf. 'Yes, I do.'

That wasn't entirely accurate. There were brief moments when Raf looked out along the heat-hazed sweep of the Corniche and El

Iskandryia felt bizarrely like home. But liking or not liking Isk wasn't Raf's big problem. His problem was Hu San and Wild Boy. They would be looking for him and when those two went looking, they found . . . All Raf had going for him was they didn't yet know where he was or who he'd become. Which meant Raf needed to keep on being Ashraf al-Mansur the way he needed to keep breathing. And, unfortunately, it looked like the two states were inextricably linked.

Disappear into the night?

That was a definite possibility. Isk was full of foreigners running bars, brothels and dubious businesses, doing the work pure-born Iski regarded as beneath them. The only flaw there was that Lady Nafisa would undoubtedly call the police. It didn't matter what version of the truth she told them. She was *someone who mattered*: they'd find him.

Killing her or staying close were his safest options, maybe his only options. Either way, he kept ahead.

'Ashraf?' The question was a whisper.

He spun, fast. 'How the fuck did you . . .'

Wide-eyed, Hani held up her hands so he could examine the grease smeared across her palms, then lifted her arms to show the oil smeared down the front of her flannel pyjamas. 'It's a bit slippery,' she said seriously. 'It gets easier when you've done it a few times.'

Like using the glass sword in *Dragon's Bane III* or writing your own level for *Imperial Assassin*. Hani didn't really seem to distinguish between what she did on screen in her nursery and what she did in life, it was all real. Sort of . . .

Raf said nothing. Telling the child that climbing wires was dangerous wasn't his job and besides, judging by the stubborn glee in her eyes it would have been pointless anyway. The danger was precisely why she did it.

'You off to feed Ali-Din?' he asked eventually.

Hani looked at him with a new respect. 'That too,' she admitted. 'But I also came to see you.'

'Well, here I am,' said Raf.

'They work like speaking tubes,' Hani said, pointing towards the lifts. 'Stand at the top and you can hear everything . . .' She paused to consider what she'd just said 'That's why we should whisper . . .'

'I'm whispering,' mouthed Raf and Hani giggled.

'Stupid.'

'Yep,' Raf glanced round the silent *qaa*. 'You're probably right.'

'Why were you in prison?'

To answer or not to answer. 'For killing someone.'

Hani looked appalled, shock swallowing her small face as she

69

struggled for something to say. And then she relaxed slightly. 'They must have done something very bad.'

'No,' said Raf. 'They just talked too much.'

'And you killed them?'

Raf shook his head. 'At least, I don't think so. But I got the blame.'

'That's not fair.'

'No, it isn't.' Raf smiled. He could remember when he too used to believe in 'fair,' right up to the day he'd been driven, aged five, through the gates of a Swiss boarding school. And he'd kept wanting to believe. Making excuses for the arbitrary beatings, cold baths, sly hands, the randomness of lesser punishments . . . He was seven the first time he ran away. The last time was the day before his eleventh birthday, but that was from a different school. Out of five attempts, three were briefly successful.

In the end, his brain had to admit what his gut already knew: there was no justice, no fairness, only rules. Those who used, twisted or kept to the rules got by, those who didn't were marked down as enemies of order. It was a very thorough training. 'Emotional institutionalization' was how Dr Millbank described it.

And in his own fashion Raf had been keeping to rules ever since. What was his taking the fall for Micky O'Brian but playing to the rules of the world in which he found himself?

'Aunt Nafisa said you were a spy,' Hani said, tugging his sleeve. 'Spies kill people. It's their job.'

'*Assassins* kill people,' said Raf. 'Spies collect secrets.' But Hani wasn't listening. She was already working out another justification in her head.

'If it was your job,' she said, 'that would make everything all right.'

CHAPTER 14

Lady Jalila rolled sideways off the couch and wrapped her gown tightly round herself. Her stomach was cramping and she wore the tension in her neck and shoulders like a heavy body cast. It hadn't been an easy final half-hour.

'You know where . . .'

She nodded abruptly at the slim Greek woman and walked hurriedly from the consulting room to the lavatory next door, squatting just ahead of a spasm that emptied her bowels in a long squirt of almost clear water. That final ritual was as much a relief as it was undignified. Lady Jalila could put up with the anal speculum and lying on her side with her knees pulled up and buttocks exposed as gravity forced water into her colon and out again, emptying her lower gut of faecal matter. She could even stand those five minutes of intolerable pressure towards the end, when a warm herbal infusion replaced cool water and Madame Sosostris locked a crocodile clip round the tube to keep the infusion inside.

It was the uncontrollable gripe in her gut immediately afterwards that upset her. Those few seconds between the couch and the lavatory pan when she feared she might disgrace herself.

As for the rest of it, Lady Jalila made a point of never considering how she looked when she was on that couch or what the Greek woman thought of her endless visits. The beneficial effects of cleansing were too valuable to give up. And though she knew her husband the Minister didn't really approve for a number of reasons, none of which included the substantial cost of her frequent visits – she could handle him. Literally, if that was what it took.

Better.

Sighing, Lady Jalila squatted again, double-checking that her gut really was empty. It was. As empty as her abdomen was flat and her stomach just slightly, attractively curved. Even her hips looked thinner now that her colon was no longer a sausage stuffed full of poisonous waste.

If only all life's complications could be flushed out that easily.

Wrapping the paper gown tight about her, Lady Jalila returned to the consulting room of the relentlessly old-fashioned third-floor clinic set between Nokrashi and Rue Tatvig, in a not-at-all-salubrious area of El Anfushi.

She'd been the first to discover Madame Sosostris, back when the herbalist was pulled in for questioning. In those days Lady Jalila had been just plain Jalila, a uniformed recruit in the *morales*. Recognizing someone useful, she'd amended the arrest sheet from performing abortion to practising unlicensed female circumcision and kicked Sosostris free with a warning. Two months later, she'd gone looking for the woman with a search warrant in one hand and a business proposal in the other.

Now everyone Lady Jalila knew came to the clinic – even Coroner Mila, the new City Magistrate for Women, who usually regarded matters faecal as being beyond mention, like sex.

Lady Jalila smiled sourly. Everybody fucked. The coroner-magistrate just withheld her approval because Lady Jalila didn't bother to hide the fact.

'All done, then?' asked the Greek woman, looking up. Tall, hipless and small-breasted to the point of clinical androgyny, Madame Sosostris had the body most of her clients secretly craved, whether or not they realized it. Her very shape gave them a target at which to aim. A reason to keep coming.

'Then I'll let you dress . . .'

Madame Sosostris always waited for the client to return before leaving them to change back into their clothes. Of course, Lady Jalila was more than just a client. She'd quickly become Madame Sosostris's dear friend and ally, an invaluable patron for a woman practising therapies not entirely approved of by Islamic mullahs. Her husband was Mushin Bey, Iskandryia's Minister for Police, respected deputy of General Koening Pasha himself.

Madame Sosostris left the room at an elegant glide.

Next Tuesday, decided Lady Jalila climbing into a white CK thong that no longer felt tight round the hips. That was when she'd visit next. She shuffled her full breasts into a sports bra and looked round for a mirror, forgetting there wasn't one. Though it didn't matter: she'd still be thin enough to check her shape in the glass when she got home for lunch, after she'd dropped in to check on Nafisa.

All in all, a good morning's work. Her white jacket now clung in the right places without bulging in the wrong ones and the matching silk skirt hugged her hips without wrinkling. Lady Jalila wore white because white went with her swept-up blonde hair and her husband liked clothes that emphasized the difference in their age. Thirty-one might be old enough for all of her friends to have large families but to the sixty-five-year-old Minister of Police it seemed positively childish. But then Mushin Bey still thought of her as the seventeen-year-old she'd been when she first joined the women's police force. All blonde hair, blue eyes and innocence.

Lady Jalila pushed her feet into a pair of Manolos, then picked up the Dior bag that contained her credit cards and smiled.

Long may it remain so.

Lady Jalila let herself into her cousin's madersa, frowning at the door Khartoum had left unguarded. Nafisa always had been slack with her house boy.

The glassed-over knot garden was hot as a steam bath, bringing Lady Jalila out in an instant flush. She knew her cousin claimed not to be able to afford air-conditioning except in her own little office. But what was the point of owning a famous garden if it was uninhabitable for most of the summer?

'Nas?' Lady Jalila used her pet name for Nafisa.

Nothing.

Passing the *liwan* with its cooling marble slab now dusty and dry, she stepped out into the open courtyard and stopped to breathe deeply. Early July in El Iskandryia was often humid and hot, but nothing like as cruel as that covered garden.

'Nas?'

The silence was complete. A lack made deeper by the absence of running water in the courtyard in front of her.

Lady Jalila started to climb the *qaa* steps, hearing her heels ring on the stone slabs. Cousin Nafisa didn't approve of Lady Jalila's kitten heels: they made scars in the marble. At the top of the stairs, she hesitated. To her left was the large tiled expanse of the *qaa* proper. While straight ahead was the cubicle of Lady Nafisa's office, cool and air-conditioned, created by filling space between arches with sheets of smoked glass.

That was where Lady Jalila went first . . .

'I don't care who he's with. Tell him I'm at the al-Mansur madersa and I need to talk to him *now*.' For once Lady Jalila didn't have to raise her voice. The urgency in her tone was obvious even to his idiot PA and, seconds later, her husband's worried face flashed up on her tiny silver Nokia. As ever, he looked just like a small startled rat.

'What's . . .'

'Wait,' said Lady Jalila suddenly, snapping off the camera option on her mobile. Something silver and sickening had just caught her eye. Let him read about it or look at the crime-scene photographs later if he must. Nafisa dead with her blouse ripped open – there were some things she didn't think her husband needed to see.

'Nafisa's been murdered,' said Lady Jalila.

'Nafisa?' His horror was absolute, obvious. There were several things the Minister clearly wanted to say. But he said none of them, contenting himself with a simple 'I'm so sorry.' He glanced beyond the edge of her screen to a group of people she couldn't see and waved his hand, dismissing them. A muted question filtered into her earbead and she heard her husband's grunt of irritation. 'Tomorrow,' he said crossly. 'It can wait.' And then she had his full attention again.

'How did she die?'

'She was stabbed . . . with her pen.'

Lady Jalila heard him punch buttons on his desk. 'Don't touch anything.' That was the policeman in him speaking. 'I'll get my best man onto it now.'

'Mushin.'

The anger in her voice stopped him dead.

'You really don't get it, do you?' She didn't care if all his calls were taped or not. Or what his PA thought when the little tramp typed up that day's transcripts. 'Nafisa was stabbed with her pen, understand? She wrote that letter and someone stabbed her.'

He understood now. She could see that from the sudden tightening of his jaw.

'You know who else signed that letter,' said Lady Jalila. 'Don't you?'

He did. He knew only too well.

She had.

'I want you to put Madame Mila on this case,' Lady Jalila said fiercely. 'It's an attack on our values.' By 'our,' she meant women's.

The Minister's lips screwed into a tiny moue of irritation but he nodded. 'I'll do it now,' he promised.

'Good,' said Lady Jalila and punched a button on her Nokia, consigning her husband's rat-like feaures to a flicker, then darkness.

CHAPTER 15

New York

It was ZeeZee's childhood therapist who first suggested that, since the small boy had hated his time in Switzerland and New York obviously didn't suit him, the best answer might be to find him a place at a specialist boarding school in Scotland.

So, four months after he first arrived in New York, the child who would become ZeeZee left again, at the suggestion of a therapist that ZeeZee knew, even then, he didn't need. And the boy knew why he was being sent away too. He kept fusing the man's neural-wave feedback machines . . .

The next time ZeeZee arrived in America he was eleven. The Boeing had come in low over Long Island and sank onto the runway at Idlewild in a simulation-perfect landing. It was the first time ZeeZee had ever flown in an Alle Volante. He travelled executive-class with his own tiny room, and though the cubicle walls were veneered from a single peel of Canadian maple and his bed had a frame made from the same extruded magnesium alloy found in Japanese racing bikes, the cubicle was still no bigger than the inside of a small van.

ZeeZee hadn't minded about the size at all. After a term in a dorm with nine other boys – the largest of whom thought Welham *sounded enough like* wanker *to be interchangeable – the privacy and silence of his cabin was enough to make him drunk with the luxury of it all.*

There was a stewardess who arrived every time he pushed the button, and who smiled and didn't mind because he was travelling on his own and looked just like she thought English children were meant to look – blond and blue-eyed, the way they did in films.

The fact he wore grey flannel trousers and a cotton shirt with a striped tie helped fix the image in her mind. As did his thick tweed jacket, which he called my coat. *His shirt even had links at the cuff made from Thai silver, with tiny dancers embossed on their black domed surface.*

The stewardess let the boy be first off the plane, passing him into the care of a second attendant, who smelled strongly of roses and took him straight to baggage reclaim.

'Is that all you've got?' she'd asked, examining the single case he pulled from the executive-class carousel.

He nodded. There was no point telling her the case was almost empty and he'd only brought the thing because leaving it behind would have been rude. The case was a leaving present from his tutor's wife.

'Over there,' he'd said suddenly as they walked into the Arrivals hall. Beyond a vast wall of glass stood a line of white Cadillacs on the slip road outside, their drivers standing by open doors while inside the hall excited families waved frantically. ZeeZee waved back.

'I'll be fine now,' he said firmly and thrust out his hand.

Any fleeting doubt the attendant might have had lost out to the novelty of shaking hands with a serious, immaculately polite eleven-year-old boy. 'If you're sure,' she said.

'Of course.' ZeeZee sketched her the slightest bow.

The woman with the warm scent smiled and shook her own head in disbelief. 'Okay,' she said, 'enjoy your stay.'

'It's not a stay,' ZeeZee said seriously. 'This is where I live now . . .'

CHAPTER 16

6th July

Felix felt like a candle melting.

He was tired, he'd had his holiday cancelled and he'd been at the al-Mansur murder scene just long enough to confirm that a woman was dead, there was a traumatized child sat wide-eyed in one corner of the *qaa* and the Minister's wife, who'd apparently called in the crime, was missing from the scene itself . . . And just when it looked like his afternoon couldn't get worse, some dreadlocked trustafarian in shades and a stupid suit came hammering up the *qaa* steps, puffing like a lunatic.

'Hold it,' Felix barked.

'I live here,' announced Raf, stopping to glance at the fat man blocking his way. From the rye on the man's breath to his thinning hair gone grey and tied back in a lanky ponytail, the man had 'American cop' written all over him. Which was weird, given this was North Africa.

'Prove it . . .'

Raf had left his office at a run, over-tipped a cab to jump two lights and pounded straight through Nafisa's knot garden, leaving shredded shrubs behind him. He'd made it from office to steps in five and a half minutes. Obstruction wasn't what he needed right now. Instead of stopping, he began to squeeze between the fat man and the door frame.

A finger jabbed his chest. 'Identity papers,' the man demanded. Even speaking bad French he had an air of authority – derived from more than just age or experience.

Raf hated him on sight. So he made quite sure he got in the first move.

Faced with having his knuckle rupture or stepping backwards, the man retreated with Raf still twisting the offending finger. Some of the moves Raf had learned on remand were so simple a child couldn't screw them up. That was the idea, anyway.

'Ashraf . . .' Hani's shout meshed with a blur of movement, the cold click of metal and the touch of a police-issue revolver to Raf's head. Very slowly, Raf let go of the man's finger and stepped back.

'You know this person?' the cop asked Hani, sounding disappointed. As if that somehow meant he wasn't allowed to beat his target to pulp.

Hani nodded, eyes wide. 'That's my new uncle.'

'Identity papers,' the man said. His left hand kept the Colt pushed against Raf's skull while his right reached for the card Raf extracted from his inside jacket pocket.

'Fucking terrific.'

Definitely American, Raf decided, watching the man return his revolver to its hip holster. First language Brooklyn, second Arabic, third very bad French. Which was one better than him.

'Colonel Pashazade Ashraf al-Mansur . . . *Pashazade?* Your dad's a fucking Pasha?'

Your dad. Now there was a concept with which to conjure.

'No,' said Raf, grabbing back his Third Circle laminate. 'He's the Emir of fucking Tunis.' Stepping round the fat man as if he wasn't there, Raf knelt beside Hani.

'You all right?'

'No.' She nodded towards an open door. 'Aunt Nafisa . . .'

'Don't let the kid go in there,' said the man heavily. 'Don't touch anything. And don't even think of getting in my fucking face.' With that he stamped his way downstairs to tape off the crime-scene entrances before anyone else decided to appear.

It took Raf nearly a minute to spot the platinum pen rammed hard between her ribs, its metal end protruding beneath one breast like a witch's third nipple; but then he was stood in an open doorway, on the other side of a rustling strip of police tape that had been hastily strung across the door.

'Shit.' There didn't seem much else to say. And besides, it was hardly the first corpse he'd seen. All the same, it was his aunt, supposedly, and he was surprised at how unmoved he felt. The wound was ugly, the small office was a mess. That was it.

'They murdered her,' whispered a voice behind him and when Raf looked back Hani was there, eyes vast as she stared up at him.

'Who did?'

'The foreigners.'

Somewhere inside Nafisa's office a lavatory flushed, a lock clicked open and before Raf could react an almost-elegant blonde stepped into the tiny room, still wiping her mouth. The door she'd used was hidden behind a Persian rug that hung on the wall from a wooden pole. Except the pole wasn't really attached to Nafisa's office wall: but to the top of a door. Behind her came the sound of a cistern filling.

'Lady Jalila,' said the woman, introducing herself.

'I'm Raf.'

'Yes, I know . . .'

They stared at each other in silence. She'd done a good job of cleaning herself up but the scrub marks on the front of her white jacket didn't quite hide vomit stains. And she very carefully avoided stepping anywhere near the desk as she crossed the dead woman's office.

Her composure held for as long as it took the child behind Raf to turn on her heel and clatter away down the *qaa* steps. Lady Jalila looked startled.

'You let Hani see this?' The woman's voice was suddenly brittle, her hands shaking. To Raf it looked like the onset of shock.

'No,' said Raf. 'That was you.'

Lady Jalila shot him a puzzled look.

'You were obviously here first,' Raf added.

'I imagine that I was in Nafisa's loo being sick when Hani appeared.' Whatever else Lady Jalila intended to say was lost in a sudden tread of heavy feet below.

'Up here,' she barked. But Felix had got there first. The two uni-formed police officers were halted in the courtyard, listening intently to whatever it was the fat man wanted to say.

'Hey, Boss,' said the younger, when Felix finally stopped talking. 'Control said to tell you you're showing up as offline . . .'

'His Excellency?'

Both uniformed officers nodded as one.

'Felix here,' the detective announced, flicking a switch on his watch and then punching a button. Other than that, he said nothing for the next few minutes, just turned a deeper shade of red. 'Yes, sir,' he said when the call was finishing. 'I'll make sure she gets every courtesy extended. And, yes, I'll remember it's easier for you if I don't turn off my connection.'

'My Lady.' When Felix looked up to where Lady Jalila stood staring down into the courtyard, the politeness in his voice was at odds with the contempt in his eyes. 'The Minister thinks it might be best if you went straight home.'

'Does he indeed . . .' Lady Jalila headed for the *qaa* steps, nodding for Raf to follow.

'Presumably he's sending a car?'

'No,' said Felix. 'He's sure one of these officers will be delighted to drive you. That is, if you don't mind travelling in a squad car?'

Lady Jalila sighed heavily. 'If I must.'

'So all I need now,' said Felix, 'is to know when it would be convenient for me to call on you . . . ?'

'On me?' The woman stopped in her tracks. Her voice made it sound as if Felix had suggested they book into the nearest Ramada for a quick afternoon of bestiality and child abuse.

'There *has* been a murder.' Felix glanced from Raf to Lady Jalila and then at Hani who was coming out of the kitchens with Donna in tow. What he thought about having his crime scene littered with a bey, children, cooks and the wife of his boss was obvious, if unprintable.

CHAPTER 17

Seattle/New York

The third time ZeeZee arrived in America he was almost sixteen and his previous trip was a memory he didn't take out of the box and dust down too often. It had begun badly and gone down hill from there . . .

There'd been no waiting stretch limo that earlier time, no one to meet him, not that the small boy had expected either and not that he minded. And besides, he'd proved quite capable of catching a Carey Bus and unloading his almost empty case outside Grand Central. He ditched the case in a gash bin on 42nd. There was nothing inside except a school coat and he didn't need that any more.

The yellow cab he stopped to take him to the apartment his mother was borrowing on the Upper East Side parked illegally while he ran inside to get the fare. And when he discovered his mother wasn't home, he borrowed the $10 from a uniformed doorman and was vaguely surprised when the elderly black man assured him that his Seiko automatic wasn't needed as security for the loan.

It seemed she'd remembered to tell the front desk that her son would be sharing the apartment, even if she hadn't remembered to meet him at the airport.

By the time his mother came home, he'd found a room he assumed was his – from an almost-new copy of Vampyre Blade III *and an old Sony console – and had a long shower, eaten a slice of cold pizza from the fridge and slept right through to the following morning.*

She came in as he was cooking toast under a grill he could hardly reach because whichever designer her latest friend had employed hadn't factored eleven-year-olds into his equation. But then, the apartment wasn't designed as living space, more as a public statement of identity. And even the kitchen was bigger than his old dorm and it was only a fifth of the size of the new living room, where one complete corner had been ripped right out and replaced with glass to look down on Central

Park. ZeeZee figured that when she borrowed the flat, she must have forgotten he hated heights.

The living-room fireplace was machine-cut from some grey stone he didn't recognize and along both of its sides stretched elegant steel shelves packed untidily with master disks of her trips and large, tattered books full of her photographs. Other disks and books were crammed sideways into the narrow gaps above.

Rugs, oil paintings and an antique leopard skin completely covered the other walls, but those didn't belong to her. On the floor itself, newspapers competed for space with empty plates, glasses and half a dozen camera bags that did . . .

'Darling. How good to see you.'

She held a pair of shades and wore a crimson scarf tied over hair that needed washing. Her black jeans and jersey looked like they'd been slept in, except that one look at her eyes told him she was too wired to have slept in days.

They had both smiled, slightly tentatively.

'You found it, then?'

ZeeZee nodded, then went back to cooking his toast, leaving her to make conversation.

'I've booked you into a school,' she said. 'It's over on the other side of the Park. There's a prospectus around here somewhere.' Her black-nailed hands fluttered at a clutter of papers covering the sand-blasted steel kitchen table. 'You can start when you want. I hope it will do . . .'

He looked at her then.

She shrugged. 'They took a year's fees up front.'

While his mother took a shower and then fixed herself a line, ZeeZee set up the reconditioned Sony console. He got as far as skimming the 'read me' before he realized there wasn't a television in his room to plug the console into. Moving the huge TV from the living room into his bedroom seemed impractical, as did moving himself and his bed into the living room, so he decided to worry about it all later and instead took a lift down to the foyer to see the doorman.

What ZeeZee remembered most about that year with his mother was watching screens with Max the doorman. Inside Max's office was a bank of video monitors linked to hidden CCTV cameras in the foyer, lifts, corridors and parking bay. The cameras were chipped for sound but Max liked to watch them with the volume turned down. Creating stories for the people he saw.

By the end of the first month, ZeeZee's mother was just one of a dozen characters ZeeZee and Max watched lock up their doors, then promptly check their hair, cleavage, teeth or waistlines in corridor mirrors. ZeeZee *learned which men were going into flats they shouldn't be going into. He saw elegant women kiss men who weren't their partners. He watched an Italian girl who didn't even know he existed hurriedly change her tampon in a lift, secreting the old one neatly in a tissue. And he stayed glued to a monitor as two drunks screwed on the hood of a black Cadillac in a corner of the underground garage, even though one of them was his mother and the other the man who lent her the flat.*

ZeeZee made it to the end of the year and then did what he'd always said he wouldn't do, went back to Roslin in Scotland. Neither he nor his mother really discussed it. Life just happened that way, as if all the necessary conversations had already been had and all that remained was to fix the ticket. It was hard to know which of them found his leaving the greatest release.

CHAPTER 18

The crime perimeter was secure, no press were present and a junior detective was out on the sidewalk, trying to determine the perpetrator's entry and exit routes. So far without success. Lady Jalila had gone and Felix was busy trying to persuade Raf to do the same.

Below them, guarding the bottom of the *qaa* steps, was a tall young man with the flawless skin of a Nubian and the upset eyes of a recruit not yet grown used to death. The young uniformed officer had given a length of tape to Hani, who was twisting it endlessly so that sunlight caught a holostrip of lettering which read *EIPD – do not cross*. As she flipped the tape back and forwards, making it sparkle in the hot sun, the child looked almost happy.

Felix shrugged. Kids weren't his area and the idea wouldn't have occurred to him. True enough, he had a daughter in Santa Fe. Only Trudi lived with her girlfriend, three tabby cats and a gun under her pillow; the last time he'd seen her she'd probably been younger than the kid sitting by the fountain playing with the tape.

These days his daughter had cropped hair, a razor-wire tattoo that wound up her arm from elbow to shoulder and nipples pierced with silver spikes, one tiny spike going across and the other down . . . He knew about those because her last but one Christmas card had a picture of her and Barbara on the front, taken at a Gay Pride barbecue in San Francisco. They were stripped to the waist and holding bottles of Bud. Only the bottles were closer to their button-flied groins than they were to their mouths and Barbara had pierced nipples too, linked together by a chain.

Trudi looked hot and tired, so he'd written back saying he hoped she was taking vitamins and that if she had to go out like that in public he hoped she was wearing lots of sun cream. That earned him a postcard of a tram. Only three scrawled lines on the back but one of them was her new e-address. They wrote to each other now, not often but a couple of brief paragraphs once every few months. And she sent him more photographs of herself, fully clothed this time, with one of the cats sitting on her lap.

There'd been a time of no photographs at all, when Trudi was in her early teens and her mother was going through a religious phase, if that was what you could call moving state and announcing to her new neighbours that no, she wasn't divorced, her husband was dead. It had taken the ghost cancelling her alimony for five months to start the pictures flowing again. Before they did, he got a stiff letter from her attorney to which he'd had his own reply in Arabic. The photographs had restarted pretty soon after that.

'It would be best . . .'

'No,' said Raf. Not waiting for Felix to finish the sentence. There were a number of reasons why he didn't want to leave the crime scene and go back to his office, only one of which he could tell Felix.

'I can't just leave Hani.'

That, at least, was true. Without Lady Nafisa the girl was a scrawny nothing. She wasn't pretty, she was way too young to be married off and, anyway, the kid was without a dowry. She had to be: Iskandryian law said girls couldn't inherit in their own right. So unless Lady Nafisa had left everything to a favourite charity someone other than Hani was going to inherit and the chances were it was him. And that wasn't what Raf wanted either.

A murder, money, the recent appearance of an unknown heir. Arrange into a winning combination . . .

Before the murder, *RenSchmiss* was just one middle-aged woman's obsession. Now it would be debated in drawing rooms and cafés across North Africa.

If the fat man wanted to keep talking about *Thiergarten* killers, that was fine with Raf but he knew what conclusion most people would draw from the evidence. And that was before he factored the press into account. The press were there to service the newsfeeds, which meant pictures, syndicated to local feeds all round the world, including Seattle.

Raf sighed.

The beard, hair and any thought of polarized contacts would have to go and the shades make a long-term reappearance. It was just a pity he didn't have time for a completely new face to go with his new name and nationality.

'I'll stay . . .' He held up one hand, stopping Felix in his tracks. 'Lady Nafisa was my aunt . . .' He was about to say something crass, like *duty demands it*, when the other man's mobile started beeping.

It kept beeping while Felix searched his trouser pockets and finally tracked the watch down to his jacket, which was upstairs in the *qaa*, slung over a silver chair.

'What?' Felix demanded. He made no attempt to keep the irritation out of his voice.

The Minister was on the other end again. Raf knew that from the way the Chief of Detectives suddenly straightened up, pausing mid-stride. One hand came up to smooth his hair, thick fingers once again slicking sweat across his scalp.

'Yes, sir. I'm glad your wife got home safely. I sent one of my best men with her . . .' If the Minister noticed the criticism implicit in the words it didn't stop his list of questions.

'Exactly when did it happen?' Ripping aside the tape that closed off the study door, Felix walked over to the dead woman's desk and half closed her paper, making sure the sticky pages didn't actually touch. It was the midday edition. 'So far all I can say is that it happened after twelve noon,' said Felix. 'Yes,' he said, 'I *can* state that categorically.' Felix listened to the next request and shook his head, sending sweat trickling down the bridge of his nose.

'No, Your Excellency. I don't think we should turn the site investigation over to Madame Mila.'

'Yes, I know the General is . . .'

'No, I'm not . . .'

'If I can just . . .'

'Yes, he's still here . . .'

It was a one-way conversation after that, Felix's protests fading into silence, broken only towards the end when he nodded abruptly.

'Whatever you want, sir . . .' Felix tapped a button to end the call, scowled balefully at his watch and stabbed a switch that put it back on standby.

'You should have got out when you had the chance,' he told Raf. 'The Minister wants you as my official witness.'

'Which means what?' Raf asked, pushing back his own hair. The wind that seeped in through the smashed mashrabiya was hot and sticky, and Nafisa's precious air-conditioning unit would probably have been reaching meltdown, if someone hadn't already ripped its thermostat from the wall, leaving wires trailing.

It might have been Raf's imagination but he was sure her body had already begun to smell.

'What does it mean? It means you stand in that doorway and watch me commit professional suicide. You don't come in the room, you don't interfere and you definitely don't talk while I'm working. Understand?'

No, he didn't. 'What am I witnessing?' Raf demanded.

'Me. While I do this.'

On the marble table where Lady Nafisa had given her lunch for the parents of Zara bint-Hamzah, Felix dumped a battered leather case with reinforced corners and a webbing strap to hold the top tight shut. The words on the strap read *Property of the LAPD – do not remove without authorization*. Yanking off the strap, Felix waved his hand in front of something that might have been a human head, had it not been made of clear perspex and filled with jumbled electronics. Chunks of crystal memory had been crudely glued to the back.

Its eyes briefly lit red.

'Meet Dr Dee,' said Felix. From the other side of the case Felix pulled a battered camera, a Speed Graphic digiLux so old it had a separate flash unit and came minus a removable memory dump, which was where Dr Dee came in . . .

'First off, I'm going to sweep the scene, do crime-scene shots, then body shots. And finally I'm going to examine the body . . . Your job is to see I don't plant or remove evidence and that I don't molest or defile the woman's corpse. You got any problems with that?'

Silence.

'Good, then let's get started . . .' Felix slid out his hip flask, flipped its lid and downed the flask in one. 'Beats holding your nose or saying prayers every time,' he added sourly, noting Raf's undisguised shock.

Only when Felix was certain that the tiles directly in front of him were clear of clues did he lie flat and sweep the floor with the beam of a tiny maglite. Two blouse buttons showed up immediately, both near the wall. Other than that, there was only debris from the mashrabiya. Lady Nafisa had been as fanatical about outer cleanliness as she had been about the inner kind.

'Why aren't I surprised?' Felix asked, but he was talking to himself. Lifting both buttons using tweezers, he dropped them straight into separate evidence bags, carefully dating and labelling each bag.

It took him no more than fifteen minutes to take positioning shots, with another ten for body shots and five for close-ups of the wound itself. In that time he stopped twice to drink from a second flask and when that ran out he calmly switched to a third and used that instead.

Perspiration rolled from the fat man's face as he worked, and the air around him stank of whisky and sour sweat. But never once did he stumble or even look drunk. He just snapped off each shot, checked the quality on the little screen at the back of the Speed Graphic and moved on, looking for the next angle, his next shot. He had a professional's tolerance for the drug of his choice. Raf had seen it before, up close and way too personal, every single day of the year he had spent in New York with his mother.

CHAPTER 19

Seattle

Hitting America aged fifteen was different. So different as to be unforgettable in a life where everything was unforgettable. No flight attendant held his hand on the trip out and he travelled regular, legs cramped into a tiny gap between the edge of his seat and the sloped chair-back of the passenger in front.

Next to him sat a black-eyed girl wired into a Sony Dance-Master, the thud of Hold Me Down *hissing from earbeads as her long fingers danced over the touchpad of a Nintendo to an entirely different beat. She smelled of toothpaste and a cheap powdery scent. Beyond her was a window seat, empty except for a Tibetan bag with an untouched magazine poking out of the top.*

ZeeZee desperately wanted to ask if she'd mind if he took the window seat but didn't know the words . . . It wasn't that she didn't speak English. She did. Confidence was his problem. His school outside Edinburgh was strictly single-sex. Which meant tarting the smaller boys was a regular pastime for most of his year: talking to girls wasn't.

PanAmerican called the seats regular but most of the regular passengers were further forward, drinking free vodka shots and eating complimentary cashews while watching Hollywood's finest on the screen in the wall of their bunks.

The seats at the rear of the Boeing were for students, casual workers, girls hoping to find work as nannies: the kind of people who didn't travel often, bought their own tickets and couldn't believe just how few US dollars they got in exchange at the bureau de change. Not that ZeeZee had forked out for his own seat.

Providence had paid for it.

Providence in the form of a man in the Lyons Coffee Lounge at Heathrow who walked away from his table and forgot a leather pouch he'd put on the chair beside him. Until then ZeeZee had been running away to Paris to find bar work. By the time the man hurried back to where he'd been sitting. Zee Zee's plans had changed and Seattle was in the cards, almost literally.

While the man filled out a form to reclaim his pouch from Lost Property, where ZeeZee had left it, ZeeZee was off buying dollars from a FirstVirtual auto-teller in Arrivals, using a deposit card he'd extracted. Selling half those dollars back to a different machine in Departures took him a minute and gave ZeeZee enough paper money to buy a cheap, one-way ticket to Seattle-Tacoma. He had to show the girl at PanAmerican his permanent US visa. But once she'd swiped his passport through a reader and the visa came up valid she was all smiles, even when he bought the cheapest stand-by she had.

The deposit card he flushed away in a men's room on the way to his gate. Some kind of warped morality made him buy a cut-price ticket. And it was only after take off that he realized the owner would just claim a full card against insurance and ZeeZee could have travelled first if he wanted.

'You wanna borrow this?' The girl was holding out her magazine, one hissing earbead carefully cupped in her hand where she'd half unplugged herself from the music. He didn't recognize the accent.

'Hold Me Down,' ZeeZee said, nodding at the bead, 'the ice-hot FP remix . . .'

She looked at him then. Glanced, without realizing it, at his white shirt and grey trousers. He'd ditched the jacket and striped tie but nothing could make what he was wearing anything other than what it was, half a school uniform.

He didn't mention that he only recognized the mix because some jerk in his common room had downloaded the Belize Sleez compilation and had played it to death.

'End of term?' she asked.

ZeeZee shook his head. 'Just had enough.' He took the offered magazine and was surprised she didn't immediately pull away when his fingers accidentally brushed her hand.

'What about you?' ZeeZee tried to make it sound like he always talked to strange girls on planes.

She smiled and named some city he didn't recognize, except to realize it was probably in the neutrality corridor between the Soviets and the Berlin alliance. 'I've got a student visa,' she added, 'but I intend to find work in Seattle. You don't know anywhere?'

He didn't, but she still told him her name and lent him a spare set of earbeads, toggling the DanceMaster onto split so they both got the full mix. Twenty minutes later, when the lights dimmed and an attendant came round with covers and all the couchettes tipped back, ZeeZee and Katia ended up under the same blanket.

The blanket was PanAmerican blue, logo-laden along all edges, with holes all over to trap air. It came vacuum-wrapped in foil and it was only after they had both struggled to rip open her packet that Katia discovered the easy-release tab.

'Dumb,' said Katia and ZeeZee smiled slightly nervously. He kept on smiling as he pulled the single blanket over both of them. And if Katia noticed his fingers shaking she didn't let him know. Instead she just rolled onto her side, facing away from him, and curled up with her head rested on her arm.

'Listen,' she whispered.

So ZeeZee did.

The new track was like nothing he'd heard before. A young boy's voice soared in a language he didn't recognize above a famine-sparse synth line that bled into a gull's cry and ended with a softly building loop of whale song. Bhagavad Gita. Not his taste, but it went with the yin/yang tattoo on her wrist and the grey titanium stud piercing the bridge of her nose.

Settling down, the girl shuffled herself backward until her bare heel just touched ZeeZee's ankle. And it seemed natural, somehow, for him to rest one hand on her leg and gently stroke the brushed surface of her chinos, feeling her warmth beneath as he moved his hand in time to the music.

When she didn't complain he kept going. And the next time she shifted, he suddenly found it easier to reach the seam that his finger had been tracing along the inside of her knee.

'That's neat . . .'

He wasn't sure that was what she actually said, but he muttered agreement anyway and shifted his fingers higher. He didn't quite have the nerve to trace the seam all the way to the top, so he settled for smoothing his hand gently up over her hip.

'No.' She tensed as his fingers reached the softness of her very slight stomach, only to breathe out again as ZeeZee hurriedly moved his hand, finding instead the swell of one breast through her thin green T-shirt.

She wore no bra.

She didn't move and nor did he, seemingly flash-frozen to the spot. Then, infinitely slowly, she moved his hand softly, letting her suddenly erect nipple write a line of fire across his palm.

ZeeZee started to breathe again.

Gently he reached under the cloth of her T-shirt to find a breast that was full and warm, smooth to the touch. Close to, her long dark hair smelled of resin and oil, unwashed and almost animal.

91

'God.' ZeeZee sucked in his breath as he found her nipple with his thumb and first finger.

'Softly,' she said over her shoulder and he nodded, even though he knew she couldn't really see him.

Much later, when the Boeing was halfway across the Atlantic and most of the other cabin passengers were sleeping, ZeeZee smoothed his hand back across her hip and ran his fingers gently up that seam. And only the fact she opened her knees slightly told him that she wasn't also asleep.

One button fastened the band of her cheap chinos and the fly was a simple nylon zip, nothing fancy or expensive like tiny straps, toggles or invisible velcro. Katia couldn't afford designer clothes, even if they'd been available in whichever unpronounceable city it was she came from.

Terrified she'd say no, ZeeZee began to ease the zip, as if undoing it extra slowly meant she might not notice. Then he popped the single button at her waist. When she still didn't protest, he let his fingertips creep gently down her abdomen, reaching for the waist-band of her knickers. What he found was tight body hair, then dampness and finally heat.

Katia wore nothing underneath, not even a basic thong . . .

She wouldn't look at him when the cabin lights came up. Her jeans were already buttoned and zipped, her T-shirt smoothed down. She'd rearranged both herself about an hour earlier, just before she drifted into sleep.

ZeeZee was more relieved than hurt by her sudden distance and put the earbead he'd borrowed politely but silently into her hand. Despite himself, he was grinning as he left the Boeing.

He was fifteen. He'd never yet kissed a girl – but he'd had one tighten frantically around his fingers and then, when her gasps were safely swallowed, push her hand back into the waistband of his trousers to squeeze until her wrist was sticky with his release.

Seattle was definitely the right place for him to be.

CHAPTER 20

'Guard the door for me,' Felix told Raf, resting his Speed Graphic on Lady Nafisa's desk and pulling a foil packet from his hip pocket. Ripping open the foil, he pulled out what looked like a large condom, shaking it between first finger and thumb until a tissue-thin glove was revealed.

'Surgical,' Felix told Raf, ripping open a second packet. 'Nanopore latex, anti-static. I get them from the hospital. The standard-issue stuff round here is crap.' Felix shrugged. 'I could always change manufacturers, but they're probably paying kickback to the Khedive's second cousin . . .'

'What am I guarding against this time?' Raf asked as he watched the man struggle to force his thick fingers into the tight gloves.

'The coroner,' said Felix cryptically and knelt beside the seated body. With his fingers out straight, he ran his right hand over Nafisa, never quite letting his fingertips get close enough to touch either flesh or clothes. It was as if he was feeling for something that wasn't there.

Taking his tiny maglite, Felix swept its beam across Nafisa's skin as she sat in the chair. 'No fibres, no animal hair . . .' He was talking to his watch, to Raf and to the weird back-up device in the room outside, but mostly he was talking to himself. Getting himself ready for the bit the coroner wouldn't like.

The leather case Felix took from his pocket contained a Saez scalpel, the old-fashioned titanium-edged kind, a handful of glass thermometers, tiny combs, surgical swabs and glass holding tubes that could freeze themselves. He only planned to use the first two.

Lifting the edge of Lady Nafisa's skirt, Felix checked the dark bruises on her buttocks and lower thigh.

'Obvious lividity . . .'

He pushed the bruising and watched the skin go pale beneath his

93

fingers as the blood that gravity had pooled in the tissue moved aside. Within another couple of hours that would be fixed in place.

'. . . lividity still blanches.' That confirmed his time frame.

All he needed now, for thoroughness, was a core temperature reading. The simplest way of getting that was to use a rectal thermometer, but Felix knew better than to even consider the idea. Instead he reached for his Saez scalpel, moved the skirt higher still and punched his scalpel through the skin of Nafisa's abdomen. Extracting the blade, Felix took a surgical thermometer and worked it deep into the tiny wound. Ninety seconds later he broke the red tag off the top of the thermometer to fix the temperature and withdrew the sliver of glass and silicon, dropping it into an evidence bag, which he initialled.

A human body lost roughly one-point-five degrees an hour, depending on surrounding temperature. The reading was within the limits he'd expect.

'Initialling postM wound . . .'

Using his pen, Felix drew a circle around the wound on Lady Nafisa's abdomen, signed his initials and added the date and time. The coroner-magistrate would have a fit about it, there'd be another strong memo to the Minister mentioning desecration of the dead and Felix would get told not to do it again.

Again.

To which he'd reply, as he always did, that if he wasn't allowed to use the orifices that Allah provided, then he'd have to make his own. As yet Madame Mila hadn't come up with an answer to that . . . Mind you, she hadn't forgiven him either.

'Toxicology report . . .' Slamming a sterile plastic reservoir into a syringe, Felix picked a vein in Nafisa's wrist and drew blood, circling and initialling the puncture mark. Let them complain about that, too.

The corpse felt warm through the latex of his glove as he lifted a breast to examine the pen buried beneath it. He felt for the edge of her ribcage and then counted up, already knowing what he was going to find.

'Penetrating wound to chest, between third and fourth . . .' The blow was perfectly placed to puncture her heart. And it was a single stab wound, highly professional. Amateur assassins often missed. Suicides left hesitation cuts, little lacerations and half-hearted weals while they jabbed or slashed at themselves to see how much it was going to hurt.

No defensive wounds were present to indicate that Lady Nafisa had even tried to fight for her life. Yet this was a woman notorious for fighting for everything she considered her due.

Lifting her right hand to recheck unbroken skin between the woman's thumb and first finger, Felix almost hissed with irritation. 'No defensive cuts to finger web, nor across palm or wrist . . .' He stopped, turned over the hand to look at her nails. The cuticles were still manicured and immaculate, that morning's lacquer as dark and glossy as a blood trickle but the nail ends were badly chipped and ripped back, all of them.

If she'd been a girl locked in a cellar to starve to death, then that was what he'd expect her fingers to look like at the end of the first day, before they stopped being something used to scrabble at a locked door and became food instead. And it did happen, even in El Iskandryia – but only among the poor, out in the slums, to daughters and sisters who hadn't been as careful as their fathers or brothers expected. It didn't happen to the middle-aged and rich.

Besides, her office wasn't a cellar and her door had been found open.

Felix shook his head, thought briefly about starting his fourth hip flask, the emergency one, and rejected the idea. Every year new morality laws made his life that much more difficult. It was hard enough being Nasrani in a North African city, even worse to be so obviously fat and pink in a country full of elegant Arabs, rugged Berbers and sophisticated Levantines. And his own Catholicism might now be almost residual, but it still made for difficulties in an Islamic metropolis where a male officer wasn't supposed to touch a female corpse.

But then, this was a city where the police test for rape in the outer boroughs was to sit the victim on a rough wooden stool to see if she squirmed with pain. If she didn't, she hadn't fought back and it wasn't rape. Most fought back. Many died rather than submit. Not surprising when most *felaheen* still chose to kill their daughters for being disgraced rather than kill the rapist and risk starting a blood feud.

Screw it. Felix took the swig anyway, aware without looking that the nail of the thumb he used to flip up the top was bitten to the quick, just like all his others. He'd have to go back on the *Sobranie* soon, whatever the medics said about ghostly shadows haunting his lungs. Logical deduction was hard enough without self-inflicted nicotine withdrawal.

So what had he got?

At first glance the attack appeared frenzied. But any attacker in a real frenzy would just have punched the pen straight through whatever clothes Lady Nafisa wore, which meant the open blouse signified some-thing. Unless, of course, what it signified was not frenzy but passion, and the stabbing came later, when the widow's defences were down.

That wasn't an avenue Nafisa's cousin Jalila or her husband would want explored with too much thoroughness . . . Or any thoroughness at all, come to that, Felix decided sourly as he listened to the sound of heels clicking regular as a metronome across the courtyard outside. That would be Lady Jalila's friend, the new coroner-magistrate.

Felix waited for the sound of her and Hani's footsteps on the stairs. Then, when they didn't come, he tuned out the distant chatter of Hani's voice and went back to examining the body, using his last few seconds of peace to search for anything he might have missed. Something obvious.

There was a tiny stigma right in the centre of her left hand, a dark crater-like indentation that bled slightly along one edge. Significant? Possibly. He grabbed a shot anyway and hurriedly thrust the dead woman's hand back in her lap where he'd found it. Then Felix smoothed the skirt down round her knees and stepped back. He left the blouse as he'd found it, torn open at the front. He didn't want anyone saying he'd been messing with the evidence.

'Chief Felix . . .' The coroner-magistrate's greeting was borderline polite, but brittle. 'No one told me you'd be here.'

'Didn't they? Then you've been talking to the wrong people.' Felix took his time to straighten up, rolling his heavy shoulders to ease their stiffness. And then, when he could put it off no longer, he turned to face the ebony-skinned woman who stood glaring from the doorway.

Madame Mila. Her hair pulled back, her nails worn short and unvarnished, her black trousers and coat cut from local cotton, not even off the peg but off the shelf from Wal-Mart.

Word was, Madame Mila dressed simply because of her job. Felix's view was that she'd dress like that no matter what job she did.

'We've done everything according to regulations,' said Felix. 'His Excellency here is my witness to that . . .'

The woman raised her eyebrows but didn't bother to reply. Instead she stepped over to the body and touched her finger to the throat of the stabbed woman, checking that there was no pulse.

'Dead,' she announced. Felix nodded. The official time of death was now, not when Felix estimated she was killed but when the death was formally recorded by a medical officer.

Carefully, Madame Mila closed the open blouse. Then she stooped for the tissue-thin modesty shroud Felix had earlier discarded and spread it over the dead body. Only after that did she turn back to the door, nodding for Felix to follow her.

'Body's released,' Felix said to his watch. Formalities complete, the corpse could now be removed and the fingerprinting brigade sent in. Felix took a last look round the crime scene, a token glance for anything he might have missed.

'Chief . . .' The voice was unnecessarily impatient.

'What?' Felix demanded. 'What's your problem this time?'

'The pashazade.'

'Using him as my witness was the Minister's idea,' said Felix flatly. 'You got a problem, take it up with Mushin Bey. Ashraf and I are out of here.'

Madame Mila shook her head. 'He goes nowhere,' she said. 'At least not with you. As of now, he's under arrest. Suspicion of murder.' She tightened her grip on the shoulder of the small girl stood beside her. 'And this is *my* witness.'

CHAPTER 21

Red on white inside, grey on grey without, where the Pacific beat on jagged rocks and gulls circled like sailors' souls over a stark concrete bunker that made the work of Mies van der R look soft and fluid.

Micky O'Brian lay inside on a white silk carpet that cost $340 a square yard and could only be ordered over the web from Beijing, cash in advance. Outside, through a long window that ran the length of his precious fast-floor art gallery, gunmetal waters could be seen lapping the shore of Puget Sound. Drizzle made the sky as dull as the sea and reduced visibility to a few hundred paces.

The jetty in front of Lodge Concret was bare. A thin strip of factory grating held above the rocking waves by anodized posts. The clinker-built pleasure boat that should have been there was long gone. So was a Matisse nude, a Christo abstract and one of the most important early works of Cézanne still to be in private ownership . . . Farmhouse at Auvers had been painted in 1873, the year after Cézanne moved to Pontoise to be close to Pissarro.

White on red.

Seepage from a bullet hole in the back of Micky O'Brian's head had formed its own abstract, more Rorschach blot than Rothko. A vivid red splash that would fade to black as blood soaked into silk and eventually dried. There was a message in the colours, and the message was that the man wouldn't be testifying to anything.

At fast glance it looked like Micky was grabbing a nap, half curled on his side in slacks, gold slippers and a Chinese dressing gown with a five-toed Mandarin dragon on the back. But that was only at fast glance. His wide-eyed glassy stare told a different story. One that ZeeZee picked up only in fragments, as he checked the long gallery and found it empty of any killer, with its picture lights turned down to 'dim' and a still-chilled bottle of Mumm Cordon Rouge open on a side table.

There were macadamia nuts and chilli olives in little bowls alongside the bottle. An open but untouched box of Partegas corona had been placed nearby, along with a neatly rolled spliff placed ostentatiously on a silver ashtray. A very Micky O'Brian touch. The air in the gallery was heavy with scent from a huge vase of black tulips. Debussy drifted from flat wall speakers. Clair de Lune *or something similar. Something lightweight, in keeping with Micky's acting abilities.*

The visitor Micky O'Brian had been expecting was ZeeZee. But someone else had definitely got here first.

ZeeZee carefully put the fat manila envelope he'd been delivering on the arm of a white leather sofa and considered his options. He could call the police or he could just leave, quietly and quickly. Returning the way he'd come, on the back of his 650cc Suzuki. And why not? He now had no one to meet. No reason for being there.

'Shit.' ZeeZee picked up his envelope and headed downstairs, the Debussy nocturne looping in his head. He made it as far as the sandblasted glass front door before someone yelled his name.

'Hey, ZeeZee . . .' The amused shout came from behind him. 'Going somewhere?'

He turned to see two bulls he knew in SPD jumpsuits flanking a woman who wore a black Chanel suit, black shoes and Shu Uemura makeup. Not that she needed it: even naked, her face would have been flawless, her eyes bright, brown and hard as glass. He had no idea who she was.

All he knew was the woman had to have practised that contemptuous, deadpan stare. It was too convincing to be real. The grins on the faces of the uniformed officers were something else entirely. Certainly not real smiles, more grim-faced got-you-you-bastard kind of expressions.

'Micky O'Brian . . .' ZeeZee began, breaking the silence.

'Yeah,' said the woman. 'Why don't you take us to meet him?'

'He's . . . When I got here . . . I didn't know . . .'

She looked at ZeeZee without saying anything. Just waited until his words stumbled to a halt and then kept waiting while the English boy skidded around in his head for the right approach to take to what was about to happen – and realized there wasn't one.

'Don't tell me,' she said finally. 'You got here a couple of minutes ago and found the front door open. You knocked but no one came, so you went inside. And guess what, you found Micky O'Brian shot through the skull . . . Or was it the throat?'

'A head shot,' ZeeZee said, without thinking.

The two uniformed officers looked at each other. As if that only confirmed what they expected.

'And you were on your way to call the police?'

99

ZeeZee nodded.

'So why didn't you use the hall phone?' The woman nodded to a Sanyo fixed to the wall by the front door, its screen black but one diode flashing lazily in the lower left corner, to signal the system was set to standby.

'I didn't see it,' said ZeeZee hastily. 'I was too shocked.'

'Which is why you were whistling . . .' She hummed back at him the main motif from Clair de Lune. *'I can see the headlines now. The whistling hit man . . .'*

'I haven't killed anybody,' ZeeZee protested.

'Of course you haven't,' she said sourly. 'So why don't you come and show us the person you didn't kill?'

Micky O'Brian's body was where he'd left it. The blood seemed a little darker, Micky a little more obviously dead. Other than that, walking into the gallery could just have been a bad attack of déjà vu.

'So you found him lying there like that?'

ZeeZee nodded.

'And you touched nothing?'

He shook his head, then hesitated.

'Yes?' she said, drawing out the word until it ended with a hiss.

'I touched the wine bottle. To check how cold it was . . . And I turned off the music.'

'How thoughtful of you.'

'But I didn't touch anything else. I didn't kill him. And I didn't take the paintings.'

The detective flicked her gaze to a blank space on the wall. Then back to the body. So far none of them had checked Micky for a pulse. But maybe they'd decided it wasn't necessary, given the very final expression on his face.

'So you're trying to shift the blame to an accomplice, right? He shot Micky, took the paintings and left you to lock the front door . . . Yeah, I know,' said the woman, as she held up her hand to still ZeeZee's protest. 'You didn't kill him and you don't know who did.'

Shrugging, she walked over to Micky and looked down for a while, then bent to free something trapped under him. 'Here,' she said, tossing it to ZeeZee. 'You left this behind.'

The fat envelope he'd been carrying hit the floor as ZeeZee fumbled to make the catch. And then, while he was still worrying about what he'd dropped, ZeeZee realized what he'd just caught. What he'd just tagged with his sweat, fingerprints and oil. An old Wilson Combat, its usual barrel replaced with a .22 conversion. The deep scar of an acid etch where the barrel's identification number should be.

'Ditch the gun.'

ZeeZee heard her words but he wasn't really listening. Had he always been the patsy: or was he only now surplus to requirements? He looked in disbelief at the weapon in his hands, knowing exactly who it belonged to . . . Wild Boy had just, very firmly, taken him out of the loop.

'Drop it.' The woman nodded to the man beside her, who flipped his service-issue Colt out of its holster and trained the sight on ZeeZee's chest before the English boy realised what was happening.

'Put it down real slow.' The man holding the revolver had a Southern drawl and a liking for theatrics. The trigger on his gun was already pulled, his knuckle white from depressing the trigger to its fullest extent. Only his thumb was holding back the hammer.

'Your choice,' the woman said coldly.

Wasn't it always?

ZeeZee kneeled slowly and placed the Combat flat on Micky's white carpet, muzzle pointed safely towards the wall. He didn't want any misunderstandings.

'I didn't kill Micky O'Brian. I didn't . . .' He wanted his voice to sound decisive and confident but instead it sounded shrill, as if he was trying to convince himself.

'Switching to .22 was a good move,' said the officer with the gun. 'But, you know what . . . ?'

ZeeZee shook his head.

'You really should have used a silencer. We got a call about the shot right after it happened . . .'

ZeeZee looked through the gallery's long window, taking in the rugged coastline, the choppy grey waters, the sheer isolation of this stretch of Puget Sound. Yeah, he'd bet there'd been a call, but not made from around here. There was no other house within miles. He couldn't wait for the part where they looked in the envelope and discovered Micky's delivery: half a kilo of uncut coke.

CHAPTER 22

300–3500 Hz (with harmonics peaking above 3500), is an average frequency-range for the human voice. And the sensitivity of human hearing is pretty smooth between 500–5000Hz, with 110dB being usually as loud as a voice gets.

The prisoner in the next cell was breaking 120dB, his screams emptying in a single breath that ended as swallowed, choking sobs. And though the air in Raf's small room now stank of sweat, everyone was being positively polite.

The bey was good – Felix had to give him that. He hadn't tried to claim immunity or demanded to talk to the Minister. He'd even allowed an embarrassed sergeant to wire him to a polygraph, fastening the band round his own wrist and placing his right hand completely flat on the plate. Not that the bey was exactly cooperating, either.

He hadn't yet removed his black jacket, which still looked immaculate after hours of questioning; and he'd only just taken off his dark glasses, after Madame Mila finally agreed to lower the brightness of the overhead lights.

It had been hypocritical of Felix to have put on record at the outset that he hoped the coroner-magistrate knew what she was doing – because he didn't hope that at all. What he actually hoped – very much – was that Madame Mila was making the worst mistake of her short but impressive career.

'Hani heard you shouting at each other.' The sergeant kept his voice reasonable. At Madame Mila's earlier suggestion, he'd tried hectoring but that only made the man in front of him shut down. Emotionally autistic.

'Arguing,' stressed Madame Mila. 'All of last night.' That was the fact to which she kept coming back, time after time. The one fact Raf couldn't deny.

'She wanted me to marry Zara bint-Hamzah,' repeated Raf. 'I refused. She was cross.'

'Oh, she was *way* more than cross.' As ever, Madame Mila's voice was cutting. 'She threatened to disown you because you betrayed that poor girl. So this morning you went home and stabbed her. Rather than take the risk . . . That's what happened, wasn't it?'

'No,' said Raf. 'It wasn't . . .'

'So how did it happen?' The young police sergeant fired his question, but it might as well have been Coroner Mila speaking. This was definitely her show.

'I was in my office all morning.'

'No,' said the sergeant, looking at a screen, 'we've been over this. You left at 11:30 . . .'

'And went straight to Le Trianon,' Raf shrugged. 'That's the same thing. You can check at Le Trianon.'

'We have. You left your cappuccino undrunk and your paper on the table.'

'While I went for a stamp round Place Saad Zaghloul.'

'Which was at what time?'

'Noon,' said Raf. 'Maybe later. As I said, I didn't look at my watch.'

Heartbeat, blood pressure and limbic pattern all held steady. Every diode on the Matsui polygraph lit a peaceful green. They might as well have been discussing the weather. *Hell*. The sergeant sucked at his teeth. *The weather might have got more of a limbic reaction out of the man.*

The officer glanced bleary-eyed down at his screen. 'According to the maître d' you were gone for an hour, at least.'

Raf shook his head. 'I got back slightly before that, then waited to catch someone's eye. I wasn't in a hurry . . .'

Madame Mila snorted.

'Besides,' said Raf calmly, 'you know there isn't time to walk there and back, from Zaghloul to Sherif, inside an hour, never mind murder somebody and fake a break-in. Which I didn't.'

'So you took a taxi,' the sergeant announced tiredly.

'Then where's the driver?'

'We're finding him now.'

'No,' said Raf, looking straight at Madame Mila. 'You're not, because there *was* no taxi. I went nowhere near the al-Mansur madersa at lunchtime and I didn't kill my aunt – as that machine has already verified . . .' He nodded contemptuously at the primitive polygraph.

Felix pushed himself away from the wall. 'Time to call the Minister,' he said. Felix was talking both to the coroner-magistrate and to a fish-eye unit she'd placed on the plastic table between Raf and her sergeant. 'You had your eight hours. You blew it . . . I'm releasing him.'

He glanced at Raf and grinned.

Raf sat next to Felix, his back to a sea wall, staring inland over the dark expanse of dust and shut-down kiosks that was Place Saad Zaghloul. The café where they'd just bought supper was the only place still serving at two a.m. and Felix had been hungry. In front of him rested a half-full bottle of Algerian *marc* and a paper plate that had, until recently, been piled with grilled chicken breasts drenched with harissa sauce. It was as near as Felix could get to a genuine McD chick&chilli burger.

Raf was improving his life with a third styrofoam cup of thick black coffee laced with rum. He didn't think of it as using caffeine to release dopamine in his prefrontal cortex, but he felt the hit all the same. This way he could tell himself the shakes weren't really about having been locked up in a cell.

'You know,' said Felix, 'you could have told me . . .'

Just what Raf could have told him the fat man left drifting on the sticky night breeze blowing in from behind then.

'. . . don't you think?'

Raf said nothing. Instead, he drained his coffee to the dregs, only stopping when his mouth filled with grit from coarse-ground beans. He wasn't going to sleep anyway. The image of Hani's guilt-stricken face was pixel-clear in his brain.

'If you had,' continued Felix, 'I could have got the coroner-magistrate off your case right at the start, before we hit the station. If only I'd known.' The conversation seemed to be going round in circles. Or maybe that was just the sky.

'Known what?' Raf asked tiredly.

'I made a call to Hamzah Effendi. You know what he told me?'

No, Raf didn't. In fact, he couldn't begin to guess. The last time he and Hamzah had talked, the thickset industrialist had been standing on the upper steps of the *qaa* and had threatened to have Raf's legs broken for disgracing his daughter.

'He said you were an attaché at the Seattle Consulate . . . Said I wasn't to mention that he'd told me.'

Raf went very still.

'It's okay,' said Felix as he leant back and drained off a beaker of Algerian rot-gut brandy. 'Look, fuck forbid I should get all touchy-feely. But I've been there . . . Smoke, flames, flying rubble. I'm not saying you should talk any about what happened but, all the same, telling me would have spared you that shit with Mila.'

'You think I killed Lady Nafisa?'

'The fucking *Thiergarten* killed Nafisa.' Felix slapped Raf heavily on the shoulder. 'All the same, until this is over I'm going to have to take that passport from you. And the gun. General's orders.'

'Gun . . .' Raf looked as shocked as he felt.

'Hani told Madame Mila you sleep with an old revolver by your bed.' Felix smiled sourly. 'Someone should tell that kid to keep her mouth shut . . . Anyway,' he shrugged, 'drop them both off tomorrow, before the autopsy.'

'Tomorrow . . . ?'

'This morning, whatever . . . All bodies get buried by the following noon, murder victims included. Shari'ah Law.' His tone made it clear exactly what he thought of the Khedive's new deal with the mullahs. 'Five a.m. then,' said Felix. 'Nice and early.' And he pushed himself to his feet, staggering off across Place Saad Zaghloul without a backward glance.

CHAPTER 23

Felix didn't mention the tattered state of Raf's beard or hair. Most of both were gone, cropped short with kitchen scissors from the madersa. The job wasn't yet finished, but then he'd only had two hours between arriving home and having to leave again, and most of that had been taken up with Hani.

'How's the kid?'

Raf paused, remembering.

At 2:30 A.M. she'd been a shaking little bundle, crouched on the *qaa* steps with a blanket wrapped round her and Ali-Din clutched tight in her arms like life depended on it. 'She'll survive.'

Felix sucked at his teeth. 'That bad, eh?'

'Yeah,' said Raf. 'The kid wouldn't sleep in the nursery because Nafisa's room is next door, the kitchens were out because Khartoum sleeps there. And she said she couldn't sleep in my room because it's on the men's floor and she isn't a boy . . . So we turned on the fountain, dragged out a carpet and she crashed in the courtyard under a tree.'

Raf didn't mention any Arctic fox he might have left curled up by her head to guard the kid while he was away. Mostly he didn't mention Tiriganaq because he didn't yet know what, if anything, the fox's dawn reappearance meant. Besides, Felix didn't look like someone who'd understand about inner ghosts. Crawling ants and pink elephants were more his style.

They were waiting outside a steel door in a dark underground corridor that was to-the-bone cold, something Raf hadn't previously felt in El Iskandryia. The occasional shop or café might be air-conditioned but this was different. Cold grey walls and cold stone floor, even cold overhead strips that had a light thinner than the washed-out blue of dawn outside. For once Raf wasn't wearing shades: Versace wraparounds didn't seem appropriate in a morgue.

106

'You know,' said Felix slowly, 'you don't really act like a bey.' From his hungover growl it was hard to tell whether this was meant as a compliment.

'Most of the time I don't feel like one.'

'Then you'd better start pretending,' said Felix seriously. He curled his fingers into a clumsy fist and punched Raf lightly on the shoulder. 'Okay?'

Raf was still wondering exactly how he felt about becoming the fat man's unofficial adoptee when Felix hammered hard on the closed door for a second time.

'All right, all right . . .' Bolts drew back inside and someone in a mask peered through a sudden gap. Over her shoulder came a blast of blood and formaldehyde.

'You're late.'

Felix checked his watch. 'It's only five a.m . . .'

'I did it at four. Still, you might as well come in and see.' The woman stepped back, then stopped dead at the sight of Raf, her face suddenly indignant behind her mask.

'It's okay,' Felix said hurriedly, before she could slam the door. 'This is the dead woman's nephew. They were very close, and he's as desperate as me to find her killers . . . Raf, meet Kamila. Kamila, meet Pashazade Ashraf al-Mansur.'

'This is not fair,' the girl protested tightly, backing away from the door as Felix gently pushed his way into the autopsy suite. 'I'm taking a risk just talking to you.'

'Kamila works for Madame Mila,' Felix told Raf. 'Her father works for me. Sometimes these things are useful.' He ignored the cadaver of an elderly woman laid out on a mobile cart and made his way towards a steel autopsy table where another ripped-open body lay covered with white gauze. Holes had been punched in the table's surface to let liquid drain down to a collecting tray underneath.

'What did you find?'

'The cause of death was a puncture wound to the chest. The mechanism of death was—'

'Kamila!'

'This wasn't what we agreed,' the girl said furiously. 'It's bad enough that you're here. As for him . . .' She glared at Raf.

'How did my aunt die?' Raf kept his question short and his voice as cold as the mortuary in which they now stood. Somehow the dark glasses in his pocket had found their way onto his face. Pretend, Felix had said. Raf could do one better than pretend: when necessary, he could *be.*

'Well?' Raf demanded. Even the fat man looked shocked at the sudden anger in his voice. 'I want to know . . . How did she die?'

'Heart attack,' Kamila said quietly. 'The pen severed her left main coronary artery. Which produced a big ischemic area. Tamponade was absent since the pericardium was punctured, but she—'

'You know what the fuck this means?' Raf demanded, swinging round to Felix.

The man nodded. 'The pen spiked her heart. Not much blood on the outside, quite a lot on the inside but, technically at least, still death by heart attack. How am I doing?'

The girl gave him a grudging nod.

'Seen it before,' Felix said cryptically. He yanked away the covering gauze without asking Kamila's permission.

Despite his best intentions, Raf looked. He couldn't help himself. All the same, he knew that from now on it would be impossible to think of Nafisa as anything other than so much jointed meat. What had once been human was human no longer. The body had been sliced open in a Y that began at each shoulder to shoulder, met below the breastbone and ran in a single slash down to a depilated pubis. The intestines were still in place but heart, lungs, oesophagus and trachea were a black and gaping cavity.

'Any signs of rape?' he asked abruptly.

'No.' The girl's answer was brusque. As if that was exactly the kind of question she'd expect someone like him to ask.

'Then why was her shirt open?'

In answer, Kamila turned her back on him. 'I'm about to repack the body,' she told Felix. 'You can indent the coroner-magistrate for a copy of my report. She may even let you have one.'

Felix nodded. 'What about other wounds?'

'What did you have in mind?' She'd spotted where Felix had lanced into the dead woman's abdomen to take a core temperature, though the fat man hoped that fact wouldn't make it into her final report. And that wasn't what he was asking about, anyway.

'Anything . . .'

The girl started to shake her head, then paused. 'Maybe this,' she admitted, lifting one of Nafisa's hands, which moved unwillingly beneath her grip. Detritus had been scraped from beneath each split nail and bagged and labelled. The tips of each finger still showed traces of staining where prints had been taken.

'Could be nothing,' said the girl. She nodded at the circular bruise that the fat man had already noticed on the dead woman's palm.

Felix nodded to a small metal trolley. 'Okay to touch this?' He lifted Lady Nafisa's Mont Blanc pen, transparent bag and all, from a metal kidney dish and held the blunt end to the bruise, without letting pen or flesh actually touch. The end was way too small.

'Anything else?' asked Felix.

Raf wondered if the Chief and the pathologist had noticed the pen was missing its top, then realized both of them must have done. Which made his not mentioning the fact significant. Some kind of inter-departmental dance was going on between Kamila and Felix that Raf didn't begin to understand . . .

But he would. Raf was making it his business. Secure the circle, the fox always said. So if the coroner-magistrate had him pegged as culprit, well, he'd bring Felix on-side as protection. And if staying close to Felix meant involving himself in Iskandryian politics then he could do that too, and play out his role of Bey. Life's absurdities existed to be milked for all they were worth. And besides, anything was better than being returned to Seattle to face Huntsville or Hu San. Which was exactly what would happen if anyone discovered who he really was.

'Answer the man,' Raf ordered. 'Anything else?'

'Nothing,' said the girl firmly.

Felix smiled. 'Normal stomach contents?'

'Chief!' Her voice was exasperated, as if she expected him to ask the ridiculous but still found it irritating. 'This is a minimum-invasion autopsy – boss's orders, minister's orders too. Simply confirm cause of death. Repack body, sew along dotted line. You know how this goes . . .'

'Simply *confirm* cause of death,' Felix said slowly, 'Sweet fuck. You know how worried I get when I hear those words?'

'Cause of death *pen*. Mechanism of death *torn heart muscle*. Manner of death *homicide*.' It was obvious Kamila considered their visit well into overtime. She'd had enough of the two men trespassing on her territory and wanted them off it, just as soon as possible. All the same, she was willing to compromise. 'Look,' she said as she herded them towards the door, 'you can indent me direct for a copy of the report.'

Felix nodded thanks. 'About those stomach contents,' he added softly. 'Just tell your father the results and let him pass them to me. Okay?' Felix smiled sweetly and dragged Raf from the room before Kamila had time to refuse.

CHAPTER 24

'La ilaha illa Allah . . .'
  . . . Glory be to the Most High.

The small hand that gripped Raf's had fingers of steel, nails sharp as glass and a palm clammy as that of a drowned child. Which was what she was, only Hani was drowning in ritual and other people's pity. The hand in his shook so rapidly that her tremors were practically invisible.

All through the funeral she'd been tightening her grip, until by the final round of prayers she was alternately hanging on as if for dear life and digging her nails deep into his skin. Though it was hard to tell whether Hani was angry with Raf or herself.

The funeral was brief: divided into four parts and quite obviously following a template that, equally obviously, he didn't recognize. The opening verses of the Quran had been read first, followed by another reading. An intercession was made and finally a plea that the gates of Paradise be wide enough to allow Lady Nafisa entry and therein that she be washed with water and ice, purified as a garment is purified of corrupting filth . . . It was a sentiment Raf briefly found himself wishing he could believe.

'Not much longer,' he whispered, reassuring himself as much as Hani. They'd arrived together, straight from the madersa, accompanied by a weeping Khartoum and Nafisa's cook Donna, who stopped at the gates of the necropolis, crossed herself with undisguised fervour and refused to take another step.

And as he stood dressed in black and waiting in the blazing sun for the interment to finish, Raf could almost feel Donna's fierce gaze on the back of his neck. But then, almost everyone was watching him – except for Hani, who wouldn't lift her eyes from the ground.

He'd shaved, trimmed the remains of his beard down to a short dark-blond goatee and taken clippers to his skull, because that was the quickest way to get rid of dreads. All of which turned out to be a bad mistake. Apparently, not shaving was a North African mark of respect, a signature of mourning. Lady Jalila couldn't even bring herself to talk to him. Unfortunately, the same couldn't be said for everybody else.

'Okay,' said a voice at his shoulder. 'Ready to go?' That was Felix, more smartly dressed than Raf had seen him before, his ponytail washed and his shoes so shined and polished. He'd even blacked the heels. Though the suit he wore, newly pressed or not, still looked as if he kept it hidden at the back of a cupboard and dragged it out once or twice a year when he had a colleague to bury or needed to attend the funeral of some victim. It went almost without saying that the cloth, colour and cut were at least fifteen years out of date.

'Come on.' Felix touched Raf's elbow. 'Time to move.'

Felix had been the one to collect them from the madersa and driven them out to the necropolis in his pink Cadillac with white-walled tyres. And Raf got the feeling it was only the fat man's presence that was keeping Madame Mila at bay. He hadn't expected to see her at the funeral. But then, Raf had naively thought it would be just Hani, himself and Felix, not realizing that fifty of Iskandryia's great and good would turn out into the airless rising heat of a Wednesday morning to see the cloth-wrapped body of Lady Nafisa carried into her family tomb.

'Ashraf,' hissed Lady Jalila, materializing beside him like a bad smell. 'You have to lead.' Dark patches of sweat showed under the arms of her white linen suit, but her make-up was still immaculate and the few strands of hair that escaped from under her Hermès scarf glinted prettily in the sunlight.

'Come on,' Raf said and turned to Hani, only to stop at the sight of her face.

The child had her legs set apart, her heels dug deep into the grit of the path. Everything about her body language roared defiance except for the hurt in her eyes. Raf recognized that, the exploding bleakness, which wasn't the same as remembering it. Though he remembered well how hard he'd had to learn to forget.

'We need to move,' Raf said softly.

Hani shook her head. No question of compromise.

'Hani.'

Heads flicked round at Lady Jalila's rebuke, until most of the mourners were gazing at the child. There was something hungry about the gathering. Lady Jalila held out her hand to Hani and waited.

Nobody moved.

'*You* lead,' Raf suggested, taking in the crowd of strangers and knowing they listened to his every word. 'You were her closest friend and you found her. Besides, you can see the child is terrified.'

He dropped to his knees on the gravel path. 'We're staying here, aren't we?'

Night-black eyes stared back at him, then arms thin as sticks fastened themselves tight round his neck as Hani clung to him and her butterfly trembling exploded into full-blown shakes. Sobs shook her body but Raf had no need to look to know the child was crying: the tears were trickling into the collar of his shirt.

When he looked up, a good half of the onlookers were gazing sympathetically at them both. The Minister of Police even had a sad, tolerant smile on his face.

'If you insist.' Something ghost-like flitted across the face of Lady Jalila as she turned to face the mausoleum door. And she walked away without waiting for her husband.

'Poor child' said Mushin Bey sadly. 'Such a loss.' Raf figured the Minister of Police was talking about Hani and not his wife, but it was hard to tell.

One by one, the other mourners followed Lady Jalila and the body until they were all swallowed by darkness and the necropolis suddenly felt empty. From a nearby bush came the bubbling call of a common bulbul and beyond a high wall cars could be heard grinding gears at distant traffic lights.

'About goddamn time,' said Felix, with feeling. The flask was out, flicked open and tucked safely back in his jacket in an instant. 'Needs must,' he said, looking oddly shamefaced. 'It's either grab the odd refuel or not turn up at all . . .' He glanced towards Hani – folded into Raf's arms, her eyes screwed tight, her face buried in his shoulder – and nodded thoughtfully. 'Good man,' said Felix softly. 'Now find out what she really knows . . .'

The al-Mansur mausoleum was elegantly simple. Its very simplicity a sign of the design's antiquity, which easily predated both the city's invasion by Napoleon in 1798 and an earlier seventeenth-century plague that had swept the streets of life and briefly reduced Isk to a handful of dilapidated dwellings occupied by obese rats.

A low door, cut into the side of a marble base, led down to a deep crypt. Rising up from the square base, basalt pillars at each corner supported a roof that rose, in its turn, to meet at a point in the very centre. A short metal spine that jutted from this point ended in a simple crescent. Though it was difficult to see from the ground what material the crescent had been hammered from, as winter storms had weathered the metal to a deep black.

Under this roof, centred on the base itself, was a simple memorial. A rough-hewn slab of stone, balanced on its side and apparently held upright at either end by a short square pillar, one of which had once been broken and repaired with stone of a slightly poorer quality.

'What are you doing?'

'Looking at the building,' said Raf, slowly stroking the child's hair. She didn't quite pull away, so he stroked again, more slowly still. Years back that had worked for a different animal, a wounded one, when no other boy at his school could get near it.

'It's a *kiosk*,' Hani said. She nodded to the mausoleum. 'And that thing's a *cenotaph* and those are *stelae*.' The upward jerk to her chin told him she was talking about the narrow pillars.

'*Yesterday I was as you, tomorrow you will be like me . . .*' Hani recited from memory the inscription on the base. 'How old do you think it is?'

Raf looked round at other, more ornate tombs. A few of which had similar square roofs, though most had little domes, cupolas of stone decorated either with starburst motifs, herringbone patterns or intricate, intertwined arabesques. Even the newest ones looked as if they'd been there for centuries.

'I've no idea,' he said, 'tell me.'

Hani's lips twisted. 'Twenty years . . . Donna told me. My aunt built it for her husband. The pillar broke in the first year and she made the builders replace it for nothing.'

'But the site . . .' Raf scanned the necrotic jumble that crowded in on itself, bent by age and gravity, some of the funerary monuments so close to collapse they looked as though they were trying to shoulder neighbouring tombs out of the way.

'Bought an old tomb and pulled it down.' The child shrugged. 'Of course, she had to pay someone to carry away the old bodies.'

'Of course . . .' Raf nodded at a heavily bent cork tree nearby. 'It's too bright for me,' he said. 'Are you all right with moving?'

They walked over to the shade together, Hani never once releasing her grip on his hand. She'd been holding on without break from the point they stepped into Rue Cif and climbed into the back of Felix's open-top car. Quite what she thought would happen to her if she let go Raf had no idea, but it was equally obvious Hani didn't intend to find out.

Just getting her out onto the street had been difficult enough. Getting the kid into the car had taken a major miracle. Though it wasn't until

Hani had appeared in a dress, her straight black hair carefully tied back, that Raf even realized he had a problem.

She'd walked easily enough from the *qaa* through the courtyard, and less easily from there into the oven-like heat of the covered garden, which was already beginning to wilt after only one day without Lady Nafisa's attention. But by the time she'd reached the madersa's final squat passage out onto Rue Cif, Hani was shaking with fear.

'Come on,' Raf had said, tugging slightly on her hand. Her answering yank almost took his arm out of its socket. And as he stared down to where her face was setting into a mask of stubbornness made flesh, realization hit.

He didn't hear her whisper first time so she said it again.

'I've never . . .' Hani's voice trailed away into silence.

'You've never left the house?'

The truth was confirmed in the eyes of the old Sudanese porter who stood watching the anxious girl stand frozen on his doorstep. Self-imposed boxes, that was what life produced, thought Raf bleakly. Simple and basic or complex and jewelled, it made little difference. Prison was still prison and exile was exile, internal or not.

'Are you afraid?' he asked Hani.

Her answer was a fierce scowl.

'Well,' said Raf, 'are you?'

'No. Of course not.' She bunched her fingers into fists and pressed her hands hard at her side. 'I'm never afraid.'

He would be. Nine years without leaving the madersa where she'd been born. Without stepping beyond the rear door into Rue Cif, never mind using the carved front portal that led from the house to the busy mayhem that was Rue Sherif. Not that anyone still used the Rue Sherif portal, of course. The sun-blasted street doors might remain in place, but the actual archway behind them had been bricked up ten years before Hani was even born, on Lady Nafisa's orders. The few visitors Lady Nafisa had allowed into the madersa since her husband's death used the entrance in Rue Cif.

Dropping to one knee, Raf forgot about his new suit. 'Not afraid?' he said. 'Everyone's afraid . . .' He was aware of Felix watching him from the waiting Cadillac. 'It's what keeps us alive.' He'd almost said *human*.

Hani looked doubtful.

Raf sighed. He didn't want to run the *duty* routine, but he was going to anyway, because that was what would work. He and the kid shared a number of the same buttons in common.

'She was your aunt . . .'

'Your aunt too,' Hani said sullenly.

114

Yeah, right. That was somewhere he didn't plan to visit. 'But you knew her properly. Much better than I did.'

The nod was tiny.

'And everyone will expect you to be there . . .'

Hani looked doubtful.

'I'm sorry,' Raf said softly. He stood up, slipped on his dark glasses and struck a pose, one hand tucked into his silk jacket, as if holding a gun. *Imperial Assassin V.*

'Hey,' he said, 'Stick with me. You'll be safe.'

Hani's lips twisted. Only the briefest twitch, but it was almost a smile.

CHAPTER 25

The long blade shone silver. Not as bright as sun on the water in the harbour beyond the shop window where a new Japanese super-yacht sat looking smug and sleek, but bright enough to make the newly arrived English boy glance away.

Behind a wooden counter at the back of the shop was a Chinese woman hard at work removing a scratch from the mirror-black lacquered scabbard of a Honshu wakizasi. *Her shop mostly sold reproduction Japanese swords because that was what tourists in Seattle seemed to want and could afford. The sword held by the boy was real, a fact reflected in its price.*

Cotton bound the ray-skin hilt, its tsuba *was pierced and simple, the scabbard was lacquered wood with traces of crazing, where an under-lacquer showed through. But it was the* shinto *blade that made that particular sword special Even the fact her great-grandfather died at Nanking wasn't enough to stop her appreciating the* katana's *stark beauty.*

Hu San Liang had already decided the young tourist would walk out empty-handed. He liked the sword but couldn't possibly afford it. If he'd had that kind of money the boy would have bought the weapon already.

Instead he was taking a last, regretful look. A few more minutes and he would be gone. Buying a coffee at Starbucks next door, most probably. Some small consolation for not being able to afford what he really wanted.

Hu San was used to it. The prices in her shop were higher than elsewhere. Partly that was because harbour-front sites in Seattle were expensive, occupied mostly by hotels, franchise chains and exclusive bars. The other reason was that Hu San didn't sell rubbish. She shipped the reproductions from Osaka to Seattle through her own small import/export company. Cheaper reproductions could be bought from Spain or Taiwan for a fraction of the price but she had her own motives for sourcing material from Osaka. Quite apart from an obvious one, which was that her lover was Japanese.

'How old is this?' The boy's voice was polite, his accent definitely not local. Hu San had watched him come into her shop every day for a week and silently pick up the same sword and pull it respectfully from its simple scabbard to examine the hamon: that wavy temper line where the blade was coated with clay before firing, so that variations in heat would produce a hard but brittle cutting edge, backed by softer but more flexible steel.

It was the best sword in the shop. Hu San suspected the English boy knew that. She also knew the boy had blanched the first time a price was mentioned, but still kept coming back.

'How old? Three-fifty years, maybe a bit more.' Hu Son's voice placed her as second-generation Chinese-American. More Seattle than anything else.

'And the scabbard?'

'What do you think?'

The boy picked up the scabbard thoughtfully. When he thought Hu San wasn't looking he flicked a thumbnail across a gold mon on the scabbard's side. The circle peeled rather than flaked away.

'New,' said the boy, looking at the handle. It was all new except the blade.

'The blade is the sword.' Hu San said shortly. She waited for the question but the boy just nodded.

'Beautiful,' said the boy. Then, to Hu San's relief, he put the blade back in its scabbard, put the scabbard back on its daisho stand and left her shop. Which was as well, because the Chinese woman was expecting a visitor. And not one she looked forward to meeting.

Taking a pen from its tray, Hu San moistened a block of ink and began to practise writing her name. She'd practised every day since she was four, which was now just over thirty-five years ago. One day she would get it exactly right, but hopefully not too soon.

Her Korean visitor wore a dark suit, white shirt and red tie. The uniform of money-men or gangsters. He came in just as Hu San finished her third attempt. Neither bowed to the other and the Korean made no effort to hide his contempt at the smallness of the shop or at how Hu San was passing her time.

'Try writing an epitaph,' he suggested, 'if you must do that ethnic crap.'

But Hu San had no intention of dying. At least, not that day and not to any timetable worked out by a Korean. She knew the Korean's name, of course, but wasn't prepared to do the man the honour of using it, not even in her head. She'd known his father and that one had also been stupid.

'You know why I'm here?'

Hu San gave the briefest nod.

The Korean put his hand into his jacket pocket. 'Agree to our terms,' he said, 'or else . . .' The rest of what he planned to say was lost in the ring of a bell as ZeeZee walked back into the shop and headed straight for the sword. Hu San had been right. The boy had gone next door to Starbucks and nursed a regular latte – at the shelf by the window – while he came up with his proposal. He would put down a deposit on the katana*, pay every week and collect the sword when its price had been met.*

He wasn't about to mention that he didn't yet have a job.

Taking the sword from its rack, ZeeZee slid free the blade and held it out in front of him, feeling the perfection of its balance. Only then did he notice Hu San was not alone and that her visitor was gaping bug-eyed at him like some fish out of water.

'Go,' ordered Hu San. 'I'm shut now. Come back tomorrow . . .'

'You heard her,' said the suit. 'Move.'

ZeeZee was never quite sure why he didn't just walk out of the shop. Stubbornness, maybe. Disappointment at not being able to make his eminently sensible proposal. Sheer chance, perhaps. Some half-remembered butterfly stamping its foot way back when he was born. Although, later, the fox told ZeeZee it had snapped awake, sniffed the air and tasted something sour. Tiri was like that, unpredictable. Whatever the reason, ZeeZee lowered the blade and started towards the counter. There was something he really needed to discuss.

'Out,' said the Korean, jerking his head towards the door. He had a gun in his hand that hadn't been there a second before.

Inside the boy's head an animal growled and ZeeZee heard a low whisper that hadn't spoken since he was seven.

Raise the sword . . .

Without pausing to think, the boy lifted his blade, cavalry-sabre-style, and stepped forward. 'Are you being robbed?'

Hu San glanced from the boy to the Korean and then nodded.

The growling got louder.

'Call the police,' ZeeZee's voice was hoarse, way too high. He took a slow breath to steady himself. 'Call them . . .'

Most of his weight ZeeZee rested on his left heel, leaving his right leg forward and heel slightly raised, as he took up the two-handed position taught at school. Man with gun versus man with sword. In theory it was a straight stand-off, but the idea he might actually have to use his blade raised questions of the kind the boy didn't want to answer.

'Fuckwit,' the Korean said flatly. He was talking to ZeeZee, or rather he was talking at ZeeZee, because his hand was already bringing up the revolver.

Sun flashed on metal, time slowed, and a katana blade slid through flesh and bit through bone, showering the boy with hot rain.

'Bow,' ordered Hu San.

For a second the Korean's severed head remained on his neck. Then it tipped forward and fell to the floor. Death smoothing away the man's sudden expression of disbelief.

The Korean would probably have crumbled forward anyway, though to ZeeZee it looked as if the blood pumping from the man's neck was what forced him to his knees. It rained down around ZeeZee as he stood staring in shock at the razor-sharp blade resting unused in his hand.

'Could you have killed him?' Hu San asked as she wiped her own blade on a corner of her jacket.

Could he? ZeeZee didn't find the question odd. But then there was very little in life that he found odd. And it was a good question, even if he didn't yet know the answer. He'd never killed anything, not a fish from a lake or a sparrow with a BB gun, and yet . . .

He shrugged.

'No matter.' Hu San, elder sister of the Five Winds Society, pulled a tiny Nokia diary from her blood-splattered jacket and flipped it open. Her conversation was soft, unhurried and authoritative. ZeeZee didn't understand a word. Just as he didn't really understand how a middle-aged Chinese woman could manage to vault a counter and unsheathe a sword in less time than it took the Korean to raise his gun.

Stepping round the blood-splattered boy, Hu San walked to the shop door and flipped round a simple sign, from open to closed. Then she pulled down two bamboo blinds and locked the door. 'Shut for stocktaking,' she announced lightly.

CHAPTER 26

7th July

Lady Jalila blinked as the crypt's darkness gave way to sudden daylight. Beside her walked Madame Mila, head turned slightly towards the older woman. There was probably only five years' difference in their ages, but the Minister's wife had a confidence that came with money, good clothes and power, even if that power was vicarious and by right belonged to her husband.

By contrast, Madame Mila was ill at ease and obviously resented the fact. She had intellectual brilliance, striking looks and an unbroken run of victories in court from her recent career as a public prosecutor. What she lacked was connections. Lady Jalila knew that. They talked, or rather the Minister's wife talked and the younger woman listened intently, occasionally nodding.

Both of them were headed towards where Raf and Hani sat in the shade of their borrowed cork tree, backs pressed hard against another family's tomb. Reluctantly Raf climbed to his feet and brushed gravel from his suit. Hani clambered up after him.

She didn't look at her aunt or the coroner-magistrate.

'You have my sympathy,' Lady Jalila told Raf. 'And, of course, if there's anything I or the Minister can do to help . . .' She smiled, then shrugged as if to stress she wished there was more she could offer. But Raf still caught the point when her eyes slid across to Hani and noticed that the child was clinging to his hand, her fingers glued firmly inside his.

'Thank you,' Raf said politely, nodding first to Lady Jalila and then at the stony-faced woman stood beside her. 'I'd better get Hani home . . .'

'Your Excellency . . .'

He was the person addressed, Raf realized, turning back. The coroner-magistrate was staring after him, her elegant face at once flawless and utterly cold. Her eyes between darkness and a void.

The woman was attractive and regretted it. Her brittleness a warning at odds with the warmth of a perfume that featured musk mixed with some botanical element so elusive Raf decided it had to be synthetic. Chemical analogues that fell midway between spices and fruit were big business, even in a city that prided itself on having the finest spice markets in North Africa. He'd seen the hoardings on his way through Place Orabi.

'. . . Yes?' Raf said finally.

'You didn't know your aunt very well, did you?'

'I hardly knew her at all.' Raf kept his voice cool, matter-of-fact. 'Why?'

'Madame Mila was just wondering,' Lady Jalila said.

The younger woman nodded. 'She must have been surprised when she first heard from you. Pleased, obviously . . .'

'She didn't hear from me,' said Raf. 'Until last week I didn't even know she existed . . .' And here came today's understatement. 'My father's family isn't something my mother talks about . . .'

'So how did your aunt know where to find you?'

How indeed?

'Good question.' Raf let his gaze flick over Madame Mila, taking in the neat row of tiny plaits, her perfect skin and her scrupulously simple suit, which was immaculately pressed but not nearly like as expensive as Lady Jalila's outfit or the suit he was wearing. It was a gaze Raf had watched Dr Millbank use at Huntsville to bring unexpectedly difficult inmates into line. And the beauty of it was that its effect was almost subliminal.

'I believe my father keeps an eye on my progress.'

This time when Raf walked away no one called him back.

Felix offered to drive them home from the necropolis. But his drive home turned out to be an extended tour of the city that involved a slow crawl along the Corniche, beginning at the crowded summer beaches at Shatby and taking them past the grandeur of the Bibliotheka Iskandryia (where a rose-pink marble façade hid 125 kilometres of carefully ducted optic fibre) round the elegantly curved sweep of Eastern Harbour so Hani could see the fishing boats and horse-drawn caleches and then north along the final stretch of the Corniche towards the new aquarium and out along the harbour spur towards Fort Qaitbey, which had once been the site of the Pharos Lighthouse, one of the seven wonders of the world.

Pointing with one hand and steering with his other, Felix kept up a running commentary that made up in jokes for what it occasionally lacked in historic accuracy. He didn't stop or even suggest they stop, except once on the return trip, when he pulled over an ice-cream van and Hani was given her first ice cream.

Heading south down Rue el-Dardaa at the end of Felix's impromptu tour they hit afternoon traffic. Squat, brightly carapaced VWs, sleek BMWs, the odd Daimler-Benz mixed in with an occasional bulbous-headed Japanese vehicle, apparently designed around some idealized memory of a Koi. By then, the kid was asleep on the backseat, her head against Raf's side, and Raf was running over his future options and getting nowhere fast.

There'd be a will to be read. Legal requirements to be observed. But he already knew from something the fat man had said that he was the sole heir. The house was his and so, it seemed, was responsibility for Hani.

'Sweet Jeez.' Felix grabbed a hip flask, gulped and put it back under his seat. 'Can't be doing with this.' He spun the wheel hard and Raf suddenly found himself out of the crawling traffic and cutting the wrong way up a one-way route. The fish van headed in the other direction very sensibly mounted the sidewalk and scraped a wall rather than tangle with Felix.

The man was right. The traffic really was tight as a nun's ass.

'Which reminds me,' said Felix. 'You saw who else was there?' He tossed the words over his shoulder.

'No,' said Raf. 'Tell me.'

Felix grinned. 'Quite pretty, very rich, spent most of her time glaring at you . . .'

Oh, *her*. 'Hamzah's daughter?'

'Yeah,' said Felix. 'I wondered who'd show.' He glanced in his rear-view mirror, catching Raf's eye. 'All respect to your late aunt and everything, but that was the real reason I went. It's the old dog-to-vomit syndrome. If killers can't manage a nostalgia trip to the crime scene they sometimes attend the funeral.'

'*Zara?*'

Felix sighed theatrically, shook his head and flipped his vast car into Rue Kemil, then hung a right into Rue Cif, completely blocking the narrow street as he killed his engine outside the nondescript madersa door. 'Not Zara. The man who wasn't there, her father. We've wanted to rattle Hamzah's cage for months.' Felix grinned. 'I'm going to be bringing him in personally first thing tomorrow. See what happens if I poke him with a stick . . .'

CHAPTER 27

'We're here . . .'

Situated out beyond Glymenapoulo in a formal garden that ran down to a rocky beach, the Villa Hamzah was a bastard cross between the Parthenon and a Sicilian palazzo. Only three storeys high, but each one heavy with grandeur, colonnaded and porticoed like a riotously expensive wedding cake baked in brick and iced with grey stucco.

At its back stood the sea. At its front the Corniche . . . though an expanse of expensive lawn and a short length of drive kept the villa and road separate. Steps led up to a huge portico that rose two full storeys, with the portico's flat roof forming the floor of a balcony that jutted from the front of the house as proud and heavy as any conquistador's chin.

Double columns on either side of the balcony rose higher than the balustraded roof of the house itself, to support a smaller portico decorated at its centre with an Italianate and recent-looking coat of arms.

The windows at ground level were small and rudimentary, in keeping with Iskandryian tradition that put serving quarters on the lowest floor rather than in the attic. It was the windows of the second and third floors that were grand; each one peering imperiously at the world from under a colonnade that ran round both sides and the rear of the house.

Villa Hamzah was the house of an industrial conquistador. Arrogant and assertive, but also bizarrely beautiful and with proportions so perfect the plans had to have been drawn up using the golden mean. Not at all what Raf was expecting – though he wasn't too sure what he had been expecting, except that it wasn't this.

'You want me to wait?'

Raf glanced both ways along the Corniche, seeing cruising cars, noisy groups of expensively dressed teenagers and an endless row of street lights flickering away into the far distance. It was late but there were empty yellow taxis every seventh or eighth vehicle and he was unlikely to be at the villa long enough for the traffic to die away completely.

'No, it's fine.' Raf peeled off an Iskandryian £10 note and then added £5 as a tip. He could always call the driver back if he needed to, and besides, it was still cheaper than having him wait.

'I'll take your card.'

'Yes, Your Excellency.' The cabbie pulled a crumpled rectangle from his pocket and handed it to Raf, who immediately scanned both sides to check that a number was given in numerals he could understand. It was.

The wrought-iron gates were already open. And there was no sentry box, bulletproof or otherwise, for a smartly uniformed guard, which surprised Raf even more. Flipping off his shades, Raf adjusted his eyes and ran the spectrum from infraR to ultraV, but got nothing unusual. So far as he could see, security was completely lacking. No linked web of laser sensors, no bank of infrared cameras, not even a single starlight CCTV mounted on one of the huge pillars.

Hamzah was either very trusting or his reputation was all the protection he needed. Which wasn't as unlikely as it sounded. Three years back, while Raf was in Huntsville, a Seattle street kid on Honda blades had put a cheap Taiwanese rip-off Colt against Hu San's head and taken her bag. From start to finish the heist took less than thirty seconds and no one got hurt. Fifteen minutes later the kid turned himself and the bag in at the precinct on 4th Street and made a straight-to-video confession.

Hu San still had his legs broken, but cleanly, and the blue shirt who took the contract doped the kid up with ketamine before he began.

Gravel crunched under foot as Raf walked to the front door and knocked hard. 'I'd like to see Hamzah Effendi,' Raf said to a sudden gap, which would have been backlit if the Russian bodyguard standing in the way of the hall light hadn't taken up the whole doorway. Raf kept his voice bored, like a man who knew he would be seen.

'I see,' said the bodyguard. 'Is he expecting Your Excellency?' It was obvious he already knew the answer.

'No,' said Raf. 'But tell him Ashraf Bey would like a word.'

The Russian grinned, the first sign that he had more than iced water in his veins. Until then the man obviously hadn't recognized Raf, not minus dreads and beard. 'Right,' he said. 'I'll just see if the Boss is in . . .'

Stepping inside the door now being held open, Raf waited politely next to a portrait of Hamzah so new Raf could smell paint drying while the guard walked solidly away across a vast chessboard of a hall paved in white and black marble.

'*Ashraf!*'

Raf opened his ears a little wider, jacked up his hearing or whatever he was meant to call what happened when he turned the volume up in his head. The outrage was Madame Rahina's and he heard Hamzah's answering growl, but not Zara . . . Voices blossomed into a brief argument that many would have missed. But Raf followed it just as he followed the Doppler effect of footsteps approaching down a corridor.

The man approaching stank of cigars and Guerlain aftershave, too much of it. His brogues had hand-sewn leather soles that creaked on the tiles. In the painting, he wore impossibly shiny black boots and stood against a balustrade, the background behind him an out-of-focus blur of green and blue. A gold Rolex was recognizable on one wrist. The little finger of his left hand sported a red-stoned, high-domed signet that could have been mistaken for a graduation ring. He wore a frock coat that reached the top of his boots and carried a rolled blueprint, signifying his profession. On his head was the red-tasselled tarbush of an effendi.

'Karl Johann,' announced a deep voice behind him. 'He was due to paint a Vanderbilt but I made it worth his while . . .'

'It's good,' said Raf.

'Given what I paid him it should be.' The industrialist glanced round his hall, checking it really was empty. Or maybe he was listening to the sound of breaking glass echoing up a corridor. If so, he seemed resigned to the damage.

'My wife wants you killed,' he said. 'Or maybe your balls removed.' Hamzah shrugged. 'I've explained you don't do that to beys. Not openly, anyway, unless you're very stupid. But that's not the reason I refused her demand . . .' Shrewd eyes watched Raf and when Raf didn't ask *What is?* the man nodded slightly, as if he expected no less.

'My daughter told me about the tram.'

What tram? Raf almost asked. But he kept his mouth shut and after a second the man twisted his heavy lips into a slight smile.

'Discreet, aren't you? Well, it probably goes with the job.'

Which didn't answer the question.

Through the haze of that morning's funeral and yesterday's murder appeared the chill ghost of a memory. Zara with the flowers. Zara vomiting neatly onto a rocking wooden floor, the worried black kid with the nose piercings who'd reached for her hand, then noticed Raf's open gaze. *That tram.*

The first time that ever I saw your face . . .

'Her mother still believes she spent the evening with a work friend,' said Hamzah. 'The kid works at the library you know . . .' Even when facing embarrassment full-on the man couldn't keep his pride in Zara out of his voice, and he *was* embarrassed. 'Thinks she got shellfish poisoning too. But I know a hangover when I see one and wherever Zara spent the night I'm damn sure she didn't sleep over with . . .'

The sentence trailed away as Hamzah forgot how he'd intended it to end. 'Don't entirely blame you,' he said finally, his voice blunt. 'You can have the pick of North Africa. Why go for trouble? But she's a good kid for all that.' He bit on his cigar and then considered the smoke for a minute as it eddied towards the distant ceiling.

'Can't tell her mother why you rejected her, obviously.'

'Wait,' Raf held up his hand. 'That had nothing to do with it,' he said. 'How old is she?'

'Nineteen.'

'Fine,' said Raf. 'I'm twenty-five. I don't intend to get married to some stranger. And nor, I imagine, does she . . .'

Hamzah's answer was a laughing bark. 'That's exactly what her mother's afraid of,' he said.

There wasn't much Raf could say.

'Now,' said Hamzah, 'you didn't come here to discuss my daughter. So what do you want?'

'First off, to ask you a question.'

'Then fire away.' The man looked darkly amused.

'Okay,' said Raf, watching a pulse point on Hamzah's temple, the man's mouth, his eyes. 'Did you kill my aunt?'

'No,' said Hamzah. 'I didn't.' His dark pupils remained exactly the same size, neither expanding nor contracting. The corners of his mouth remained firm and the pulsebeat on his temple stayed regular as a metronome. Raf didn't need access to a polygraph to be certain the man hadn't killed Lady Nafisa.

'Of course,' Hamzah added, 'I could always have hired someone else to do it for me . . .'

They sat in a panelled study overlooking the Mediterranean. Waves broke on a headland away to the right, ancient blowholes spewing white plumes high into the air: while on a beach below the window, waves just lapped against the sand and then retreated, soft as a caress.

The coffee they drank was laced with cognac. Raf could taste it on his tongue, though the alcohol wasn't mentioned when a uniformed maid brought in a silver jug on a heavy silver tray. Raf refused the offer of a cigar, waiting while his host bit off the end of a fresh Partegas only to swear when he remembered he was meant to be using a cigar guillotine.

'So,' said Hamzah, trimming the ragged edges of his cigar into a crystal ashtray. 'What else do you want to know?' Smoke swirled around his head like evaporating dry ice around some pantomime devil. The effect was studied, Raf understood that. Everything he'd seen told him Hamzah was making a Herculean effort to be something he wasn't – quiet, urbane and softly mannered. What interested Raf was *Why?* He was already impressed: the house and its very location saw to that.

'Well,' Hamzah growled, 'you going to ask? Or just sit there and look at my decorations . . . ?' A flick of his hand took in the dark oak panels and carved marble fireplace, the polished floorboards and Art Nouveau windows that stretched from ceiling to floor.

'It's about my aunt . . .' Raf drained his cup and sat back in a red leather chair. Intelligence told him to approach the matter obliquely, so he did. By asking a direct but different question.

'What did she hope to get out of my engagement?'

'You're a bey,' Hamzah said flatly. 'I'm rich. What the hell do you think she got out of it?' He was no longer smiling.

'But the dowry gets held in trust,' said Raf, trying to remember what he'd learned from an afternoon in front of Hani's screen, skimming legal sites. 'To be returned in case of divorce, if the marriage is unconsummated or not blessed with children. All that's on offer is interest and that would have gone to me . . .'

'She had heavy expenses.'

'You paid her?'

'In this city,' said Hamzah, 'everyone takes commission.' He stubbed out his cigar and took another one from the mahogany humidor. This time, though, he remembered to remove the end using his little gold guillotine. 'She took two and a half million US dollars.'

'Two and a— What proportion of that was her commission?'

Hamzah Effendi just looked at him. 'That *was* her commission. The dowry itself was a billion . . .'

Raf whistled. As responses went it was entirely instinctive.

'And you,' he asked. 'What did you get out of it?' Given the massive villa, the Havana cigars, the uniformed maid and frock-coated bodyguard, it seemed extremely unlikely that Hamzah's need was anything physical.

'Respectability,' Hamzah said bluntly. 'You'd be surprised what a title can do . . .'

No, thought Raf, thinking back to Felix's reluctance to let the coroner-magistrate sweat him properly, he wouldn't be surprised at all. 'The Khedive can't take the *effendi* back?'

Hamzah's grin was wolfish. 'I'd like to see him try . . .'

Raf nodded, slowly, carefully considering his words. 'I've got a problem,' he said, 'and so have you. Actually, I've got two problems, both complicated. But yours is worse.'

'Tell me mine first, then.'

'The police. Khartoum heard you threaten Lady Nafisa.'

'I threatened you, too,' Hamzah reminded Raf. 'That was my daughter you rejected.'

'But I'm still alive,' said Raf. 'And Nafisa's not. The police are going to pull you in at dawn tomorrow. See what they can pin on you.'

'How do you know?'

'Chief Felix told me.'

'And now you're telling me . . .' The man paused to stub out his second cigar and didn't light another. 'You're certain?'

Raf nodded.

'Get me Sookia, Son and Sookia.' The order was barked at a Sony unit on a table by the wall. Seconds later a little flat screen flickered into life. The conversation was short and one-sided, and ended when Hamzah clicked his fingers so the screen went dead, cutting off a pyjamaed young lawyer in mid flow. The man would arrive at the villa within the next half-hour as Hamzah had demanded, Raf had no doubt of that.

'What will you do?' Raf asked.

'Go down to the station tonight, with my lawyer, and sort this out. What do you think . . . Okay,' said Hamzah. 'Now it's my turn. You've got thirty minutes to tell me your two problems and if I can help I will, whether my wife likes it or not.'

'First off,' said Raf, 'do you know if Lady Nafisa had debts?'

'No idea. Why?'

'Because her account is empty.'

Hamzah blinked. 'Gone?' he asked. 'Two and a half million just gone?'

'One million in and out on the same day, according to her notebook . . .'

'Through a one-use-only blind account?'

Yeah, according to Nafisa's book that's exactly how it was done. Raf nodded his agreement. He didn't stop to wonder what Hamzah knew about one-use accounts because he'd realized instantly that it was probably rather a lot.

'And the other one and a half?' Hamzah asked.

'Not even mentioned.'

The industrialist nodded. 'Those were drafts from Hong Kong Suisse,' he said. 'Redeemable anywhere.' And for a few seconds they both thought about redeemable bankers' drafts and didn't like where it was leading.

'What was your other problem?'

'Can you recommend a good builder?'

They talked for the remaining ten minutes about what Raf wanted done in the *qaa*, which was to get rid of Nafisa's office altogether. For all its smoked-glass pretensions it was no more than an expensive pre-fabricated hut dumped down in one corner of a large living space. He'd like to have moved Hani out of the madersa completely but Felix thought that would look bad. Besides, Raf had another problem that made it a bad idea.

When it came down to it, Raf's salary from the Third Circle was no more than token. He had no money and owned nothing except the suit he wore: at least, not until the will was granted probate and, even when that went through, all he'd have would be a ramshackle house and no means to maintain it.

None of which he mentioned to his host, the man who'd put the price of a billion dollars on his daughter's dowry. With Hamzah, he stuck to practicalities like explaining what he wanted doing with the *qaa*, and why . . .

So when Hamzah suggested getting the *qaa* blessed and then immediately amended his suggestion to getting the whole house blessed, Raf was surprised. He didn't have the industrialist pegged as religious. It turned out that Hamzah wasn't, but it was a good point all the same.

'My mother died in a fall,' said Hamzah. 'It was only after a mullah blessed the site I could bear to go back into the garden. I was nine. At nine you can see things that aren't there.'

And at twenty, thought Raf ruefully, *and twenty-five*. And, for all he knew, thirty . . . Maybe for life. Maybe with some things, once they were in there, they were in there for ever, like Tiriganaq. Further conversation was cut off by a distant bell. The lawyer had made it from one side of the city to the other inside twenty-five minutes.

'Look,' said Hamzah, 'I can't pretend I liked your aunt but Hani's okay, so here's what I'll do for you . . .' He smiled at his own words. 'I'll get a team over there tonight. Because what's the use of owning a construction company if you can't rustle up a few builders?'

Walking over to a pair of French windows, Hamzah shot two bolts, then neutralized an alarm by tapping five digits into a small keypad next to the window frame. Raf's time was up. 'Leave this way,' he said, opening the door to let in a warm night wind. 'You'll find the walk more interesting.'

CHAPTER 28

7th July

For the girl in the water, illumination came not from the city lights strung out along the shore nor from far-distant stars whose distance was measured in countless millennia, because those were half hidden behind fit clouds. No, illumination dribbled from her fingertips in fractured Morse and spun in nebular swirls around her feet. Whole constellations burned around her shoulders and flowed over her skin like glittering smoke in a high impossible wind. She was the night and the night was her.

Zara had been coming to this beach to swim at night since she was seven, though it wasn't until three years ago she'd started smoking blow to make the liquid constellations come closer.

She'd brought Avatar out here once, one evening just before she went to New York. Some ideas needed to be left as ideas and that was one of them. He'd hated the water, he hadn't wanted to get undressed in front of her and one of his new ear-studs had rusted and given him an infection. And later, when she was on a plane and it was too late to say sorry, she realized he'd resented being asked to come out to the villa anyway. So would she, if she'd been born in a slum and Villa Hamzah was where she wasn't allowed to live.

So Zara went back to only coming here late and only ever alone.

Getting here from her room was easy. A short drop from her window, little more than her height even back then, five easy paces across a strongly made tiled roof, then down a short length of heavy iron drainpipe, the old-fashioned kind complete with regular brackets bolting it to the wall. Chance worked in her favour sometimes.

Swimming like this had been the one thing she'd missed while living in New York. No pool came close. As a child, she used to believe that she'd have been happiest being a street kid, if she could still have come here at night. Now she knew it was only money that gave her the freedom to swim like this, in the salt dark, alone, naked . . . But even money had its flip side, though you probably had to be there to believe that.

This was her world. Alone, untroubled, with the whole amniotic Mediterranean as an immersion tank. Her mother hated the sea.

Zara sank under a wave, letting warm blackness close over her head as air dribbled from her lips, and felt herself slip slowly until her toes touched the bottom. The rocks were velvet with algae, seaweed flicked around her calves and ankles like sharp grass.

Raf was shouting, only he didn't shout, he never shouted . . . He stopped, thought about that for a split second and then started shouting again. Waves lapping dark rock were his only answer.

Triangulation: he had the concept before he had its name. Noting where he now stood, Raf next glanced back to where he'd been standing, triangulating the position of the head when he first saw it.

It should be . . .

Eyes skimmed the dark water until they saw a figure break surface. Somewhere nearby the shouting started again. And inside his head came a rolling litany, mostly composed of *Oh, fuck, shit* and *God* . . .

'Present and correct,' said the fox.

Raf's suit ripped across the shoulder as he yanked off his jacket, sleeves revealing red silk as they turned inside out like snake skin. Kicking off his shoes Raf pulled the black tee over his newly cropped head, dropping cloth onto wet rock without thinking. His heart was a steady hammer.

'Chill,' ordered the fox and Raf's cardiac rhythm steadied. He couldn't see the animal but it sounded near. Sounded full-size, too, as tall as he was, with a voice that stuck its claws into his memory and ripped.

'Nictate your inner eyelids.' Raf did what the fox suggested. Experience showed this was usually safer. 'Now get out there.'

The water was warmer than Raf expected, salt like blood, and phosphorescence clung to him as he swam. The swimmer was further out than Raf had thought and the heavy cloth of his trousers dragged Raf back like a chute, slowing him down. But he swam steadily, closing the distance between them.

Clear the mouth of vomit, lift the chin . . . pinch the nose, take a deep breath and blow . . . take your mouth away and watch the chest fall . . .

He was pretty sure he could do mouth-to-mouth. Resuscitation too, if necessary. *Find the top of the arch of the ribs . . . two fingers on it and heel of the hand on breastbone . . . press hard on the lower half of breastbone* . . . The number of apparently random facts Raf could pull out of his head always surprised him. Not least because he'd never been that good at turning up to lessons.

When Zara broke the surface she was behind him. She didn't stop giggling until Raf turned and moonlight suddenly lit his face.

'*You.*' Zara sounded genuinely shocked.

'Yeah,' said Raf tightly. 'Me . . .' He was about to say something truly vicious but Zara's shoulders broke the surface as a wave sucked back in the undertow. Bare skin, no strap for her costume. It took Raf a second to process what his eyes had seen and his adrenal system had reacted to already.

She swam naked.

'Who did you think it was?' Raf demanded.

She didn't answer, not at first. 'This is my beach,' Zara said finally. 'You're trespassing.' That's who she thought it was, some idiot trespasser.

Raf shook his head. 'Your father told me to . . .'

Shit and double shit.

Did Hamzah expect this – and what did it say about him if he did? Raf lent back into the water and kicked for shore, still swearing at his own stupidity. Back on shore, he didn't bother with shoes, jacket or tee-shirt, just rolled them into a untidy ball and stamped off towards the villa. He didn't care how many lawyers the man had in there.

'Where are you going?' Zara shouted from the water.

'To get a lift home,' Raf said angrily. 'You think a taxi's going to pick me up in this state?'

'Try walking,' she called. 'It's what ordinary people do.'

Raf turned back and stared. 'Hani's at home,' he said coldly. 'Her aunt got murdered yesterday. This morning Hani left the house for the first time ever, to watch her aunt be buried. We're sleeping in the courtyard because she's too frightened to go back indoors. It's late. I've been away longer than I said I would. Which bit of that don't you understand?'

Raf's face was ice, his words utterly uninflected. He could have been talking to a particularly stupid child, except he would never talk to any child in that way.

'Five minutes,' said Zara. 'Meet me at the gate.' When she hit the beach it was thirty paces up shore, where her clothes waited in a neat pile. Then she was running for the villa and swearing inside her head, mostly at herself.

It was the sun that did it. Sports convertibles were big in North Africa, even locally made ones. Morocco had its own air-cooled Atlas, Algeria imported a three-wheeled Soviet Benz knock-off and the Ottoman countries made do with a sub-licensed Ford that leaked oil, belched smoke and was so simple to service it could be stripped back by a ten-year-old and repaired by a blacksmith.

Of course, almost everybody who could afford something more upscale imported a Japanese machine. One of those enamel-and-chrome cut-down copies of old American beasts, all retro fins and goggle headlights. They looked great, told you when they needed gas and practically booked themselves in for servicing, never mind downloading their own tweaks for tuning. Which, with twelve tiny cylinders and forty-eight valves, was just as well.

Zara's car was different. Its 240-horsepower V6 engine had been turbocharged way up beyond three hundred. The headlights were sharp multi-element clusters, using light-guide technology. A speed-tuned aerofoil in the nose and a fixed diffuser tunnel at the rear kept the wheels glued to the road.

It was low, silver and spartan inside. The two-seat cockpit was stripped back, a simple array of controls with an unmistakable utilitarian elegance. The fascias, fillings and switches were machined from solid aluminium. It was the first racing F-type Jaguar that Raf had seen outside of the one in Seattle Museum.

'Get in and hold on.'

Raf grabbed a side handle and she was away, ramming the clutch through a crescendo of rapid gear changes rather than use automatic. Then it was near-silent running all the way, the Jaguar's engine never rising above a growl as the F-type burned up night traffic on the Corniche, hung a tight left into Place Orabi, tyres leaving burned rubber on the blacktop.

Khedive Mohammed Ali appeared and vanished in a blur of grandeur, the Place des Consuls streaming by on either side. A right skid down a short alley between Catholic and Greek Orthodox cathedrals fed her through to Rue Kemil, the unlit shops on either side reflecting only each other in darkened glass windows, until the car roared between them, headlights picking out peeling script over locked doorways.

'I didn't do that for you,' said Zara firmly, as the car screeched to a halt at the entrance to Rue Cif. And then she was crunching her way through the gears again, leaving him alone on a street corner, fifty paces from where Hani waited on the other side of a wall.

CHAPTER 29

All matter moved. At a basic, base level atoms resonated, electrons could simultaneously occupy contradictory positions in space. What the eye regarded as solid was anything but . . . Of course, at a human level, movement was also what you got when people were too empty to stay still. That was the fox's opinion, anyway.

Wild Boy rode a red 650cc with a custom-built exhaust pot no larger than the silencer on a Ruger rifle. The bike was Japanese like Wild Boy himself, which had no significance (the same bike was ridden by ZeeZee, standard issue for all lieutenants in Hu San's street militia). And Wild Boy was on his way to see ZeeZee, which did . . .

The Japanese kid dressed smart but flashy in silk suits that flattered his rough-cut hair and emphasized his slim shoulders and narrow hips. At the front, Wild Boy's hair was razored to frame wide eyes and high cheek-bones. That was the way Hu San liked it.

He wore a brushed-steel Tag Heuer, lace-up Louis Vuitton boots, cotton shirt from Abercrombie & Fitch, a white Moschino coat over his dark suit and wide Alain Mikli spectacles fitted with tinted glass. Even his cigarettes were Gitanes, carried in a black enamel case with a Gucci clasp. Everything about Wild Boy had a label except the position he occupied in the Five Winds.

It took ZeeZee two months to work out what Wild Boy did. At first he figured Wild Boy and Hu San were somehow family, then that Wild Boy was her bodyguard. Though why Hu San would need a bodyguard when she could wield a blade that way wasn't clear. Unless it was a matter of face. As it was, ZeeZee didn't really work it out for himself at all. Hu San's Croat enforcer Artan told him. 'They're lovers, fuckwit, he's her pretty boy . . .' Wild Boy didn't protect Hu San. She protected him.

Wild Boy hated ZeeZee from the start.

Maybe it was simply the fact that Hu San took ZeeZee on at all. He was the only Caucasian in Five Winds, except for Artan, and Artan didn't count. Hu San got through enforcers like Wild Boy got through Chinese take-out, which was often how her enforcers ended up looking after she'd sent them to a disputed area of town. Though those areas got fewer by the day.

The only branded thing ZeeZee carried was a small .357 Taurus, with a rib grip and two-inch ported barrel, in matte Spectrum blue. And even then he carried that in a cheap $10 neoprene holster from Gunmart. He didn't want the revolver and only carried it because Hu San insisted. Unlike Wild Boy's gun, ZeeZee's weapon was legal, clean, licensed and never-before-fired, and ZeeZee aimed to keep it that way.

The job Hu San had chosen for him was pig-simple. A hundred years back, in a harbour-side bar, an English ex-policeman called Charles Jardine met a Seattle attorney named Angus Bannerman. Several whiskies later they came up with Jardine&Bannerman, an agency that would handle both the legal and investigative sides of life's personal problems, plus deliver subpoenas and do a little underwriting of bail bonds on the side.

By the time ZeeZee became a junior partner, the legal and investigative side was a memory held only in mouldering ledgers in the basement, bail bonds were a minor sideline and thrusting subpoenas into dirty hands made up the bulk of the business, especially subpoenas that were hard to deliver. On paper, which really meant on microfiche at a warehouse out on the city edge and on a thumb-smeared DVD in City Hall, the company was recorded as stand-alone and independent; majority-owned by its partners. In practice, Hu San owned and ran it, and always referred to the company as Jade&Bamboo, smiling at the words. As with most of her jokes, ZeeZee didn't get the punchline.

All ZeeZee had to do was dress neatly, present himself at the reception desk of some gilt-edged outfit in Houston, Los Angeles or Seattle (though mostly it was Seattle) and talk his way up to whatever floor was necessary. Either that or stroll casually through the doors of some exclusive club as if he belonged. His English accent and manners usually did the rest.

Once inside, he apologized for disturbing his quarry, handed them the court order and, whipping out a tiny Nikon, immediately apologized again for snapping a shot of them holding the papers. There would be a click, a faint ping and the evidence would be uploaded to J&B's secure databox before the person holding the subpoena had even worked out what was happening.

And all the time, ZeeZee thought people were polite because he was polite, not realizing until he was in Huntsville that the bulge of a revolver slung under his left armpit said more about him than a floppy haircut, elegant clothes or any credit card ever could.

135

For a year or so, what Hu San got out of owning J&B eluded ZeeZee. Until he began to realize that for every fifteen or twenty supposedly difficult subpoenas he managed to deliver, there was always one job where the target had vanished like early-morning mist before the sun. Sometimes the target left his or her old life behind in uneaten toast or unwashed clothes. And sometimes their possessions were gone as well, gutted out of an apartment or house that echoed with absence.

There seemed no logic, at first, to which person on the list would suddenly vanish but slowly ZeeZee began to develop a sixth sense. So one autumn morning he reversed the order of two jobs and turned up early at an art brut *concrete lodge outside Seattle.*

ZeeZee left his red Suzuki and black crash helmet at the top of a rough earth track that fed off the crumbling backtop and walked down towards the house and Puget Sound's pale waters beyond.

The man on the jetty wasn't expecting to see him. That much was obvious from the way he froze, heavy suitcase still clutched in one hand.

'Sorry to disturb you . . .' ZeeZee held out his hand and when Micky O'Brian put down his suitcase, ZeeZee slipped the court order into the hand that reached out, watching the fingers close from instinct. ZeeZee relied on that reaction a lot in his line of work.

'Smile.'

By lunchtime the sudden breakdown of Micky O'Brian was leading the local news and had third slot on Sky. A feeding frenzy was about to begin. Ravaged by drugs, or maybe by pleurisy brought on by AIDS, by alcohol and painkiller addiction, by paradise syndrome . . . Journalistic diagnoses were made from positions of absolute ignorance; conflicting, contradictory, as many irrefutable facts offered as there were commentators.

Shots of a private ambulance with blackened windows appeared fast on Celebrity Update. *As did footage of a grey-haired woman in a white coat who spoke sincerely and at great length to the camera without actually giving out any information at all.* Confidentiality *got a name check, so did* courage, hope *and* recovery. *The name of the clinic got mentioned three times, but that information was redundant. Everyone watching the CU channel already knew where celebs got their lives, health and shit back on track.*

The fact was, Micky O'B would be in there forty-eight hours max, seventy-two hours at a push. The clink operated a high-profile arrivals policy, while arranging the world's quickest and most discreet departures.

The only thing on which every single commentator agreed was that Micky O'Brian's agent had signed him into a clinic that morning and the head of the clinic was now refusing to let cameras past the gate. That

Micky had recently been served with a summons regarding a major drugs bust went unmentioned.

Wild Boy slid to a halt outside ZeeZee's apartment as dusk hit, rolling darkness and soft mist through the streets. Hanging his helmet from a handlebar, the Japanese boy took the stairs two at a time on his way up to the third floor. He didn't knock, just kicked the door out of its frame with some fancy footwork and stood in the gap, glaring.

'Hey, fuckwit . . .'

Been here. Fear filled ZeeZee's throat like mercury rising in an old-fashioned thermometer.

'. . . Who the fuck do you think you are?'

It was the wrong question. But only because ZeeZee couldn't answer it. So Tiriganaq answered it for him. Using the English boy like a puppet.

'I know who I am . . .' said ZeeZee's voice, 'and I don't give a fuck who you think you are.' Then ZeeZee found himself scrambling off the bed to grab his holster and yank free the Taurus.

When ZeeZee woke up he was standing in an approximation of Wild Boy's usual stance, shoulders relaxed and one hand hanging loose at his side. In the background, on a screen next to the damaged door, the newsfeed kept running unwatched; flickering like a sad ghost at the edge of his vision. It was old footage of Micky O'Brian, back when he could still act.

Wild Boy looked at the gun and smiled. 'You don't have the balls.'

The click of a hammer being thumbed back was ZeeZee's answer. Some of Hu San's people filed their hammers flat to stop the point snagging on clothes. Not ZeeZee. His revolver was factory-perfect. And when ZeeZee had first started working for Five Winds, Wild Boy had delivered a box of fifty bullets. Only seven of them were missing. They were the bullets in his gun.

'Try me,' said ZeeZee, and raised the gun. The Arctic fox's growl behind his eyes was enough to make the world resonate like a struck glass. He could feel Tiriganaq's grin leaching through onto his own face.

'I've got a message,' Wild Boy said. 'Hu San is very disappointed in you. And she thinks you should be disappointed in yourself.' He hooked a long strand of dark hair out of his eyes, concentrated on delivering his message and tried not to worry too much about the weird smile on ZeeZee's face.

Then he left.

CHAPTER 30

8th July

Hamzah kept his promise. The builders arrived at five the next morning in a Mack diesel with *HZ Industrial* logoed down the side. They parked up in the Rue Sherif and a Taureg foreman in a striped jellaba walked round to the back where he hammered on the door until Raf appeared, bleary-eyed and squinting.

Khartoum should have gone but he sat unmoving in one corner of the courtyard, not far from where Hani slept. From what little he'd said, Raf gathered he was terrified the killers might come back.

The young Taureg glanced doubtfully at Raf's tattered dressing gown, which came from an old wardrobe on the second floor and was a testament to the late Lady Nafisa's private frugality. Anyone else would have thrown it in the bin. 'Your Excellency?'

Raf smiled. 'Ashraf al-Mansur,' he agreed. 'Hamzah Effendi sent you?'

'Yes, Your Excellency . . .' Shrewd eyes glanced over Raf's shoulder at the madersa's narrow entrance with its porter's bench and traditional blind ending. Getting building supplies in that way would be next to impossible. As for removing the walls of an upstairs office once it had been taken down . . .

'Does Your Excellency . . .'

'On Rue Sherif,' said Raf. 'Bricked up.'

Five minutes later, the foreman came back with two workmen who looked even younger. Each carried nothing more sophisticated than a crowbar.

Next to arrive were the police. Two officers came at dawn, stepping over rubble to pass through the freshly opened front door. No one had reported noise or called in with suspicions about a truck parked on Rue Sherif. And they didn't come to check that builders were meant to be ripping out a wall to make space to remove bits of a crime scene. They

138

came for Raf. It was a measure of Felix's fury that he didn't come himself.

Five minutes after the two officers appeared, Madame Mila arrived in a long blue Mercedes with tinted windows. The kind of car that screamed *important government official*. Raf could put the sequence together in his head. Hamzah had turned up at the precinct with his lawyer, quoting Raf as his reason for being there. Hamzah had left the precinct. In a fury, Felix had woken the Minister to get permission to bring in Raf.

The only thing Raf didn't understand was why the Minister had immediately called Madame Mila or what Madame Mila could want from him. It turned out to be his signature.

'Sign here.' The woman thrust out a notepad and a stylus.

Raf glanced at the screen and shook his head. 'Not without knowing what it says . . .'

'You can't read?' The woman's voice was incredulous.

'Not Arabic,' said Raf, 'though I can speak it . . . How well do you speak English?'

The woman said nothing.

'Well, then . . .' He reached for the pad and passed it to Hani. 'You tell me,' he said. 'What does it say?'

The girl skimmed the swirls of Arabic, then read them again slowly, her lips twisting as she mouthed the words to herself. 'I don't want this,' she said to Raf, her eyes suddenly enormous with fear.

'Why not?' he demanded. 'What does it say?'

It was Madame Mila who answered. 'An order is being issued for Hani to be made a ward of my office and given into protective custody.'

'An orphanage?'

The coroner-magistrate looked at him as if he was mad. 'Lady Jalila has offered to stand guardian to this child.' She glanced at Hani. 'You are a very lucky young lady.'

'If that's a court order,' Raf said slowly, 'why do you need my signature?'

'A formality,' said the woman.

'And without my signature . . . ?'

'The girl will still be taken.'

'Just not yet,' said Raf, nodding to himself. He handed her back the pad. 'I'm afraid I can't sign this . . . The child will stay here with her nanny.' He pointed to where Donna hovered in a courtyard doorway, scowling at the noise. The old woman was cook, housekeeper and mopper-up after Ali-Din. Being the child's official nanny should add no extra burden.

'So,' said Raf. 'Am I under arrest?' He fired off his question at the elder of the two police officers. 'Well?'

'Of course not, Your Excellency, but we have been told to bring you in for questioning.'

'In that case,' Raf said. 'I'll be with you as soon as we've all had breakfast.' He paused, to look at their doubtful faces. 'Don't worry,' he said. 'You can get on the blower and tell Felix I'm not going anywhere.'

The meal Donna provided was simple: *'aish shamsi* bread warmed on an oil-fired range in the kitchen, which was where they ate. It was served with a thin dribble of sweet butter and a large mug of chocolate dusted with cinnamon. Donna also made chocolate and warm bread for the builders, then carried another tray out to the waiting police car.

'Woman's gone,' Hani told Raf, translating from Donna's Portuguese without missing a bite. The child looked less frightened now that daylight had arrived and she had a plate of warm food in front of her, but she was still obviously worried. 'Do you really have to go?'

Raf nodded.

'But you'll come back?'

'Of course,' Raf said firmly. 'They probably just want to talk about the stuff I did in America.'

'When you were an assassin . . . ?'

'I wasn't an assassin.'

Hani actually smiled. A faint flicker as if she was the only one to get the punchline to a particularly obscure joke. 'Of course not,' she said. Grabbing a whole slab of *'aish shamsi*, Hani started peeling off strips. 'I'm off to feed Ali-Din,' she announced and slipped from the table. Seconds later, Raf heard Hani's feet clattering on the stairs up to the *qaa*. It was the first time she'd stepped inside the house since her aunt was murdered.

Raf was distraught, apparently . . . Having missed out on Tuesdays murder *and* Wednesday's autopsy plus funeral, Thursday's tabloids had decided to make up for missing time by running the killing, autopsy and funeral as one breathless story, with endless sidebars of comment and very few facts. Actually, it was mostly comment or conjecture, with little blind URLs at the end of each paragraph to remind readers that they could always download more of the same.

He was also desolate, missing and strangely unmoved, Raf discovered. A little-known figure in Iskandryian society, rumour now had him as one of the most-influential fixers in North Africa. His work in America was so secret that every justified request to the Minister of

Police for official information had been met with an impenetrable wall of silence.

There was a long-lens grab of him sitting on the gravel next to Hani outside the al-Mansur mausoleum and a standing shot taken at such an extreme angle it had to have been lifted from a spysat.

'Lies' snarled Felix, sweeping the papers from a table. 'Like most of the crap you've told me.' Felix jerked his head at the officer standing beside Raf and the man stepped backwards, looking doubtful. So Felix jerked his head again and the officer scuttled from the room.

That left Felix and Raf together in a cell no more than ten paces by ten paces. All the light was artificial, glaring down from a single strip crudely screwed to a filthy ceiling. Blood – or what looked like blood – was splattered up one wall and around the chair in which Raf sat. A relic of earlier encounters.

The fat man's bunched fists were shaking with anger.

Raf stood up and stepped away from the table.

'Oh, don't worry,' Felix said bitterly, 'No one would dare get heavy on *your* ass. We're not that stupid.' He slammed a file on the table and nodded to Raf to open it. Inside was a single sheet of A4 paper. At the top was a pixelated mugshot of Raf, still wearing dreadlocks and beard.

'We received this while you were on your way in,' said Felix. 'Only it was crypted so we couldn't immediately get it open. But that was okay, because five minutes after you arrived we got sent a neat little 4096-bit key. Nothing too complicated, right? Because we're police and we're stupid . . .'

Felix pulled a packet of Cleopatra from his pocket and tapped loose a cigarette. Ignoring the 'No Smoking' sign glued to the door, he lit up with an old 7th Cavalry Zippo and dragged carcinogenics deep into his lungs. 'You know, it's hard to believe anyone of twenty-five could have built up this kind of record.'

Raf ran his eyes down the sheet with rising disbelief. It was hard to imagine how anyone could have that record, full stop . . . Personal envoy from the Sultan in Stambul. Weapons training at Sandhurst. A spell in Paris, counter-intelligence at Les Halles. A level of security clearance so high its name was blanked out because no one at the precinct had authority to know it existed. Throw in genius-level IQ, eidetic memory, weapons-grade negative capability and it read like a biofile straight out of . . .

'Yeah,' said Raf, 'I find it hard to believe myself.' Every year of his life was covered, from leaving school to arriving in Iskandryia: he just didn't recognize any of it.

'Mind telling me why you warned Hamzah?' Felix ground his

cigarette butt out on the table top and promptly lit another one, inhaling hard. His jacket stank of cigarettes, whisky and disappointment. 'Unless, of course, it's a secret.'

'No secret,' said Raf. 'He just didn't do it.'

'And you know who did?'

'No.' Raf shook his head. But he did know it wasn't Hamzah.

'Let me see,' said Felix. 'Your aunt arranges a marriage that comes apart before it happens. Hamzah threatens to kill her. She dies. We decide to bring him in for questioning. With me so far . . . ?'

Yeah, he was.

'And then, very strangely, you tip him off and a few hours later his boys are demolishing large chunks of the al-Mansur madersa. Conveniently destroying a crime site in the process.'

'It gets worse,' said Raf. 'My aunt took Hamzah for $2,500,000 in commission on that deal. It's missing.'

'Sweet fuck.' The fat man's cigarette went head first into the table, dying in a shower of sparks, and out came a hip flask. Felix examined the thing as if he'd never seen one before and thrust it angrily back in his pocket, 'You wanna coffee?'

An old Otis hauled them up to ground level and they left together, walking under the oppressive grandeur of the precinct's entrance portal. On their way through, every officer at the front desk stared at Raf until he stared back and ten people looked away at once. 'Get used to it,' said Felix. 'Where do you want to go?'

'Le Trianon.'

'Should have guessed,' said Felix and clicked his fingers for a taxi. It was only 9:30 in the morning, but Felix still recognized when he was right over the limit.

Raf was shown to his table only seconds after two Americans were ejected to make space. The New Yorkers stood on the other side of the red silk rope, glaring and muttering until Felix went to talk to them. They left quickly after that.

'What did you say?'

'Me . . . ?' Felix waited until the maître d' had finished arranging his plate so one octagonal edge exactly aligned with the table.

'Which one would Sir like?' The man asked, nodding to a trolley filled with pastries.

'All of them,' Felix said bluntly. 'But I'll take those three.' He pointed out three pieces of baklava dusted with crushed almonds. 'And bring me a proper-sized cup of coffee . . .'

'Well?' Raf asked.

142

Felix looked down the street as if he might still see the departing New Yorkers through the press of bodies filling the sidewalk. 'Said you were the Khedive's personal hit man and they'd been hogging your table . . . You're not, are you?' Before Raf could answer, Felix flipped up his hand. 'Don't feel you have to answer that, obviously.'

Huntsville had been simple. Raf had understood the rules. Most of which he'd kept and a few of which he'd broken. He'd taken who he'd become on remand and kept the identity, because it worked. The freaky hair and biker beard had been good protective camouflage. But trying to understand his new life was like pushing water up a hill. Every time he got near the top the fox curled up inside his head warned him it was the wrong hill or the water was gone. Raf was tired, more scared than he dared admit and he was alone in a city that got more, not less weird the more he knew about it. And then there was Hani . . .

'Look,' said Raf, 'can I tell you something?'

Felix bit off another chunk of baklava and Raf took this for assent.

'That piece of paper,' said Raf, 'it's crap, all of it. I don't have weapons training. I'm not in the Sultan's employ. I've never even been to Stambul . . .'

'Yeah, right.' Felix asked, swallowing his mouthful. 'So what *were* you doing in America?'

Raf didn't answer. He couldn't.

Felix sighed, but whatever he wanted to say was cut dead by a sudden buzz from his watch. 'You'd better get home,' he told Raf as he tapped the *off* button. 'Madame Mila's turned up again.'

'*She* called *you*?' It sounded unlikely even as Raf said it.

'No, that was Hani.'

'How did she know I was with you?' Raf asked.

Felix scooped up the last sticky crumbs of baklava and stuffed them into his open mouth. 'More to the point,' he said, 'how did the kid get my number?'

143

CHAPTER 31

'And where do you think you're going?'

ZeeZee paused on the steps while a doorman raked him with the gaze that hotel staff everywhere reserve for tramps, hawkers and delivery boys who've come to the wrong entrance.

'Got this.' ZeeZee lifted the cardboard crate a little higher and waited. What people expected to see was usually what they saw: it cut down on thinking time. ZeeZee had been about five when he'd worked that out. The doorman expected elegant diners and the occasional delivery boy too idiotic or ignorant to find his own way to the service entrance at the rear.

Which was what ZeeZee gave him.

'Where do you want it?' ZeeZee might sound stupid but he was being intelligent, more than intelligent . . . Unintelligent people who disappointed Hu San usually ended up having accidents. While people intelligent enough to be disappointed in themselves mostly decided to suck on a gun barrel, to save Hu San the trouble.

ZeeZee didn't intend to do either: but nor was he stupid enough to try to hightail it out of Seattle. His only route to safety was to face up to Hu San in such a way that he was both alive and forgiven when the confrontation ended. And since getting to Hu San before *Wild Boy* had been an impossibility, success depended on meeting the woman later, in a place *Wild Boy* didn't go.

That Hu San knew nothing about the upcoming meeting was obvious. Her evenings at SHC were private, a shrine of calm in the busy wilderness of her day, and it had never occurred to her that anyone might dare interrupt.

Getting unnoticed into SHC took a pair of overalls, a Mariners baseball cap worn back to front, bad attitude and a case of vintage Mumm. Not that ZeeZee could afford twelve bottles of champagne, but any price that saved his life was cheap.

'Round the back, idiot.' The doorman glared at ZeeZee, then stepped quickly back as a thin woman in Arctic fox climbed the steps and nodded for the doorman to start the revolving door.

'Good evening, Madame. I do hope you have a pleasant—' That was as far as the man got before ZeeZee pushed forward.

'Just tell me who gets this, okay?'

Both fox-fur and doorman turned in shock.

'Look,' said ZeeZee. 'Somebody has to sign for this crap.' He shifted the clinking box higher still, until it half blocked his face. 'Come on . . .'

The woman stared at him. She had the taut manner of a judge or maybe an upstream divorce lawyer. Someone prosperous, someone who expected lesser species like delivery boys to show her respect. 'Who do you work for?'

'Why?' ZeeZee borrowed the look he gave her straight from Wild Boy. A hard-eyed stare that ended in a deceptively gentle smile. 'What's it to you?'

The doorman was giving ZeeZee directions and a name before the boy even had time to return his attention to the uniformed flunky. 'There,' said ZeeZee, 'that wasn't too hard . . .'

Darkness, silence and cats. His three favourite things. Or maybe the three things that made him feel safest. The stink he could have done without. Scrawny grey shadows fought over an empty foie-gras tin fallen from a sodden cardboard box, pencil-thin backs crooked in anger. Along one side of the courtyard was an open loading bay, along the opposite side were trashcans, all overflowing.

Either the garbage union were on strike or SHC hadn't heard of recycling. Whichever, the courtyard stank of rotting food and cat piss. Seattle's most exclusive dining club had two faces and this was the other one.

'Elmore,' ZeeZee demanded of an elderly Hispanic sitting on the edge of the loading bay, pulling heavily on a cigarette. Dead butts littered the ground below his dangling feet like empty cases from an overactive machine-gun.

The man jerked his thumb behind him, towards darkness.

ZeeZee adjusted his eyes. The darkness was large and empty, overlooked by internal windows and stained across its scuzzy floor with food spills and scabs of old chewing gum.

Choosing a door at random, ZeeZee kicked it open and staggered down a passage past the open door to a kitchen, case clutched firmly in his hands. Heat blasted out at him, along with the stink of grilled fish. Somewhere inside the kitchen a radio was playing an ancient Daniel Lands track, the soft rock drowned beneath a crash of plates and the clatter of table silver.

145

A swing door at the end of the passage flipped ZeeZee from one world to another: the back-of-house peeling green paint changing to distressed wooden panelling, as the old linoleum underfoot became carpet, not deep pile but expensive and exactly matched to the pale colours that swirled down the room's long handmade curtains. He was staring across a foyer and through a revolving door, straight at the back of the uniformed doorman.

It was time to change identities.

Dumping his overalls in a swing-top bin next to old-fashioned porcelain urinals, ZeeZee crammed his champagne crate in an under-sink cupboard beneath the powder room's row of stone basins. Of course, he had to flip the cupboard's brass lock with the blade of his pocket knife, but the damage was minimal and a twist of torn-off paper jammed the door shut again.

The figure that straightened up in the mirror was smart Unquestionably young but neatly dressed in white shirt and Hermès tie bought for the occasion. His blond hair was just slightly too long but combing was enough to turn the look from unacceptable to merely louche. A fat cigar was all it took to finish the part of rich boy about town . . .

'I'm sorry to trouble you, Madame.'

Hu San looked up from her notebook to see an Armani-clad barman hovering nervously at her elbow.

'One of our new members is most insistent about joining you.' The Turkish boy's nod was discreet, but there was no mistaking he meant the young man who stood at the bar, smoke spiralling up from a Romeo y Julieta held tightly between the fingers of one hand.

Dark eyes locked onto ZeeZee's face. There was no shock or outrage, barely even surprise. It was, thought ZeeZee, like looking into a deep well and not even knowing if there was water at the bottom. 'Send him over,' said Hu San. 'But tell him to lose that cigar first . . .'

Around the edge of the room, on black leather banquettes, slouched Seattle's wealthy. Tall and blond or dark, handsome and unfortunately not tall at all, elegantly dressed or expensively dishevelled, both women and men talked intently or stood to shake hands and air-kiss briefly. The Brownian motion of money.

The woman with the fox fur was repeating her story of meeting a horrible delivery boy on the way in. She was telling it for the third time and her partner was still pretending to be shocked.

Only a few of those in the room showed their age in a surgical tightness around the eyes, the regrettable side effects of having reached middle age before the start of nanetic surgery. The rest had that youthful permanence

146

which came from being able to afford faces that were constantly rebuilt from the inside.

Hu San sat in the middle of the room, in her own exclusion zone. Expensive hair, simple jewellery. Anyone who was close enough to her table to smell her scent or see the tiny silk characters embroidered on her black jacket was too close. And getting too close to Hu San was dangerous. Only, in ZeeZee's case, staying away was more dangerous still. She was vaguely impressed that the boy had been able to work this out for himself.

'What will you drink?' Hu San demanded.

'A Budweiser.'

'Green tea,' she told the waiter, 'and bring a glass of house white for our newest member.'

'So, tell me why you're here,' said the Chinese woman once the drinks had arrived and ZeeZee had pulled up a chair of his own.

Very carefully, the English boy placed his long-stemmed glass onto the white tablecloth between them and – despite being seated – put his hands together, bowing as best he could. 'I wish to apologize,' ZeeZee told Hu San. 'Haruki has told me how badly I have disappointed you.' He used Wild Boy's real name when talking to Hu San, but then, everybody always did. 'I am truly sorry.'

Hu San nodded. 'Drink your wine,' she said. 'I'm going to make a call.'

No mobiles allowed, not even in the bar. ZeeZee could understand that, especially in a dining club that thought stone basins were smart and didn't serve beer. And that was the last thing he bothered to think until her return was signalled by a hand resting lightly on his shoulder, the merest brush. Probably no more significant than reaching out to pat a stray.

'I've booked us a table for supper . . .' said Hu San. 'A waiter will bring your drink.' And she nodded to the Turkish boy behind the bar who watched them go. Not openly but almost proprietorially, as if noting, with slight bemusement, that two rather disparate people had made friends in his bar.

'Wow,' said ZeeZee, stopping in the doorway of the dining room. A low ceiling was hung with swathes of cream silk that made it look lower still. The floor was blond wood, probably beech, the gold walls anything but straight, rippling round the large room in soft, almost Gaudiesque curves. The effect was of dining within a vast, impossibly expensive tent.

Hu San smiled. 'I own both this club and the hotel,' she said, answering a question ZeeZee hadn't asked. 'The city may not like me, but without my money this place would have shut years ago.' She nodded towards a window and the dark glittering water of the harbour beyond it. 'Five floors, original building, right on the waterfront, less than two hundred members . . . It costs me over a million a year in lost revenue.'

147

'So why do you do it?'

'Work it out.' Hu San's smile went cold.

'Influential people, increasingly valuable location . . .' The boy stood just inside the door and watched money rise off the other diners like steam. 'And inside information,' he added finally, afraid that Hu San would be angry. Instead the Chinese woman just nodded.

'Good,' she said, 'Not just a pretty face after all. Now,' she clicked her fingers lightly, 'let's eat . . .'

Hu San ordered for both of them. Anorexic food for anorexic appetites. It certainly wasn't what got served in the cafés and bars he used. The soup was Savoy cabbage, a teaspoon of sour cream swirled into a tablespoon's worth of lightly puréed cabbage, the whole thing covered with fine shavings of black truffle. It came in a large white bowl that appeared badly chipped round the rim but was probably meant to look like that. After the soup came a sandwich, except that Hu San ate hers with a fork, so ZeeZee did the same.

Mimic, reflect, replace – if nothing else he knew his own strengths. Mind you, that was because he'd seen them laid out – boxed off and numbered – in a guarantee the fox had shown him. It was all there, zipped up tight inside his own head. And, given his mother's belief in the purity of nature, he was lucky she hadn't gone for high design, or he'd probably have had bug eyes. Except that all his augmentations seemed to be mammalian. Well, almost all of them . . .

'Eat,' said Hu San, spearing a sliver of warm pork that had been hidden under a paper-thin square of bread slow cooked until it was dry enough to crumble at the touch. Holding together the pork and bread like glue was a mustard mayonnaise mixed with shredded rocket.

Hu San drank a Californian Chardonnay with the Savoy cabbage, switched to an Australian Shiraz for the pork and finished with a chilled '38 Sauternes, which she used to wash down a tiny vanilla cream baked with armagnac prunes. She drank one half glass from each bottle and left the rest, without offering any to the boy who sat opposite and nursed his house white until its contents were blood-heat.

Occasionally she'd look at him and smile. And at the end she leaned forward and brushed his hair out of his eyes with a single finger. 'It's time for you to go,' she said. 'Remember to leave the way you came in . . .'

They were waiting for him in the loading bay. Which he could have guessed, had he bothered to think about it.

They were fast, efficient and professional. But then, that was their job. ZeeZee didn't get in even one blow, one kick . . . He was too busy fighting the length of wire that had been flipped over his shoulders from behind and now held his arms helpless at his sides.

'Fuckwit.'

Until a punch caught him in the stomach, ZeeZee had assumed the person holding the wire was Wild Boy. But Wild Boy was working the gloves. Stepping out of the shadows in best street-punk fashion, his leather collar turned up against the night wind, his hair elegantly dishevelled. Both fists wrapped in neoprene gloves that were weighted along the knuckles with lead shot.

'Wrong place, wrong time . . .' Wild Boy took ZeeZee's face between thumb and finger and squeezed, gouging the pressure points. 'You know what you did? Wrong, wrong, wrong.' The first two punches caught ZeeZee in the stomach, the third slid between the English boy's rib cage and hip, causing a blood-red poppy of pain to flare inside ZeeZee's head and then wilt slowly, from the petals inwards. Only the wire kept him on his feet.

'Bastard.'

'Aren't I?' Wild Boy drew back his fist and grinned.

'Not the face,' snapped the man holding ZeeZee upright. Fear was behind the sudden anger in his voice. 'You know what she said. Not the face.'

'Shame,' complained Wild Boy, stepping up to ZeeZee to knee him through a breaking scream into . . .

In the beginning there was darkness and the fox comprehended it not. So it ran some diagnostics and the darkness was revealed as syncope, relating to abrupt cerebral hypoperfusion. A quick and dirty check on syncope and hypoperfusion convinced the fox that the problem was both local and diminishing, so it shut down again to save energy. The fox fed off neon mostly, because its nine other power options had failed.

Of course it featured telemetry, self-check integrity and various other measures designed to ensure permanence (with five intra-optic LEDs to warn the carrier in case of a system fault) but these had also failed. But then the Seimens-Oakley was a very early model and only intended to run for seven years in the first place.

So now it worked in the background on a need-to-know basis. If the host needed to know, it popped up, otherwise it could run silent for months, even years. The fox lived in ZeeZee's skull. Not his brain but his actual skull, housed in a compact ceramic case because ceramic allowed uninterrupted transmission and had high mechanical strength and identical hardness to the surrounding bone.

It had numerous functions, expressed in its own guarantee as a complicated menu of sets and subsets. But its primary function was obvious. The fox existed to keep its host alive. 'Well balanced' and 'happy' hadn't been options on the early models. And anyway, the marker for genius doubled as a marker for dysfunction: that had always been made quite clear.

ZeeZee took a shower, long and hot enough to bring out the bruises, then walked over to the mirror to take a look at the damage. He had a flowering of broken skin over his ribs and above one hip. His balls felt the size of oranges, though they looked no worse than dark and swollen plums. And dark weals circled his upper arms where the wire had held him tight.

What interested him most, though, was a raw, weeping graze down one cheek of his depressingly adolescent face. A surface wound only, probably from where he had hit the filthy concrete floor on blacking out. That seemed most likely. But wherever the injury had come from, it was bleeding – which was a start.

The tub of ibuprofen in his bathroom cabinet suggested one 200 mg tablet, increased to two if the pain didn't go. ZeeZee gulped four, washed them down with a couple of bottles of cold Bud from the fridge and waited impatiently for both beer and analgesic to bite on his vomit-emptied stomach. He wasn't brave enough to beat himself up while sober.

The first blow ZeeZee threw did no more than make his eyes water, which was less than useless, so he went back to the fridge. Maybe you had to be furious or drunk to be able to hurt yourself properly.

As a fourth Bud followed the third down the boy's gullet and the alcohol finally began to flood his veins, ZeeZee found the courage to punch his own face. Or maybe it was the idiocy. Whichever, he slammed his face down into an upcoming punch and felt an eyebrow split.

When he stopped swearing and trying, he watched the eye socket beneath the split brow close up front of him, as he looked into a wall mirror, seeing a naked boy squint hazily back. Now was the time to wrap ice in a dishcloth or use a pocket of frozen peas. But ZeeZee did neither. Instead, he took an old Opinel knife out of a kitchen drawer and yanked open the blade. Without giving himself time to think, ZeeZee lifted the knife to his face and slashed across his chin, opening a two-inch long cut that curved under his jaw.

All he needed now was a plaster and sleep . . .

Winter rain against the window of ZeeZee's bedroom woke him with a steady roll of sound, too fast to be defined as drumming. Occasionally the clatter rose as gusting wind hurled droplets like gravel straight against the glass. The temperature inside his apartment was cold enough to make even him huddle under a fourteen-tog quilt.

It was partly that his only radiator was broken, but mostly the cold came from an open window. He had his years at Scottish boarding school to thank for that. In Switzerland there had been individual rooms, shower cubicles and underfloor heating. None of his Scottish dormitories had even been heated and all the windows were forever open, even when snow was falling. Fresh air and healthy living were the reasons given. Neither was true. Shut the windows and the stink of fifteen adolescents became unbearable; made worse by clouds of cheap deodorants and too much aftershave. Open windows made up for lack of washing and a once-weekly bath.

Rolling slowly out of bed, ZeeZee pulled back the curtains to give himself light and white walls that had been lost in darkness washed yellow, in the sudden sodium glare of the wet city outside. All he needed was enough light to piss – that, and another dose of analgesics. One day, of course, he'd get a real life. Probably around the time he got measured for a coffin.

Underneath its plaster, his cut had joined cleanly, the edges already lightly bound together by insoluble threads of fibrin. And now that his hands were steadier ZeeZee took time to cut and apply the neatest possible butterfly plasters. Hu San liked neat so that's what he'd give her. As promised on the box, the plasters slowly took on the colour of his skin until they were almost invisible. All the boy could now see was a clean, neat edge to the cut beneath.

Better than perfect.

What came next? Ribs, transport and clothes. Winding a long crêpe bandage round fractured ribs wasn't something he recommended. Mostly the pain just froze his lungs but sometimes, as ZeeZee reached for the unravelling roll of bandage, neural lightning caught at his heart as well. By the end, pinpricks of sweat prickled his hairline and his whole upper body felt as if it had been bound into a nettle corset. So he chewed yet more ibuprofen, though this time round he passed on the iced beer.

Usually ZeeZee had no trouble with stuff like which clothes to wear: he bought five of everything and rotated it. But today was different. Hu San wouldn't be expecting him at the breakfast meeting and, even if she was, she'd expect him to turn up in the usual dark suit, white shirt and red tie like he always did. Well, he was going to borrow a few of Wild Boy's feathers.

'Seattle Taxi Service,' said a woman after he punched nine digits on his home phone from memory. 'How can we improve your day . . . ?'

'A cab from here to the Seattle Harbour Hotel,' said ZeeZee. Then told the woman where he was and when he wanted the car, which was right then.

The line went silent. 'Yeah, we can do that. You going to let me see you?' This was a sight check, to see if he looked like some dustout or merely sounded like one.

'Sure.' He hit visual on his phone and the woman yelped.

'You're naked.'

'Yeah,' agreed ZeeZee. 'But I'll be dressed by the time the cab arrives.'

Her laugh was abrupt but not really unkind. 'You'd better be. Five minutes max . . .'

Which was what he needed, ZeeZee told himself. A countdown. He skipped on shaving because one, it would hurt and two, Hu San was obviously into rough trade. All the same, he took a razor to his jaw line. Black jacket, because that was the only colour he wore. A PaulSmith leather job, tailored but not tight. From right at the back of his small cupboard, he pulled a slate-grey silk shirt he'd bought but never worn and matched it to a pair of deep red trousers some Polish girl had given him two weeks before they split. She'd also been responsible for the silk shirt. He couldn't recall her name but he remembered the snakeskin bag he'd bought her, the by-product of one of his random attacks of senseless guilt.

Black shoes, black tie, and finally a pair of Armani shades with smoke-grey lenses that he'd found left forgotten on a café table near Hu San's shop. ZeeZee was dressed before the taxi arrived.

A porter rushed to open his taxi door and ZeeZee slipped the man $10. Maybe it was meant to be more, but that was what he had and it seemed quite enough to do the trick.

'HS Export,' he told the girl at the desk.

'They've already started,' said an older man, materializing behind her from some cubbyhole where assistant desk managers lived. He was trying hard not to stare at the cut on ZeeZee's face and not doing a good job.

'No problem,' said ZeeZee lightly. 'Have they actually started breakfast yet?'

The man looked at the girl who picked up an old-fashioned desk phone. 'Yes,' she said, 'I'm afraid so.' She nodded as she spoke, emphasizing the fact.

'Then perhaps you could order me Earl Grey and toast and have it brought straight in . . .' ZeeZee smiled before turning away. He knew which door to head for because there was a sign on it saying HS Export – meeting in progress and, besides, it was the same conference room every week . . .

'My apologies.'

Hu San looked up, saw the English boy standing stiffly in the open door and almost smiled. Saving face was something she understood.

Safe behind his shades, ZeeZee skimmed the room, editing out Victorian landscapes, Persian rugs, a large silver samovar and other examples of instant antiquity, probably bought by the yard. What ZeeZee was interested in was his audience. The one he was about to wow by doing precisely nothing.

Mostly they were suits. A couple of enforcers. Plus Wild Boy and Hu San. All sitting round a table in front of their almost-finished breakfast. Same as it ever was.

'You're late . . .'

'I overslept,' ZeeZee's voice was languid. The kind of drawl for which he used to beat up kids at school.

'Overslept?' Hu San did smile at that. 'Sit down,' she told ZeeZee shortly and he did, taking the only place still free. At the other end of the long walnut table, directly opposite her.

Timing was everything in life, so the fox once said. ZeeZee waited until Hu San was in mid flow, running down a list of recent successes and the very occasional failure, pulling facts and figures alike out of her head, and then he slowly and silently took off his shades and watched her words slow, falter and finally dry up.

When she spoke her face was utterly impassive. That was how everyone sitting round the table instantly knew she was furious, though most of them still assumed it was with ZeeZee.

'What happened to your face?'

'My face?' ZeeZee's fingers came up to caress the slight graze on his cheek, the understated scar across his chin and the dark and swollen eye that removing his shades had suddenly revealed. 'I came off my bike.'

'Did you?' Hu San stood up and walked the length of the table. She didn't even make the boy come to her. Gripping ZeeZee's chin between her first finger and thumb, she twisted his face towards the light, only to drop her hand as pearls of blood oozed between the butterflies.

'You came off your bike?'

The boy nodded. 'Sure. I had supper with a friend, drank too much and slid the Suzuki on my way home. These things happen . . .'

'Is the bike damaged?'

'No.' ZeeZee shook his head. 'Like me, there's hardly a scratch.'

Hu San opened her mouth to answer but whatever she intended to say was stopped by a knock on the door.

'What . . .'

A waitress stuck her head nervously round the doorway. Her cheeks had gone red before she'd even stepped into the crowded room. In her hands was a tray. 'I'm sorry, Madame. It's the tea and toast that—'

'Over here,' indicated ZeeZee, flipping up one hand.

The girl walked over to where ZeeZee sat at one end of the table and silently put down the tray, leaving just as quietly. ZeeZee knew that everyone was watching him, especially Hu San. That was why he made sure his fingers didn't shake as he carefully poured the tiniest splash of milk into his cup and followed it with Earl Grey. Then, very slowly, he started to butter his toast.

The Japanese weren't the only people who could conduct a tea ceremony.

CHAPTER 32

8th July

'Okay,' promised Raf. 'Everything's okay.'

'No,' said Hani crossly. 'It's not. How can it be?'

It was true that Madame Mila had finally gone, taking with her two uniformed policewomen and the court order she'd been trying to wave in Raf's face. But it had taken threats to get rid of her, even if they were largely unspoken and involved not her life but her career.

'You can't win,' Raf had said as he'd entered the courtyard and stepped between a furious Madame Mila and Hamzah's Taureg foreman who was resolutely blocking her way.

'Can't I?'

'No,' said Raf. 'You can't.' Leaning forward, he lifted the RayBans from her nose and smiled as the magistrate-coroner blinked in the sudden glare. 'And before you try you should make sure you understand who you're dealing with.'

'Yes. I know,' she said. 'You're a pashazade.' The anger in her voice was cut with contempt that Raf could pull rank quite that crudely.

'No,' said Raf, thinking of the fox. 'I mean . . . Who am I? What do I do? Why am I here . . . ?' He paused. 'I suggest you have one of your pet policewomen call the precinct to find out.'

At a nod from her boss, the nearest officer flicked a switch on her belt and tapped a throat mike twice with her finger. Raf didn't hear the question or answer but he saw the woman's mouth tighten. Then she leaned across to whisper bad news into Madame Mila's ear.

By now half the precinct would be claiming they'd known he was special forces all along, while a couple of the more out-and-out fantasists would be remembering when they'd met him before. Their lies turned to truth by simple unquestioning repetition. Of course, it just meant that if someone did decide to come after him they'd come carrying heavier guns . . .

After Madame Mila left, Raf rode the lift up to the haremlek, intending to ask Hani where she wanted to live, since she didn't want to live with Lady Jalila and her other aunt was dead. He also intended to suggest that Donna went with Hani to wherever it was. He'd keep Khartoum on to run the madersa. The old man knew which souk sold what and, besides, Raf needed someone else around. The ramshackle building was far too big for one man to live in on his own, even someone as antisocial as Raf.

By the time Raf reached Hani's door he'd amended his plan to asking Lady Jalila for advice on good schools. There were worse places to live than away from home; and, in Hani's case, boarding was probably her best option. Particularly as the only realistic alternative Raf could think of involved sending her to his father in Tunis or trying to find her a foster home.

'And the Djinn who was of the Only True Faith looked closely at the child asleep on the golden bed and marvelled at the loveliness of her hair that was like midnight spun into thread. And the cloth on which she lay was embroidered with pearls like tears and her nightdress was as white as moonlit clouds.'

Hani hiccupped and her screen stopped recording. Carbon dioxide cured hiccups, or so Hani had been told, so she exhaled into her cupped hands and breathed in again, inhaling cinnamon-scented breath. She didn't really want to tell Ali-Din a story but she'd finished *Golden Road III* for the second time and she was bored. Or rather, the afternoon dragged more slowly than ever if she left it unfilled. And talking to herself kept the hurt at bay, mostly.

Hani clapped to get the computer's attention.

'And when the Djinn saw her, he unfolded his mighty wings, saying "Glory to the True God. This is a creature from paradise." And he flew heavenwards until he met the Ifritah and said, "Marvel at the poor child who sleeps here in innocence. For you will see none more brave . . ."'

On the plate beside Hani's screen were a few cake crumbs, not really enough to bother with but Hani scooped them up crossly, squeezed them into a sticky mass and then pushed them into her mouth. She had heard the lift whine noisily as its wire dragged over the ungreased wheel at the top of the shaft. Aunt Nafisa had promised to get the lifts serviced. That was another thing which wouldn't come true.

'And the Ifritah spiralled down from the star-studded firmament, alighting on the balcony of a marble palace in old Cairo and did as the Djinn bade. And, Glory to the True God, the child who slept in innocence in the golden bed was every bit as beautiful in loveliness as the tattered beggar boy asleep in the old graveyard by the grave of his father . . .'

Hani knew he was there, but she didn't stop telling her story and she didn't look round. To do so would be to admit that a man had entered the haremlek. And that was something that never happened. So, instead, she kept telling her story to Ali-Din and the puppy told it secretly to her screen, which wrote it down in flowing letters, with ornate calligraphy for the names of God and less ornate but still beautiful capitals for the names of humans, locations, ifrits and djinns. She'd chosen the lettering herself from a database at the Library. Accessing the script had been easy; she'd just pretended to be a professor of literature from Cairo University. Cairo was Hani's favourite city. She'd never been there, but in *The Arabian Nights* that was where the most beautiful girl ever born was discovered, sleeping, by a djinn.

Lady Nafisa hadn't liked Ali-Din and she hadn't liked *The Arabian Nights*. But then, Lady Nafisa was dead. So that showed what *she* knew.

'Hani.'

Raf could have told her a story of his own. Maybe he would, one day. Maybe soon. On the red-tiled floor, beside the girl's small chair, a robot dog sat in what looked like a puddle of spilt tea. The dog was silver, leather and tattered felt, with floppy plastic ears and a long tail that ended in a blue glass button. Instead of eyes the dog had a black plate stretched over the top third of its head like a motorbike visor, behind which were twin video cameras.

What the dog saw she saw, in a tiny window open on one corner of her screen.

'Ali-Din's made another mess,' Raf said quietly.

Hani's eyes slid to the rag dog and she nodded doubtfully.

'He's not real.'

'I can see that,' said Raf. 'But then, nor is my fox.'

The glance Hani flicked at her screen was to check she wasn't dealing with a complete madman. *Been there*, thought Raf. *Felt that* . . . 'We need to talk,' he said apologetically.

It took an effort, but Hani made herself turn round; made herself wait until she had Raf's whole attention; made herself ask the question, even though she already knew the answer . . . 'You're going to send me away, aren't you?' Her words were little more than a whisper.

'Hani, I can't . . .'

'Knew it.' She almost stamped in frustration. 'I can help here. I won't get in the way.'

'It's not about—'

The girl didn't let him finish that sentence, either. She wasn't interested in his reasons any more than Raf would have been if he'd

157

been her: adults could excuse anything. Even things they didn't really believe in. They both knew that.

'Why, then?'

'Because . . .' He didn't have a *because*. Or, rather, he had dozens, from local tradition to his own convenience, all of which he could justify, in none of which he actually believed. But then, believing in things got you hurt. And if the thing you believed in was a person, that could hurt you worse.

'We'll talk about it later,' he said. Remembering that that was what adults had said to him.

Next morning was Friday and the city was shut. Gathered together in the early-morning cool of the kitchen, Khartoum, Raf, Donna and Hani ate breakfast, before Raf and Hani started work cleaning up the rubble that Hamzah's builders had left behind. Hani insisted on cooking and gave Raf a plate piled high with flat bread and sticky chunks of comb honey. Her own she left empty except for a peach and a handful of grapes.

Only when Raf had finished did Hani pile up the dishes in the sink. After that, she made a second bodun of java, even though Khartoum and Donna drank only mint tea and Raf insisted he was wired enough already. Then she went to fetch a broom, the room echoing to her footsteps.

Outside the kitchen window Rue Sherif was almost empty, missing its usual heavy grind of traffic. And the few taxis that travelled moved unhindered along almost deserted roads that saw the trams stilled and most shops locked tight. Loudspeakers everywhere were calling the faithful to prayer, from minarets dotted like spindly rockets across the humid city. Raf ignored them.

'Isk wasn't always this quiet,' said Hani. She spoke with the absolute certainty of someone aged nine. 'But it all changed last year. Now you aren't allowed to drive unless you're going to the mosque.' She carefully swept a pile of crumbs from under the table into a plastic dustpan and, just as carefully, tipped the pan into a metal dustbin. Which was fine, except that blowback sent a swirl of dust and crumbs up into the girl's face and started her sneezing. 'Not funny,' she said fiercely.

All of the major rubble from the hall had already been removed by Hamzah's men who'd left behind only dust, grit, fist-sized chunks of brick and the fine white bones of dead mice and an unlucky kitten. No treasure, but Hani was getting to grips with her disappointment.

The wooden double door on Rue Sherif now opened onto a newly revealed entrance area, tiled in black. To right and left, running round the edge of the hall, an elegant split staircase hugged the wall, alabaster balustrades rising around its edge, the ever-increasing gap between floor and stairs filled in with what looked like a smooth fall of ice that turned out to be white marble.

The actual walls were bare, stripped of whatever paintings, tapestries and hangings had originally cut the monochrome severity of the black floor and white staircase.

The style was Third Empire, which was undoubtedly one of the reasons why it had been bricked away. At a time when Iskandryia's Nazrani contingent had been building ornate villas in the High Moorish style, Ottoman families were having their own ancient houses demolished to be replaced with buildings better suited to Faubourg St Germain. Two hundred years later both communities were still embarrassed by their earlier enthusiasm. The hall might be the only part of the Madersa al-Mansur to be reworked in Third Empire style, but its European influences would have been enough of an embarrassment to Lady Nafisa for her to have it bricked away. But then, this was a woman whose outward acceptance of *in-shallah*, the surrender to God's command, had been such that she avoided using the future tense in public, because it presumed on the will of God . . .

At the top of the marble stairs, Hamzah's builders had un-bricked another archway, one that led to an alcove. Without being asked, they'd demolished a wall between that alcove and the *qaa*. Of Lady Nafisa's smoked-glass office nothing remained but a bad memory.

Just how Hamzah's team had done the work they had in the brief time they'd taken was beyond Raf. All the same he was grateful, and looking round at the new entrance, the rebuilt *qaa* and the replacement mashrabiya he felt more at home than he'd felt . . .

Forever was the answer, if he was honest. And Raf kept on feeling right at home, even when someone rapped with a cane on his new front door and a tall, instantly recognizable man strode in. Or, at least, strode as much as anyone could with a damaged leg and a walking stick. The resurrected hall was swallowed in a single ironic glance.

'You've wasted no time.'

Behind General Saeed Koening Pasha walked Lady Jalila, a scarf wrapped demurely round her hair. Then came two bodyguards from, the General's personal cadre who silently took up positions on either side of the front door. The General's face had that stony-eyed glare usually found only on statues. His skin was dark, not from the sun but from heritability and his cheeks were hollowed out with age and lack of sleep. Piercing eyes examined Raf from under heavy brows.

'You and I need to talk,' he told Raf, his gaze sweeping the hall until it reached Khartoum. 'Leave us,' the General ordered. 'And take the child with you.'

He pivoted round to face Raf, malacca cane thrust hard on the floor. 'I take it this is the way up?' The tiles were crossed in a clicking of walking stick and boot-heels before Raf even had time to answer.

Lady Jalila followed, demurely.

Walking directly behind Lady Jalila, Raf got the full benefit of the sight of her buttocks as they flexed with each step she took, sliding beneath the shot silk of a sand-coloured suit. If she wore underwear it was only a thong: he knew that because the afternoon's heat and humidity made her skirt fit tighter than any second skin.

The woman climbed the stairs slowly, one at a time, in a stride that almost let Raf catch a flash of inner thigh and waiting darkness. There was a sleekness to her legs and bottom that spoke of personal trainers and whole days spent working out in some exclusive gym of which he'd undoubtedly never even heard.

At the top, General Koenig Pasha walked through the spot where Lady Nafisa's office had been and clattered his way to the balcony to stare at the darkening sky. A storm was coming in, but not fast enough for his satisfaction. It was left to a slyly smiling Lady Jalila to do the social chit chat.

'So,' she said, 'how are you?' With a practised sweep, she pulled the scarf from her head and shook out her blonde hair, then casually smoothed the front of her jacket, full breasts briefly obvious beneath thin silk. She was watching Raf watching her and her smile faded the moment she realized it wasn't being returned. The unspoken offer, if that was what it had been, came and went before Koenig Pasha even had time to turn round.

'I thought we should talk about your niece,' said the General.

'Hani?'

'You have others . . . ?'

Not that he knew about.

'You see,' said the General. 'There's a problem. It seems Lady Jalila and your aunt had an agreement. If anything should happen to Lady Nafisa, then her cousin was to look after Hani. In fact, I gather the Minister and Lady Jalila had actually promised to adopt the child.'

'And Lady Jalila has this in writing . . . ?' Raf's voice was polite.

He could have spat in her face and her disgust would have been less. 'No' said Lady Jalila tightly. 'I don't have it in writing. Neither of us imagined a situation where that might be necessary. Of course, I didn't know about you then . . .'

'Or I about you . . .' Raf said simply and watched her hesitate.

160

'Hani will be better off with Lady Jalila,' said the General. 'A country estate, the best schools . . . And, of course, she's known Hani all her life.'

Whereas Raf barely even knew himself. Okay, so only he knew that . . . but a country estate? 'I thought Lady Jalila lived in the *Quartier Greque*?' Raf said contemptously, naming an overpriced area of mercantile houses near Shallalat Gardens. Vast and ornate, the houses had gone from fashionable to slum tenements and back again in a century. Leave anything long enough in Isk and eventually its time would come round again – that seemed to be the rule, anyway.

'We're selling the house,' Lady Jalila said crossly. 'I've got an architect drawing up plans for a summer villa out beyond Aboukir. I'm sick of the city in this heat.'

'And the Minister?' Raf asked politely. 'Is the Minister of Police for Iskandryia really planning to live in the suburbs?'

'He's got his flat over the precinct. Next to your fat American friend. And I've already got my eye on a new winter house, though I'm not sure what business it is of yours . . .'

Raf stood up, just as Donna brought in a tea tray. One look at the old woman was enough to confirm how terrified she was to be in the presence of the General. Raf didn't feel too special about making matters worse. 'I'm sorry,' he told the old woman. 'But you'd better take it back. Lady Jalila is just leaving.'

And the most feared man in North Africa who, as a young military commander, had shot his own brother for disobeying an order to retreat, raised one heavy eyebrow and padded silent as a leopard after the furious woman. He nodded once at Raf and then again to Donna, scaring the old Portuguese maid almost witless. The famed anger that Raf had expected to see break like thunder across his patrician face was entirely absent. If anything, Koenig Pasha seemed almost amused.

'Felix called,' said Hani, as soon as Lady Jalila had gone. 'He wanted to talk to you so I told him you were with her . . .'

'What did he say?'

'Something very rude.' Hani grinned. 'I don't think he likes her. Mind you, I don't think anyone likes her.'

'So you definitely don't want to live with Lady Jalila?'

Raf regretted his suggestion the moment it was spoken. Hani's answer was a rising babble of outrage that died only when he grabbed the child and scooped her up, ignoring the fists that tried to hammer at his head. When Raf looked round, Khartoum was standing in the doorway, glaring.

He had his answer.

'I had to ask,' Raf said gently.

'Never.' Hani's voice was fierce, her chin held high. 'I'd run away first.'

'But she was Aunt Nafisa's best friend . . . ?'

'That's not my fault,' Hani said crossly.

CHAPTER 33

Seattle

'Sorry to trouble you.' The voice was scrupulously polite, the accent so floppy haired that Hu San knew immediately who was on the other end before the boy had even announced his name.

It was late and an ice-cold wind blew in off the Sound, throwing white spray against the harbour walls. Up in her penthouse, Hu San sat listening to Nyman's Piano Concerto and drinking jasmine tea. The rain outside and the churning sea below didn't bother her. Weather only made Hu San feel more real.

Though ZeeZee had never called her before, at home or at her office, which was how she still thought of her small waterfront shop, Hu San had been expecting this phone call. She'd been expecting it for three days, during which the English boy had gone calmly about his work, serving court orders and reporting back any information that he thought the Five Winds Brotherhood might find useful.

Now he would want to complain about Wild Boy. She knew her staff called Haruki 'Wild Boy' behind her back. What they didn't know was that it had been she who first came up with that name, back in the days when Wild Boy was a scruffy street kid who trawled the strip with a gravity knife in one back pocket and a tube of KY in the other. It had been an easy trade. She liked his looks and he liked her money. Besides, any scraps she could offer him from her life were better than the one Haruki already had.

'I hope you're not about to give me a problem,' Hu San said shortly.

'I don't think so. I was hoping for an address for Haruki?'

Half question, half request . . . Still, it threw Hu San off guard.

'What?'

'I owe him an apology.'

For what, exactly? *Hu San wondered. Maybe the English boy had heard about her anger with Wild Boy and held himself responsible. If so,* the boy was right: he was responsible for Wild Boy's current disgrace. But that still didn't mean it was his fault. Hu San clearly remembered saying Not the face. *Wild Boy hadn't listened and she couldn't accept that.*

Wild Boy was on ice until he grovelled properly. Screaming fits and protests wouldn't do, and nor would sulking. And yes, sex complicated things, no one could deny that. All the same, she expected obedience, even from the boy who sometimes spread her legs.

'Tell him to quit sulking,' said Hu San and rattled off the address for an apartment block two streets back from the harbour. She paid the rent, she paid his bills and she paid the woman who went in once a week and cleaned up. In fact, she paid the woman double, once to do the job, and once again to ignore the discarded roaches and the gun Haruki could never remember to hide away in a locked drawer.

Let them make friends, *thought Hu San tiredly.* Or she'd get rid of both of them. Besides, both their sets of bruises should have started to fade by now. And anger faded like bruises, or it did in people wise enough not to nurse it. As to whether Haruki was as wise as the English boy obviously was, that was something Hu San reckoned she was about to find out.

Payback time.

ZeeZee blipped his bike into life, let out the clutch and felt his tyres squeal on the wet tarmac. Rain had cleared the harbour road of everything except a delivery truck, a police car and him. Spray from his back wheel rose behind the Suzuki like a wave. And by the time he reached Wild Boy's apartment, rain was vaporizing off his single exhaust to add its own fog trail to the spray. It was cold and undeniably wet but ZeeZee was seriously enjoying himself.

Hidden strips lit the foyer inside Wild Boy's building. A wall of glass separating the warmth of the foyer from the dark and rain of the sidewalk where ZeeZee had left his bike.

'Going all the way,' he told the clerk behind the desk, pointing his finger at the ceiling. Inside a lift, he checked his gun. Full load, seven shots. Flipping out the cylinder and then flipping it back. Only then did he realize a video camera was positioned in the top right corner of the lift. Too bad. Besides, he had a license for the gun, because delivering court orders meant not everyone liked to see him coming.

ZeeZee counted off the floors as each number lit and the lift shot past, headed for the penthouse. What was it Wild Boy always used to say? *It ain't over till the fat lady pings . . .* The English boy took a fold of paper from his pocket and looked at it. Wild Boy lived on this stuff – that, and Mexican red. Hu San – he wasn't too sure what she used, but something

164

more than just life regularly reduced her eyes to dark pinpricks. He, on the other hand, didn't even smoke. The fox didn't approve.

Not usually.

Weighing the twist in his hand, as if it might actually have a weight rather than being too light to feel, ZeeZee shrugged and carefully unwrapped the chemical origami to reveal the grey, salt-sized crystals inside.

'Have a great evening,' said the lift.

'Thanks,' said ZeeZee as he put his nose to the paper and inhaled, hitting it with both barrels. 'I intend to . . .'

A creak of the apartment door tugged Haruki away from his dreams. Far away – in the world inside his head, which was less safe even than the world outside – he registered first the click of a lock recessing itself and then a door creaking open on hinges that needed oiling.

The next click was closer and dispelled his dreams like wind through smoke. It came a microsecond ahead of the cold kiss of metal on his forehead. Revolvers that operated on double-hammer action were increasingly rare but Haruki knew of at least one person who owned a model like that. The cold-eyed English boy who walked alone and mostly talked to himself.

'Get up.'

Haruki opened one eye. His other was too badly swollen to open. Around the eye he could, there were distinct bruises, left by a bony knuckle.

'Out of bed.'

Slowly, very carefully, Haruki eased his feet out from under the covers, toes feeling for the floor. The cold made him reach instinctively for his silk dressing gown.

'You won't need that.' A hand flicked Haruki's fingers aside before they could touch fabric. 'Walk over to the window.'

Haruki did what he was told, trying to ignore both the cold and his own nakedness. Most of all, he tried to ignore the revolver and a rising fear brought on by questions he suspected it would be stupid to want answered.

'Open the curtains.'

He did that, too. Seeing the pinprick lights of Seattle flicker in the falling rain. The carpet felt sticky under his bare feet and the room stank of incense, empty beer cans and half-finished Singapore noodles. The sheets were dirty and his Toshiba wall screen was running nothing except static, but the view out over the harbour was heart-stopping. So beautiful it almost made up for dying surrounded by his own squalor.

'Now open the window.'

The glass slid back silently and a sudden gust of cold raised goose bumps on Haruki's naked skin. 'Why are you doing this?' Wild Boy asked. His voice sounded small, even to him. 'We didn't touch your face.'

The English boy shrugged. 'Did I ever say you did?'

'You let Hu San think so . . .' Wild Boy's hand went up to touch the bruise below his eye and his fingers came away wet.

'How sweet,' said ZeeZee. 'You're crying.' He raised the gun and sighted along the top, seeing a naked Japanese boy no older than he was. 'Any last requests?'

Haruki just looked out from under his fringe.

Zee Zee sighed. The fox was right and he was wrong.

'I don't know about you,' ZeeZee said as he lowered his gun. 'But I'm not finding this nearly as much fun as I thought.' Stepping back towards the bed, he threw Haruki a dressing gown.

'You don't love her,' Wild Boy said fiercely.

'And you do?'

Haruki nodded, sliding first one, then another arm into the gown and knotting the belt loosely round his narrow waist. 'And she loves me.'

'Not any more,' said ZeeZee.

He closed the apartment door behind him and left Wild Boy to lock up the window and call Hu San, if he was that stupid. Not that he would – call Hu San, that was . . . ZeeZee knew Wild Boy. Shame would prevent him.

Haruki was right about one thing, though. ZeeZee didn't want a lover, certainly not a Chinese gangster in her late thirties. A mother – now, that was something different. But that was one place even Wild Boy couldn't make him go.

Shoving his gun back into its holster, ZeeZee zipped up his black biker jacket and hit a button to call the lift. He didn't know how well Wild Boy would sleep but as soon as he got back to his own room he intended to crash out like the proverbial log, cooking sulphate or not. And then, first thing tomorrow he planned to get up and go visit Micky O'Brian. Hu San wanted a small package delivered. Something by way of apology for the recent misunderstanding . . .

Sitting on the edge of his bed, knife in hand, Haruki remained awake for the best part of five hours while he went over what had happened. What he'd said, what had been said to him. It was as if black and white had suddenly reversed. Maybe he could have handled matters differently. Perhaps he really should have launched himself at the English boy and not even thought about the gun.

Except that if life had taught Haruki anything it was when to lose

166

fights. Most times he fought hard and won but occasionally he knew to give in. That knowledge had saved his life as a kid. He wasn't proud of how he'd made his living before he met Hu San but never once had she shown anything but sympathy. Until now . . .

Sadly, Haruki put his hand to his swollen eye and then touched the edge of the blade to his throat. No use, he didn't feel brave enough for really grand gestures. Reversing his grip, so that he held the blade securely, Haruki dragged its point across his wrist, feeling sick. The wound should have been deeper but two glistening sinews blocked his way.

The tears that started up ran unchecked down his face as he sat there on his bed, his one good hand wrapped tight round his damaged wrist, trying to hold the edges of the cut together. For all his front, it seemed he couldn't even kill himself properly. Haruki had a decision to make without being sure how much time he had left in which to make it . . . In the end, shame or not, Haruki ordered his mobile to call Hu San and keep calling until it got through. He wanted to apologize or say goodbye, whichever seemed appropriate.

CHAPTER 34

Saturday began hot, the early-morning sun turning the Corniche to a burning silver strip that flared along the shore and separated the city from its beaches and low-lying headlands. But even early, with the sun hanging low over Glymenapoulo to the east, the air was too heavy and too sticky for blue sky to last.

A headache settled over the city, dogs growing restless and feral cats slinking from the shade of one shabby tenement to another. Policemen pulled at their high collars as they tried to relieve the itch, women scratched discreetly and men at café tables casually adjusted their balls. Through endless shuttered windows came the sound of toddlers whining, being slapped and whining louder still.

Under their glass roofs the souks overheated, peaches turned bruised and rancid in the open markets and at the taxi rank on Place Orabi a driver killed two passengers in an argument over his tip.

The storm came in at noon, as muezzin were calling the faithful to prayer. It fell on Iskandryia in a rolling landslide of dark clouds that slid down the coast, vast and soot-hued, banked so high that the outer edge of each cloud turned back on itself and still kept climbing. Looking up was like staring down into a bottomless canyon.

And with the clouds came a chill that cooled the air until the only heat was latent, radiating back from, alley walls and parked cars. Hani didn't notice the sudden chill at the time because she was too busy in the haremlek throwing 'rubbish' clothes into a black plastic bag . . . Rubbish meant anything neat, anything fussy, anything that Hani's aunt had made her wear . . .

Now they were up in the attic, rubbishing that without quite saying so, Raf had decided to get the al-Mansur madersa swept clean of ghosts and rearranged by the close of the weekend. Some ghosts need exorcism.

Some die, shrivel in the daylight or let time brick them off into the little-visited rooms of memory.

His own were mostly sterilized and labelled, neatly hidden away by the fox or secure behind emotional safety glass as the regime at Huntsville had demanded. But Hani's ghosts . . . Raf intended to kill those with a bucket and mop, black bin liners and the scrape of clumsily moved furniture.

'It's dark . . .'

'I know,' said Raf, glancing round. 'The electricity's out again.'

'No.' Hani stood in a doorway, holding a torch. 'I mean it's dark outside. The whole sky's gone black . . . Come and see.'

'Let me just finish this,' said Raf, picking up a chair. He was sorting through an attic, which led out onto a flat roof. A room stuffed with ancient china, wall hangings, carpets and old chairs, domestic detritus to which people had been too attached or too lazy to discard. The space was also home to a wasps' nest, high in one corner, and a tribe of mice that left markers in a spread of oily seed-like droppings.

They'd gone up there to find new furniture for the *qaa*, after Hani had rejected the original stuff on the basis that Aunt Nafisa liked it. Raf had seconded her opinion on the grounds that the silver chairs, at least, were unbelievably uncomfortable.

There were undoubtedly very good reasons why it was a psycho-logically bad move to let Hani discard her smart clothes and the *qaa* chairs on the sole basis that they had been liked by an aunt whose death she should have been mourning. And no doubt any child psychologist could have told Raf exactly what those reasons were but, since he'd had enough of psychologists as a child to last both of them a lifetime, he didn't care.

As Hani waited, the first heavy droplets of rain hit the flat roof outside. 'It's beginning,' she announced and then she was gone, stepping though a sudden steel-grey sheet of rain that closed off the open doorway like a bead curtain.

'Hani!'

He was too late. By the time Raf reached the door, Hani's hair was plastered to her face and her green tee-shirt had turned dark and heavy with rain. She was laughing.

'Come on.'

The water was warm and the drops huge, falling so heavily that they bounced off the tiles until the guttering that drained the roof could no longer cope and a skim of water built up across the surface of the roof to swallow the rain.

'Does this happen often?' Raf had to shout to make himself heard above the noise.

Hani grinned. 'Not like this.' She spread her arms wide. 'This is wild.' And it was.

Walking to the edge, she leant over the parapet to watch rain racing through a storm pipe at her feet and fall in a heavy stream on Rue Cif below. Waves of racing water drove down the middle of the road, sweeping rubbish before it.

'The carpets,' said Raf, suddenly. 'Come on.'

With Hani's help, he dragged a heavy roll of cloth out onto the flooded flat roof of the madersa, discarding his shoes and socks to trample back and forth across the unrolled bokhara until grey water seeped between his toes and was washed away by rain. By the time he'd dragged out his second rug, Hani had ripped off the Nikes he'd bought her the day before and was trampling hell out of a small carpet of her own.

It rained . . . and then it rained some more. Fresh clouds rolling in over Iskandryia to replace those that were empty. Until they too were spent. By the time the storm had burnt itself out, four carpets were clean and two wall hangings were refreshed enough for the dark smudges across their middle to be revealed as mounted archers chasing what might have been antelope.

'It's over,' Hani said, looking up at the clearing sky.

Raf nodded. The air was cool – and smelt completely clean for the first time since he'd arrived in El Iskandryia. The pressure was gone, too, the city's headache lifting, with the storm clouds. Above the street swallows swooped, nymphing on newly hatched insects. Coming in low and fast, flying in formation, their shrill cries rising and falling as they swept by.

Felix rolled up the next evening in his Cadillac and dumped the car with its keys in the ignition, two wheels on the road and two on the sidewalk.

'You trying to get it stolen?' Raf demanded, opening the new front door to greet the fat man.

Felix glared at the nearest fellaheen who stepped into the road rather than try to push past him or his car. 'No one would dare,' he said. It took Raf a moment to realize Felix wasn't joking.

'We've got a problem,' said Felix. He dug his hand into a pocket and pulled out a black G-Shock special, the kind people bought on planes. 'This yours?'

Raf nodded. Anything else seemed pointless.

'Thought it was hideous enough. Want to tell me when and where you lost it?'

'I didn't even . . .'

'. . . Know it was gone. So I take it you don't admit to making a quick trip to my HQ in the last twenty-four hours?'

Raf just looked at him.

'We've lost some plastique,' Felix said flatly. 'It happens. Someone at the precinct cuts a block in half, amends the evidence docket and usually sells it back to one of the crime families. Or to someone with a grudge . . .'

He was speaking openly, Raf realized, because the reality of who Felix saw was obscured by a fantasy CV that let the man treat Raf as more than equal.

'The problem is the plastique was lifted from Mushin Bey's office.' Felix paused, long enough to let that sink in. 'And your watch was found in the corridor outside.'

'Shit.'

'Oh, it gets worse,' said Felix as he pushed past Raf and started up the recently uncovered stairs. Raf was still wondering how everyone who came in knew exactly where to go when the answer hit him in the face. All large houses of a certain period followed a rigidly defined floor plan. There was nowhere else those stairs could go.

'Coffee?'

Felix grunted, which Raf took for *How kind. Yes, please* . . .

'Got any cake?' Felix demanded when Raf put a tray in front of him. By the time Raf had returned with baklava, Felix was emptying the last drop from his biggest flask direct into the brass coffee pot.

'You're going to need it,' he said, seeing the look on Raf's face. 'You're officially off the hook regarding this.' He tossed the G-Shock onto a table. 'Though privately General Koenig Pasha himself says tell you not to be so bloody careless. And to listen very carefully to what I've got to say before you go take a private pop at the *RenSchmiss* brigade . . .'

Raf sighed.

'You remember the broken mashrabiya?' Felix said.

Yeah, he remembered it.

'We took a couple of bits off Hamzah's boys and ran them under an electron microscope. The carving was ripped apart from inside. Not smashed from the outside. You understand what that means?'

Raf had a pretty good idea, and he didn't like it one little bit. 'That I'm back to being the main suspect?'

'No,' the fat man shook his head. 'Not with polygraph readouts as flat as a boy's tits . . .' He pulled out a leather-bound notebook and flicked it on, buying himself time as he pretended to read off the results. He could actually recite them from memory and had, in fact, only just done exactly that over his mobile to the Minister for Police.

'The mashrabiya was destroyed from inside. There were no finger-prints other than Lady Nafisa's on the pen. The scrapings from under her nails contain skin, but it's her own, and that bruise on the palm of her hand . . .'

'Matches the missing top for that make of pen.'

Felix nodded.

'And the stigmata on the other palm?'

'Is an impression left by the diamond ring on her other hand.'

Raf lifted his right hand and put it over his chest, then placed his left hand over the top of that, trying to imagine jerking down so hard that the sharp edge of a ring on his right hand sliced into the hand above as he drove a pointed object into his own heart. He couldn't.

'And I know there were no hesitation cuts,' added Felix. 'But there were no defensive cuts, either – no stabs into her hands, no slashes between thumb and fingers. And her shirt was open . . .'

'Which means what, exactly?'

'Murderers usually stab through cloth. Suicides don't . . . I'm really sorry.' Felix looked from the coffee cup in his hand to the newly cleaned *qaa*. There was a freshly washed carpet on the wall. A recently polished leather Ottoman in one corner. Donna had even put a vase of wild roses on a marble side table. He could recognize an exorcism when he saw one. Even when it was all for nothing.

'I don't know how to say this . . . But in Iskandryia suicide is a crime. One with severe penalties.'

'She's already dead,' Raf said flatly.

'I know,' said Felix. 'By her own hand. And that means her entire estate becomes forfeit. This house now belongs to the Khedive. By law, you have thirty days to make other living arrangements.'

'No,' Raf said.

'That's the law. But I've discussed it with the Minister and the Minister's discussed it with the General. We're prepared to say it wasn't suicide if you're willing to back up an announcement that your aunt's will names the Khedive as sole heir.'

'I mean, no, she didn't kill herself.' Raf knew his voice was shaking but, try as he might, it was impossible to keep it steady. 'She didn't kill herself . . . She wouldn't . . . Why break the mashrabiya, why use a pen?' More to the point, why bring him over from Seattle if she planned all along to kill herself?

'Distraction, maybe?' Felix shrugged apologetically. 'Someone decides to off themselves, who knows what goes through their mind?'

'She was murdered,' Raf said firmly. 'You tell your Minister that.'

'That's what Mushin Bey told me you'd say,' Felix muttered.

'Yeah? Well, you tell him I'll nail the killer . . .'

Felix looked deeply unhappy.

'He said you'd say that as well.'

CHAPTER 35

Club CdH was hidden at the bottom of a well.

And on clubnite its crowded spiral staircase stank of cheap lager, expensive scent and musty groundwater. This last was because the shaft fed down to a vast cistern strung with steel walkways and ratchet joists, with a bar and JVC sound system at one end, both on a raised area where half the water-filled cistern had been paved over centuries before with stone slabs.

Underwater lights, sunk to the bottom of the cistern, up-lit swimmers so that they cast huge black shadows onto the vaulted ceiling overhead. Only a few clubhards swam naked. They went naked not because it was that kind of club but because public nudity was banned in Ottoman Africa and even being at CdH made a political statement.

That, at least, was how Zara justified it, if asked. Besides, everyone knew $E=MC^2$ was a cuddle clone. It made dance-heads love each other. It also made them way too chilled to be able to do anything about it . . .

The electrics were working, the bar was stocked with Star, memory on the sound system had been loaded for tonight's mix. Come midnight the place would be rammed to the rafters, the crowd split unevenly between the majority on the dance floor and those, like her, who would be swimming. Zara grinned and adjusted an earbead, scanning bands until she found the voice for which she'd been searching.

Av was out there, spreading the good word.

'That was Vertigo Voudun, the Blue Ice mix. And don't forget tonight – CdH goes naked.' He spoke through a button mike slicked to his throat. Inside his helmet Avatar had true quadsound, aural grooves cut into the lining to channel music to his ears. Stacked into one of the drag-resistant side panniers on his cut-down Yamaha DarkStar Racer was a hit-and-run sound system. The other pannier held a kit that uploaded to a pirate satellite channel.

174

It was an old Balearic cliché to wire the bpm of a mix to the DJ's heart rate but Av didn't do cliché or tradition. He had the bpm wired direct to the engine of his bike. Every blip of the throttle upped tempo, every increase in tempo upped speed. And hard/Trance didn't even kick in until his speeds were strictly illegal.

'This is LuxPerpetua with *Escape Velocity*, the FNM 90–2 mix . . . And remember, naked at CdH . . . Enjoy.' Avatar slammed open his throttle and blasted the DarkStar and himself clear over the red line.

Zara locked the door behind her. *Danger* read a rusted sign. *40,000 volts. Keep out.* Avatar had lifted it off a substation at the North End of Rue Ras el Tin and Zara had epoxied it to the door hiding the way into the well. So far, no one from the city's electricity board had turned up and tried to read their meter.

Known as *CdH*, the *Club des Hachichins* could only be reached by the red spiral behind that door. The staircase was six months old and ceramic, bolted together with green screws, each one the size of someone's finger. Rumour said Av had stolen it from a hotel in Shatby that was looking for it still.

Zara had no idea of the age of the stone-lined shaft behind that door but she assumed it was at least five hundred years. Anything younger than this in Isk was regarded as almost new. Besides, newer than that and she'd have been able to find it on the city maps at the Library.

Zara was the club's promoter, organizer and owner. That was, she owned it if anyone did, inasmuch as the medieval cistern was below a multi-storey car park owned by HZ International – which was her father by another name.

Once there had been hundreds of cisterns below the city, with arched roofs and stone-lined holding tanks. Every important family, every mosque or madersa had had one. Sometimes they had even been owned by individual streets or one of the souks. Most had dried up, collapsed or been forgotten. Of those that were known still to exist, twelve were mentioned in Fodors. CdH occupied the thirteenth.

She'd found the cistern before she went to the US but she'd only started up CdH on her return. And already Avatar and a posse of doormen were having to turn punters away. Clubnite ran one day each month, the date chosen at random by software on Zara's notebook. All clubs went out of business eventually, but she and Avatar were doing their best to lower the odds against theirs doing the same.

Av was pretty freaked about not being followed, but Zara knew that was just kiddie shit. Meanwhile, tonight was another clubnite and it was her job to go collect the brain candy.

CHAPTER 36

28th July

'Find the man. Deliver the package. Do it on time . . .'

This was his first day in the job and Edouard wanted to get things exactly right: because that way he'd have a better chance of getting chosen again tomorrow. Employment in Iskandryia was difficult. Upset one man and ten potential employers could slam their doors in your face. Edouard spent a lot of his life trying not to upset important people who might one day employ him. And the important person he'd visited this morning ran a courier service out of an office above a haberdasher's at the back of the tram station on Place Orabi.

Now Edouard had a day's work, with the chance of more work tomorrow if he was efficient. And he hadn't even had to do this first day for nothing to show he was adaptable.

What he had to do was deliver a package, but not until 11:30 A.M. Edouard pulled his old Vespa back onto its stand and waited. He'd found the right café, on the edge of Place Gumhuriya just as he'd been told, and had spotted the man in the photograph. Now he just had to wait for the right time . . .

'And that was LuxPerpetua and this is Isk's own Ahmed Shaabi with *Jules&Jeel* . . .' Slap bass began to stumble in and out of a drum track that sounded more Bedouin than anything else. To Raf it was just weird-shit music from a radio taped to the seat of some scooter parked up at the lights. Three weeks had passed since his aunt had been found dead and in one week's time he would have to move himself, Hani, Donna and Khartoum out of the madersa.

He was doing his best to think about something else.

On the notebook in front of him was a list of names. The notebook was the old-fashioned kind with paper pages because that was safe. Short of looking over his shoulder or using a seriously hiRez satellite, no one

176

could see what he was writing and he was secure in the knowledge that no pet geek of the Minister's was sitting five tables away with a hidden Van Eck phreaker, recording everything he put up on screen.

Most of the names were crossed out, but half of them had then been written in again. In the centre was his aunt, circled heavily. Radiating out from Lady Nafisa were lines leading to Hamzah, Jalila, the General, Mushin Bey, Zara . . . Lines from these names led to other names until the page was a matrix of connections – all leading nowhere.

What he had was a diagram as hermetic as any kabbalistic chart and about as informative. When it actually came down to it, Raf had to admit what he'd been avoiding admitting even to himself: he couldn't prove for certain it was murder. And even if it was, what chance was there that he could solve a crime from scratch and with no obvious clues.

He'd followed them all except the General, who hadn't left his house in weeks. Bought himself a digital scanner he couldn't really afford in Radio Shack and fed it Zara's number and then, in desperation, the number of the Minister and finally of Felix. The Minister hid his calls behind heavyweight crypt, Felix seemed to leave his mobile off most of the time, and from Zara, once his scanner had cracked the crypt, he'd learned only that she ran a club and the GSP coordinates she gave out to selected punters indicated it was in a multi-storey garage. Which was vaguely interesting, if not helpful.

It was Wednesday, 28 July, 10:48 A.M. and his heartbeat, blood pressure and alpha count were almost normal, if maybe a little on the high side. No one at the office had yet tried to call him and he'd sat outside the Gumhuriya café for thirty-five minutes – which, in direct sunlight, was thirty-five minutes too long for his genetic make-up. The heat was thirty-four degrees and for once humidity was low. All this he read off from the face of his watch. None of it really interested him.

Missing from the report was a record of the complex organic molecules gating through myriad alveoli in his lungs, flooding his blood system each time he sucked the plastic mouthpiece of a small sheesha.

Tetrahydrocannabinol . . .

The brass water pipe had bright edges. As if someone had traced neatly round its undulating body with light. The trunk of a eucalyptus, in whose shade Raf sat, was split in two at head height, then split again and again, time branching, until it ended as a luminous three-dimensional schematic, the answer to some important question no one had ever remembered to ask. He had a feeling the 'no one' might have been him.

Raf wasn't sure if he should have accepted the water pipe or not.

'Fuck it.'

A minute or so later, Raf repeated himself.

Later still, he rested the sheesha's purple tube and mouthpiece on the café table in front of him and checked his wrist. Not as much time had passed as should have done.

Swirled a glass of cooling tea with a spoon, Raf watching its brief vortex slow and die. Entropy. He was hot, his shirt was sticky and a thumb print smeared the lenses of the shades that kept the city at bay.

He was breakfasting at a felah café on Place GH, incongruous among thickset moustachioed men wearing striped shirts or long jellabas. Everybody in the place was male, apart from an elderly Tunisian woman in black who appeared every few minutes carrying plates from the kitchen, which she left at one end of the counter for a waiter to deliver. It was a face of the city he hadn't seen, where full breakfast cost half the price of a croissant at Le Trianon and the first sheesha came free.

The only reason they accepted Raf at all was because of what he wore. It had taken him several mornings to understand that. The jacket was long and black, and it came from the back of a cupboard on the men's floor at the madersa. It was old and had a collar of the kind that turned up rather than folded down. People glanced at him oddly in the street whenever he went out, but they still moved politely out of the way.

New clothes. The thought was random but true. However, thinking it and achieving it were different matters, because his credit card had expired along with his aunt. A fact he'd only discovered when he had tried to use it in the French boutique near Place Orabi. What little money he had was borrowed against his salary from the Third Circle, which was looking more token by the day. Apparently working for S3 was an honour; it was just a pity it wasn't one Raf could afford.

Of course, he could always ask Hamzah for a job.

Or not.

The kif in his pipe tasted sour, even though it had been cured in honey. *But that's just me,* thought Raf. The whole of life had turned sour the moment Felix barged into the madersa more than a fortnight back, dropped his bombshell and then gone, leaving Raf with the job of telling Hani she'd lost her aunt and now she was losing her house. Which wasn't a good thought, because it just made Raf remember that he still hadn't told her. And he really should have done.

God help her.

He couldn't eat for worrying and he didn't want to drink, no matter that spirits could probably be found in half a dozen illicit bars within five minutes' walk of somewhere like Le Trianon. As for drugs . . . Leaf cured with molasses or honey was hard to avoid in this part of the city.

Kif was sold ready-rolled by hawkers on every street corner and as huge, wood-stamped blocks in the *suqs* around el Magharba. But despite today's sheesha, dope had never really been his style and when he did break with the fox's good intentions, he used amphetamines. The basic kind cooked up in basements. Speed made him feel the fox more strongly.

But Isk ran at the wrong speed for sulphate. And while coke could undoubtedly be found behind the black glass doors of expensive night-clubs, just as dance drugs could be had in the tourist haunts, which filled nightly with German kids whacked out on substances a mere molecule away from MDMA, finding fuel to feel the fox had proved more difficult.

Besides, the fox was dying. Raf was pretty sure of that. It spoke less and less often and mostly after dark. It didn't talk to him the way it used to and it had offered no advice on how to find his aunt's killers, not even bad advice. Most of the time, when Raf went looking inside his head for the animal, he found only flickering facts and an emptiness where the voice used to be. And all taking the sheesha had done was add an echo to that emptiness. An echo of silence at odds with the street noise around him.

To Raf's right was the neo-baroque monstrosity of Misr Station, terminus for the A/C turnini that ran through from Cairo. From above, the tracks looked toylike and the dusty square seemed small, crowded and dirty, set between an overflowing taxi rank and a sprawl of flat roofs broken occasionally by the spiky minaret of a mosque, the breastlike dome of a Coptic basilica or the spire of a Catholic church.

Higher still, the individual buildings blurred into a street plan that revealed only roads and blocks of solidified city life. The darker alleys, where the sun daily lost its battle against shadow, faded out until even el-Anfushi's widest streets showed only as hairline cracks that finally blurred and vanished. Raf's throat was too tight and getting tighter as he fought against the thinness of atmosphere, fought for breath.

'Your Excellency?'

The city spun up to hit him, hard and fast. And Raf had to slam one hand on top of the other to stop both from shaking, He didn't feel very excellent about anything.

'You all right?' The boy's voice faltered as Raf glanced up. 'I'm sorry, sir. I mean, can I get you anything else?'

A new life, a proper childhood, the answer to who really killed his aunt because, sure as fuck, she *didn't* do it herself . . .

'Felix,' Raf told his watch, popping in an earbead in time to hear the number being dialled. There were things they needed to talk about. Like the fact Raf had recently warned Mushin Bey that Lady Jalila and he would have to take Raf to court before they could get their hands on Hani.

'Get me some fresh tea,' said Raf, peering at the waiter. 'And take this away.' He pointed to the sheesha, now growing cold on the table in front of him.

Felix arrived just after the tea, running his pink convertible up onto the sidewalk and stepping straight out to stand beside Raf's table. 'You look like shit,' he said, as he yanked out a chair. 'But I imagine you know that.'

Without asking permission, he lifted the notebook out of Raf's hand and snorted at the chart. 'Very pretty,' he said, about to hand it back. Then he paused, and jabbed his finger at one of the names. 'We're raiding her dance club tonight,' he added as an afterthought. 'You might want to come . . .' The gravel in his voice was a legacy of too many cigarettes, years of alcohol and the fact Felix regarded anything before noon as early morning.

The fat man ordered hot chocolate with whipped cream and two almond croissants. 'Falafel or cakes,' he said to Raf in disgust, when the waiter had gone. 'No one in this godforsaken pit knows how to cook proper food.'

'Why stay, then?'

Felix looked surprised. 'You think anyone else is going to employ me on that salary?' he asked. 'Anyway, I'm too old for Los Angeles and too high-rent for some burb. And besides . . .' The fat man paused, choosing his words with care. 'There's fuck all real crime here.'

Raf wanted to laugh. Or maybe cry. Or just go to sleep . . . He wasn't certain which. Maybe all three.

No crime . . .

'Oh, sure,' said Felix. 'Twice a year the winds come and the murder rate doubles, but that's keep-it-in-the-family stuff. The odd drunken Russian gets rolled, but only occasionally and then only if he's stupid. There's rape, but no more than anywhere else, the occasional mugging, the odd drugstore heist, predictable low-level stuff. But the real shit? Forget it.'

'Gangs,' said Raf. 'Drugs running, organized crime . . .'

'What about it?'

'. . . It must exist . . .'

Felix smiled. 'You want to know what my boss does about organized crime? He invites the heads of each family to dinner once a year and reminds them – politely – to keep paying the General their taxes.'

He shut up after that, but only because his chocolate had arrived in a cup the size of a bowl. When Felix resurfaced, the bowl was empty and cream ran across his upper lip in a tide mark.

'Message direct from the General,' he said. He picked up a croissant, looked at it and then put it down again, carefully dusting sugar from his fingers. 'He thinks it would be nice if you gave back the plastique.'

'Didn't . . .' said Raf, '. . . take any explosive.'

'Then who did?'

'How the . . .' Raf couldn't remember the rest of that sentence so he finished the next one instead. 'Who . . . stole . . . my . . . watch?'

Who . . . stole . . . my . . . ? Felix leant in close and lifted the dark glasses from Raf's face. Swearing in disgust when the bey threw up one hand to protect his eyes from the sudden light. The pupils gazing back at him were vast and empty, black as dead stars.

Fucking terrific: he was Chief of Detectives. He was meant to notice these things. 'Get trashed, why don't you . . .' Flipping open his brief-case, Felix reached inside for a Bayer-Rochelle inhaler and went back to swearing. His police issue THC inhibitor was almost empty.

'Use the rest of this,' Felix told Raf. 'And then go to the pharmacy . . .' He pointed across the square to a neon green cross. 'And buy another. Then we'll talk.' He tossed Raf the almost empty inhaler, sighing as Raf fumbled the catch.

'A package for Ashraf Bey.' Edouard stood at the man's elbow, shuffling nervously. Despite the heat Edouard was dressed in a cheap Kevlar one-piece and wore a smog mask. His one-piece had *atlas cares* scrawled across the shoulders in a kind of casual, outdated corporate scrawl that fifteen years earlier had probably taken some account exec three breakdowns and most of a week just to brief.

Edouard was worried. He'd been told to follow his instructions exactly. And it was unquestionably noon, because the square echoed with the cry of a muezzin, and he definitely had the right café – but now the right man wasn't here any longer. Edouard had decided he'd better deliver the package to the right place at the set time and then wait for the right person to return.

'I'll take it.'

Edouard was about to protest when the man flicked open his wallet and flashed his gold shield. 'I said, I'll take it . . .'

'You'll still have to sign.'

The fat man scrawled his signature across a pad and reached for the envelope. 'Go,' he said and Edouard went. Unhappy but resigned. A second day's work looked increasingly less likely every time he ran what had just happened through his head.

181

Glancing across the square to the apothecary, Felix checked Raf was still out of sight and gently shook the envelope which was brown, padded and looked very much like government issue. From habit, Felix held the envelope by its edges, so as not to leave fingerprints. The only obvious anomaly he could see was that its flap was tucked in rather than glued, as if the sender had been too lazy to gum the thing shut.

'What the hell.' Felix rattled the package until a flat box slid out onto the table. It wasn't like he'd actually opened the thing. What he got was a chocolate box, the expensive kind. Charbonel & Walker. Stuck to the top was a small white card with kittens on the front and a laser-printed message.

'If you get this, I'm already dead – Aunt Nafisa.'

Which wasn't what Felix had expected the card to say. For a split second he almost slipped the chocolate box back into its envelope. That way he could watch Raf's face for surprise or horror, for any clue at all as to what was going on. Because, as far as Felix was concerned, liking Raf and trusting the guy were two separate things entirely.

But not even taking one peek was asking too much and, besides, knowing exactly what was inside put Felix in a still stronger position. Particularly if it was letters, maybe a diary, even photographs . . .

Felix lifted the lid and a sweet smell grew. Not flowers, chocolate or marzipan. Something he knew so well the stray hairs had risen on the back of his neck before his brain even made the connection. RDX/C3. High-brisance plastique explos—

Glass into diamonds, shattering.

But by then a hundred eight-millimetre ball-bearings had already taken off half of the man's face and removed his right arm at the shoulder, though Felix hadn't yet grasped that. Where his cheek had been was living skull, yellow and glistening, one eye socket a smear of beaten egg white. A fist-sized hole in his temple exposed his brain and across his upper chest wounds had blossomed like blood-red poppies. The blast area was both precise and limited: the chocolate box little more than housing for a simple claymore.

Fractured jaw opened impossibly wide, Felix began to scream silently at the world. He tried to stand, found his leg was broken and crashed sideways, taking the table down with him.

And still no one moved until Raf came running through shock-stopped traffic. Doing the other man's screaming for him.

Sightless and almost deaf, gravity dragging the last shreds of identity out of his shattered skull in a heap of folded jelly, Felix still managed to make it to his knees, then spasmed and fell forward, grit sticking to flayed flesh.

It was pointless even trying to talk to a man whose throat was ripped open, whose cerebral fluid oozed from an open skull and whose pumping blood was creating tiny cascades that branched left and right down cracks in the sidewalk, taking the shortest route to the gutter. Yet the pointlessness didn't stop Raf shaking Felix. Shouting at him.

In the distance the wail of an ambulance fought the siren of a racing police car. But the ambulance, at least, would be too late. Felix was a corpse, his body just didn't know it yet.

'*Do it.*' The words came suddenly, cold and clear.

Raf wanted to ignore them. To pretend he hadn't heard. '*Do it,*' said the fox, who never usually woke in daylight. So Raf did.

Unclipping the holster from the man's belt – badge, spare clip and all – Raf slid free Felix's Taurus and checked the cylinder. It was loaded with ceramic-jacket hollow-point.

'Back,' he ordered. And, watched by a retreating crowd, he untangled the man's coat from a broken chair and wadded it into a bundle to act as a pillow for Felix. Then, rolling Felix on to his front almost as if for sleep, Raf put the muzzle to the point where the man's skull met his neck and softly squeezed. What was left of Felix's head exploded, along with a chunk of pavement below. It was only luck that stopped ricocheting fragments taking out Raf's own eye.

Friendship came with a price that both of them had just paid.

Sirens split the shocked silence that followed. Jellaba-clad gawpers scattered suddenly as a cruiser slid to a halt kitty-corner to Place Gurnhoriya. Out of its doors came two armed officers in flak jackets, assault rifles at the ready. But by then Raf was already gone: retreating through the crowd, the fat man's gun thrust into one pocket.

He jumped a tram, standing at the back on its open wooden platform, slipping off at a crossing to cut through a narrow alley full of empty shops and boarded-up houses. A builder's board promised total redevelopment. The completion date for the project was two years before Raf had arrived in Isk.

The smell of urine and damp earth filled his nostrils, coming from houses that had fallen in on themselves to become gardens kept lush by sewage leaking from a shattered pipe. The area was full of blind alleys and cluttered yards. Sometimes two blocks was all it took to slide from comfort to abject poverty – or vice versa. Money clung to the boulevards and the coast. Cut back from those and the city of the poor was always there. The cities of darkness, of brothels and lies. Old beyond meaning or memory, desolately grand and running by unspoken rules.

Raf was beginning to feel horribly at home.

He stepped through an open door into a deserted house and kept going until he reached a locked door at the rear. One kick opened it and Raf found himself watched by an old woman as he crossed her courtyard and stepped out into a crowded street.

It was only when Raf stopped, looked round and tasted the sweetness of blood at the corner of his mouth that he realized a sliver of pavement had opened his cheek clean as a blade.

RenSchmiss

CHAPTER 37

28th July

The water lights were off, the house lasers down. Somewhere at the other end of the vaulted room, a band was tuning up. And here, where tiny waves splashed against the rough stone of a cistern wall, Zara had wrapped herself in the darkness. Below her feet had to be the bottom of the cistern but she had only a sense of hanging over emptiness.

Three months before, a stoned-cold immaculate Danish boy had gripped tight to a rock and let the water close over him. Only to drop his ballast and kick upwards. He claimed to have seen a skeleton on the bottom, arms crossed over its chest. And people did disappear in Isk. Disappear completely. But Zara didn't really believe the story of the skeleton. Something had gone wrong with a batch of E/equals that month.

All the same, she did believe the darkness was occupied. Because whenever she left other swimmers behind and slid herself into a dark corner far away from the safety of the steps leading up to the dance floor, she could sense that something down there was aware she was there, hanging in the water above whatever it was.

Though maybe that was just E/equals too, from way back . . .

Now was chill-out time. Av's decks were deserted. The huge bank of smart lights rippled rather than throbbed, stilled by the lack of strong beat to catch and follow. Up on stage, out of her sight, four elderly black guys were coming to the end of an acoustic set – well, mostly . . . Something intrinsically West Coast ethnic that mixed Cape Verde with Mbalax and Soukous. A click track hiccupped from a child's beatbox, almost lost beneath balafon and sabar.

And the fit sounded loose but was actually tight and Zara felt relaxed for the first time in weeks, though that could have been from mixing Mexican with Moroccan.

Zara sighed. And kept sighing until the water closed over her again and bubbles like large pearls rose from her lips as she raised her arms and slid deeper. She would have gone deeper still but the pearls were gone. So she kicked once and glided to the surface.

'Going down, floating up . . . Guess you could call that an Ophelia complex,' said a voice right beside her. 'Oh no,' it countered, 'because then you'd be wearing some clothes . . .'

Instinct made Zara cover her breasts, and water made her choke as her head bobbed below the surface. When she'd finished coughing, she concentrated on swearing. She knew who it was.

What she didn't recognize was the voice of whoever spoke next.

'That was rude.'

Arms splashed up to snake round Zara's neck and Hani was suddenly glued fast like a limpet. She was grinning in the darkness. Breathing hard, though at first Zara thought that was from the swim. Then she realized the child was excited, dangerously excited.

'He hit a big man at the door,' said Hani. There was a horrified fascination in her voice.

'He wouldn't let us in,' Raf said apologetically.

Zara snorted, her face hidden in shadow until Raf adjusted his eyes and she came into view as cleanly as if someone had toggled the brightness on a screen.

'He didn't get up,' Hani added.

'Unconscious,' insisted Raf hastily, 'nothing worse. I had to see you . . .'

'Why?'

Of all questions it was the simplest to ask and the hardest to answer. Had Raf been thinking clearly, or even at all, he might have known he was in shock from Felix: seeing someone killed did that to you. But he wasn't supposed to do shock, at least not according to the wretched genetic-heritability guarantee. And anyway, he had more than one reply to her question.

Club. Felix. Hani . . . which came first?

Raf had to remind himself that Zara couldn't see in the dark, that her hearing was probably only average. So she might have missed the thud of heavy boots as bouncers crisscrossed the club searching for him. Pretty soon one of the bone clones would engage his brain and decide to fire up the water lights.

Except that they were about to be cornered themselves, if the distant clang of a door and abrupt trill of sirens at the high edge of his range was any clue.

'You're being raided,' Raf told Zara.

'Shit . . .' She sounded almost grateful. 'That's what you came to tell me?'

No, he'd come to beg her to look after Hani and to tell her that Felix was dead. Just like his aunt was dead. This city was turning into a personal war-zone and he was still busy trying to spot the enemy.

Raf shook his head, remembered she couldn't see him and opened his mouth to speak. But it was already too late. Up on the spiral, a riot cop using a throat mike attached to the kind of bass-heavy public hailer that turns your guts to water and dribbles them round your feet was demanding that *Someone Turn On The Lights. NOW . . .*

'How many ways in?' Raf felt an adrenaline rush kick-in with a vengeance. The fox was back on line.

'One,' said Zara.

Even Hani groaned.

'Two,' Zara amended, then corrected herself again. 'Three . . . Do storm drains count?'

Hani grabbed her tee-shirt from a corner where she'd left it and scooped up Ali-Din while Zara went looking for her clothes, which should have been folded neatly beneath a bench. Raf's own suit was sodden but at least he was wearing it.

'You need new clothes,' Raf ordered.

Zara opened her mouth to protest but Raf was gone, sliding off in a different direction towards a blonde girl in spray tights, a snakeskin waistcoat that might once have slithered and a long trench coat cut from wafer-thin *faux* ocelot. Zara couldn't hear what Raf said but the girl handed over her coat without comment.

'Use this.' He stood between Zara and the worst of the crowd while she struggled into the coat. Searchlights were in use but the house system seemed down. If Avatar had any sense, thought Zara, he'd have pulled the fuses.

'Over there . . .' Zara said, nodding to a wall that lit and vanished as a hand-held hiLux hit the stonework and then swept back over the restless crowd. The crash squad were still looking for the main switch.

'. . . We need to get over there.'

Covering part of the wall was a swirl curtain that shimmered with an infinitely ridiculous number of infinitesimally small fluorescent beads trapped between its wrap and weft. Raf didn't really have time to admire the effect. His brain was rich with theta waves that rolled across his cortex, firing neurones. Behind his eyes was a memory of Zara naked, soft hips and no body hair. Her legs long, her stomach almost flat. Water rolling in droplets between full breasts.

Sweet memories that stopped him remembering ugly things. Like blood turning black in a gutter or a breeze-blown fragment of ribbon fluttering across the road towards him.

'He wasn't listening,' Hani said.

Zara sucked her teeth, crossly. 'This way,' she ordered and ducked under the curtain. Her fingers twisted and fluorescence blossomed from a broken trance tube. They were inside a packed alcove that was arched over with crumbling red brick, and around them was rubbish, mostly broken beer boxes or empty industrial-size containers of still mineral water. Someone's knickers lay discarded on the floor.

Beyond the alcove was a gap where a storm drain fed into the cistern from the street. Clearly visible on the wall were crumbling iron hand-holds, rusted with age.

'You first,' Zara told Hani, 'Me next, Ashraf last . . .'

That was the order in which they went and that was the order in which the *morales* arrested them in the narrow side street where the drain began. Raf climbing out to find Hani silenced by a hand over her mouth, while Zara stared furiously at a *gendarme* officer with skin the colour of pure chocolate and a bottle-green uniform so immaculate it must have come straight out of a box.

Overhead an ex-Soviet copter, with a searchlight now fixed to the side of its gun bubble, pinned Raf in its beam, then flicked its attention to another street as soon as the officer moved in, Colt held tightly in her hand.

'*Ashraf Bey*,' she said, looking in shock at Raf's still-dripping suit.

'Yeah,' said Raf. 'Me.'

Behind the officer were two privates and at the end of the narrow street was a green van the same colour as the woman's uniform. Its rear doors were open and waiting.

Been here, thought Raf, *done that. Not doing it again.*

There were three ways it could go. She could let him walk, try to arrest him, or call for advice and back-up. Only the first was any good to him and Raf didn't see it happening. Not if the screen-splash he'd caught at the madersa had been right and the IPD were busy nailing Felix to his forehead like the mark of Cain.

Crunch time came as the officer lifted her wrist to her face, ready to call HQ.

'Don't even think about it.' Raf had the fat man's gun out of his sodden pocket and in his hand before she had time to do much more than flinch. Her own weapon still pointed lazily at the ground. She'd got the uniform all right, she just hadn't got the moves.

'Fuck up and I'll kill her,' Raf told the two privates. 'Understood?' The gun wasn't the only thing he'd borrowed from Felix. The sudden hard-ass drawl also belonged to him.

'Your watch,' Raf demanded.

Bottle-green handed it over with a scowl that turned to distilled hatred as Raf tossed her elegant mobile straight down the storm drain. Now her HQ could pinpoint it all they liked.

'Going to shoot *me* too?' The woman's voice was cold, her contempt unchecked. Raf didn't know quite what she saw when she looked at him but it was something she hated. He wasn't too sure he liked it that much himself.

'Felix was dying,' Raf said shortly. Which was true. Half of the man's skull was gone, his brain a fat slug that gravity enticed towards the pavement.

'This man murdered Felix Bey.'

For all the attention the officer gave the gun in his hand, Raf might as well have been unarmed. Except then, of course, he'd have been under arrest already.

'There was a bomb,' said Raf, seeing shock explode in Zara's eyes. 'Felix took the full blast.'

Zara pushed hair out of her face and stared at Raf. 'You finished him off?'

'Yeah.' Raf nodded. 'What was my option? Let him exist on life support, wired up and quadriplegic, surviving on sugar-water and vitamins?'

With definitely no alcohol, no illegal porn channels and no working gearstick to engage even if he did. 'He'd have hated it.'

'So you got to play God?' That was the officer.

'Someone has to . . .' Raf spun the Colt round his finger, stepped in close and jammed the gun under bottle-green's chin.

'Ashraf . . .' Zara's voice shook. 'Don't . . .'

'I didn't kill Lady Nafisa,' Raf said slowly. 'And I didn't murder Felix.' He was talking to the officer, but Zara was listening and so was the kid; so really he was talking to them too. 'But I'm sure as hell going to hunt down whoever did. And I'll shoot anyone who gets in my way. You make sure everyone gets that message.'

Lifting the gendarme's Colt from her lifeless fingers, Raf tossed it after the watch and then walked her to the rear of her van, with the two squaddies following meekly behind. She climbed into the riot van without being asked.

'Now you,' he ordered and the squaddies scrambled inside, jostling each other in their haste. They stank of sweat, fear and kif. Which was what you got if you conscripted *fellah* who just didn't want the job. Still smiling, Raf slammed the rear doors, locked them and dropped their electronic key through the grille of a storm drain.

'Coming . . . ?'

Watchful and unhappy, Zara shook her head. 'No,' she said. 'Running away only makes things worse.'

Raf's laugh was sardonic. 'You've obviously never tried it.'

CHAPTER 38

Sudden and abrupt, Raf's kick echoed off the side of a derelict Customs shed, booming out over rusty tracks to the night-time emptiness of the docks beyond. No lights came on anywhere, no security guard ambled out of the darkness to find out what was going on.

The stretch of crumbling tenement south of Maritime Station was that kind of area. Low concrete housing with rusted bars for shutters and blank squares of chipboard where glass should be. Cancerous enough to make every project block Raf had ever seen look suddenly rich.

'For me . . .' Raf told Hani as he kicked again at the steel door of the deserted warehouse, under a peering signboard that read *Pascarli & Co, Cotton Shippers*, 'Aunt Nafisa's timing makes no sense. That's the problem.'

He'd talked his way through the first two diagrams in his notebook, skipped the autopsy data as being much too upsetting for Hani, and was back to chasing timescale round in his head. Who was where, when?

He was talking to Hani because it beat bouncing ideas off thin air and the fox was back in hiding, or dead. Or both. At least the kid had Ali-Din to talk to, not that she spoke much to her rag dog either these days.

Hani was worried about something but asking her directly about it hadn't worked. Though he'd tried that several times, starting when he'd got back to the madersa after Felix flat-lined. All he'd got in return was sullen silence.

Back then, Raf hadn't told the small girl Felix was dead: any more than he'd told her they had to leave the house. Just asked his question and regretted getting no answers. But scaring kids wasn't his style. And besides, Raf could remember a time when he too had shut right down, until the adults round him began to say his lights were on but no one was home. And he *had* been home, of course – he just wasn't answering the door . . .

'You see,' Raf said. 'Aunt Nafisa went to a committee meeting at C&C at 10 A.M.' He used *a.m.* because that was what Hani knew. Lady Nafisa had thought the 24-hour clock vulgar. 'She left her meeting at eleven, but didn't get home until one. So where was she . . . ?

'Now,' said Raf, answering his own question. 'She could have been shopping.' He kicked one last time at the door and it flew back to reveal damp-smelling darkness. 'But then, what happened to her parcels?'

But it wasn't shopping, because Lady Nafisa didn't buy things when other people were about. She made stores open for her specially, at night, when she could count on the manager's full attention.

'Through here,' Raf told the girl and stepped into a musty darkness, nudging the door shut with his heel. Her fingers in his hand felt as fragile as twigs and almost as dry. She hadn't yet asked Raf why he'd really shot Felix. But as she'd trotted through the night towards the docks, the child had tossed possible answers around in her head and not liked most of them.

It had been Ali-Din's job to find the warehouse. And the way it worked was that every time a crossroads appeared, Hani would stare at the eyes of her rag dog and then nod left or right depending on which eye blinked. If neither lit then the route was straight ahead. The puppy ran on some kind of satellite positioning system matched to a template of Iskandryia.

Hani's slight thaw had lasted until they reached the end of Fuad Premier, where a narrowing boulevard intersected with Rue Ibrahim and rattling midnight trams ran southwest from Place Orabi towards a rail terminus and the Midas Refinery stockyard.

The address Zara had given Raf was on the far side of the tramline, in an area where ramshackle souks gave way to near-derelict tenements before ending in a stink of sewage, rotting fish and diesel that leached from rusting dockside cranes dotting a cancerous concrete wilderness at the southeast end of Western Harbour.

It was dog-shit city.

A whole area of festering poverty that the *Rough Guide* didn't mention, other than to suggest that visitors should keep to the main routes during the day and avoid the place altogether at night. The official city guide omitted any mention of the area.

And, in a sense, the tenements and sprawl of empty warehouses *didn't* exist for most people in Iskandryia: for them, the slums were invisible and unnoticed, except by *felaheen* who didn't vote or would only have voted the wrong way if they did. America might stack its urban poor one family on top of another in high-rise blocks but in North Africa the poor were marginalized in a more literal sense . . . They lived at the

barren edges of its cities or occupied unwanted spaces like this one –
which existed between a tramline and the dockside railway, was edged
along its third side by a canal and slid, on its one good side, from squalor
through poverty to the almost picturesque as it finally meshed with the
souks of the El Gomruk . . .

'Up here,' said Raf, reaching a ladder. His voice echoed inside the
empty warehouse the way kicking down its door had echoed off derelict
buildings outside.

Above was a prefabricated office, slung between two steel girders
originally added to strengthen the brick walls of the warehouse. The
spiral staircase that should have led up to it was missing, so maybe Zara's
tale of an upset hotel was untrue.

'Can't see,' Hani protested. She sounded cross and upset, but at least
she'd started talking.

'I can,' said Raf. 'I'll go first and you follow after.' Part of him wanted
to do it the other way round – so that he could catch Hani in case she
slipped – but it was impossible to know what he might find in the office,
so he went first. He could have made her stay below, of course, but he
knew the child would like that even less.

'How can you see?' Hani asked scornfully. 'It's dark.'

'Ali-Din can see in the dark.'

'That's different.'

'Why?'

'Because Ali-Din is only . . .'

Her voice trailed away and Raf started climbing. Left hand pulling
him up the ladder, his right tightly gripping the revolver.

The prefab was empty of people and full of kit. Each wall was
smothered with cheap Ikea shelving, the bolt-together kind. Metal tables
were pushed hard against the shelves. The only gap on the walls was a
window, that would have looked north along the dockside towards
Maritime Station if someone hadn't covered it over with tar paper and
taped along all the edges. There was a sourly mechanical, almost
chemical stink to the place, underlaid with stale tobacco.

Most of the kit in the room was instantly recognizable, like two stand-
alone Median PCs and an Apple laptop with a fold-out satellite dish,
which was definitely illegal. Plus a stack of vinyl piled next to a
Blaupunkt mixing desk. The rest of the apparatus was far weirder.
Starting with a full scuba suit, matching quadruple oxygen bottles and a
shrink-wrapped box of sterile 1000ml beakers stacked next to the
entrance hatch.

And someone had gone to the trouble of dragging plastic drums of
distilled water up to the office. But that was the least of it. In one corner

was a Braun freezer, wired to a bank of car batteries. In the opposite corner, a cupboard made of glass had an extractor hood taped and double-taped to its top, with a duct leading straight out through an outside wall.

On a table by the cupboard a long glass spiral of tubes fed down to a sealed beaker and every ring in the spiral was joined to the next with a ground-glass joint. Jammed between two of the rings was a half-smoked packet of untipped Cleopatra, while a battered paperback copy of *Uncle Fester's Organic Chemistry* leaned against the beaker. The *Fester's* was the edition with a skull on its cover.

Inside a medical chest placed on the floor next to the table were bandages, burn salve, spray skin, surgical glue, a small canister of Japanese oxygen and a box of surgical gloves. There were also a dozen more packets of untipped Cleopatra.

'What have you found?' Hani demanded.

'A kitchen,' said Raf as he returned to the trap door and put out a hand to help her up, 'but not the kind you know.' He tried not to mind that the child flinched away from his grip.

'*Wake up*,' said Hani.

Raf came to on his feet. Banging into shelving as he spun, hand going for his shoulder holster before he remembered he didn't wear one these days and the gun was in his pocket.

Instinctively, he checked the fat man's revolver, fast-flipping the cylinder. Out and in. The weapon was one shot light – as if he could forget.

Still, with luck, whoever Ali-Din said was coming wouldn't know that.

'*Ali-Din* . . . ?'

Raf stopped.

'How does Ali-Din know someone's coming?'

In answer, Hani put her puppy on a table by the taped-over window. The rag dog shuffled round and swung its large head until its eyes stared at where the tenements would be visible in the early-morning daylight, if only plyboard and tar paper hadn't replaced the glass. When its head stopped swaying, its blue-buttoned tail started to wag, like a faulty metronome.

'Don't tell me,' Raf said. 'The nearer the person, the faster the wag?'

Hani nodded.

'So it's a friend?'

Hani's eyes went wide, impressed at his grasp.

'A friend?' Raf stressed, even though he already knew the answer.

Whoever had given the toy to Hani had chosen an expensive model. Though the mechanics couldn't be that difficult. To greet or growl the unit wouldn't even need satellite tracking – not the visual kind, anyway. Simple band scanning could check numbers on a mobile against basic visual recognition software and have the wag or growl defined either by how the child had reacted visually to that person before, or else, if the unit was really expensive, by reading off stress levels or beta waves.

There'd be a time lag of a few seconds but nothing too difficult to hide.

'Tell me,' said Raf, as he pocketed the revolver and headed for the trapdoor. 'Wag or growl? Which did Ali-Din do when he saw Aunt Nafisa?' Hani still hadn't answered when he reached the bottom of the ladder . . .

'Sweet fuck.' Raf forgot all about saying hello to Zara. Instead he stepped out into the morning glare, scrabbling for his dark glasses. He still couldn't get used to the North African sun, not after the grey skies of Seattle and the equally soft skies of Switzerland and Scotland before that.

Zara was dressed in tight black jeans, matched with a white silk shirt with long sleeves, no bra and only flip-flops on her feet. But it was her split lip he noticed.

'Leave it,' she said, when he tried to check the swelling. She stopped outside the warehouse door, refusing to go any further. 'I want to know why you shot Felix . . .'

'He was already dying. I just sped it up.'

Zara sighed. 'How very macho.' She pulled a print of *Iskandryia Today* from under her arm. 'You sure it wasn't because he told the truth about Lady Nafisa's suicide?'

'How do you . . . ?' Raf demanded.

'The whole city knows,' said Zara and shoved the front page in his face. Felix stared out, looking fifteen years younger and a hundred pounds thinner than when Raf had last seen him. There was no picture of Raf, though the words *Suicide, Lady Nafisa*, and *Ashraf Bey* made cross-heads down two columns on the right.

'Nafisa didn't commit suicide,' Raf said flatly. 'She was too devout, too *respectable*.' He put heavy stress on the last word, and knew it to be true. Delete and discard were functions his unconscious had never had to master. He could actually *see* Lady Nafisa, alive inside his head, retiring to her room five times a day for prayers. See her reprimanding Hani for playing with Ali-Din that first Friday when the child should have been reading quietly or practising needlework.

Suicide was a sin.

Besides, she was too selfish, too in love with who she was to throw

195

over wordly grandeur without a fight. Lady Nafisa didn't cast herself into darkness. Someone forced her through that door . . .

'There's been a couple of people on the radio who agree it wasn't suicide,' said Zara. 'They say it was you.'

'Me?' Raf stopped, shook his head and stared at the picture of Felix. He hadn't murdered the man and he hadn't killed his aunt. And Raf didn't need to stake his life on it, because he already had.

The raid on CdH also made the front page, but much smaller. And the picture of Zara was a paparazzi shot, snatched outside the Precinct as she clambered from the back of a riot van.

The copy didn't actually need to say she'd been naked beneath her coat when arrested, because the valley of shadow just above where the *faux* ocelot buttoned told its own story. Which hadn't stopped the paper stressing her nakedness three times in three paragraphs.

'What did they do to you?' Stepping forward, Raf took Zara's chin gently between first finger and thumb and turned her cheek to the light. A heavy bruise could just be seen beneath carefully applied concealer. One eye was also bruised and bloodshot, though Zara hadn't bothered with belladonna drops. No amount of eye brightener would be enough to hide her puffy eyelids or the redness where tears had dried.

Without thinking, Raf put an arm round her shoulder to help Zara into the warehouse, and felt rather than just heard her intake of breath and sudden hiss of pain.

'Forget it,' said Zara, brushing his apology away with a sour smile. 'No one else seems to think it's important. So what do you think of the place?' She stepped past him and into the warehouse. 'The collective use it. I just pay the rent.'

'The collective?'

'Friends . . .'

'But you all share the profits?'

Zara shook her head. 'I let them sell stuff at the club, at their own risk. CdH takes nothing off the top . . . Took,' she corrected herself. 'We *took* nothing off the top.'

'Doesn't look like that made a difference,' said Raf, one finger tracing a raw welt that ran round the side of her neck. Its edges were puffy and pinpricked with blood. This time Zara didn't flinch.

'Bastards,' said Raf.

Zara laughed. 'You think the police did this?' There was a slow-burn anger in her voice, like slightly damp black powder getting itself ready to hiss and flare. 'The *morales* were politeness itself. Even drove me back to Villa Hamzah in an unmarked car. This is my mother's handiwork.'

'Because you were arrested?'

'Because I was naked. Because I was with you. Because no one worth anything will ever marry me now . . . How many fucking reasons do you think she needs?' Zara took a deep breath, steadying herself. 'Why do you think I was so desperate to get away to New York?'

There was no answer to that.

Raf eyed the ladder doubtfully. Seeing Hani crouched at the top, watching them with a blind intensity.

'I'm up here,' she told Zara. 'Do you want me to come down?'

By way of reply, Zara began to pull herself up the ladder, wincing at every new rung. By the time she reached the top, pain had her breathing only through her mouth, though she tried to hide the trembling in her hands.

'Antiseptic,' Hani told Raf, 'and cotton balls.' She put them into his hands and returned with a spray that read *plastic skin*, another of analgesic and a small bottle of mineral water . . . Ripping a stained blanket off a lopsided camp bed, she nodded for Zara to lie down, which the young woman did, being too tired to disagree.

'This will hurt,' said Hani, her voice serious.

'Really,' Zara said dryly. 'What a surprise.' For the first time in hours the child almost cracked a smile. But that vanished the moment Zara tried to take off her shirt and found it was stuck to her back.

Hani proved to be more than adept when it came to dressing the wounds, which she did with minimum fuss and maximum patience, stopping every time Zara swore or jerked under her touch. When one blast of analgesic proved not enough, Hani resprayed Zara's bare back and counted up to fifteen before she began again to lift off dried blood with wet cotton balls.

Hani's proficiency wasn't what held Raf's attention, however. What gripped it – so tightly he had to remind himself he'd actually seen Zara naked, not just without her shirt – was the curve of one full breast as it pressed out at the side, as she lay face down on that rickety camp bed. He'd seen his share of naked women, although none of them quite that beautiful; but this was heartbreakingly different, and he felt the breast's shape in his head like a shiver.

Somewhere in his psycho-profile files at Huntsville there was probably an explanation. Which, no doubt, Dr Millbank would have been happy to expound. Back there sex was something to be talked about, analysed and discussed, preferably in open meetings. In return, Huntsville ran 'access weekends' in a block of log cabins that looked like a bad lakeside motel. Every window had red checked curtains, little beds of nasturtiums prettied up both sides of the front door and books stood in neat rows on shelves inside, along with framed prints of snow-capped mountains and a fridge full of Miller Lite and that pale Mexican beer. The low-rent kind that made it hard to get drunk.

But the *normalizing* touches were irrelevant. All anyone was really interested in were the big Shaker beds with their disposable sheets that got replaced each morning.

It hadn't mattered that Raf had no one to come visiting. At the end of his first month Dr Millbank signed him off as in need of ongoing psychosexual therapy. His designated therapist was a blond academic in her early thirties who was writing a thesis on *regressive institutionalization*. One weekend the academic didn't arrive and a dark-haired serious Canadian student of hers turned up instead. All the Canadian wanted to do was heavy pet and then take breaks to make notes. It was from the student that Raf learned his therapist had been working on the same paper for eleven years. Which sounded pretty institutionalized to him . . .

When Zara's welts were clean, Hani sterilized the area with antiseptic, waited for it to dry and then graffitied over each one with a thick line of plastic skin; and all the while the child's face was frozen into a mask, seconds away from dissolving into tears.

'Hey, it's okay,' Zara insisted. 'It just stung a bit, you know?'

Slowly, Hani nodded. And the movement was all it took to tip the drops from her eyes and spill them down her cheeks: rendering Raf instantly irrelevant, though he didn't know why.

The two girls looked at each other, then back at Raf.

'South of here,' said Zara, 'you'll find a boat, just before the railway jetty.' She pushed herself up on one elbow, revealing a flash of breast as she dipped one hand into her jeans pocket. 'You'll need this,' she said firmly. The card she gave him was grey, scratched and dull with age. It was blank on either side. 'We won't be long.'

'What about . . .'

'Hani's going to clean up my face, aren't you, honey? And then we're going to talk, in private. Then we'll do our prayers. After that, we'll come and find you . . .'

The first vessel Raf came to stank of oil and rested so low in the water that any half-decent wave could lap over its side and finish the job of sinking it. The next two were small tunny boats, battered red hulls and peeling oak decks warped and split with heat. Old-fashioned steel padlocks locked tight their cabin doors.

After that was a long gap of jetty where rusting bollards waited vainly for bow ropes from container ships that would never come back. The new boats docked in the deeper waters behind him. Ferries and cargo vessels from Marseilles and Syracuse, roped fast to the jetty of Maritime Station. And beyond those were anchored sleek grey cruisers and an elderly aircraft hangar that stood off from the entrance to the naval base at Ras el-Tin. The General was rumoured to keep certain prisoners aboard the *Ali Pasha*, held below decks in conditions of both sumptuous luxury and restraint.

Ahead of Raf, where shallows condemned the water to near-emptiness, the main dock came to an abrupt halt as the dockside jerked back onto itself to become a long jetty which angled out towards the middle of the harbour. The glint of wheel-hammered tracks confirmed that the spur was still in use. Probably to shunt containers out to Soviet cargo carriers too vast even to dock alongside Maritime Station.

Raf was still looking for the right boat when he realized he'd been staring at it for the last ten seconds without registering the fact. It was there, all right, in a vee of greasy water where the dockside folded back to become the jetty. Only what Raf first saw as dead water beyond the boat turned out to be the mouth of Mahmoudiya Canal, feeding from a large hole in the side of the dock.

Two centuries before, twenty thousand *felaheen* had died in three years digging the fifty miles of waterway that now linked El Iskandryia to the capital. The canal was built on the orders of the Khedive, so goods could flow from Cairo to North Africa's greatest port, while fresh water from Iskandryia could be diverted to irrigate the hinterland. First started in 1817 on the orders of Mohammed Ali, it was built by a French architect – as was much of Iskandryia from that period.

For the first hundred years the canal, or at least the bit that circled the city, was lined by some of Isk's grandest houses, each with a luxuriant garden leading down to the water's edge. But the houses crumbled and the rich left. The clear water clogged with madder rose, effluent and finally bodies as Spanish Influenza hit the city and, for ten weeks or so, Iskandryia emptied of the living, leaving only the dead.

Now Zara's black boat rested in the shadow of that canal mouth, lying so low in the water it too might have been slowly sinking; except this vessel was designed to ride almost level with the waves. Fifty feet long, ten wide at the stern once its chisel-edged prow had finally flared out, the boat was an ex-UN-issue combat craft. Stealth-sheeted and proof against infrared sensors.

Its retractable glass antenna was just visible at the rear. Turned off, the antenna was transparent to radar. Only in the brief periods when it was broadcasting or receiving did the inside of the hollow glass whip turn to plasma, as a single metal electrode at its base stripped electrons from gas.

The last time Raf had seen a VSV had been ten years before on CNN when one of the 15,000bhp craft had been in the middle of being freighted aboard a McDonnell Globemaster V to be air-lifted to some emergency in Indonesia. If he remembered correctly – and, as always, he did – out of the water it looked like a cigar tube that someone had pinched flat at the front end. That, and the fact it had once been the fastest ocean-going vessel in the world.

'Well . . .' Raf glanced from the old VSV to the grey card in his hand. 'Why not?' There was a lot about Zara he didn't know. In fact, he suspected that there was a lot about her that a lot of people didn't know, starting with her parents.

A slot next to a small door at the rear of the long cockpit swallowed the card and then spat it out again. Without any sound, without a single diode lighting or any other clue that the VSV's computer even knew he was aboard, the door frame scanned Raf for weapons and confirmed the card was real. The multiple check-sums matched those in memory and Felix's revolver was judged not hazardous.

A lock clicked and the door opened outwards. The cabin inside was a clean as the boat's outside was filthy and Raf realized the litter on the decks, the tide marks and oil smears were intentional. Someone had ripped out the original bucket seats that had run down both sides of the cabin and replaced them with two metal beds, a small fridge, a bank of comms, kit and, most bizarre of all, a shower cubicle.

The only other thing in the stripped-bare cabin was a white telephone, the old-fashioned kind with a handset that needed to be picked up. The phone was busy taking a message and a read-out on its base announced that its memory was already backed up with ten others. Probably all from the same man by the sound of it . . .

'Zara.' Anger fought worry in the caller's voice, worry winning. 'Your mobile's turned off and I've tried everywhere else. If you're there, pick up . . .'

'Zara, are you there? *Zara* . . .'

For a second, Raf was tempted to leave the receiver in its cradle and let Zara deal with her father when she finally turned up: assuming she did and that sending him ahead wasn't her ploy to get Hani away from a dangerous maniac. But there was something approaching desolation in Hamzah's gruff voice. His fury a flip side to a love he'd probably never put into words but which was there all the same.

Raf lifted the receiver. 'She's not here.'

'*Not* . . .' Hamzah sounded stunned. 'Who is . . . ?'

Realization hit him a second later.

Zara refused to use the word *beat*. Grown-ups either hit children or they didn't, in her opinion. Calling it something else might soothe an adult conscience but it made little difference to the child.

'It's okay, honey. You're allowed to tell me.'

Hani didn't answer. Partly because she'd never really seen another person naked and she was looking at Zara with the disturbed fascination of someone who knew that, one day, strange things would happen to her body too. And partly it was because Hani didn't know the right answer.

Hani tried very hard to give only right answers, even if other people thought that wasn't true. *Other people*, had always been Aunt Nafisa and Donna, but now her aunt was dead and Donna was still at the madersa and *other people* were Ashraf and the woman standing in front of her, struggling to get into her filthy shirt without letting the cloth scrape her back.

'Do you want me to do that?' Hani asked.

Zara nodded, and sat back on the edge of the camp bed.

'This arm first,' Hani said.

Obediently Zara threaded one arm through the offered sleeve.

'Now this one . . .'

'Did she?' Zara asked, gently moving Hani round so the child stood facing her. The child blushed, though at what Zara wasn't certain.

'She did, didn't she?'

Very slowly Hani nodded.

'Often?'

'Sometimes.' By now the child was gazing anywhere but at the young woman in front of her.

Zara didn't need to ask if the blows were hard. She'd faced that question for herself and could answer as a child. All blows were hard when it was someone who was meant to love you and someone you were meant to love – did love – until you finally taught yourself not to . . .

'Something happened, didn't it?' Zara said gently.

Hani shook her head.

'Yes,' said Zara. 'When Lady Nafisa came home . . . You saw her come in and something happened. Was she angry?'

'No,' Hani said, nodding. The answer was there on her tongue but her mouth was closed into a bitter, troubled trap, holding in secrets too heavy to speak.

'Tell me,' Zara said. 'She came home and you were where . . . ?'

'In her study,' Hani's voice was a whisper. 'She'd taken Ali-Din.'

Hani clutched the rag dog tight, as if someone might be about to confiscate the toy again.

'So she hit you . . .' Zara could understand the child's hurt. She'd inhabited that world until first thing this morning. Now her world would be different.

'No,' said Hani. 'She missed. So I ran away.'

'She missed?'

Hani nodded. She was thinking. Remembering, but not quite understanding. 'Aunt Nafisa was falling over. She shouted at me because her head hurt.'

'What?' Zara asked quickly. 'What did she shout?'

'To get a doctor – and to leave her alone.'

'So what did you do?'

Wide eyes regarded Zara. 'I shut the door and locked it . . . She was drunk. It's wrong to be drunk.' Hani nodded intently, reassuring herself. 'When Donna got drunk Aunt Nafisa slapped her and said next time she'd call the police . . .'

So you didn't call a doctor, thought Zara, *because you didn't want the police to come. And then your aunt was killed and the police came anyway. No wonder you're traumatized.*

'Honey,' said Zara as she stroked Hani's cheek, 'it's okay. You did right. And I promise we won't let anyone know she'd been drinking.'

The anger coming down the line was almost palpable. Hamzah's fear had finally found a target it could hate. 'I will kill you if you've hurt her . . . Do you understand?'

'Me, hurt Zara? I thought that was your wife's job.'

That earned Raf stunned silence. Raf could do misdirected hatred too, better than most. Raf and Hamzah were two minutes into what passed for a conversation and were already headed for a brick wall.

'You shot Felix Bey,' Hamzah said finally. As if that was proof Raf intended to slaughter his daughter as well.

'News travels . . .' So did a memory, sliding out of the past. Felix discussing the General. Felix bad-mouthing the Minister. Felix talking about skimming his percentage off men like Hamzah, but still not looking the other way. In a city like Iskandryia anyone could have sent that bomb.

Raf ran tired fingers across his scalp, feeling stubble. It needed washing along with the rest of him. He felt old and tired, centuries older than when he had first arrived in the city. His face was narrower, his dark blond beard made his lips look thinner and chin more pointed. There was a vulpine cruelty to his own face that Raf didn't recognize.

The prince must make himself feared in such a way that, if he not be loved, at least he escapes being hated.

An old memory.

Well, okay, if the fox said so.

'Let me tell you about Felix,' said Raf angrily. 'He had cancer of both lungs and a liver with more holes than a sponge. He drank a bottle of whisky a day and had a daughter he hadn't seen in years. What he didn't have, when I last saw him, was medical insurance covering lifestyle choices or losing half his head . . .'

The words were ice-cold, burning with blue fire. Raf didn't really know the person who spoke them or recognize the anger that shot them out of his mouth and down the line to the suddenly silent industrialist. He only knew that, this time, that person was him.

'He told me he was the only really honest cop in that place and I believed him. And, yes, I shot him,' said Raf. 'I put a gun to what was left of his head and pulled the trigger. And I'd do it again. Right now, tomorrow, next year, whenever . . . He was the closest thing I'd found to a partner in this stinking sewer of a city and I owed him. What part of all this don't you understand?'

The man on the other end broke the connection quietly. Seconds later the windows darkened to an impenetrable black, the interior of the boat brightened as bulkhead lights came on and the dashboard lit with a dozen different readouts. Over on one wall a window came to life, revealing a rolling news programme. *Ashraf Bey trapped.* Below it, a wall-mounted keyboard beeped once to show it was live.

A tiny voice from the VSV's console announced the craft was shielded, operating fooler loops and running overlapping stealth routines. It also told Raf that he had visitors.

'Well, now,' Zara said, as he opened the door to her and she saw the live array of the console beyond. 'You want to tell me exactly how you managed that?'

CHAPTER 39

The aged *felah* behind the make-shift counter looked as old as a twisted olive tree until one noticed his eyes. Then it became obvious that although hot summers and wild winter storms had beaten his face to the colour and consistency of cheap leather, the man's eyes revealed his true age: which was still old enough to have seen almost everything the city could offer, except the sight of police openly surrounding the madersa of a bey.

And he knew it was Friday afternoon and his street licence banned working, but the crowds were out – and when the crowds were out they needed feeding.

'*Taamiya . . .*' Falafel. On the cart in front of him was a stack of aluminium bowls, three wine bottles now filled with some kind of sauce and a ladle. The wide neck of a metal jar stuck through the flat top of his cart. Inside the jar, already-cooked falafel were slowly cooling.

On a separate cart, in a huge metal container of bubbling oil, bobbed more taamiya ready to be scooped out and transferred to the main cart. Next to the bobbing taamiya was a smaller bowl of beaten egg into which they'd been dipped, before being rolled in bread crumbs ready to fry. Here too were kept piles of pitta, which a slash of the knife converted from simple flat bread into a pocket waiting to be filled with taamiya, chopped salad and sauce.

The younger man took the food he'd asked for and gave the cart owner a handful of change, half of it adorned with the profile of the Khedive, the rest featuring His Imperial Majesty. Only the poor still used small change and it didn't matter to them whose head was on the coins, so long as agreement existed about how much each little circle of metal was actually worth.

'La.' Raf waved away an even smaller coin the falafel seller offered as change and bit into his warm pitta bread, tasting fresh coriander and feeling oil run into his beard. He hadn't felt hungry when he ordered the pitta, had merely needed something extra to help him blend with the restless crowd gathered around the taped-off entrance of Rue Cif. But now, with his striped and tattered jellaba – that cloak of invisibility worn the length of the North African littoral by the dispossessed – and taamiya in his hands, Raf felt ready to begin fighting his way through the crush.

There was a knot in his stomach and it wasn't all hunger, though more than twenty-four hours had gone by since he'd last eaten, maybe longer. Raf wasn't sure, because he wasn't wearing a watch, and that was part of blending in too. If he could find a street stall he'd pick up a *faux* Rolex, something obviously cheap and not real.

What he needed was something suitable for a jellaba-wearing felah, like a cheap Thai fake or the kind of flamboyant G'Schlock copies garages gave free with gas . . . Just as he'd needed the budget wrap-arounds he'd picked up from a 24/Seven in Place Orabi which made the people he was pushing through look amber and ghostly. Some of the crowd had been brought here, like him, by newsfeeds or radio. Most had just followed neighbours or stopped off on their way back from a mosque.

'What the fuck happened?' Raf asked, offering a tiny coin to a woman hawking plums from a woven satchel. 'An accident?' For all he knew the felaheen used ornate politeness when talking amongst themselves but, if so, the woman didn't seem to notice. And if she looked at the stranger with the torn jellaba in surprise it was at the fact he even had to ask.

'They're searching Ashraf Bey's house.'

'He won't be there . . .'

The woman spat. 'Of course he won't. He's under arrest. They're looking for proof the pig killed his aunt for the money . . .'

'What money?'

'There was money,' she said shortly. 'And there's a reward for information. That's what I heard.' The next time Raf looked, the woman was shuffling towards a uniformed officer, ignoring outstretched arms that offered coins for her remaining fruit.

'Out of there.'

Raf was moving in the opposite direction before he realized what the fox had ordered his body to do. *Too fast*, the fox told him, its voice faint. And Raf halted his panic-driven trot to a slow stroll, pushing his way to the front of the crowd. He was helping kill off the fox, by making it appear in daylight. They both knew that. But the fox had never said anything about it, never criticized.

'*Head for Mushin.*'

The man he'd come looking for stood like a poisoned dwarf just inside Rue Cif, staring hard at the rear door to the madersa. What did the man hope to find? Raf had no idea. Unless the Minister was just there to be seen by the news 'copters overhead and the ground crews.

'*Shield*,' whispered the voice in his head and then it was gone, fading to static that fizzled and died. Raf was alone again.

Tossing his half-finished pitta into the dirt, Raf flashed Felix's gold shield at a surprised police sergeant and stepped over the tape before the man had a chance to check the name or protest. The fact that Raf headed straight for Mushin Bey was enough to make the sergeant step back, muttering bitterly about plain-clothed shitheads.

'Hey, you,' said the Minister. 'Back behind the line.' The small man didn't just look like a cinema usher, he sounded like one too.

Raf grinned and flipped open Felix's pass to show the shield and then, as the Minister's eyes widened, rammed the barrel of the fat man's revolver hard into the small man's thigh. 'I've got his gun, too,' said Raf, relying on their distance from the crowd and the long sleeve of his own jellaba to keep the revolver hidden.

'You won't . . .'

'I just did,' said Raf. He nodded towards the middle of Rue Cif, where the closed-off street stood dark and empty and the crowd and police looked very far away. 'Take a walk.'

Raf could tell that Mushin Bey wanted to complain, to threaten, to promise Raf that he'd be hunted down like a dog – but one look at the hard edge to Raf's face told him not to waste his breath. This man would kill him if necessary. And all that Raf knew about the Minister, he read written in fear on a weasel face and deduced from panic rising from the man's skin, unsweetened by courage.

He was no more a real head of police than Raf was a real bey. Mushin Bey was a politician, which put him off the list where killing Felix was concerned. The man had needed Felix, rotted liver and all.

'Okay,' said Raf. 'It's murder now you think you can pin Nafisa on me, but it was suicide when you couldn't. So tell me, who are you protecting?'

'No one,' said the Minister. 'As you well know.' He sounded like he believed it. And he tried to stare back, but his pale eyes slid away from the wraparounds bisecting Raf's face, fear subverting any real anger.

It was a feeling Raf suddenly recognised. Already there was a fragment of worry inside his head telling him to put down the gun and surrender. To give himself up to authority as he always did eventually, once the brief flare of anger had burned out to leave only the taste of failure in his mouth. A death penalty existed in Iskandryia as it did in all Ottoman cities, even the free ones, but he could cut a deal. He didn't doubt that . . .

'We know about Felix fixing the autopsy,' the Minister said flatly. 'What did you have on him? Little girls, drags, payoffs . . . ?'

'No one fixed that autopsy,' Raf said crossly, jostling the Minister further back towards an empty area of the street. 'Unless it was you?'

Without intending to, Mushin Bey answered with an instinctive shake of his head so minute it was almost subliminal. Raf believed him. What he found impossible to believe was that the man wasn't covering up for someone else.

'Tell me,' said Raf, 'when did you switch from being certain it was suicide to being certain it wasn't?'

'When you had Felix killed. I assume you suddenly realized he'd stuffed you up with that suicide verdict.'

'When I . . . ? He was dying,' said Raf. 'It was a *coup de grâce*.'

And then the Minister explained something that stood Raf's day on its head and made a mockery of the scribbled and intricate chart of connections carried deep in Raf's pocket. Mushin Bey wasn't talking about the shooting. He meant the bomb. They'd found the man who'd delivered it and he was happy to help. The Minister paused for a second and amended that to *very* happy to help. And what really impressed the Minister, and he was prepared to admit this, was Raf's idea of arranging for the bomb to be delivered to himself. What better way to divert guilt . . .

'It was meant for me?'

'Don't . . .' The Minister didn't get to the next word because by then Raf was bringing up his gun.

'You know what I think?' Raf said as he flicked back the hammer and positioned the muzzle carefully under the Minister's chin so any bullet fired would be guaranteed to remove most of the back of the man's skull. 'I think you know who killed Lady Nafisa.'

'Me?' Anxiety shrivelled Mushin Bey's face. Panic blossomed until it was only a matter of seconds before the Minister either soiled himself or else started pleading for his own life. And every emotion inside the man was stripped naked except for the one that Raf actually sought.

Guilt would have been enough to make him pull the trigger.

'I didn't murder Felix and I certainly didn't murder Lady Nafisa.' Raf's voice was hard. 'I'm not so sure you didn't, but you get the benefit of my doubt . . .' That was the kind of crap Dr Millbank used to speak all the time. 'But *someone* killed them, and if that turns out to be you . . .

'Remember,' Raf told the man, 'I trained in places that wouldn't even let you through the fucking door.' And with that, he leaned forward and dropped something soft into the Minister's pocket, smoothing the jacket neatly into place.

'The remains of that plastique I didn't take,' Raf said simply. 'Take you off at the hips, no question.' He thrust one hand into his own pocket and kept it there, closing his fingers round a tube with a spring-loaded button on top. 'I'm going to walk out of here. You cause me *any* problems and I'll leave you as chopped steak all over the street. You understand me?'

The minister did.

Idly clicking the button on a breath-mint dispenser as he walked away, Raf wondered how long it would take Mushin Bey to discover that the object burning a hole in his pocket was actually one uneaten plum.

'Yes, I shot him . . .'

Two wheels bit and the bike was flying. Hot summer wind rammed its way through ventilation ducts cut into the bike's aerodynamically perfect fairing, cooling the Japanese v-twin as DJ Avatar red-lined his whole way down the sweep of the Corniche.

'And I'd do it again.'

He was too fired up on the mix, too wired to check his profile in the smoked windows of expensive cafés lining the final stretch of road.

'Right now, tomorrow, next year, whenever.'

Av didn't recognize the man's voice – because they'd never spoken – but he knew who it was. Just as he knew for sure it had to be Zara who'd dumped the file into his postbox. Her way of apologizing for who the *morales* drove home and who they kept locked up in a basement for forty-eight hours with a pisspot for company. Though where a murderer and his half-sister fitted together . . . Well, that was some place he definitely didn't plan to go for too long.

All the same, the mix was sweet and its message sweeter still. Pure and illegal as the fragments of meth still burning the back of his throat. The police had cracked the club but this was his revenge.

Simple bass went nowhere slowly. The synth line looped colder than liquid nitrogen, crackling with static.

'Believe it. This is DJ Avatar and that was *the Bey*. Coming at you from the wrong side of the mirror . . .' The boy hit a button on his handlebar: manic laughter drowning out the track and then it was back, sucking its way inside his brain and the brain of everybody else listening, which by now was most of the city.

'Enjoy . . .' The bass dropped out to be replaced by a double heartbeat and the sound of pure anger, expertly mixed.

'Let me tell you about Felix . . .'

CHAPTER 40

31st July

A wave rolled over Raf's shoulder, leaving droplets that shone like opals in the noon sun, their salt still prickling his factor 40-coated skin. *Let me tell you about . . .*

He couldn't get Av's mix out of his skull but had moved beyond minding.

Behind him, the moored VSV operated at half stealth, which gave it the radar profile of a small fishing boat. Raf didn't even know where he was, only that the vessel was nestling between two rocky headlands off a low island that lacked any fresh water. And that didn't matter: Zara had brought her own supply and, anyway, VSVs carried small desalination units at the stern.

The sea was wine-dark, the sky a blue so impossible that, even through shades, it looked as if some unseen hand had ditched the presets and started messing with both saturation and brightness. Umber-hued shrubs lined the lower reaches of a stunted hill, their gnarled roots clawed into the thin dirt that had collected between huge rocks – and Raf could smell the scent of lavender blowing towards him on a warm wind.

They were there because Zara had announced that going there would be a good idea. And, without being told, Raf got the feeling that she'd visited the island many times before, though with whom she didn't say. All Raf knew about her island was that it was three hours from Iskandryia – three hours, that was, if one travelled in a boat that cut through waves the way light skewered darkness.

'Hey, look at me.'

Raf watched as Hani launched herself, head first, off the side of the boat to sink below the waves in a stream of bubbles. She was diving, if it counted as diving to sit on the very edge of the deck and bend forward so far that her arms almost touched the waves.

'Did you see?'

Raf nodded and trod water as Hani splashed her way towards him with clumsy strokes. 'Got you,' she said, her arms coming up round his neck, so that Raf found himself carrying her slight weight. The child's hair spread in rats' tails across a face that was suddenly split by a knowing grin. 'Are we running away?'

'Only for today.'

Hani nodded thoughtfully. 'Better do some more dives, then.'

From the deck of the VSV, Zara smiled as the child unhooked her arms and paddled back towards the boat. Her father, now – he ran in the opposite direction from responsibility and called it work.

Watching Raf with Hani was like seeing storm clouds clear. Zara knew exactly what had burnt out the storm, because she'd orchestrated it. Well, sort of . . . It began when Raf was out, checking exactly what was happening at the madersa and she'd started going over all the men she'd known, which wasn't many. Whatever his reasons, her father had little to do with his brother and so she'd never met her cousins on that side. And her mother was an only child, as if that wasn't obvious.

Boyfriends: there'd been two in New York. She'd chucked one of them and one had chucked her, but both times it had been over the same thing. Speaking to her friends in student halls, Zara had taken to referring euphemistically to the reason as *cultural differences*.

Both boys had been white, both Protestant, both uptight and angry but too repressed to discuss it, do anything about it, except glower or sulk. She saw the same repression in Raf, for all that he was meant to be half Berber. He could undoubtedly do both in-your-face or reserved – violence being the flip side of stepped-back – but a straight-out raise-your-voice hand-waving argument? Zara didn't think so. Which was why, after he finally got back from talking to Mushin Bey the previous night, she hadn't given him any option . . .

And for a while she hadn't been sure she was right.

Sitting on the floor of the VSV, darkness falling over the Western Harbour outside, Raf had rubbed one hand tiredly across the back of his neck and asked the kind of question you ask when your anger has been coming out of every radio in every cab in the city. And when getting home means walking unnoticed and unknown past slum kids chanting your words in the street.

It was too late to stop Avatar's mix burrowing worm-like into the city, because *InnerSense/Fight Bac* was racking up heavy rotation, roughly every fourth play. But Raf still wanted to know one thing:

'How the hell did he get it?'

Zara swept the hair out of her eyes and hugged Hani closer. The child was curled up into a little ball, her head on Zara's knee and the rag dog clutched between sleeping hands.

'Own the streets,' said Zara, quoting a liberation theosophist currently serving twenty-five years solitary in Stambul, 'and you've got the city . . . He does it from the back of a bike, you know. Doesn't need to, that's just the way it's developed.'

'Who does?'

'Avatar. My brother . . .' Zara made it a point of principle never to add the *half*.

'Your . . . ?'

Zara nodded, 'Yes,' she said. 'Av. You met him on the tram. I gave him the sound file.'

'You what?'

Their argument went from there. And at the point when Hani scrambled off Zara's lap to cower against the bulkhead, her chin legs tucked up to her chin and her eyes wide with fright, having everything out in the open no longer seemed such a good idea to Zara and the damage looked done.

Zara had just finished accusing Raf of being an arrogant, over-bred, emotionally retarded inadequate and Raf was explaining to Zara in over-simple words why it wasn't his fault if she was some spoilt little rich bitch who'd got done for stripping off at an illegal club.

As for marrying her . . .

'*Stop it.*' Hani's voice was fierce, her chin jutting forward and her mouth set in a determined line. She was way too cross even to acknowledge the tears that rolled down her face. '*Stop it.*'

The small cabin was loud with their sudden silence.

'I'm sorry,' Raf said quietly and he got up to leave the VSV.

'Don't go far,' Hani ordered. 'You'll only get lost.'

Darkness he liked, and silence. Both of which he got, staring out over the shimmering black expanse of the Western Harbour. There had been drunken shouting from Maritime Station as a party of Soviet sailors were escorted back to a destroyer by police: and Customs boats were making great play of criss-crossing the water at high speed, their searchlights cutting across the waves. Only, the sailors had got safely back on board and the cutters had given up sweeping the waters on the dot of midnight and returned to base, leaving the way clear for small, unlit boats to sneak out of the harbour mouth.

'That's the thing about night-time,' Zara said behind him. 'It makes even something as ugly as Maritime Station look beautiful.' She put a chilled beer into his hand and Raf was glad he'd pretended not to hear the door open.

'You know,' said Raf, 'I've probably got a head full of hardware I didn't ask for and, yeah, I can see in the dark but I don't think I'm over-bred, though I'll agree the emotional stuff . . .'

By way of answer, Zara ripped the top off her beer. As apologies went it raised more questions than it answered, but it was still better than she expected.

'I'm pretty sure I'm not even a real bey,' said Raf. 'I don't have finely honed battle skills and I wasn't working for the Seattle Consulate when it got bombed or even before that . . .'

She held out her beer and, after a second, Raf realized he was meant to take it. Then she waited, while he worked out he was meant to give Zara his unopened can in return. The beer felt melt-water cold and tasted clean and slightly sweet. So he concentrated on tasting it, not taking a second mouthful until he'd properly savoured the first.

'What were you doing in America?'

'I've been in prison,' Raf said simply. 'Outside Seattle. I was there for a while.'

'Why?' Zara demanded.

'I was charged with murder.'

'Don't tell me . . .'

'I didn't do it.'

Zara felt her lips twist into something that was almost a smile. 'But they arrested you anyway.'

Raf nodded. 'The thing is,' he said, 'I don't really know what I'm doing here. And there's something else. Why are you . . . ?'

'Why am I helping you? Let me see,' said Zara, counting off the points. 'You jilt me publicly, you shoot the fat policeman, I'm not wearing any clothes when I'm arrested and you're accused of murdering your aunt for money . . . I don't know, you tell me.' She looked at him, then looked again when she realized he really *didn't* understand.

'I'm tainted,' she said flatly. 'No one will marry me. I probably don't even have my old job any more. I need you to be innocent . . .'

'And you came out to tell me this?'

'No,' Zara shook her head. 'I came to tell you that Hani wants to say something.'

What Hani wanted to tell him was that Aunt Nafisa had had a big argument on the phone months before Raf even arrived. And Hani knew who with because her aunt spent a lot of time calling the man *Your Excellency* and *General*.

'So,' Zara kept her voice low. 'What do you think the argument was about?'

Raf shrugged. They'd been talking about it all day, whenever they got a second to themselves. And the only idea he'd come up with was too ludicrous to share.

'Well,' said Zara, 'tell me this. Do you think she was drunk?'

The VSV was on its way back from the island, steering itself and running every routine in its armoury. This time round, it was Zara who leant against Raf's shoulder, while Hani slept on the bed opposite, a sarong pulled tight round her like a sheet.

Did he think his aunt drank? No, even though the child had seen her staggering round the house. And Raf was sure narcotics were out, but equally he didn't believe it was suicide. Which brought him back to murder. And if the *Thiergarten* were left out of the equation, and Raf really didn't believe she'd been assassinated on orders from the Khedive's advisers, then nobody seemed to have a motive, unless it was hothead students at the German School in Iskandryia, and Raf didn't believe even they'd be that stupid.

General Koenig Pasha might be half Prussian, but from what Felix had said, the General tolerated *Thiergarten* activity and that was all. And the students at the German School were unpopular, as young men with no real cares and excess money usually are: they knew full well the debt they owed Koenig Pasha for their protection.

'Drunk?' Raf said. 'I don't know . . . I'm losing the thread.'

'Assuming there is one.'

In less than two hours' time they were due to enter Isk's western harbour by running parallel up the coast, sliding between the shore and a breakwater, using a route firmly fixed in the boat's memory.

The VSV would take a route close to the rocky shore, running low in the water and silent, staying well away from the naval base at Ras el Tin. And yet the naval base would still see them on screen.

But it wouldn't matter.

Because, as she'd already told Raf, the boat belonged to her father who had an understanding in place with the General himself. A dozen passenger liners a day might dock at Maritime Station and still the western harbour's single biggest commercial activity was smuggling. Hashish, vodka, Lucky Strike, Nubian girls . . . It didn't matter. Cargo passed in and out through Western Harbour and the General's men took his ten per cent off the top of the lot. To simplify life, boat profiles were logged at Ras el Tin and somewhere in a subset of a subset of the Navy's housekeeping routines was a constantly updated record of how many runs each boat made.

It kept everybody honest.

'Want to tell me about that hardware in your skull?' she asked Raf.

'No,' he shook his head slowly. 'I don't think so.'

Some days he wasn't even sure the fox was real. Although the malfunctioning hardware was, obviously. And somewhere in the soft stuff he had filed away a perfect memory of promises from a genome sub-contractor in Baja California that went belly-up two years after he was born. Infrared sight, ultraviolet, seven colours, nictitating eyelids – the 8,000-line policy said plenty about effective night vision and very little about retinal intolerance to sunlight.

Originally humans possessed four colour-receptors, only they weren't human then, or even mammal. The fox had once explained it all, sounding almost proud. Most primates now had three receptors only, which was still a receptor up on the two that early mammals originally had, being nocturnal. Raf had a guaranteed four, with his fourth in ultra-violet. Something he had in common with starlings, chameleons and goldfish.

Later clauses dealt with extra ribs to protect soft organs and small muscles that let him close his ears. Only now probably wasn't a good time to mention that.

Idly, Raf kissed Zara's hair and smiled when she gently pushed him away . . . If she really wanted him to stop she'd say so. Her forehead tasted of salt and so did her bruised lips when she finally raised them, her mouth opening until he could taste the olives and alcohol on her breath.

'Wait,' she said.

When Zara had finished tucking in Hani, the thin sarong completely covered the sleeping child, resting lightly over Hani's face so that it quivered with each breath like the wing of a butterfly. 'That's better,' said Zara.

'Lights lowest,' she added and the cabin dimmed.

The next time they kissed it lasted until he moved Zara gently backwards and she winced. 'God, sorry.' Raf had seen the bruises again when Zara swam briefly, letting salt water sterilize the whip marks.

She shrugged. There had been worse. 'Guess what?' Zara said lightly. 'You're the oldest man I've dated.'

'I'm twenty-five!'

'You look older.'

'I don't feel it,' said Raf, 'except on the days I'm a thousand.'

She wore no bra that he could feel and, when his hand finally found them, her breasts beneath her shirt were fuller than he remembered, tipped with soft nipples that promptly puckered against the cloth.

Raf kissed her lips, as if kissing might take her attention off where his hand had strayed, and when her lips melted he risked smoothing his palm softly up over a hidden nipple, his touch feather-light.

'How long before we're back?'

Zara smiled. 'Not that long.'

He wasn't sure which question Zara thought she was answering; but reckoned this was the point where those *cultural differences* came in. Except her fingers were already undoing enough pearl buttons for him to slide back the sides of her shirt and reveal one full breast.

It tasted of the sea, so Raf's tongue traced the taste in a salt circle around her nipple, feeling her flesh pucker and harden, then turn soft as his tongue lapped wave-like over the top.

Zara shivered.

So Raf undid a few more buttons for himself, bringing up both hands to grip her newly freed breasts. His balls ached, his brain swam with alcohol, cheap drugs and cheaper memories but he knew that on this boat, with this person, he'd finally discovered where he belonged, where he always wanted to be.

'Let me try this,' said Zara and she shuffled him sideways, off the long seat until Raf was kneeling between her open knees with his hip pressed hard into her. Her knees locked and she wrapped both arms around Raf's hips to pull him tighter still. Her movements were deliberate, intense and shockingly private: as if, despite the fact Raf was kneeling in front of her, his hand gripping one breast, she was somewhere else, alone.

He couldn't see her in her eyes. And yet Zara wasn't totally in that urgent, rocking darkness between her knees. A darkness so intense he could taste a different salt rising to drug him. She was rocking, pushing herself forward and grinding hard against him. Each movement faster and harder than the one before. Breath hissed between her teeth like pain as she muttered something over and over. Some command or order that finally spilled her over the edge into a sudden gasp that she swallowed, muting it to a low moan that died as the rocking ceased and she pushed him away.

She was crying.

CHAPTER 41

1 st August

The Sunday-morning air held more smells than a spice market – baking bread, an open drain, wood smoke from a *hamman*, turmeric from a locked warehouse . . .

All the scents mixed in her nostrils as Zara ploughed her way across the city, down starved alleys that turned right, then left, then right again. She was walking the bottom of a dark crevasse. Guided not by daylight, which was confined to those brief patches of sky visible between roof edge and a forest of satellite dishes or aerials, but by her inbuilt, almost perfect sense of direction. Not to mention anger, barely restrained irritation and killer PMS.

There were 150 districts in Iskandryia. Cities within the city, villages within towns. Some were rich and some crowded, a few almost deserted, backdrops to a play with no characters. Rotting houses and crumbling souks emptied of the living by the influenza attack of '28. Her grand-mother had died in the epidemic and so had an aunt. That so few members of her family had been taken, and those old and ill, was regarded by her father as a kindness from God.

Other districts were too poor to have been mapped. They went untaxed as well, because no one earned enough to make taking direct taxes worth the trouble. Where that happened, other groups levied tariffs instead, in the name of religion, protection or some banned nationalist ideal kept alive by crowded housing, open sewers, infrequent water and nonexistent Medicare.

These groups paid protection in their turn. And those they paid had their own dues to pay. And somewhere high above them, like a hawk looking down disdainfully at vermin on the ground, hung the shadow of her father . . .

Ashraf Bey knew nothing of this city. He thought he did because he knew Place Zaghloul from Place Orabi and could walk from Le Trianon to Rue Cif without consulting a map or needing to stick to the grand boulevards. He believed Isk was a European city lodged on the edge of North Africa.

Anyone who knew anything knew that this was at least as untrue as it was correct. There *was* an elegant European city of red-brick apartment blocks, stuccoed villas and vast palazzos. But it made up only one layer and that was mostly confined to the sweep of the Corniche, the apartment blocks both sides of boulevards like Fuad Premier and an area around Shallalat Gardens where irrigation kept manicured lawns preternaturally green.

The *real* El Iskandryia had more layers than baklava, more layers than time itself. There was the expatriate-Greek city, the city of visiting Cairene families who appeared at the start of summer and vanished just as promptly. And the city of Jewish shops and synagogues, of rich Germans and infinitely less rich Soviets. And below all that the invisible, the Arab city from which her father hoped to remove her and his family . . . Money could do that, if it was used well. Take you from *felaheen* to *effendi* in three generations.

The city moved across time as well as cultures. A single turn from one alley into another could throw you back a century, to spice markets and dark warehouses where herbs hung from wooden poles, drying in the hot breeze. Another turn, a different alley and the present receded further, as the scent of herbs changed to the rawness of uric acid, of dressed hides hanging in a tannery while raw skins were trampled underfoot in urine-filled vats by men with jellabas pulled up round their hips.

She loved El Iskandryia, its uncertainties and contradictions. Its outward self-assurance and inner darkness. It was the politics Zara didn't like. But then some things in life were beyond change: that was what her father said. She still hoped to prove him wrong.

Zara shook her head, still troubled. She believed Ashraf Bey when he said he'd been in prison rather than working at the Consulate; at least, she did most of the time. What she didn't believe was that the Emir wasn't his father. She knew that was a double negative but didn't care. She needed to see her father and, since she couldn't go home, she was on her way to meet him at Hamzah Plaza, though he didn't yet know that.

Her hair was perfect. Her make-up so immaculate that no bruises were visible. Even her lip looked normal.

Straightening her shoulders, Zara adjusted the lapels of a dark Dior suit she'd just charged at Marshall & Snellgrove – having woken a personal buyer to get the relevant boutique opened early – and stalked across the square towards a building she'd never before bothered to visit, her father's HQ.

The building she approached was black, with pillars of white marble and a three-storey entrance carved from red sandstone and modelled on a horseshoe arch in M'dina. Her father was very proud of his building. The architectural critics had been less kind. *Ersatz Moorish* was one of their gentler comments.

What sounded like rain turned out to be an alabaster fountain set in the middle of a sunken garden. A thing of elegant lines and stunning simplicity, the fountain had been carved a millennium before for one of the princelings of Granada. Her father had never mentioned its purchase, far less what it might have cost.

Zara swept past the fountain and through a revolving door that began to spin just before she reached it. Ahead of her waited a bank of elevators with glistening mahogany surrounds and brass doors polished to a shine. Any one of them would take her up to the top floor.

'Miss . . .' A rapidly approaching security guard almost but not quite raised his voice as he glided across the foyer. In his face politeness battled with exasperation. Politeness won. His eyes had already priced her suit and noted her air of confidence but he allowed himself a second glance as he got closer, to confirm what he already suspected . . . He didn't recognize her.

Zara stopped.

'Visitors have to sign in.' He motioned towards a distant reception area where a young woman stood watching them. 'You do have an appointment?'

'No,' said Zara, 'I haven't. But my father will see me.'

She punched the button on a lift and watched the doors slide open, almost silently. The security guard was still looking suitably appalled when she stepped inside. He probably had a kid, Zara reminded herself, plus a wife who was bound to be pregnant, a mortgage . . . He needed the job she was busy losing him.

'Ring my father,' said Zara. 'Tell him I'm on my way up. Say you couldn't stop me.'

The man nodded and stood back, instantly relieved. He'd remember her kindness and not the arrogance that had let her walk through him, Zara knew that. And he wouldn't realize what he'd just told her – that her father was already in . . .

Which meant he'd had an argument with her mother. Zara smiled Her father only ever came in early on days following an argument. Some weeks he forgot about going to the office at all. Why should he, when anyone he needed to see could be ordered to come to him? His office on the top floor existed mainly to remind people who was in charge.

Hamzah didn't do lunch with visiting foreigners – he had staff to do that for him – and he didn't take taxis or even use his chauffeured stretch much. He walked, because money bought time and that created space for him to walk if he wanted to, which he invariably did. More people saw him that way. Remembered he'd begun as one of their own.

She loved him, of course. Feared him, too. More than she feared her mother, if she was honest. Checking her hair in a mirror, Zara brushed one sleeve to remove dust from where she had touched an alley wall and stepped out, head high, when the lift reached its destination and the doors opened. She expected to see her father waiting at the top but he wasn't. Instead she got a small woman with tightly cropped grey hair and large amber beads.

'Miss Zara?'

'Olga Kaminsky?'

The woman's eyes widened and Zara smiled her best smile. 'My father mentions you,' she said lightly. 'Always compliments.' Zara could almost see the woman reassess her, as she took in Zara's suit, her immaculate hair, the discreet and appropriate jewellery and the folded newspaper tucked under one arm. She didn't look like a spoilt brat who got herself on the news for being in trouble with the *morales*. Which was precisely the point.

'I'm sorry to turn up unannounced, but I was hoping to see my father.'

Olga Kaminsky nodded. 'He's expecting you.'

The door to her father's office was ebony carved into arabesques and inlaid with leaves of pink or pale blue marble. Olga knocked once and went in without waiting to be invited.

'Miss Zara,' she announced, stopping in front of a huge desk.

Duty done, Olga Kaminsky turned to Zara and smiled. 'How about some coffee? And maybe a croissant . . . ?'

'Well,' said Hamzah as the door shut. 'Coffee *and* croissant – and I'd always been under the impression that Olga didn't approve of you.'

'How could she not approve?' Zara said. 'She hadn't even met me . . .'

Hamzah laughed. Neither of them mentioned the fact that Zara hadn't been home for thirty-six hours. Or why. All the same, he saw how carefully his daughter carried herself as she sat back in a large leather chair without being invited.

'Nice place.'

His office was everything Zara expected. Huge, with windows along two walls, the longest looking north over the Corniche and a blue splash of the Mediterranean beyond. The other looked out over the red-brick edifice of St Mark's College, where Hamzah had swept floors when he first arrived in Iskandryia.

A mountain of printouts balanced on one of the leather chairs, while an old Toshiba notepad sat open on the sofa. On the wall behind his desk an out-dated assault rifle balanced on two nails. It was old, rusty, stamped out from cheap, sheet steel. A Kalashnikov AK49. Like the fountain outside the office, Zara had never seen it before.

The whole room was a mess, which didn't surprise her. His study at Glymenapoulo was the only room her mother wasn't allowed to have cleaned. Here, he didn't even have someone to nag him about the mess – unless that was Olga's job.

'Coffee . . .' The door opened ahead of the knock and his PA walked in holding a tray. 'Your Excellency . . .' Olga served Hamzah his tiny cup of Turkish coffee and beside it she put a plate of rosewater Turkish delight, studded with almonds. 'And here's yours,' said Olga. Zara got a long cappuccino and a croissant, along with a linen napkin.

As the woman turned to go, Zara realized her father was blushing. For a horrified second she considered that there might be something be-tween Olga and him and then realized that it was the honorific. He'd wanted *Your Excellency* so badly and now it made him blush. Zara smiled. Her father would get used to *effendi*, just as he'd got used to living in a villa surrounded by European antiques. And once he was used to it he'd start to enjoy it. That was his way.

'I suppose you've come to tell me you're not coming home?'

'No,' said Zara. 'I've come to ask for your help . . . But you're right,' she added. 'I'm not.'

'Do you want to return to your friends in America?'

'No.' Zara shook her head. 'I'm not going to run away. Not even if that's what you want . . . This is my city too.'

Hamzah's nod was approving. 'It's not easy, an unmarried woman living alone. You'll need an apartment, a driver. I can supply those.'

'Let's talk about that later,' said Zara, in a voice Hamzah knew meant she would do anything but. 'Right now I want to talk about Ashraf Bey.'

Hamzah thought about mentioning his daughter's face had suddenly gone red and decided against it. The picture of her on the news in that idiotic coat was too clear in his head. Instead, he glanced out of a window, then reached for his cup. The coffee was too hot but he drank it anyway, chasing away its mudlike bitterness with a piece of Turkish delight. 'Eat your croissant,' he said, 'or Olga will be upset . . .'

They were negotiating, silently without words: he knew that. Even in

El Iskandryia the gap between what could and what couldn't be said was vast, and Isk was the most relaxed of the Ottoman cities. A free port and a micro-state. The personal fief of its owner the Khedive – unlike Cairo, which the Khedive held in trust for the Sultan in Stambul.

But freedom was relative. And the gap between father and daughter still wide. In many families it was unbridgeable. The woman he sat opposite knew less about him than he actually knew about her, which was almost nothing.

He feared she'd taken at least one lover while in New York. But the only real thing he knew about her was what she'd told him the night before she flew, when they were talking obliquely about the three months she'd just spent in a Swiss clinic. Which was that she wasn't proud of everything she'd done, but she was ashamed of very little.

'I can give him money,' Hamzah said simply. 'A route out of Iskandryia if that will help. But I can't protect him . . .' He wanted to say more, to ask obvious questions, but for Zara the only question that mattered was the one she asked.

'Why do the police insist he killed his aunt?'

'Maybe he did,' said Hamzah, chewing the edges off a cube of Turkish delight. He smiled sadly when Zara handed him her napkin. 'Have you thought of that?'

'He swears he didn't.'

'And you believe him?'

Zara bit her lip and nodded, not trusting herself to speak.

'Olga.' He punched a button on his desk. 'Tell legal to call me.' Seconds later a screen beeped and the face of a small bald man squinted out at Hamzah. 'Excellency?' The voice was reedy, the accent cut-glass Cairene.

'Beys,' said Hamzah. 'They have complete *carte blanche*. I'm right, aren't I . . . they can't be arrested?'

The elderly lawyer hesitated. 'Up to a point, Excellency . . .'

A small smile lit Hamzah's face and he jerked his chin towards the screen to indicate to Zara that she should listen carefully. 'What are the exceptions?'

'Two types of murder – of a mullah or a family member – gross blasphemy before two reputable witnesses, and gross outrage of a minor, witnesses ditto.'

'So Ashraf al-Mansur can be arrested?'

'Given that he murdered his aunt, yes . . .'

Hamzah held up his hand to still Zara's protest and she suddenly realized she was out of the screen's line of sight. The lawyer couldn't see her and so didn't know she was there.

'Thank you.' Hamzah blanked the screen. 'My first question,' he said to Zara, 'is why do they *really* want Ashraf al-Mansur? And my second is, who exactly is *they* . . . any ideas?'

He sat back in his chair. 'No? Then I suggest you find out or I suggest your friend does . . .'

The meeting was over, Zara realized. And what was more staggering than her father treating her as an adult was his treating her as an equal. She'd asked him a question and he'd given her two relevant questions in reply. Either one of which might be the key. Going to America had been a good move, whatever work friends might say. And returning had been the right move too, whatever Zara might sometimes think herself.

'What do I tell your mother about why you're not coming home?' Hamzah's voice was neutral. But his eyes widened as Zara pulled off her silk scarf, to reveal that she wore no shirt beneath her Dior jacket, and began to undo her jacket's black glass buttons. At the last minute, she turned her back on her father and slid the silk jacket down over her shoulders, revealing the marks.

'Tell her what you like.' Ten minutes after Zara left her father's office and headed on foot towards the General's mansion, Hani crawled out of her bed, looked round and went to shake Raf. 'Zara's gone,' she said.

'Has she?' Raf sat up, groaned and slid his legs over the edge of the couch. He did his best to sound unconcerned but he needn't have bothered. Hani was too busy pointing at his feet.

'You're wearing shoes,' she said.

Yeah, he was. Both of them fully dressed was one of Zara's conditions for sharing the VSV's narrow bed, though even being dressed wouldn't make a difference if Hani told someone he and Zara had shared a mattress. Zara was under twenty-one and behaviour likely to corrupt a minor would be the least of it.

'After I went to sleep,' asked Hani, 'did you argue?'

'No,' said Raf, 'we talked.' *And got nowhere*, he added silently. At least he didn't think they'd got anywhere. It was hard to remember with his mind full of Zara's breasts and the taste of her in his mouth. Maybe she'd believed Nafisa's death really wasn't his responsibility. Maybe not. He'd try to work it out when his hangover took a holiday.

Where Zara had gone was solved by a brisk call from Hamzah. 'Zara dropped by,' he said, sounding amused. 'She said I should give you this.' Hamzah reeled off a string of numbers that became letters towards the end. 'Your aunt's bank details,' he added, seeing the blank look on Raf's face, 'From when I paid Nafisa's commission . . .'

'Where's Zara now?'

'I don't know,' said Hamzah, 'not officially. But unofficially I gather she's headed in the direction of Shallalat Gardens and the General's house.' He clicked his fingers and the screen went blank.

Raf groaned. 'Coffee,' he begged Hani.

'Tastes horrible,' she replied. But she went hunting all the same until she found tins of cappuccino stacked in a locker at the stern. Peeling back the lid on a tin, Hani took a mouthful and spat it at her feet. 'If that's what you want.' With a shrug and a sigh, she tipped the remains of the can into a saucepan and lit a small ring in the pull-down galley. When the sweet liquid was hot she poured it carefully back into the can.

'Here,' she said.

Raf drank it while she watched, her eyes alert for any hesitation. 'Perfect . . .' He sat back and put his hand behind his aching head, thinking about his aunt's bank details. 'You had a computer at the madersa, didn't you?'

'LuxorEON,' she said. 'Broadband access, running Linux.' Her voice was a dry imitation of Nafisa's at its most patronizing. Then she shrugged, bony shoulders hunching beneath her tee-shirt. 'Why?' Hani asked. 'What do you need . . . ?'

Numbers rolled up the screen so fast they made Raf feel even more hungover than he already was. These were dead accounts at Banque de Lesseps. He had Lady Nafisa's account details scrawled on a scrap of paper but Hani wasn't interested in that. The numbers on the VSV's screen were scrambled and she had an animated on-screen helper doing something with algorithms at lightning speed as she searched for Lady Nafisa's old account.

The computer aboard the VSV was an old stand-alone, the kind that used a satellite modem and made up in sheer memory what it lacked in speed or connectivity. It had taken Hani all of two minutes to junk every default setting and come up with a configuration she actually liked. But then, as she pointed out with a surprising lack of bitterness, if you've spent nine years trapped in the same house with only a computer for company, you get good at it or you get bored.

'That one,' said Hani as a 28-digit number lit red and the screen froze. Everything else on the screen disappeared and the number shuffled itself until Hani was left with the same 8-digit/3-letter sequence Raf had scrawled in front of him. She made a couple of passes with the cursor, her thumb moving lazily over a trackball, and the number disappeared. 'Don't worry,' she told Raf, just as he started to do exactly that. 'It's checking we're legal.'

She smiled and Raf tried to smile back. He'd no idea what Hani had just done.

'Here we go,' said the child as a bank logo began to animate on screen and the account went live again. There was quiet pride in her voice and an air of competence about her that would have looked impressive on someone three times her age.

'You're good.'

Hani nodded, taking Raf's compliment as a statement of fact. Fingers dancing and thumb rolling her trackball, Hani opened and shut screens at the speed of thought, collecting passwords and opening and closing trapdoors. She rode a rhythm that drummed inside her own head until her fingers suddenly faltered and Raf could almost feel the child's confidence vanish. When Raf looked round, a photograph of Lady Nafisa stared at him from the screen, arrogant and imperious.

'I'm going to use the—'

Hani slipped out of her seat before Raf could say anything and so he sat there, trying not to listen to the child throw up her breakfast. The water in the heads ran, then ran again and she came out wiping her mouth. Neither of them said anything but the first thing Hani did when she climbed back into her seat was to make Lady Nafisa disappear.

'She said she was living on her savings,' Hani said, nodding at a seemingly endless list of red figures. 'She always did lie.'

Nothing in Nafisa's accounts made obvious sense, but Raf expected that. And he was beginning to see the pattern. His sense of self might be fucked, but he could knit connections from nothing and call it logic. Just as the madersa had rich public rooms and the private rooms had been bare even of furniture, so ran Nafisa's accounts. Money had been spent lavishly on clothes but almost nothing on food. No payments at all for Khartoum or Donna. Very little on electricity, none on Hani's broadband connection, which meant it was either illegal or someone else was footing the bill.

So far, so predictable.

The surprise was in the brackets that ran like a sour river along the bottom line. Picking 1 January as a date and flicking back year on year showed that her account had been overdrawn for at least ten years, which was as far back as Raf bothered to check. Not huge amounts in someone like Hu San's terms, but getting larger and literally in the red. Until this April.

'Shit.' Raf was talking to himself but Hani squinted at the screen as he highlighted a figure. Hamzah had lied. She hadn't taken him for $2,500,000: her commission had been double that. $5,000,000 from Banque Leventine in Cyprus. Straight in and straight out again, almost immediately, only this time in two amounts. $4,500,000 to an account in El Iskandryia and $500,000 to Havana.

'Let me . . .' Small fingers flicked over the keyboard, numbers resolving. The name that came up meant nothing to Raf.

Caja de Cuba.

'Want me to chase it?' Hani's voice was neutral.

'If you can.' Raf had no intention of asking when she'd learned to crack files – or how. He was far too worried she might stop.

'Okay.' And with that Hani squared up to the screen, smiled slightly and let her fingers loose, chasing one link after another, running searches and routines she seemed to pull out of the air. Beside her sat the rag dog, a mechanical *whirr* coming from its guts like a low growl.

'What . . .'

'Back up,' said Hani. 'The screen talks to him and Ali-Din remembers.' She sucked at her teeth to signal that Raf shouldn't ask any more questions and went back to work.

'Got it,' Hani said finally. 'Started here/ended Seattle. You want to know everywhere the $500,000 went in between?'

Raf didn't, so Hani cross-referenced the new account number to a customer bank database, which took almost no time at all because – unlike with Banque de Lesseps – the data at the Seattle end wasn't double-encrypted. This time the name meant something. Clem Burke, lately of Huntsville, registered as sole owner of Seattle's newest detective agency.

'Now the next one,' Raf told Hani. But she was already on it, leaning in close as if trying to crawl right inside the screen. Raf was forgotten, he realized. The world outside did not exist. There was a hunger to the child's face, an intensity that reflected pure concentration. Her brows were knit, her lips clamped tight. This was the other thing in her life over which she'd had control. What she ate and what she did on screen were ring-fenced for her alone. A thin slice of a life that everybody else was parcelling up and deciding for her own good.

Ali-Din was a side issue.

'Got it,' said Hani. Numbers resolved as the screen on the VSV talked via uplink to a datacore at Banque de Lesseps and data fed back, anonymous and cold, nothing but presence and absence of electrical charge until on the other side of the screen to Hani an electron beam rastered down the glass and Hani swore.

H.E. Saeed Koenig Pasha. The General's own personal bank account. Shit indeed. Fear played inside Raf's head like a whistle off the walls of an empty courtyard, heard every day without really hearing, until one stumbled over oneself, sat cross-legged in the dust. Hani broke the connection without being asked.

Next they looked at payments that had come in. And the first and most obvious point was that until the $5,000,000 from Hamzah there had been nothing for at least nine months. Before that, going back five or six years, there had been regular payments, spaced maybe four or five months apart, starting big and getting less and less.

To Raf it looked like someone selling off the family silver and waking up one morning to find it was all gone. Maybe her outgoings would be more use.

'Try that,' he suggested, pointing to a small, fairly regular debit in Nafisa's account. The last time it had been paid was the day he'd arrived in Iskandryia.

Hani went back to her screen.

CHAPTER 42

'You must be Zara bint-Hamzah,' said the boy who opened the door to her. Before she could ask how he knew, the boy had stepped back and was ushering her through the front door of the General's palatial mansion on Rue Riyad Pasha.

He was about her age, maybe slightly younger, dressed in a simple shirt and tan chinos. A faint – a very faint – beard could just be discerned on his face.

'This is where I ask you if you have an appointment to see the General and you say no, but it's very important . . .'

Zara nodded.

'A pity. You see, the General never receives anyone without an appointment. It's a matter of principle . . .'

'I thought anyone could petition the General?' Zara said. She didn't mean to sound as upset by his news as she did.

'Of course,' said the boy with a smile. 'Anyone can. Just write a note and leave it. In five weeks' time, when the secretariat have worked their way down the pile, someone will read your note and, if necessary, bring it to his attention.'

'What counts as "necessary"?' Zara asked.

'A threat to his life. A threat to the life of the Khedive. News of an uprising . . . We get a lot of those.' He ushered her though another door into what looked like a dining room, then another, this time into a small study. On the wall was an oil painting of the old Khedive and a smaller – if only slightly – portrait of the General wearing full uniform, with a curved sword hanging from his belt. The sword in question stood in the corner of the room, balanced upright like an old umbrella.

'Better not stay here too long,' said the boy. 'He doesn't really like people in his office.' From the top drawer of an ornate desk, he selected a key and used it to open French windows that led out to a garden.

'Come on,' he said, then paused. 'Have you been here before?'

Zara just looked at him until he shrugged.

'I'll take that as a *No.*'

Tall cedars rose from a lawn that was emerald green. The kind of lawn that old people talked about when they mentioned the mansions that used to line Mahmoudiya Canal, even though they'd never seen the lawns themselves and had only heard of them from their grandparents.

'Underground irrigation,' said the boy. Beds full of red and blue flowers that Zara had never seen before lined the path the boy chose. 'Come on,' he said, so Zara followed. Until he stopped at a metal bench set in the shade of a bush topiaried into the shape of a perfectly crenellated wall, and indicated that Zara should sit.

'No,' she shook her head. 'Not here.' A quick, almost embarrassed flick of one hand indicated him, then herself, the bench and its obvious seclusion. 'How can I?'

The boy looked surprised, but not irritated. 'We can walk,' he said simply and so they did: down another path until they reached a small lake with a fountain. Three stone women wearing very little stood, facing out, with their backs to each other. One of them held an apple and the other two, who were without the first's discreet stone drapery, used their hands to hide stone pudenda.

'Nakedness is not always a sin,' said the boy lightly. Then he smiled and shrugged, before adding, 'But, of course, that sentiment is probably heretical . . .'

He led her round the fountain and then down another path that doubled back inside the vee of greenery that the General had carved for himself out of a section of public gardens.

'So tell me,' said the boy. 'What is so important that you need to see the General?'

'I'd prefer to tell him . . .'

'No,' he said seriously. 'You misunderstand. The General is unable to see you, so I am seeing you instead. Now, what did you want to say?'

Haltingly, occasionally exasperated with herself, Zara began to tell him about Ashraf. Not everything, because she didn't mention his time in prison or Raf's belief that he wasn't really a bey. But she told the boy about Felix, about how Ashraf swore that his aunt's death was neither suicide nor his doing. Zara talked about how he'd cleaned up the house and asked her father to get rid of the office where his aunt had been killed so as not to upset Hani. And she spoke of Hani and how the child was afraid to leave Ashraf's side . . .

Halfway through, the boy insisted they find a bench and walked away without waiting to see if Zara followed, though the bench he found her was out in the open, unscreened by hedges and in full view of the house. 'This man,' said the boy, when Zara finally finished. 'You know where he is hiding?'

The boy sighed at her silence, then shrugged.

'You don't know, and if you did, you wouldn't tell me?'

'Right.'

'Wrong. You do know and you still won't tell me . . .' He looked at Zara, his gaze steady. 'I guess that makes it love.'

After he'd listened to all the reasons why he was wrong, they changed the subject and Zara sat down again. 'America,' said the boy. 'You've been there. What's it like?'

'New York,' she corrected, and then she explained in detail why the two were completely different. How New York was really a part of Europe that Europe had mislaid. Explaining this took more time than she intended.

At the front door, as he was showing her out, Zara paused. 'You *will* tell the General what I said about Ashraf being innocent . . . ?'

'Of course.'

'And there's no chance of my seeing the General himself?'

The boy sighed. 'What do you want with Koenig Pasha,' he asked, sounding slightly wistful, 'when you've already seen the Khedive?' And he shut the door, politely but firmly in Zara's face.

CHAPTER 43

'Ashraf Bey,' said Raf into a brass grille set in a white pillar on one side of a large metal gate. Above the grille a discreet *se vende* sign from an exclusive realty agent in Rue de L'Église Copte had a simple strip neatly glue-gunned across the top. When Raf put his hand up to check the *sold* sign, he discovered the glue was still sticky.

There would be a small CCTV watching his every move. Up in a tree, probably, though he hadn't been able to spot it. Unless, of course, the Minister linked direct to a spysat, which was possible. At least ten private houses in Iskandryia were meant to be protected that way.

That it was only ten said something . . . On the Upper East Side whole blocks relied on nothing but spysats and a direct line to one of the top-end private police units. His mother had given him the details in one of her last e-mails, he forgot how many years before. She might have written a few more times, of course. Raf didn't know, he hadn't bothered to check that account much.

Static cracked from the speaker grille. 'Ashraf Bey,' said Raf for the third time. So far no one had shown much interest in letting him in. He could scale the gate, no problem. Even the spikes along the top wouldn't give him trouble unless he actually managed to fall on one. Weather, old age and too many coats of paint had made them blunt, almost rounded.

'The Minister isn't here.'

'I know that,' Raf said. 'I want to talk to Lady Jalila.'

There was another burst of static and then silence.

'The question,' said a different voice when it came, 'is whether Lady Jalila wants to see *you* . . .' The words were cool, ironic.

'I don't know,' said Raf. 'Do you?'

The click of a bolt recessing was his answer, though no one appeared to show him the way and the mastiff that lolloped across a gravel path towards him seemed not to have been told he was allowed to enter.

'Heel.' Letting his hand brush the mastiff's head, Raf kept walking and heard rather than saw the animal fall into step beside him. No fear, at least not of animals. Let Lady Jalila make of that what she liked.

The house was old made modern. Once-stuccoed walls stripped back to stone and a roof retiled in pale grey slate. Old-fashioned windows had been sandblasted back to bare metal frames, glazed with smoked glass and covered with wrought-iron bars that were ornate and obviously handmade to order, but were bars all the same.

The front door was heavy and studded, pale oak polished to a shine. This could be her taste, or maybe not. It seemed a little too self-consciously modern and American for the Minister but perhaps Raf had misunderstood him.

'Your Excellency is most welcome.' It was obvious from the quiver in the maid's voice that he was anything but . . .

'I don't bite,' Raf told her, 'whatever you've read in the papers.' He waited for the French girl to stand aside and when she didn't he pushed gently past, eyes instantly adjusting to the darkness. The decor within was as ruthlessly modern as without. Black floors, glass walls, the only nod to classical taste being two large abstracts, one each side of the hall, on walls that were otherwise bare.

'Rothko,' said Lady Jalila. 'Mid-period. Not his best work but that's all locked up in museums.' She had a glass of clear liquid in one unsteady hand and a tiny pearl-handled revolver in the other.

'Medicinal,' Lady Jalila said, holding the glass up to the light. 'You can ask my doctor.'

'And the gun?'

'Safety, darling. You're a dangerous killer – or don't you catch the news . . . ?'

'I've been busy . . .'

'Tell me about it. Apparently that little girl you almost married now thinks you're innocent . . .' Lady Jalila lowered the revolver and took a gulp from her glass. When she surfaced the glass was empty and even at a distance Raf could smell the gin on her breath. 'But we both know different, don't we?'

The only thing Raf knew was that she was drunk and armed. And if anyone had come up with a more lethal combination than alcohol and a gun then Raf had gone through remand with his eyes closed. 'Look,' said Raf, 'I need to ask you some questions about my aunt.'

'About Nafisa?'

'That and a few other things . . .'

Lady Jalila laughed. 'Oh,' she said as she gently touched the barrel of her gun to Raf's cheek, 'I can talk about *things* for ages. You'd better come up.' She turned towards a rise of open steps, only to turn back. 'Take the afternoon off,' she told her maid.

'In here.' Lady Jalila threw open an upstairs door and Raf found himself in a drawing room with a white suede sofa, a long onyx table and floorboards of stripped cedar. Another, much smaller painting decorated one wall. A simple slash of red above a slash of dark blue, the paint thin, uneven and not quite covering the canvas.

'Unique,' she said heavily. 'Worth more than both of the ones in the hall. He didn't see it, of course. Thought it should be cheaper because it was smaller.'

He was the Minister, Raf decided, not Rothko.

Lady Jalila sighed. 'You have no idea how tiresome life can be . . .'

Raf looked round at the tiny but priceless Persian rug hung in one corner, the impossibly rich Moroccan burgundy of a leather beanbag big enough for a giant. At the single sprig of flowers in a Venetian vase filling the whole room with a perfume headier than incense.

'No,' he said. 'Probably not.'

Lady Jalila poured him a gin and tonic, dribbling Bombay Sapphire over three lumps of ice and adding not enough tonic. A dash of bitters from an unmarked bottle finished the preparation. There was a fresh lime cut into slices on a saucer at the side but she didn't bother to add it to his drink or hers. 'I'd ask you to make them,' she told him, 'but you'd probably only get it wrong. Men do.'

Lowering herself carefully onto the suede sofa, Lady Jalila crossed one leg over the other. She wore a tight blue jacket and matching skirt which rode up enough at the side to show a long expanse of nylon from knee to hip.

'Well, do you like it?'

Raf dragged his eyes away from her.

'What do you think?' Casually, Lady Jalila uncrossed her legs and leant back, head turned towards the tiny Rothko. Her knees parted. Only slightly, but enough for Raf to see clearly the white thong beneath her tights.

'Interesting,' said Raf.

'Mmmm,' Lady Jalila smiled slightly. 'Public exhibitions bore me, but there's always something about private views . . .' She shifted lower in her seat, arms coming round to hug herself until her full breasts were pushed together and outwards.

Raf wanted to keep talking, to keep up the pretence that this was just a conversation but proper words wouldn't come so he just nodded sagely. And all the while, Lady Jalila squeezed at her breasts and squirmed forward on the sofa until both gusset and thong edged up between swollen folds of flesh.

'The Rothko,' asked Raf shakily. 'When did you buy it?' But Lady Jalila wasn't listening. He could see her nipples hard beneath her jacket and each time she hugged herself they scraped against cloth, making her hiss between open lips.

Her foot rubbed his ankle and before Raf could protest her heel had climbed the side of his leg and rested on his groin, grinding down against him. He could have touched the dampness between her legs just by reaching forward. But all he did was watch as she shifted on her seat until the thong stretched so tight it vanished altogether. She was gasping, breathing through her mouth as she stared blindly at a ceiling fan. Lost to the gin and to what was going on between her legs and inside her mind.

She came silently, biting down on a cry as she jacked forwards and then sprawled back, knees wide and arms still clutched across her front.

A lavatory flushed and water ran. A hammering in the pipes went on for too long for it to be a basin being run. Which meant Lady Jalila was taking a bath or shower. For a moment, Raf wondered if he was meant to have joined her under the water, but decided that was unlikely. Most probably she'd forgotten he was even there. She'd certainly forgotten her revolver which rested on the white sofa next to a sweat patch in the shape of Lady Jalila's buttocks. Just as she'd forgotten the handbag beside her discarded shoes on the floor.

Driving licence, snakeskin wallet with mid-denomination notes and three credit cards. Gold but not platinum. So either they weren't as rich as she pretended or else the Minister was less lavish with his bounty than Raf had imagined from seeing them together. There was make-up – Chanel and Dior, predictably enough. A packet of sterile tissues, a packet of Durex Vapour with one condom missing and a half-empty plastic tube of breath mints.

Raf made a note of Jalila's credit-card numbers, wondering as he did so whether Hani would be able to do her magic with them. He looked inside the wallet for a photograph of the Minister, but she carried nothing sentimental except a small colour shot of herself standing on the Corniche. She was a teenager and the smiling woman behind her looked familiar. It was only after Raf had slipped the picture back into Lady Jalila's wallet that he realized the woman was Lady Nafisa, looking younger, happier and almost coy.

Putting aside the wallet, Raf sorted quickly through the remaining objects. A Lotus organizer, a penknife with a mother-of-pearl handle, a pepper spray and a little suede case for holding business cards. Inside were three cards of her own – *Lady Jalila, deputy head, Cross & Crescent* – an official laminate for entering the Precinct, one of the Minister's own cards, tattered at the corners, and an even more tattered card belonging to Felix.

And then Raf got the information he'd come for, without even having to ask. The last card in the holder advertised an alternative-heath clinic and five dates were scrawled on the back, four of them crossed through, with one due the following week.

Raf slid the card into his pocket, just managing to scoop the rest of the contents back into Lady Jalila's bag and get the bag back on the floor before the door opened.

'How thoughtless,' Lady Jalila said. 'Anna's forgotten to bring you coffee.'

'You told her to take the afternoon off,' said Raf.

'Did I?' Lady Jalila sounded puzzled. She wore black slacks and a white sweat shirt that might have suited a teenager if that teenager were drunk, over-developed and vacant. 'How odd . . . So what was it you wanted to ask me about Nafisa?'

There were a dozen places he could start. Beginning with the fact that his aunt had apparently been refilling her personal account with money from a charity of which the woman opposite was now acting head.

The first sum taken had been repaid in full, with interest. The second sum had just been repaid. Half of the next sum was still outstanding and Raf doubted that even Nafisa had been able to convince herself that the following sums were loans only . . .

'Well?' Jalila asked. 'What was your question?'

No one Raf recognized stared out of her eyes. The wanton who'd sat opposite him with open knees had gone to be replaced by a prim but slightly swaying woman who smelled of soap, mouthwash and toothpaste.

'Probably not worth troubling you,' said Raf. 'But I'm just tying up odds and ends and I wondered if you knew of a Madame Sosostris?'

'No. I'm sorry.' Lady Jalila shook her head, her blonde curls still damp but already falling perfectly around a face innocent as an angel's. 'That rings no bells at all.'

Raf shrugged. 'Worth a try,' he said. Then he told her he knew exactly who had killed his aunt and asked her to fix him a meeting with her husband. Somewhere neutral. When he let himself out, she was still reciting digits to her wall phone.

CHAPTER 44

'I'm armed,' said Hani. 'And I'll fire.'

In trembling hands, the child held a vast pistol with rubber handle and fat red barrel. The kind used to launch distress flares. Pulling the trigger would be enough to toss her backwards across the cabin, if not break both wrists. That it would leave a large hole in whoever was on the other side of the door was a given.

The door to the VSV stopped opening.

'Hani,' said Zara, her shock at meeting the Khedive suddenly forgotten. 'It's me . . .'

The door started opening again and Zara put her head through the gap, her glance taking in the flare pistol and the tears streaming down Hani's face. 'Hani, put that down, okay?'

The child shook her head. 'Step inside, slowly.' It sounded like something Hani had heard while playing *Killer Kop IV*.

Zara stepped forward, her hands held up where Hani could see them.

'Right inside,' said Hani. 'Then shut the door.' She was watching not the woman who'd just entered but the space behind her.

'You're alone.' Hani's words were pitched somewhere between statement and question. Only Zara didn't need to reply because Hani was her own answer. Slumping to the floor, Hani pulled her knees up under her chin and wrapped her arms tight round them, the flare gun still held in one hand.

Whatever the fear was, it had the child rocking backwards and forwards, eyes screwed shut.

'Honey.' Zara kneeled in front of the girl. 'What's wrong?'

One eye opened. 'It's been h-h-hours,' Hani said furiously. 'I thought you were d-dead.' She stopped rocking and somehow her absolute stillness was almost worse. 'Lady Jalila called me . . .'

'Here?'

'Called Ali-Din.' She nodded to the rag dog thrown in one corner. 'The Germans are coming to kill me. You're to take me straight to her house . . .'

Which Germans . . . ?

'No one's trying to kill you,' Zara said firmly. 'She's got it wrong.'

The flare gun wasn't even loaded, Zara discovered when she finally worked out how to flip down its barrel. The sobbing child had discovered the device in a watertight cupboard set into a bulkhead. What she hadn't found were any flares. But then, maybe there weren't any, because Zara couldn't find them either.

'We'd better leave,' announced Zara, after she'd wiped the pistol with a rag and put it back in the cupboard, pushing the door so that it popped shut. Quite where they were going was another matter. She only knew it wasn't anywhere near Lady Jalila's house.

CHAPTER 45

No signal. No up-link. Nothing.

Raf should have started getting worried when he noticed his Omega had stopped receiving, he realized afterwards. But at the time he figured it was just the usual crap connection.

So he kept heading north towards the address on the card he carried deep in his pocket, cutting through an area northwest of Place Orabi where child brothels used to be, back in the days Constantine Cavafy wrote his poems and Isk was where every would-be aesthete from New York, Berlin and London gathered to savour the exotic. Which usually translated into a taste for young Arab boys, rot-gut arak and opium.

Now the district was filled with hip boutiques, where the swipe of a credit card and the purchase tax-free of this season's Nikes gave jet-trash travellers a similar, more legal thrill.

Half hoping to get a working connection, Raf made his way up a side street towards the Corniche, passing an ancient mosque and a school, coming out at the fish market where picturesque boats were moored off shore to bobbing floats of blown glass. His phone functioned no better there than it had before.

The boats were mostly clinker-built and wooden, brightly coated in blood reds and deep blues, with painted eyes that stared forward. It didn't matter that some had satellite navigation and a few used echo-location to hunt bonito and shark: every family knew that the boats needed to be able to see their way home when the fishing was done.

It made sense to Raf who, by then, was standing with his back to the market, glancing between the card in his hand and a bank of buzzers on a wall. What was Tiriganaq if not his version of those eyes?

No one had answered when he pressed the right button, so he punched five or six wrong ones at random, ignoring the increasingly irritated voices demanding to know what he wanted until eventually someone hit enter, just as Raf knew they would, because someone always did.

He took the back stairs up to the fourth floor because, once again, most people always used the lift. Then he took the lift down a flight to the third floor and knocked on an unmarked cream door.

When no one answered that either, Raf whipped a new screwdriver out of its packaging and positioned it over the point where a strip of wooden frame obscured a Yale lock. One hit with the heel of his hand and the lock was sprung. Which told him two things. Not everything taught at Remand University was bullshit, and Madame Sosostris was nearby. Out for a coffee, maybe, or collecting laundry – whatever . . . People gone for longer usually remembered to double-lock their front doors.

A quick glance inside revealed a reception room that could have been for a brothel, a therapist or a chiropractor's. Copies of glossy magazines, a handful of leaflets, mainly about acupuncture. A blank screen on one wall, two crystals dangling on thongs from its bottom corners. Wicker armchairs that looked newish but were already well used.

Then a treatment room, which looked like a coprophiliac's paradise. Raf headed for a filing cabinet, ignoring the four polythene barrels atop metal scaffolding, with gravity tubes that fed down to end in surgical-steel twist joints, just as he ignored a kidney dish – next to a couch – that held various sizes of chrome speculums, each one double-tubed so water could feed one way and bodily waste the other. He needed more proof than a business card that Lady Jalila had been lying.

Raf found what he wanted in a bottom drawer, marked *dead accounts;* though he didn't think that was meant to be a joke, sardonic or other-wise. Lady Nafisa had been a client for ten years and there was a long and obsessively regular list of appointments to prove it, written by the same hand using a wide variety of different pens. There was a pattern, Raf realized, and an easy one to break. The pen used to record payment was inevitably the same pen used to make a note in the diary of the next appointment.

But the note declaring the file dead and the line scrawled through Nafisa's records were in the same ink as the last record of payment, dated the morning she died. Madame Sosostris had known Nafisa wouldn't be coming back.

And Raf didn't know if it really surprised him or not, but the person who'd originally introduced his aunt to the clinic was the person who said she'd never even heard of Madame Sosostris.

So all he needed to find was—

'Looking for something?'

The question came from behind him and the voice was confident. Which was probably reasonable, given the automatic in the blond man's hand. Though maybe the gun-toting woman at the man's shoulder was also a factor. Both were tall and fair and the last time Raf had noticed either of them they'd been standing by the harbour wall, studying a fold-out map headed *Ägypten–Kairo & Alexandria*. Something in their smiles told Raf they'd always known exactly where they were heading. And, more to the point, where he was headed as well.

Dancers, Hu San would have called them. Or rather, a dancer and a ballerina.

The woman kicked the door shut with her heel. She wore a straw Panama tipped over one eye and a pale scarf tucked into her silk blouse. They shared the same wiry build, the same almost white hair cropped short at the sides and left to flop forward over pale blue eyes . . .

In fact, they looked just like him. Give or take the slightly longer hair and his beard.

'Can I help you?' Raf asked politely.

Neither answered. Neither moved. But it didn't matter, because the fox was awake. *Disarm yourself, disarm your enemy*, said a tired voice in his head. It sounded cracker-barrel, but Raf recognized it as a koan from the old rasta he'd trained with while on remand.

Raf put up his hands and watched both dancer and ballerina suddenly relax.

'Yeah,' said the man, coming closer. 'We were told you'd be sensible.' He sounded disappointed.

'That's me,' said Raf, stepping forward to sweep aside the man's automatic with his left hand, while swinging in with his right elbow, catching him across the throat.

Sometimes you've just got to dance.

Raf uncoiled, right elbow returning to spread the man's nose sideways across his once-handsome face. Balance Raf took out with a simultaneous clap to both sides of the man's head, rupturing the eardrums. He was spared having to thumb the dancer's eyes because the man was already headed floorwards, Raf following hard behind.

As they landed, Raf put one elbow through the dancer's rib cage, driving a fat splinter of bone deep into a suddenly very shocked heart. The stink of open bowels filled the room but by then Raf had rolled sideways across the carpet, the dancer's automatic already in his hand, coming to rest beside a filing cabinet. Either it would give him cover or fill him with shrapnel, depending on what loads the ballerina carried in her gun. It gave him cover, though the only thing to be said for the sudden stench of cordite was that it swamped the smell that came from the body between them.

'Hey.' Raf's voice sounded better than he'd expected, given someone was using him for target practice. 'You want to tell me what this is about?'

He wasn't fussed about giving his position away. She already knew exactly where he was, she just couldn't reach him. 'Well?' Raf said.

Her answer was another slug, slammed into the filing cabinet. In at the front but not, thank God, out at the side. Her big problem was her slugs were small calibre, their load almost subsonic. She'd come carrying brass designed to fire at close range, then rattle round inside Raf's skull magimixing.

'You can put that gun down or I can kill you,' said Raf. It was, he realized, probably the wrong time to start enjoying himself; but knowing that didn't change a thing. His thoughts felt as clear as they'd ever been. And for the first time in years, he wasn't standing on the outside watching himself.

'Make your choice,' said Raf, noisily jacking back the slide on his newly borrowed automatic. 'It means nothing to me.'

A slug fired into the filing cabinet gave Raf his answer.

Shaking dust from his short hair, Raf took a look around him. The ballerina had a door behind her to give an exit, if that was what she needed: this he already knew. He had a wall, a filing cabinet and a blind corner without door or window. Not good at all.

On the other hand . . . Raf smiled. 'I hope they're paying you well,' he said, doing his best to sound genuinely concerned. 'And I hope you've got insurance. Because the hospitals round here are likely to slice you up for body parts if you look like you can't meet their bill . . .'

He paused to let the silence build, thinking himself inside her head until he finally, briefly became her. 'You've still got a chance,' he said. 'Which was more than your friend ever had.'

The answering shot that Raf expected didn't come. And it didn't sound like the ballerina was changing position or anything, because he could hear silence, devoid of even the faintest tread of feet moving carefully over a carpet.

The woman was listening to him, which was her first mistake – probably the only mistake Raf needed. 'Look,' said Raf. 'You've been set up.' He paused again, as if hit by a sudden thought. 'You got a mobile there?'

The woman would have, undoubtedly. A Seiko wrist model or a Paul Smith wallet, the chrome flip-open kind. Something classy but anonymous to let her call in the cleaners when her job was done.

'Call home,' he told her. 'Have your handler access the precinct files, check out Ashraf al-Mansur.'

Nine, three . . . three, nine, two . . . two, two, five, four, zero, three. She was using something with a keypad and it was a local number, Raf decided, following the dial tones in his head. What was more, she got a connection first time which told him all he needed to know about his own situation.

The woman spoke rapidly, her intonation rising towards the end. Twice she stumbled over her words. Being scared made her unpredictable, which made her dangerous; and Raf seriously didn't want to be on the wrong end of a gun held by a frightened ballerina. Not when more triggers got yanked in panic than ever got squeezed with intent.

'*Schisen.*' The word was soft, spoken with feeling.

'Ashraf al-Mansur,' said Raf, 'special forces, explosives expert, advanced weapons training . . .' He paused, trying to remember what else the kid had put on her list, because it was Hani who'd faked his CV, Raf was certain of that. 'Crack shot, proficient in close combat.' And there was other stuff, real facts that Hani didn't know or couldn't imagine.

'Acute hearing,' said Raf, 'enhanced vision, eidetic memory . . . How am I doing?'

He wasn't expecting an answer yet and didn't get one. All the same, the woman's breathing grew shallower, more ragged. Right about now should be when she'd start thinking about how to bring this deal to an exit.

'There's a door behind you,' said Raf. 'Feel free to use it.'

'And get killed on the way out? Spend the rest of my life looking over my shoulder?' The blonde woman spat out her words, bitterness battling fear. 'You killed Marcus.'

'I'm sorry,' said Raf. What was more, he meant it. Killing the blond man hadn't been an accident but equally it hadn't been entirely from choice. 'You were set up, both of you. Because whoever sent you knew you wouldn't walk away from this alive . . .

'Think about it,' he said as he stood up, staying pressed back against the wall. 'You're disposable. Not to me but to whoever hired you.'

'That goes with the territory.'

'Yeah,' said Raf, 'but what was the franchise? To kill me or get killed yourself? Think about it,' he repeated. Surrendering the protection of his filing cabinet, Raf stepped carefully over the dancer who lay face up, blindly staring at a cracked ceiling. And the bullet he'd been waiting for all his adult life never came.

She was smaller than Raf had thought. Older, too. Her eyes were only half watching Raf's gun.

'Your husband?'

'My brother.' She tossed her own weapon onto a nearby chair and peeled off latex gloves. Glancing at Raf for permission to approach the body.

The woman didn't touch the corpse, just kneeled beside it and looked. Her eyes were as dry as her face was impassive. But when she spoke her voice was cracked with tension and raw with anger. And the anger was not directed at him.

'Bastards.'

Raf gave a long low, silent sigh of relief and put the dead dancer's automatic in his jacket pocket. What he'd just achieved was the cerebral equivalent of reversing a throw hold. 'You want to tell me who hired you?'

She didn't, which was exactly what he expected. He wouldn't have believed her anyway. That would have been too easy and these things never were.

'Fair enough,' said Raf. 'But I'd like you to be very clear on one point. I'm already dead. And I'd like you to pass that on . . .'

The ballerina glanced up at that and saw Raf's smile. A smile so wintry she wanted to shiver. Very briefly, she wondered what his face would look like without those shades and decided she didn't want to know. Never would be too soon to see him again.

From the bullet-riddled filing cabinet Raf took the files for Nafisa and Jalila, ripped the page that contained Lady Nafisa's last appointment from the clinic diary and grabbed a manila envelope as an afterthought. When he shut the door behind him, the ballerina was carefully picking up her spent brass. One fewer calling card for forensics to consider.

Time to change camouflage, Raf decided. The building's elevator only ran as far as the fifth floor, after that it was stairs all the way up to the eighth. On the sixth floor was a communal bathroom for men and a separate one for women, which probably meant no hot water at all on the floors above where the hall carpet grew stained, the paint peeled and the doors became narrow. More importantly still, the locks became old and cheap . . .

Raf posted the files and appointments page to Zara, c/o Villa Hamzah. Then, wearing his new washed and untorn jellaba, he ordered a coffee at a café next door to the apartment block and waited. When the dregs of the first coffee got cold, he ordered another and took the offer of an ornate sheesha and the evening paper. For once he wasn't on the front page or on pages two and three. Page four had a small paragraph, no picture. Someone somewhere had taken a decision to turn down the heat.

Raf smiled.

An hour after he'd left the clinic, a black van turned up outside. Largish, oldish, anonymous . . . The man in the driving seat clambered out, brushing cake crumbs from dirty blue overalls. Licking the suction strip on an on-call sign, he slicked it to the inside of his windscreen and wandered up to the main door, large toolbox in hand.

Cable repairs . . . air-conditioning experts . . . 24-hour electrics . . . From city to city, the cover rarely changed. The only thing unusual was that it had taken the van an hour to arrive. Since it was unlikely that the firm for which the dead dancer worked was that inefficient, it meant the woman had needed time to say goodbye to her brother. Which was a good sign. At least, Raf thought so.

The coffee was bitter and what little Raf had of the hashish was home-grown and too sweet. But when the man in overalls reappeared Raf knew it had been worth his wait. So he tossed a couple of notes onto his café table and pushed back his seat.

What was left of the dead dancer was being carried out, cut up and jointed in those black bags. And from the frozen stare on the blonde ballerina's face as she trailed after the clean-up man down to his van, it was equally clear she'd been present when the butchering had been done.

That was love of a kind.

Cleaner and woman held a fleeting discussion on the sidewalk. More a quick question and an emphatic answer, really. The man wearing overalls shrugged and pulled himself up into the driver's seat. The ballerina didn't acknowledge his nod or even glance at the vehicle as it slid into the traffic, positioning itself behind a rattling green-painted tram.

She was good at blending, Raf had to give her that. From the flash of a packet, it was obvious her cigarettes were local. Except that no local woman would have smoked untipped Cleopatras; but then, no local woman would have smoked in public. Only she was a tourist, wasn't she? And tourists did stuff like that out of ignorance. Showed their bare arms on the streets, didn't cover their hair, smoked in public. What she didn't do nearly so well was validate her surroundings.

Her gaze slid over Raf. A man, a striped jellaba, spent sheesha in front of him, settling up with the waiter of an Arab café. It wasn't what she was looking for and so she didn't see it. In non-eidetic people, the cortex was wired weird like that.

Cigarette in hand, she flipped open her wallet and made a call, light-ing and discarding a second Cleopatra before her handler called her back with whatever information she'd asked for. An address, most probably, given the way she promptly yanked the map from her bag.

Raf and the ballerina moved off together, joined by their invisible thread of anger and need. Raf following twenty paces behind, his head half buried in an evening paper. Moscow Dynamos had destroyed Belgrade Eagles, Danzig had drawn with Naples. Montenegro had been thrashed by Tunis. That particular game was being replayed on café screens everywhere, the fact the score was known in no way diminishing the cascade of outrage when a player from Tunis got fouled inside the penalty area.

The Ottoman provinces kept their dislike of Berlin under control but their contempt for Austria-Hungary was legendary. The significant difference being that the Kaiser had few, if any, Islamic subjects while whole areas of the Austrian Balkans were Muslim . . .

The woman went in through one revolving door and came straight out of another, barely bothering to pause in the foyer of the Suq el Meghreb. She was checking for a tail, but Raf was so far back that he'd barely turned towards the first door when she reappeared from the other muttering angrily.

She was coming unravelled in front of him, the slow burn of her shock overriding common sense to such an extent that she patted a bulging pocket and tossed her map into a bin, doubling back barely fifty paces before hanging a left into a blind alley so narrow it was more of a gap between the Suq el Meghreb and a neighbouring warehouse.

There was no way Raf could follow her into the gap without being seen, so he strolled past its narrow entrance, counted sixty and doubled back, glancing in as he walked by. The ballerina had vanished, the *cul de sac* was now empty.

Raf really didn't like what that said at all, because what it said was that she'd gone upwards and he was going to have to climb . . .

CHAPTER 46

Only tourists ever bothered using the black carriages that plied their trade along the final sweep of the Corniche. Which meant that no one paid much attention to an ancient caleche being pulled past the fish market by an elderly mare: one of a dozen carriages working the Golden Crescent, that strip stretching up from the new Bibliotheka towards the headland and the heavy grandeur of Fort Quaitbey.

'What are we going to do?' Hani demanded, as the leaf springs of their carriage squeaked ratlike over the cobbles. 'Well?'

Zara said nothing. She just watched fishing boats depart, their square nets raised and the lamps that would lure catch to their net unlit, but Hani wasn't fooled for a minute.

Behind them, Place Orabi burned its eternal flame in the tomb of the unknown warrior, up ahead was Shorbagi mosque, famous for lacking a minaret. Its muezzin called from arcades that looked out over a market square. Just another useless fact her aunt had insisted she know. Hani shrugged. None of it mattered now.

'Well?' she demanded.

'I don't know,' Zara said crossly, but she did. They would go to the address they'd been given. Maybe she should have taken Hani to Lady Jalila's house when the first message came. That way, maybe Raf would still be . . . Surreptitiously Zara checked the text she'd copied across from Ali-Din fifteen minutes before, even though she already knew it by heart. *Raf murdered. Hani in terrible danger. Meet me at . . .* No key accompanied the words and at the top the *from* field was blank. But the text itself was signed LJ, which Zara took to be Lady Jalila. The only relative Hani had, now that Raf was . . .

'You're crying again.' Hani said.

Zara shrugged. So what if she was? Stranger things had happened.

246

'Thought so . . .' Hani swapped seats so she could sit next to Zara and put one arm round the elder girl's sore shoulders. 'I'm sorry.'

I don't know how to handle this, thought Zara. She desperately wanted to tell Hani it was all right to cry. Only then there would be two of them turned inside out, exposing their bare flesh to the world. It was unbelievably selfish, but Zara didn't think she could cope with that.

Beyond the mosque was the fish market, shutting up for the night. The cobbled square already hosed down and the kiosks locked shut. What vans were there waited for morning and the new catch. The hum of their refrigeration units a reminder that come dawn the bustle would begin again. Then the catch would be gutted, packed in ice and trucked out along the desert road to Cairo, where it would go on sale in the kind of fishmongers that required those serving to wear striped aprons and use French names for everything. The kind of place her mother talked about without ever having been to one.

'Faster,' Zara told the coachman, who scowled but still cracked his whip at the grey. He'd spent a good hour taking his caleche slowly up and down the Golden Crescent at Zara's request and now she wanted speed. Reluctantly, the grey rose to a trot.

'Turn here,' Zara ordered but the coachman shook his head, reining in.

'Can't leave the Corniche,' he protested. 'Regulations. I can take you further up or I can take you back, but I can't leave the esplanade.'

'Great,' Zara muttered, but she was talking to herself.

'It's all right,' said Hani, stuffing Ali-Din into a new rucksack, bought that morning. 'We can easily walk from here.' The child wore new jeans that matched her rucksack, and a white Hello Kitty tee-shirt still creased from its packet. Her usual buckle shoes had been replaced with stack-heel orange flip-flops and her long hair had been cut until it was as short as Zara's own.

Zara wasn't sure about that last touch. But Hani had demanded it, sitting on a stool in the VSV until Zara hurriedly used scissors to send long dark strands tumbling to the floor. And, in a way, Zara was flattered: they looked more like sisters now – and that had made shopping for clothes less risky.

Normality was difficult for both of them, Zara discovered. Almost everything Hani knew about life she'd learned through a screen. The crowds worried her, the noise worried her, the street smells she found so fierce that she took to holding her nose until Zara told her to stop. Too many people were watching. She didn't understand that money had to change hands before something could be taken from a shop. Somehow, it was as if many of the most basic rules weren't in her book. On the other hand, she could date buildings just by looking at the brickwork. She knew exactly who or what every street had been named after. And passing a Radio Shack with a flickering screen in the window, Hani dashed in to reset it almost without breaking stride.

As for her, Zara knew she belonged to Isk, but the Isk she belonged to didn't yet exist. Hers would be a city where men of her own race didn't expect her to step into the road so they could pass. Where robed clerics didn't glare to see a woman and child out on the streets alone. And where shopkeepers didn't look over her shoulder to see who was paying.

But they tried hard to be normal and blend in. Together they ate crêpes from a market stall like tourists, drank warm mineral water that fizzed from its bottle and glued their fingers together with sticky almonds. Standing with their backs to Place Zaghloul, they'd watched grown men crash stunt kites into the waves and then jerk the kites skywards, swirling tails scattering silver drops of water.

Happy almost.

Until news of Raf's death came and their fragile, almost-happiness fractured down the middle as Zara suddenly found herself more scared and more alone than she dared admit . . .

Seventy dollars for a caleche along the Corniche was outrageous. Snapping shut her wallet, Zara took Hani by the hand and walked away without a backward glance. Less than five minutes later they both stood in front of an oak door so sun-blasted the last traces of paint had peeled away to leave only bleached wood cut by darker grain.

'Is this it?' Hani asked doubtfully.

Zara checked. 'Yes,' she said, trying to sound confident. 'We're here. Do you want to ring the bell?'

Hani shook her head. 'You do it.'

Zara didn't recognize the grim-faced blonde woman who answered the door. But it was hard not to notice that she was holding a flick knife and that there was blood on the blade.

CHAPTER 47

Hell didn't reside below any more than paradise resided above, whatever stories that child spun her rag dog. Hell was being suspended, like pain, between dirt and a darkening sky.

Someone up there was screaming, but Raf kept telling himself it wasn't a voice he knew. A bloody cut disfigured his mouth where he'd chewed his bottom lip ragged with frustration. He wanted to climb higher, needed to. He had to follow the ballerina, but his arms would no longer work and his legs were far too busy holding him fast to pay too much attention to any orders his mind might send.

Raf wasn't afraid of heights. He'd never been afraid of heights. What he was afraid of was falling. Falling and flames. But above and beyond need and fear, what he really wanted to know was just where the fuck the fox had gone now . . .

He was breaking into a spice house by levering himself up a narrow gap between the spice house and the facing wall of an adjoining suq: that was the theory, anyway. Proper climbers had a name for gaps like that. Only, proper cumbers also carried equipment and, on the whole, didn't spend their entire lives terrified of falling from high places.

Sweat stained his shirt. He could feel the perspiration beneath his hair, under his arms and in his groin. A long slick of wet enamelling his spine.

Beyond scared, you reach a place that is almost beyond being ashamed. But only almost. Hani was up in that room, Zara too. From the moment Raf had recognized their voices he'd known that up there was where he had to be, desperately had to be, and only a memory of silver rain was stopping him.

And the really sick joke was, Raf wasn't even sure the silver rain was real. He, who never cared enough about anyone to be truly afraid for them, was terrified that Hani might be killed. And as for Zara . . . If he hadn't vomited already he'd be doing it again, beyond doubt.

Below him, between the suq and the spice house, was the tiny blind alley down which the ballerina had vanished. At its end was a tiny courtyard belonging to the spice house. One back door, padlocked, one CCTV camera for security, nothing fancy; even adjusting his eyes across their whole spectrum hadn't revealed any trace of hidden beams.

As for dealing with the camera, Raf had justified being there by clumsily yanking up the front of his jellaba and unlacing his fly, at the same time as snatching a quick look around. To his right had been the red-brick wall, to his left the yard, little more than a token reminder of a larger one that had existed back before the suq was built. Above him a distant cast-iron loading boom jutting from the side of the spice house, its wheel rusted tight. The open window just below it had looked very far away.

Ambling back up the alley until he was out of camera range, Raf had jumped, feet jamming against the wall on both sides. He'd seen it on screen, mountaineers straddling a gap and climbing effortlessly, leaving the ground far below them. He managed four, maybe five awkward hops.

It wasn't pain in his ankles or lack of skill that stopped him. It was looking down. Down onto a drop of no more than three metres, but it was enough. Vomit rose barometer-like in his throat, spewed between rictus lips and trickled to the ground below, leaving memory etched on his palate as an aftertaste.

Open the door.

Can't.

Open the door.

No.

The voice of waves, other children shouting. Later on, in another place, he'd had to push one of them downstairs to cure that. Threw a knife across a crowded dining room so that it nailed a wooden beam beside another's head. Sheer luck but impressive.

Fear of heights or fear or falling? They were different. That difference had been explained to him at length by a psychiatrist at Huntsville, who masked her stink with cologne and scuttled sideways into rooms like a crab, because that was the only way she could fit through the door.

Apparently the height/falling difference mattered. Until he recognized which one it was, nothing could be done to cure what was a simple, almost boring phobia. All he had to do was watch some films and tell the fat woman what he felt.

Only Raf felt nothing as he looked at pictures of smiling children climbing frames or slides, shinning up ropes and leaping off walls. He didn't know any of them. And how he felt when he looked down couldn't be described. Not in words a child might use and certainly not by the adult that child became.

If he fell now and rolled on landing, he could walk away with nothing worse than a few bruises. Every shuffle upwards increased that danger. A few more shuffles and it would be a broken ankle rather than bruises, then a leg or hip. Much higher than that and his spine would concertina. At the top, where he needed to go, where muted screams broke through the open widow – fall from *there* and his vertebrae would be, crushed on impact. He knew that for a fact.

Very carefully, Raf twisted round until his back pressed against the suq's brickwork and his feet jammed hard against the crumbling warehouse wall. It felt safer than straddling the emptiness. By shuffling his back and straightening his legs he might be able to inch his way higher. All it would take would be for him to conquer one simple, irrational fear.

All. Darkness swept in against the edge of his thoughts every time Raf glanced down. And the alley floor sucked in his concentration like a singularity swallowing light. Until looking away became nearly impossible, climbing ditto.

Crying with frustration, Raf made himself stare up at the window, its shutter swinging slowly in the evening breeze. Everything he needed to become was on the other side of that. Zara, Hani, the ballerina . . . And whatever the ballerina was doing, that was something he needed to know about.

Hey, dead boy, the voice in his head was mocking. *Recognize where you are?*

Raf did. He'd been there before.

CHAPTER 48

Switzerland

Outside was silver rain.

Inside a fox cub coughed, thin shoulders heaving and skull flat to the floor. The door stood ready to be opened, buckled by the noise and anger of what waited on the other side.

He touched the handle.

Skin seared and the boy's fingertips vaporized, fragments of skin left sticking to the red-hot door knob as he yanked back his hand. He wanted to cry but he was doing that already.

It was nothing, he'd been telling himself . . . Nothing seeping under the door, nothing pushing past the sodden towels he'd used to close out the gap; but he could no longer pretend. Tears dripped unnoticed onto his red wool dressing gown.

He could smell burning and the smell came from him.

All the boy had to do if he wanted to live was turn the handle and yank back the door. It was that simple. The alternative was to die in peace, letting go any last shred of hope that stuck to his soul the way his burnt skin was glued to the door handle. Die, or walk out into the silver rain. Into the Hell pastors talked about in chapel.

Water still trickled from the cold faucet but it was boiling now, steam rising from the basin as he turned on the tap. A gravity-feed cistern in the roof behind him supplied water and the noise had not yet reached his stretch of attic.

Stripping off, the boy screwed up his dressing gown and held it under the water, burning his already burnt fingers. When the cloth was completely sodden, he wrapped it around his body. The dressing gown wasn't long enough to protect his ankles or calves but it would cover the rest of him, for what that was worth.

He opened the door by gripping its handle through cloth from his gown and twisting. And when steam hissed from beneath his fingers, the boy knew he should have dealt with the door first, when the dressing gown was still dry, rather than this way round. Logical rather than lateral, he wasn't as good at that as his mother's friends expected.

But this wasn't a test.

Taking a deep breath, he threw back the door and stepped out. There was no ground, no walls, no roof above him. Only a red glow. A darkness of night sky held back by flame. The silver rain had almost finished, thick drops of lead trickling down from gutters to evaporate into dark smudges on fire-scarred walls. Surrounding him was what was left of one attic and between him and the next surviving attic lay nothing but a smouldering pit of fire bisected by a black steel girder that stretched over empty space.

The noise of the flames had grown softer. Burnt out, along with the west wing of the school. There was fire behind him, scavenging its way like cancer along the building, shattering walls, melting lead and eating through wooden beams to drop the blazing remains noisily into orange cinders below.

Firemen had seen him now. That became obvious when a spotlight almost bowled him backwards with shock. Someone swore, their words made puny by distance and flame, and the light snapped out. So the boy shut his eyes and let them adjust, calling up darkness in his head. Waiting until the extraneous noise died and the orange glow behind his eyelids slid away.

When he looked again, the pit was back, framed round with darkness and night, while tiny grey bats of ash spiralled high into the air.

'Stay there.' Words loud enough to come from God bellowed from a hand-held loudspeaker somewhere below. 'You're safe there.'

The boy shook his head. The man lied, probably not intentionally. But only because the man wasn't where he was, so didn't know any better.

He was going to die or he was going to live: the choice was his. Not their choice, his choice. He and the fox were the ones who had to walk the abyss.

On the far side of the attic, a tall ladder was sliding upwards in a fluid sweep of hydraulics, a man balanced at its top. The man wore dark blue overalls and a yellow helmet with a bump across the top like a ridge of bone. A night visor covered his eyes and nose, and on his back was an oval oxygen tank. One of the new models, doughnut-shaped with a hole in the middle. He was mouthing words the boy didn't wait to hear.

'Time to go,' said the boy.

Claws needled into the flesh of his shoulder as he tightened his grip on the scrabbling animal. Of course the cub wanted out of there, so did he, and that meant crossing the iron beam. He didn't blame the fox for not being happy, but it wasn't helping.

The iron beam was recent: put there within the last seventy years to brace internal walls of a Swiss arms dealer's mansion originally built for show rather than quality. The beam and its bracing were the only thing stopping the wing of the Swiss boarding school falling in on itself.

Flames flickered below him, held in check by fire hoses but waiting, gathering themselves to explode upwards and sweep away the last fragments of his attic. This was life.

He shook his head crossly, flipping blond hair into already stinging eyes. He didn't like the school and didn't want to be there. He couldn't see the point of useless tests or running through brambles in the rain. It wasn't even the exercise he minded. It was the other pupils. The ones who never saw what he saw.

There were tears in his eyes again, but he couldn't work out why. Maybe he was just scared. That was allowed, wasn't it?

Except it wasn't.

Boys like him weren't scared. They did the stupid, the splendid and the impossible without making a fuss. They walked out along red-hot—

'Enough already,' said the fox. 'Move it.' The beam was sticky underfoot. But that was the soles of his slippers melting, each step leaving a black footprint on the beam behind him.

Heat rose as if from a furnace, billowing his dressing gown until it blew out like a limp balloon. It was hotter than the wall of heat he'd hit that time stepping off a Boeing onto the tarmac in Singapore.

His mother had been photographing tigers then. Not the original singha after which the island had been named, but the new ones, the reintroduced ones that kept dying because there was nothing in the wild for them to eat. The director had offered to pay for her to bring her kid along: it added human interest to the other sort.

Bubbling step followed bubbling step. The next one would take him to the middle of the scorching beam, then he would have to do what the fox said. Not that he could turn round; any more than he could stop the soles of his slippers bubbling, molten rubber blistering the bottom of his feet.

Going on was his only option. The burning pit wasn't there. The beam was just a line he'd scrawled on a floor to amuse himself, a crack along the edge of some floorboard. Reality was what he wanted it to be, what he made it.

Staring straight ahead, the boy wrapped the struggling fox tight in his arms, buried his cheek into hot fur and walked across the remaining stretch of beam onto the front page of next morning's papers.

Fox Saves Boy – only the Enquirer got it right.

Fear, shadow and tears gave his childish face the tortured beauty of an

El Greco saint. No one mentioned that he owed the anguish which twisted his mouth to a terrified fox cub chewing chunks out of his shoulder.

By the time a tee-shirt was being faked in sweatshops in Karachi and sold on street stalls in London and Paris, he was gone. No longer aware of the fuss, no longer watching the screens. He had more important things to talk about – his mother was coming herself to collect him.

She flew into Zurich first-class on Lufthansa and the ticket was free, like the cars and hotels. Reporters met her at Kloten and photographs of him being hugged by a thin woman in a long black coat with shades, were syndicated worldwide. There were some long-lens pap shots from a brief stay-over at the George V in Paris – all flat surfaces and squashed depth of field – but no one got real access until London.

A man Raf didn't recognize – who called his mother Sally a lot and looked at her ankles – sat on a chair in a BBC studio on the outskirts. Hot lights blazed above the boy, raising beads of sweat under his newly cut hair. The fox cub sat on his lap, pinned by his hand to the grey flannel of his school trousers.

The trousers and tweed coat were a compromise. He wore school uniform for the interview and the school in Zurich didn't charge a term's notice for removing him as a pupil.

Everyone won except Raf.

On the studio wall was a bare blue screen. On it the people at home would see whatever the producer wanted them to see. Mostly this was a long shot of the boy balanced high on the iron beam, his face raised to heaven.

When the man had finished asking his mother how she felt about having a child who was a hero . . .

She was glad he'd rescued the fox.

What was she photographing now . . .

An endangered seal colony on the Falklands.

What would she and Raf be doing next . . .

Spending some quality time together at a friend's apartment in New York.

When all that was over, the man who called his mother Sally turned to the boy and, pasting on a sympathetic smile, asked how he'd felt up there on the beam.

The man wasn't happy with the boy because the producer had already halted the interview once, after a sound man complained he kept unclipping the button mike fixed to his school collar.

'Well?'

What had he felt? He wasn't too sure he'd felt anything at all. Mostly he'd been busy keeping his head empty.

255

'Were you scared?'

Only of having nearly killed the fox. Despite himself, despite not allowing himself feelings, the boy's eyes misted and for the first time since he'd reached the top of the fire truck's ladder, his mouth trembled.

It was like punching a button. Repressed irritation segued into instant sympathy as the interviewer's face softened. The man rephrased the question, glancing only once at the camera.

The boy thought about it. He still didn't know how he felt but now everyone was waiting, his mother's pale eyes fixed on him, her face tense.

'I can't sleep,' said the boy finally. That at least was true. Always had been. Darkness unravelled in front of his eyes in minutes that ticked by so slowly it was like living inside freeze-frame.

'Dreams,' said the interviewer. 'I can understand that.' He glanced at Raf's mother, his look conveying just the right amount of compassion mixed with an unspoken question.

'He'll be seeing the best child therapist in New York.'

The interviewer nodded. Debated the propriety of asking his next question and asked it anyway. 'When you do sleep,' he said, 'what exactly do you see?'

Nothing, that was the real answer. A brief darkness that swallowed emotion, fear and guilt. But, glancing round the studio, Raf knew that wasn't the right answer and he was learning fast that 'real' and 'right' were different things.

'Flames,' he said simply. 'I see flames.'

The producer brought the interview to a quick halt after that. Time was needed in the cutting suite and they had an actor from the National standing by to voice-over the links needed to tie the interview into existing footage of the fire.

In the hospitality room afterwards, hardbitten hacks wrapped heavy arms round the boy's tense shoulders and told him how brave he was. And all the while, the boy stood clutching a glass of orange juice and wondering why none of them had thought to ask him how the blaze got started in the first place.

CHAPTER 49

Some sense of meaning was there, just about. Hidden beneath animal howls that ended in choking silence. *Stb pzzz.* But the German ballerina had no interest in stopping, not yet. Not until Madame Sosostris told the ballerina why she'd been hired. Only Madame Sosostris wasn't saying, because refusal was the only thing keeping her alive – although that definition was becoming increasingly loose.

Sighing, the ballerina lit another Cleopatra and inhaled deeply, letting the smoke dribble from her mouth. Then she inhaled again, and stubbed the cigarette out in the screaming woman's navel.

Zara put her hands over her ears.

Ashraf was dead. Someone she knew and liked had been murdered. Maybe more than liked, if she was honest. Now she'd walked Hani straight into a trap. Zara had brains, she had courage, she should have been planning their escape but somehow . . .

All she wanted to do was cry. Zara was disgusted at her own cowardice. The kid, on the other hand seemed almost oblivious, only glancing up from where she squatted beside Ali-Din whenever another cigarette went out.

Outside, late evening leeched daylight from the sky. Lights would be coming on along the Corniche, the fish restaurants shuffling tables as tourists finished their supper and locals arrived to eat, children in tow. And, sitting alone in his study, nursing an illegal whisky, her father would be checking his messages and trying not to worry. She could look after herself, that was what he would tell himself because that was what she'd spent the last five years telling him, every opportunity she got.

She was sorry to have let him down.

'It's okay.' Hani squeezed Zara's hand. 'Raf will be here soon.'

'Raf's dead, honey.'

257

'No,' said Hani, as she tucked her wriggling rag dog tight in her arms and stroked its ears. 'He's just late, as usual . . .'

They both waited at one end of a spice-drying attic, or maybe it was a mezzanine. Whatever, it filled a third of the length of the building and was a simple platform, hung under the roof and anchored to an end wall. Slit windows in that wall let in air and would have looked down onto a street if only the street hadn't been so narrow or the windows set so high. That was the end where rickety stairs led up from ground level. At the other end of the platform, a simple rail separated the edge from a drop to the floor of the warehouse far below.

Light came from a single bulb that hung like a fat water drop at the end of an age-blackened twist of flex. The room it revealed was functional. A place of sour-smelling leaves drying on canvas tarpaulins, of peppery herbs hung from crude beams, each brittle bunch lashed together with rough string. The same type of string bound the elbows of Madame Sosostris tight behind her as she lay quivering face up on a medical couch, knees wrenched back and ankles lashed to her elbows so that her arched body was taut beneath a short Muji vest, which was all that she now wore. In Berlin that position was called 'Teasing the Rat.'

The more Zara tried not to think about what that couch was actually doing there, the nastier her suspicions became. Full pharaonic circumcision, which used to be called female infibulation was illegal in Iskandryia. But then, so was abortion and the little silver trolley with the surgical trays could have been for either – or even for both.

Beside her, Hani suddenly sneezed at the dust in the air.

The ballerina paused. *'Gesundheit,'* she said, sounding distracted. And then went back to heating the tip of her flick knife with a Zippo.

Black carob, henna and oregano, chilli and ginger. Their scents clashed with each other and with the smell of cumin, coriander and frying garlic that drifted up from a distant street stall. But rich as the mix was, it wasn't enough to hide the stink of fear that rose from the tethered herbalist.

'Tell her,' Zara pleaded.

The ballerina smiled.

'Please.'

'Ja,' said the blonde German, as she pressed red-hot metal into the inside of the bound woman's thighs. 'Explain who really hired me and maybe I'll let you live . . . But then again, maybe not.' She jerked the blade sideways.

Blood ran between Madame Sosostris's legs in a trickle like scarlet tears.

'Tell me,' suggested the ballerina.

'What's to tell . . . ?' The question bubbled between bitten lips. 'I hired you. I didn't know he was dangerous . . . I made a bad mistake.'

'No,' said the ballerina. 'Not you. Someone else ordered you to hire me.' She pivoted on her heel and buried rigid fingers into the side of the arched woman, ignoring piss that spread across wipe-clean leatherette and dribbled floorwards, following blood down a crack in the boards. And in the silence between falling drips Zara heard a knock at the door below and then the sudden jagged trill of a bell, so loud that even the ballerina jumped.

'Expecting someone?' she demanded, holding her blade close to her victim's eye. Madame Sosostris shook her head.

'Well?' The question was shot behind her, at Zara.

'No,' said Zara.

The ballerina turned back to her victim. 'Well, now,' she said, listening to a second, more impatient ring from below. 'Maybe we can kill you, after all. Okay, *you* . . .'

Zara nodded.

'This is how it works . . . You answer the door and the child stays there. Any problems and . . .' She flicked her knife sideways, leaving Zara no doubt what would happen to Hani's throat.

Zara went. Walking slowly down the ancient stairs until she reached the main door to the spice house. A big part of her wanted to keep walking, out of that door and into a world where upstairs wasn't happening. But she knew, stupid or otherwise, she'd probably die rather than leave Hani.

'Who is it?' she demanded.

'Me.' Lady Jalila's voice was scared or furious, but through an inch of sheet steel it was hard to tell which. *'Now open up, quickly . . .'* She pushed at the door, then visibly jumped when she saw it was Zara. 'Where is Madame Sosostris?'

Zara pointed to the ceiling.

'And you brought Hani?'

Of course she'd brought Hani. This was where the message had told them to come. Zara nodded.

'Good.' The woman pushed past Zara and headed towards the stairs without needing to be shown the way. 'I'll be taking her with me.'

'Lady Jalila . . .'

'What?'

What indeed. Zara thought of Hani upstairs and the blonde woman with her cold northern eyes and hot blade and said nothing. Besides, something was wrong. What did Lady Jalila mean, asking if Hani was there? Here, still? Here, now? Where else would the child . . .

'Lady Jalila.'

'Well?' The woman's eyes flicked from Zara to dark drips on the floor behind her. And when she stayed silent, Lady Jalila sighed. 'Leave it to me,' she said, reaching into her pocket. 'Just leave it to me.'

The rest Hani and Zara reconstructed from memory. Remembering most a *pas de deux* faster and more intricate than any they'd seen on a newsfeed.

Sound travels relatively slowly but, being cool-loaded and thus subsonic, Lady Jalila's first bullet travelled more slowly still, which meant it wasn't quite the surprise to the ballerina that it might have been. Though by the time Hani looked up, the German's blonde hair had finished streaming out behind her in a sticky white, grey and red plume.

The .38 hollow-point entered the ballerina's head just below the jaw, passed through her soft palate and removed what had until then been the back of her skull, sucking out blood, bone fragments and grey jelly to splatter them over the brick wall behind.

A split second after her head flicked back, the woman's bowels and bladder loosened and her body stepped back, exploded blue eyes staring blindly at nothing. The crash the ballerina made as she hit the boards was loud enough to echo through the almost empty building.

'Mid-period,' muttered Lady Jalila, surveying the wall. 'Maybe mid-to-late . . .' Her eyes swept over the attic to take in Hani with her rag dog, the dead ballerina and finally, scornfully, Madame Sosostris hogtied on the couch.

'Murderer.'

Before Zara could protest, Lady Jalila brought up her gun and yanked the trigger three times. Hollow-points took Madame Sosostris in the upper body, splintering ribs into bone fragments. Lungs collapsed as the first two bullets blossomed into sucking wounds in her side, the final shot taking Madame Sosostris sideways through the heart and blasting her off the couch onto the floor.

The gurgling stopped.

'She hired the German to kill Ashraf,' Lady Jalila said as if that explained everything, though whether it was said to Zara or herself wasn't clear. Walking over to the dead woman by the bed, Lady Jalila lifted a scalpel from a metal dish and slashed the twine binding her arms and feet. Then she rolled the sticky twine into a neat ball and dropped it into her pocket. She placed her own .38 in the dead herbalist's hand.

'We'll tell the police they shot each other.'

It wasn't a suggestion.

'Just leave the official stuff to me,' said Lady Jalila. 'Okay . . . ?'

Without waiting for Zara's answer, Lady Jalila walked across to where Hani sat, hugging her knees and clutching her rag dog.

'Time to take Ali-Din home.'

Hani shook her head. 'You killed her,' she said, voice empty.

'Of course I killed her,' said Lady Jalila. 'There was no choice.'

Only the child wasn't talking about the blonde German, Zara realized. Or about Madame Sosostris. And everything fell into place as if the answer had always been right there, just waiting for Zara.

Cold.

Staggers.

Hallucinations.

'The pen was a side issue,' Zara said without thinking. 'Lady Nafisa died from poisoning.' And she suddenly knew exactly how the woman standing in front of her had done it. Except that by then Lady Jalila was crouching beside the dead herbalist, taking back her own gun.

The next bullet she fired took Ali-Din through the head.

CHAPTER 50

Always count the guns.

Crouching by the window, company to fat-toed geckos that had grown used to his stillness, Raf whispered it again – just in case he forgot. Counting the guns had been rule one, according to Hu San; and Raf had made a special point of remembering the things Hu San told him.

The automatic would belong to the ballerina, only she was dead. Raf had heard that happen. Lady Jalila had the revolver, subsonic slugs but unsilenced barrel; silencing a revolver was a contradiction in terms. From an empty plastic Coke bottle taped to the muzzle to the most expensive hand-turned tungsten mutetube, nothing actually worked. Some of the shock wave always forced its way between cylinder and chassis.

If you needed to mute a revolver then the answer was to self-load the brass and use less charge, which was what she'd done. Whether or not in imitation of *Thiergarten* dogma, Raf didn't know. But, either way, just knowing how to do it made her a professional in his eyes.

The ex-ballerina had a gun, so did Jalila and so did he . . . Three in total, if he didn't count the one he'd lifted from the dead dancer. Which made it four functioning weapons. Quite how knowing that helped him Raf had forgotten.

'Enough already . . .'

Old words but true ones. Bats echo-located around him through the warm night air, taking moths in mid-night, each curving strike almost surgical in its precision. Their echo bounced off shutters, refracted from high walls or vanished through open windows to return milliseconds later. Cold and mysterious, like some distant music of the spheres.

There was a tom cat lurking in the dirt of the alley floor far below, its heavy shoulders hunched and thick muscles locked in anticipation as it walked, oblivious, round Raf's discarded jellaba and shades, tracking whatever vermin hid behind the rubble. If the cat was dimly aware of the spiralling almost-mice, it didn't allow them to put it off the prey within reach.

Yet another city within a city, world within world. A metropolis of wild dogs and feral cats, rats breeding beneath grain silos and mice infesting the cotton bales that waited to be loaded into containers along the dock. Spiders, scorpions and millipedes fat as callused thumbs, safe from the frail, fly-hunting geckos that haunted the twilight edge of street lights.

Raf twisted his head to one side, easing an ache in his neck. Just holding himself secure in that gap between walls took effort. And if he waited much longer he'd have no strength for what must happen next.

Dead boy . . . It was an odd nickname for a man to give a child. He remembered the man well, with his faltering monitors and flat-lining neurofeedback machines. Remembering never had been Raf's problem. His first identity number, its position over a battered metal hook that took his school coat, the exact marble pattern of tiles along a hospital corridor – he knew them all. Far better than he knew himself, because Raf had been afraid there was no self.

We are the hollow men . . . Maybe now, but not back times . . . Back then he was just a hollow *child*, not English/not American, not rich/not poor, not wanted except for his logic skills. He could easily have passed that test. But he thought that if he failed they'd let him go home.

Live with it, as the fox would have said.

The silver rain was finished, almost twenty years before.

While Hani was in there. Zara, too.

And he was out here.

And they both undoubtedly believed he was dead and some days he still was. Some days it surprised him he even had a shadow or that when he stared in the mirror there was a reflection waiting to scowl back. But those days got fewer.

And the fear was gone, burned out. The fox dying too. He was going to have to make his own decisions. And this was the first of them . . .

Grabbing the rusty metal bar that had once supported a pulley, Raf kicked off from the spice house wall and let gravity swing him through the open window towards which he'd been climbing.

Things to do, people to become.

Hani was sure she saw a smoke-grey animal leap into the room, becoming Raf as it hit the ground and rolled. When he came upright, Raf's gun was already cocked, its muzzle pointed straight at Lady Jalila's stomach. What Raf didn't do was pull the trigger.

'*You.*'

He nodded.

'*You're . . .*'

'Dead,' added Hani and Raf nodded, watching the revolver pointed at his chest. Small, elegant, with pearl handles and an over-fussy blue finish that definitely didn't match the dark purple nails of the hand holding it.

Lady Jalila smiled. Her full lips twisting prettily.

'Darling,' she said. 'You kill me, I kill you . . . Such a waste, don't you think?' Lady Jalila meant it, too, Raf realized. Her greeting was real. In some warped way she really *was* pleased to see a man who only that morning she'd arranged to have killed.

'You murdered Felix,' said Raf.

Lady Jalila shook her head. 'Murder has to be intentional. That was an accident.'

'And you expected to get away with it?'

'Oh,' said Lady Jalila, 'I already have . . . And I'll get away with this too. As will you. You and me, we're different.' Her pale blue eyes swept the room, taking in the dead ballerina and herbalist, then Zara. 'Whereas people like her . . .'

'What about people like me?' Zara demanded.

'Disposable.' Lady Jalila shrugged elegantly. 'What on earth made you think you deserved a pashazade?'

'Who said I wanted one?'

Lady Jalila ignored that. 'You know what you lack?' Lady Jalila said as the girl turned away. 'Breeding . . . That's why people like you never amount to anything. Ashraf, however . . . Who knows? With my help he could be the next Chief of Detectives.'

Looking deep into Jalila's pale eyes, Raf finally recognised the truth. She was barking, completely off the Richter scale. Dysfunctional, deluded, sociopathic . . . Exactly the kind of ally someone like him might need to reach the top of the pile.

'Jalila.' He nodded discreetly towards the far end of the mezzanine, where light from the single bulb barely reached.

'Tell me how I could get Felix's old job,' Raf said quietly when they got there. 'And then tell me what it's going to cost.' Both of them still held their guns, only now the muzzles pointed at the floor.

'The cost?' Raf could almost see Lady Jalila calculating, dividing the cost of a box of bullets, deducting the ten per cent discount she got at government shops and dividing the remainder of it by fifty. 'In cash terms, about thirty-five cents . . .' Her tongue dipped out to lick her bottom lip, its tip moistening already glossy lipstick. 'The *how* should be obvious.' She glanced towards his gun.

'Kill Zara?'

'Too easy,' said Lady Jalila. 'I'll do that myself.'

The floor far below was in darkness. Hollow. Empty. She saw nothing and he saw the same. But with two more colours and in sharper focus. 'Why just Chief of Detectives?' Raf said. 'Why not Minister for Police?'

'What about my husband?'

'Accidents happen,' said Raf. 'Ask Felix.'

'You'd really kill Mushin if I asked?' For a moment Lady Jalila sounded almost interested.

'Why not?' Raf's voice was blunt. 'He's not that rich and I doubt he's much use in bed. What have you got to lose?'

Lady Jalila roared.

'Try me,' suggested Raf, seriously.

'Maybe I will,' said Lady Jalila laughing. 'Once you've met my reserve.'

'No problem.' Raf broke open his revolver as if checking the load. Blued, lightweight and virtually indestructible, the Taurus was a beautiful piece of work. It was also so much useless ceramic and tungsten with its cylinder nipped out to the side like that. Now was the time for her to shoot him if she wanted.

Lady Jalila just looked amused. 'When did you know?'

About the pen being Jalila's inability to resist an artistic flourish? 'Right from the start,' said Raf. He lied. It wasn't until the night on the VSV he'd realized his aunt had been poisoned first, then stabbed later. Two different methods, two different places, same person. And as for Jalila being responsible . . . Originally he'd been sure it was the General.

'And you know the really ironic touch?' Lady Jalila's eyes sparkled.

He didn't.

'Nas was mean as sin, but she still paid good money for that colonic . . . Of course,' said Lady Jalila, as she reached out with one finger to brush the back of Raf's hand. 'In the end she left me no choice. And she would keep sleeping with my husband.'

'*That* was your reason,' said Raf. '*Jealousy?*'

'No.' When Lady Jalila shook her head, burnished curls brushed her shoulders and framed an angel's face. 'But it didn't help.'

She stretched lazily, her silk shirt pulling tight. Hani and Zara were invisible to her, Raf realized. All her artfulness was reserved for him.

'Why, then?' Raf prompted.

'The Autumn Ball. No one's meant to hold the chair at the C&C for more than two terms. Nafisa had five and wanted six. It was my turn but she wouldn't resign . . .' Lady Jalila sighed, then brightened. 'You really must come. I promise you, this year will be the best ever. Everyone will be there.'

Of course Nafisa wouldn't resign. She couldn't, Raf realized. Not without admitting she'd plundered the accounts.

But what Jalila wanted, she was given. And if she wasn't given it, she took it. He'd known someone else like that: his mother. Raf flicked the cylinder shut on his gun, hearing it click into place.

'And the price I have to pay?'

'Don't be silly,' said Lady Jalila. 'You know it already.'

So he did. Hani.

'On the count of three,' said Lady Jalila. 'Okay?' Tightening her grip on the handle, she turned lazily to face Zara, trigger finger whitening at the knuckle. *One, two* . . .

She made it to the start of *three* before Raf thumbed back the hammer on his own revolver, swung round and watched Lady Jalila's baby-blues explode with shock. Very slowly, the woman tripped backwards over one kitten heel, and met the rail that might have saved her if Raf hadn't reached down to scoop both feet out from under her.

Time expanded, so that every action took longer than it should have done, including the fall. If she wasn't dead when she went over the rail, the wet thud as she hit concrete confirmed that she was once she reached the ground.

Raf stared briefly down at the smashed body, then back at the child who squatted by a broken rag dog and held the dead ballerina's smoking gun in her hands. She'd understood every nuance of the conversation. Which had been a risk Raf had to take.

'You missed,' Raf told her fiercely. 'Okay?'

Hani weighed next to nothing when he reached her. A bundle of sinew and bone. Terror holding her body so rigid that her arms and legs practically vibrated with fear.

'You missed,' Raf said more softly, stroking the back of her hair. 'I didn't. The police will tell you the same . . .' He kept his words simple, hoping that repetition would be enough.

'Do you understand? You missed . . .'

Disbelief slowly left the child's eyes and then vanished completely, replaced by tears as her sticklike arms snaked up to superglue themselves round his neck, almost choking him.

Later, when Hani's sobbing had stopped, Raf gently unpeeled her arms and sat himself back against the end wall, his spine pressed hard against rough brick.

Life felt real. This was who he was. He was Ashraf Bey, guardian to Hani al-Mansur and friend of . . . Raf looked across to the crude window where Zara stood staring at the wall opposite or half watching bats flitter over the rooftops without really seeing them. Well, maybe 'friend' was the wrong word.

'You should talk to her,' whispered Hani from where she sat next to him, knees drawn up, back also pressed to the wall. At her feet was what was left of Ali-Din. Scraps of rag, smashed memory, a cracked lens, fragments of ubiquitous phenolic circuit board . . . All that remained of the only real proof that Lady Jalila had stabbed Nafisa.

'Zara?'

When the girl stayed silent, Raf sighed and slowly pushed himself up off the boards. It was evident that she heard him coming from the way her shoulders stiffened at his approach. 'I thought you were dead,' Zara said. 'And then, when you finally turned up, I thought *I* was dead. I really believed you intended to let her kill me . . .'

Underneath the overwhelming smell of past fear was the residue of some cologne, oxidized and turned sour from sweat. But then, God alone knew how *he* stank – or looked, for that matter.

'So did I,' said Raf.

Zara glanced round at that and their eyes locked, her own dark with *felaheen* DNA, his chilly and pale as any dawn. He couldn't help it: that was the colour his pre-natal contract had specified.

'Only for a second, towards the end.' Raf shrugged and spread his hands in a gesture as old as humanity. 'Sometimes, believing is the only way to play a part.'

'And I'm meant to accept that?'

'Yeah,' said Raf. 'If I can I don't see why you can't.'

'So what happens now?' Zara's voice made it clear she reserved the right to disagree, whatever his answer.

'We tell the truth.'

'We *what* . . . ?'

'We tell the truth,' said Hani sadly. 'It's the one thing nobody can stand.'

EPILOGUE

Hani's spoon froze in mid-air. 'Zara would like this . . .'

'Probably,' said Raf, glancing at his Omega a second ahead of it beeping to remind him that he should be somewhere else.

Pashazade Ashraf Bey was in demand. Three weeks after the shocking murder of Lady Jalila by a renegade *Thiergarten* assassin, he was still a hero for the daring rescue of his niece, Hani al-Mansur, and of the daughter of Hamzah Effendi, a well-known industrialist. Charities begged Raf to be on their committee. There was the rumour of a Japanese miniseries. General Saeed Koenig Pasha called him almost daily. He had until two p.m. to decide if he wanted to be Iskandryia's new Chief of Detectives.

He didn't.

The only person not interested was Zara; not interested in Raf and not interested in the polite, handwritten little notes the Khedive had taken to having delivered to Villa Hamzah. As soon as she'd been poly-graphed, her statement taken and affidavit signed, she'd stormed back to Glymenapoulo Bay. Not to the Villa Hamzah but to a small summer house in the grounds. And since then she'd met Raf only once. At the office of her father, where she'd stood stiff-backed and formal while Raf politely refused Hamzah Effendi's offer of a reward for rescuing her and the big bear of a man had tried hard not to be offended.

'Look,' Hani said, spooning down another mouthful of ice cream hand-beaten from fresh milk, egg yolk and Caribbean vanilla pods. 'She's not going to call you. So you call her. It's not difficult.'

'Maybe . . . Later . . .'

Hani sighed and turned her attention back to her pudding. No matter how cold the vanilla ice was when Hani's bowl left the kitchen at Le Trianon, it still melted before she could take more than a dozen spoonfuls.

Still, they were small elegant spoons and she ate slowly. Her attention taken mainly by tourists who strolled the length of Rue Missala. Some smiled at the small girl sitting at her roped-off pavement table. Others glanced away, having decided the child in the Armani shades was famous and the man beside her was a bodyguard. In their next few steps they invariably decided who they'd just seen.

She'd been variously the child-model Isabella Cloud, a violin prodigy called x'Tra Sweet, known never to leave her compound in Wako, and HRH Yasmine, only cousin of the young Khedive.

'Ready to move?' Raf folded his afternoon paper. He'd had the vending machine include downloads of anything personal and there were three snippets about him in the paper, none of them true and all of them highly complimentary.

'Sure.' Hani nodded at her bowl of melting ice cream. 'You want some?' She knew full well he'd say no.

Two small coffees had already gone cold in front of Raf, but he didn't mind and they weren't really cold. In Isk, in high summer, nothing was unless it came straight out of a freezer like Hani's endless supply of vanilla ice.

Originally, Raf had thought Hani insisted on coming with him to Le Trianon every day because of the ice cream, but he'd got that wrong. What she really liked was the bustle of the brightly dressed crowds, safely kept at bay by a rope that separated her table from the busy street beyond. And when she wasn't there, she was up in his office, being spoiled by Raf's assistant who'd suddenly revealed a side no one had ever before seen. It turned out the man grew up with three younger sisters and, bizarrely, had liked them all.

'Okay,' said Raf when his watch complained again. 'You need me to take you up to the office?'

She didn't. Not if her snotty look was anything to go by. Finding her own way from the table up to his office was child's play to Hani. For a start, the Third Circle had its own private lift. And, as Hani had pointed out more than once, she didn't even have to climb the wire.

The girl was fine, Raf knew that. It was only anxiety that made him ask each day and that wasn't Hani's problem, it was his . . . Some day he'd have to stop trying to protect her. Not to mention stop letting her eat nothing but ice cream. But that time wasn't yet.

'You can get me—'

'. . . On your mobile. Yes, I know.' Hani sighed. 'Look, I'll call you if I need you. Okay?' She had to have borrowed that line from Zara.

'Make sure you do.' Raf watched as the kid threaded her way between two pavement tables and disappeared into Le Trianon's air-conditioned darkness. Maybe she knew he was watching her go, maybe not. Either way, she didn't look back.

'Car,' said Raf and seconds later the fat man's Cadillac rolled up to the kerb, white-walled tyres freshly washed. 'The precinct,' Raf told his new driver, 'and then home.'

'Whatever you say.' Skin like chocolate, eyes hidden behind mirror lenses, black cap balanced at an angle on his dreadlocked skull, Avatar nodded.

Zara's half-brother had recently got the Cadillac's shell sandblasted back to bare metal at a fly-by-night bodyshop out at Karmous. Then he'd had the twelve-cylinder super-turned somewhere different. So now it roared like the devil and every surface burned with sunlight. The boy was arguing for a quad Blaupunkt sound system, flat speakers set into the leather door trim. To date Raf had been holding out, but it wasn't an argument he was about to win.

'You called my sister yet?' Avatar demanded.

Raf shook his head.

'You plan to call her?'

'We've got ten minutes to get to the Precinct,' Raf said firmly and pretended not to notice Avatar's grin.

It was only when the shining car overshot the turn and kept gunning down Iskander el Akhbar towards Glymenapoulo that he realized the boy intended that Raf should make a meeting all right, just not at the Precinct, And not with the Minister.

Raf could live with that.

EFFENDI

PROLOGUE

27th October

'Of course,' said Ashraf Bey. 'We could just kill the defendant and be done with it . . .' He let his suggestion hang in the cold air. And when no one replied, Raf shrugged. 'Okay,' he said. 'Maybe not.'

It was getting late and autumn rain fell steadily on the darkened streets outside, while inside, sitting around their table, Raf's visitors continued to chase the same argument in tight circles. A Grand Jury was in session. If three judges plus a senior detective in a damp, third-storey office could be called anything so imposing, which seemed doubtful.

'An accident,' suggested Raf. 'The steps in this precinct are notoriously slippery. Or perhaps suicide . . . Shoelaces, an unfortunately overlooked belt . . . ? One of my people would have to be reprimanded, obviously.'

Raf looked from Graf Ernst von B, the German boy, to a sour-faced politician from New Jersey who insisted everyone call her Senator Liz, neither of whom met his eye. There was also an elderly French oil magnate, but he sat so quietly Raf mostly forgot he was there. Which was probably the man's intention.

'Alternatively,' said Raf, 'I could have him taken out to the courtyard and shot. Or, if you like, we could lose the body altogether and just pretend he never existed. One of the old Greek cisterns should take care of that.'

They didn't like this idea either; but then the young detective with the Armani wrap-rounds and drop-pearl earring hadn't expected them to . . . He was acting as *magister* to their judges. And no one as yet, least of all him, seemed very sure what that actually entailed.

'*Justice*,' Senator Liz said loudly, '*must be seen to be done*.' Her voice remained as irritating as when the session had begun several hours earlier.

'Lord Hewart.' Raf pulled the quote from memory. 'One of the worst

273

judges in history. And even he never suggested putting a North African trial on American television.'

'That's not . . .' Ernst von B's protest died as Raf flipped up a hand.

'Let's hear what St Cloud thinks,' he said, and turned to the Frenchman. 'Do *you* think justice needs to be televised?'

'Me?' Astolphe de St Cloud slid a cigar case from his inside pocket. And though the iridescence of its lizardskin was beautiful, even by the light of a single hurricane lamp, what they all noticed was the enamel clasp: an eagle spreading its wings, while jagged thunderbolts fell from between the bird's sharp claws.

As if anyone there needed reminding that St Cloud would have been Prince Imperial, if only his father had bothered to marry his mother.

'It depends,' said St Cloud, 'on what Your Excellency means by *justice* . . .' Shuffling a handful of prints, he stopped at one that showed a young girl with most of her stomach missing. 'If we decide the evidence is convincing enough, then obviously the prisoner must stand trial. Like Senator Liz, my only reservation is that, perhaps, El Iskandryia is not quite . . .'

Raf caught the wry amusement in the Marquis' voice and glanced round the room, trying to see it through the eyes of a man whose own business empire was run from a Moorish palace overlooking Tunisia's Cap Bon, and who now found himself in a third-floor office, without electricity, on the corner of Boulevard Champollion and Rue Riyad Pasha, in a tatty four-square government block built around a huge courtyard in best Nationalist Revival style.

At street level the exterior walls to Iskandryia's Police HQ were faced with cheap sheets of reconstituted marble, while glass hid the exterior of the two floors above. Black glass obviously. The architect had been on loan from Moscow.

It showed.

As for the level of comfort on offer . . . A fire burned in a bucket in the centre of the floor, filled with logs from a dying carob. Apparently, the tree had been not quite alive and not yet dead for as long as even Raf's oldest detectives could remember.

Two men from uniform had hacked it off just above the roots, using fire axes. Now chunks of its carcass spat and spluttered as thin flames danced across the top of their makeshift brazier.

Directly above the brazier, suspended from the centre of the ceiling like an inverted red mushroom, hung a state-of-the-art smoke detector. Like almost everything else in Iskandryia since the EMP bomb, it no longer worked.

And behind Raf's head, a window unit that once adjusted

electronically to lighting conditions had been rendered smoke friendly, also with a fire axe. Through its shattered centre came flecks of rain and a salt wind that blew in from the Eastern Harbour.

'Justice,' said Raf, 'is whatever we decide . . .' His voice lost the irony, became serious. 'And since the killing occurred within the jurisdiction of the Khedive, I demand that the trial take place in El Iskandryia.'

Senator Liz shook her head. 'Absurd,' she said. 'We have to change the location. You cannot expect us to work in these conditions . . .'

'I don't remember anyone asking you to work on this at all.' Wrap-round dark glasses were turned to the woman. The other two he'd chosen. The Senator was different, she'd practically demanded to sit on the Grand Jury.

Actually, there was no 'practically' about it.

On her breath Raf could smell gin, while a none-too-subtle miasma of sweat rose from her compact body. If von Bismarck and St Cloud could manage to bathe in cold rainwater, then so could she.

'Your Excellency,' said Ernst von B, 'Senator Liz has a point. It will not be easy . . .' The young German spoke slowly, in schoolboy Arabic, supposedly out of respect for Ashraf Bey's position as *magister*, though Raf suspected his real reason was to annoy the woman, who spoke no languages other than her own.

'Nothing is ever easy. But the decision is made.' Raf stood up from his chair. And it was his chair because they were in his office. His was the name engraved on an absurdly long brass plate on the door. *His Excellency Pashazade Ashraf Bey, Colonel Ashraf al-Mansur, Chief of Detectives*.

He'd told his assistant a plastic nameplate was fine but that wasn't how things were done in El Iskandryia. The long plaque had turned up the day after Raf took the job, and once a week, on Thursdays, a Cypriot woman from maintenance came up from the ground floor to polish the sign.

'Excellency?'

Raf turned to find that St Cloud stood next to him, leaning on a cane with a silver top.

'You *were* joking about those steps, the accidents . . . I have your word this trial will actually take place?'

Raf nodded. 'You do.'

The trial would happen and it would happen soon. In all probability the defendant, one Hamzah Effendi, would be convicted. Raf just wished Hamzah wasn't father to the girl he should have married.

CHAPTER 1

18th October

Nine days before the Grand Jury met in an upstairs office at Champollion Precinct, Ashraf Bey sat through a warm Iskandryian evening, bombed out of his skull, at a pavement table outside Le Trianon, drinking cappuccino and listening to DJ Avatar wreak havoc on the words of a Greek philosopher.

The afternoon call to prayer had finished echoing from the mosque on Boulevard Saad Zaghloul and the bells from l'Eglise Copte had yet to begin. If it hadn't been for a sense of dread hanging over El Iskandryia, this could have been a Monday in October like any other.

Horse-drawn calèches, their brasses shined and wheel bosses polished, rumbled up the Corniche, from the fat seawall known as the Silsileh all the way north to Fort Qaitbey, where the ancient Pharos lighthouse once stood.

And at both ends of the sweeping Corniche, at Silsileh in the shadow of Iskandryia's famous library, and at Fort Qaitbey, groups of tourists watched as fishermen set hooks or mended and untangled nets, waiting for the evening tide.

It was a tourist who'd taken the taxi that stopped outside Le Trianon, with its window down and sound system up too loud, giving Raf the chance to hear the city's favourite DJ one more time.

'And remember . . .' Avatar's voice was street raw. 'Rust never sleeps. Coming at you from the wrong side of those tracks, this for the Daddy, the Don . . .'

Most of Raf's officers thought DJ Avatar came up with *SpitNoWhere* on his own; if they thought at all, which Raf considered unlikely. So they happily stamped the corridors at Police HQ, humming along, not knowing that the unchopped original went, 'In a rich man's house, there's nowhere to spit but his face.'

Raf hadn't known that, at least not until recently, but the fox in his head did. And while the fox couldn't say why, the General's *aide de camp* had just delivered to Raf an engraving of hell, inscribed with the words, *'At its centre hell is not hot.'* It had at least been able to identify the picture as late Victorian, unquestionably by Gustave Doré . . .

'. . . ou know,' said the fox, before all this happened. *'. . . ese things, they occur.'*

The fox had a grin like the Cheshire cat, except that no cat ever owned so many teeth or carried its tail wrapped up round its shoulders like a stole. Come to that, few cats took afternoon tea at Le Trianon.

These things could have been Raf becoming Chief of Detectives by default, or his recent refusal to marry the daughter of a billionaire.

'Why?' Raf asked. *'Why* do they occur?'

But the fox didn't answer.

Sighing, Raf took a gulp of cold cappuccino to wash away the taste of cheap speed and fixed his gaze on the pedestrians who streamed past his café table, separated from the terrace where he sat by a silk rope and the assiduous attention of two bodyguards.

The only pedestrians to meet Raf's stare were those, mainly tourists, who didn't realize who he was. They just saw a blond young man in dark glasses, wearing an oddly old-fashioned suit, the kind with a high collar.

'Come on,' said Raf, searching inside his head. 'You can tell me.'

He ignored his two guards, who looked at each other, then hurriedly looked away. Raf didn't doubt that they could see tears trickling from under his glasses, but he didn't much care either.

The fox was saying good-bye.

The beast had been dying for years. Its abilities limited by memory conflicts, failed backup and the fact that, these days, the animal could only feed on neon light.

Once Tiri had been state of the art. Feeding on daylight, infrared and ultraviolet, or so it told Raf. White light, black light – back then anything went. The fox sharpened Raf's reflexes, steadied his nerves and gave him good advice. It was what Raf had instead of parents . . .

A small ceramic box set into his skull behind one ear which kept him sane, sort of, and gave him a definable centre. And once, when Raf was very young and in another country, it had helped him walk out across a steel beam through flames and crumbling walls.

Only life wasn't simple; because the fox, of course, refused to admit that it existed. The fox's view was that Raf had a number of unresolved issues.

'Your Excellency . . . ?'

Someone hovered at his shoulder.

'Go,' said Raf and the waiter went, grateful to have been waved away.

Raf went back to watching the tourists who fed from Place Saad Zaghloul, and headed south down Rue Missala, searching for bars and theatres or just in a hurry to get back to their hotels.

After a hundred and eleven days in the city, Raf could now identify tourist groups as clearly as if they wore labels: waddling Austrians, dark-haired Frenchmen, the odd bunch of shore-leave Soviets in mufti and, rarer still, an occasional pink-skinned Englishwoman with silk scarf and sensible shoes. But mostly Iskandryia got nice couples, as befitted a famously romantic city.

The fuck-me singles, with their piercings, tattoos and trailer chic, came out only after dark, and then only in closely defined areas. Places like PeshVille, where Scandinavian kids hosed lines of coke off toilet rims, while girls shuffled, in darkened corners, on the unzipped laps of boys too blasted to know they weren't safely hiding out in student halls back home.

But that wasn't really Iskandryia, just how it went, with the limo-delivered international DJs as interchangeable as the clientele. It could have been Curitiba or Berlin, Punta del Este or Kota Baru. And anyway those clubs weren't Raf's business. The tourist police dealt with that stuff.

'You in there?'

Raf counted off the seconds, listening carefully for an echo inside his head. One winter night, when he was maybe ten and feeling sorry for himself, something that happened less often than Raf remembered, he'd asked the fox if he (Raf that was) had a soul . . . And the fox had gone all silent.

That was the weekend Raf refused to go to chapel. For five weeks he'd been made to run round a field in the sleet at the back of his school, while the others sang hymns in the dry. And the fox's only comment, months later, had been to point out that he should have waited until summer to lose his faith.

Maybe it was one of his schools that first put the fox in his head. Or perhaps it was his mother. Alternatively, just maybe the fox was right and it didn't exist, maybe it had never existed outside of Raf's imagination.

Raf sighed. 'Do I get an answer?' he demanded. 'Or do I sit talking to myself like an idiot?'

'Your Excellency?' It was the maître d' this time. Raf tried to wave away the thin man but the maître d' stayed rooted to the spot, urgency winning out over embarrassment. 'The General is on the line from New York . . .' In his hand the man held an old-fashioned telephone. 'He says it's very urgent.'

Raf shook his head and almost laughed as shock flooded the maître d's face. No one refused to talk to General Saeed Koenig Pasha, not even His Excellency Ashraf Bey.

'What do I tell him?' The maître d' begged frantically.

Raf thought about how to answer for so long that the thin man holding the telephone actually began to squirm with agitation.

'I know,' said Raf finally. 'Tell him my fox is dying.'

CHAPTER 2

An early tram rattled up Rue Moharrem Bey towards Misr Station, jinked around the silent taxi rank at Place Gumhuriya and continued west along Boulevard Sherif, passing the open front door of the al-Mansur madersa.

On the madersa's second floor, in a small room in the haremlek, a nine-year-old girl, nicknamed Hani, slept badly while a Catholic cook watched over her. The cook spoke just enough Arabic for her closest friend to be the skeletal Sudanese porter who sat, cross-legged, on worn stone steps at the front of the house talking slowly into an ancient cell phone.

'Yes, Hamzah Effendi,' he said, watching the almost empty tram go by. 'I know where His Excellency is. He's still at Le Trianon.' Khartoum listened again. 'Wrestling with evil djinn,' he answered and broke the connection.

Two of the tram's fares were tourists late home to bed, the other three Iskandryian, headed to work. A short-order cook, a chambermaid, a stall holder from a minor souk. Travel was cheap in the city. For most of those who worked in the service industries it needed to be.

At some hours of the day gulls could be heard everywhere across the city, but this early in the morning they circled tightly over the Shambles, rabid for any entrails that might be tossed from gutting table to harbour.

Years before, when the women with their razor-edged filleting knives had been children, or maybe it was when their mothers had been children, the Khedive had declared it illegal to discard the guts and tailings of each night's catch. Every scrap not sold had to be ploughed into the barren edges of the delta to improve the soil. Then came the first flu epidemic and with too few *felaheen* to gather in crops that lay spoiling in the existing fields, increased maize yields ceased to matter. So now the entrails went back into the water.

And when the gulls finally dispersed and first light finished staining the horizon, the sun rose out beyond Glymconapoulo Bay and another Tuesday morning began.

Shutters were opened, doors unlocked. In red-brick tenements everywhere, middle-aged women looked at potbellied men and remembered dark-eyed boys, marriage vows and lost virginity. Men mourned the slim-hipped girls they'd married and, catching sight of themselves in the mirror, wondered how they'd never noticed they'd become someone else.

And on the edge of Glymconapoulo Bay, in a stuccoed villa as arrogant as any conquistador's palace, a barrel-chested industrialist turned off his phone, sighed heavily and picked up a revolver.

Again.

In front of Hamzah Effendi was a naked angel, wings spread wide and breasts full, like those of a distantly remembered mother. Except that the angel was pale and fair-haired and elegant, things untrue of anyone in his family.

She hovered within a page torn from a book, written in a language he couldn't read and inscribed on the back, *'Only here will you find peace'* and *'Apollyon.'* General Koenig Pasha had penned these in his immaculate copperplate just below a half title that read *'Divina Commedia di Dante Alighieri: Paradiso.'*

With the engraving came a gun. They were the governor's answer to Hamzah's desperate plea for help.

Shooting himself would ruin his looks, Hamzah knew that. Regretted it. A long succession of twentysomething mistresses had assured him that he had the dark eyes of a hunter, the mouth of a poet and the profile of an emperor: the founder of a dynasty, not one of those weaklings that came later, slope-chinned and nervous, the kind who got strangled with a golden rope as they slept.

Hamzah's chin jutted so proudly that the eye almost slid past his heavy jowls and neck. His face had a flabbiness now that business partners seldom recalled when they thought back to meeting him; somehow imperfections got forgotten, leaving only a memory of his strength.

A gulp from his crystal tumbler later, Hamzah put down the gun.

Again.

'Coward.'

Alcohol tells the truth. *'I didn't mean it,'* that's the lie. People do mean it, every time. Hamzah did, even if the person at which he swore was himself. Of course, he'd have preferred to bawl out Ashraf al-Mansur but the recently appointed Chief of Detectives wasn't taking calls.

Downing another gulp of neat Laphroaig, Hamzah topped up his glass and carefully hid the bottle in the bottom drawer of a burr-walnut desk. Alcohol was illegal in Iskandryia, except for tourists and in certain bars attached to the bigger international hotels, or unless one had written permission from the General. It was a prohibition of which Hamzah heartily approved since one small sliver of his diverse interests involved supplying illegal alcohol to illegal clubs, many of which he owned anyway.

There were no early memories for him of a high-breasted, thin-hipped girl. Any more than his wife had memories of a smouldering-eyed boy who turned her body to fire. Their marriage was arranged and the only thing odd about it was that, in theory at least, Hamzah did the arranging. Rahina's useless father had owed him a debt and she was part payment.

Hamzah would have preferred the money.

He wondered, but only briefly, how well his wife would cope as a widow. Maybe her life would be improved? Money would be no problem and Villa Hamzah had never been Rahina's first choice as a home, so his guess was that she'd leave the city entirely. Either, to live on a country estate in the delta or else move to Tunis or Algiers, where his disgrace might not follow her.

Hamzah ran through the checklist in his mind.

Will, signed and witnessed.

Accounts, doctored obviously; the real ones were bleached to NSA standards, overwritten and bleached again.

Deeds to the villa.

Share certificates . . . Those were mostly for Hamzah Enterprises, the Midas Refinery, Quitrimala Industries and the offshore and Sudanese oil fields. The French and the Germans had recently offered to buy him out, but any deal could be done with his executor.

Bank accounts, both known and previously hidden.

Suicide note. Words had always given Hamzah trouble. So he'd quoted from a poem he learnt once, long ago beside a river, when he was a boy. *'I loved you so I wrote my need across the night in stars . . .'* He'd probably got half of the words wrong, but they'd expect that.

Everything was in place for what came next. Shares in Hamzah Enterprises would dip on the Bourse but bounce back. Oil prices were rocketing and the Midas Refinery would continue turning crude to cash, whoever owned it. Only in the illegal clubs, brothels and dance halls would there be a fight for succession, and that would have happened someday, whatever . . .

The revolver he held stank of oil, which was his own fault. Every gap

282

in the previous week he'd spent cleaning and re-cleaning the .38, until the rifling shone metal-bright and the cylinder spun as cleanly as if the weapon was new rather than a hundred and twenty years old.

Now was the point for him to suck silence from its muzzle.

Only he couldn't.

He'd been maybe ten years old when he acquired his first gun. *Felaheen* back then didn't know their ages. Often they didn't know their families either. Some nights he'd wished he was one of them. But later he found excuses for the beatings as he tried to imagine what life must have been like for his uncle in Abu Simbel at the height of the little war, to be penniless, illiterate, with a dead wife, dead sister and a small nephew.

No, Hamzah shook his head slightly – children, responsibility, the past – those were places he wouldn't revisit. Because then he'd start thinking about . . .

Bite on darkness.

The revolver's handle looked odd, held upside down like that, with three of his fingers wrapped round its ivory stock and one curled tight across the trigger. All but one of the chambers were empty, because he'd only need the single bullet, the one waiting for the fall of the hammer.

Watch the knuckles whiten.

Every step of his life had been leading to this point. From a shack on the Nile's bank to a study panelled in pale English oak in a vast stone villa, on the edge of Glymconapoulo Bay. Symmetry was what his daughter Zara would have called it. Perhaps a paradigm. She was fond of big words and bad politics.

From nothing back to nothing.

Only he couldn't do it, for reasons as ugly as the reason he had to do it in the first place. All that was left for him was to accept what came.

Hamzah yanked the taste from his mouth, spun his study chair in a half circle and blasted the head off a taut-hipped marble girl with the blank eyes of a victim and the tight buttocks of a Renaissance catamite.

Flying splinters from her crystalline hairdo ricocheted off bombproof glass in the far window and splintered English oak panelling. Alarms exploded and before the marble dust had even begun to clear Hamzah could hear running footsteps in the corridor outside.

Alex would be upset. His wife would be furious. And her French chef would be quietly disapproving. The only one Hamzah cared about was Alex. Good bodyguards were hard to find in North Africa and he was going to need one.

'Boss.' The big Russian skidded to a halt, automatic already drawn and laser sight lit. A red dot danced across the walls, coming to rest when Hamzah's bodyguard realized the wrecked study was empty.

'Nothing to kill,' said Hamzah. 'Unless you want to slot her?' He jerked his heavy chin towards the damaged dryad and blinked as Alex blasted off first one arm, then another. Finishing with two rapid shots that took the statue off at her knees.

'Okay?'

'Yeah.' Hamzah coughed. 'Pretty good.'

The statue was a fake, a Victorian copy of a Renaissance original, provenanced from the Russell-Coates museum in Bournemouth, which apparently was a spa somewhere in England. Hamzah had loathed the carving on sight, buying it only when he realized how much it would upset his wife. She thought all statues were an abomination in the eyes of God, never mind naked ones, and still hadn't forgiven her husband for having his portrait painted.

'You bored, Boss?' The ex-Soviet *Spetsnaz* had taken in the empty glass on the table. 'You want maybe we should have some fun . . . Check out one of your clubs?'

'*What clubs?*' The small woman in the doorway glared at Hamzah's ruined statue, then at Hamzah. 'You told me you'd got rid of the clubs.'

Madame Rahina wore her wealth in gold bangles up both arms and in large sapphire earrings that made up in sheer worth for what they lacked in elegance. And even over the acrid dust, her cologne was heavy and obvious.

All her irritation was focused on her husband. Somewhere down life's journey from local schoolmaster's daughter to wife of a major industrialist she'd learned the essential Iskandryian art of walking into even the most crowded room and seeing only people who mattered.

Five years on, she was still smarting from the only time she'd been invited to one of the General's soirées and Koenig Pasha had chosen not to see her.

'Well?' demanded Madame Rahina. 'Did you sell the clubs or not?'

Hamzah nodded. Yeah, he'd sold them all right. To himself in another guise, then leased them straight back.

'Yes, of course I did.' Well, the *himself* in this case was actually a DJ called Avatar. Partly his choice of the boy was sentiment, and Hamzah knew he was sentimental (he'd yet to meet a gangster who wasn't), but mostly it was plain common sense. He'd needed to reward Avatar for an essential service the kid had performed three months earlier, one summer night near the beginning of July. When the shit was still waiting for someone to switch on the fan . . .

CHAPTER 3

7th July

At the eastern end of the city's sweeping Corniche, where the expensive Palladian villas built from imported limestone boasted gardens that reached down to the sea, a girl swam under a warm dome of summer stars.

She was naked and out of her head on redRiff. Which was better than a few years back when her crutch of choice had been amphetamine sulphate, the pharmaceutically pure kind dished out by the sort of diet clinic that double-checked your credit rating and forgot to measure your weight.

The blond man leaving the grandest of those villas had yet to notice her because he had other things on his mind, like being wanted for murder. But he would.

Inside the villa that Ashraf al-Mansur had just left, a boy tossed silver dreadlocks out of eyes that were angry and forgot about the flick-knife he'd been using to clean his nails.

Avatar had stolen that habit from an old film, but Hamzah already knew this. Recognizing his own faults in somebody younger either made for Hamzah's losing his temper or keeping it. He was working hard to keep his.

'Zara's out there. You got that?'

Hamzah Effendi nodded.

'And you know she's, like . . .'

Hamzah said nothing but, yes, he knew. She was naked. They were discussing Hamzah's only daughter, the one who was meant to be upstairs in bed, asleep. The girl who'd recently been dumped, very publicly, by the very man Hamzah had just sent down to the beach.

'Well . . . whatever.' It was Avatar's turn to shrug. Things he thought would worry the old man sometimes didn't . . . And things Av considered nothing often did. So the boy trod carefully but tried hard not to reveal the fact.

'You heard what Ashraf Bey said?' asked Hamzah, his voice hoarse with good cigars and better whisky.

Yeah, Avatar had.

'You believe him?'

The boy shrugged. How did he know who looked like a killer and who didn't . . . ? The bey was some blond-haired princeling, half Berber and half something *nasrani*; all silk suits and Armani shades. That put him way outside Avatar's frame of reference. Until Hamzah's daughter, in the early days of her 'Comrade Zara' phase, had tracked Av down and dragged him off the street, he'd thought sleeping in his own bit of doorway was posh.

'Me,' said Avatar, 'I believe nobody.'

Hamzah smiled.

Avatar had entered via a window seconds after Raf exited through the French doors, headed without knowing it towards the rocks where Zara swam, phosphorescence smoothing across her adolescent body like slipstream.

'Kamil . . .'

'DJ Avatar, Av, Avatar, 2Cool Kid,' the boy corrected his father without even thinking about it. The options tossed out machine-gun fast. He didn't answer to Kamil, any more than he used the door at Villa Hamzah. This last was his present to the man who sat on the other side of the desk.

Four years back – after Avatar had kicked her – Madame Rahina, the woman who very definitely wasn't his mother, had made her husband promise never to let Avatar through the door of Villa Hamzah again.

So Hamzah hadn't.

'Av . . .' Hamzah Effendi paused and picked a cigar. Remembering just in time to use a tiny gold guillotine to circumcise its end. A life's worth of biting off the end and spitting was a habit he found hard to break. Hamzah wanted to explain to Avatar exactly why he'd sent the bey out of that door, down to where his daughter swam naked: but he couldn't put *'needs must'* into words. At least not words he found acceptable. So instead, the big man took another pull on a Partegas and thought about his lawyer waiting nervously in the hallway.

He could wait. Whatever it was Avatar had come to say wouldn't take long.

'You need money?'

Avatar grinned. Of course he needed dosh. Didn't everyone? Apart from the industrialist who sat in front of him. All the same, that wasn't why Avatar was there.

'Some journalist's been asking about you . . .'

'A *nasrani*?' It had to be. Hamzah already kept most of the local press in his pocket, and the few who were not lapping up his hospitality missed out, not from any misplaced moral backbone but because he already had them by the balls.

'English. Well, probably. You know . . .'

Hamzah knew. It was unfashionable to say so, but telling one from another was difficult until *nasranis* started flashing round their passports or local currency.

'So let me guess.' The big man smiled and let cigar smoke trickle towards the ceiling, though the smile didn't reach his eyes and a breeze through the open window dissipated the smoke before it reached the height of a picture rail.

'Organized crime the Ottoman way?'

Avatar shook his head.

'Well it can't be the refinery because then they'd just go through my press office . . .' His refinery was situated to the west of Isk, at the point where slums met desert. In an industry working hard to improve its image, Midas Oil was an entire lap ahead. Bursaries, research grants, third-world scholarships, a whole marine-biology, antipollution programme at Rutgers.

Accidents got apologized for the moment they happened, critics were greeted with open arms, research papers were put to peer review and released, copyright free, straight onto the Web. It was a long-term game and, as Hamzah had hoped, it was driving even the softest ecological pressure groups insane.

'What then?'

'Your childhood . . .'

To the man's credit, Hamzah did little more than blink.

'Think you can deal with this?' Hamzah asked Avatar.

'Sure,' said Avatar. 'You want him killed?'

Hamzah raised his eyebrows, amusement driving out the last echoes of anger.

'No,' he said with a smile. 'I don't want him killed. Whatever you've heard, whatever the police whisper, that's not how I do things.'

Avatar looked for a brief second like he wanted to disagree. Then he shrugged. 'It's your party,' he said. And left without glancing back, exiting through a window larger than the front door of most of the places in which he'd lived.

CHAPTER 4

Sudan

'Safety off,' said the gun.

Standing beside Sergeant Ka, Zac said nothing. He'd spoken little enough when he was alive and now he was dead he talked even less . . .

Ka thought that strange, because Zac's sister Ruth had also said little from the time she'd been captured to the moment she died. But now she talked so much that Ka couldn't concentrate on watching the growling trucks that rolled across the scrub towards him.

'Distance?'

'Half a klick and closing . . .'

Status and range. That was all the plastic H&K/cw could manage. It was an incredibly stupid weapon and the boy with the bone cross, feather amulet and boots several sizes too big didn't know why the manufacturer had bothered.

There was meant to be some way to turn off the voice but to do that you needed to be able to read. So instead Ka had ripped the tail from his shirt and tied it to the stock, right over the little plastic grille behind which the speaker hid.

Before Ka began this mission, Colonel Abad had ordered him to be sure to check his weapons each morning. Then, when that was done, to inspect the weapons of the rest of his troop. Only there was no rest any longer. At least, Ka didn't think so.

He was it.

So Ka inspected his own weapons, trying to remember what he was meant to be looking for . . . Dirt, maybe, and rust. Except rust wasn't a problem because it hadn't rained in a year in this part of wherever he was, somewhere between Bahr el-Azrek and the At-barah. At least, that's where he thought he was.

Untying the lanyard that fastened a revolver around his neck, Ka checked it. It was as clean as any weapon could be in a country where most

288

of the earth had turned to red dust and half of that had been stripped away from the rock beneath. The revolver was his favourite. He'd have liked it even more if any of the bullets he carried in his truck had been the right calibre.

H&K21e clean and freshly oiled. Tripod fixed and belt ready. H&K/ cw . . . spotless. His knife wasn't clean but that was because Ezekiel's blood had ruined the leather of its handle. Everyone had warned Ezekiel not to pick up bomblets, but the boy was six and the cluster bombs came in red, green and yellow.

Ezekiel had always loved bright colours.

Their most junior soldier had been left under a blanket of stones where he died, on the side of a hill just below the cracked eggshell memorial to where a functioning mosque once stood. Ka had refused to kill the boy until the others stopped talking to him. He was the sergeant, they said. Stuff like that was his job. In the end, Ka had given in, gone back to where he'd rested Ezekiel in the shade of a broken wall and found the small boy already dead.

But he buried the blade deep and carried it back to camp to show them the deed was done. Things had been different after that. They all wanted to be with Ka but he no longer wanted to be with them.

Now he was alone, with his back to the empty village. Well, it was two villages really. One built from grey brick that looked heavy but turned out to be solid froth, like ossified spit. That version had been constructed ten years before by the government and destroyed by them as well, a few years later.

The older village was behind the new one, jammed into a space between the start of a hill and a scar of rock. But most of its mud-walled huts had fallen in, from age this time. According to the Colonel, there was no water for miles, what with the wadis drying up and the nearest bore hole being both barren and filled with corpses from an earlier battle.

Ka lifted his H&K/cw and snapped free the lower clip. It was loaded with 5.56mm, each kinetic round dipped in holy water and polished with snakeskin. His old AK49 had been altogether better, less flashy. But an older boy had wanted Ka's AK49 and given him the plastic gun in return. That boy was dead now. Ka didn't feel too bad about it.

CHAPTER 5

'You need to be here . . .'

Avatar's call came through as Hamzah was getting ready for bed. His wife was upstairs sleeping, and his daughter . . . Wherever Zara had gone after her swim, she'd taken her little F-type Jaguar and left a wet towel on the hall floor by way of good-bye.

'Where's here?'

'Sarahz . . . Corner of Place Gumhuriya.'

Hamzah knew exactly where the club was. There might be a dozen bars and restaurants he owned without knowing exactly where they were, but Sarahz had been one of his early acquisitions, maybe the first.

'I'm about to turn in.'

'Not now, you're not . . . Believe me, I've got something you'll want to see.'

Avatar put down the club's pay phone and went back to his decks. Building on a breakbeat *sambassimba* anthem that cut the heavy over-dub/techno fusion that was ol'sko drum'n'bass with lighter Sao Paolo rhythms, weirdshit polka, vicious Fender licks and syncopated snare.

'SpecialBeatService,' the near original PatifePorto mix.

He was working a late-Wednesday crowd, upstairs at Sarahz. Mostly poor little rich boys from St Mark's plus a handful of overdressed, hard-eyed kazuals from Moharrem Bey. The girls were tourists, mostly. A smattering of au pairs, exchange students, teenagers glad to get away from their distant families.

Avatar got the gig on merit. The manager didn't know his new DJ was the bastard of Hamzah Effendi. Until ten minutes ago, Amici hadn't known that his club was owned by Avatar's father – and he was still getting over that shock.

*

Hamzah sighed and pushed himself up off his *bateau lit*. The mahogany bed had been imported eighty years earlier from Marseilles, found the previous year in a souk in El Gomruk and repaired for Hamzah by a sullen carpenter from Mali who spat, chain-smoked and forgot to wash but had the hands of an angel and the eye of an Italian polymath.

Hamzah forgave the carpenter his bad habits because he actually made things by hand, instead of using machines. Madame Rahina hated the *bateau lit* but that was fine. As Hamzah frequently pointed out, nothing required her to sleep in it.

Habit had made such things easy for them; and Hamzah's practice of working late justified his need for a bed in the room off his study.

Within the standards set by culture and religion, he was a good husband and he tried to be a good father. He'd never once raised his hand to his daughter and had only occasionally slapped his wife, and that not recently.

It would never occur to him to hit his mistress, but then Olga used to assassinate Americans for a living, in the days before she came to work as his PA. Olga was *Organizatsiaya* and also a Soviet spy, but she knew that Hamzah knew, and they both understood that Commissar Zukov at the Soviet Consulate now required little more than a daily report on Hamzah's movements.

Tomorrow she'd report that, after a good breakfast, he voluntarily presented himself at Champollion Precinct, the Police HQ in Rue Riyad Pasha, to be questioned about the murder of Lady Nafisa, aunt of Ashraf Bey. She'd mention that he'd taken his lawyer and been released without charge . . . Because Hamzah would be released, that was why he kept tame lawyers.

Quite apart from the fact that, for once, he was totally innocent.

Hamzah hit a button beside his bed and waited.

'Boss?'

'I'm going out.'

'Very good. I'll get the car.'

It was obvious which vehicle Alex would select. Hamzah's Rolls-Royce Silver Ghost. Like Olga, Alex was Soviet and so, bizarrely, was the Rolls. At least its modifications were . . .

'If you're ready, Boss.' The big man slammed shut the rear door and Hamzah felt, rather than heard, the solidness of bombproof steel and a thud as heavy locks slid into place. The car was originally built for Lenin, one of six that the revolutionary leader ordered from London when the fledgling Menshevik Alliance was at its lowest ebb.

With Cossacks advancing from the Crimea and Siberia already lost to Admiral Kolchak, Vladimir Illych had ordered his secretary's secretary to write to Charles Rolls ordering six models of his latest car, the cars to be paid for in advance, in gold. Three weeks later, the British PM reluctantly agreed to the dismemberment of the old Tsarist empire . . . Prussia, France and America followed.

Hamzah had purchased the vehicle at Commissar Zukov's suggestion during one of the CCCP's habitual bouts of bankruptcy. And had spent the first six months having various illegal listening devices taken out. Alex had come with the vehicle.

'We got trouble, Boss?'

Good question. And if he did have trouble, was it the kind that mattered? Hamzah hired people to keep trouble at arm's length but Avatar wasn't one of them. The boy was grief of a different kind.

'Let's find out,' said Hamzah and leant back against black leather, remembering the boy's mother, a dark-skinned slip of a girl who spoke three languages and didn't know her own age. Hamzah did, knew it to the very month, but never admitted it, except occasionally to himself.

Rammed was how tourists described Sarahz. Rammed to the rafters, to the gills, rammed tight. The same thing happened every Wednesday, the El Anfushi clubs closed up and hardcore clubbers headed south looking for the real thing. Sarahz gave it to them. Neo retro, classic house, random darkwave . . . even trance, so epiphanic it came with a built-in halo. Chemical sainthood.

And DJ Avatar bestowed the radiance, from battered Matsui decks that had been rebuilt so many times that the only original component left was a cheap plastic logo glue-gunned to the front. Av learnt fast. His first real sound system comprised a triple deck, reconditioned 303 and original theramin. The lot got ripped off his second week playing clubs, at some cellar behind Maritime Station.

Now he had a deck that looked shit and sounded like it was wired direct to God. And when he wasn't riding his Wild Star, Avatar drove an old VW camper with one side caved in from front arch to rear fender. Prayer beads hung from the front mirror and the back window was stickered with quotations from the Holy Quran. No one looked twice. Certainly no one looked and thought, 'Ah, there goes enough rare vinyl to open a shop.'

Which was the point, obviously.

Sarahz had an all-night licence. The result of astute blackmail, a little bribery and the impossibly convenient fact that it was directly opposite

Misr Station, with a huge taxi rank to one side and Place Gumhuriya to the front. Since the nearest apartment block was a hundred metres away and inhabited by people who really didn't matter, there were no complaints. At least none that made it onto the record books.

'*D'bozzizzere* . . .'

Which Avatar quickly translated as, 'The Boss is here . . .'

Nodding, Avatar killed the lights in his booth and slid a disc into one slot and a slab of samples into another and put the deck on auto. He didn't figure on being gone longer than it took to build up and break down and, to be honest, most of the floor were so caned it was doubtful they'd even notice.

'Out of here,' he told his throat mike and heard an acknowledgment through his earbead. If whatever looked like taking longer than it should, Smugs would work the crowd. Smugs was a house regular, ten years older than Avatar, with half the following. Av tolerated the other guy's lack of skill and in return Smugs didn't object to Avatar claiming the decks when fancy took him.

'On the roof,' said the manager as Av unlocked the booth's rear wall and stepped into a darkened corridor. All shaved skull, pearl stud and shiny black suit, Carlo Amici stood back politely and Avatar sighed. This afternoon the man had regarded Av as a lower form of life, some kid who got overpaid for pushing buttons and spouting crap. Now, suddenly, he'd discovered that Av had a direct line to Hamzah.

There went another good gig.

'I'll find my own way up,' said Avatar, heading for a steel door.

'You could use the lift . . .'

'No, this is quicker.' Cooler too, more in keeping, though Avatar didn't mention that.

The fire escape brought Avatar out on a flat roof that overlooked a darkened square. Over on the far corner of the roof, a small man was lashed to a radio aerial. The aerial was illegal but, equally obviously, no goons from Radio Authority came by with angle grinders and chopped $15,000 of pirate transmitter into metal spaghetti as happened in other clubs. Next to the naked journalist stood Hamzah Effendi, elegant in Homburg arid camel-hair coat.

'Old man.' Avatar stepped out of the darkness.

Hamzah smiled and held out a hand. The big man's grip was firm but controlled. What he offered was a greeting, not a test of strength.

Avatar was being publicly acknowledged in front of Alex, Carlo Amici and a couple of the doormen. Without wanting to be ungrateful, he did wonder why . . .

'Okay,' said Hamzah, 'I'm here. Who's this . . . ?'

'Remember the shitweasel I was talking about . . .' The boy nodded towards the naked man. 'His name's Mike Estelle. He came in earlier, still asking questions. So I figured it might be a good idea if you two actually met. You know, socially . . .'

'You did this to him?'

'Did what?' Avatar looked at the quivering Englishman who was lashed to the mast by his testicles. There wasn't a bruise on the man. And the only blood came from where the little shit had chewed out the inside of his own mouth.

'I barely touched him . . .'

Hamzah smiled. 'You,' he said to the man. 'Here I am. You want to tell me what this is about?'

A sniffling silence was Hamzah's only answer. Sniffling silence and frightened eyes that stared back, wide and defenceless. Well, Hamzah had news for the Englishman. Defencelessness didn't impress him and it certainly didn't punch any buttons.

'No questions?' Hamzah sighed. 'Your choice . . . Throw him off the roof,' Hamzah ordered in English, turning away.

The rising thud of a bass loop from the floor below mixed neatly with Mike Estelle's rising scream. And apart from Alex, only Avatar saw the tiny, sideways chop of Hamzah's hand, which negated the order.

'You hear me?' Hamzah demanded crossly. 'Do it now.'

'Sure, Boss. Sorry, Boss.' Alex produced an evil-looking pair of pliers from his pocket. 'Let me just snip this wire.'

Between them, Avatar and Alex freed the struggling journalist and dragged him to the edge of the roof. The fall was barely twenty feet but the ground below was concrete.

'He should be dressed,' Avatar said suddenly. 'Less suspicious.'

'No,' said Alex, voice casual. 'Foreign tourist gets blasted, weirds out and jumps from club roof. Check out the local newsfeed. Happens all the time . . .

'Yeah, really,' he added, seeing Avatar's doubtful look. 'Besides, no problem, the Boss will tell the police what to decide . . .' Alex began running the sobbing man backward and forward, like an athlete limbering up for some Olympic event. 'Okay,' he said to Avatar. 'You ready?'

That was when the *nasrani* shat himself.

Hamzah sighed. 'Okay,' he said heavily. 'Let's try it a different way.' He took a fresh Partegas from his pocket and paused as both doormen bounced forward with lighters. Waving them away, Hamzah bit off one end and spat it over the edge. Only then did he nod to the one nearest.

'Last chance,' Hamzah told the journalist. 'My name is Hamzah

Effendi. I own the company that owns this club. I also own an oil field, the Midas processing plant and a shipping line. All this you can get from any trade directory . . . So tell me, who sent you and what do they really want to know?'

CHAPTER 6

Sudan

Sergeant Ka turned towards the truth and raised a fist above his head in formal salute:

> *I will ascend to heaven.*
> *I will raise my throne above the stars.*
> *I will sit on the mount of assembly . . .*

Before the silver talisman he wore around his neck became an amulet, it was briefly a bride piece in a dusty city with empty streets and a broken-down bazaar. South of the city lived the Dinka, cattle people, who once roamed the cracked earth between here and the upland forest, where fever trees glow and scrub lies lifeless, until rains come and the underbrush explodes.

Originally, the talisman was recognizable as a Maria Theresa dollar, but the touch of a thousand hands had worn it flat. The coin, however, was never Austrian. It was minted in Stambul, a hundred years after the empress died, at a time when silver dollars were a common currency in the Sahara, Arabia, and the Sudan.

Having been taken south as payment for slaves, the coin become a bride price before coming north again, around the neck of a child who stabbed the grandson of the Dinka who originally received it in marriage.

She used a blade because that day's bullet ration was gone . . . Later, she swapped the talisman for a bone crucifix taken from a nun; but that was months later, long after the little war started in Abu Simbel. Mostly Ka avoided thinking about the little war and how he became a soldier.

And sometimes he forgot.

Before Ka was a soldier, he was a camel boy, which was an easy job and one he liked. Foreigners came by gleaming barge to the great temple and he and boys like him led them by camel up the thorny slope from the river's edge to the foot of the cliffs, where great carvings had stood undisturbed for well over three thousand years.

Back then, Ka wore tattered shorts and no top or shoes, because that way the tips were better. Once he'd worn a Pepsi T-shirt and a pair of Nikes that a pink-skinned girl had left behind and hardly any of the foreigners chose him. They rode with the barefooted boys.

He'd have learnt his lesson from this, even without the beating he got from his uncle. Next day, Ka went back to no shirt or shoes. He also began to listen to the guides when they were too busy to notice.

Soon he knew all the best stories about the great king and his wife. He could explain why the four big statues all wore the double crown of Upper and Lower Egypt, while inside the cliffs, in the darkness of the inner chamber, the king wore only the white crown of Upper Egypt or the red crown of Lower Egypt, depending on whether he was in the northern or southern part of the temple.

And he learnt what interested the foreigners, those people who wasted water as if it was endless. Who washed under flowing showers, shat in unused water and giggled as they tipped full bottles over their heads and let clean water drain away into the dust.

He told them of kings marrying their daughters, brothers sleeping with sisters, mothers with sons. It kept the magic sacred, kept the river flowing and renewed the dark silt that lined the banks and fed the kingdom, but he didn't explain that. The reasons were never as important to the nasrani as the actions themselves.

When Ka told of battles where the king's army collected testicles to help his scribes count the number of captured, the men would look sick and the bareheaded women either quizzical or appalled. And Ka would smile and look happy when they tipped him, pretending to be surprised. As if he'd spend his whole morning telling them tales just because he loved foreigners.

No one loved the foreigners, not really. Except, maybe, the government because they brought in francs, marks and American dollars. The poor, the felaheen, would rather the foreigners didn't wander unasked into mosques, still wearing their shoes, that they didn't choke the desert roads with coaches that threw dust into the faces of those walking and, most of all, that they didn't need endless hotels along the river, because now the areas richest in silt were closed to those who used to sharecrop them and landlords got their money from the tourists instead.

In one month, at the start of the little war, the army beat to death forty-eight people because they came from a distant village where the headman's son had gunned down five foreign tourists. Forty-eight for five. That was the exchange rate.

The son, Samir, whose name meant one whose conversation in the evening is lively, but who was never heard to say more than two words together, lived away from his father's village in a brick house on a rocky islet somewhere unimportant between Aswan and Wadi el-Sebua. He was a strange man, educated first at a local school and then at el-Azhar College in Al Qahirah. He left el-Azhar to work for the Société de Géographie d'Egypte, only to leave that in turn a few months later.

After his reappearance near the village, Samir adopted a family of ungainly chicken-sized birds. There was nothing very special about the birds other than the fact that they lived in a reed bed and were entirely purple, except for their stiltlike legs, which were pink. They weren't even rare.

Before he died under torture, Samir was questioned by a major from the Al Qahirah military police. The local police were happy to do the job themselves but had been ordered to leave the job to an expert. One reason, some suggested, for their lack of action after the dead Samir's cousins ambushed the major's car, shot dead his eighteen-year-old driver and cut off the major's hands, then beat him to death.

By then, the disc of Samir's questioning was on its way to regional HQ at Aswan for transcription and analysis. It made no sense at all.

Splashing water, that came fast. The clank of something, probably an empty bucket hitting a concrete floor. A slap. Another slap.

'I'm asking you again. When did you join the Sword of God?'

'Never. I'm not a member.'

'Then why kill foreign tourists?'

The sound of a ragged sigh. Part pain, part exasperation.

'They shot the gallinule . . .'

'The tourists?'

'No, the contractors. They cut down the acacia, grubbed up the tamarisk and shot my . . .'

A thud, leather on flesh.

'NO, WAIT.' The voice is foreign, the accent atrocious. Whoever is wielding the whip, they do what they're told. Silence follows.

'You want me to believe you shot five tourists because contractors killed a few wading birds?'

'The river doesn't need another hotel and it doesn't need more tourists. Besides, the birds were there first.'

'So you are Sword of God.'

'No, I'm an ornithologist . . .'

That was the start of the little war, which lasted a month. The big war came afterwards and went on for much longer, but Sergeant Ka never quite worked out who the government were fighting. No one important, obviously. And most of the fighting wasn't in Egypt anyway, it was in Sudan.

The little war, which was what his uncle called it, didn't seem so little once the tourists stopped coming to Abu Simbel and the soldiers arrived. Inside of forty-eight hours the whole of Ka's village had been rounded up and marched into the desert. Only a handful of adults survived the first week's march. Most died of heat or succumbed to the cold at night. Very few made it into the second week to reach the holding pen at El Khaschab.

Ka's uncle was one of those. With his wife, parents and own son already dead in another place, the man no longer believed in God, only this lack of belief was so shocking that all Ka's uncle registered was an emptiness as his midday prayers escaped between parched lips and ascended to a silent heaven.

Above him the same cruel sun that turned half-fertile earth to dust and killed the crops in the year Ka was born blistered his skin. A swarm of freshly hatched flies draped his shoulders like a heavy mantle but he hardly noticed them. Just as he failed to notice the watching boy or the white-plumed vultures that hopped and shuffled through the dirt, a handbreath away.

They are excluded by a single question. Should he shoot himself or should he shoot his nephew. With only one bullet remaining, it was impossible to do both . . .

CHAPTER 7

Zara got arrested for indecency on the 28th July. The first Hamzah knew of it was a day later, from a local paper. Front page, single column.

Rebel Daughter Restrained.

Since Hamzah relied on bribes, blackmail and his fearsome reputation to ensure such things never happened, never mind got reported, he was obviously furious: particularly since the shot used in *Iskandryia Today* showed his daughter crop-haired and naked under a tight coat.

It would be fair to say that he was also troubled. The police were paid handsomely to leave anything that might connect to Zara or her friends well alone.

So far as Hamzah was concerned, *leaving alone* meant not arresting his daughter at some illegal/political dance club. And if the Club de Hashishan really was hers, and the police were probably right about that, then that was even more reason for letting things be.

Unfortunately, the offending picture of Zara turned up again, slightly larger in *Iskandryia on Sunday*. This was the paper that his daughter had just tossed in the bin, before stamping out of his marble-and-red sandstone office . . .

'Well,' said Olga Kaminsky, 'you deserved that.' Hamzah saw her smile as she removed Zara's cup from his desk and wiped away icing sugar with one easy sweep of a linen napkin.

Stating the obvious to Hamzah was living dangerously, but he paid Olga to tell him the truth and so Olga did. Besides, he was too shocked to fire her. Which he did about once a month, only to say nothing when she turned up the following day, as if their fight had never taken place.

Another PA might have convinced herself that this was because he prized her opinion, that the unusual leeway he gave her had nothing to do with those half dozen occasions each year when he took her to bed, but he knew Olga lied neither to him nor to herself. All the same, their relationship wasn't based on anything as simple as sex.

It was her lack of avarice that first captured his imagination. Other mistresses had taken the diamond chains he offered, the Cartier watches, the inevitable mink. Olga took nothing but her salary and returned every gift, opened but unused. She seemed to want nothing from him but his company and, occasionally, his presence in her bed. And it was *her* bed, a single one with metal frame, because she'd refused his offer of a flat as well.

'Olga, where did I go wrong?' Hamzah's grin was rueful but admiring. There couldn't be another daughter in Iskandryia who'd stamp unannounced into her father's HQ, spin on the spot and slip off her jacket to show her naked back, lash marks and all, when asked why she refused to come home.

But then, daughter and mother had never been close. And it hadn't helped that Rahina's only advice to Zara before her abortive engagement to Ashraf Bey was, 'Never undress in front of your husband.'

If Hamzah could have stopped the whippings, he would have done so years back; but mothers dealt with daughters and fathers with sons. And his boast that he'd never lifted his hand to Zara lost out to the fact he'd never actually raised his voice to protect her either. Tradition strangled him, Hamzah knew that. Under the silk shirt and Gucci suit he was still a *felaheen* at heart.

Zara, however, was not a *felaheen* daughter. Proper schools, two years in New York and a career at the Bibliotheka Iskandryia had seen to that. She was brave, beautiful and smitten with Ashraf Bey, although Hamzah was prepared to bet almost anything she hadn't let Raf know that.

He understood what drove his daughter. What was even weirder, he actually admired her while knowing full well it was meant to be the other way round.

'Olga, I've got a problem . . .'

Her laugh was instinctive. 'You've got lots of—' Then she stopped. 'You mean you've got a problem I don't know about?' Olga paused in the doorway, then quietly came back to where Hamzah sat. She didn't perch on the edge of his desk or casually grab a chair and straddle it. She waited for Hamzah to nod towards a leather sofa. And when she sat it was elegantly, with her stockinged legs crossed at the ankle.

Hamzah wondered what Olga saw when she looked at him. A filthy capitalist? A self-deluded gangster? A parvenu so desperate for baubles he bought his own title? Or a father unable to safeguard a daughter who refused all protection?

'Okay,' said Olga briskly. 'Problems I do know about . . . Your daughter's been busted by the *morales* for running an illegal club. She's in love with some spoilt little princeling who doesn't know his arse from his elbow. There are rumours of a strike at the refinery. And, despite a full and frank talk, someone's still asking around about your childhood, according to Kamil . . .'

'Avatar,' Hamzah corrected, without even thinking about it. 'He calls himself DJ Avatar.'

'Whatever. He could still become a problem . . .'

'No,' said Hamzah. 'Ashraf Bey's a problem. Avatar just wishes he was.'

'You believe the bey's for real?'

'I know he is,' Hamzah said heavily. 'And he's a trained killer, government issue . . . A bit damaged round the edges but still under guarantee.' The big man laughed. 'Well, that was how he described himself.'

'And you actually *wanted* this man to marry your daughter?'

'*I want*,' Hamzah corrected her. 'More than want, *I need* this man to marry Zara.'

'I see,' said Olga. 'Can I ask why?'

Hamzah shook his head. There were, in his experience, immutable laws about how fathers felt regarding the suitors who sent flowers and elegant cards to their daughters. The first feeling of hatred gave way to one of regret. Third, and finally, came loss as the daughter became a woman. So was it written.

Laws, equally immutable, governed the behaviour, if not the actual feelings, of those courted. Whoever came calling, daughters pretended to despise them. Presents were returned unopened, letters sent back unread. Mashrabiya shutters were slammed tight against each and every serenade. No touch was sought or permitted.

Yet Hamzah knew beyond doubt that his own daughter had spent a night with this man. And while he should have been furious, he was merely worried and oddly sad. It was hard to know if his tenderness for Zara and her willingness to turn to him was a sign of success or proof of failure.

And beyond these things he barely ever thought about, like his own feelings, was a real threat to his wealth, his happiness and to his own and Zara's lives. Because when Iskandryian newsfeeds began running stories they shouldn't and the police stopped contacting him at the first sign of trouble then the threat was real.

Someone somewhere reckoned they could change the balance of power.

'Look,' said Hamzah, relenting slightly. 'At its most basic, I need Ashraf to marry Zara to give her protection . . . Protection I may not be able to provide for much longer. And if she doesn't marry the bey, I have to find someone else. The big problem is that I may not have time.'

Behind her heavy spectacles, Olga's blue eyes were large. She understood exactly what he was saying. If Hamzah could no longer protect his daughter, then he couldn't protect her either. If he couldn't protect her, then what hope had he of protecting the refinery, Hamzah Enterprises or any other of the myriad shells within shells making up the story that justified the last thirty years of his life . . .

'Have you upset the General?'

'No.' Hamzah shook his head. He and Koenig Pasha had a better understanding than most people realized. All the General required of Hamzah was that he recognize who was in charge of El Iskandryia, which, wasn't the young Khedive and wasn't him. In return, the General kept Interpol at bay, played Washington's investigators off against those from Moscow, and shamelessly ignored or flattered Paris.

'Tell me,' said Hamzah, 'is there such a thing as a normal childhood?'

'No,' Olga replied immediately.

'Then, even allowing for the fact no one has a normal childhood,' said Hamzah, 'mine was different.'

Standing up from his desk, he walked to a window, leant out and watched a sweeper in the playground of St Mark's College. The fact that Hamzah's marble-and-red sandstone office was built next door to the college was not an accident.

He'd worked the kitchens at St Mark's, long ago, when he first arrived in the city. The name *Hamzah* came from a faded board listing every pupil killed in the war of 1914–15. The *Quitrimala* that became his surname was borrowed from the gilded spine of a book in the library.

He wasn't meant to leave the kitchens but no one saw a young boy in a jellaba with a split broom in one hand and a dustpan in the other. To the pupils and masters of St Mark's, Hamzah was so invisible that he might as well have been made from glass.

No one would ever look through Zara.

'Follow her,' Hamzah demanded.

'Me?' Olga sounded surprised.

The thickset man briefly considered that option. There were advantages but the disadvantages were greater. 'No,' he said, 'get someone from security. Have them report back every five minutes.'

At noon Hamzah received a report that Zara had been admitted to the General's house and had seen not the General but the young Khedive himself. Two hours later she was shopping for children's clothes accompanied by a small girl, described as anxious and scrawny. The child had just demanded a haircut, one enough like Zara's own for them to be taken for sisters.

At six, both Zara and Raf's niece Hani were being driven aimlessly back and forth along the Corniche in a calèche, one of those open-top, horse-drawn carriages loved by tourists. Shortly after that, they disappeared through the door of a warehouse at the back of an old market near Rue Tatwig.

A quick and dirty skim through the land registry revealed that it was owned by a holding company. An even dirtier skim anchored the ownership to Madame Sosostris, a known agent of the *Thiergarten*, Berlin's infamous intelligence service. An organization with whom Koenig Pasha was believed to have close, if occasionally fractious, links.

But it was only when Zara was joined by Lady Jalila, wife of the Chief of Police, aunt to Hani and cousin to a woman Ashraf Bey was rumoured to have murdered, that Hamzah began to get really worried.

CHAPTER 8

Sudan

'Don't be ridiculous.'

'I'm not.'

'Yes, you are . . .'

It was Zac who came up with the idea of turning off the river, a few days after antiquated F-111s bombed Masouf Hospital with his brother inside.

Ka had found a small radio and a pair of spectacles. The radio was one of those old, windup things made of blue plastic. Like the spectacles, its case was cracked, and the dial didn't work too well, but it still got Radio Freedom, which was the government, and Radio Liberty, which wasn't . . .

An old woman was talking about war. She sounded cross and upset. Close to tears. She didn't think the hospital had been an arms depot at all, she thought it was a hospital.

Did she have any proof she was right?

Did anyone have any proof that she wasn't?

How long did Madame Ambassador think the war would go on? The woman asking all the questions was younger, her voice brittle.

'As long as there's water to be fought over,' replied the old woman tiredly. 'As long as . . .'

'. . . the Nile flows,' Zac repeated, for about the fifth time. 'That's what she said.'

'Rivers aren't taps,' said Sarah, flicking long black braids out of her eyes. Being reasonably open to new ideas, Sarah wasn't contemptuous like Saul, just doubtful. She looked across their small campfire to where the sergeant sat, and casually asked Ka what they were all wondering . . .

'What do you think?'

It was Ka's job to know.

'Well' – Ka poked at the embers with a stick, sending sparks flicking

skywards – 'rivers get bigger, right, Saul?' That was what he remembered being told.

Saul shrugged. He was older than Ka and bigger, only not as clever. And Saul wasn't his real name any more than Sarah was Sarah or Bec was actually Rebecca. But they'd fought with Ras Michael and those were their given names. The shoulder patches might have changed after they swapped sides at Aswan, yet the biblicals had stuck. Mostly because they'd been with Ras Michael for so long their original names were lost.

'Gets bigger? Says who?' Bec's voice sounded aggressive but then it always sounded aggressive. Hers was still a real question.

'I do,' said Ka, more confidently. 'Rivers start as streams and then get bigger on the way down the mountain. So they must begin small.'

'What mountain?' Zac asked.

'There's always a mountain,' Ka said. 'Or a hill. So if we find the start we can block it . . .'

'And just how do we do that?' Bec demanded.

It was Zachary who answered. 'With ash,' he said, then blushed. 'You build the dam with stones, put twigs behind it and then throw ash in the water. That blocks the small holes.'

'Okay,' Saul said heavily. 'Suppose we decide to turn off the Nile . . .' His tone made it obvious how stupid he found that suggestion. 'How do you suggest we get to where it starts?'

'Follow it,' said Sarah, as if that was blindingly obvious.

'Rivers wiggle,' Zac protested.

Sarah looked at Zac, trying not to be cross with the small boy. 'Then we'll just have to follow the wiggles, won't we?'

'Not necessarily,' said Ka, then stopped. Only he'd said too much already. And Sarah was looking at him, openly interested.

Reaching into his shirt pocket, Ka pulled out the dark glasses. They were warm beneath his fingers. From the moment he'd found them, day or night, whatever the temperature in the desert they were always slightly warm. As if their temperature was controlled by a tiny spider's web of gold threads that ran beneath the surface of the frame.

'Wow,' said Saul. 'He's got shades.'

Ka kept his temper.

'Where am I?'

'What . . . ?'

Flipping up one hand, Ka cut dead Sarah's question. He could still see the others but now the fire had become a white blaze. A split second later, the flames fell into focus and it was the others who backed into shadow. And then in front of Ka's eyes, the picture changed. Maybe it altered inside his head or maybe the new picture happened on the lenses. It was hard to tell.

All Ka knew was that suddenly he looked down at himself. A boy with too-big boots sitting at a crude fire beside a girl in a vest and combats. Opposite sat another heavier girl, a small boy hugging a gun, and a large boy who was clearly the eldest but whose poorly mended arm put him at an obvious disadvantage.

Around them were dotted other fires, other groups. Ka was slightly shocked at just how many fires there were. Further away began real tents, where the real soldiers slept, their campfires fuelled by gas, not scrub or camel dung. Beyond this, a slope began and at the bottom was a wide river. And though the water level was low, fat hippopotami still hung heavy near the muddy banks, ignoring the jackals that slunk out of the darkness to drink.

Black birds with white crowns roosted in the ruin of an old tomb, its broken walls split apart so long ago that it looked like a natural formation, an outcrop of crumbling mud brick.

Lions were meant to sneak down from the highlands, ridden by white-whiskered monkeys who spoke a real language and lived high on a cliff face, secure from humans. Ka could see neither of these.

Though he could see movement, away to his right, human movement where dry wadis fed from mountains that ran along the distant coast like a spine. Beyond this, a thin strip of towns and small cities separated the spine from more water than Ka could imagine.

RED SEA.

The letters lit across his vision, but he didn't need to read them because the name was spoken softly into his ears. Which was as well because Ka hadn't been taught reading, though he could remember anything if he knew it was important. And sometimes he remembered things anyway, just in case they turned out to be useful later.

So he knew, without being told, that the white markings on the bonnets of the 4×4s racing down the dried oueds towards their camp belonged to the government.

They left their fire banked up and burning brightly. Their rucksacks made a huddle under Saul's old blanket. At ground level it looked like they were still there and sleeping.

Ka led them through the early morning, heading west. Pickets were stationed at regular spots around the camp, but those on guard duty sat talking or smoking kif, which they hid in their hands so that ends stayed hidden from the grown-ups. Who, if they were wise, stayed away. Two nights back a ten-year-old picket had fragged a one-bar, ostensibly for refusing to give the password. Word was, she'd tried to confiscate his cache.

307

'This way.' Ka slid down a gravel bank to where silver water spread away into forever. Reality was less far than it looked, but far enough. Now was where he learnt if he actually had control over the group or not.

'We have to cross the river,' said Ka, his voice calm. As if asking them to brave the water was a perfectly reasonable request. For a second, he wondered whether to mention the armed trucks racing across the desert on the other side of the camp, each one filled with a dozen heavily armed soldiers.

Saul might want to stay to fight and Ka could live with that. It mattered very little to him what Saul did, or where. But Sarah might stay too, and that mattered much more. Bec, as ever, would do what was the least effort.

'What about crocodiles?' Zac asked.

'There aren't any,' Ka said firmly.

'How do you know?'

'I just do.'

Obviously enough he was lying, because he could see at least three. Loglike flickers that grew brighter the harder he looked. Crocodilus niloticus, according to the glasses, five hundred paces away. With luck, the reptiles would remain asleep. Without luck . . . Well, that applied to everything.

'Come on,' insisted Ka. 'Move it. And hold your weapon over your head so water doesn't go down the barrel.'

'I can't move it,' said Saul quietly. Sounding, for once, less than certain.

'Why not?'

'Because I can't swim.'

'Oh . . .' Ka hadn't thought of that. 'Anybody else?'

'I probably can,' Zac said brightly. He paused, suddenly aware that Ka, Sarah and Bec were staring at him. 'I mean I've never tried but . . .'

Bec sucked at her teeth, crossly.

'Sarah?'

She was the only one Ka was really bothered about.

'Of course I can swim. My father was a fisherman.'

'So?' His father had kept camels and Ka hated the animals and they hated him. He never rode when there was an option to walk.

'So I can swim,' said Sarah. 'Okay?'

'Well, I can't.' Saul's voice was getting angry.

The picture shifted and tightened, an overlay of wavy lines hanging ghost-breath in front of Ka's eyes. Some spoke of height, being set tight to the edges of scars and cliffs. Others mapped the river. It took Ka a while to realize that these indicated depth, but that was because his attention was on something else.

Sarah volunteered to get the boat.

'Turn your backs,' she demanded, waiting until they had. Beneath her vest and combats she wore nothing except a ragged thong cut high at the hip. A Norwegian nurse had given the thong away, along with the rest of her spare clothes the day before returning to a family farm outside Namsos. The new owner died of a gut shot. Sarah had swapped the thong for a half packet of Cleopatra and an amulet from the person who owned it after that.

'Be back soon . . .'

Ka heard the slight splash, as they all did: but he was the only one able to watch as Sarah struck out across the dark expanse of water, head bobbing and legs kicking to the side. Except it wasn't her head he watched but her back and buttocks, flesh thinned by hunger and endless marches that trailed the Ragged Army up and down the river.

Fifteen minutes later, Sarah was on her way back, puffing slightly but happy. Although what the others saw was a boat that glided towards them as if by magic.

'Turn round,' she demanded, scrambling up the bank and into her dusty clothes, ignoring the water that ran down her legs and between her small breasts.

'What's with you?' Saul demanded.

Ka jumped.

'You're standing weird . . .'

'I was listening,' Ka said hastily and regretted it the moment Saul asked him the obvious question.

'To trucks,' said Ka.

Which got their attention. Zac went fly-catcher, mouth hanging open, Bec looked round and even Sarah shot him a sideways glance as she squeezed water from heavy black braids. That was when Ka remembered he wasn't going to mention the government.

'Blue hats?' Saul's voice was raw.

'No idea,' said Ka, although he had. There were blue hats, militia and regular government troops. Plus two open trucks full of nasrani wearing black uniforms and swirling face paint. 'But I don't plan to hang round to find out.'

'You just going to run away then?'

Ka stepped back. 'Which is more important?' he asked Saul. 'Staying here or going to turn off the Nile?'

'We can do that later,' Saul protested.

'What if we're dead?' Ka said. 'Who'll go then?'

309

The deck of the tiny felucca had been bleached white from a lifetime's sun, the sky sail was rotten and the sycamore sides were warped. Cracks above the waterline had been ignored but any gaps below were stuffed with rope and crudely gummed over, both inside and out, with dollops of bitumen.

'It looks great,' Ka told Sarah.

Together they launched her boat, then stood back, up to their hips in the wide river as Zac pulled himself up over the side. Bec followed, hooking her dress above wide hips to keep it out of the water. Ka guessed she knew she wasn't wearing any pants.

CHAPTER 9

The earlier collective gasps of a city in orgasm were silent, although the crunch of exploding fireworks still tripped car sirens, providing a counterpoint to the dogs that found themselves tethered for the evening.

October 7 was *Ashura*, tenth day of Muhram and the date of El Iskandryia's biggest fireworks display. A night when rockets rose so often from parties along the Corniche that they ceased to attract the eye; and only the grandest waterfalls of silver sparks raised even slight interest. At midnight, having fasted for two days, the city turned its attention to feasting.

Cafés spilled out onto pavements, restaurants were overbooked months in advance and only money or influence could get you a late table.

Heading west on Boul Isk, a dining car swayed over rails beaten silver with use and water slopped from a carafe. In a kitchen so small that the evening's menu was limited to only five dishes, a sous chef dropped his steamer of asparagus . . .

But all of that was only background. Maxim's was still the only place to dine at the end of *Ashura*. A single restaurant car with, bizarrely enough, its own liquor licence; crowded out with people who mattered. Which, in Zara bint-Hamzah's considered opinion, meant monied *and* stuck up, as opposed to her dad, who was just obscenely rich.

As of that morning, Zara's hair was blue, almost purple; cut extra short, like a stevedore's, in solidarity with the dock strike in Tunis. Needless to say, the razor cut cost more than any stevedore earned in a week.

It did, however, suit her, now that a month of dieting had given Zara back her cheekbones. And she understood the absurdity of her unstinting support for lost causes. Zara shrugged, then sighed, then shrugged again.

The final shrug was to annoy her mother.

Zara was dressed head to toe in a very grown-up *Atelier Azzedine* creation that revealed almost no flesh while clinging tightly to every curve. The gown had been worked up from a single sketch, then cut and corrected on the body of an appropriate house model. A notoriously slow and expensive way to work.

The honeymoon might not have happened, but Zara still appreciated her father letting her keep his present. Another of his surprises, altogether more unexpected, sat in her Gucci bag. The new Amex was not a top-up job, like the one that held her six-monthly allowance, nor a secondary card drawn against one of her father's banks. This was different, tied blind into a megainterest account in Zurich. Just how mega only made sense once Zara had called Switzerland, read off the account number and had someone tell her just how many dollars sat with the gnomes.

So she was both beautifully dressed and absolutely terrified. Because what her father had promised her, right after she nearly got murdered that evening in the warehouse, was her own flat . . . So she no longer had to live at Villa Hamzah.

Instead, he'd kept her at home and given her a one-off, nine-digit payment in US dollars, made to an account in a city where women having capital was obviously not against the law.

And for Zara, the real problem was not that her father had given her so much money, not even that he'd obviously changed his mind about letting her live alone, it was that she could no longer get close enough to him to find out why.

Later, was all he could say, *when things are sorted out.*

Taking a single caper from a nearby bowl, Zara sucked out the salt and reduced the flower bud to pulp with her tongue. She was reaching for another when a waiter materialized at her shoulder.

'Champagne?'

'Please.' Zara smiled and held up her glass, making someone at a table across the aisle snort with contempt. At the sight of a woman drinking, at the fact she'd lifted her own glass or just because she'd smiled at a waiter? It was hard to know and Zara told herself she didn't care. So she kept the smile in place and waited until her glass was full, then carefully thanked the man.

There was a Starbucks in New York at the intersection of Morningside and West 123rd, catercorner to Central, where Zara had wasted every weekday evening for nine months waiting tables for basic plus tips rather than call home and admit the allowance she'd asked for wasn't enough to cover living in Manhattan, not even in a fifth-floor walkup.

The day she started being rude to waiters was the day she would shoot herself.

Still smiling, Zara looked across at the other table and raised her glass . . .

Millions had gone on Maxim's last refurbishment. Designers from Prague and Dublin had specified chairs that were, apparently, Arts and Crafts, ergonomically corrected to reflect modern requirements of comfort. The floor was smoked glass and the walls pale Burmese silk, taken from lava genetically fixed to excrete gossamer-thin strands of gold. Every painting was original, expertly provenanced. Mostly they were a mix of sombre Klee and Matisse, with the occasional August Macke. All this was the stuff of travel features.

What wasn't common knowledge was that a substantial proportion of the refurbishment costs went on bombproofing the restaurant car to US Army standards. Hamzah Effendi, however, knew the security specification exactly. Safety Unlimited was a subdivision of Martini & Gattling, now a wholly owned subsidiary of Quitrimala Enterprises.

Around the restaurant, interchangeable notables picked at roast turbot marinated in lime on a bed of cucumber, or prodded sautéed duck liver with fenugreek and Thai chilli. Maxim's was resolutely uncompromising in its allegiance to traditional fusion.

Personally, Hamzah would rather have been at home eating eggs fried with halumi but, as well as being *Ashura*, tonight was to celebrate Zara's escape from the clutches of a rogue *Thiergarten* assassin. That had been the idea anyway.

Only Zara sat gazing listlessly out of a window, Rahina was furious about something and their guest, a major who'd practically invited himself, was halfway through a boring description of the luxuries to be found aboard a liner called the SS *Jannah.*

'Do pay attention.'

Hamzah opened his eyes but Zara was the one being scolded. Somehow his wife's voice got the attention of everybody in the restaurant except her daughter.

'Zara, please pay attention.'

'To what exactly?' She smiled coldly at her mother.

'To what the major is telling you, darling.' The endearment was at odds with the anger in the dumpy woman's dark eyes.

'And what is the major telling me?' Zara asked, sweetly. She batted her eyelids at the man, who looked away, finally embarrassed. Quite at which of the many embarrassments on offer it was hard to say.

'Well?' Zara asked. When the major pretended not to hear her question, Zara went back to watching the shops go past.

According to the *Guide Michelin*, two Parisian chefs were first responsible for the idea of converting the tram into a moving restaurant. Where other entrepreneurs might have tried to cram in tables, they'd bought two wooden tramcars, linked them together and used the front car as a restaurant and the rear as offices and a kitchen. That had been 120 years before and, with only eight tables ever available, Maxim's had been booked solid for months ahead ever since.

'Just how did you get a reservation?' Zara asked suddenly.

The next table stopped talking. Maybe they were interested or maybe she'd just interrupted their idiot conversation; Zara didn't know and really didn't care.

'I mean,' she said bitterly, 'you couldn't know I was going to be *rescued* by Ashraf Bey, could you? And it wasn't like you knew he was going to turn out innocent.'

'I never believed that Raf . . .' began Madame Rahina.

Zara snorted.

Ignoring the look of outrage on her mother's face, Zara turned to her father. 'The table,' she reminded him, just in case he'd forgotten.

'I never,' repeated her mother loudly, 'I never . . .' But she didn't get to finish that sentence either.

'You did,' said Zara. 'You told me execution was too good for him and that you knew, just as soon as you saw him, that he was an evil . . .'

'I got a list of everyone who had a table booked,' said Hamzah flatly, his voice cutting through the blossoming quarrel. Zara bet he pulled that trick at business meetings, not that he'd need to do it often. Most people he met owed him their living. 'Then I called them up in turn and made one of them an offer.'

'Which one?' The major's French carried a Cairene intonation that went with his hawklike nose and high cheekbones. His skin was as honeyed as her own was dark, and skilful tailoring on his dress uniform showed off his elegant figure. Zara reckoned she might even like him, if only he'd lighten up a bit.

'I mean,' he said, 'how did you choose?'

Hamzah laughed. 'Oh, that was easy. I told each one that I had every intention of eating here tonight and offered a token sum for his table to the one who sounded most horrified.'

Despite herself, Zara smiled, though it was obvious that the major was startled by the joke Hamzah made against himself. Which begged a big question, why was he' really here? When she'd first walked into Maxim's and seen his name on a place card, Zara was sure he'd be her new suitor. Some well-born, near-bankrupt staff officer her mother had found to make her respectable . . . As if anything could make her respectable in Iskandryia's eyes after Raf had publicly jilted her.

Her father's money in return for social cachet. Class for cash, that was the deal Raf was offered. And it almost worked. Would have done in fact, if Raf's now-dead aunt and her own decidedly undead mother had had anything to do with it. Only thing was, Raf had other ideas.

'Well,' said Zara, 'you got the table. So when do we actually get to eat?'

'There's plenty of time,' Hamzah said calmly.

'Really?' Zara looked at her watch. 'Maybe my Rotary's fast.' She tapped the side, shrugged and went back to staring out of the tram. So what if she was behaving badly? She'd said the meal was a bad idea when he first suggested it and repeated herself when her father announced he'd booked a table. Nothing had happened since to make her change her mind.

The ornate offices of Thomas Cook and the Olympia building slid past, Café Athinios and the stuccoed Palais de Justice following after. Place Zaghloul let her look out over a dusty square to the dark sea beyond, until the view was cut off by a bus station. They were still headed west, one block back from the Corniche.

Coming next was the tomb of the unknown warrior, where tramps slept against marble walls, tattered booths sold sticky almonds and foreign tourists walked hand in hand, seeing only beauty. Beyond that, the Corniche curved north towards the brooding weight of Fort Qaitbey.

Another road would herd the tram along the top of the promontory to Ras el-Tin, then steer south towards Maritime Station and the start of the old dockyards.

Seen on a map, the jutting promontory looked like a fat apple core. But the district's rocklike solidity was an illusion. Once, the area had been mostly underwater. Then a causeway joined an island to the shore. Eventually the causeway had been thickened, then thickened again with rubble until finally El Anfushi was created, with its narrow streets and weird, inward-looking Turko-Arabic houses. Houses that must be . . .

'Why couldn't you just invite Hani by herself?' Zara demanded suddenly. Hani might be nine but she could still date a building just by looking at it.

'Well?' Zara asked crossly.

'Perhaps she was the one who didn't want to come.' Madame Rahina's words were brittle. Her anger at Raf's snub not quite offset by the pleasure she got from blaming Zara.

'You asked her?'

'No, of course I didn't *ask* her. You don't *ask* children. She was included on the invitation to Ashraf Bey.'

Terrific. Zara's glance slid to the empty chairs. Place names still showed who should have sat in them, though the maître d' had insisted on whisking away the table silver when he realized that Hamzah's missing guests were likely to remain that way.

'You didn't really expect him, did you?' Hamzah asked his daughter gently. There was no anger in his voice, no accusation. Just the acceptance of basic facts. Chief among them was that the last time Ashraf drove out to Villa Hamzah, she'd flatly refused to see him. Actually, Raf hadn't driven himself at all, Avatar was the one behind the wheel and she'd been cross about that too.

Expect him? She expected nothing.

That Av was missing was a given, Zara knew that. Her father only ever saw the kid if he knew her mother was busy elsewhere. And even that was a recent development, poor little bastard. Which was what Av was. In a city where polygamy was normal, to be illegitimate was by definition to be poor, one of the unwanted.

'Here,' said the major as he handed her a linen napkin, spotless and uncreased, 'you might want this . . .'

Zara looked at him blankly.

'You're crying,' he said.

She was too, which might explain the soft edges to the streets outside.

316

CHAPTER 10

The girl at the window was unmistakable as the restaurant car trundled by. Her desolation so real that Raf could almost taste it through glass.

Been there, felt that.

He wore dark glasses from habit, a leather coat lined with spider's silk and boots with toe caps and black metal heels. Behind the Armani shades his eyes had four colour receptors, as they had done from birth, one more than strictly human. His fourth was in ultraviolet, though he could recalibrate across the entire spectrum.

Sound he adjusted by opening and closing his inner ear. So far, so predictable, if somewhat simplified. Unpredictability started with the fox, which now spat static, swore and raged inside his head.

The police bike on which Raf sat came with twin headlamps, featuring the very latest in multielement cluster/light guide technology, but he'd disconnected them at the same time as he cut the wires to the brake light and both sets of indicators. The reflectors he'd ripped off by hand. Matte black alloys went with a racer-noir engine cage and a light-swallowing paint job. The whole bike was gloriously transparent to CCTV.

The paint job was fresh and done by a garage at cost. A lot of people in the city suddenly wanted to be friends with the new Chief of Detectives. As it was, Raf practically had to order his local store to start charging full price for groceries and only the threat of taking his business elsewhere had convinced the manager Raf was serious . . .

'*You certain some fuckwit intends to snatch her?*'

Raf wasn't sure whether to nod or cry, so he nodded. The fox might be back but it had rebooted to a default personality. And Raf had always thought the fox was the stable one while he suffered the glitches.

'*Says who?*' demanded the fox.

Said every snitch on the precinct's payroll, every cut-rate whore

317

trying to cop a plea, even a few semihonest members of the public too afraid to leave their names. Rumour had hit the streets on steroids and been breaking lap records ever since.

The *why* changed with every telling, but the *what* was rock-solid, whispered from under veils and escaping like smoke in the cafés from between half-open lips; somehow, and it was a very indeterminate somehow, tables had been turned on Hamzah, the man himself had been made the proverbial offer that can't be . . . only he had, and as of now, Hamzah's kid was a walking target. Everybody but everybody who was anybody, who knew that kind of thing, already knew it. Hamzah included.

'*Daddy's rich?*'

'Come on,' Raf muttered crossly.

For a while the fox said little, so Raf went back to worrying about Hani, because some days that felt like what he did best.

Just before leaving home, Raf had asked the kid if there was anything she needed, meaning toast or hot chocolate before bed, and she'd looked at him, her arms like sticks and small face serious, flicked her dark fringe from darker eyes and said, '*more time.*'

So that was what he was trying to give her. Time and space. Life's great shortage for those who already had the luxury of water and food. Since the incident at the warehouse, Zara hated him, fair enough. Raf could live with that, but Hani's mistrust really hurt. He saw it in her every silence, her refusal to eat when he was in the madersa's huge kitchen, in sideways glances and half-conscious flickers of fear.

Most of the time Raf managed to convince himself that it was just his imagination. And then he'd come home to some unguarded look or catch a muttered reassurance from Donna to Hani, as the kid was sent to kiss him good night before trundling off to bed.

Puddles, Hamzah had said, surprising Raf, the one time they talked. Adults might labour upstream against their grief but children step in and out of sadness, trailing it after them in damp footprints. Only to step back into misery when the ground behind them begins to look dry.

CHAPTER 11

7th October

'I'm fine,' Zara insisted.

'No, you're not.' There was a determined expression on her mother's face. 'Major Halim's absolutely right. What you need is some air.' Madame Rahina glanced at her husband for support but Hamzah was staring pointedly into the bottom of a brandy glass.

One of the advantages of dinner at Maxim's was that it held an international drinks licence. Alcohol might be frowned upon, but it was not illegal.

'Air,' said Madame Rahina. 'A good idea . . . Don't you agree, my love?'

Hamzah pretended to wake with a start. He knew exactly what was going on and had done from the moment his wife first mentioned inviting the major, but he trusted his daughter to do only what she wanted.

'I think it's up to Zara,' Hamzah said carefully. 'Personally, I'm going to concentrate on pudding.' The thickset man picked up a leather menu and held it in front of him like a shield.

Despite herself, Zara smiled.

The major smiled back and inside her head Zara shrugged. He was handsome in a flinty, movie-star kind of way, what with his granite jaw, brown eyes and hair just a little longer than Army regulations allowed. And he probably hadn't expected his off-the-cuff suggestion to be pounced on quite so hard by her mother.

Besides, some problems were best got out of the way.

'Sure,' said Zara, pushing back her chair. 'Why not?' She waited for a second while the major tried to catch the attention of the maître d', then shrugged. 'No sweat,' Zara said. 'I can stop it myself.' And with that she reached for the emergency chain, which looped its way down one wall, and yanked.

Crockery hit the floor. Some from their table or others, but mostly from the arms of a stumbling waiter who'd been stacking plates in an opposite corner.

A woman screamed.

The tram stopped.

'Is there a problem?' The maître d' was white-faced with anxiety, his French accent as broken as the Limoges china around his feet.

'Of course there's a problem.' Zara grabbed the menu from her father. 'Look at this. You haven't even got chocolate ice cream . . .'

'Cut his engines now.'

'No.' Raf shook his head.

'Come on.' The fox sounded disgusted. *'It's a clean shot.'*

It was too. The man stepping down from the abruptly stopped tram had paused to scan Ibrahim Square, one of his hands on Zara's shoulder, the other thrust deep in his jacket pocket. He said something to the girl and she nodded carefully, but moved away the moment he tried to take her arm.

What reassured Raf was that Zara looked irritated rather than afraid.

And yet Place Ibrahim Pasha was deserted, the restaurant car obviously planned to make good its escape and somewhere below Zara's feet were catacombs, cut into limestone a thousand years before the birth of the Prophet. Rumour said they spread beneath Pharos in endless dark passageways, rough-hewn chambers and deep oubliettes. Had Raf been Zara, he'd have been terrified.

'Just do it,' said the fox. *'Or maybe you're afraid?'*

Of killing if necessary? No, Raf shook his head. He didn't think so . . . If it wasn't necessary? Then yes, very. And something else was worrying Raf, worrying him enough to make him rewrite his plans on the fly.

'That uniform . . .'

'So?'

'You recognize?'

'Maybe it's fake,' suggested the fox.

'Yeah, that makes sense,' said Raf. Dress in the flashiest way possible. A bottle-green cavalry tunic with gold braid and sword knots to sleeves and collar. The kind of outfit guaranteed to make people look and remember. Rather than choose something anonymous like *sécurité*, whose black uniform made most people glance away, whether it was intended to or not.

Raf stood up, brushed dust from his knees and walked back to his bike.

'*Where are you going?*' the fox demanded.

'To talk to Zara.' Breaking stock from barrel, Raf folded his borrowed police-issue nightSniper in two, twisting off the tiny laser sight and dropping that in his pocket. The rest he clipped into place down one of the Honda's front forks.

'*Very dinky . . .*'

Ignoring the fox, Raf stalked across the square, a figure dressed in black moving across an expanse of unlit ground. He was impressed the major spotted him so quickly.

'Zara.'

She turned when he called, the smile freezing on her face. Her eyes raked over him, seeing nothing in the darkness but distant light reflecting off the emptiness of his shades.

'Still wearing disguises, I see.'

'You know him?' Major Halim took a hand from his pocket.

'Oh yes.' She turned to the watchful major, her eyes bitter. 'How could I possibly forget Ashraf al-Mansur . . .'

'The *bey*?'

Raf put out his hand, then lowered it again, unshaken. The police had a file on the General's *aide de camp*, but then they had a file on pretty much everyone. 'Whatever,' said Raf.

Major Halim had both hands clenched into fists, something Raf doubted the man even realized. And busy emotions worked their way across his movie-star face. Distrust battling doubt, caution fighting mistrust.

Caution lost.

Looking at the major's handmade uniform, his immaculate leather boots, the careful disorder of his dark hair and a discreet signet ring on his left hand that signalled membership in a family known for its closeness to the Sultan in Stambul, Raf knew what was coming. He'd heard those rumours too . . .

'I have a brother at court,' said the major flatly.

'An elder brother,' Raf agreed, 'Faud Pasha.' Facts collected themselves for use, the structure of the Sublime Porte's directorate, the rank therein of Faud Pasha. 'Second Minister for Internal Affairs.'

'First Minister,' Major Halim corrected.

'Acting First Minister,' said Raf firmly. 'Married well. Trusted notary to His Sublime Majesty . . .' He could do this. He'd always had the skill, right back to when he was a kid. Every fact in his head was filed, cross-referenced, graded for likely importance. When he was seven Raf failed an exam. He did it to prove to himself that he could. There were other reasons too, but time was teaching Raf that it didn't pay to dwell on those.

He glared at the major. 'As for you . . . Unmarried, this year's mistress in Al Qahirah, last year's in Abukir, neither serious. An adequate trust fund but no capital and currently no way to pay your share of the extortionate repairs to the roof of Miclavez Court . . .'

Zara's eyes when Raf checked were wet. For a woman who'd once told him she never cried, she'd taken to doing a good imitation.

'. . . Oh yes, and you once shot an eleven-year-old *fellaheen* rioter.'

'He was . . .'

'Holding an empty starting pistol,' said Raf. 'Something cheap, generic and Taiwanese.'

There were files on every member of Koenig Pasha's staff. Even one on the General, though the ex-Chief had drawn the line on keeping one on the Khedive himself. Either that, or it was so well hidden Raf had yet to find the thing.

Keeping those files up-to-date had turned out to be simplicity itself. All Raf had to do was nothing. The web of informers put in place by his predecessor, Felix Abrinsky, kept spinning, once they realized they'd continue to get paid for each snippet of information. 'Anything else you'd like to know about your friend?' Raf asked Zara, who promptly turned her back on him.

'What about you . . . ?' Raf asked the major. 'With me so far?' He watched uncertainty replace anger in the major's eyes. Rumour might hurt but hard information was actively dangerous and Raf tossed it around like a throwing knife.

'There's no record of . . .'

'Look,' said Raf, 'let's simplify things. Your brother checked me out in Stambul and found no record of my being an honorary attaché in Seattle . . .' He ticked points off on his fingers, trying not to miss any. 'No one in special forces has heard of me, Sandhurst say I'm not on their files, St Cyr ditto, I'm not on the Sultan's official payroll and so far as your brother can find out, I don't exist.'

Raf's cold smile was wasted in the darkness, but his voice carried enough ice to make even Zara shiver. 'Have you any idea of the level of security clearance that signifies?'

Slowly, reluctantly, Major Halim shook his head.

'Did you check me with my father?' Raf continued.

'The Emir?'

Yeah, the Emir of Tunis, apparently. That was what his aunt Nafisa had said, just before she got herself stabbed; Raf still didn't believe it, and it was hard to know in retrospect if she'd believed it or not. Whatever, no one had yet come out and said it wasn't true.

'Well? Did you?' said Zara, sounding suddenly interested.

'Yes, I did.' The major looked nervous. 'He wasn't able to answer.'

'Why not?' Raf asked, and knew he'd won when the major actually shuffled his feet, looking like the small boy he must once have been back before Zara was born.

'He was unwell.'

'You mean my father's mad,' said Raf. 'Stark raving.' That was what Iskandryian intelligence had down in their files. The Khedive's second cousin lived in a tent near Nefzaoua Oasis, surrounded by heavily armed girls in green jumpsuits and guarded at all times by an elderly Frenchwoman. In private the Emir apparently favoured simple wool jebbas, but his public dress never changed from a striped jellaba, worn with a general's peaked hat.

He lived for hawks, grew generation after generation of saline-resistant grasses in a biodome on the edge of Chott el Jerid, Tunisia's salt-crusted inland sea, and had once hired a Soviet cryptographer and one of Caltech's most brilliant geneticists to extract meaning from the randomness of junk DNA.

Political decisions the Emir made after consulting the heavens. Not listening to a pet astrologer, though that would have been bad enough, but asking questions of the constellations themselves. And when he spoke, in public or private, reports had it that he spoke only in complex couplets, perfectly cadenced and delivered after long thought.

Among the Berber tribes, who still traversed the empty sands and rock seas with little care for international borders, he was regarded as North Africa's sole sane ruler. It was a minority opinion and one with which it was obvious Major Halim didn't agree.

'So tell me,' said Raf, 'who am I?'

The major looked at the young princeling in the black leather coat, the dark glasses and black gloves whose pale hair blew in the slight night breeze. 'The son of the Emir of Tunis,' he said without hesitation.

Raf nodded and offered his hand. This time they shook.

'Very touching,' said Zara. 'Now if you've both finished with the male-bonding shit, perhaps Major Halim could escort me home. Of course,' she added crossly, 'if this wasn't El Isk I could get myself home. Since I'm perfectly capable of walking, chewing gum and looking where I'm going at the same time. But since this *is* Iskandryia and any woman alone at night is *obviously* a prostitute . . .'

Raf grinned. Then smiled some more at Major Halim's discomfort. 'This is nothing,' he said, 'you wait until you know her better and she gets really cross.'

'*Better* . . . ?' The major executed a tiny bow in Zara's direction.

'Much as I'd welcome the chance to get to know Miss Quitrimala better, I'm afraid that's impossible.' His tone was genuinely regretful.

'Don't tell me,' said Zara, 'you couldn't cope with a third mistress.'

'It's not that,' the major said, looking shocked. 'I'm leaving for Berlin next week, on secondment to the *Thiergarten*. After that, if everything goes smoothly, I hope to become Iskandryia's attaché to Stambul.' For a moment, admitting this, the major seemed almost bashful. But Zara was too cross to notice.

'Then what,' she asked furiously, 'was gate-crashing my supper about? All that sucking up to my mother. And the crap about me needing air and taking a walk . . .'

'This is difficult,' said the major and glanced at Raf. When it became obvious that Raf refused to take his cue to withdraw, Major Halim sighed. 'The Khedive intends to take a holiday . . . Well deserved obviously.'

Zara opened her mouth to speak, then closed it again. A sudden tension locked her shoulders, which refused to budge, even when she twisted her head from side to side. Zara had a nasty idea she knew exactly what was about to come next.

'His Highness was wondering if . . .'

'Have you talked to my parents about this?'

'Of course,' the major said nervously. 'Your father said it was your decision where you took your holidays and with whom. Which was not, to be honest, the reaction I was expecting. Your mother thinks it's an excellent idea.'

I bet she does, thought Zara. Somewhere in her mother's finely gradated misunderstanding of Iskandryian society, the woman undoubtedly believed that being mother to the Khedive's mistress was even better than having a bey in the family.

Zara had been spot on about her mother's desperation that she take this walk, totally wrong about the motives. 'It's not going to happen,' she said calmly.

So calmly that even the major could hear her keep the anger in check.

'Tell the boy I'm not interested. Just that, nothing else. Don't make it polite, don't give my apologies or regrets because I'm not sending them . . .'

'You misunderstand,' the major said carefully. 'You misunderstand completely. The Khedive's intentions are entirely *honourable*.' He stumbled over the word, not certain how much he could actually say. In his own mind, before supper, when he'd been running through how to approach the coming evening, he'd seen them both taking a moonlit stroll through the terraces of the Palace Ras el-Tin while he proffered the Khedive's invitation and she accepted gratefully.

'He doesn't want to get me into bed?'

The major's lips twisted. 'Let me repeat myself. His intentions are strictly legitimate.'

Zara's eyes widened. Impossible visions of palaces, sleek yachts, long holidays aboard the *SS Jannah* opened like flowers before her.

'And if I go on this holiday?'

'Then he'll propose,' said Raf, 'won't he?'

Major Halim looked pained. 'You can't honestly expect me to comment.'

'God.' Raf laughed. 'Koenig Pasha must be climbing a wall . . . Only my cousin could decide he needed to marry a hard-line republican. Not to mention occasional communist.' They had files on Zara too, back at the precinct. Files he could recite from memory.

'Have you spoken to my parents about that bit as well?' Zara asked the major.

Major Halim shook his head. 'Only tentatively about the holiday. Enough to make clear that you would be an honoured . . .'

'Well, don't,' Zara stressed. 'Speak to them, I mean. It's nothing they need to know.'

'They're your parents.'

'Talk to either of them about this,' said Zara, 'and I guarantee I won't go.'

'But the Khedive is determined to do this properly. By the book.'

'You do realize,' Zara interrupted crossly, 'that if the Prophet had been a woman, there wouldn't even have been the Book, because no one would have listened, never mind written it down . . .'

CHAPTER 12

8th October

The first of that Friday's calls to prayer found Raf leaning against a seawall, watching smugglers run empty cigarette boats into Western Harbour under protection of both darkness, which came free, and the Commander of Ras el-Tin, whose protection came anything but . . .

And the Terbana Mosque's definition of dawn seemed open to debate. The Mufti had defined it as the point not when light first touched the sky but when the absolute utterness of the night first lessened.

Raf thought the man was being unduly optimistic.

Hamzah's call came four hours later, just as Raf was about to shower away the black dog of his wasted night. Because even blasting his police Honda to Abu Sir and back, fifty klicks along the shore, had done nothing to improve Raf's mood, even though early mist had hung over the Mariout marshes and the Mediterranean had still worn her night colours.

'For you,' shouted Hani, her call echoing up the lift shaft from the haremlek below. 'It's Effendi.'

Raf had warned Hani not to call Hamzah that, but currently the child was paying zero attention to anything he said.

'Tell him I'll call back.'

'He says it's important.'

Sighing, Raf picked up his dressing gown from the floor and pulled on some old leather slippers that Khartoum insisted once belonged to Hani's grandfather. When Raf made some glib comment about dead men's shoes, the old porter had pulled deeply on the wrong end of a cigar and nodded like it was obvious.

'This alone is true,' he'd told Raf. 'This here, at this time, for this person.' Khartoum had announced it like that was also obvious. Three days later Raf was still puzzling over that one.

'Uncle Raf . . .' Hani's voice was tight with exasperation.

'I'm on my way.'

'. . . You could always get comms installed up there.'

Raf nodded and slid back the metal grille to step into the lift. He could indeed, but he wouldn't. His floor was the only level of the madersa not fitted with a screen and he liked it that way.

'. . . or you could try turning on your watch,' added Hani, when he finally reached her floor.

'But then you wouldn't have an excuse to complain, would you?' Raf said and punched a button to activate a screen. Hani stalked off in silence, chin up and shoulders rigid, and though Raf heard the slam of her bedroom door he didn't call her back.

Just after their Aunt Nafisa was murdered, Raf had made a promise to Hani not to send her away to school. Keeping his word was proving harder than he'd imagined. Particularly as everyone else seemed to think the girl would be better off living somewhere different, somewhere he wasn't. Until recently he'd have disagreed.

'Hamzah.'

'Your Excellency.'

'You don't need to call me . . .'

'This is official.' The industrialist's face was tight, with a greyness that suggested acute shock.

'Zara.'

'My daughter is here,' Hamzah said. 'And she's fine. Although for reasons I don't understand, I gather you met her early this morning.'

'And Avatar?'

The man looked embarrassed. 'Avatar's gone,' he said simply. 'Kidnapped . . .'

'*Avatar?*'

Raf's explosion of anger brought Hani out of her room; or maybe it was the way he slammed the wall with the side of his fist. 'How do you know?'

'I've had a note.'

'Demanding what?'

The man on screen took a deep breath and slowly released it. 'That doesn't matter.'

'I'll need to see the note.'

'It no longer exists,' said Hamzah, staring out at Raf. 'I burned it . . .'

'So what do you want?' Raf asked tightly. 'Since you obviously don't consider you need police help to get Avatar back . . .'

'I want you to come out to the villa and take a look at something my gardener's just found . . .' With that, Hamzah fumbled at his end of the connection and the screen in the haremlek went dead.

Even ripped open and with her feet washed by the waves, the girl might have shown signs of lividity had she been dead for much longer than a few hours. As it was, the skin was waxy and slightly warm, but gravity hadn't pooled blood along the underside of her legs. Both rigor and early, nonfixed lividity had yet to occur.

That gave Raf his time frame.

The killer had opened the blonde girl from pubis to sternum, then slashed again, straight across her rib cage, the cuts forming a cross. Smaller incisions, made at right angles, acted as stops to the cross. Her heart was missing, which was often the case in crimes of *mutilé*, so were both her lungs, and the killer had cut the initials *H.Q.* into her wrist.

Not a single print could be taken from her pale skin. Whoever had wielded the blade had worn surgical gloves, and from the cleanness of the incisions Raf put odds on her killer using a scalpel or filleting knife.

Mind you, since what little Raf knew of forensics came from reading notebooks left by Felix Abrinsky, the previous Chief, and since the fat man's notes were often impossible to decipher, Raf fully accepted that the sooner he brought in professionals the better.

'Sir, you might want to take a look at this . . .' The young police-woman carrying a camera kept her voice level, almost businesslike. Raf hadn't met her before but she looked about twelve and wore a black *hijab*, the traditional headscarf, checked along its edge in the blue and white of the WPF.

Her boss, Madame Mila, coroner-magistrate for women and head of the WPF, had obviously already warned her in general against talking to other departments, and against talking to the Chief of Detectives in particular.

Raf's way round this prohibition had been to point out the obvious.

'*Touristica,*' he'd announced on seeing the body, mere seconds after arriving on Hamzah's beach. It didn't matter what gender tourists were, they still came under the *poliz touristica*, who reported to uniform; uniform automatically reported all unsolved serious to Raf.

'How do you know, sir?' Stuck between a rock and the proverbial, Raf thought, looking at her heavy face. Upset Madame Mila or upset Iskandryia's new Chief of Detectives.

'What's your name?'

'Leila, Your Excellency.'

'Take a look at her breasts.'

The young woman blushed but did what she was told. The breasts in question were small and pale brown.

'What do you see?'

Leila stayed silent, staring desperately.

'It's okay,' said Raf, 'take a look at her . . . lower half.' The dead girl was completely naked, draped backwards across a rocky outcrop on Hamzah's beach. Her feet were underwater, the rest of her was beginning to mottle in the early-morning light.

'What do you see?'

The police officer peered closely, looking for abrasions or thumb marks, something to say the woman had first been raped, but her flesh was unbruised and nothing obvious sprang to mind.

'She . . . has a tan line round her hips?'

Raf nodded and Leila almost sighed aloud with relief.

'What else?'

'That's the only tan line.'

'Neatly done.' Raf flicked on his Seiko and hot-keyed Champollion Precinct. Not bothering to announce himself, he rattled off time, place and crime code. 'The first official on the scene was Officer . . .' He glanced quickly at Leila.

'Durrell.'

'Officer Durrell from the Women's Police Force who recognized immediately, from the tan mark of a bikini bottom and a corresponding lack of a tan mark for the breasts, that the victim had to be a tourist. Accordingly the crime scene was handed over to me as the most senior detective present.'

Mind you, thought Raf, Officer Durrell was more impressed with his abilities than she need be. This was the second mutilated body to be found in a week. And since the first one was now on her way back to Austin in an icebox and the second was also blonde, young and obviously Western, it was difficult not to assume a pattern, albeit slightly unprofessional; since, having only two cases, the most Raf should be positing was a basic similarity.

Unfortunately, the police didn't know if the first victim had been raped. The pathologist had apparently forgotten to check.

In short, bleak sentences Raf ordered in a scene team and told the handler to notify Madame Mila's office of the change of responsibility. Only once did Raf's voice hesitate. Having just ordered that the tourist go to the nearest morgue, as soon as the site was swept and the crime-scene shots completed, Raf had a change of mind.

'No' he said, 'send it to Dr Kamila . . .' Kamila didn't work for his division but she could be persuaded, and she knew what she was doing. She was also a woman. In crimes like this that could count.

'Okay, Dr Kamila it is. The pickup location? That's . . .'

Raf waited for the question, which never came. Instead the handler muttered a hurried Ten4 and broke his connection. Within minutes the fact that a naked tourist had been found butchered in the grounds of Villa Hamzah would be round Police HQ. Within half an hour the outer precincts would know.

The fact Raf had called in the crime would only make the titbit more juicy.

Turning on his heel, Raf stamped through the salt grass, which separated the rocky headland from the villa's terraces, and entered Hamzah's study through its garden door, without knocking. There was a conversation that needed to be had and Raf wasn't looking forward to it.

The industrialist was sitting at his desk, just as Raf expected. And he didn't even frown when Raf strode in from the garden.

'Where were you two hours ago?' Raf made little attempt to keep the anger out of his voice. This was the man who'd burned the note sent by Avatar's kidnappers. The man who'd pimped his naked daughter the night Raf walked out of that door, who was now pimping her again to the Khedive.

'Still dining with my wife at Maxim's.'

With my wife . . . Raf looked for the slightest hint of irony in Hamzah's face but there was nothing. 'Can you prove that?'

Hamzah nodded. 'I think they'll remember us,' he said sourly.

'And this was a long-standing arrangement?'

'No,' said Hamzah, looking up. 'It was very last-minute. Why?'

'Because there's a butchered girl in your garden, round about where your daughter usually swims, and your initials are carved into her wrist. So what I want to know is the usual stuff . . . Who is she/where did she come from/who did it . . . ?'

'And if I tell you I have no idea?'

'No idea,' said Raf as he pulled a square of card from his pocket and tossed the Polaroid onto Hamzah's desk. 'No idea who did this?'

Hamzah Effendi picked up the photograph and began to tremble. The movement started in his fingers and spread like fever until his whole body shook. And his body kept shaking, even after he'd turned the photograph facedown and pushed it away from him.

His body was still shaking when he pushed back his chair to rush to the lavatory. And it was doing the same when he came back after vomiting up his breakfast and what had remained of the previous night's meal.

'She was facedown,' he said. 'When I saw her she was facedown.'

CHAPTER 13

8th October

'Eduardo?'

Eduardo nodded from instinct. It didn't matter that the person talking was half a city away and Eduardo's watch wasn't toggled to visual. He still nodded.

'*Na'am* . . . This is me.' Eduardo folded his broadsheet and placed it carefully on the table. He would have preferred one of the Arabic-language tabloids but he had his position to consider, so he always downloaded *L'Iskandrian*.

The Frenchman and Frisco were watching him from the corners of their eyes. He knew they'd both decided his watch was a fake and his new job just empty words, but they were wrong. Instinctively, Eduardo straightened in his café chair and ran one hand though his thinning hair, then discreetly rubbed his fingers clean on the side of his black chinos.

He listened in silence, nodding seriously now and then like a man agreeing with a particularly pertinent point. Not everyone had an elegant Silver Seiko that double-encrypted conversation and screened itself from vanP hacking.

'*Na'am*, I understand.' Eduardo did too – really – but just to be sure he asked the man to repeat his instructions more slowly.

Eduardo liked his new job. He even had an office, a third-storey walk-up off Place Orabi, above a haberdasher's at the back of the bus depot. With the office and watch came new shoes, new trousers and a zip-up leather jacket that looked old and tatty unless you got really close, when it was possible to see that the scuff marks were printed onto the animal hide.

The man who gave Eduardo the jacket had pulled out a gravity knife, dropped its blade and driven it hard into the leather. The sharp point of the blade hardly even left a mark.

'Mesh,' he told Eduardo, 'ultrafine, from spiders that shit steel.'

Eduardo didn't know whether the man was making fun of him or not. All the same, Eduardo liked what he now did. Which was mostly sit in cafés and talk politics, something he wasn't sure he really understood. Listening to the counterarguments, Eduardo had discovered a talent for separating half-truth from mere wish. A cast-iron, built-in bullshit detector, the man called it, speaking as if such a machine might actually exist.

Eduardo imagined it as small, with cogwheels that whirred and narrow brass pipes that grew hot from circulating water. When Eduardo was a child he lived in a small burg in Namibia and the local train, to Windhoek and back, had run on coal and wood, dried dung too when the shortages began, though dung didn't work that well.

'Mmm . . .' Eduardo said, nodding. 'Sure thing.' He tossed a handful of silver onto the table. Time to go. His watch didn't need him to shut down the connection, because it did that for itself. It did other things too, like bring him the latest football results and forecast that it was going to rain.

'Things to do,' he said to Frisco, speaking Ladino. 'Deals to make.' Iskandryia was a city with a number of languages that might claim to be the lingua franca, of which Spanish Hebrew was just one. The other man nodded. Frisco had told Eduardo his real name but Eduardo kept forgetting, though he remembered that the man claimed his forefathers were *moriscos*, expelled from Spain.

When Eduardo started coming to the café, he and Frisco had played a few games of chess but now the old man made excuses not to play, probably because Eduardo kept losing.

Inside Eduardo's office the air was cool, which was a miracle given his desk fan had fused and the October sun beat direct on an outside wall; but the walls were thick, built decades before from limestone blocks stolen from a Coptic church three streets away. And anyway, closed shutters kept out much of the brightness. There was also an air-conditioning unit attached to one wall, a brown box that stuck its metal arse out into the street, as if threatening to shit on pedestrians beneath. Unfortunately that had been broken ever since someone hid a wank mag up the air outlet. When Eduardo first took the box apart to see if anything obvious was broken, he'd been left with frayed wires, rusting iron pipes and mildewed, disintegrating pictures of pale nipples and shaven pudenda.

So he'd put the casing back together and pushed the mags back where he found them, and now tiny mushrooms grew in clusters on the grey carpet, right below where the unit dripped water.

A Sony Eon3 sat on an otherwise clear desk. A simple Luxor

terminal, he'd chosen it at random in a souk at the back of Rue Faransa. Glued to its side was an anonymizer, which had been given him by the man. On the 'mizer was a label, PROPERTY OF EL ISKANDRYIA POLICE DEPARTMENT: NOT TO BE REMOVED FROM CHAMPOLLION PRECINCT UNDER ANY CIRCUMSTANCES.

Punching a key, Eduardo started random number software and waited. Without him having to ask, the terminal popped up a comms screen and Eduardo keyed in the number he'd just been given. Then he did what the man had told him to do.

Eduardo didn't know that he was being rerouted or that, at the receiving end, his call was logged as having come direct from Fez; all Eduardo knew was that a tiny icon on the screen's task bar lit green and a connection got made.

The person who picked up at the other end said nothing to introduce himself, which was fine, because that was what Eduardo had been told to expect.

'I'm taking the contract.'

'Who gave you the details?' The voice was gruff.

'That doesn't matter.'

'What guarantees do I have that the job will be done?'

'None.'

'By the day after tomorrow or the line of credit closes.'

'Tomorrow night,' said Eduardo and broke the connection.

CHAPTER 14

'Don't you like pastries?' Hani sounded puzzled instead of angry. She'd been ploughing her way through a dozen *basbousa*, stuffing them into her mouth with sticky fingers at the start, then eating more slowly and finally nibbling, mouselike around the edge, once she realized Raf wasn't going to tell her to stop.

Her lunchtime vitamin stood untouched by her plate.

'What?'

Raf glanced up to find dark eyes staring at him from a pinched face. He tried to make sure he and Hani ate together at weekends, while Donna bustled around in the background, banging together pans and clattering knives into a double stone sink, each side large enough to be a horse trough.

The kitchen took up most of the ground floor of the al-Mansur madersa. Outside was a tiled courtyard with a fountain and beyond that a stone garden house, then a walled garden, roofed over with glass.

Above the kitchen was the *qaa*, where important guests were greeted. This had a large marble floor and smaller indoor fountain. The haremlek was a suite of rooms above the *qaa* and Raf's floor was at the top, above the haremlek.

The madersa was vast, old and badly in need of repair, but no other room was as large as Donna's kitchen, which seemed to spread in all directions.

It had taken Raf a while to realize that Donna's clattering wasn't irritation at finding him cluttering up her space, which was so big a crowd couldn't have cluttered it; she objected to his presence for different reasons. People like Hani and His Excellency were meant to eat upstairs, at a marble table in the elegant *qaa*, waited on by others.

'You're not listening to me . . .' Hani said crossly.

'I'm sorry . . .' She was right. He wasn't.

335

There wasn't much else Raf could say. But Hani wanted more. Something dismissive of her concern, something adult. He could see that in her eyes, the wish for a fight so that she could stop being worried for him and go back to being angry.

'Look,' he said softly, 'let it go, okay?'

By the time the noise of her falling chair had finished echoing round the kitchen, Hani was out of the room and racing up the outside steps to the *qaa*. Raf listened to her shoes slap the floor overhead, then heard Hani slam a hand against the button for the lift. Seconds later the madersa's ancient Orvis creaked into action.

Raf put his head in his hands. When he looked up again Donna was sitting on the other side of the table and in front of him was a tiny cup of Turkish coffee. It was the old woman's cure for everything.

'The child's young, Your Excellency.'

Raf nodded.

'And she's scared.'

'That I will send her away?'

Donna shook her head and discreetly rubbed her crucifix. 'That you will die.' The old woman's voice was matter-of-fact. 'Since her aunt . . . She dreams all the time. That you die and she be left here alone.' Donna shrugged. 'They would not let people like me look after Lady Hana. They would not let me live here . . .'

Only Donna got away with calling the child by her real name. Everyone else had to use Hani. Named for the boy the child resented not being.

'Go to her, Excellency,' said Donna, 'and talk.'

'And say what?' His question sounded weak even to him.

The old woman shrugged. 'That you will not be going away. That you don't plan to die.' Her lips twisted into a sour smile at Raf's expression.

'Well, does Your Excellency?'

Raf shook his head.

'No,' said Donna, crossing herself. 'Somehow I didn't think so.'

'Go away.' Hani didn't bother looking up from her screen. On the floor beside her chair sat an untouched toy dog, still in its packaging. It was the most expensive model Raf had been able to afford.

'It smells in here,' said Raf.

She did look round at that.

'Old clothes,' he said, gesturing to a bundle on the floor. 'Old clothes and misery . . .' Raf pulled back the inner shutter of a mashrabiya and autumn sunlight washed into Hani's bedroom, through her balcony's ornately carved screen.

'Now I can't see my monitor.'

'You can use it later,' Raf said, 'but first we need to talk.' He sat on the red-tiled floor, his spine hard against the edge of her metal bed. The springs were rusted and the mattress so old that horsehair poked through holes in its cover. Changing the thing was absolutely but of the question, apparently.

'Sit by me . . .'

Hani sighed and made a great show of turning off her machine, even though they both knew it would have gone to sleep at a simple voice command. Then, surprisingly, she did as he asked and parked herself next to Raf, her own back pressed into the side of the bed. Dust flecks danced in the afternoon sunlight in front of them. Their ersatz randomness actually the result of immutable laws of heat and motion.

'I saw a body yesterday morning.'

Hani grew still.

'It was at Zara's house. A stranger . . .' Raf added hurriedly.

'You've seen bodies before,' Hani said.

He nodded, they both had. Aunts Nafisa and Jalila. Those deaths were one of the things that bound them together.

'When you were an assassin . . .'

'Hani!' They'd been through this before. 'I was an attaché . . . Nothing more.'

'Attachés are spies. Spies kill people. Everyone knows that.'

Raf sighed.

'Who was he?' Hani asked.

'*She,*' Raf corrected. 'And we haven't found out yet.' Obviously enough, he didn't mention the mutilation, which was actually a *cross potent* according to the pathologist, who'd looked it up.

Toxicology showed heavy traces of an mdma clone in the victim's blood and alcohol in her stomach. The girl had been alive and conscious from the start of the attack until near the end. And swabs taken from her oral, anal and vaginal mucosa indicated that she'd first been raped, then cut. So Raf now had a file to read on *crosses coupe*, which had apparently been the mutilation of choice during something called 'the little war.' There was one bite mark, below her right breast, but that was faded and the bruise yellow. So either it happened before she arrived in Isk, it was the result of a casual holiday romance or her boyfriend had come with her but had yet to step forward.

Which, at least, would give Raf one sensible suspect. Provided the boyfriend could be shown to have nerves of steel and a reasonable grasp of anatomy.

'The trouble,' Raf told Hani, 'is in realizing when facts aren't related . . .'

He halted himself there, wondering whether to begin again and decided not to bother with the talking. With luck, sitting next to Hani would be enough, because when he was a child, the point at which adults started in on explanations was the moment he stopped listening.

'Everything is related,' said Hani. And glancing sideways, Raf realized her face was screwed up in thought. 'That's what Khartoum says . . .'

The kid was nine, whipcord thin, with the body of a child younger still and eyes old before their time. Lack of sleep, bad dreams and night sweats, he remembered them all well. Although, these days, if Raf worked at it, he could go for months without recalling them once.

'Maybe he's right,' said Raf finally. 'Maybe everything does connect.'

'You don't know?' Hani looked interested.

'No.'

'I thought spies knew everything.'

'Not me.' Raf shook his head. 'Me, I know nothing, except that I'm not going to send you away, I'm not going to leave you and nobody is going to kill me . . .'

'Aunts Jalila and Nafisa were killed . . .' She waited for Raf to nod, which he did. 'But the reason's a secret . . .'

Raf nodded again.

'Why?'

'Because . . .' Raf stopped. 'Because that's the way things work in Iskandryia.' He ignored the doubtful expression on her face. 'What can I tell you? What the General says goes.'

'Koenig Pasha?' Hani looked suddenly relieved. 'Not Zara's idea? Not yours . . .'

Raf shook his head, his half smile a reflection of hers.

Hani nodded. 'I was worried,' she said, 'that it was Zara. If it's Koenig Pasha who says we must lie, then that's different . . .' Her shrug was almost comically adult. 'Lying is his job.' For a second, she sounded almost exactly like her late unlamented Aunt Nafisa.

There were, it turned out, two entirely separate levels of morality in Hani's world. One occupied by those, like him, her and Zara, who weren't meant to lie, and another given over to those destined to massacre the truth.

Pushing himself to his feet, Raf wondered what would happen when the child finally realized that if he was a spy, then she'd got him filed under the wrong group.

338

'Where are you going?' Hani demanded.

'Out,' said Raf.

'The murder?'

Raf shook his head. 'Something else . . .'

Hani regarded him carefully. 'I thought you were going to leave finding Avatar to someone called Eduardo?'

'Hani!'

'So I listened,' said the child. 'Anyway . . . you need me to help with the search.'

'I don't.'

'Yes you do,' said Hani.

'There is no way,' said Raf, his voice firm, 'that you're coming with me.'

'Who wants to come with you?' Hani said dismissively. Scrambling to her feet, she waved one hand in front of her screen and watched it blink back to life. A pass of her thumb over a floating track ball and the active window closed, revealing an aerial shot of the city.

'He's locked in a cellar,' said Hani, voice casual. 'There's stale water outside.'

'What kind of stale water?'

'So you *do* want my help?'

Raf sighed.

'Ali Bey ordered the Mahmoudiya Canal built in 1817,' Hani said carefully. 'On the far side, a green tram comes towards the window, then turns left . . .'

'Anything else?' Raf didn't know what else to say.

Hani nodded. 'Turbini. No.' She stopped, correcting herself. 'Not turbini. Freight trains, long ones that rattle, somewhere behind the room. Which means he's . . .' She touched the picture, pulling up a tight lattice of streets, where tramlines ran south along Rue Amoud, before turning into Avenue Mahmoudiya. At the bottom of the picture, on the other side of the canal, a fat ribbon of track ran towards a rail yard. 'Somewhere round here.'

'And you know this how?'

Hani nodded to a toy tortoise gathering dust in one corner of her bedroom. It was old, with overrounded edges and what proved to be fractal patterns playing constantly across its shell, like swirling clouds. Someone had applied a sticker of a cartoon rabbit, then tried to peel it off sometime later, leaving a sticky patch and half a smug, bucktoothed face.

The tortoise was so ancient that it connected by cable to the wall feed, with another cable run round the edge of Hani's room to her screen.

'I used Herbert,' said Hani.

It was possible . . . In theory, CCTV cameras covered all the main streets in the city. Trams, trains, even licensed taxis carried vidcams by law. Face recognition software was notoriously flawed, but could probably just about pick a dreadlocked DJ with facial piercings from the crowd of suits or jellaba-clad market traders.

'Really?'

Hani turned away, killing her terminal with a snap of her fingers. Conversation over.

'Hani.' Raf dropped to a crouch in front of the small girl, and she let him take her pointed chin in his hands and turn her face back, so they stared straight into each other's eyes. Dark brown and palest blue. Strange cousins.

'I need to know, honey. Please?' *Honey* was what Zara had taken to calling Hani, before Zara and Raf's quarrel meant Hani stopped seeing the older girl.

'Not fair,' said Hani, her voice suddenly cross. She shook free her head. 'Do I ask you about the fox? No, I don't. Ever . . .' The child was unmistakably upset.

'Sorry,' said Raf, backing away. It looked like an impasse, pure and simple, except that nothing would ever be pure in Hani's life, or simple. And they both knew she'd already answered him, in her own way. What Hani saw when she looked inside her head was not what he saw, obviously enough, but it was not what anyone else would expect to see either.

With one final apology, Raf left Hani to her tight and angry silence.

CHAPTER 15

9th October

Eduardo was worried about his Vespa. It was genuine Italian and had belonged to his uncle. The torn seat had only just been replaced with a new one made from red leather, while the old two-stroke petrol motor had been swapped for a Sterling unit that ran on pretty much anything. Mostly, Eduardo had been feeding his Vespa with the cheapest grade of *jaz*, a brandy so rough that even Frisco refused to drink it, but the unit seemed happy to work with anything vaguely flammable.

He'd left his bike near the canal, watched over by an urchin in a blue jellaba who squinted badly and carried a stick too small to frighten away anyone. Five lila, the boy had asked. *Five.* Grandly Eduardo had offered him ten to keep an extra-special watch and the small boy's smile had been vulpine, as if seeing straight through Eduardo's generosity.

This was the first time that Eduardo had visited a proper brothel and it wasn't nearly as grand as he'd been hoping. For a start, the huge entrance hall tickled his nose with dust and carpet cleaner, rather than with rose petals or expensive Parisian perfume. There were no chandeliers, few paintings and the Iskandryian rugs were old but not valuable. Though there were looking glasses, great big gilt ones on the walls, but these just showed Eduardo back to himself, a small man in a too-big leather coat.

At least the small cubicles above the bus station were easy to reach. Even if the beds were dirty and bare. Maison 52, Pascal Coste, was so out of Eduardo's way that he'd got lost just getting there.

'Excellency.' The voice came from a narrow doorway, one Eduardo had dismissed as belonging to a cupboard. In it stood a blonde woman with a face so white she could have walked out of one of those Japanese pantomimes. Her mouth was a slash of Chanel, red as a wound. Behind her shoulder bobbed other heads, fair-haired and fair-skinned and way, way younger.

'Our girls, Excellency.'

He wasn't an *excellency* and it seemed cruel to Eduardo to keep calling him one. True he wasn't exactly a *felaheen*, but neither was he rich or well connected. No one called on him for patronage. He was just some *pied noir* who'd recently found work and been told by the man to come to 52 Rue Pascal Coste.

'I'm due to meet . . .'

'All in good time, Excellency.' The old woman swayed into the room, her feet compressed into tight pumps and her body wrapped in a fringed cocktail dress nearly as old as she was. A matching shawl hid most of the crepe lines that marked her shoulders, chest and neck. 'First you need to choose one of our delightful girls . . .'

They trooped silently into the hall. A few looked at him with vague curiosity but most just stared at the carpets or examined their nails. There were ten in total. Blonde or brunette. Two of his age and five somewhat younger. The last three were almost children and the prettiest had a dark frown on her face and a bruise across one soft cheek that no amount of make-up could hide.

All except the youngest were bare-breasted, two of them completely naked, the rest wearing thin pants or white petticoats, mostly with tight elastic that cut into their middles. The youngest was dressed in a white nightgown with Maltese lace round the neck. Eduardo could recognize the stitching – his mother had worked in a sweatshop for most of his childhood. And when she wasn't at the machines, she sewed at home at a window until the light faded.

The young one in the nightdress glanced up, scowled at Eduardo and Eduardo quickly looked away. Straight into the resigned face of a brunette.

'That one,' said Eduardo and the chosen woman looked surprised at his choice. She was not quite the oldest, with heavy hips, small breasts and full derrière. A half-smoked Ziganov hung from between her fingers, its gold band stained pink from the lipstick she used. English, Eduardo decided, that was how she looked . . .

'I'm Rose,' said the woman.

Eduardo gave his card to the waiting Madame without being asked. The gold Amex was only to be used in emergencies or when so ordered by the man, like now.

He signed with a flourish, not bothering to look at the amount.

'Excellency.' There was new respect in the old woman's voice; and for the first time since she'd started using the honorific, it sounded like she might mean it.

Taking back his card, Eduardo smiled and started up the wide stairs.

Then stopped to indicate that his choice should go first. He wanted to look at Rose's buttocks as she walked. She climbed slowly, apparently only too aware of his gaze. And at the top she paused, as if trying to remember which chamber the Madame had told her to use.

'This one,' she said, opening a battered door.

'Eduardo,' said a voice Eduardo recognized. It was the man, dressed in black and wearing shades even though the chamber was shuttered against the evening light. Behind him sat a short-haired girl in a white shift, her breasts full enough to be obvious beneath the cloth and tipped with nipples that showed like shadows.

'Boss.' Eduardo bowed, feeling stupid. Nothing about the man suggested he wanted Eduardo to shake hands, but bowing still didn't feel quite right.

'Come in and lock the door behind you,' ordered the man. He said something in a language Eduardo didn't understand and Rose went to sit quietly on a large *bateau lit* beside the other woman.

'You made it,' said Raf.

Eduardo looked puzzled. Of course he'd made it. 52 Pascal Coste was where the man had told him to come.

'And you bought the things I asked for?'

Eduardo nodded and pulled a heavy package from under his coat. For extra safety he'd tied it tight with string, which suddenly seemed unwilling to untie.

'Later,' said Raf. 'Put it down there for now.' The chest of drawers he indicated was cracked on one side and scratched across the top. 'No, even better, put it in a drawer.'

Eduardo did what he was told.

The chamber was the largest in the brothel by far, with two leather divans and a big *bateau lit* filling most of its space. Most of the *maison*'s other rooms featured narrow single beds to discourage lingering. It had taken Raf nearly forty-five minutes of trawling the datacore at Police HQ before he finally found a brothel within easy distance of the corner of Mahmoudiya and Rue Amoud el-Sawari. Hani could undoubtedly have done it in a fraction of the time, but Raf just hadn't felt right asking her.

This room had been the choice of visiting couples, back in the days before the General did his deal with the Mufti and the *morales* suddenly became a problem. It was somewhere wives could buy their jaded husbands a whore or two for their birthday, to do things that didn't get done at home. Most of the visiting women just watched, a few joined in. All were married, rich and decently connected. Respectable members of the kind of families who donated funds regularly to the police.

The *accord* had changed all that.

For the first time in a hundred years girls from poor families returned to wearing the *hijab*, while Iskandryia's *mesdames* made do with head-scarves and dark glasses, altogether more elegant and not remotely to the Mufti's liking. The property laws were revised to exclude female heirs, driving alone after dark became a criminal offence for women, and to go out with bare arms was to invite some fanatic to scratch his disapproval into your skin with a metal comb . . .

Raf had heard Zara on the subject. She was old enough to remember the city before it started to change. Felix too, the old Chief of Detectives, had been less than impressed with the General's decision to sign an *accord*.

All trades had been hit, brothels included. Not that they actually closed. The brothels of Iskandryia were both an institution and tourist attraction (which was altogether more important). Along the Corniche several could be found in the grander houses, where chambers were by the night, cash was forbidden and anything less than a gold card strongly discouraged.

Of course, visiting tourists were billed variously for cultural excursions, theatre groups or an art exhibition. That way everybody was kept happy, from the punters to the card companies and the brothels. Especially the brothels, because embarrassed punters had a habit of getting home, then denying they'd ever visited the place that billed them and that made the card companies very unhappy.

This *maison* was different, though . . . Somewhere for Iskandryia's own residents. It paid its local taxes, plus a little extra to Police HQ and in return found itself on the police database as an information source, which gave it some protection should the *morales* decide to call. The fat man had approved identical deals with brothels all across the city.

Raf and Eduardo were lovers, at least they were according to the Madame downstairs. That was how she'd explained Raf's request for a double chamber to her girls. Officially, of course, homosexuality didn't exist in Ottoman North Africa. In practice, it was almost universal, if staunchly illegal: a society that placed a premium on female virginity, made premarital sex a killing matter and then made it too expensive for most men to get married before their midtwenties was bound to need an easy acceptance of the inevitable, whatever the law said. And that was quite apart from the one in ten men born with little physical interest in women.

'What do we do now?' Eduardo asked.

'We fill the time,' said Raf. 'Until it gets dark.' Walking over to the window, he examined the chamber's mashrabiya, which looked out over the canal, taking in its two sets of shutters. One set closed it off from the street directly below, the other closed off the actual balcony from the room in which he stood.

'You,' said Raf, pointing to the girl he'd selected at random when he first arrived. 'What did you say your name was?' She didn't, or he'd have remembered it.

'Justine.' It was meant to sound French, Raf guessed. From her skin and the black roots to her short hair, he'd have said *moriscos*, but he'd been in Isk less than four months and he wasn't Felix. His predecessor had been famed for his ability to read origins at a single glance.

'Can you get me a drink?'

She looked doubtful. 'What would Your Excellency like?'

'Wine,' said Raf, 'white and chilled, something dry.'

Justine looked more doubtful still.

'Anything you can find,' Raf said and she fumbled at the lock, then scurried from the room.

Raf sighed. He was tired of people being afraid of him. Maybe she was afraid because in her terms he was rich . . . To be honest, in Justine's terms he was probably beyond rich. Even though he could barely afford Donna's and Khartoum's wages and repairs to the al-Mansur madersa were beyond his wallet. Maybe she realized he was police. Or perhaps it was just that he dressed in a suit and wore dark glasses indoors.

Probably it was all of those things. The girl was afraid of everything – of the punters, of her Madame and of time's winged chariot – he could see it in her eyes. If he asked, she'd say she was seventeen, but Justine had a good ten years on that. She was older than he by maybe three years, older than she could afford to be in her trade.

'Will this do?'

Justine held up a dusty bottle of Cru de Ptolémées, two tooth mugs and a handful of ice cubes. Her breathing was ragged from having run upstairs.

'Thank you.' Raf smiled at her and nodded towards the balcony. 'We're going out there,' he told Eduardo. 'I'll see you in an hour or so.'

'What do I do?'

Raf glanced round the chamber. 'Whatever.'

The wine tasted as sour as Raf expected, but all the same he smiled as he poured some for Justine.

'*Salut.*'

'I can try again?' Justine suggested, having tasted it.

'No.' Ice cubes clinked as Raf dropped a few into her glass. 'Who knows?' he said, giving her mug a quick swirl. 'This might help.' In fact, chilling it made no difference, but Raf finished his glass anyway and, when the sourness was gone, refilled. When that was done, he drank most of hers as well.

Sitting back against a shutter, the one he'd told Eduardo to bolt from inside the chamber, Raf examined the balcony, as he examined everything . . .

Straight ahead, beyond an intricately carved screen could be seen fragments of the darkening city; while folded back, against the sidewalk of the mashrabiya were plain shutters that could be used to close off the screen against afternoon heat or cold night air.

He sat in a little world, boxed in on all sides.

'Your turn,' said Raf, handing back Justine's glass.

She drank a little and gave him back what was left. 'You can tell me,' she said finally, when the weight of his silence got too heavy for her to bear. 'Some men find it easier to talk.'

He was not *some men*, Raf wanted to tell her. He was *him*, however unsatisfactory that was. And there were days when he wasn't even sure he was that. When the noise inside his head reached out for the rest of him and his fingers froze and his neck ached and a knot that writhed like an injured snake appeared in the pit of his stomach, leaving him breathless and filled with dread.

Those were the days he needed the fox most. And now the fox was dying and it looked like for good this time.

'Tell me,' Justine said, taking the empty glass from his fingers to put it carefully on the floor. 'What's troubling you?' Her question was as practiced as the butterfly touch of her fingers on his wrist. Even the slight tilt of her head looked like something she'd learnt. All the same, Raf felt a need to answer.

'I'm going to kill someone,' he said flatly.

'When?' Justine kept her expression masked and her question simple.

'Tonight,' said Raf.

'Me?'

He shook his head and felt a single tear slide under his shades. 'Not you, not me. Not those two.' He nodded his head backward to the room behind. 'Just a man.'

'One man?'

'With luck . . .'

'Without luck?'

He thought about it. 'Several,' Raf said slowly, 'maybe more.'

Justine nodded as if this was to be expected. 'And this makes you sad?'

Raf shrugged.

Later, when he'd finished staring through the carved screen at the canal which ran wide and slow between concrete embankments, Justine helped him remove his jacket. And then, having folded that and placed it carefully beside his empty glass, she pulled up her slip and straddled him.

She turned away when he folded his fingers into her pinned-up hair to pull her forward into his kiss, then let him turn her back. They tasted the sourness on each other's lips, their kiss slow, almost thoughtful. Not what she was expecting and not what Raf had intended. Putting up one hand to hold a breast, he felt Justine overflow his fingers.

A boat low in the water. A girl with her shirt undone. The salt of tears and the sea on her lips . . .

'Your Excellency's paid for me,' Justine said, seeing his sudden hesitation. 'You might as well have your money's worth.'

And he'd paid for Zara too. Or was it that her father had paid for him? Either way, breaking the deal had cost Raf almost as much as it had cost Zara. Which was too much. And how could he tell himself his choice of Justine was random? She had the same dark skin and eyes, the full breasts and smooth shoulders.

'Fuck me,' he said. So she did; her fingers reaching down to undo his old-fashioned fly. Over her shoulder, Raf could see a boy fishing in the shade of a felucca. A makeshift house had been built on the felucca's deck out of sheets of galvanized iron, laminated cardboard and what looked like the remains of a plywood tea chest. A scar on the trunk of a squat palm nearby, where it had almost closed round the felucca's mooring rope, said the boat had been there a lot longer than the boy.

Occasional barges piled high with hessian sacks slid in front of the felucca, obscuring it. Perhaps cotton from the fields or a date crop. Raf hadn't yet read up on the seasons in the Delta, what got gathered when.

'What's in the boats?'

Justine stopped moving on his lap.

'The barges,' Raf said, nodding towards the canal behind her.

'Cigarettes,' Justine said without looking. She named two brands of cheap cigarillo made from a dark locally grown tobacco, then shrugged. 'Why sell to the kiosks when you can sell at three times the price to tourists?'

Wrapping her arms round Raf, she pulled him in close, so he could no longer see the canal over her shoulder. And rocking gently, she pushed down against him, and pushed and pushed, until she finally came, or at least pretended to . . . insides tightening as she ground her face into the side of his neck.

'Enough.' Raf slid hands under her buttocks to help her off him. She was breathing swiftly and he could hear her heart pound against her ribs. The sudden satiety seemed real enough. As did the musklike stink of her body.

'What about you?' she asked eventually, sitting back on her heels.

'I'm okay.'

She smiled. 'You don't look like a man who lies.'

Raf's grin was foxlike. 'I seldom do anything else.'

Justine raised a carefully painted eyebrow. 'As Your Excellency wishes.'

Bending forward, she took one of his nipples between her teeth and bit, then released it and backed away until she lay almost flat. After a while, Raf forgot everything except the ache in his groin and a building tightness as her mouth opened, swallowed him and withdrew, time and again. She was good, better than good. Experienced.

He came hard and fast, his fingers reaching out to grab her head as he emptied his fear into her mouth.

'Sorry,' he said, letting go.

Justine's shrug said it all. He wasn't the first to grab her like that and wouldn't be the last. He was a man, her expectations of the breed were no higher.

'I mean it,' said Raf. Over her shoulder, he could see that someone had lit a hurricane lamp aboard the felucca and that the boy with the fishing rod was gone.

Eduardo sprawled, snoring soundly while Rose stared at the cracked ceiling, her slip rucked up round her wide hips. She heard Raf use a knife to lift the bolt on the shutter and turned her head, but other than that she made no attempt to move.

He nodded and Rose nodded back. Watching as he walked slightly unsteadily across to the battered desk to take Eduardo's parcel from its top drawer. Cutting the string with a single swipe of a black glass knife, Raf returned the blade to the scabbard Velcroed to his ankle and spread the contents on the nearest Ottoman.

One automatic, one spring-loaded cosh, one chilli spray, taken from a thin man with a head wound found floating in the hyacinth-infested shallows of Lake Mareotis. Also found on the man was a small pouch, impregnated with the residue of what looked like a dance drug, and a razor-sharp knife. The pouch was still with toxicology, but the knife was the black one Raf had just been using.

The pistol was a clone of a Sturm/Ruger KV95d, a ten-shot, 9mm double action with manual safety, weighing in at twenty-seven ounces and featuring a matte blued finish and black rubber grips. It had one bullet missing. The element that interested Raf was not that the KV's serial number had apparently been filed off, but that it had never been there in the first place, according to the armourer at Champollion. Best guess was that the gun had come out of a black weapons factory somewhere Soviet, without undergoing any of the internationally pre-scribed security checks. Given this, it was no surprise that the history chip embedded in the handle had never been initialized.

As for the cosh, it was a basic model of a type found in souks across North Africa, only this one had been machined with a titanium spring and shot-heavy neoprene head. The chilli spray was mass-produced in Morocco and sublicensed from the US. It could have come from a corner shop almost anywhere.

The body itself had been dragged from Mareotis by a netsman, who dumped his unwelcome catch in the reeds on the bank rather than deal with the police. The old man had only retraced his steps after a local station reported that the German Consulate was offering a reward for information on a missing second secretary.

Sometime between then and the body being delivered in a handcart to the gates of the German compound every one of the dead man's possessions went missing. Raf knew this because a furious liaison officer had put a call through in person to find out what Ashraf Bey intended to do about the outrage.

Raf's promise to have a uniformed officer add the crime to that day's roster just as soon as someone came in from the Consulate to fill out the requisite forms didn't improve matters.

Eduardo had tracked down the old fisherman to a café at the end of a narrow main drag in a marsh village too poor to have more than one street anyway. Eduardo might have suggested he was from the police, though he never actually said so. He did, however, say there was a reward for the return of anything taken from the dead German's body. Since the sum Eduardo mentioned was significantly higher than any sum the fisherman might have got selling the dead man's possessions, the deal was swift and satisfactory on both sides.

Since then the package had been where Raf had told Eduardo to put it, sitting in a desk drawer in Eduardo's walk-up office above the haberdasher's, waiting for a use.

'How do I get onto the roof?'

'First left,' said Justine, 'then up the stairs.' She glanced at Rose, then at the sleeping Eduardo and back at Raf. 'What about him?'

'Let him be,' said Raf, and the woman beneath Eduardo nodded, like she expected no less.

'This is for you,' Raf said to Justine and peeled off twenty hundred-dollar notes. 'And this for Rose.' Raf handed across another ten. It was more money than either would earn in a year. When he turned back, the money had vanished from Justine's hand though she stood exactly where she'd been standing before. 'If I don't come back,' said Raf, 'then I threatened to kill you both if you dared tell the Madame I was gone . . . Which is what I will do,' he added, as an apparent afterthought. 'And if I return, then none of us ever left this chamber, understand?'

Both women nodded.

Justine did one final thing for Raf. She opened the chamber door, looked round to check that the passage really was empty, then walked to the women's bathroom, flipping the bolt on the roof door as she went past. She bolted it again on her way back, returned to the chamber and locked its door behind her. Then, job done, she lay back on one of the leather ottomans and listened to the silence overhead that said His Excellency had already left the brothel roof.

CHAPTER 16

9th October

Raf saw the grey kitten first. So he stopped, swaying slightly, and waited for the suddenly frozen animal to unarch its back and walk away. There were mice nesting in attics, geckoes so still they could be dead and desiccated and bats that spiralled like embers in the hot night, dancing through the air to a tune that only they and Raf could hear.

Bats liked old buildings and El Iskandryia was nearly as full of old buildings as it was of bats. It was one of the things that Raf . . .

Enough scribble, Raf told himself, *you need to concentrate.*

Crossing the darkened roofs without problem, Raf moved silently from one pool of shadow to another, until he was almost where he needed to be. Then he stopped and began the breathing.

He had a dozen triggers. Single words, snatches of song . . . But the long slow breath that emptied his head was the one he liked most. The facility was already there long before he first met I & I. And although the old Rasta had found it hard to believe how fast Raf picked up *rabo de arraira, querxada* and *esquiva,* killing moves disguised as Latin American dance, Raf never told him that he was designed to learn. He just left the old con where he'd found him, still in the yard at Remand3/Seattle.

Occasional cars prowled the street in front of the derelict house, fuelled by petrol, natural gas or alcohol. The signature from their exhausts mixed into a heavy soup of sugar and hydrocarbons that made his sinuses ache. And there were stronger smells, coming from somewhere closer. Food cooking, mixed with something raw and potent, like burning leaves, which is what it was . . .

Retracing his steps until he found a low wall that edged a roof terrace, Raf used this to clamber onto the tiles of a spice attic running the width of the next two houses. A couple of seconds of silence later, Raf was looking down on a thin man smoking in the shadow of a door, his hand curled round the end of his joint to hide its gleam. At the man's feet was

351

a discarded copy of *Hustler*. Three cans of Diet Coke had been drunk, then crushed flat, before being lined up on the edge of a plastic table.

Careless, the fox would have said.

Beside the crushed cans was an empty automatic. Handle angled away from the man's reach, with its full clip resting alongside. The guy was standing guard because that was what he'd been told to do; not because he was expecting visitors.

'*Really careless*,' said Raf, dropping in from the low roof. And as the thin man spun round, Raf flipped out his cosh and tapped the side of his head, hard to medium. Catching the guy before he hit the tiles was the only difficult part.

A battered hiPower, an old Opinel lock-knife with a broken tip to its blade and a handmade garrotte constructed from fishing line and toggle handles. Not exactly *Thiergarten* issue. Raf still pocketed the lot, pushing the oversized Browning through his belt. The unconscious body he rolled against the wall.

Braised mutton, Raf decided as he stood near an open doorway. Mutton, coriander and bread cooking on a skillet. Somewhere in the house a radio was tuned to a pirate station, raw *al-jeel* mixed with a thin synth loop that scratched at the back of Raf's mind. If there was anyone in the rooms directly below, then they were either very still or fast asleep.

No one was there, although Raf checked each room to make sure, finding them all empty. At the top of the next flight of stairs, he stopped to listen. The radio was closer and there were too many people for him to work in silence . . .

It was time to make another plan.

Up above the tiles, bats ran tight circles, losing their feat of the silent figure who stood frozen while they scooped insects from the warm wind.

Ten minutes was what Raf had allowed himself. Ten minutes of stilling his heart and breath and thoughts. Chasing away the sour fog in his head. And then, as one soft fragment of blackness lurched in too close, made clumsy by a struggling moth, Raf flipped out his hand and pulled the bat from the air. Breaking its wings, he tossed the animal down at his feet to watch it flap helplessly on the red tiles.

He was going to kill a human in a minute. Life's price for getting Avatar back. Both for the person who paid and the person who took. So it was, he realized, unutterably childish to be upset about hurting something with a brain the size of a grain of rice, especially something that made its living killing other things.

Red in tooth and claw, his mother would have said. It was humans who were unnatural, having placed themselves outside evolution from choice, which was bad for the world as a whole. He'd read her paper, *Restoring the Balance*. Pretty good for a woman who accepted cash from, a Swiss multinational in return for stepping down as head of *Nature-First*. Of course, they'd given her something extra as well, him . . .

Or perhaps it was the other way round. Maybe funding her films was extra and he was the deal. The fox was better at this kind of stuff. All Raf knew was he came with an eight-thousand-line guarantee from a company that went belly-up after he was born.

So no one got to collect on anything.

'Hey.' Raf's whisper was low, but easily heard by a scrawny stray that watched him from, the next roof, its back prickled with doubt as hunger fought its mistrust of Raf.

As ever, hunger won.

Raf knelt beside the twitching bat, watching the stray approach, its whiskers spread. Very slowly the small cat came within range. Not adult, but no longer really a kitten. The soft fur was gone and with it most of one ear.

And as the hungry stray shot forward to take the dying bat, Raf reached out and placed one finger on a broken wing, preventing the cat from dragging away its prey. 'Eat it here.'

The animal did so, killing the bat with a bite to the neck. By the time the cat realized Raf had released the wing, its meal was almost finished and all that remained was a smudge of soft leather dark against the cooling roof.

'I'd get you another,' Raf said, as he took the animal by the scruff of its neck, 'but we don't really have time.'

From the floor below came the sound of rats. Somewhere below that a water pipe banged and a conversation started up, then died as a door opened and shut. In the background a three-chord special died mid-thrash, feeding into a jingle for Peugeot. All in all, it sounded like the backing track to utter normality.

'Okay,' said Raf, 'this is what we do . . .'

The cat landed at the bottom of the stairs, flipping itself over in midair to land on the bare boards. One glance said its route back to the roof was blocked so instead the animal ran towards an open door, stopped at the top of those stairs and froze as someone at the bottom looked up and swore.

'Ismail?' A gruff voice called up twice and, when hissing was the only answer, the questions turned to swearing. Raf heard the Arabic for *useless* and *idiot* several times. Confident steps on the stairs said the man expected no trouble and at the point he understood it was trouble that expected him, he was already heading for the floor.

353

'Two down,' said Raf to the cat, which did little but swish its tail in silent agreement.

Under his tatty jacket the unconscious man wore a shoulder holster and nestled inside that, still locked in place by a Velcro strap, was a snub-nosed revolver, with letters engraved along its chassis that read **genuine Colt, made in USA**. The sharp edges to that lie made it obvious that the actual place of origin was some local sweatshop.

Which worried Raf a lot.

That there were two sides to Hamzah Effendi was common knowledge. The family man and the crime boss, Jekyll Effendi to Felaheen Hyde. Offend the first and he'd buy out your company and close it down. Offend the second and he'd slaughter your children, bulldoze your house into the ground and sow that ground with rock salt. There was something very biblical about some of those reports on file.

Kidnapping Hamzah's child, even a bastard born without property rights, was the crime-world equivalent to standing on the rails at Masr Station and trying to hold back an incoming train. There might not be quicker ways to commit suicide but there were undoubtedly a dozen ways that were more pleasant.

So why do it? And why do it with cheap labour?

'Up you go.' Raf waved his hand at the cat, which had just taken to sharpening its claws on the edge of a banister. The grey cat left via the roof stairs without a backward glance.

Raf telescoped the cosh and put it in his pocket. The fake Colt got stuffed into his belt. One cosh and three guns – his own, the Browning from the roof and now the fake – plus a black glass blade, its edge ground so sharp as to be almost fractal. That was what the advertising promised anyway. The fawn jacket he stripped off the unconscious man and shrugged his way into, feeling the cloth flop round his shoulders.

Holding a gun in each hand, Raf stamped his way down the flight of steps, pulling the clumsy tread of the other man from memory. He remembered in time to bang into the upright at the bottom and casually shoulder open the kitchen door rather than use its handle. Two men and a boy glanced up, boredom becoming alarm when they realized that whoever Raf was he wasn't one of them.

'No,' said Raf, twitching one gun, 'don't get up.' He spoke Arabic, his accent understandable if atrocious. 'And there's no need for anyone to die . . .' Just for a second the dark void of his gun's muzzle hovered over the heart of the boy.

'Unless that's your choice?'

They'd all shaken their heads before Raf had time to finish his question.

354

'Good,' said Raf, and found that he meant it. He also found he'd been wrong about them cooking. It was takeout he'd been able to smell.

In front of them, on a cracked pine table stood a foil plate filled with gristle and mutton bones, beside an even larger container that had held couscous. A half-empty jar of harissa sat nearby. As did unleavened bread and a jar lid's worth of stubbed-out roaches and twists of torn cardboard.

Carbohydrate and kif, two good ways to waste one's edge. Not that any of the three gave much sign of having had an edge to start with.

'Weapons on the table . . .'

A motley collection of go-faster revolvers and flashy switchblades piled up next to the foil containers. All fake pearl handles and fuck-me electronic sights that looked great and did nothing constructive.

'All of them.'

A couple of boot knives and a pair of brass knuckledusters joined the growing pile. It reminded Raf of the trash that he used to take off teenagers at the door of BonBon, back in Seattle, in the days before Raf fell out with Hu San, leader of the local Triad, and had to become someone else.

'And the rest . . .'

The middle one, whom Raf had figured for the boy's father and the old man's young brother, pulled out a one-shot throw-down from the back of his belt and sullenly placed it next to his knife.

'Now put them into this,' said Raf, pushing across the foil container that had held couscous. Obediently, the three began piling up weapons, taking care not to point the guns anywhere near Raf.

Sit down, stand up, sit down . . . Every time they did what Raf ordered, the imprinting got stronger; that was how the human psyche worked . . . Had Raf been about to kill them, it would have been the right time. He assumed they were bright enough to understand that. And yet they were still way too casual.

'You do know who you've kidnapped?' Raf looked at the boy, the one who'd shivered under the gaze of Raf's gun. Not only was he the youngest, he was also less obviously stoned. What Raf got by way of reply was a slight shake of the head. Though that turned out to be not in answer to the *who* part of Raf's question but the *what*. The kid was arguing definitions.

'We didn't kidnap anybody. We're just guarding him.'

'And that's meant to make a difference?'

The boy shrugged.

'It's DJ Avatar,' Raf said. 'Hamzah Effendi's kid.'

The kid looked suddenly shocked. But even that wasn't straightforward. It turned out he liked Avatar's music. Hamzah didn't figure.

'He's been fucking arrested,' said the old man. 'For torturing a *nasrani* to death.'

'Raped her first,' the boy's father added. 'He's in prison.'

'Really?' Raf asked. 'Who arrested him?'

'Ashraf-fucking-Bey. It happened yesterday.'

'No,' said Raf. 'That's not what happened. Believe me.'

'Yes it is . . .' The old man's pupils were dilated beyond their natural limit, expanded so much they looked like the eyes of someone with a fatal head wound, fixed at that point when the pupils explode. Whatever the man's poison, it was serious stuff.

'On his own beach,' added the boy, sounding suitably outraged.

They left via a back door into a rear alley, having collected both their lookout and Ismail, two men with evil headaches but no worse. The kind of small-time fry, all of them, evolved by every ghetto to fit the niches that others reject. Life's bottom feeders; too disorganized to mastermind their own events, at least not ones that worked, and not hard enough to handle real trouble. That they'd been hired to guard Avatar made no sense at all.

Pulling his automatic from its holster, Raf prowled the house, leaving the locked cellar until last. The roof was deserted and the attic empty. So Raf took the few remaining bulbs from their sockets and locked the roof door before sweeping the level below, where bedrooms had once been. Four empty rooms, filled with acrid dust and silence. Broken chairs filled the far corner of one. In another, some *clochard* had started a small fire on tiles that had cracked. A handful of Thunderbird cans lay blackened in the ashes. Taking each bulb in turn, Raf locked those doors too, using the iron mortise locks common to North Africa. Just to be on the safe side he pocketed the keys.

Empty houses were a familiar sight south of Mahmoudia. At least they were on that stretch west of Rue Menascae, where an area of almost sufficiency surrendered to the dank touch of institutionalized poverty. For streets to be derelict there was as normal as finding crack houses at crossroads, or overcrowded tenements that overlooked unsafe playgrounds, dead trees standing reminder to unmet aspirations.

Travel companies did a good line in offering the 'real Iskandryia' from the safety of air-conditioned coaches. As if the *arrondissement*'s simmering resentment somehow made it more real than the old wealth of the Greek District or the comfortable red-bricked mansion blocks near the fish market.

356

'Enough already,' said Raf, adding his varied collection of keys and bulbs to the weapons discarded by Avatar's guards. There was nothing he needed in the empty kitchen. It was time to find the cellar.

The Daimler-Benz parked below the FOR SALE sign had smoked windows and whitewall tyres, newish but dusty from trawling through too many back streets. The vehicle had *hire car* written all over it.

Seconds after its headlights died, the near-side rear door opened, briefly lighting the inside. What interested Raf was the woman who got out.

'You know her?' Raf asked, yanking Avatar to his feet and dragging him across to the cellar's high window. Had he had more time, Raf might have been kinder, gentler . . . The story of his life really.

'You're drunk!' Avatar said, belatedly realizing the obvious. He sounded surprisingly shocked.

'Not entirely,' said Raf. 'Now . . . you know her?'

Avatar shook his head.

'Well, I do. Last time I saw her she was standing behind your sister, waiting to climb onto a restaurant car.' The boy didn't ask what Raf was doing watching Maxim's. Which was a fair trade-off, because Raf didn't ask what made Avatar throw in his job as Raf's driver.

Zara had that effect on both of them.

'So what happens now?' whispered Avatar, watching the woman walk towards the house, her silhouette looming large above the bars of the cellar's only window. Behind her walked a driver.

'We dance,' said Raf. 'Then I go find whoever dumped a dead girl in your dad's garden.'

He saw surprise on Avatar's face. 'This is just the sideshow,' Raf explained apologetically, looking at the drugged and swaying boy. 'Just a sideshow.' Quickly drawing the black blade from its sheath on his right ankle, Raf checked the point and tried out a couple of steps.

'Well,' he amended, 'I dance.'

Raf hauled Avatar over to a soiled mattress opposite the door. 'You lie down here and *pretend* to be ill.' Flipping round the blade so that it pointed upwards, Raf stood with his back to the doorframe. All it took to embed the blade lightly in the wood was to flip up his hand and step away, leaving the knife protruding from the frame behind him. There were probably better ways to guarantee having a blade ready for use while leaving both hands free; this just happened to be the one that I & I had taught him.

The next few minutes Raf reconstructed later from sounds alone, beginning with the scratch of a key. The Yale on the front door was oiled but even so the tumblers grated a little. There was the click of a light switch, followed immediately by a grunt of irritation. A snatch of Arabic fired into the darkness was repeated, louder this time, irritation becoming anger as the woman caught her hip on the corner of a table in the hallway, the table scraping across tiles.

Already her breathing was less steady.

Raf caught the exact point her anger turned to worry. It came just after her driver banged open the kitchen door and found the room deserted, silent and dark. What little light came through the front door obviously revealed nothing except the fact her guards were gone.

'Fetch a torch.'

Heavy treads crossed the floor above Raf's head, then came the clash of metal heels on the front steps. The creak of a car door. A slam. Moments later the driver was back, his tone apologetic.

The woman swore, louder than was wise. And Raf heard the click of a gas lighter, then heavy footsteps descending towards the cellar door.

'Fucking ragheads,' said the woman. 'You can't get them to do anything . . .'

The driver muttered something that might have been agreement. He was still muttering as he stepped through the door and dropped his lighter. Screaming was out of the question given that Raf's garrotte had already crushed the cartilage of his larynx, so the man gurgled instead.

'Come in,' Raf told the woman. 'Unless you want me to finish off your driver . . . ?'

Not a problem apparently.

Finding her wrist in the darkness, Raf pulled her hand, gun and all, from her side pocket. The weapon she held was tiny, impossibly elegant and looked very expensive. Twisting it from her rigid fingers, Raf tossed it into Avatar's slop bucket, adding a splash and liquid clank to his collection of sounds.

Everybody did something well, that's what the fox used to insist when Raf was small. It was just that some people took longer than others, to discover their real talent. And this, it turned out was his . . . Not caring about the doing until the doing was over. Of course, given his guarantee, Raf probably shouldn't have cared at all.

Blood had strung a necklace round the throat of the driver, although Raf was the only person in the cellar who could see the dark pearls. And the wire was too tight to be clearly visible even to him.

'Slip off your jacket,' Raf told the woman, 'then step away from it.' He waited while she shrugged off her dark coat and put it carefully on the damp tiles, folding it first. Did that signify strength or weakness? The fox would have known.

358

She was thin; dressed in a white silk blouse, thick black belt and a knee-length skirt that matched the folded jacket. As upscale and anonymous as the guards had been obvious and down-market.

'Turn around.'

Tucked into a small holster on the back of her belt was a tiny Colt. The almost invisible bulge on her thigh was undoubtedly something predictable like a derringer or throwing knife.

'Disarm,' Raf said simply.

The Colt she placed carefully on the floor. The bump remained where it was, which was her choice. Stupid, of course, but still her choice.

'This is where you tell me who you are,' said Raf.

The shake of the woman's head was so slight as to be almost subliminal.

'The alternative,' said Raf, yanking the garrotte, 'is that I finish strangling your driver.'

'Poor driver,' was all she said. And as the big man lurched in panic at the tightening of the wire, the woman dipped one hand towards her thigh, sliding back raw silk to reveal a razor-edged blade.

Now.

Without thought, without prior intention, Raf dropped the borrowed garrotte and reached up and back, his fingers folding around the handle of his own blade, which tumbled rapidly through the darkness; the woman's right eye emptying onto her cheek like broken egg as vitreous humour slid down tight skin.

Stepping into her scream, Raf slammed palm against hilt and drove the knife through the woman's parietal lobe and into her cerebellum. Somewhere in that sequence the woman's brain stem got sliced and she stopped being strictly human. Though the whimpering only stopped when Raf put thumb and first finger either side of her throat and squeezed.

He was in the process of lowering her to the ground when a mobile rang. Raf found it in the inside pocket of the woman's discarded jacket. The little phone was clumsier than he'd expected from someone of her erstwhile elegance.

'Na'am?'

Raf listened for a few seconds and shook his head.

'No,' he said, slightly breathless. 'Fraulein Lubeck can't come to the phone. Yes, I'll ask her to call you back . . .' He listened hard. 'No,' he said finally, 'I'm sure she's never heard of someone called Ashraf Bey.'

CHAPTER 17

Each Seraphim 4 × 4 had a blade at the front designed to dig into dunes and turn over sand, which is what they did. Within minutes the dead were ploughed under, enemy trucks torched and camera crews invited in.

Trucks burning weren't exactly hot news but new shots still got added to stale ones. And trustworthy faces in pale suits stood under the blistering sun and reassured the doubtful that after a bitter fire-fight rebel militia had been defeated with almost no loss of life to PaxForce.

'Zero loss of life . . .' corrected a voice in Ka's ear.

'Then why say almost?'

'What?' Sarah glanced round, then shrugged and turned her attention back to Saul. They were moored under an overhanging thorn that kept the afternoon at bay, while lapping water cooled their hiding place and tossed sunlight onto the underside of its spiky canopy.

Ka was ignoring all questions. He was getting good at that. Ignoring the others meant not facing questions he couldn't answer.

'Well?' Ka asked the voice.

'No dead would mean an unfair fight. Strong against weak. A few dead equals luck, skill, better weapons . . . It's about presentation.' The voice paused and, without having to ask, Ka suddenly found himself looking down on a thornbush rather than at a battlefield.

'Who are you?' the voice demanded.

Ka sighed. 'You've asked me this already . . .'

'Humour me,' said the voice. It didn't sound very humorous at all. 'That's a basic rule, okay?'

'Sergeant Ka,' said Ka. 'We were part of the Army.'

'Were?'

Ka thought of the ploughs turning over sand and blinked as his p.o.v. changed. The 4 × 4s were done now, even out at the edge of what had been Ka's camp. Some trucks were even leaving, helmeted troops waving to a

360

blonde woman who stood atop a dune, laden down with power pack and portable satellite dish.

Ka turned off the radio. 'We can't go back,' he told the others, as if that was an end to the argument.

'Oh yes we fucking can.' Saul's voice was deeper than Ka's own. His superior age showing in its gruffness and the ease with which he dropped swear words into his conversation. 'We just turn this shitty boat around.'

'They'd flog us publicly,' Sarah reminded him. 'Maybe shoot us.'

'Yeah.' Bec flicked her gaze from Sarah to Ka, then back again. 'We'll need an excuse.'

Lifting his shades, Ka stared at Bec. 'We can't go back,' he said slowly. 'You know why we can't go back? Because everyone's dead.'

Mouths dropped open and Zac instantly flung his hands over his ears, as if to block out Ka's lies. Both his sisters were in that camp, Ka realized; had been, rather . . .

'It was quick,' Ka insisted. 'Instant,' he added hurriedly. 'It was instant. A bomb made a small bang and everyone just fell over.'

'Yeah?' said Saul. 'And how do you know . . . ?'

'I just do. Then the 'copters came and trucks full of soldiers.'

'Why did they send soldiers?' Bec asked. 'If the bomb had already killed everyone?'

Ka didn't have an answer to that.

'Because the bomb doesn't exist,' said the voice in his ear. 'That's why . . . In a moment your radio is going to come on. Talk to it direct.'

My radio is switched off, Ka wanted to say, but the blue box was already noisily swooping hi-to-low at exactly sixty cycles a minute, like a miniature police siren.

'Sergeant Ka,' said the boy, holding the radio to his ear and feeling stupid.

'Lieutenant Ka,' corrected the voice. 'As of now. Lieutenant Ka, Sergeant Sarah, Corporal Bec . . .'

'What about Saul and Zac?'

'Zac's a baby. And Saul . . .'

Ka waited.

'He's a spy, you understand?'

'I understand,' said Ka, sitting up so straight his hair almost caught in down-hanging thorns.

'I understand, sir.'

'Sir.'

'And you know who I am?'

Ka shook his head. Somehow that was enough.

361

'Colonel Abad,' said the Colonel, introducing himself. 'You've heard of me?'

Oh yes. Ka grinned stupidly at the badge on his shirt. Those shades, the cigar, that black beard. The Colonel.

'Where are you exactly?'

The boy looked round him. Cliffs tight on both sides of the river and white-headed vultures overhead. But then there were always vultures circling thermals over this stretch of the Nile. Above the vultures, made smaller both by reality and distance, hovered raptors. Black-winged kites, most probably.

Sarah's felucca was tied at the river's bend, on the side where floodwater flowed less fast and silt almost buried rocks that were pale and strangely square. Three thousand years earlier, during the flood season, a cargo boat had run aground there. Staying with his freshly hewn sandstone, the captain had sent slaves downriver to get help. He died in the night waiting for their return, killed by an adder as he sat by a small fire lit to keep jackals at bay.

Colonel Abad knew these things. The hieroglyphs of the pharaohs cartouched below their statues, the genera of birds and animals, even the molecular structure of each rock that made up the crumbling cliffs and temples, statues and ruins.

Ka could identify concrete, sandstone and polycrete, the frothy stuff that set hard and could be coated with sand or gravel, provided any covering was whacked on before the crete had time to dry. Both sides used it to make HQs that blended into any background.

'We're upriver from the camp,' Ka said, 'on a bend near low cliffs . . . And we haven't eaten all day,' he added as an afterthought.

'You got grenades?'

'Yes,' said Ka. At least Saul had. Zac, Sarah and Bec had two rifles, a knife and a pistol between them. He had the plastic gun. What his dead lieutenant called a doublePup. He didn't like it very much.

'Swap it,' said Colonel Abad. 'First chance you get. Right . . .' The radio crackled for a second. 'Listen up. Food first. That means losing a grenade to the river. Get Saul to throw and Bec and Zac to collect the fish . . . All of them.'

'Do we eat them raw?'

'Sushi.' The voice sounded amused. 'Only if you want. Personally I'd suggest a small fire and usually I'd recommend dry twigs, but today we want smoke, don't we?'

'Do we?'

'Oh yes,' said the voice, 'very definitely.'

*

Ka shuffled backward, then stopped when his foot hit Sarah's shoulder. The girl didn't move but she did glare, waiting while Ka edged sideways to give her space. They were alone together in the desert, on an important mission . . . That was how Ka had explained it to the others.

'Accident,' said Ka.

Sarah nodded. Opened her mouth as if she was about to say something, then shut it. She had perfect teeth, Ka realized. Tourist's teeth. All in a neat line and with no chipped edges.

'How old are you?' He'd asked the question without thinking. 'I mean, really?' He knew Sarah said she was fourteen but then he said he was thirteen.

'Fifteen,' Sarah said firmly.

'Me too . . .' Ka smiled, then shrugged. Questions were never welcome, he should have known that. Ka just wanted to be the one who persuaded her to open up and talk. Already he could describe how she looked without looking. Hair as black as her eyes, braided into long plaits. Her skin somewhere between dark chocolate and purple, not café noir like his. She'd taken grief for that in the camp; grief, comments and idle slaps. Mostly from the older girls.

There were more girls than boys in the Ragged Army. That was because they fought better, according to Saul, having more to fear if captured. Although Saul was the only person Ka had ever heard say this and, besides, both sides chopped off the hands of those who wouldn't change and it was hard to think of much worse than that.

'What are you thinking?'

'About these,' said Ka and flexed his fingers. 'Sometimes . . . about being captured.'

Sarah nodded. 'Right,' she said. 'Scare yourself, why don't you?'

Sighting along the barrel of her rifle, she began to tighten her finger on the trigger.

'Not yet,' protested Ka. He had orders from Colonel Abad and he intended to obey them. 'I'll tell you when.'

'I can do it from here,' Sarah said crossly.

'I'm sure you can,' Ka agreed, 'but the Colonel . . .'

He'd told Sarah about Colonel Abad. He'd told them all. No one any of them knew had ever seen the man in the flesh, but even having talked to the Colonel by radio raised Ka's importance with the others.

'The Colonel?'

Ka had nodded.

'He spoke to you?' Zac's small face had been bright with wonder.

'Yes, he wants me to go on reconnaissance . . .' Ka stumbled over the word. 'After we've all eaten.' Ka gave them their new ranks, pretending

not to see the anger in Saul's eyes. 'You,' he said to Saul, 'throw your grenade into the river and we'll grab the fish as they float to the surface.'

'It's my last one.' Saul's voice was suspicious.

'You were the person complaining you were hungry.' Which was true enough. He'd complained louder than anyone. 'Throw it into the middle,' Ka ordered.

'Wait.' That was Sarah.

Ka stared at her until she looked away, suddenly unsure. 'I mean,' she said quietly, 'perhaps you think he should throw it over there.' Sarah pointed to a gravel spit a hundred paces up river. 'So we can catch the fish as they float towards us.'

Agree with her, said a voice in his head.

'You're right,' said Ka. 'That's a much better idea.'

'Really?' Sarah suddenly looked more unsure than ever.

The explosion boiled the river and echoed off the cliff face, sending egrets skywards in a wheeling cloud. In total they collected fifty-three fish, with Ka just missing a loglike Nile catfish that came to the surface, then rolled over and sank. Most of the catch were fat perch sporting heavy lines like makeup around their eyes. And mixed in with the perch were a handful of deep blue talapia.

Sarah told the others that talapia collected a better price at market but, to Ka at least, both fish tasted equally good. In a flourish that surprised everyone, Bec ripped handfuls of leaves from a spindly bush and stuffed them inside the gutted perch before letting Sarah bake them on her smoking fire pit.

'Corporal Bec is in charge until I get back,' Ka announced when everyone had eaten more than they should. 'Sarah comes with me. The rest of you remain here.'

'Says who?'

He could pretend not to hear Saul or he could answer. And for once the truth was a better reply. 'Colonel Abad,' said Ka, 'those are his direct orders . . .' He turned to where Sarah was washing her fingers in the river.

'Sergeant . . .'

Ka had led the way up a wadi, coarse gravel giving way to grit as rare grass scabs grew more spiky and vanished altogether. Walking in the heat of the afternoon was insane but that was what the Colonel had wanted. And the man had been sympathetic, his voice understanding but firm as it crackled through the radio.

'I only ever ask for the necessary,' he had said. 'And you and Sergeant Sarah can do it. I'm certain you can.'

364

So Ka kept walking into the shimmering haze, with the low cliffs two hours behind him and miles of low slope ahead. Plus a dark line at the horizon that could have been mountains but was probably low cloud. And if not cloud, perhaps a trick of the heat haze. Whatever it was, that thin smudge of colour was further than either of them could walk.

'Give me the bottle . . .'

'No.' Ka shook his head and kept going. One foot in front of the other, his plastic rifle held firmly in front of him. They'd stopped twice already for water. If they finished their bottle now how could they manage the return?

'You don't even know where you're going . . .'

That was true.

'Colonel Abad will tell us,' said Ka. 'When he's ready.'

Sarah sucked at her teeth and pushed past Ka, forcing her aching legs to carry her over a crescent-shaped dune. Sweat had glued her vest to her back and drawn dark circles under her arms. Even her combats were sticky with perspiration and those were made from a special kind of cloth that breathed for itself. She knew that because it said so on the label.

Ka let her go on ahead. Sometimes when Sarah got angry it was best to leave her alone. But that wasn't the real reason Ka was happy to let her walk on. Ka liked watching the way her thin hips swung as she walked. And he liked the changing gap of nakedness between the top of her loose combats and the bottom of her vest. Also . . .

Any further thoughts were cut off by the crackle of his radio.

'Lieutenant Ka here.'

Ka noticed Sarah turn back but he was already intent on new orders that were simple and precise. Walk half a klick straight ahead, climb to the top of a vast mound and wait until their target was too close to miss. No more than fifty paces max . . .

'Load your rifle,' he told Sarah.

She shifted her Martini Henry so that it was angled across her body. 'It's already loaded,' Sarah said, as if she couldn't believe he'd say something that stupid.

'What about the sights?'

'What about them?'

'Set them for fifty . . .'

Obediently Sarah adjusted for distance. Then she licked her finger and tested for wind, even though she knew there wasn't any. Satisfied that she was right, she made another slight adjustment and worked the bolt, pulling a bullet into the gun's chamber.

'What now?' she asked.

'We wait . . .'

The truck looked like a child's toy. That might have been a side effect of a yellow Tonka-toy paint-job that was intended to make it blend in with the desert, or it might have been the balloon tyres, which bulged with each jolt across the broken ground.

'The Colonel knew this was coming?' A look that Ka recognized began to creep across her face, smoothing away all expression. She didn't even glance over when she spoke. Instead, she wriggled her body down into the sand, shuffling one knee outwards until it gripped the ground like a rider's leg locked tight to the side of a mount.

'Well?' she said.

'Yeah,' said Ka, 'undoubtedly.' Right on cue Ka heard his radio crackle to life. They both guessed what the orders would be but Ka told her anyway. 'Shoot the driver.'

Sarah wanted to suggest taking out a tyre instead. Only, so what if she killed the driver and the truck crashed? The hardest thing it could smack into was the side of a dune and besides, shooting people was her job. She never got the shakes, at least not in advance and she always held the moment.

Ice in the soul, her uncle had called it. The feeling had come after Kordofan, which was when she'd first been captured, towards the end of a battle with her brigade already retreating and the scrub full of bodies and abandoned weapons. One of Sarah's own officers had unwittingly provided camouflage and she'd almost got away with hiding in a ditch beneath him. And then the stripping crews had come and yanked away his body, intending to strip it of everything valuable and found Sarah crouched beneath.

Faced with five men who had wrists heavy with Rolexes and Tag Hauers worn like bracelets, she'd stood up, straightened her shirt and recited the first verse of the Holy Quran.

She'd been learning the words for weeks. Everyone she knew had been learning them in secret, when the officers weren't around; friends testing each other until their recitations were perfect.

The men still raped her, of course, but not that violently and when she crawled to her knees afterwards to find her clothes, she buttoned her shirt around a throat that was uncut and over a stomach that still had its guts where they should be, on the inside.

They'd taken nothing she couldn't afford to lose. At least that's what she told herself as she limped away towards her new camp. Equally it was nothing she'd wanted to give them either. And so the ice froze inside her and hardened around her like a shell, unnoticeable to everybody except those who got too close.

366

'Now,' Ka told her.

Close up it was possible to see blue lettering on the bonnet and a whip aerial that flew a blue pennant, which cracked and flicked in the afternoon air. Two white men sat together up front, both wearing shades and talking to each other rather than keeping watch on the rough track.

North European or American. Or that other continent that began with A. There were a lot of those. Pulling in a breath and holding it, Sarah aimed her rifle high, then slowly lowered the barrel and fired the moment she dropped through her target.

'Clean shot,' she said to no one.

Ka was already up and running. He rolled once at the bottom and came upright, then crashed forward, his doublePup already sighting itself in . . . Not that Ka needed hi-tech to cut down the uniforms scrambling from the back of the truck. Those he missed with his first magazine were too stunned to do anything but panic as his next reduced them to noncombatant status.

Only one man, an elderly sergeant, hit the ground and racked back the slide on his own submachine gun. Which was as far as he got. Ka's third magazine took off the top of the man's skull in a single burst.

'Got it.' It was the man's battered AK49 Ka wanted. A cookie-cutter buzz gun stamped out of cheap metal, idiotproof and unbreakable. Just getting that made his whole trip worthwhile.

'Lieutenant Ka,' he answered his radio without consciously realizing it had buzzed. The voice on the other end was quietly impressed. 'I knew you could do it. Heap sand over the bodies and drive back to the river . . .'

'What about the cliffs?' Ka said.

'You can get to within three hundred paces. Walk the rest. Now open the passenger door and check the glove compartment . . .'

Ka pulled the door open and yanked out both bodies. He must have missed hearing Sarah's second shot. The jelly splashes he wiped off everything with Kleenex taken from a pack on the dashboard. The blood puddles, urine and shit proved more difficult so Ka did what women used to do in his village and scrubbed handfuls of sand across the plastic seats and floor.

The tissues he burned and the sand went back to join the other sand and the bodies Ka lost under the crusting edge of an overhang. It wasn't hard. Ka just dragged the dead over one at a time, then crumbled away the overhang by stamping along the sharp edge of its crust.

All the while, Sarah sat and watched and Ka let her, even though he was senior. She got like that after a firefight. Most of the time everyone else pretended not to notice. It was safer.

'Open the glove compartment,' said the Colonel. Ka could hear from his voice that he was preparing to be patient. 'It's that grey handle . . . That's right, on the dash . . .'

Inside was a map the Colonel obviously expected to be there, plus a big bar of chocolate and two cans of real Coke, both chilled.

'A map,' said Ka, 'sweets and two cans of Coke, they're still cold.'

'The compartment doubles as a chill cabinet,' the Colonel told him. 'What else?'

'Nothing.'

'Lift out the base.' There was additional static to the voice this time. A bigger distance.

'Tiny glass bottles,' Ka announced as he pulled out a handful of ampoules. 'With needles.' Each one was the length of his smallest finger, with a hollow needle the length of his thumbnail fixed at one end. The needles had plastic safety caps. Red lettering and a picture of two twisting snakes were printed on the side of each bottle.

'Well done,' said the Colonel. 'Now break a line of squares off the chocolate for Sarah and eat another yourself, then put the rest back in the cool compartment along with the ampoules . . . You can have the Cokes,' he added as an afterthought.

CHAPTER 18

That Raf cried worried the cat not at all. Tears salty as blood ran into his neat beard and trickled across his chin. The cat would happily have dined on the puddle of fresh vomit between Raf's knees, but the tiny bats the man plucked out of the air were richer and warmer. And besides, they were *being offered*, the almost-kitten didn't even have to steal or beg. All it had to do was kill and eat.

Leaving Raf to his own memories . . .

'T-cells down fifteen percent again.'

'Will he die?'

One could almost hear the shrug. Well, Raf could from where he sat in a window, staring out at the crooked tip of the Matterhorn. It was late spring and the lower meadow was alive with dog violet, speedwell and ladies smock. If he pushed his sight until his eyes hurt, he could just see a dark hawk frozen on the edge of the upper slopes, waiting to hit its prey.

'You know, sir,' said the first voice, 'I'd really be tempted . . .'

'Would you?' The answering laugh was sour.

'Well, suppose . . .'

'Don't suppose,' the second voice was suddenly cross. 'Think instead. We can either carry over the costs or close the project and put the costs against this quarter's bottom line. Which one do you suggest?'

The other person thought about that.

'Fit one of the new synthetics,' said the cross voice. 'Ditto on the bone marrow.'

'Sir, we're already over budget.'

The senior man sighed, heavily. 'Take it off R&D. Slap a couple of new patent numbers on the chart. The usual . . .'

Twelve weeks followed in a blur of morphine until reality finally drip-fed its way into the analgesic fog and ruined the next three months of Raf's life. The three months when Raf didn't have to remind himself to eat or worry about whether or not he could get to sleep, because the snakes did that for him. They wove themselves under his skin and up his nose, into his throat and up his pee-pee. A fat one even came out of the side of his stomach.

One time when Raf grew bored exploring the walls inside his own head, he woke himself up to find a girl he didn't recognize sitting on the end of the bed, crying.

'What's wrong?'

She jumped and squeaked at the same time, and Raf smiled.

'You're awake . . .' The girl sounded shocked. She checked the readout from a grey box sitting on a bedside cabinet. 'It says you're asleep.' Her words were to herself.

'Look at this,' said Raf and jerked the dancing line so that it peaked right off the screen, then he levelled it out until it looked like the flat bit at a valley bottom. 'See, you just make it do what you want.'

The nurse looked at the small boy wired into the surgical slab. Her name was Anne Rigler and she was Scottish. The medical brokers were paying her less than nurses usually earned in Switzerland but much more than she could earn in Aberdeen now that the oil was gone.

'It's a disgrace,' she said, sounding furious.

Raf stopped playing. 'I'm sorry. Does it break the machine?'

'No, no . . .' Pink fingers folded over his own, swallowing them. Her grip was so tight that it hurt. 'I don't mean what you're doing to their machine.' Anna's voice had a sob in it. 'This.' She jerked her chin towards the electronic bed, then round the small room. 'All of this.'

'They're mending me,' Raf explained patiently.

'Mending you?'

The boy nodded. 'New kidneys,' he said, 'improved breastbone and something to make my body mend faster when I get hurt. I don't mind, it's better than lessons.'

'Lessons?'

'I have to do lessons . . .'

She smiled. 'I wasn't mad about school either. Why don't you like yours?'

'Boring,' said Raf. *'Boring, boring, boring* . . . No one ever says anything new. It's just what's already in the textbooks.'

'You can read?'

He looked at Anne as if she was mad. 'Of course I can read,' he said. 'I'm five.'

The nurse thought about that for a while. As she did so, she jotted notes on a chart and swung her foot, so her sole scuffed the floor with each swing. Wherever the thoughts went, they didn't lead her anywhere she wanted to go.

'Do you like it here?'

Raf shrugged. 'It's okay. Better than the *Tigris* . . .'

Her look was a question.

'My mother's ship. It smells dirty and I get sick. All that static . . .'

'She's a sailor?'

'No,' Raf laughed. 'She saves whales . . .'

She did too. And cut together award-winning films from hours of footage taken with a tiny camera taped to the side of her mask. The whales were killers and ate seals like Scooby snacks. Raf often wondered why she didn't save the Scooby snacks instead.

CHAPTER 19

'Enough,' Raf told the cat, wiping vomit from his shoes with a handkerchief taken from his jacket. Somehow a fresh one materialized in his top pocket every morning. Like eating lunch in the kitchen, it seemed ordinary tissues weren't for people like him.

Raf shrugged and screwed the soiled linen into a ball, pushing it deep into a trouser pocket. He was alone on the roof, Avatar having agreed to take the dusty hire car only after Raf marched him to the front door.

Av had been too weak to go, even after Raf had put back the lights, wiped down the door handles and carefully explained exactly why he should. So, to save time, Raf had cheated, ramping the kid up on a foil twist of speedballs taken from the driver's wallet.

'This will help you walk,' Raf told him. 'You want that, don't you?'

Avatar nodded, eyes huge.

'Yeah, figured.' Raf had dropped to a crouch beside Avatar's soiled mattress, with the driver's dropped lighter in one hand and the foil twist in his other. 'Suck the smoke,' said Raf and put a flame to the foil.

Avatar gagged.

'Slowly.' Raf's voice was soft, its tone soothing. He needed the boy out of the house and soon. Which bizarrely meant stopping Avatar from taking in too much smoke at once.

'Who are you?'

Raf stared at the boy, whose skin was as smooth as Italian leather in the overhead light. High cheekbones had become visible where there'd been adolescent softness only months before. The kid was Renaissance beautiful and part of that beauty was that Avatar didn't yet know it. To make matters more complicated, Avatar had his sister's eyes. Hurt and all.

Raf sighed. 'I'm your boss, remember . . .'

'You fired me!'

372

'You kind of fired yourself.'

'Well.' Avatar's smile was sad. 'Maybe.' He rolled sideways off his mattress and stood unsteadily. Around him the cellar seemed to rock and then settle. 'I could work for you again,' Avatar suggested.

'As of now, you do,' said Raf and turned the kid towards the door, watching him walk away, weak from hunger and dizzy with smoke.

'About Zara . . .' Avatar said over his shoulder.

'What about her?'

'She's . . .' Avatar searched in vain for the accurate word. 'Cool, I suppose.'

'So everyone keeps telling me.'

'She's also in love with you.'

Raf sighed and tossed Avatar the car keys. Adding an inevitable clang to his collection of sounds.

CHAPTER 20

Sudan

Ka could see Sarah's mouth open but her words were gone. Tears ebonied her cheeks and snot ran from her nose. His one attempt to put an arm round her had seen Sarah push him so hard that he almost fell over a small cliff.

It was Zac, Ka realized, tiny and doll-like in the river amid silver flashes.

Leaving Sarah where she stood, Ka ran through the wadi until, halfway down, rock crumbled under his feet and for a few blessed seconds all Ka's attention went on staying upright.

Then he was at the water's edge and reality came flooding in. Half-smoked perch were pegged out on twigs over the fire pit; but the real stink came from the humans, who had all been dead for hours by the look of it. Those bruises dead people get were already present wherever flesh touched ground.

Their fire pit was sodden with urine and Zac's ripped-open rucksack had been tossed on top of the cold embers. Everywhere had been searched and nothing found; because what the soldiers wanted still shaded Ka's eyes from the sun.

Bec had two bullet holes, one in her stomach and another below a breast. One shoe was missing and her rifle empty. Saul had a bullet through his good shoulder and another in his leg. He'd been finished with a rifle butt to the temple. Zac was a head shot, close up and through the back of his skull. The kid had fallen where he knelt.

UN-issue, 90–2 ammo meant nothing. All sides took weapons where they could capture them, ammo too. As for Sarah's felucca, a tossed grenade had reduced that to kindling, sending more dark-eyed perch to the surface.

'How did they get here?'

'Combat hovercraft, Thornycroft Mk 11, grade 5 stealth profile . . .'

Ka didn't listen. He'd been talking to himself anyway and since there weren't any track marks or, come to that, any tracks down which trucks could have come, he'd been on the point of working out that the enemy had used some kind of boat.

'We have to bury them.'

'No,' said Ka and held up one hand, as if that was enough to hold back her bubbling anger. 'The Colonel says we can't take that risk.'

Her answer was a glare.

'I want to,' said Ka. 'They were my friends too.' Which wasn't quite true. Saul was a bully and he'd never got to know Bec, but Ka knew the three of them had been together since Kordofan. And Zac . . . Zac had been Ka's responsibility. 'But what if the troops come back to make another search . . . ?'

Sarah said nothing.

'They'll know some of us are still alive and come looking with planes. What . . . ?' said Ka, seeing Sarah's face suddenly harden.

'You're afraid.'

'Afraid? I'm scared shitless. You, me . . . it's just a matter of time.'

'The will of God,' Sarah said.

'You believe that?'

She thought about it. 'I used to, kind of still do. Maybe I just want . . .'

'Yeah.' Ka put his arm round her shoulders and this time she didn't push him away. . . .

In the back of the truck was a thermoflage net, fitted with a pocket at each corner that could be filled with stones or loaded with sand, for when the terrain was impossible to peg. As well as blanking out thermal signatures, the huge net stealthed radar. Or so the Colonel said and whatever that meant, it sounded good.

The smashed boat was far behind them and night had come in. Heat still radiated from the sand but the temperature of the air was in free fall, latent heat losing out to the sprinkling of cold stars overhead.

'We'd be better sleeping inside . . .' Ka made it almost a question.

'Front seat?'

'That's still sticky. It should be the back.'

Sarah's grunt was doubtful.

'It's going to get colder,' warned Ka. Something experience had told Sarah already. Being out in the emptiness without a bag or fire was no joke and her survival blanket was back with the . . .

'Hey' he reached out, 'it's okay.'

She cried when they lay side by side enfolded matting in the back of the yellow Seraphim, hot tears for what she'd lost. Though crying made no

375

real sense, because everything she'd ever had to lose, Sarah had long since thought gone. Except her life maybe, and she was finding that increasingly hard to care about.

And so Ka held her tight and muttered his desolate promises into her ear. That he would look after her and any soldiers who came after them were dead, that the war would stop once the river dried up . . .

And she let his words wash over her and by the time Ka stopped promising and climbed clumsily on top, she'd stopped crying. It was his tears that fell into her face and breasts as he moved slowly above her, his quiet sobs the last thing she heard before they both fell into sleep.

CHAPTER 21

'Present,' said Raf, tossing the scrawny animal at Hani so that it landed claws out and stuck to her bare shoulder. 'This one doesn't need batteries.'

'Ouch.' Grabbing the cat by the scruff of its neck, Hani yanked back its head and glared. The animal glared right back and five seconds into their staring contest it began to purr.

'The sound of nine lives,' said Raf.

Hani raised her dark eyebrows.

'Purring is a healing mechanism. 27–44Hz. That frequency helps bones mend and heals cuts. It works on humans too . . .'

Sunday morning, at a stone table in the madersa's walled courtyard, the splash of the marble fountain Raf had paid to be mended cutting through the clatter of Donna working nearby in her huge kitchen. Breakfast was spread out in front of them, almost untouched.

Coffee for Raf, orange juice for Hani.

Having drunk her juice, Hani had swallowed a token mouthful of balila and been on the point of getting down when Raf beat her to it and went to get his apology. Which was what the almost-cat was. For asking Hani how she found Avatar . . . Right question, wrong way.

'For me?'

Raf nodded.

'What does it eat?'

'Well . . .' He considered her question. 'Bats are its favourite . . . That's a joke,' Raf added hastily, when Hani started to look worried. 'Tell Donna to get it some meat.'

'What's it called?'

Raf shrugged.

'Uncle Ashraf,' Hani's voice was mock sweet. 'If it's a boy can he live in the haremlek?' Hani still had problems getting her head round the

377

idea of anything male being allowed near the second floor of the madersa. Centuries of tradition were a hard mind-set to break.

'It's a girl,' said Raf, 'and she can't *live* there . . . but she can visit, all right? She lives in the courtyard . . .'

'. . . or the kitchens.'

Raf pretended to think about that, knowing already that he would let Hani have her way. 'Maybe,' he said. 'Provided you clean up any mess and Donna agrees.'

'She will,' said Hani, with the absolute certainty of a child who knows she has the winning hand in a particular relationship. With that, Hani slid from her seat, not to go ask Donna but to find Khartoum. She needed to have a serious discussion about a sensible name.

Having taken the dirty breakfast plates back to the kitchen, Raf stopped to check an update on the ISK rolling news channel, which was all Donna ever watched. Bodies had been found in a derelict house near Mahmoudiya following a tip-off, and a nightclub called Sarahz, on the corner of Gumhuriya, had been firebombed, although the damage was less than it could have been.

According to Ferdie Abdullah, the channel's elegant if elderly anchorman, these events were not related.

CHAPTER 22

13th October

Changing down a gear, General Koenig Pasha slung his favourite car around a corner and glanced at his passenger. 'We got the murderer,' he said casually and smiled to see disbelief freeze the Senator's face.

'When?' Senator Liz was so shocked she forgot to be polite.

'A couple of days ago. My Chief of Detectives . . .' The call from Raf had come the previous evening. It seemed the killer had been killed. According to a cross-crime/evidence-sifting algorithm run that afternoon, seminal fluid taken from the girl butchered on Hamzah's beach gave an exact DNA match to a man found murdered in a deserted house in Mahmoudiya. Ashraf Bey proclaimed himself as surprised as the General.

'This man,' said the American. 'When will he stand trial?'

'Never,' the General announced airily.

'But surely . . .'

'I'm afraid not.'

If the boxlike black Bentley lacked the élan of the General's two-tone 1936 Rolls-Royce Phantom III or the racing lines of his green 1937 Hispano-Suiza, it made up for that in raw power, being a two-handed broadsword to the others' rapier.

The General liked cars much more than he liked people, most of whom lacked a quarter of the Bentley's character. And he decided that if Senator Liz Elsing had been a car, she'd have been a Ford, reliable, bland and irritating. He, however, would have been this Bentley.

'It seems the murderer died,' added the General. For propriety's sake, this was the point at which he should have said *under questioning*, because the woman would expect no less. However, as her traditional Western prejudices could be relied upon to fill in that gap for herself, the General changed gear instead and heard the motor slow to a throaty, law-breaking roar. A roar that impressed him more than anything the Senator might say.

Originally made in 1931 and totally rebuilt in 1993 at the orders of a Sudanese drummer whose fingers could coax rhythms from goatskin that defied simple mathematical definition, the eight-litre vehicle had been presented to the General by Hamzah Quitrimala. A small token of the industrialist's appreciation for being given permission to build the Midas Refinery.

The red leather driver's seat on which Koenig Pasha sat was as battered and shiny as a club chair. The walnut trim on the dash was solid, not veneer, and years of careful hand-polishing had produced a patina that would enhance the most elegant antique.

Which it was, the General reminded himself. Though it was hard to remember that fact when the car's 7,983cc of inline power could still accelerate its bricklike body to 110 mph. Only one hundred had been built and most of those with the 144-inch wheelbase. The General's featured the 156.

And in fourth gear, the car could range from walking speed to the ton, vibrations kept to a minimum by rubber mountings to the engine and gearbox.

'What do you think?'

'Very colourful, Your Excellency,' said his passenger, watching as a small Citroën three-wheeler laden with peppers pulled over to let the General pass. He knew her researchers had told the Senator that, unfortunately, the current vegetable crop would be bumper. Which gave her one less way to get leverage.

'I meant the car . . .'

'The car, Your Excellency?'

By now protocol demanded that Koenig Pasha ask the Senator to call him *General* or maybe even *Saeed*; at the very least it should have been *sir* . . . General Saeed Koenig Pasha, however, had no intention of obliging. Senator Liz, as she insisted he call her, was known to the General as an international busybody so afraid of her own vices that she'd turned the magnifying glass of her insecurity on the virtues of everyone else.

He also doubted, strongly, that her fact-finding mission to El Iskandryia involved the finding out of any facts. In his long experience, special envoys from the White House or Berlin were only interested in trade, polishing their spheres of influence and issuing threats, usually disguised as a once-in-a-lifetime, one-off opportunity.

'Bentley, eight-litre, 1931 . . . Superb machine.'

The small woman looked embarrassed. Too clumsy to make small talk like the diplomat she was supposed to be and too worried about getting it wrong to pretend she knew about vintage cars, Senator Liz retreated into silence, which was something of a first.

Smiling grimly, Koening Pasha put his foot to the floor and swung the heavy Bentley out into the middle of the road to overtake two Army jeeps and a tractor, which were the cause of their slowness. Let the soldiers catch up with him if they could.

Of course the Senator didn't like his car. Americans expected cruise control, air-conditioning and a basic AI, all of which the General regarded as utterly redundant. If the General got hot, he opened a window, and if that failed to work, he just went faster . . .

As for directions, if he got lost he stopped and asked the *felaheen*. It was worth it for the shocked look when they realized to whom they were speaking.

'Finally,' said the General, 'we're here.' Stamping on the brakes, he swung his wooden steering wheel and aimed for a farm track, accelerating into the skid so that the car's rear barely missed shunting one side of a crumbling set of gateposts.

After that, the heavy car ate up the dirt road, bouncing in and out of potholes and past row after row of walled terraces cut into the sides of the hill, until the jeeps were just distant plumes of dust behind it.

His own trail would be visible for miles, an almost biblical column of smoke ascending to heaven. All the same, Hakim and Ahmed would be worried, but then being his bodyguards that was their job, and his new *aide de camp* would be sweating blood and cursing under his breath. It had better be under his breath, because the General would hear about it if it wasn't.

'Here we go,' Koenig Pasha announced, skidding to a halt in a slick of gravel that popped like small-arms fire.

Here was a farmhouse cracked open like an egg. Red pantiles lay scattered across the earth, mostly in shards but with the occasional half tile. All the really good ones had been taken, then the not-so-good. What was left were discards, tiles too damaged to make stealing them worthwhile.

A single doorway stood doorless, while wooden shutters hung loose from shattered windows that had never known glass. And from inside came a scuttling like rats picking their way across broken crockery.

'Outside,' demanded the General. 'Out of there now.'

'Yes, Excellency . . .' The anxious voice probably called everyone *excellency*, just to be sure. But the General had to call again before its owner appeared.

'I'm coming, Excellency.' With his eyes blinking at the sudden glare, a moon-faced boy materialized in the dark doorway. His gaze slid to the old man's face and for a split second the young *fellah* didn't recognize who was standing there.

Then he did.

'Stand over there,' ordered Koenig Pasha, nodding towards an outhouse wall. The boy was almost drowning in fear and yet he did what he was told, moving dreamlike towards a point indicated, like a swimmer fighting the current. His feet were bare, just visible beneath an oversized jellaba, which sagged from narrow shoulders and scraped the ground.

'Your brother's clothes?'

The boy looked blank.

'The jellaba.'

'My father's old one, Excellency. I . . .' He stopped. 'I don't have a brother.'

The General nodded thoughtfully.

'And who else is in there?'

'In where, Excellency?' The voice was tight.

Koenig Pasha looked round at a row of ancient olive trees that time and war had reduced to splintered stumps. Once there'd been a retaining wall holding up their terracing, until its collapse had let red earth spill onto the level below. There'd been a well too, only that had been filled with rubble and capped off with polycrete. He'd given the order himself, years back.

'Where do you think I mean?' he asked.

'There's no . . .' The boy's voice slid an octave and halted.

'Come on,' said the General, directing his order to the empty door. 'It's not safe in there.'

A ratlike scuttle inside turned into a second face, dark-skinned and broad-cheeked. The girl was maybe thirteen, roughly the same age as the boy. Her black hair was pulled back under a *hijab* tied hastily round her head, so that only her face could be seen.

'We were looking for Hussein's goat.' Her words were a whisper she didn't really expect him to believe. Resignation and fear expanded eyes already darkened with charcoal. Red was smeared crudely across her lips. Pomegranate juice, probably. That was what girls used when he was young.

Koenig Pasha looked from one child to the other and back again. 'No brother,' he said to the boy. 'But this is your sister, right?'

Puzzlement met hope in the boy's thin face. As if the child was watching for the catch, for a trap that would snap shut on his lies. He said nothing, not even when the General repeated his question.

The old man sighed. 'I thought so,' he said and waved them away. Neither moved.

'Go,' Koenig Pasha ordered. 'Go now, before I change my mind.'

When they reached the edge of the ruined olive grove, the General suddenly stepped forward and shouted for the boy to stop. He did, as rooted to the dusty earth as the broken stump next to him.

'Good luck.'

Again those puzzled eyes, distant and uncertain.

'With finding your goat.'

The boy grinned fit to burst and snapped a ragged salute. Then, grabbing the girl's hand, he hurried her out of sight down a slope.

'Truants,' said the Senator.

'Who might have died,' the General agreed flatly. 'If their being alone up here was reported to the *morales* . . . Everything has a price,' he added, leaving blank which *everything* he had in mind.

'They die. That's the law?'

The old man shook his head. 'I am the law,' he said. It was a statement of fact, nothing more. 'The boy would have been badly beaten by his father. But the girl . . .' He shrugged. 'Locked in a cellar. Maybe even bricked in to starve or tossed in a ditch with her throat cut. Not stoned to death, not yet. Though that may come . . .'

If you don't support me. He imagined the Senator could read his subtext easily enough. *Stick with me because what comes next will be worse.* She'd have heard it before. Hell, she'd probably heard it all over. Mostly in Central America. Apparently half of her research staff agreed. He knew too that the other half thought she was breaking rule one of foreign affairs. *Never ask for what you know cannot be delivered.*

'What was it you wanted to tell me?' she asked the General.

'Tell you . . . ?'

'This is about achieving deniability, isn't it, Your Excellency?' Senator Liz indicated the empty terraces surrounding the sunlit farmhouse. In the near distance dust plumed as a pair of jeeps juddered their way up the dirt track road towards the crown of the hill. She and the General had another two, maybe three minutes to themselves at the most.

'No.' The General shook his head and fished in his pocket, finding a box of Sobraine and his Zippo. Engraved on one side was an eagle over crossed thunderbolts, badge of the Fifth French Foreign Legion. Koenig Pasha's capture of the lighter was a long story and he was resigned to no one ever getting it right.

'I didn't bring you here to talk,' said the General. 'I wanted to show you this . . .' He waved a hand at the ruined farmhouse and the terraces with their collapsing walls and uprooted vines. 'You know what this place is?'

He watched Senator Liz struggle to remember all she'd been told about the General's history, about Iskandryian politics. Sometime in the last week, before the woman landed at Ali Pasha, spooks from Langley would have briefed her. After the briefing, she'd brushed up on her protocol.

Those lessons had been only partly successful. At least that was the General's opinion. Her manners at the table were impeccable and practiced. Small amounts of food got left at the side of her plate to acknowledge the richness of her hosts. She never showed the soles of her Manolos when she sat. Her right hand only was used to present her card and eat or drink, the unclean hand she kept to herself.

The Senator even kept eye contact longer than most Westerners and her handshake was gentle, lacking that bone-crunching grip most Americans believed indicated decisiveness or virility. But like most of her kind, her grasp on history was so slight as to be dangerous. And though she could *salaam* with grace, touching her hand to her breast and then forehead, before lifting it away, she lacked the wit to realize that in El Iskandryia no woman ever used that greeting.

Saeed Pasha sighed. He was prejudiced against Americans. Mind you, he wasn't that fond of the English either. The Germans and the French, now you knew where you were with them. The first were brutal, the second devious. He had the blood of both in his veins.

'This place,' said the General. 'You know where you are now?'

'No, I'm sorry . . . I don't.'

'They came up that track . . .' Koenig Pasha pointed to a strip of road. 'Wearing rags that had once been uniforms, their bare feet soled with tar from the desert road. Many of them were younger than your granddaughter.'

He'd been briefed too. On the woman's background and tastes, which were both predictably American.

The Senator knew what Koenig Pasha was talking about now. 'What did you do?' she asked; though he could tell she wasn't really sure she wanted to know.

'What could we do? We killed them. We gunned them down in their thousands as they shambled towards us. All the amulets in the world couldn't hold back our bullets, despite what the enemy had been told. They carried ancient Kalashnikovs, spare magazines duct-taped together, pangas blunt with overuse, Martini Henrys . . .' The General stopped. '*Martini Henrys*. British revolvers taken by the Dinka, the barrels and cylinders drilled out to take current ammunition. It was a bloodbath.'

He could see it still in front of his eyes. A hot morning in early summer with the Nile only just on the rise. The mercury hitting 110F. No rain for six weeks.

Ten thousand strong they advanced up the desert highway with limp banners aloft in the hot and breezeless air. The dust from those in front had turned to khaki the ragged clothes of the ranks behind. Now, all that many of them had by way of uniform was a red ribbon tied to one of their upper arms. Behind them, at the rear, marched their officers, five hundred veterans of a ruthless campaign fought in the deserts around Meroe and the foothills of Abyssinia. They carried laser-sighted rifles, mortars and portable rocket launchers. Most wore lightweight body armour, air-conditioned helmets, ear-beads and throat mikes. Men and women alike, their hair was cropped short and their eyes hard with satisfaction at how easily Al Qahirah had fallen.

Major Koenig Bey, as he was then, had three hundred men left from his regiment. Some had died but more had deserted in the face of assurances that to oppose this Ragged Army was to oppose the absolute will of God. In vain the local Mufti had insisted in proclamation after proclamation that this was untrue. The Sublime Porte, His Imperial Majesty Mehmet VII, in his role as religious leader of the Osmali empire issued an edict stigmatizing the Mahdi. No one paid any attention.

Winning was left to a twenty-eight-year-old sapper, a half-Egyptian, half-German who had reached regimental rank solely because every other officer had resigned, deserted or was already dead.

This was a man whose first action on arriving at his new HQ in a farmhouse overlooking the desert road was to send for a flame-thrower, have the pressure tank converted to take emulsion and order that the walls, floor and ceiling be sprayed white. While teenage officers advised by elder NCOs set up gun encampments and mortar pits, Major Koenig oversaw first the removal of all furniture from the downstairs of the farmhouse, then the removal of its two cheap overhead strip-lights and the light switches. Only then was the converted flame-thrower used to redecorate the rooms to suit the major's taste.

Back in went a table and chairs, the overhead strips and a potbellied charcoal stove that the major took everywhere, for when he wanted fresh bread or coffee.

People might mutter but not when he was within earshot. And besides, the major knew exactly what he was doing as he stood in the middle of the redecorated room and told his officers not to bother setting up charts.

They were outnumbered and outgunned. All they had on their side was their command of a hilltop. That and strategy. And in the end Major

Saeed Koenig Bey won by retreating. Though first he shot his favourite brother through the head for refusing to follow an order.

Amil was young, handsome and the undisputed favourite of both his parents in the way that only youngest sons can be. Bizarrely, despite their difference in age, Major Koenig adored him.

With the Ragged Army marching uphill, into the fire of the major's machine guns and with every death being recorded by CNN drones hung high enough overhead to be out of rifle shot, Major Koenig ordered a retreat.

'Why?' Amil's question had been simple.

Because we're being filmed. Because we're turning ourselves into murderers. Because I won't order the deaths of a thousand twelve-year-olds who think that dirty feathers and dry twigs in a totem bag can stop bullets and that paradise waits with open gates for those who die, and see nothing contradictory in those two beliefs.

All of these would have been honest answers. But his senior sergeant and the other NCOs were watching the major, their uncertainty as to the wisdom of his order curdling to doubt. And orders were orders, that was what he'd been taught. The rules of engagement demanded it.

'Because I say so . . .'

'But we command the hill.'

'Not any longer.'

Amil opened his mouth to protest and bit back the words as his brother pulled a Luger from his belt.

'We retreat now. Understand?' Major Koenig glanced round his command group, which comprised a couple of hardened NCOs and a dozen subalterns so young they hadn't yet had time to grow a first moustache. The Ragged Army advancing up the hill was forgotten momentarily. The crack of return fire from his own men outside the farmhouse gone from the major's mind.

'We pull back to the crossroads and stop.'

'Sir,' his senior sergeant had raised a hand.

'You have a problem, Sergeant?' Words sharper than flint and cold as ice. Disdain, derision, mounting disbelief that any NCO might dare question an order. All of those and more were in the five words.

The senior NCO swallowed a smile. He was old enough to know the voice of his old commander, the major's father, a ruthless bastard but a highly efficient one. As commanding officers went he was good, but the sergeant wouldn't have wanted the man for his father.

'No, sir. Absolutely not, sir.' He snapped out a salute like the rawest, most frightened recruit and swung on his heels, the other NCOs straightening up, reassured now the decision had been made.

And there matters would have ended if Amil hadn't insisted on taking a step forward to object. The rest had gone down in legend. Muttered by the General's enemies as proof of his ruthlessness and spoken openly by his friends as proof of the same. Amil died with a mocking smile on his face and a bullet between the eyes from his brother's gun.

Major Koenig left the body where it dropped.

By the time the major returned to the farmhouse that evening, walking under a white flag of truce, Amil's body had been carried away and dumped with others in a pit dug into the terraces by a thin girl on a tractor. He came alone, unarmed, and stood silent and uncomplaining as rough hands searched him before letting him inside.

The ground floor of the farmhouse was crowded with the cream of the Ragged Army's generals, their own uniforms anything but that. Some of the junior officers wore battle-dress stripped from UN observers but most had uniforms cut and sewn by local tailors along the way.

A few were imported, bought via middlemen from military tailors in Algiers, Berlin or Stambul. Two officers were even dressed in the uniform of Major Koenig's regiment. One had, until that afternoon, been his *aide de camp* and the other the major had thought dead. Certainly the man had never returned from the morning's reconnaissance.

Amused eyes watched him notice them.

A charcoal fire burned in the potbellied stove he'd been forced to abandon, heating a brass jug of fresh coffee. A hurricane lamp lit the room against advancing night.

Against centuries of tradition, Major Koeing was not offered a small cup of sweetened coffee or a brass sheesha filled with apple tobacco. He sat unasked on the only chair not in use and when he requested a glass of water to wet his throat this was refused. The major was pleased. It made what came next easier.

He was there to negotiate the surrender of El Iskandryia to the Ragged Army. General Mahdi had not bothered to come in person. Rumour said the jihad leader was too busy imposing his rule on Al Qahirah, where cinema doors had been bolted tight, bars burned and women whipped in public for going out with their heads uncovered. Schools for girls had been closed, female doctors banned from working, and aid workers of both sexes given twenty-four hours to leave the country.

Berlin, Paris and Washington were too busy being outraged to have time for what was about to happen on a hill to the south of Iskandryia.

Camped on terraces that had been cut into the slope before Islam or Christianity even existed, the Ragged Army crouched round fires lit with dried dung or branches ripped from the ancient olive grove. Food had been plentiful in Al Qahirah and most were no longer hungry. But they lit fires and killed any goats they could scavenge because that was what they did. Habit can take only weeks to become tradition and they'd had years. First in the Sudan, then moving north.

'Tomorrow and the next day we march,' their leader told Major Koenig. 'The evening after that we arrive at El Iskandryia. Friday we pray. Saturday you bring out the old man to make his surrender.'

Fat chance, thought the major. The Khedive was too ill to leave his bed. Besides, he was Khedive, the old man would die rather than surrender his city. 'And the terms?' Major Koenig asked.

There were no terms. The city surrendered. That was all there was to it. Those whom the Ragged Army let live were those who would live. No promises would be made.

Same terms they gave Al Qahirah.

'I agree.' Major Koenig held out his hand and when this was not taken, bowed slightly and clicked his heels, Berlin style, purely for the pleasure of seeing hatred flood the faces of his enemy. 'The city will be ready for you,' he added.

Snapping a drill-perfect salute, he walked to the door, stopping only to reach into the emptiness where a light switch should be and touch together two wires.

The resulting blast broke the major's right ulna in two places and dislocated his shoulder. Though what really hurt was the length of light fitting that scraped its way across his hipbone, fracturing his pelvis.

The bomb in the empty striplight was technologically primitive. All the same, it worked better than the major had been expecting. And while the West had at its disposal numerous kinds of self-firing *plastique*, not to mention those little synthetic viruses they were so busy denying, he'd had to rely on a block of Semtex, a basic detonator, ball bearings, batteries from a mobile and some recycled flex. All of it, excluding the ball bearings obviously, well past its use-by date.

The light fitting killed everyone standing under it; just not all at the same time. The luckiest deaths were immediate. Necks snapped or skulls broken open, hearts pierced by shattered ribs. Under heavy fire from his own side, who'd advanced as ordered at the sound of the explosion, the major got trucked to a camp in Al Qahirah, a shard of light fitting still embedded in his hip, his broken arm locked tight in a battle dressing. The *fellah* from the Ragged Army who'd pulled Major Koenig from the rubble thought the officer was one of her own.

'And General Mahdi. If I remember . . .' The Senator paused, wondering how she should put it delicately. 'Had his hands cut off . . .'

'Among other things.'

That was three weeks later, in Al Qahirah. By then the Ragged Army had mostly surrendered, its mercenary core either dead, under arrest or rapidly selling each other out in return for immunity. Major Koenig was right. Taking out the enemy's generals had been the solution.

And Senator Liz had finally remembered enough of the General's history to wish she was somewhere else. What type of man took visiting dignitaries to see where he'd shot his own brother? The answer was obvious. Someone like Koenig Pasha.

'They never did find who murdered General Mahdi, did they?'

'No,' said the General, his eyes holding those of the American woman, 'you're right. They never did . . .'

'And Colonel Abad?' She named Mahdi's infamous adviser, Washington's *bête noire*.

'In paradise, no doubt,' said Koenig Pasha. 'Or maybe hell.'

CHAPTER 23

14th October

'Hey.' Hani sounded so cross that Ifritah's ears flicked back and Hani had to stroke the cat to get her purring again. 'I was watching that . . .'

'Sorry,' said Raf, clicking his fingers to change channels. 'I need to see what other people are saying about what's happening.'

'Happening where?'

'Here.'

Hani raised her eyebrows but stayed put as Raf banged down his briefcase and turned his attention back to the screen. *Heute in Berlin* had nothing and neither did the US feeds, but that wasn't surprising; both countries were notoriously insular. And Iskandryia's own Ferdie Abdullah was concentrating on a second arson attack on a nightclub opposite Misr Station.

Raf found what he wanted on *Paris – la Ronde*, which segued straight from a snippet on the Prince Imperial's first term at St Andrews to a moderately gloating roundup of problems to be raised when representatives of the Kaiser and the Sublime Porte finally held separate meetings with a US arbitrator, to discuss renewing the Osmanli Accord, the treaty that defined spheres of economic influence in North Africa, the Middle East and the Balkans.

Berlin wanted the spheres expanded, as did Moscow. Paris was reserving its position. US Senator Elizabeth Elsing was on record as saying she thought spheres of influence were undemocratic. The French anchorman smirked when he reported this.

'Boring,' announced Hani, so Raf told the screen to find another cartoon and soon a bug-eyed, yellow whatsit was bumbling round being kind to small animals. And while the whatsit ran rescue missions or fried scary monsters with its awesome magic power, Raf boned a leg of lamb, cubed the meat and braised it in a heavy pan.

'What are you making?' Hani asked in the ad break.

390

'*Hunkar begendi*, kind of . . .'

'Sultan's delight.' Having just discovered McDonald's, Hani's tastes had telescoped. Anything that failed to come between two bits of bun with reconstituted french fries didn't count.

For the sauce that gave its name to the dish, Raf needed to puncture tiny holes in four aubergines so they wouldn't burst when he grilled them in Donna's gas oven until their skins went black and blistered.

'You want to do this?' Raf picked up a fork and nodded to the uncooked aubergine.

Hani shook her head. So Raf punched holes in the purple skin instead.

'What *is* happening?' Hani asked. She was back with Ferdie Abdullah, who was running through the main headlines. Behind him a minor oil pipe bled crude onto gravel and hot sand while a huge billboard reading MIDAS REFINERY blazed like an advertisement for chaos. Before setting it on fire, the arsonists had taken time to stencil a row of red fists along the bottom of the sign.

Against a background of flames, impossibly young soldiers loaded two trespassing Ishies into a police van. With their faces hidden by goggles and belts studded with drives and umbrella modems, the freelance newshounds stumbled towards confinement like vintage astronauts traversing some monochrome lunar plain.

The masks were all affectation. A decent digital lens could be mounted onto the side of ordinary glasses and still be so small as to be almost invisible. As for the drives, anything bigger than a packet of Cleopatra was either outdated, third-world cheap or intentionally obvious.

On-screen, Ferdie Abdullah was explaining that, according to Iskandryia's bright new Chief of Detectives, the apparently random, wide-ranging attacks of the previous week *were* connected after all, having been carried out by the Sword of God. Which was the first Raf had heard of it.

'*I never said that . . .*'

'What?'

'I never said the attacks weren't random.'

'No?' Hani looked up from stroking Ifritah. 'What does random mean?'

'Not related.'

Scooping the grilled aubergines out of their skins with a fork, Raf put the pulp to one side while he got butter from the fridge. Then all he needed was to add flour to the molten butter and beat hard as milk went into the mixture.

'So they are related?'

Raf stopped looking for a skillet. 'I don't know,' he said.

Hani sighed.

After he'd added mashed aubergine to his roux, Raf ground in a twist of pepper, a twist of sea salt and sprinkled on a handful of grated cheese. The lamb went onto the middle of an already warmed serving plate, with the aubergine sauce swirled in an elegant circle round the outside.

'You hungry?'

Hani shook her head.

'No, me neither.' Raf passed the serving dish to Hani. 'See if Khartoum wants this, then I'll buy you a burger . . .'

'For you,' Hani announced from the doorway of the porter's quarters at the rear of the madersa's covered garden.

'For us?' Khartoum glanced up from his game of Go as did his opponent, the owner of a small stall in Rue Cif, which ran along the back of the madersa. 'You made this?' Khartoum looked surprised. Also disbelieving.

'No, Uncle Ashraf made it.'

'His Excellency . . .' the stall holder looked surprised. 'The bey cooks?'

Hani smiled at the man whose knee-length coat and white cap announced he'd made the ritual pilgrimage to Mecca. 'His Excellency does a lot of strange things,' she said shortly and backed out of the room. If either man thought it strange that the child had a flea-bitten cat slung round her neck like a collar, they didn't mention it.

'You'll be fine,' promised Raf when Hani hesitated in the madersa's ornate marble hall. For reasons neither Khartoum nor Donna could properly explain, her late Aunt Nafisa had felt it necessary to keep the child indoors. Which meant the funeral of her aunt was the first time Hani had ever left the house.

'Of course I will,' Hani said and yanked open the front door. She smiled as she took Raf's hand, though her nails dug hard into his palm as they stepped from the quiet of the madersa into the noise of Rue Sherif.

Raf dug back and Hani's grin turned vulpine. When they reached the corner she was still grinning and still trying to dig her nails through his skin. They both knew she was only half-joking . . .

That night, the fox came as clouds blocked off the stars and the sky moved closer to the earth, imposing an obvious but impressive boundary, like that loss of focus at the edge of a dream or the distant strangeness of the world beyond an aquarium as seen by some captive angelfish.

And as all this occurred, outside of the world outside the al-Mansur madersa, Raf sat on the edge of Hani's narrow bed and watched the small child sleep, badly . . . She mewled half words and broken sentences that matched the fluttering behind her closed eyes. Panic glued strips of damp hair to her forehead and every so often she'd roll her shoulders as if fighting her way through a crowd. Raf watched and waited in what should have been darkness and would have been were he anyone else. At no point did he allow himself or the fox to sleep.

CHAPTER 24

Sudan

It was Sarah who taught Ka how to catch the birds that flocked south. While the ghosts of the others hunted lizards through the ruins of J'habite, she sat in the shade of the truck, sharing her pipe with Ka and refusing to talk.

Smoking always made Ka talkative. Sarah was the opposite. This was a month after Zac died and Ka was still afraid of Sarah's long silences and the sudden thunder bursts of her anger.

As she stared blankly at the blue sky, Ka risked an occasional sideways glance at where the top button of her shirt had come undone. Not her collar button, which was missing, the one below that.

Through the slight gap he could see the start of a breast, shadow against shadow. And on the wrist of the hand holding her steel pipe, fine hairs lit in the light that dappled through the thermoflage covering their truck. His own skin had gone dark in the desert, yet hers was darker still. Almost purple, like al-badingan, a plant carried from Africa to al-Andalus by the army of Islam, though Ka didn't know that. He just knew his uncle had grown them one year. Soft fruit that spoiled easily and was eaten as a vegetable fried with mutton oil and salt.

The pipe was Sarah's own. Bent and scratched, it had been filthy when she took it off a dead nasrani *photographer. Which meant Sarah had wasted hours meticulously scraping tar from the mouthpiece with a thorn stripped of its bark.*

The last person to try taking the pipe from Sarah had ended up with two fingers of his right hand bound together for a month, to help his bones knit. But these last few weeks she'd taken to sharing her pipe with Ka and her food too, though only when there was enough to spare.

Everything about that afternoon was normal until a small dark bird swooped overhead and Sarah suddenly sat up straight. A minute later other birds followed, heading south.

394

'Netting,' Sarah demanded, her voice urgent.

Ka looked puzzled.

'Netting,' she repeated and pointed to an unused roll of thermoflage that still lay where they'd dumped it five days earlier. 'Hurry.' Sarah grabbed his hand and pulled Ka to his feet.

Ka knew better than to refuse. 'What are we hiding?' Ka asked. 'And what are we hiding it from?' Hiding themselves from the planes was the usual answer but the truck was already netted and the sky was free from silver specks.

'We're going to catch food,' she told Ka and the boy stopped fussing.

'Do what I do,' said Sarah. So Ka did.

Together they unrolled the net and laid it flat in the road. Then Sarah cut two long lengths of electrical flex from a cardboard roll in the back of the truck and gave one to Ka.

'The net goes there,' Sarah said, indicating a dark slit of alley between two broken houses. 'You take the one on this side and I'll take the other.'

Reaching the roof on his side of the alley was easier than Ka expected, mainly because the stairs were in place and neither floor had fallen in. Sarah's climb took longer and when she finally appeared on the roof opposite, sweat had fastened her shirt tight against her back.

'Broken stairs.'

Ka nodded, silently threading one end of his wire through a gap in the parapet when he saw Sarah do the same. When she tied one end tight, he did that too and obediently tossed the rest of his flex over the edge, watching as it fell into the street below.

'Okay,' said Sarah. 'Now we do the netting.' She disappeared from view and it took Ka a moment to realize she'd started the return climb. Although he still made it down before she did.

'You've got stairs,' Sarah said.

Ka nodded guiltily.

'Some people . . .' Crouched back on her heels, mouth slightly open and face fierce with concentration, Sarah carefully tied her wire to a corner of the net and waited for Ka do the same. After that, all they had to do was climb back to the top and haul on their wires until the net was in position.

She smelt of kif, as always, but beneath the smoke Ka could smell sweat as it dried into her shirt and a feral stink that he also carried, but mostly forgot to notice. All of the other girls he'd met had washed with sand, disappearing behind a wall or bush to scrub it into their skin. Sarah was different. If the river was nearby she used that; otherwise she used nothing.

'Why are you sniffing?'

'I'm not.'

Sarah looked at him.

'The pipe,' said Ka. 'I like it.'

Sarah nodded, like she understood. But a few minutes later she got up to make a hard-to-see adjustment to one corner of the trap and when she came back, she sat somewhere else.

Later on, the blue sky turned pink along its edge. Pink turned to purple and purple to a blue so deep it was almost black. And stars hung silent as Sarah lay back and wondered at their unimaginable distances.

Sitting on the other side of the fire, Ka held a spit-roasted bird, one of a dozen that he'd eaten as the evening wore on and the flames burned low. Two more tiny birds cooled on a length of aerial near his feet. The wings he'd taken to discarding as hardly worth the bother, throwing them back to sizzle in the fire while he concentrated instead on pinching strips, of hot meat from the tiny carcass.

When the fire was done and the night turned colder, they retreated to the back of the truck, Sarah to clean her pipe and Ka to talk to the Colonel. He was still talking when Sarah fell asleep. Though she woke once, later on, to remove his hand from inside her shirt.

CHAPTER 25

15th October

It was a job and someone had to do it. Shutting his eyes briefly against a flickering beam of red laser, the man calling himself Mike Estelle opened them again, then smiled through the yellow afterglow at a young American dancing opposite.

Wide face, fair hair, a turned-up nose that looked natural; sweat darkening the valley between her breasts and beading her throat like glitter dust. Trousers slung low enough at the back to expose the black waistband of a thong.

Her name was Dawn, apparently.

'Okay?'

She grinned back and danced closer.

And closer.

When Mike jerked his head at an exit, she nodded. And when he put one arm round her shoulder to steer her towards the door, she smiled and let his hand slip forward until it hovered above her shiny bra. With a sideways glance, he grabbed a handful, ready to make a joke of it if she protested but Dawn just giggled and turned her head, mouth opening as she raised her face for a kiss.

A crowd of students pushed past on both sides, jeering at the thirty something man with his arms locked round a teenager, though no one actually seemed to mind that he blocked the door between the main dance floor and the loos at Neutropic. The last of the students, a kid with a magenta dread wig, silver contacts and a vest that read DEEP AND TRIBAL, glanced back, noticed that the girl now had one breast completely out of her bra and grinned. So Mike twisted his lips into a smile and nodded to the student, a ubiquitous knowing nod that the *Thiergarten* agent hoped said *sorted*.

From the floor came the gut-crunching, ear-bleeding thud of bass bins overlaid with a wasplike electronic loop that wound itself up and up but went nowhere, endlessly . . .

Mike hated the noise but then, he hated nightclubs, which was why he'd been so happy to firebomb the last one. To really like the music, he'd decided, you had to be out of your head and Mike was teetotal everything. Unlike the Friday night crowd around him.

That any clubs opened on a holy day upset the mullahs; so those which did made sure their licences were up-to-date, closing times were met and the local uniforms paid off. The *morales* themselves were mostly beyond bribery, though blackmail could work.

The other thing Neutropic did was weed out locals at the door. Anyone who didn't do a convincing impression of a well-dressed foreigner got bounced by the fashion police. Letting in Iskandryia's own just wasn't worth the grief.

Which was fine with Mike Estelle. The last thing he needed was to hook up with some local kid who had an angry elder brother and five uncles.

'You know what I like about this place?'

He didn't.

'Everyone's always off their heads.'

Yeah, he liked that too. Mind you . . . 'You know, it's a bit noisy . . .'

'What?'

He started to repeat himself and then realized she was grinning, so he grinned back and gently steered her through the door and towards some fire doors.

'Wait.'

He looked at her.

'Rehydration,' she said, pulling three tiny pink hearts from the pocket of her white jeans. 'Need a bottle for these.' Actually they weren't jeans, they were some kind of paper-thin trouser, bias-cut from acetate, belted with a silver sheriff's star on a leather thong threaded through loops. And she didn't need water . . .

'You ever tried a kite?' He dipped his own hand inside his shirt, reaching for a small pouch that hung on a silver chain round his neck. Shaking out a tiny purple lozenge, he dropped it into her open hand.

'No need for water with these,' he said. 'They just melt in your mouth.'

'What's in them?'

He smiled and named a cat valium analogue mentioned earlier at the bar by some girl he'd bought a drink. She had been older than this one, not yet close to being drunk and there was a hardness to her, a neurotic edge that made him nod politely, knock back his Diet Coke and disengage. Places like Neutropic didn't exist for people like her to waste his time. Besides, she'd been Swiss and he needed a Yank . . . Or at the very least some Yank wannabe from the American university.

What he actually fed the kid was something else, obviously; but the chemical formula would mean nothing to her and no one had bothered to name this drug something snappy. She didn't yet know it but she was about to be reeled in on something none of her friends even knew existed.

'They're great,' said Mike, closing her hand around the lozenge, the chemical formula of which was just one molecule off an anaesthetic that had been briefly popular fifty years earlier. This version had remained on paper – well, disk – in a Swiss lab until a May evening three years earlier when a Sudanese research student working up something for the weekend had screwed over one of her sequences.

Asked later that night at Zurich's Apocalypse if she was carrying drugs, the research student had said, *yes, lots.* Ordered to empty her bag, she laboriously took out everything. Credit chips, tram tickets, vapourthin condoms, a tampon, loose change, the fluff in the bottom . . .

Standing in the queue watching all this happen was a very junior opportunities exec from the research division of Bayer-Rochelle. A thousand US dollars to the largest of the door staff saw the girl, plus her emptied bag, in a taxi headed out of Zurich towards an elegantly landscaped campus beside Lake Lucerne.

They talked, at least she did. About everything she'd ever done that had embarrassed her. They ate supper at the campus canteen and then, much later, after a romantic walk beside the lake they went to bed via a quick detour to his open-plan office. She remembered nothing of the chocolate torte or *Wiener Schnitzel,* the moon glistening on cold water or the sex but she woke bandy-legged and raw, having signed a contract relinquishing any intellectual rights she might possess in whatever chemical had induced such a chronic attack of honesty and obedience.

It was a good story, true or not. And amnesia was one of the more useful side effects of the drug. Amnesia, anaesthesia and obedience. What more could any person want?

At the moment nothing. That would come later.

'Real rush,' said the man, mouthing his words over the background noise.

'If you say so.' Dawn shrugged, smiled and put the lozenge on her tongue, looking like a child with a sweet. Within seconds her smile had become a grin, then her personality imploded, her pupils widening into vast black circles through which she fell.

It was 3.45 A.M. Exactly one hour and forty-five minutes after he walked through the door. With a satisfied smile, Mike reset the alarm, on his Rolex and checked that it was off-line for all functions. It would be extremely inconvenient if some overzealous Iskandryian cop was to use station switching to check Mike's progress across the city at a later date.

'This way.'

She nodded, her face so unguarded as to be almost infantile. Wrapping his arm tight around her shoulders, Mike steered her through the emergency door at the back of Neutropic and into a parking lot packed with cars but empty of people.

'Which one do you like?'

Dark eyes regarded him gravely.

'Tell me.' It was an order.

'That one,' said the girl without hesitation. The red Mazda to which she pointed was exactly what he'd have expected of her. Flash without being that well made. This was the difference between him and the girl. He'd have gone for something expensive but understated. Which, obviously enough, was why he'd got her to make the choice. That way police had a harder time trying to construct a profile.

Pulling a thin grey card from the pocket of his trousers, he rested it against the lock of the little Mazda, and let the internal electronics do their magic. Commercial versions of the universal key did stupid things like ping when the right combination was found or have diodes that flashed up the side in sequence, as if part of some scanning routine.

His version had no diodes and made no noise. So the only way to know if the lock was disengaged and the alarm disabled was to listen very carefully to the tumblers.

'Get in.'

Without waiting to see if the girl would do what she was told – she would – Mike climbed into the driver's seat and slid his card into the key slot. Lights lit on the faux-metal dash and the engine fired up. So did the sound system, which the owner had left tuned to some shit station that pumped dance.

'Find something you like.'

'I like this,' said the girl, nodding towards a speaker.

He sighed. 'Something else,' Mike said and waited while she found some woman singing about the taste on her tongue.

Whatever . . . First gear meshed into third, then fifth, as he skipped second and fourth. From where they were to where he needed to be was next to no distance. Except that it would be best if the clock showed he'd driven somewhere else first, especially if he hadn't . . . Or at least nowhere that mattered.

A rip out along the Corniche added some distance, the little Mazda nipping in and out of the sparse traffic, hugging in behind trucks or bigger cars every time a camera came into view. One of them might actually have picked out his licence plate but, chances were, it wouldn't matter. He'd be gone and the car dumped.

As for her . . .

'Enjoying yourself?'

The girl nodded. She had goose bumps on her bare arms and her slight tummy pushed its way over the waist of trousers not really designed for sitting, but her smile was still happy and he believed her.

'Good.' He flipped the Mazda off the Corniche and down a side street, overtaking a VW camper. The traffic was thinning to nonexistent and the sky looked less dark than it had.

'We've arrived,' he told the girl, parking alongside a metal gate set in a heavy-duty fence. A rusty iron padlock hung from the bolt. 'Time to get out . . .'

Obediently she climbed from her seat and stood beside the car.

'In here.'

The padlock looked tight but since it only shut on itself and the casino's rear gate was actually closed off with a twist of wire, that didn't matter. Only one security light lit the gate and that badly, the other two lights having been vandalized. But then everything in life was down to preplanning and, before he'd retired, the man calling himself Mike Estelle had been extremely good at that.

The best in fact. Most controls were pure amateurs when it came to setting the stage and arranging the props. Both of those he could do without thinking. It was the wet work he didn't usually handle.

'Where are we?'

The man glanced round at the smiling girl, noticing again her pale hair and the wide face of someone whose ancestors farmed a bleak edge of the fjords. She shouldn't have been asking him questions, only answering those he asked and doing exactly what she was told . . . Which, pretty soon, was going to involve taking off that silver bra and climbing out of those stupid trousers.

'We're at another club,' he told her. 'A different kind.' Which was the truth but wasn't about to set her free. 'Here,' he added, pulling a second purple kite from his pouch. 'Take this, you'll like it.'

She looked at him, puzzled, her eyes trying to look past something inside her head.

'Go on.'

Obediently, she swallowed the kite without waiting to let it dissolve on her tongue. Again that grin. And anyone inside her head who might still have been at home switched off the last of the lights and moved out.

'This way.' He snipped the wire holding shut the gate with tiny, orange-handled clippers and discarded them on the gravel, secure in the knowledge that the latex gloves he wore were surgical specials. In the ordinary run of things, his prints might still have been visible to forensics, but each fingerprint had been softened earlier that evening, using a simple solution of household bleach.

Just inside the gate stood a security hut, mirrored glass in its only window, looking out at a road that led from the gates to a loading bay, where a pull-down shutter was locked to a clasp set in concrete. The loading bay clasp was properly padlocked.

Mike shrugged. The key would be where those keys always were. Hung on a board inside the hut, should he need it, which was unlikely. So far so predictable . . .

The grey card he'd used on the little Mazda also worked for the door of the security hut. Whoever had decided to replace a standard Chubb with a Japanese box had made a bad mistake. It was still way harder to pick an old-fashioned mortise than jazz some chip, probably always would be.

Inside, the hut was the usual clutter: a microwave, so old its inside was enamelled with fat, a stained Braun coffeemaker, five mugs, none of them matching, no saucers and more discarded packaging around the plastic swing bin than inside it.

The man sighed. This was why he'd never taken to field-work . . . 'Clean the mess up,' he told the girl and she nodded.

'All done now.' Her voice was matter-of-fact, as if she found nothing odd in having happily picked up someone else's rubbish, scrubbed down all the work surfaces and cleaned out the inside of an old microwave; but then the drugs ensured there was nothing odd about the situation for her to find.

'Good girl.'

Closing his borrowed copy of *Hustler*, illegal in all of North Africa, if slightly less illegal in El Isk than most other cities, Mike stretched, pushed himself up from where he sat and walked across to where the American girl stood smiling.

At 5.49 A.M. Saturday morning. The Quitrimala Casino. The call to prayer had come and gone. It was time, more or less.

CHAPTER 26

16th October

Dawn had broken by the time he locked the hut door behind him.

Dawn had . . .

Mike smiled tightly at his own joke and stretched the fingers of one hand, like a concert pianist doing post-performance exercises. Then he turned his head from side to side, trying to reach the pain in his neck.

In his other hand he carried a heart and two dripping lungs; they weighed more than he expected.

'Hey, dipshit . . .' The insult was light, contemptuous. The accent a mix of street rough and faux polite. What was most unnerving was that the boy behind him chose German, Mike's original language.

Slowly, very slowly, Mike turned. As he did so, his free hand swung down, reaching for a holster hidden on the back of his belt.

'I don't think so . . .' The boy with the magenta dreads jerked his own automatic and Mike's hand froze. He was remembering.

'The club,' said the boy with the noisy gold earbead. 'In the corridor.'

The man remembered. The group of students, with one lagging at the end. Their eyes meeting, that knowing nod. It hadn't been about the girl, or rather it had, just not in the way he'd thought.

'And before that,' said Avatar. He popped silver contacts from his pupils and dumped them and a magenta wig onto the tarmac. 'On a roof at Sarahz, remember? You were pretending to be English.'

Adjusting his earbead, Avatar faded out some weirdshit track about dogs, boats and guns.

'You're not police?' Mike's eyes widened.

'*Les merde?* You'd be so lucky . . .' Avatar's smile was grim. 'I command a brigade of *Action Directs* . . .'

'You're military . . . ?'

Avatar sneered, with all the arrogance of someone whose fourteen

403

years had seen things that made growing up fast the only safe thing to do. 'Anarcho-Marxist-Syndicalist. If anyone strips this city back to its machine code it's going to be us . . .'

'You're too late,' said Mike. 'Another dead American. Another burst of outrage.'

Avatars gaze flicked towards the grisly relics in the man's hand. He'd been working on the assumption that rape would precede killing, probably carried out slowly and methodically given the almost feline cruelty of the man's earlier behaviour.

Making a wrong call wasn't something Avatar liked.

'Drop the offal and empty your pockets.'

Avatar waited while the man took out a disposable camera, cigarettes, the flat electronic key, a cheap lighter and a small Japanese sushi knife that looked just like a child's chopper.

'And the rest . . .'

'That's it,' said the man, puffing his coat pockets inside out.

'Travel light, don't you?'

Action Directe approved of travelling light. No baggage, emotional, literal or political; all three were known to slow down the response time between opportunity and action. And yet, personal was political, according to Zara.

How was Avatar to know if his decision to act owed its driving force to the fact this man was obviously *Thiergarten*, and thus an enemy of progress, or to the fact that the girl butchered on the beach at Villa Hamzah had, in some way, been a warning to Avatar's father, whose politics were definitely not Avatar's own?

And then there was Raf, who was *merde* himself but who had saved Avatar's life, something Avatar hadn't yet admitted to the old man.

The boy shook his head.

'Just give me the pills,' said Avatar and waited for Mike to unbutton the first two buttons of his shirt. They both noticed that Mike's hands trembled as he handed over his pouch.

'Open wide.' Avatar held out a tiny purple kite and raised his gun until it touched the underneath of Mike's chin. The metal was cool against the German's early-morning stubble.

The man swallowed his fate.

'Pick up the offal and walk,' said the boy.

The door to the cargo bay opened easily, though the man no longer had the capacity to be surprised when the boy produced a spare key from his own pocket and unclicked the padlock, sending the metal shutter scrolling skywards in a rattle of metal machine music.

'*Rust Never Sleeps . . .*'

Avatar had named his brigade after an ancient CD found in a market. Weird shit, of the best kind. He'd sampled the tracks he wanted and given the CD to Zara. She'd said nothing about it since, so he figured it just wasn't her taste.

It took Avatar and the man more than ten minutes to find spare cylinders of butano and drag them from the kitchens up to the loading bay. There were seven in total. Each one large, orange and as heavy as Avatar, maybe heavier. After that came huge blocks of lard to be smeared around the casino, vats of margarine and a couple of industrial-sized containers of ghee. Then methylated spirits on the stairs, used to fuel fondue heaters, the flashy old-fashioned kind.

'You see those?' Avatar pointed to cans stacked against a kitchen wall, each one full of maize oil. The casino might boast two world-class chefs, poached from the SS *Jannah*, but half of the visiting punters still stuffed themselves with freshly cooked chips sprinkled with paprika. The Soviet half . . .

The German nodded.

'Pour them on the hall carpets and come back here when you're finished.'

Avatar's first idea had been to let the man do all the work, but carrying the butano had been a job for two and time was running out . . . For himself and the city, for his father, even for the General if the word in the alleys was true. And Avatar trusted what he heard on the streets because that was where he belonged, no matter how much Zara wished it otherwise.

As for this casino. He didn't approve of casinos or the people they attracted. And he didn't want it.

'. . . Finished now.'

Avatar smiled at the German and beckoned him closer. Childlike eyes looked into his as the man smiled back. He'd just gutted a girl, Avatar had to remind himself. A girl whose ripped-open corpse was in a hut not fifty paces from where he stood, probably with his father's initials cut into her wrist.

'Here,' said Avatar as he passed over a bottle of cooking brandy. The name was French, the label printed in Isk and the grapes grown in Algiers. Ersatz identity. Coming from nowhere. As fucked up as the city. 'Take a drink.'

The man did, gagging on the raw spirit.

'And again.'

When the bottle was almost empty, Avatar walked the man up the darkened stairs to the loading bay and stood him in the middle of a concrete floor that was by then awash with spilt oil, methylated spirits and smashed bottles of brandy. The gas cylinders stood like sentries around the edge.

Using coins, Avatar jammed open the butano valves and, as soon as the smell of gas was strong enough to overpower the stink of evaporating alcohol, he told the man to count down from a hundred and then, when he reached zero light himself a cigarette. The other thing Avatar did before he slammed the bay doors and hiked the volume on his earbead was skim the sushi knife across concrete so it came to a halt beside the bloody relics at the man's feet.

It was only later, when Avatar was driving his camper van back to Club Neutropic, alibis already building in his mind, that he realized he should have questioned the German before killing him.

CHAPTER 27

If anybody else in the computer room had been stuffing their face with a Big Mac and large fries, chocolate shake and a side dish of onion rings, Madame Roden would have thrown her out, if not banned her altogether.

Because it was Hani, who'd knocked first, asked if she might come in and then smilingly thrust a carton of fries at the fastidious systems manager for the night shift, Madame Roden had politely taken a lukewarm reconstituted fry and chewed it as if sampling a priceless Perigord black truffle.

'Shouldn't you be at home asleep?' No sooner was the comment made than Madame Roden winced at her own lack of tact. If she'd been recently orphaned like that, she'd have wanted to follow her new uncle everywhere too.

'Uncle Ashraf came back to get some papers,' said Hani, apparently oblivious to the woman's *faux pas*. They weren't really papers, of course. Most of the bey's day-to-day files downloaded direct to his watch. But a few, the really important ones, he had to sign for with a handprint before collecting them from the precinct's central datacore.

Madame Roden was responsible for the night running of the core, but it more or less ran itself and most of her shift was spent stopping uniforms from slopping coffee on their keyboards and preventing them from trying to reach unsuitable photographs archived by the *morales*.

Pictures snatched by police photographers played a big part in most immorality cases. Though, of course, to the *morales* the grabs were just evidence. Well, to most of them.

Madame Roden shook her head. She shouldn't even be thinking such stuff with a small child around.

'Could I use a terminal?'

The elderly woman was doubtful. Nothing in police regulations actually forbade it, but then, nothing said it was all right either. As for previous precedents, nine-year-olds wanting to use her computer room were a novelty. Come to that, civilians this side of the front desk were a novelty, full stop. Children or not.

'I saw Kamila on the way in,' Hani said suddenly. 'I told her I was coming up here and she said to say hello . . .' Hani grinned. 'Hello.'

Madame Roden smiled. She could remember when Kamila was this age. More than ten years ago, though it seemed far less. These days her daughter was a pathologist, reporting *direct* to Madame Mila, unbelievable though this was.

'Can I?'

Madame Roden blinked. 'Yes, of course,' she said, slightly bemused. Hani had that effect on her. Actually Madame Roden had noticed the child had that effect on most people.

'Thank you,' said Hani and scrambled up onto a seat to tap the space bar in front of her, waking the terminal.

'Do you want me to help you find something to play with?'

Hani shook her head. She liked the neatly dressed elderly woman, but that didn't mean she felt guilty about tricking her. Life had long since taught her that all adults existed to be tricked, except maybe Ashraf, but her uncle was different.

'No, thank you,' Hani said politely. 'I'm going to write another fairy tale.'

'Another?'

Hani smiled. 'About Suliman the Magnificent and the angry djinn . . .'

As soon as she had the screen to herself, Hani went to her postbox, grabbed a half-finished story she'd started months before and pasted it into the precinct's basic word-processing package over a scuzzy parchment background. Rubbish page texture and rubbish font. At home she had fifty-three kinds of illuminated capital alone, most of them lifted from a university archive in Al Qahirah.

Minimizing *Suliman's Dream, trope III* and twisting her screen slightly so that it was no longer overlooked, Hani did a double log-in, remaining as a guest but adding a window that knew her as Mushin Bey, husband to her dead aunt Jalila, not to mention Minister of Police, thus Ashraf's theoretical boss.

One rumour said Uncle Mushin was at home, sitting in darkness grieving for his dead wife, another had him in a clinic getting over a long-term alcohol habit. Hani preferred the second theory.

No one had thought to cancel Mushin Bey's network access. No one had even changed his password, which inevitably was *Jalila*.

Top access, obviously. Superuser status. Hani doubted her uncle even knew what that meant or entailed. Flicking her fingers from key to key, Hani called up a current crime list and highlighted only the ones that had been mentioned on the news by Ferdie Abdullah.

Then she decided to read about the girl found on Hamzah's beach and changed her mind two paragraphs in. A lot of the medical words were strange to her, but enough of the others made sense enough for her to close the file.

'I wonder,' said a voice, 'have you seen . . .'

'In the computer room, Ya Bey.' Madame Roden never quite knew whether or not to smile when she met Ashraf al-Mansur. True, he was her husband's boss, which meant she should. But then there was all that sad stuff with his dead aunt. And Kamila's boss Madame Mila apparently hated him. And it was said poor Mushin Bey couldn't hear the name al-Mansur without falling into a rage. As if the bey could have saved everyone from those terrible assassins.

His Excellency looked positively ill with exhaustion, poor man.

At the door, Raf turned. 'I should thank you,' he said. 'For letting Hani use a machine.'

'A pleasure.' The small woman blushed.

'Do you know what she's doing?'

'Writing another story, Your Excellency, so she says . . .'

'That sounds about right.' Raf nodded to Madame Roden and went to his office, where a black bakelite phone was trying to wake the dead. The telephone had to be some kind of joke. At least, Raf assumed it was. Felix had definitely been making a statement of some kind.

Raf had moved straight into the fat man's office. Not bothering to get the place redecorated first. Claimed the man's desk too. In the bottom right drawer, behind a box of nanopore gloves, was a bottle of Jack Daniel's, more than half-full. Four empty bottles occupied the drawer on the left. That seemed to be about the extent of the old Chief's filing skills.

Raf was about to pick up the receiver when the phone went dead and a bulb lit, signifying that his assistant had finally arrived. He checked his Seiko – 8.30 A.M., Sunday morning. Raf sighed.

'Caffeine,' he demanded, punching a button on a bulky office inter-com. Another of Felix's joke purchases, presumably. 'Please,' Raf added as a belated afterthought.

'Your coffee, Excellency . . .' The thin girl put down a tray and straightened it, so that the marquetry along one rim aligned exactly with the edge of his huge desk. 'And you have . . .' Her voice was nervous. 'You have three calls to return.'

'Is that all?' Most days, even Sundays, he had several dozen backed up and waiting not to be answered.

'Three you need to deal with, Excellency,' said the girl, as she carefully poured a tiny brass cup of coffee. He thought her name was Natacha Something. The fox had spotted her coming out of an interview room carrying papers and got Raf to ask someone her name.

Quite why, Raf still wasn't sure; except that the girl had deep eyes, skin the colour of dry chamois and a body toned from evenings spent in an expensive gym. But what both he and the fox had really noticed, on their first glance down the corridor, was long dark hair, falling to her narrow hips. Utterly straight and midnight black.

Next time Raf had seen her, the girl was opening the door of his office for him and handing him a coffee and that morning's crime sheet. Someone, somewhere in the precinct had translated his casual enquiry into the fact he wanted the girl as his new PA. So now she handled his post, made him coffee, kept his diary and did other stuff he knew less than nothing about, all the while watching him nervously from the corner of her eye.

Wondering when I'm going to proposition her probably, Raf thought with a sigh.

'Trouble, Your Excellency?'

Raf looked up. She was . . .

'How old are you?'

Natacha blushed. 'Eighteen, Excellency.'

And now working for the new Chief of Detectives, even if she had fallen into that job by accident. No doubt she dressed carefully outside the office, but in here she wore black jeans and a white cotton blouse, black leather shoes with lowish heels and matching belt. The neck button of her blouse was unfastened and her sleeves folded back, like in the magazines, to make it obvious that she was ready to work hard.

A year ago, from what Raf gathered, those bare wrists would have been fine. Now they were only just acceptable. A year from now, dressed like that, she might well be breaking some official code. Of course, a year from now she could be unemployable in any office in the city, just on the basis of her gender.

'What are the important calls?' Raf's voice was more abrupt than he intended and he could see the girl try to work out exactly what she'd done to offend him.

'Hamzah Effendi was the first. Then his daughter Zara.' The girl paused. 'She left a new number. Apparently she'd had the old one changed and forgotten to tell you.' Was there an element of disapproval in that face?

Raf thought that, on balance, there might be . . .

'And the third?' he asked gently.

'The General.'

Just what he needed. Raf glanced at the report open on his screen. Stomach ripped, heart and lungs missing, slashed stops to the long strokes of the cross, the initials *H.Q.* cut into her wrist . . . It was getting so Raf could recite the litany of wounds in his sleep. Only sleep wasn't currently an option. Not if it meant letting the fox disappear again.

'Tell them all I've gone to breakfast,' said Raf. 'That is, should they call back.'

Natacha's shock almost made him smile. Hamzah Quitrimala was rich and everyone in Iskandryia knew Raf had been meant to marry Zara. But the girl's horror was reserved for the fact that he might refuse to jump when the General ordered. Koenig Pasha's main advantage was that no one dared underestimate his power, with the result that the old man barely had to use it.

'Just tell them,' said Raf.

Felix's old Cadillac sat in the fat man's bay. That is, the sign still read FELIX ABRINSKY, CHIEF OF DETECTIVES because the paperwork needed to change the sign was sitting on Raf's desk awaiting his signature. Since Raf wasn't too sure about sticking with the job, he'd been ignoring the forms. And besides, he got some weird kick out of seeing the sign still there. Like Felix was about to come shambling out of the lift onto the garage level and head for his car, trailing whisky fumes, litter and bad advice.

CHAPTER 28

The arms were those of El Iskandryia, their use on a pennant restricted to the governor, though almost anyone on Rue Missala would have announced confidently that the flag was that of Koenig Pasha himself, such was the immutable link in most people's minds between the General and their city.

The last time Raf had seen the young officer at the Bentley's wheel was months back, the day Raf arrived at Iskandryia's airport. At the time, Raf was being bumped up a chain of command like the problem he was.

'. . . *sef*,' said a whisper in Raf's head.

'Captain Yousef.' Raf offered his hand.

The man looked pleased to be remembered but slightly embarrassed all the same. 'Major Yousef, Excellency. I've been promoted.'

'Congratulations. For services rendered . . . ?'

Major Yousef looked more embarrassed still. He obviously didn't think it was appropriate to explain what Raf already knew. The major had come to the General's attention by refusing to take responsibility for deporting Ashraf Bey as an undesirable and been promoted because this turned out to be a wise decision . . . the fact this promotion had been over the head of older men, including a senior captain the General disliked intensely was, of course, not to be mentioned.

'Coffee?' Raf asked, as Le Trianon's headwaiter materialized from within the café, 'Or perhaps mint tea?'

'Neither, I'm afraid, Your Excellency.' The major nodded towards the waiting Bentley. 'You're expected.'

'The General . . . ?' Raf did his best to look surprised.

Major Yousef nodded. 'There's been another murder. A dead American. But apparently Your Excellency already knows that . . .' Gesturing towards Raf's Cadillac, parked on the pavement where the fat man used to park, he added, 'I'll have someone bring your car.'

At the oak door to the mansion in Shallalat Gardens, Raf was met by a young boy who glanced once at the Chief of Detectives' haggard face, raised his eyebrows and nodded towards a door behind him.

'He's in there . . .'

The boy paused, as if he intended saying more, then shrugged, mostly it seemed to himself.

'I know,' said Raf tiredly, 'he's upset.'

'Upset.' His Highness Mohammed Tewfik Pasha, Khedive of El Iskandryia and also ruler of Egypt, at least in name, stopped dead. 'Upset,' he said, staring at Raf with large eyes. 'Upset doesn't cover half of it . . . Oh yes.' The boy paused, remembering something else. 'And apparently he knows the truth about your origins.'

Raf hammered on the study door, waited for a couple of seconds, then hammered again. Instead of hitting it a third time, he straightened his shoulders and walked into the governor's office, only to find the small room deserted.

Panelling, mirrors and a floor of white marble, all that came as no surprise. Every high-ranking office in El Iskandryia seemed kitted out with variations on ersatz European, although Islamicist mosaic did at least replace wood panelling in some. What was surprising was a new oil painting taking up most of one wall, its brushwork bright and its heavy gilt frame positively pristine.

In it, the boy who'd met Raf at the front door wore a bottle-green uniform with three gold loops of braid knotted around each wrist. Other than that, and a thin gold stripe down each side of his trousers, the uniform was bare apart from star and crescent badges either side of its high collar.

At the boy's side hung a simple sabre, with a single gold knot on a double length of braid. On his head was a red fez.

'Dressed like some *mutahfiz* . . .'

Which wasn't a word Raf recognized, though it was obvious from the voice behind him that it wasn't a compliment.

'. . . and now apparently you want to lose him his city.' The old man stood swaying at the French windows, white knuckles gripping the top of a Malacca cane. Over his shoulder Raf could see a preternaturally green garden of monkey puzzle, rhododendron, bronze statues and tightly clipped box hedges.

'Having a bad day?' Raf asked.

Eyes dark as any storm glared back at him.

Olive trees. Red earth. A boy falling backward, face shocked.

Raf blinked.

'Afraid?' demanded the General.

'Always,' said Raf.

The old man looked surprised at that. 'Of what . . . Me?'

Raf shook his head. 'Not just of you, of everything. Waking up/falling asleep. Looking in the mirror. Losing a bit of me I'm not even sure exists.'

'The usual . . .' The old man nodded and absentmindedly put his brandy balloon on the immaculately polished surface of an antique desk, creating a ring. That was how Raf knew Iskandryia's most famous teetotaller really was drunk. 'The condition of life,' said the General. 'We live, we die. In between we're afraid to admit we're afraid. You know the real definition of courage?'

'There are dozens,' said Raf, picking up the General's glass and wiping the desk with his sleeve. 'Most of them contradictory.' He swirled the cognac until it coated the inside of the glass, then watched the pale liquid break into rivulets.

'. . . egs,' said the fox. '. . . gn of a good VSOP.' Raf could remember being told about *legs* by one of his mother's lovers, the Animal Channel producer probably. Speaking to the boy about brandy while really trying to impress a drunk obsessive, being too stupid to realize the only thing likely to impress Raf's mother was money to fund her films.

'What . . . ?' Raf looked at the General who stood waiting.

'My definition of courage,' said the old man. 'You know it?'

'Dying well?'

'Acting as if you believe, even when you don't.'

'Same thing,' said Raf as he put down the General's glass, this time on top of a folded paper that sat on the desk between them.

A fuzzy picture showed a missing teenager, her long blonde hair uncovered as she stood grinning on a street corner in some city that wasn't El Iskandryia . . . Paris, maybe, judging from a sugary white basilica behind her.

What little text there was screamed its certainty that this girl was the butcher's most recent victim. No underlined links pretended to go somewhere, because *Saiyidi* wasn't downloaded from a news vendor. It was run off an old-fashioned press in a cellar somewhere in Karmous and read by those without paid access to newsfeeds or money for vendors. The same kind of urban poor who listened to pirate stations and recognized souk rumour for the truth it was.

'You promised me the killer was already dead.'

'She is . . .'

'*She?*' Koening Pasha raised his eyebrows at the pronoun. 'Whoever told you that was wrong. Sack your informant.'

'No one told me,' Raf said crossly. 'The woman's dead. I killed her.'

'So who did it this time?' demanded the General. 'Her ghost?' His laugh was bitter, tired also. 'Drink,' he said.

Raf shook his head, then realized that wasn't an invitation but an order. Glancing round, he found a large bottle of Hine sitting on a semicircular marble table, balanced on top of a fat pile of intelligence reports.

Half the cognac was gone and its cork was missing. Raf was still looking round for a glass when the General grunted with irritation.

'Not you, idiot, me . . .' He held out his brandy balloon while Raf filled it halfway to the top. Then, turning unsteadily towards the French windows, the old man stamped back into his garden, not bothering to check that Raf was ready to follow.

Which he very definitely wasn't. Raf was too busy skimming an intelligence report, the one under the bottle. It was concise, factual and loaded. According to some second attaché at the temporary Consulate in Seattle, a local triad, represented by a button man named Wild Boy, was offering $1,000,000 for news of someone known as ZeeZee. The man had been tracked to an Ottoman Airways flight bound for Zanzibar. Unfortunately, enquiries at the Ottoman Airways office in SeaTac/Seattle had failed to identify the name under which ZeeZee had travelled or whether his journey had been broken en route.

What was known, was that the man had travelled on a diplomatic passport, probably issued by Stambul. Though, regretfully, the woman on the check-in desk had not actually looked inside.

'Remind you of anyone?'

Raf looked up to find the Khedive standing in the hall doorway, face quizzical.

'No,' said Raf. 'Afraid not.'

The boy smiled. 'Me neither.'

Under the biggest cypress tree was an ornate bench. Between the cast-iron bench and a nearby oak stood a rain-streaked statue slightly taller than Raf. The statue showed a rudimentary metal tree with a naked girl falling headlong between its stark branches.

'Pike sverer mellom grenene,' said the General. 'Gustav Vigeland – 1907. You know what it represents?'

Eyes wide, mouth open, small fists clenched. Raf could take a reasonable guess. But the General got there first, answering his own question as if he'd been the one asked.

'Whatever you want it to represent . . . So the next question,' said the General, 'is who decides exactly what *we* represent?'

He didn't wait for the answer to that either.

'Because I don't and you sure as hell don't . . .' The old man raised his brandy balloon and suddenly the dark eyes that stared at Raf over the top of the glass were anything but drunk.

'The city decides.'

Raf thought he should do something about now, so he nodded.

'You've probably heard them all. Isk the whore and Isk the virgin. The city of glass. Solid and ephemeral, transient and timeless. The city within the city. Every cliché from every guidebook. The old man used the analogy of a card house as belief . . .'

Koenig Pasha was talking about the Khedive's father, Raf realized. The man who sat for fifteen years in a small teahouse on an island off El Muntaza, which was how long it took him to die. The teahouse became his bed, the island his ward and the Haremlik across its narrow bridge became his hospital, filled with specialists from around the world.

'And he stole the card-as-belief metaphor from his father . . . An old-fashioned, outdated man.' The General's voice was uncharacteristically bitter. 'But one who was nonetheless intelligent.'

Seeing the blank look on Raf's thin face, the General began to explain himself, his long fingers and narrow wrists twitching as he mimicked adding and subtracting playing cards to a card house that wasn't there.

'Knock down a couple of cards at the top and only the top rocks. Maybe the top falls, maybe it stands. And if that level falls, it can be rebuilt, using the same cards if you must. But take a card from the bottom and the whole edifice is in danger. No matter how secure the top. Once the lowest level goes, everything goes. The old man knew this. I know this. Felix knew this. Even the boy in there knows this. It seems you don't.'

'Iskandryia isn't a pack of cards,' said Raf.

'No, it's myth layered with history, so stiff with legacy code that life barely runs. A free city that half the free world would like to see abolished. Berlin mistrusts us, Paris too . . . Washington. Well, Washington hates us. The only thing still keeping us standing is that we're too stupid to know we're dead. You know what our Unique Selling Point is?'

Raf shook his head.

'Inertia. Iskandryia's been a free city for so long no one can quite imagine how North Africa might operate if we weren't. Well, take a look at the newsfeeds. People out there are beginning to imagine it . . .' The General swallowed back the last of his cognac and breathed in, inhaling the fumes. By the time he'd finished coughing he'd apparently reached a decision.

'So far as I can see,' said the General, 'as Chief you have three main problems.'

'I have?'

'The first,' said the General, 'is personal. The way life works is public virtue, private vice. You keep doing it the wrong way round. The remaining two problems are more serious . . .' Koenig Pasha's voice was harsh but thin, its determination at odds with an old man's frailty. 'One big problem, one slightly smaller. First, find out why tourists are being butchered.'

'We think . . .'

The old man sighed heavily. 'The problem,' he said, 'is that you don't . . . You're going to tell me the killer's dead, again. Burned up in that fire. You think I don't get reports from your office? Forget finding out who carried out the latest atrocity. I told you to find out *why* it happened.'

'And how do you suggest I do that?'

'Break heads. Use the Army. Take whatever you need from the treasury . . .' The old man looked for a moment as if he might be about to rescind that last suggestion, but instead he shrugged. 'Just find out. And keep it out of the papers and off the newsfeeds.'

'That's the big problem, right?'

The General's smile was wintry. Flicking a curled leaf from the arm of the bench, he followed its brief and twisting fall. Then he told Raf what Senator Liz really wanted and exactly why he, the General, couldn't give it to her.

With trembling hand, the General took a crisp sheet of paper from his desk drawer and reached for a fountain pen, the black Mont Blanc inlaid with a silver cartouche bearing the arms of Prussia.

The old man was still writing laboriously when a knock came at the door. A second knock followed and when the General didn't answer it was Raf who said *enter* and watched the door open a little. The boy who'd let Raf into the gubernatorial mansion slid sideways through the narrow gap, only to stop and glance anxiously between Raf and the General.

'General Koenig?'

The old man nodded but kept writing.

If the Khedive minded his chief minister sitting while he himself stood it didn't show. In fact, nothing about the boy suggested he found the situation in any way odd, and only a glance at the ornately framed painting on the wall convinced Raf that he stood opposite El Iskandryia's absolute ruler.

'. . . The newsfeeds.'

Without looking up, the General tapped one corner of his desk and a long glass with an opalescent Murano frame lit to reveal a worried woman standing outside an old-fashioned mansion, built in an early-twentieth-century style dismissed as High Arabesque. In an open sub-frame in one corner, fire engines hosed down the broken shell of something sheet glass and concrete.

Raf caught the words *casino, firebomb* and *US negotiator*. And then the main picture flicked to a woman in a black suit behind a large desk. On the front of the desk was a large seal displaying the American eagle. *Chaos, lawlessness* and *organized crime* cropped up in almost every other sentence. Just in case Senator Liz's anger wasn't obvious enough, C3N had thoughtfully run Arabic subtitles along the bottom of the screen.

'Don't underestimate that woman,' the General said, 'she flew UN 'copters back in the little war.' He reached for another sheet of paper and scrawled two lines across its china-clay surface, then signed the sheet with spidery handwriting and pushed it across the desk towards the Khedive, his fingers shaking. 'All I need now is your signature for these . . .'

The boy signed without dragging his attention away from the news, which showed a crime team sifting the wreckage of the smouldering casino. A voice-over was talking, guardedly, about rumours of a dead girl found nearby. Raf got the feeling that more was intentionally being said with the gaps than with the words.

'Enough,' said the General, tapping his table to blank the screen. 'We need to concentrate on getting His Highness out of here . . .'

'I'm sorry?' The Khedive looked startled, then stubborn. 'No,' he said. 'I can't possibly . . . Not now.'

'Your holiday' said Koenig Pasha. 'What time's your flight?' The voice was little more than a cross whisper from an old man. And he did look old, if one looked past his immaculate uniform to the liver spots speckling his trembling wrists or the carcinoma scars that puckered one side of his neck, below his sunken jaw.

'Fik, what time . . . ?'

Mohammed Tewfik Pasha blinked, tears prickling up until he had to look away. *Okay*, thought the General, *maybe that was a little unfair*. He couldn't quite remember the last time he'd used Tewfik's pet name. Maybe when he was ten, that time the boy caught scarlet fever and was confined for days to a darkened room with curtains soaked in vinegar, much to the disgust of the palace's English doctor . . .

'Early evening,' said the boy. 'The flight's collecting me at seven P.M.'

'And you *are* going alone?'

The Khedive shook his head.

'She's the wrong choice,' said the General tiredly. 'You know that.' He stared at the boy, seeing anxiety turn to stubbornness, and sighed. 'Do what you have to do . . . Just remember, your job is to be on that flight. And yours,' he said turning to Raf, 'is to make sure His Highness goes.'

Folding his resignation into three, Koenig Pasha gave the sheet of paper to Khedive Mohammed with a slight bow. The letter to Raf, the General folded just the once and handed over with a nod. Then the old man waited until they'd both read and then reread what he'd written.

CHAPTER 29

17th October

Nothing so slight as a mere ring. Instead, long bursts of increasing frustration filled the large hall.

Raf had been ignoring the bell for a while.

Sighing, he looked round for someone to answer the General's front door and realized there was no one but him. So he went to answer it himself.

Another bad mistake.

While he and Zara stood, staring in disbelief at each other, the study door swung back and the young Khedive stormed out, tears of frustration streaming down his soft face.

Whatever final retort the boy was about to make died when he spotted Zara, with her cases. For a moment, it looked like the boy might walk across to where Zara stood, but then he shot Raf a bitter scowl, turned away and ran up the stairs. Somewhere a door slammed, then there was silence.

And as Zara stared between her suitcases and the emptiness on the landing above, Raf glanced into the study, his eyes meeting those of the General. What Raf got was an abrupt nod and an amused if wintry smile. And then the old man stretched, stood up from his desk and walked resolutely to the door, which he closed. The General didn't even pretend to need his cane.

'What are you doing here?' Zara's query was curt.

'Leaving,' said Raf. 'To visit a crime scene.' He looked at her. 'Oh, yeah, and trying to keep your father from being arrested for murder . . . Take your pick.'

Zara practically threw her suitcases into the boot of Raf's Cadillac, stamped round to the passenger side and climbed in, shutting the door with a slam. As an afterthought, she reached behind her for a seat belt and found nothing. Felix had never got round to having them fitted and Raf hadn't bothered to make good their lack.

Still seething about this stupidity, Zara stared resolutely ahead.

Which was how she missed seeing Raf clamber into the driver's seat of the big Bentley, ram the huge car into reverse and spin it round on protesting tyres until it faced the mansion's wrought-iron gates.

'What the . . .'

Zara never got to finish her question because Raf was already gone, all eight cylinders powering the Bentley out into traffic that skidded and stalled rather than risk scratching the General's car.

My car, Raf corrected himself, watching his gubernatorial pennant crack in the afternoon wind. My car, my city, my problem. My world coming down around my ears. And Hani's too, if he wasn't careful.

Up ahead was where Zara's club had briefly been. Now CdeH was gone, and the venue had reverted to its original existence as a deserted cistern beneath a rain-stained, multistory car park; the famous arrest and bust relegated to part of Iskandryia's rapidly receding good times.

The number of clubbers who now swore they'd been there that night would fill the third-class stands at Iskandryia stadium.

He could have taken a direct route, east onto Faud Premier, then cut south, just before Shallalat Gardens, but instead Raf concentrated on working the big car round narrow back streets marked on the GPS in red, too narrow for the vehicle in which he drove.

So far he'd done little more than scrape one fender on a wall. Although this changed once he reached the car park at Casino Quitrimala. Of course, if he hadn't spotted Madame Mila's blue government Renault on his way in, he probably would have missed that concrete gatepost as well.

Madame Mila stood next to her car, back straight and eyes fixed firmly on the Bentley. Exactly a pace behind her, at a distance obviously laid down in regulations, stood two officers from the women's police, both wearing the familiar police-issue *hijab*. Madame Mila, while obviously the most senior, was also by far the youngest. In place of her *hijab* she wore a simple blue scarf.

'General . . .' Her voice faltered as Raf climbed from the huge car, and Raf decided that maybe his morning wasn't going to be so bad after all. Unfortunately, his optimism lasted only as long as it took him to reach the crime scene.

Right in the middle of the sodden wreckage of what had once been a casino stood a handful of uniforms, including a grey-haired lieutenant, a crime-locale technician in whites, two members of the *morales* made obvious by their bottle-green jackets, and three plainclothes in matching black jeans, blue shirts and long leather coats. From what Raf could see, it was a typical Iskandryian crime scene, five times as many officers as needed, with interdepartmental rivalries and demarcation disputes guaranteeing that no one was doing anything useful.

'Boss.' An elderly plainclothes stepped forward, all heavy moustache and combed-over greying hair.

'You've got something?'

'Looks like it.'

Beside him, the uniformed lieutenant snorted. The hyena-like grin on his youthful face didn't even pretend to reach his eyes. 'I think you'll find *we've* got something.' There was an unsubtle stress to his words.

Raf raised one hand to chop dead an immediate protest from his own man and saw hurt pride and irritation swamp the old detective's heavy face, only to be wiped. It was a reaction Raf had begun to recognize.

'What's your name?'

The detective looked at him, judging the danger inherent in the question, while knowing he'd answer it anyway. 'Osman, sir . . . Ibrahim Osman.'

'And what's your job?'

Ibrahim Osman looked at him. 'I'm your deputy.'

Raf sighed.

'What,' Raf asked the uniform, 'makes you think this man was the butcher?'

The young lieutenant frowned. 'We got his murder weapon,' he said defensively and reached into his pocket, pulling out a blackened hunk of metal he'd probably trampled all over a crime scene to find.

'. . . *fic*,' whispered the fox. '. . . *taminated evidence . . . ow original.*'

Raf beckoned for the two *morales*. 'There's nothing for you here,' he told them. 'You can go too,' he said to the lieutenant. 'Take your men and leave the blade . . . In an evidence bag,' he added tiredly. Not waiting for the man's reply, Raf turned on his heels and headed back to Madame Mila.

Inside his head, the fox's grin was thin and mostly invisible.

'*Excellency . . .*'

Heavy clouds crowded the horizon and according to Raf's watch the temperature had fallen to 53° Fahrenheit, making it the coldest October for eighty-seven years. Mind you, according to his watch, he'd also missed three calls from Zara, who apparently needed to talk to him about her father. And one from Hani, which Raf found infinitely more worrying.

Toggling his Seiko to sound/vision, Raf added vibrate for any call coming in from the kid, while beside him the officers waited expectantly. Way too expectantly.

When Raf looked up from resetting his watch the coroner-magistrate was standing directly in front of him. A small and intense woman with braided black hair, minimal jewellery and shoes that were immaculately polished, for all that they were obviously cheap. She was, as Felix had once said, probably the most beautiful woman in the city and the most implacable. One who wore her disapproval of Raf like cheap cologne, flooding the moist air between them, colouring her every emotion.

'Madame Mila . . .'

It was obvious from her eyes what she saw when she looked at Raf. A rich, spoilt and overprivileged young notable who'd fallen into the job of Chief of Detectives. The dark glasses he wore permanently glued to his face she took as affectation, the rumours of his combat skills, exaggeration, nothing else. Which was true enough, they were exaggeration. But the ever-present shades were down to retinal intolerance and rich was the last thing he was. As for overprivileged . . . He could argue that definition with her all day.

'Well?' The woman was waiting for some response from him. So was the tight little group of uniforms, gathered on the edge of Madame Mila's conversation.

'I'm sorry' said Raf tiredly, 'what was your question?' Behind him, one of his own men sniggered and Madame Mila's scowl grew, her face darkening and perfect lips setting into a bitter line.

'A whole day's been and gone,' she said finally.

'And your point is?' said Raf, then realized what she meant. They were back to Sharia law. 'You want proof the dead girl wasn't local . . .' He was talking to himself but a plainclothes who stood nearby took it as a question and nodded, careful not to meet Raf's eye. Which meant that was undoubtedly *exactly* what Madame Mila had just told Raf.

'Where's the body now?'

'Still on ice.' It was Madame Mila who answered. 'She'd been spring cleaning a guard hut when she died, apparently . . .' Her voice made it silkily obvious she wasn't about to accept that fact without further proof.

'Wearing what?' He saw the sudden tension in Madame Mila's face and qualified his question. 'Before she was murdered,' he said, gently enough to surprise himself. 'I've read the preliminary report. I know she was naked when found.'

'White trousers,' said Madame Mila stiffly. 'Thin, like silk. And a silver . . .' Her hands sketched a slight, embarrassed double circle, well away from her own body. 'A metal brassiere . . .'

'Friday night. Wearing almost nothing. You think someone from this city would behave like that?'

Madame Mila thought about it. 'No,' she admitted finally. 'Probably not.'

Raf did, but he wasn't about to say so. 'And the wounds,' he said, 'no change at all?'

A blank look.

'Upward slash from pubis to throat, a right to left across the rib cage, entrails disturbed . . .' And if ever there was an appropriate word *disturbed* was it. Three psy-profilers had been busy from the start trying to explain exactly what that shit with the ripped guts might signify. So far, their sole conclusion was that the mutilation was historically interesting.

Madame Mila nodded, tight-lipped.

'You took a close look?'

Another nod.

Which probably explained the tightness in her eyes, thought Raf. She had slight sweat marks under her arms and tiny beads of perspiration where her dark hair was pulled into a shape nature never meant it to hold. By anyone else's standards Madame Mila still looked immaculate: judged by her own, the woman was a wreck.

'Go on,' said Raf. 'Get out of here.' He meant it kindly but that wasn't how his comment was taken.

Instead Madame Mila bridled. She actually pulled herself up to her full height, slight though that was.

'Out,' Raf said, finally losing his patience. 'I want all of you out of here . . . Except for you,' he added and pointed to a uniform at random. 'You get to finish taping off the crime scene and chase sightseers away.'

The uniform glanced at his young lieutenant, who glared at Raf, caught between outrage and a growing unease. Madame Mila just felt the outrage, which was how she got her question in first.

'Just who do . . .'

'. . . *oes he think he is? . . . interesting question.*' The fox had Raf take out his two-line letter and hand it to the furious woman. '. . . *erson giving orders, like it or not.*'

Raf shut his eyes.

He was standing, dead on his feet, in an almost deserted car park, outside a firebombed casino, in a city undergoing meltdown, with five different flavours of police, none of whom knew his real name, his record or that he was meant to be serving time for . . .

Well, welcome to the Apocalypso . . .

Except that was a club, wasn't it? Somewhere in downtown Zurich. He used to be driven past it on his way from the airport to school.

'. . . *ap out of it,*' hissed the fox.

'Why?'

Madame Mila stared at him. 'Why what?' Somehow she managed to add *Your Excellency* to the end of that sentence, as she handed back his letter. Though she did it through gritted teeth.

Raf ignored her. 'Why?' he demanded, only this time when he spoke it was inside his own head.

'. . . *ause you need to sleep and I've got to go.*'

'No.' Raf's silent refusal was loud enough to set his own teeth on edge. 'You can't go.'

'. . . *y to stop me,*' the fox whispered, its voice fading. And Raf wasn't sure if that was a threat, a plea or a simple suggestion. Whatever, he had to try.

'You,' Raf said, turning to the lieutenant. 'You carrying any meth?'

'No, sir.' The shake of the head was emphatic.

No use asking her.

Stamping past Madame Mila as if she didn't exist, Raf reached one of the cherry tops just as its driver slid into gear. The crime-locale tech pulled back into neutral when Raf rapped on the glass. A whir of electrics and cigarette smoke billowed from a suddenly open window. Smoking was illegal on duty for all ranks in all departments, but neither of them bothered with that.

'Meth, got any?'

Dark eyes looked at Raf from behind dark glasses. If the tech thought Raf couldn't see his expression, then he hadn't allowed for the Chief recalibrating his vision.

'Me, personally, Your Excellency?'

'Evidence, stuff on the way to a lab?'

'I'm not . . .'

'Redeem yourself,' said Raf and held out his hand. Sometime or other, he was going to have to find out their names, what jobs they did, official stuff like that.

Raf weighed the evidence bag, appreciatively. Fifty ready-made origamis of . . .

'What is it?'

'Dunno, Your Excel . . . Boss.' The techie shrugged. 'We haven't taken it to the labs.'

'You mean,' said Raf, 'you haven't taken it to the labs *yet*.'

The techie nodded.

Ripping open a fold, Raf tasted the earth-grey powder and felt the tip of his tongue disappear. 'Ice,' he told the tech, 'about sixty percent pure . . .' Raf debated cutting out a line and finding himself a clean note to roll but that seemed too much like hard work. So he just tipped the entire origami into his mouth and chewed, crunching crystals like sherbet. There was a synthetic sweetness that said someone had cut the dose with sorbitol.

Great, so tomorrow or the next day he was going to get the runs as well as suffer some hideous come-down . . . Or maybe not. There was enough in that bag to keep him up for . . .

Lights wrote themselves round fire-twisted trees. Broken casino walls suddenly became brighter, almost fluorescent. The slow sweep of the revolving cherry top looked positively alive, lambent. Even the rain fell like music.

Raf took a look at the plastic bag he was holding. There had to be enough ice in there to keep him up until the end of the world, which, according to Koenig Pasha, came the Tuesday after next, or some such. Raf still needed to get to the bottom of that one.

'You know Kamila?' Raf pulled the name from memory. 'Works at the mortuary.' They had to know her, the woman's father was one of them. A uniform. That was what Felix had said.

He took their silence for assent.

'Tell her to expect a couple of bodies. Tell her not to start without me.'

CHAPTER 30

Avatar slid his finger under the flap and ripped.

He wasn't sure what he anticipated from the envelope addressed to his sister on the cabin's dressing table . . . Not a love letter from the Khedive, because even the Khedive wasn't that stupid. Maybe an invitation to something aboard the SS *Jannah* that Zara would now miss.

Which would worry her no more than it would worry Avatar, so long as the Khedive didn't expect him to attend instead. It was bad enough that Zara had suggested that Avatar take her place aboard.

And she was wrong to try to remake him; to force on him the opportunities she felt he needed. Avatar belonged where he belonged, he knew that. And he was much too proud of what he'd learnt in his fourteen years to change.

Shaking the contents of the envelope out onto his cabin's pink bedspread, Avatar's eyes widened. Whatever else he'd expected Zara to be sent, an engraving of a naked, full-breasted woman bent backward, scuttling across the dirt on limbs that turned to those of a spider was not on his list. On the back in elegant copperplate pen was the word *Judecca*. Beneath this, *Welcome to limbo.*

Nothing else whatsoever.

With a shrug, Avatar screwed up the envelope and tossed it out of a porthole, watching the wind that caught his crumpled offering and kept it for a few seconds from the embrace of the waves.

Maybe he should do the same with the naked spider? Avatar had dismissed the possibility before he'd finished thinking it. He was going to send the pervy engraving to Zara. As her just reward for getting Hamzah to agree he should take her place.

Avatar sighed heavily and wished he was somewhere else. The palm in the corner of his cabin was hideous. The size of a child and planted in a Chinese container that was painted with a ridiculous number of waterfalls and colts kicking their heels on a mountainside.

Pot or palm by itself would have been bad enough, but together they constituted an insult. It was all Avatar could do not to tip the plant, pot and all, after the envelope into the Mediterranean below.

Avatar was pretty sure Zara would have loathed the palm, not to mention the cabin's kitsch Victorian screen plastered with pictures of children cut from old magazines; both of which had been meant for Zara, because this was to have been her cabin. And Avatar had been assured, by a very shocked steward, that everything in the suite had been selected personally by the Khedive himself.

If so, the Khedive had even less idea of what made his sister tick than Avatar imagined. And that included sending her a naked spider.

Avatar looked round his cabin for a scanner, realized there wasn't one and took a lift down to the bleached-blond retro of the SS *Jannah*'s business suite. After he'd got over his shock at being told everything was free to a guest of the Khedive, he found and made do with a fax.

CHAPTER 31

Hell was a circle with bars and walkways, guards and unseen voices: level after level of honesty, each level more brutal than the last. Endless faces that Raf knew intimately and had never before seen. A cold that filled his mind and chilled the inside of his bones.

'Ice,' he heard someone say. 'A massive dose of methamphetamine. Close to fatal.'

'And the voices?'

'Cerebrospinal tests show viral RNA associated with schizophrenia.'

'He's caught a virus?'

The voice was amused. 'Someone did. Twenty million years ago. All we've got are molecular footprints.' And then the voice and the white coat it wore went away and the darkness came back in.

Sometime later, a small hand slapped Raf back to life, then cross fingers swung his head from side to side, like a physiotherapist checking mobility.

'Come on,' demanded Hani.

She sat perched on top of his quilt, knees bent either side of his chest, her face almost touching Raf's own. The blur of movement Raf saw when he finally opened his eyes was Hani moving away, shifting backward.

For a fleeting second she looked relieved, but when Raf checked again that expression was gone. 'About time,' Hani said, scrambling off his chest. 'You won't believe the trouble you're in.'

'I can't be in trouble,' said Raf, 'I'm . . .'

'. . . the new governor.' Hani rolled her eyes. 'I wouldn't try that one on Zara.'

Over Hani's shoulder Raf could see a distant blue sky, small white clouds and rays of golden sun that reflected on the skin of flying babies. Next to a cluster of pink cherubs floated an even pinker woman dressed in a strategically placed wisp of cloud.

The room, in which he lay must have been thirty feet high, maybe more. Its ceiling was domed, the dome supported on marble pillars that, when he looked closer, turned out to be painted onto plastered walls.

'Late Victorian, trompe l'oeil,' Hani told him, following his gaze. 'The dome's earlier. You should see my room.'

The child slid off the bed and onto the floor. 'I brought you coffee,' she said. 'Proper coffee.' She indicated a cafetière and a china cup resting on a salver. The small tray was silver, a length of gold twisted like rope along its edge. Next to the salver was a sprig of bougainvillea stuffed into a tooth mug, the French kind with a slablike base and heavy sides.

Its smell was sickly.

'I picked it in the garden.' Hani's eyes were open wide. 'You should see the statues,' she said, 'they're all . . .'

'Naked.'

She nodded. Then carefully put the cup on its saucer . . . The thing that really worried Raf was just how hard Hani was trying to pretend that everything was normal.

'Why are they naked?' Hani asked, as if an afterthought.

'Perhaps it was warmer in the old days.'

'Yeah, right. But what about . . . ?'

'Coffee,' suggested Raf and Hani smiled.

Pushing hard, she managed to wrestle the plunger to the bottom without spilling any onto the tray. Equally carefully, she poured Raf half a cupful, then her face came apart and tears overflowed her eyes.

'Milk,' she said, between sobs. 'I forgot the . . .'

Raf let Hani pour him a second cup of black coffee. Her tears over and not to be mentioned. At least not yet.

'You blacked out,' said Hani. She used the term confidently, something overheard and assimilated. She seemed about to say more but instead lapsed into thoughtful silence, glancing at Raf when she imagined he wasn't looking. Whatever she saw seemed to reassure her.

'Here.' She passed him the cup but he was already asleep. He slept for another day.

'Excellency . . .' Khartoum stood in the open doorway, the chewed stub of a cheroot in one hand and a tea glass in the other. It took Raf a few seconds to work out that the old man was waiting for permission to enter.

Permission given, Khartoum shuffled past Raf's bed to put his tea glass on the floor in front of a huge sash window. Yanking back the velvet curtains and throwing up the bottom sash, Khartoum carefully repositioned the glass until it stood in the centre of a patch of brightness.

'Sunlight increases strength,' he told Raf, as the bey scrabbled for his dark glasses. 'And green glass is good for added serenity.' The man paused. 'As for fresh air . . .'

'What about air?'

Cupping his hands, Khartoum indicated the empty space within. 'This one handful contains more power than every single substation in El Iskandryia . . . No, in the whole of North Africa.'

'Nice idea,' said Raf.

'One person's mysticism is another's zero-point energy.' The old man shrugged. 'I have a message for you from Koenig Pasha in America.'

'You?' Raf said it without thinking.

'Donna was scared to take the call and Hani is too young . . .' An element of disapproval tinted Khartoum's voice. 'So I talked to him. Ya Pasha says three things. The first is that next time you are to take his calls. The second is that he hopes you found your picture instructive . . .'

The old man nodded to Raf's bedside table and the yellowing engraving ripped from Dante's *Inferno*, with its naked man clutching at his slashed-open chest. It took Raf another few seconds to remember the solemn *aide de camp* who'd delivered it to him outside Le Trianon, the night his fox finally died.

'The third and final thing,' said Khartoum, 'is that His Excellency is most impressed.' A smile crossed the old man's face. 'The networks are waiting. The UN is waiting. C3N is going insane. Senator Liz has started talking about you as a new force in North Africa.'

'Why?' Raf pushed himself up on his pillows.

'You've kept them all waiting for three days.'

'I've . . .'

'That's how long you've been . . . asleep.' Scooping the tea glass from the floor, Khartoum carried it across the room and offered it to Raf. Black slivers of bark floated in water thick with sediment, some of which had settled at the bottom of the glass.

'Take it,' Khartoum said. It wasn't a suggestion.

Raf did. At least he took the tea glass, but that was all. 'Is this going to make me sleep again?'

The skeletal man snorted. 'You've slept enough,' he said. 'It's time you woke up . . .' He paused on the edge of saying something, glanced at Raf huddled under a thin quilt and said it anyway.

'Demons are useful,' said Khartoum. 'They keep us respectful of the dark. But you let yours ride you like djinn.' He stared long and hard. 'I see them look out of your eyes. You think we don't know why you always wear those dark things?'

Walking over to the window, the old man stared out at the mansion's famous garden. From behind, he looked as fragile as a dying tree and as solid as rock. 'Hani's asleep outside your door,' he said, tossing his words over one thin shoulder. 'That's where she's slept since she got here, but you know that, don't you?'

Raf didn't, although something in Khartoum's voice warned him he should have. 'Three nights she's slept there. Her and that cat. She thought you were dying . . . Ya Pasha thinks you're being clever. Hani thinks you're going to die. The noisy American thinks you're refusing to see her out of spite. But God knows the truth. You been hiding. Most of your life has been hiding.'

'And you are who?' asked Raf.

'Who's anyone?' said Khartoum. 'So much dust. There are people in this city who would give all of what they own to see you dead . . .'

'Me?'

'Iskandryia's governor,' said Khartoum. 'That's you, isn't it?'

'And you represent them?'

'No,' said Khartoum, 'I represent the woollen cloak.' He shook his head at the boast, amending his words. 'No' he said. 'Not true. No one represents anyone, other than themselves and the will of God.'

The taste of Khartoum's medicine was bitter, somewhere between burned earth and crushed aniseed; but it flowed down Raf's throat and spread through his veins like creeping light, as the headache he forgot having lifted like burning mist.

'Good,' said Khartoum, and nodded grimly. 'Now you eat . . . I'd bring you something myself but then Hani would be upset.'

'Bagels,' announced Hani. 'And I remembered milk for the coffee . . .' There were three already split bagels, untoasted and minus schmeer piled into a mound on a plate so fine that Raf could see Hani's fingers through the bone china. The coffee was the colour of dishwater, its cup narrow at the base and wide at the top, so that tiny globules of goat's milk floated slicklike on the surface.

'This is what they eat in Seattle . . .' said Hani.

It was a question, Raf realized, not the statement he'd thought it was.

'You're right,' he said.

'I looked it up,' she explained defensively. 'Bagels and milky coffee, it's traditional.'

Raf nodded.

'And I downloaded you some papers to read with your breakfast.' Hani paused. 'I'm not sure you'll want them,' she added, resting her bagel plate on the side of his bed and taking a huge bundle of papers from under her arm.

They were worse than Raf expected. Monday's *Die Berliner* dealt with leaked documents suggesting that outgoing governor Koenig Pasha had once taken a five-million-dollar bribe from El Iskandryia's beleaguered industrialist, Hamzah Effendi. Nowhere was it mentioned that this was for facilitating Raf's marriage to Zara, the one that didn't happen.

The word *anarchy* featured heavily in the leader column. Questions were apparently being asked in Geneva, forcing Berlin, however reluctantly, to agree with the position of France and America . . . El Iskandryia had become a liability.

City in chaos, he'd read that one already.

Koenig Pasha rushed to New York hospital . . . That was new. Raf skimmed Tuesday's *Times* and grinned. So the old man had got himself out of the country, strapped to a stretcher and wired in to more machines than looked strictly necessary. In the picture his eyes were closed, his face even more sepulchral than usual.

Raf wouldn't put it past the old bastard to have starved himself for a day or two, just to make it look more convincing.

The General's arrival at Mount Olive Hospital in New York was as low-key as any arrival that was greeted by a hundred chanting, placard-waving protesters could be. An old man, frail as melting snow, in a borrowed wheelchair, being pushed up a ramp by a young staff nurse.

'Is Koenig Pasha really dying?' Hani asked.

Raf shook his head. 'Doubt it,' he said. 'I doubt if he's even really ill.'

'A trick,' she said, smiling. Hani could appreciate that.

Wednesday's *New York Times, Le Monde, Frankfurter, El Pais, Herald Tribune* . . . Hani had downloaded the lot and the story they told was the same. The General was ill, El Isk was in chaos, no one knew anything significant about the new governor.

There was, Raf was sorry to say, very little significant to know.

'You had a call from Zara,' said Hani. 'And from . . . Kamila.'

It took Raf a moment to pull the name from memory. Kamila was the young coroner he'd told not to go ahead until he was there. That was what, four days ago?

Hani caught up with Raf after he'd shaved and dressed and was preparing to go tour the city. Although the words *fiddling, Nero* and *burns* came to his mind.

'I need to show you something,' she said.

'Later.'

'No,' Hani insisted. 'Now.'

Her fingers grabbed the pocket of his jacket and held fast. One of the guards by the front door looked as if he didn't know whether to be amused or appalled. A glance at Raf's face convinced him to be neither.

'What is it?' said Raf with a sigh.

Hani squinted at the guard, then at Raf. 'It's a secret,' she said. 'You'd better come with me.' The room she led Raf to smelled of dust and damp, of rotting wall hangings and ancient books going musty on oak shelves. But the data port in the wall by the window was working.

'Should it be able to do this?' asked Raf, watching figures scroll lightning-fast down the screen of a toy computer shaped like a seashell.

Hani shrugged.

'I made some changes,' she said, then went back to her screen. Figure followed figure, ever faster as Hani's fingers danced over keys, never quite touching.

'Okay,' she said, 'here we go.'

They were in Tiny Tina zone, apparently. Occupying an impossibly frilly bedroom constructed from, wavy planes and pastel colours. Stuffed toys sat on the fat bed. In one corner of the virtual room sat a pink chest of drawers, decorated with stuck-on pictures of Hani's cat Ifritah.

Making some kind of pass over her keyboard, Hani popped out one of the drawers and clicked on the emptiness. Instantly the childish bedroom was gone, replaced by thumbnail pix of five wrecked buildings.

'See,' she said, 'they're not *random* at all.'

Lines radiated from thumbnails to various logos, from those logos to offshore shells, back to different logos. All the lines eventually ended in the same place, with one logo, that of Hamzah Enterprises GmB.

'They've all been burned,' said Raf.

'And every burned building belongs to Effendi,' stressed Hani. 'All five.' She was grinning at her own cleverness.

That was when Raf realized something. Usually his ideas came fast, pulled from memory in a flurry of facts, with the connections ready-made; but this came slowly, like a fish rising to the bait, and it came not formed but uncertain. Becoming certain only when he thought about it.

Over and over again, Hamzah's refinery had also been attacked and each time the harm was minimal. Highly visible, usually photogenic, but not even close to serious damage. Someone badly wanted the Midas Refinery kept in the news but not broken.

That ruled out the Sword of God, who abhorred Hamzah's links with St Cloud. One of the ironies of the Midas Refinery was that Europe saw St Cloud as the refinery's acceptable face, while the fundamentalists regarded him as degenerate. And if SoG weren't really behind the attacks

434

on the refinery, then Raf found it hard to believe they'd bothered to burn Hamzah's other buildings.

On the way out of the first-floor room, Hani dragged Raf over to a long, fly-specked looking glass. 'Are you meant to be dressed like that?' she asked.

Raf took a look and saw a pale man in a high-necked suit, wearing Armani shades and carrying a silver-topped Malacca cane in one hand. A bit thinner than before he iced himself, but otherwise not that different. Swept-back blond hair, neat beard, high cheekbones, drop-pearl earring. He saw the person he expected to see, people mostly did; until the day they looked in the mirror and saw somebody else.

'You're dressed like the General,' Hani said patiently.

'That's the plan,' said Raf. 'If I dress like the General, then maybe people will treat me like the General.'

'Yeah, right,' said Hani. 'They'll probably try to shoot you.'

CHAPTER 32

22nd October

Next morning, a couple of hours before dawn, Khartoum woke himself and went to fetch Raf. He waited in silence while the surprised bey sat on the edge of his bed and pulled on a pair of trousers, buttoned his shirt and slid into a black coat.

Sitting to dress was ordained. Something the bey had not understood until Khartoum explained this. Dressing in the pitch-dark was the bey's own choice.

Khartoum had nodded to a Sudanese guard standing outside Raf's room on his way in, and when he nodded again on his way out, the guard fell into step behind them. Two more soldiers fell into step at the front door. They were five minutes from the sleeping mansion before Khartoum saw Raf realize that not one of his escort carried a weapon.

South through the sodium of Rue Ptolomies, across Faud Premier's hard neon and into a darkened alley little wider than a shop doorway, one city giving way to another as Khartoum knew it would. Some people thought it was the *arrondissements* that mattered, because those were what got shown on maps. It was a simple enough mistake to make. The same people divided their lives. This is my job, this is my wife, my friends from the market, my other friends, my family, this is the emptiness that should be occupied by my God.

Life didn't work like that. It was layered, not separate. Woven together into a hidden script that few knew existed and fewer still ever got to read.

Woodsmoke drifted from mean doorways. There was a whining of sleepy children. A thrown-open wooden shutter swung so hard it bounced off the wall. Someone hawked and spat noisily in a room nearby. The further into the alley they walked, the sourer the air and the more battered the front doors. Until finally beaten-earth walls, stripped of their render by time or rain, framed doorways closed only by blankets.

Beneath Raf's feet, shattered tarmac scabbed the damp earth like broken skin.

Khartoum was watching him in the near darkness.

'Where are we?' Raf asked.

'Undoubtedly almost here,' said Khartoum and kept walking.

There were others in the darkened alley. Figures slipping from the curtained doorways, their jellabas poor, their faces sunken with hunger. Scars went uncorrected and poor eyesight unimproved. They had the dark skin of those who had migrated from where the rivers met. They were the city's incomers. The city's invisibles.

Lacking shoes, history, a voice.

For most of those who joined Khartoum, Raf's escort were invisible. Although at least one man did hesitate, seeing uniforms lit from an open door. And two or three slunk back into darkness and safety.

A few of the men smiled at Khartoum, most just nodded a simple *marhaba*. One or two, mainly the older ones, gave the *salaam*, right hands sweeping up to touch their heart and then that little finger-flick out from the head. To those alone Khartoum replied formally, *wa 'alaykum assalam*.

One of the smallest boys reached out to touch Khartoum's robe and was instantly yanked away by his father. Khartoum appeared not to hear the slap that followed or the muffled protests that followed that. In total there were no more than fifty people, all men and mostly young.

Occasionally, when light spilled out from a high window some of them would stare at Raf when they thought he wouldn't notice. Mostly they just trudged in silence, until the narrow cut ended, opening onto a gloomy scar of scrubland and railway track.

Away to their right, arc lights bathed the vast neobaroque business that was Misr Station, its exuberance curtailed only by distance and intervening darkness. And somewhere nearby was a truck depot, where a diesel crunched its gears, but other than this, the only sound was of feet shuffling over gravel as the group left the tracks behind to slip through a hole cut in a link fence.

An unbroken line of blank-faced, five-storey tenements faced them across a deserted road, all that separated them from a small *zawiya* built in the courtyard of the tenement opposite. The *zawiya*'s minaret was little more than a squat tower. And Khartoum's voice, when it echoed from the top, was thin and quavering against the amplified magnificence coming from grander minarets across the waking city.

The small mosque looked out of place but that was just appearance, reality was the other way round. The mosque had been there first. Once,

437

in fact, it had been a Coptic church, home to a famous Gnostic, but that was before the armies of God burst out of the desert, bringing blood, coffee, decent cooking and the truth.

'In the name of God, the Merciful, the Compassionate . . .'

The *Fatiha* gave way to other prayers, then a Bible story that Raf didn't recognize from Sunday services at school. One in which Satan was cast out for refusing to bow down before Adam and in which Adam repented of eating the Apple.

Original sin did not exist.

Vicarious atonement was not required.

To find the law, logic had only to be systematically applied to situations not explicitly mentioned in the Holy Quran . . . *Hadith* and *Ijma'*. Raf pulled the terms from memory and meaning came tumbling after. *Hadith* was a database of oral law, second only to the Book and more important than *Ijma'*, agreed precedents. Together, with logic, they made up the four classical roots of jurisprudence, which all rulers must use . . .

Hunched on his heels at the back of the crowd, Raf understood instantly why he'd been brought. Why Khartoum was so insistent.

Raf dragged his eyes away from the cracked dome overhead with its constellation of tesserae broken by the tiny darkness of fallen stars. Stained glass filled with morning light at one end of the mosque and below the window was a wooden minbar, a kind of carved pulpit in which Khartoum now stood. To one side was a niche, richly decorated with polychrome marble and painted tiles. At the top of the niche were carved stones of alternate colours, dark red and pale sandstone. It was an ancient technique known as . . .

Ablaq, Raf said to himself.

Next to him, a middle-aged man frowned, suddenly recognized Raf as the new governor and looked hurriedly away.

'This is the truth.'

Now Khartoum sat facing the crowd, telling them the story of a famous mystic who challenged a Caliph and was crucified, his ashes thrown into the Tigris. Somehow the tale of al-Hallaj developed into one about a mullah who rode his donkey backward, waving a lighter and a mug of water. When asked why, he announced that it was to ignite heaven and put out the flames of hell.

After that the stories became lighter. The poor mullah and the rich beggar. The night the mullah fell down a well. The time he announced, when presented with a pregnant woman, whose husband had died falling off a cart five years before, that the fault lay with the lazy foetus who'd been sleeping, not the mother. And then, while the men were still thinking about that, the stories ended . . .

'They are the city,' Khartoum said to Raf later. 'You forget this at your peril. And besides' – he smiled – 'what's that phrase *nasranis* have . . . ? *Seeing is believing* . . .'

'You wanted me to believe in them?'

Khartoum looked at Raf as if he was a complete idiot. 'No,' he said heavily, 'I want them to believe in you.'

CHAPTER 33

22nd October

She wasn't the first person to decide that Raf had engineered the departure of Koenig Pasha . . . Dr Kamila was just more obvious about her suspicions than most.

'A poison-induced heart attack?' Raf raised his eyebrows. 'Who said anything about a heart attack?'

'The local news. Were they wrong?' Kamila kept her tone several degrees below comfortable. One degree above the autopsy suite.

'Yes,' said Raf, 'undoubtedly . . . For a start, to have a heart attack you need a heart.'

Behind him a man snorted, but when Raf glanced round the General's old bodyguard, Hakim, was busy staring straight ahead.

'I'll be with you when this is done,' Kamila said stiffly and returned to her scalpel and a plump woman largely hidden under a green sheet.

It was three months since Raf had been in Kamila's autopsy suite. Then there'd been two bodies, one of them a stranger unrelated to his own narrative, the other the woman he was meant to have murdered. Now there were half a dozen. In El Iskandryia these days, even death was suffering from inflation.

'That man I sent . . .'

'In a minute,' said Kamila crossly, turning back to where the plump woman's scalp had been sliced around the hairline and pulled forward, so it hid her face. A section of yellow bone beneath had been cut away. Whatever was in the stainless-steel dish beside the half-empty skull might look like minced jelly but was, Raf decided, undoubtedly something nastier.

'Now,' said Raf.

'As soon as this is finished.'

Raf clicked his ringers and pointed to the electric scalpel. 'Take that toy away from Ms Kamila.'

440

'Sure, Boss.' Hakim squeezed between two trolleys and held out a meaty hand. 'If you would, miss . . .'

Very carefully, Kamila put the bowl and her scalpel on the nearest table, the double clink of metal on metal momentarily drowning out Raf's sigh. She obviously hadn't forgiven him the last time they'd met.

'The scalpel . . .' Hakim's hand was still outstretched.

'Let it go,' said Raf and the sergeant padded silently back to his place. Ahmed, Raf's other bodyguard, waited at ground level, at the top of the stairs. In the street outside, his official driver stood by the Bentley. It seemed that the only place Raf was to be free of guards was on the loo. And even that had been a battle.

At the mansion itself, he had anxious secretaries, keen assistants, more staff than-hours in the day and all awaiting orders, with only Hani willing to disagree with him if she thought his ideas were bad. Raf seriously doubted if an idiot supported by a nine-year-old was what the General had in mind when he resigned and appointed Raf in his place. So far, it seemed, his greatest successes had come from doing nothing . . . Zero-input shadow play.

'Hakim,' Raf said. 'Go join Ahmed. Understand?' The big man nodded doubtfully, then looked at Raf and shrugged.

'Is that an order, Boss?'

'Whatever it takes,' said Raf.

Hakim gone, Raf turned his full attention to Kamila. He was pretty sure the pathologist's face showed open contempt, though that could have been his imagination, given that she wore a green surgical mask over her nose and mouth.

'You know why the General appointed me governor?'

The shake of her head was quick, abrupt.

'You want to know?'

She thought about that. Her face tilted slightly to one side. Dark eyes flicked over his shoulder to the shut door beyond. No, she shook her head again, she didn't . . .

'Good,' said Raf, 'because I haven't a fucking clue.'

'That makes two of us.' He wasn't meant to hear her aside, but he did. Just as he heard a raggedness in her heartbeat, the rush of her breath and the crackle of paper as she pushed her hand through a slit in the side of her surgical gown, searching for a cigarette.

Ignoring a dozen NO SMOKING signs, Kamila tapped a Cleopatra straight from its packet to her mouth and zapped the end, tugging smoke down into her lungs. She put the crumpled packet back without offering a cigarette to Raf.

Nicotine-heavy and carcinogen-free, the smoke mixed with

formaldehyde and almost swamped the underlying signature of slowly decaying meat. And while a clock on the wall ticked off the seconds, an air purifier scrubbed at the smoke and a humming wall unit kept the tiled room not far above zero.

The morgue was fifteen feet below the sidewalk, soundproof, cut out of solid rock. Back times, before it was used for dead bodies, it had been a prison for live ones. Then the soundproofing had been more useful. Before this it was a charnel house for dry bones. Earlier still, Gnostic heretics had hidden there from the might of Byzantium.

History backed up inside Raf's head like memory, ghost after ghost, silent and hopeless. Some days he could almost taste it.

'Ever read any Ibsen?' Raf asked.

She hadn't.

'Small town gets poisoned, everybody wants to keep it quiet. I've forgotten the end . . .' Behind her mask, the girl's face remained impassive.

Raf sighed. 'Show me the bodies,' he said.

Kamila nodded. They were back to a relationship she understood. He gave orders, she quietly resented them. 'This way,' she said, walking across to a trolley that was on its own. 'This is the man you insisted we take . . .' Pulling back a body cloth, she indicated something with the stink of stale embers and the consistency of twisted bog oak.

Clothes had fused in places to flesh, where flesh was left, legs were bent at the knees, the body angled forward, fists raised, as if fighting an invisible enemy . . .

Occasional flakes of barklike flesh dotted onto the trolley's top but mostly what remained of the man was polished anthracite. The thread of a toe tag had been looped round one ankle, the actual toes having fused together.

'PA,' said Kamila, indicating the twisted limbs. '*Pugilistic attitude*, it happens when strong muscles cook in the heat. Muscles tighten, spine expands, head goes back. You find it in everything from house fires to the dead at Pompeii. He got caught in a fireball, then fell beneath the worst of the flames. You got lucky.'

Raf looked at her.

'If the heat's intense enough, the brain boils and the skull explodes . . . looks like a gunshot. Well, if you don't know what you're looking at. Instead,' said Kamila, 'the skull's in one piece and X-rays show not all of the fillings melted. And he did have fillings, rather than replacements. Which makes him a traditionalist.'

Or an idiot.

'And fillings will tell me what?'

442

'Country of origin, if God wills . . .' She shrugged. 'I'll take a look as soon as the surface work is complete.' Kamila stubbed out the remains of her cigarette and picked up a UV rod, flicking its switch.

'Forget that,' said Raf, quietly taking the rod from her hand. 'I need his nationality now. Anything that's not now is already too late.'

'Okay, you're the boss,' Kamila said, the tightness around her eyes contradicting the politeness of her words. Picking up a scalpel, she hacked open one blacked cheek, swapped instruments and reached in with a pair of tiny snub-nosed pliers. 'Already heat-cracked,' she said to herself. To Raf, she said, 'We can do this professionally or we can do it fast.'

Not waiting for his answer, Kamila crushed the tooth and used the pliers to extract a minute shard of amalgam from deep inside. The fragment went into a glass dish, the dish into a little spectrometer and Kamila punched a button. Behind smoked glass, a laser vaporized the amalgam and data began to scroll down a tiny flat screen.

'Austro-Hungarian,' she said, 'maybe German. Could be American, just about, though slightly wrong composition for US amalgam.'

'So he's not Iskandryian?'

'I'm talking about the fillings,' said Kamila.

'I'm not,' said Raf. 'What about the girl?'

'That's all you want on this one?'

'It's enough.'

It was too. *Tourists butchered by tourist.* The dead man was a foreigner. If necessary, he could be made into a tourist. That gave him something to give the newsfeeds. And the earlier deaths could also be put down to this man. Raf was still writing headlines in his head when Kamila walked over to another trolley and pulled back the sheet, exposing the face and shoulders of a blonde teenager.

She treated this corpse with more respect. Maybe because the victim was female or this was a victim, not a killer. Perhaps just because the body was more obviously human. A jigsaw of a human, true enough, with some pieces missing, but still more obviously like her, even when dead.

The dead girl looked unnaturally thin beneath the cloth, and then Raf realized why. Both her large and small intestines were already in a surgical chill bucket beneath the trolley. The bucket tagged and numbered. The more Raf looked at the corpse the more it reminded Raf of himself. He could swear there'd been one time he was across the other side of an operating theatre looking at his body as it lay on a table, figures in white coats standing around it.

'She's American,' said Raf. 'Nineteen, a politics major, doing well at university. Originally from Kansas City. Her father works for

Hallmark . . .' Raf caught the pathologist's look and held it. 'I was talking to the poor bastard half an hour ago.'

And saying nothing of any consequence, obviously enough, the meeting brief and painful. A jowly middle-aged man, still jet-lagged and pale with shock, accompanied by a vodka-sodden woman whose anger was barely in check. First they learn their kid is missing, then – once they arrive where she's meant to be – no one in authority will even take their calls. And then twenty-four hours later, just as they're ready to flip, Iskandryia's chief muckety-muck turns up at their hotel, accompanied by three armed guards.

In the end, Raf had apologized to the Haugers and left, trailing his guards behind him. And the parting glare from the dead girl's mother made it obvious she held him personally responsible for every injury inflicted on her child.

Only manners and being in a foreign city made Mrs Hauger swallow her words. On his way out of the hotel, Raf had met Senator Liz coming in. From the look on her face she also held Raf accountable.

All he'd learnt from his uncomfortable encounter with the Haugers was that their daughter Dawn didn't drink, didn't do drugs and wasn't interested in boys . . .

Pulling the modesty cloth back to her hips, Raf looked down at what was left of their daughter. She'd been beautiful in an ordinary sort of way and she was someone's child. And those someones were trying to hold their life together in a Hyatt hotel room, in a city so alien it might as well have been on another planet.

He tried to see Dawn as her parents would remember her, if they got lucky. Not as this emptiness with its faint tinge of decay, but as she'd been: blonde, pretty, with high cheeks and eyes of speedwell blue.

'Talk me through the injuries,' said Raf, folding the modesty cloth into a strip and positioning it carefully. His attempt not to offend Kamila more than circumstances required. 'How much preliminary work have you done?'

'None,' the pathologist said flatly, 'apart from X-rays. Those were your orders, apparently . . . Hold everything until you were here in person.'

'Yeah, I know. Sorry . . .'

Not the response Kamila had been expecting but then, in part, that was Raf's intention. The fox had a tag from Machiavelli covering emotional sleight of hand, but unfortunately the fox was missing, assumed dead.

'Well,' said Kamila, more embarrassed than mollified, 'you're here now.'

444

'True enough,' Raf said and wondered why he shivered. Then he remembered that he'd thought a lot about such places when he was a child, around the time he got his second kidney replacement.

Speed had been essential according to his doctor. And it had been this time constraint that made the clinic go through an organ broker. Searching for a matching kidney from someone dying or freshly dead. Of course, going this route was cheaper than growing a new one, but they'd assured his mother that wasn't an issue.

Raf had given up trying to remember which bits of him were retreads. Although, occasionally, he'd catch a slight seam of scar where he didn't expect to see one. Across his ribs or down one arm, and think, *what's that?*

Shadow memories.

'You all right?'

Raf glanced up to find Kamila staring at him, eyes anxious.

'I'm Iskandryia's new can carrier,' he said. 'What do you think?'

'I don't,' said Kamila. 'I'm not that stupid.' Reaching into her pocket, she produced a floating camera, which she tossed into the air, waiting while it ran self-diagnostics.

'Friday, 22nd October, 2:38 P.M.,' she announced once a diode lit green. 'I am Kamila bint-Abdullah, city pathologist, second grade.' Kamila's tone made clear what she thought about that. 'Also present at the autopsy is His Excellency, Ashraf . . .' She cleared her throat. 'Delete that . . . is His Excellency, the Governor of El Iskandryia.

'This is case number 49-3957, Jane Doe . . .' Kamila's smile was almost apologetic and Raf realized she'd need a formal identification before the corpse earned itself a name. 'The body is that of an apparently healthy, well-nourished female, Caucasian, late teens/early twenties. The body is sixty-four inches long and in total, but minus lungs and heart, weighs . . .'

Taking a readout from the autopsy table and the bucket that held the girl's intestines, Kamila added the two figures together in her head. '. . . 115 pounds. Blonde hair, blue eyes . . . The skin is of normal texture. There are no scars, moles, subdermal chips or tattoos.

'Preliminary X-rays and scans reveal no bone fragments, fractures, bullet tracks, knife wounds, needles or objects embedded beyond point of entry. No foreign objects in throat, anus or vagina.'

Kamila lifted Dawn Hauger's right hand and examined each finger. 'Nails painted, neatly filed and unbroken, no indication of embedded foreign material. No defensive cuts to palm, dorsal side of arm, no damage to webbing between fingers . . .

'Which should suggest suicide,' Kamila tossed the comment over her shoulder. 'At least it should according to the textbooks.' Her voice was darkly ironic, animosity briefly forgotten. She was good at the job, Raf realized. Her manner professional and assured.

'Initials *H.Q.* inscribed on inside of left wrist,' Kamila announced, finishing up the other hand.

A quick sweep with a UV rod produced no significant areas of flare, though Kamila still took swabs from one corner of the dead girl's mouth, her nasal area and just outside the vagina. She also swept the pubic area for foreign body hair, despite the fact this had already been done once at the crime scene.

Using a plastic ruler, Kamila began to measure the wounds, her voice emotionless. The longest cut ran from throat to pubis, the second longest traversed the ribs, just below heavy breasts. Together the gashes formed a cross potent. And it was a cross potent rather than a mere cross, because once again wounds showed short lines cut at either end of each slash. The top one conveniently opened the girl's throat and the bottom one bisected her pudenda, the other two scored down both sides of her ribs. Though the terms Kamila used to describe their position were *cephalic, caudal* and *lateral.*

'This is too neat,' Kamila said. 'Much too neat . . .' The pause that followed was to let Raf ask a question.

'I had a look at the crime-scene report,' she added into his silence.

'How did . . . ?' Of course, her father, sat at his front desk, proud of how well his only daughter was doing. 'What did it tell you?'

Kamila hesitated, replying with a question of her own. 'Wouldn't you expect increased disorganization?'

'Expect what?'

Kamila shrugged. 'This is the third death. Personally, at this point, I'd be looking for proof of greater risks run, not enough time allowed, less safe crime scenes, fewer escape routes . . .' She ticked the points off in her head. 'Yet, if anything, this killing is more meticulous than the last, which had inherent differences in MO to the one before.'

'You're absolutely certain?'

'Sure.' Kamila nodded. 'I pulled out all the files,' she said, pointing to a distant wall screen. 'Examined the earlier crime shots. Identical wounds, different MOs. The discrepancy just didn't get logged.'

'Why not?'

Her shrug was expressive. In it was everything Kamila felt about her opposite number at the *polizia touristica.* But what she said was, 'Maybe he's overworked . . .'

On average 1 percent of a city dies each year. Iskandryia had 4 million people. Which meant forty thousand deaths, a quarter of which might merit investigation. Setting aside the poor and the unimportant reduced that figure to three thousand, the vast majority of whom had to be buried by noon (if they died in the previous twenty-four hours), or by the following noon (if they died at noon or after).

So far this year *polizia touristica* had dealt with seven bodies. Four drownings and the three butchered tourists, on the last of which she was doing the work for them.

'My unofficial opinion,' Kamila said hesitantly, 'based on observation and on having sight of the autopsy reports of the earlier killings . . .' She was picking her words with care. 'Despite obvious similarities, my unofficial belief is that victim three was not killed by the same person as victim two, because, in the case I've examined, the positioning of each cut is more, not less, precise.'

Kamila nodded to the dead girl's opened throat, then indicated the matching cross wound at the other end of the upright. 'Exact,' she said, reaching for her ruler. 'Exactly halfway between chin and breast bone, exactly halfway down the length of the genitals. And again, the ribs . . . Identical length of cut, identical positioning. Of course,' she said, 'I'm not in a position to refute that murders one and two were committed by the same killer.'

'What are you trying to tell me?' Raf asked; it seemed a fair enough question.

'On the record,' said Kamila, 'I'm highlighting disquieting aspects of a crime. More than that it's impossible to say without further work.' Her smile was bleak. 'Off the record, I reckon Dawn Hauger was bled to death, then mutilated by someone who lacked the nerve required to butcher her while alive . . .'

'You're saying,' said Raf, 'that we've got a series of copycat killings . . .'

Kamila looked at him. 'You disagree?'

'Yes,' said Raf, nodding. 'I think what we've got is atrocity by numbers.'

CHAPTER 34

What was it with the missing mirrors? The last time the Senator had been invited to meet Iskandryia's governor, half a dozen ornate Murano looking glasses had covered the walls, making a large room look even larger. Now the old man and his mirrors were gone, their memory etched in lighter patches on age-darkened silk. So what was that about, and was it safe to ask?

Was it even safe to be alone with this man?

In front of her sat a killer. Senator Liz couldn't get that fact out of her head. Not a killer like the General, when war or political expediency dictated, but the real thing. Ashraf Bey had put a revolver to the head of the previous Chief of Detectives and pulled the trigger, claiming humanitarian reasons. And the really weird bit was, no one in the city seemed to find that remotely odd.

But then that was Iskandryia for you.

It seemed the bey might also be behind the assassination in Kabul of Sheik el-Halana, the man who authorized the bombing of the Ottoman Consulate in Seattle. Then there was the death of a *Thiergarten* agent. And the bey's rumoured links with the Sultan himself.

As far as Senator Liz was concerned, the sooner a deal was done and she was out of his company the better. Her only problem, and it was a big one, was that the ostensibly polite young man sitting opposite was obviously not listening to a word she said. And she really did need him to get behind the plan.

'Your Excellency . . .'

Twin ovals of dark glass. Somewhere behind those lenses was the man himself, whoever he was. And White House opinion was divided on that.

'Tell me,' said the man. 'Do you like our wallpaper?'

'Do I . . .' Senator Liz looked as put out as she felt.

448

'It's Turkish,' he said. 'I was thinking of having it painted. Only that's going to take gallons of emulsion and I can't decide on a colour.' He lapsed back into silence, leaving Senator Liz to look around while she decided what, if anything, his comment actually meant.

Added to the main building in 1803, the chamber they used was too large for a withdrawing room, too small to qualify as a proper ballroom. And at exactly one and a half times the height of every other room on the ground floor, it guaranteed that the roof space above was so cramped as to be useless for anything but storage, but Raf still liked it more than any other room in the mansion.

Somewhere, hidden beneath its floor covering, were marble tiles, hacked from a quarry by slaves. But none of the tiles could actually be seen because most of the space was taken by two vast Chinese silk carpets, with Bokhara runners and Isphahan rugs filling in the gaps.

'It's very nice wallpaper,' Senator Liz said carefully.

'You're right.' The man sitting opposite her nodded. 'The question is, would it look better painted? And if so, should that paint be white?'

Senator Liz swallowed a sigh. Pashazade Ashraf al-Mansur looked frighteningly like his father, the Emir of Tunis, and it appeared the similarity might go more than skin deep. The last time the Senator had been allowed into the Emir's presence, the man had been camped deep on Jubal Dahar, guarded by dark-eyed girls carrying snubPups. His Highness had taken all of thirty seconds out of that evening's routine to tell Senator Liz that the answer was *no*, whatever her query was, except for those bits to which his answer was *yes* . . .

Behind the Senator stood an interpreter, redundant from the moment she'd discovered that Ashraf Bey spoke English. Since the interpreter's day job was actually second intelligence attaché at the US Embassy in El Qahirah, Senator Liz had intended to get on-the-hoof briefings as her meeting with the bey progressed. Now, of course, that was impossible.

The Senator would have felt much happier if the impressively bulky file in front of her had contained even one sheet of usable information on the man sitting opposite. But he had no vices, apparently. Having saved the life of the Quitrimala girl, he took no reward, though the sum offered had been vast, astronomical . . . He'd turned down a marriage worth billions, apparently because he wasn't in love with the girl. He belonged to no clique, no cabal.

And he had to be insane.

Three days he'd kept the world waiting. The President in Washington, the Kaiser . . . Hell, even his own Sultan in Stambul.

'Your Excellency . . .' The entreaty stuck in Senator Liz's throat. But she had a job to do, even if that job wasn't easy. 'Iskandryia . . .'

'. . . is fucked,' Raf didn't even let her finish the sentence. 'You hear that . . . ?' He cocked one ear to the sound of a cherry top blasting past the grounds of the mansion. 'Riots in Karmous. One of the co-op banks has folded.'

'Bad news, nothing but bad news,' said Senator Liz, her voice mournful. It was a sadness that didn't quite reach her pale eyes.

'Not necessarily,' Raf said lightly. 'For example, we've established beyond doubt that Hamzah Effendi is not implicated in the murder of the second girl, the one found on his beach. Unfortunately, the real murderer was killed . . .'

'By me,' added Raf, under his breath, in the basement of a deserted house in Moharrem Bey. But he didn't say that aloud, obviously enough.

'We also know that the murderer of the first girl shot himself at Lake Mareotis . . .'

Raf didn't know that at all, but a chemical residue impregnating the pouch found with that man apparently matched the drug used to sedate Dawn Hauger at Casino Quitrimala. So it was a reasonable guess.

'Which means,' said Raf, 'three murders, three butchers, each carrying out a near-identical crime to order. Of course, now the third one is also out of action . . .'

Elizabeth Elsing blinked, but it was the reaction of her man standing behind her that interested Raf. 'You have him under arrest?' he asked, before he could stop himself.

Raf stared at the interpreter, who looked very much as if he'd like to take back the question, but when Raf answered, he took care to address his words to the Senator.

'Unfortunately,' said Raf as he put down his coffee cup and leant back, 'he also died . . .'

'He died?' So intent was the small woman that she almost fell off the sofa from bending too far forward.

'Sad, isn't it?' said Raf. 'I can, however, tell you that he was German.' Raf flicked open a leather notebook and hit resume, watching as words scrolled up the page. Yet another message from Hani by the look of it and two missed calls from Zara.

'We'll be releasing his name later . . .' Raf flicked shut the notebook and put it back on the table.

'Advance notification of which,' Senator Liz began to say, 'would be very . . .'

'*Useful*. Yes,' said Raf, 'I'm sure it would.' Whatever froideur might be about to fall ended as double doors crashed open and Khartoum staggered in, carrying a heavy silver tray.

Double loops of gold tied themselves in knots up the front of his frock coat. A cravat of yellowing Maltese lace frothed from his neck. And beneath the large silver buckles of his shiny shoes, grey showed against black, where Khartoum had missed patches of dust on their freshly cleaned patent leather.

'Fresh coffee, Your Excellency.'

Raf took one look at the old man's face and swallowed his smile. If Khartoum was dressed like that, then there was a reason. Just as there had to be a reason for the parable Khartoum had told Raf before the meeting began. It had begun by Khartoum asking him if he'd read any of Hani's stories.

The answer to that had been *no*. Although he'd had some read to him.

'Good.' Khartoum smiled. 'Here's another. A thief creeps into the enclosure of a Sufi master and finds nothing there but sand and dry crusts. As he leaves, understanding his disappointment, the Sufi tosses the thief the tattered blanket from his bed, so that he should not go back into the street empty-handed.'

'That's one of Hani's tales?'

'No,' the old man had said. 'Not yet . . .'

Raf watched in fascination as the old man lowered his heavy tray carefully onto the table. A small gilt jug was accompanied by two tiny gilt cups, a Limoges platter of rose-water Turkish delight, dusted with sugar, and a smaller plate, piled high with tiny crescents of pastry. An open cigarette box, made from beaten silver but lined with rosewood, was filled with Balkan cigarillos.

'I trust Your Excellency needs nothing.' Khartoum gave the tiniest bow and walked backward from the chamber, as if he'd been a majordomo all his life.

Coffee, tiny croissants, Turkish delight . . . Limoges dishes and an *English silver tray*. Somewhere in there, sure as mathematical certainty, was an answer to their sum. Concentrate, the fox would have said. So Raf did, starting with the *nothing* that Khartoum considered he needed.

Zero had been an Arabic understanding. The *nasrani* who came with their heavy mail and what passed for cooking grasped the numerical concept of *something* plus *something*, but zero, the addition, subtraction and definition of *nothing*, had to be explained.

The French, the English, the Germans, now the Americans. And before that the Mamelukes and the Arab invaders. He had it! What Khartoum was saying was, given the chance, Isk would again re-create itself. No one ever truly conquered this city . . . They either passed through or were adopted by the city they thought had fallen to them.

'What do you want from us?' Raf demanded.

'Us?'

'With the city, with me . . .'

He faced her across a low table and both of them understood that they'd finally arrived at the real reason why they were there.

'Iskandryia . . .' said the Senator.

'Is in chaos.' Raf shrugged. 'We've had this conversation. What matters is . . . Why are you here?'

'To offer help.' The Senator sat back, forcing herself to relax. Unfortunately, Raf saw her do it. Which just made her stressed again.

'Help?' Right, thought Raf. Obvious really. 'And in return?'

For a second it looked as if Senator Liz was about to say, *there is no 'in return.'* But something in Raf's smile stopped her. 'The situation is tricky.' She began again . . .

Your carpet is moth-eaten, hardly worth buying, the quality is poor, besides it is too small, too expensive and I don't need a carpet anyway . . . Raf had heard it often, that opening position in every negotiation. The one that said, *out of the goodness of my heart I'm going to agree to rob you blind.*

Tuning out the low drone of the Senator's explanation, Raf traced the Doppler spore of a cherry top as it raced down Fuad Premier, passed through Shallalat Gardens and vanished along Avenue Horreya. Orders had gone out that afternoon locking down the city. Leave had been cancelled across all divisions of the police, even the *morales*. The military were on standby, confined to barracks but ready. His Sudanese guard patrolled the streets around the mansion.

Raf could imagine tomorrow's headlines.

'. . . does that sound acceptable?'

Yanking his attention back to the chamber, Raf smiled at the American woman seated opposite. 'Run through that last part again,' he said. 'I think I might have missed something . . .'

Unsweetened by its sugar coating the pill was bitter. On behalf of PaxForce – read Washington, Berlin and Paris – Senator Liz demanded the right to station armed observers within the city to keep the peace. But there was worse, infinitely worse. And finally Raf understood why Hamzah had been desperate to see his daughter safely married, so desperate that he'd been prepared to bribe Lady Nafisa to achieve it.

'We have evidence,' the Senator was saying. Flipping open her old-fashioned file, she pulled out a stack of 10 × 4s, all of them copyrighted to 'Jean René' and dated decades earlier.

The photographs might have been arranged in chronological order, or by level of atrocity, or maybe the order was as random as the place names printed on the back and war really was God's way of teaching geography.

Mostly the dead were children, some almost old enough to count as adults, if that threshold was sufficiently flexible. They varied in race, skin colour, age and sex. And the only thing they had in common besides a gaping cross cut into each chest was the bareness of their feet and the raggedness of ripped uniforms . . . Inasmuch as T-shirts and cargo pants could count as uniform. Most of the dead also wore amulets, small leather bags, metal charms and badges, lots and lots of badges.

Cheap and plastic, black on red. The eyes of a saint above the beard of a prophet.

'Colonel Abad,' Senator Liz said redundantly.

Raf already knew that. He'd had a tri-D of the man on his study wall at school. Between the plastic badges, dark poppies blossomed against dark skin, wounds from the bullets those amulets were meant to stop. Flies hovered frozen around faces that stared blindly into a sky that time had long since left behind.

'Hamzah was involved in this?' Raf's question was hesitant. As if he couldn't quite believe his own suspicion, but the crosses that disfigured each corpse were unmistakable.

'No,' said Senator Liz, 'this was done by Ras Michael's Church Militant. Those responsible were tried and executed or jailed. These are Hamzah's responsibility . . .' She took the remaining photographs from Raf and discarded the top third, handing back the rest.

They were no less ugly. Children still lay faceup to the sky, their feather-and-bone amulets as impotent as the combat patches tacked to their shirts. **God Rules**, read one T-shirt. Below the slogan someone had sewn a star, cut from red cloth.

'Don't tell me,' said Raf, reaching for the original photographs. 'This is one side.' He flipped over a photograph. 'And this is the other . . .' Side by side on the table, a dead girl and a ripped-open boy stared back at him.

Senator Liz nodded.

'So why go for Hamzah rather than Colonel Abad?'

'Because we know where Hamzah is. Anyway,' she said, 'our best intelligence suggests Abad's already dead.'

'Already . . .' Raf tossed down his photographs. 'If you'll excuse me.' He didn't wait for her answer, just stood up and strode out of the chamber. On his way through the door, he flicked off the lights. Maybe she'd learn something about the nature of darkness.

Raf had an office full of researchers back at Third Circle, an Intelligence Department based out of the barracks at Ras el-Tin and a dozen detectives, one or two of whom might even be able to do their job; but he found the information he needed in the kitchens, holding a skillet in one hand and a wooden spatula in his other. Flames roared from a gas ring as the gaunt man shuffled coffee beans backward and forward, like a skeleton mixing concrete.

'There was a war,' said Raf. 'When Hamzah Effendi was a child.'

'Before *you* were born?' Khartoum sounded amused by his own question. 'Yes, there were many wars. All unnecessary. What of it?'

What indeed?

'Who was in the right?' The question sounded stupid even as Raf asked it; but sometimes questions need to be asked, even stupid ones. And he knew the Sufi's answer would be honest, no matter that the old man was partisan.

'No one was in the right,' said Khartoum.

'Then who was in the wrong?'

'No one.' Dark eyes regarded Raf, as piercing as those of a hawk. 'They were children,' said Khartoum. 'Not men, not women . . . You should ask who armed them. Who had an interest in seeing them fight? Or maybe this is a question you too think best left unasked . . .'

CHAPTER 35

'Hey you . . .' Hani grabbed Ifritah by the scruff of the neck and pulled so that the cat's head yanked back and its purr stopped as rapidly as if somebody had flicked a switch. 'That's better,' the girl whispered, hugging the cat to her chest. Immediately the scraggy animal started to purr again.

Hani sighed.

One of her arms ached from cuddling Ifritah, her foot had pins and needles and the narrowness of the window ledge on which she perched had sent her behind to sleep. The long velvet curtain she hid behind was both old and dusty, so half the time Hani had to hold the bridge of her nose just to concentrate on not sneezing because sneezing would ruin everything. Besides, as it was, her own breathing was almost too loud to let her hear what was being said by the cross American woman.

It should have been easy. But something in one of the woman's pockets was interfering with the tiny microphone Hani had stuck to the bottom of the table. Or maybe the microphone was broken. After all, it came from a Tina Tears whose head she'd cracked open with a paper-weight when the plastic proved too tough to cut using a kitchen knife.

Hani knew she shouldn't be there. Just as she knew she was in trouble if Ashraf found out. And he probably didn't even want her help. She was a child, as everybody from Zara to Khartoum kept telling her. But she also had an IQ of 160 for real, could do crosswords in French, English and Arabic and had forgotten more about computers than Raf knew, even if she couldn't see in the dark.

Hani wasn't meant to know about his night vision or maybe she was meant to have forgotten – but she did know. She knew other things too, dark swirling facts that waited at the edges of her mind, wanting to come to her if only she'd let them.

On the other side of the curtain, the small woman was arguing again.

She'd been angry since Raf came back to finish their conversation, only this was worse. She wanted Raf to give up Effendi, that was how she put it . . . Effendi had to be given up, like cigarettes.

Ashraf refused, of course, and Hani hoped he'd go on refusing. She liked Zara, and Effendi was Zara's father. Hani didn't like Zara's mother, but then Zara didn't like Zara's mother so the Senator could have her if she wanted.

'I'll leave the photographs,' the woman said crossly, climbing to her feet. Hani knew that was what she was doing by the creak of a sofa. Footsteps padded across carpet, then stopped. The Senator was turning in the doorway, wanting to say something. Only the threat or retort never came. Instead the woman and her interpreter let themselves out of the governor's chambers.

That was bad. Khartoum should have been there to let her out. Hani knew this from living with her Aunt Nafisa, notables never opened their own doors. A creak from the other sofa told her that Raf was leaving. After the creak and steps came the slam, of a door and then nothing.

'You can go now,' said Hani, yanking open her nearest window to release the struggling cat. With Ifritah gone the room became more silent still. So Hani padded across the silence and picked up one of the famous photographs. The gutted boy was little older than she was, though his skin was darker and his black hair scraped back into a fat ponytail. The two girls in the next photograph were about Hani's age. One of them was missing her hands.

Looking down, it wasn't the boy's face that gripped Hani's attention but that of the bearded man on the badge pinned to his dirty shirt. Except for a beret and a small cigar clamped between his teeth, the man could have been the *nasrani* God, the one who got himself killed.

'Abad,' Hani said to herself and picked up the photograph, tucking it down the side of her jeans and smoothing her T-shirt back into place. No one stopped her as she left the chamber or saw her in the corridor outside. All the same, as Raf sometimes said, better safe than sorry when being sorry wasn't an option.

The girl blanked her screen. 'It's nothing,' she said hurriedly.

Raf glanced from Hani's face to the photograph she was trying to slide into an open drawer. She had it turned upside down, but he could still see some of the caption. **Kordofan, 30th March. Investigators** . . .

Inside his head Raf swore.

'You got that from downstairs?'

Hani nodded. 'I'm sorry.' There was a haunted look on her face and she'd chewed one corner of her lip until it was raw. What upset Raf most was the way she leant away from him, hunching her shoulders without realizing it, in preparation for the slap that would never come.

'No,' said Raf, stepping back. 'My fault. I apologize . . .'

'Why?' the small girl asked suspiciously.

'Because I shouldn't have left those out for you to find.' He wanted to add, *because this is a world from which I can't protect you, a world that may get worse*. Instead, he scooped up the child and carried her over to her bedroom window.

Standing there, they looked out at the darkened city. As ever, her legs were bony against his arms, her wrists round his neck as thin as sticks.

'You need fattening up,' said Raf and the next question asked itself. 'Where's Donna?'

'At home.' There was a smile, fleeting and slightly exasperated. 'She won't sleep here,' said Hani. 'Apparently someone has to look after the madersa, but really she's afraid.' Hani indicated her new bedroom, the gesture taking in oil paintings, Chinese vases and a bronze dryad whose verdigrised shoulders and upturned breasts carried a faint sheen of dust.

Hani was right of course. The mansion would have frightened Donna even if it hadn't belonged to the General.

'So who feeds you while I'm working?' Raf asked.

'Me,' said Hani crossly. 'I can cook.'

'And when did you last eat?'

'I've had breakfast.' Hani scrambled out of his arms but stayed close. Away from the desk and her pink plastic laptop.

'Today?'

The child looked at him.

'You had breakfast today?'

The eyes opposite suddenly bruised with tears. 'Leave me alone, all right . . . And take your stupid photograph.' She left the room without looking back, slamming the door for good measure.

As always, adults got it wrong. It wasn't the photograph she'd needed. Hani had wanted the face on the badge.

And besides, all that look-at-me-I'm-hiding-something routine was to stop Uncle Ashraf noticing what she really had in the drawer. The Doré engraving of hell she'd borrowed from his office.

457

CHAPTER 36

23rd October

Outside on the beach, *Zara's beach*, October waves exploded against the headland and draped dark rocks with seaweed. And on the French windows to her father's study, a stray leaf trapped in a dying spider's web released its ribbon of rainbow down the glass as gasoline or herbicide slowly leached from its pores.

Zara saw neither because the curtains were firmly drawn. She wore a nightdress, dressing gown and fur slippers. The warmth of those nursery clothes at odds with the arctic cold in her heart.

'Tell me it's not true . . .'

She wasn't meant to shout at her father. She wasn't even meant to swear either, but the rules were gone, left in a corridor along with her wailing mother and a discarded copy of the *New York Times*. And all her father could do was huddle in his leather chair, a tumbler of whisky beside him and an old-fashioned revolver lying on a weird etching on his lap. The glass was Soviet crystal. Zara didn't recognize the weapon – revolvers weren't her thing. Come the revolution, she'd always seen herself using *plastique*.

Shutting her eyes to block out the world, Zara nursed the darkness until she could hold on to it no longer. Needless to say, when she looked again nothing in the study had changed, but then it never used to work for her as a child either.

'So it's true?' Zara said.

Of course it was. She could see it in his face. And even the smell of fresh vomit couldn't hide the whisky fumes. A whole bottle was gone. Enough to reduce him to childish tears without lifting the horror from his eyes.

Top Industrialist Charged with Genocide . . .

He should have warned her. Before the American papers and the downloads and rolling newsfeeds began, before Trustafarian Ishies with their headsets and cameras started churning the lawns to mud. She could almost feel the hunger out there, calling its questions and tapping at windows, hammering on the big brass knocker and ringing the bell. News was a commodity to the *soi-disant* Free World, not a duty. And the bear-pit growl of its news gatherers could be heard through the study's double glazing, through windows closed and locked, curtains drawn and shutters bolted.

'Dad, come on . . .' Dropping to a crouch in front of his chair, Zara rested her forearms on his knees and felt her father flinch. That was all it took to turn anger to tears. Zara began crying then, sorrow rolling down her cheeks. Somewhere she had a tissue, but couldn't remember which pocket, and it didn't seem to matter.

They cried in silence together.

She'd taken to asking herself a question a few years back. What was the worst it could be, the secret of her father's rise from nothing? She'd searched for clues to the answer. Once, aged fifteen, she'd riffled through his desk, using a key taken from his jacket. All she'd found was a small leather case containing pornographic photographs of a young man and two girls even younger . . . Apart from a wood-handled knife, a handful of Sudanese coins and a bone crucifix, that had been the sum total of her find.

She hadn't been able to look him in the face for weeks afterwards.

The worst she could say, until recently, was that he kept Western erotica in a drawer in his study. Now he was less than that, a man diminished. Zara was rapidly coming to realize that, just maybe, she'd never actually known who he was, not really. Her father, the industrialist Hamzah Effendi.

He broke the law for a living, she accepted that. Only he broke it less than he used to do and nothing like as much as when he was young. And anyway the free market was a crime in itself. As a good Marxist she did believe that. Of course, he also killed, or had done, at least once . . .

When she was nine she had overheard two servants discussing this and been proud. The dead man had been bad, obviously. Someone who attacked her father, forcing him to defend himself. It was all so clear in Zara's head. Only when she tried asking her ma about it she'd been slapped for her pains. By the next morning both her nanny and the maid were gone.

Now nothing she could say to her father would change what was about to happen. PaxForce wanted him to stand trial and, according to the *New York Times*, Iskandryia's new governor had agreed to hand over Hamzah, subject to agreeing upon a timetable.

What more was there to say?

Plenty. And such was the shallowness of the Western press that *how* it was said would be as important as *what* was said. Picking up his revolver, weirdshit etching and whisky bottle, Zara slammed Hamzah's study door behind her and went to get changed. Already she was rewriting elements of her plan.

'Zara . . .' The voice that met her on the landing was angry and bitter, but then it would be, it belonged to her mother.

'What?' Zara demanded.

It had been a joke among Zara's friends that they could hear Madame Rahina long before they could see her, such was the clatter of gold from her wrists. Noisy bangles and an almost permanent scowl were Zara's memories of her mother. Sometimes the gold had been so loud Zara hadn't been able to hear the slap that followed.

'How could he . . . ?'

'I thought you knew everything there was to know about him,' Zara said, her voice contemptuous. 'Wasn't that what you told everyone? Soul mates. Apart from his endless mistresses, your tranquillizers and the whisky . . .'

'Zara . . .'

Zara covered the outraged face with the spread fingers of one hand and pushed. Which was all it took to throw the woman backward. Zara didn't bother to check how she landed.

Some of the men even had little ladders so they could peer over the heads of other photographers in front. Many wore pale safari suits of the kind carried at airports by ignorant *nasrani* journalists, who expected to land somewhere blisteringly hot. Only now their suits were dark with rain and hung with all the elegance of rags on a line.

'Miss Zara . . .'

She turned, saw Alex and sighed. The huge Soviet bodyguard stood like a scolded child, head down and fists clenched so hard that veins made freeways along his wrists. An hour earlier, while her father was still drinking himself into a stupor, Alex had been faced with a highly tenacious member of the press, who took bolt cutters to the gates and challenged Alex to shoot him. Without orders, Alex had retreated.

'You took the correct action,' Zara said, for about the third time.

Alex looked doubtful.

'Examine the options,' she said. 'You think you should have shot him?' He did too, Zara could see it in his broad face. 'Sometimes retreat is necessary,' Zara told Alex carefully. 'But now someone must guard the front door. And that must be you.'

Zara watched the cogs whir as Alex glanced from her to the heavy wooden door, then back again. He was nice in his way, but monolithically slow. Still, each according to his talents . . .

'The door, right.' He nodded agreement and turned away, shoulders straightening.

'Comrade . . .'

'Yes, Miss Zara . . . ?' He paused, shoulders broad, back straight, a Makarov 9mm bulging under one arm.

She smiled. 'Nothing.'

Nothing will come of nothing, that was a line from a play she was in, back when she went to college in New York . . . A city of high-rise boxes where the girls around her fucked anything with a pulse and a penis and quality control seemed to be a contradiction in terms. But something always did come from nothing. The universe, for a start. Time itself. All that other shit Raf talked about that one night on the boat, stuff she didn't understand and guessed he didn't either, not really . . .

Zara sighed and went back to working on her plan.

The bell was made from beaten silver and had an ivory handle. Its clapper was a narrow twist of iron that ended with a small ball of soft metal the size of a pea. For as long as Zara could remember, the bell had been used by her mother to summon the nearest maid. Her father thought the bell unnecessary, he just shouted.

'Come on.' Zara rang the bell until the first maid appeared, then kept going until she had every member of staff mustered in the hall. There were seven in total. Five housemaids, a French chef and a Sudanese gardener. A surprisingly small number for a house the size of Villa Hamzah.

'I want coffee,' she told the chef. 'A large pot.'

'Of course, Miss Zara.' The little man nodded. 'I'll have Maryam bring it to the back drawing room.'

'No,' said Zara. 'You're missing the point. I want a *lot* of coffee.'

The chef blinked. 'How much?' he asked, his voice neutral.

'Jugs of the stuff. Enough for two hundred people. And *semit* . . .' Zara named the soft sesame-covered pretzels sold everywhere in the city. 'Can we do that?'

'Of course I can.'

Zara smiled. The Parisian would be baking all afternoon, mixing dough and waiting anxiously for his yeast to rise. 'Make the coffee first,' she suggested. 'I'll take it outside myself.'

461

That got their attention.

'Ridiculous,' said the chef. 'It'll be far too heavy. Maryam and Lisa can carry it.'

'All right,' said Zara. 'We also need as many umbrellas as you can find . . . Start with my mother's dressing room,' she suggested, remembering a line of them hanging in a row along the back of a cupboard.

'Oh . . . and Alex.' She left out her usual *comrade*, not wanting to embarrass the big Russian in front of the others. 'Order me a marquee. Something vast, but without sides . . . We don't want to overdo it.'

CHAPTER 37

The air was warm, the afternoon sun a haze of ultraviolet through cloud. The heavy rain didn't bother him. Not like back in Seattle.

'*Ashraf Bey* . . .'

Raf kept going, while behind him Hakim took it upon himself to punch the photographer to the ground. Providing the world with another picture.

The new governor's face already fronted *Time, Paris Match* and *Newsweek*. Cheeks hollow, eyes hard behind dark glasses, hair swept back. It was a face that Raf didn't recognize, even when he stared hard in the mirror.

As to why a mere handful of journalists clustered around the mansion in Shallalat Gardens . . . That was easy to answer. The rest were camped out on the lawns at Villa Hamzah, from where talking heads currently reported seriously on nothing very much.

Zara's offer of coffee and *semit* had been a flash of brilliance, but ordering a marquee and then staying outside to watch while a hundred journalists struggled with poles and wet ropes was beyond genius. And as they struggled, Zara had watched, not offering to help or saying anything, just standing on the lawn of Villa Hamzah, while photographers captured her guarded amusement at the chaos.

When the marquee was finally up and the journalists were out of the rain, Zara had walked into the middle of their group, without a bodyguard, without having to ask anyone to move out of her way. And then she stopped, watching them as they watched her. Meeting their lenses and the bursts of flash without blinking or looking away . . .

'*Where to, Boss?*'

Raf came awake in the back of his Bentley.

'Villa Hamzah.' Same as it ever was.

463

Then Zara had spun in a slow circle, meeting their eyes, one person at a time. At least that's what they thought; but really she'd been looking for a single logo among dozens.

Raf knew that now without doubt.

The journalists might have thought Zara was there to talk to them, only they were wrong. She'd stopped turning, stopped smiling the moment she saw someone from a local newsfeed. After that, her words had been for Raf alone.

'I am waiting to hear back from the governor. I'm sorry, but until then there is nothing more I can say . . .'

So now the governor was on his way, through a city that flickered by like the backdrop to some film he vaguely remembered preferring the first time round. The statue of Mehmet V, which once seemed so impressive, now looked tatty and grandiose, more parks than ever looked empty, windows to shops were unlit or shuttered tight with steel grilles: the rococo mansions of the Corniche that once seemed so magnificent behind their wrought-iron gates now looked defeated, held prisoner by their own defences.

We define ourselves by our own limitations. The fox had said that to him once, in Seattle, shortly before it pointed out that on this basis Raf should be very defined indeed.

But am I? Raf wanted to ask, only the voice in his head refused to answer and the voice in his heart that Khartoum talked about was missing, absent without leave. So maybe he was just the sum of his parts, few though those were. A face that looked like someone else, a fake identity and a job he hadn't asked for . . .

'Ahmed, do you know who you are?'

The bigger of his two gun-toting bodyguards turned his head, while the driver and Hakim kept staring straight on: watching the Corniche unravel through the car's ancient windscreen. 'Do I what, Boss?'

'You know who you are?'

Ahmed nodded.

'You ever think you might be somebody else . . . ?'

Raf saw the answer written in the other man's puzzled frown. 'Doesn't matter,' he said flatly. 'Just forget it.'

There was silence in the Bentley after that as the driver concentrated on the road and Hakim and Ahmed eyeballed the sidewalk and beach respectively, their fingers never leaving the triggers of their H&K5s.

'Your Excellency . . .' It was the driver. 'Five and counting.'

Koenig Pasha was the one who'd originally demanded five minutes advance warning of when he was due to arrive. And there was a hierarchy of address too. Apparently Ahmed and Hakim got to call him Boss, while the driver was required to be more formal. It was a city of rules, from opaque to transparent. Every city was.

Opening his eyes, Raf sat up and watched the coast become familiar. That café, a swimming hut on stilts, then the beach where . . . a galaxy of stars had skimmed across bare shoulders to be swallowed into darkness between perfect breasts. The hunger brought on by the memory corroded what was left of his pride.

He was no use to Zara as he was, that much Raf understood. No use to anyone; not even himself. Certainly not to the city or to Hani, which was what he mostly cared about these days.

And that meant it was time to change.

'We're here, Boss.'

They were too, passing through heavy wrought-iron gates that had been yanked open and pushed back. Lawns that had been immaculate the last time Raf saw them were crude scars of dark earth, trampled to mud by the same journalists who now rushed the huge Bentley. Already photographers were scuffling for the best shot as a 'copter overhead suddenly dropped height, its specially adapted gun pod swinging a long lens in Raf's direction.

'Take it down,' Raf ordered.

Ahmed looked doubtful but wound down his side window and started to unsling his machine gun all at the same time. Instantly the camera crews moved closer, unleashing a firestorm of flashguns and shouted questions.

'Not like that,' Raf said as he slapped down the gun. 'Get on the wire and ground that piece of shit.'

'Sure thing,' said Ahmed, tapping his throat mike. 'What do I tell them, Boss?'

'Tell them that, as of now, airspace over El Iskandryia is a no-fly zone. No overnights, nothing. Tell the pilot if he's not landed in one minute we'll blast him out of the sky. Final warning.'

'No overflights . . . What about the airport?'

'Close it.'

The flash and arc lights didn't bother Raf, he just recalibrated his vision and kept walking towards the blank-eyed cameras. *Reptiles* was what the General called Ishies, that and other things. Watching them watch him reminded Raf of his mother's early films; not the cuddly shit she shot for money, the tooth-and-claw stuff that made her name. He couldn't remember their titles now, but all those films had blood in them. Red blood on white snow. Zhivago shots, she called them, she was big on those.

'Governor . . .' A thin woman thrust a microphone in his direction and a dozen shouted questions cancelled each other out, leaving only babble.

Raf waited. And when one photographer came in too close, Raf just stared until the man took a step backward.

'Ashraf Bey . . .'

'Excellency . . .'

The shouts kept coming until everyone finally realized that Raf still hadn't said a word. And then came silence. It stretched out, distorted by the crowd's expectation and broken only by the rhythmic thud of a grounded Sikorsky chopping to a halt on the Corniche behind him. He milked the silence, because that was exactly what the General would have done: and at the point their expectation was about to curdle into anger, Raf pointed at random to three people near the front, snapping out the order . . .

'One, two, three . . . Okay, your name, your station, then the question.'

As it turned out, number one was a good choice. She was American, on staff, not a freelancer, and represented C3N, biggest of the news channels. Or so Raf gathered from the gabble with which Helen Giles introduced herself.

'Excellence . . . Will you agree to hand over Hamad Quitrimala?' She managed to trip over both Raf's honorific and Hamzah's name.

'So that he can be tried in America and jailed?'

She nodded.

'Why would I do that?' Raf asked, his voice clear but cool.

'But PaxForce . . .'

'Are you saying we don't have courts in El Iskandryia?'

That got another babble of questions, which ended the moment Raf chopped at the air for silence. He was beginning to enjoy this, Raf realized with something approaching shock.

'Well?'

The woman's worry lines deepened.

'If Hamzah is to be tried,' said Raf, 'he'll be tried here in Iskandryia. And if the evidence goes against him, he will be found guilty . . . and shot.'

Raf walked through their shocked silence, while behind him Ahmed and Hakim ported their H&K5s and glared at anyone who got too close. As they approached the villa's heavy front door it swung back and Raf found himself staring at the girl he should have married.

466

Flashguns firestormed.

'Excellency.' Zara stepped back to let him pass through into the hall.

'Zara . . .'

'Yes, Your Excellency?' She stood ramrod straight, chin up. Only the rawness that rimmed her grey eyes spoke of privately spilt tears. And one look into their cold depths was enough to tell him that the tears had been dried by hatred.

'Feeding them was a good idea.'

She said nothing in reply. Just waited, unmoving, for Raf to announce why he was there. Except that they both knew he was there because she'd said she wanted to talk to him – and now it seemed she didn't.

'I'll go,' said Raf and turned for the door, Hakim and Ahmed falling into position behind him. It was strange how quickly one could become used to having a shadow.

'Do you really intend to . . . ?'

'Intend to what?' Raf asked, one hand on the door handle. He knew exactly what Zara was asking but he made her ask it all the same.

'Execute him . . .'

Not if I can help it, but somehow that didn't seem the appropriate thing to say.

'If they extradite him,' said Raf, 'you'll never get your father back. You know that, don't you?'

'At least they won't kill him . . .'

'No,' Raf said, 'they'll just lock him up until he dies. Surround him with guards twenty-four/seven. Dismantle Hamzah Enterprises and break up the Midas Refinery to pay for court costs and reparations. You think that's what he wants? Your father knew this was coming . . .'

'I'd worked that out,' said Zara, tears starting up in her eyes. 'That's why he wanted you to marry me.'

Raf nodded.

'The Khedive,' her voice was a whisper, 'that meal.'

'He was trying to protect you in the only way he knew how,' said Raf, his smile rueful. 'He even tried sending you back to America, he told me you refused . . .'

Her shoulders beneath his fingers were bony and she wore a scent he didn't recognize and undoubtedly wouldn't have been able to afford, had he wanted to buy her some more. And up close, with her arms tight round his neck and her face buried wetly in his shoulder, Raf could tell that Zara wasn't wearing a bra. It was a shit time to notice something like that, but where Zara was concerned he always seemed to notice things like that at the wrong time. Like right then was a really lousy time to realize that he loved her.

467

Raf pushed Zara away, very slowly, until they stood a handbreadth apart, facing each other, their eyes locked. There was something she wanted to say.

'Anything you want,' said Zara. 'I'll give you anything you want, if you can save him.'

CHAPTER 38

'Safety off,' said the gun.

Lying beside Lieutenant Ka, the ghost of Bec's little sister said nothing. She'd taken to appearing at odd moments when Sarah wasn't around, but now Sarah was gone and so Bec's sister was smiling but silent. In fact, the whole world was silent except for a couple of green parakeets that squawked from a telegraph wire overhead, pretty much right above where he'd set up the thermoflage netting.

Of course, Ka knew what Bec's sister wanted to say. What she'd been saying every night in his dreams, before she did what she once did, stood up from a long-dead fire and shuffled out beyond the big camp's pickets to find a thornbush. Only it wasn't her bowels she needed to empty but her head, which she did by sucking on a revolver.

They weren't going to reach the source of the river. Nobody was going to turn off the Nile. The war and the river would keep flowing: the river wherever geography took it, the war wherever it wanted logo.

'Distance?'

'Five klicks and closing . . .'

Status and range. That was about all the H&K/cw could ever manage. And Ka really didn't know why the manufacturer had bothered. Ka had a feeling he might have got cross about that before. He was finding it increasingly hard to remember.

The Nile was out of sight, across rock and thorn. Last time he'd seen it, the river had still been grand even though Ka was now south of Omdurman City, where the Bahr el-Abiad and Bahr el-Azrak joined to become the life-giver everybody knew.

Somewhere still further south, the river split again but either Ka hadn't reached that point or he was past it.

The Colonel could have told him, only Ka wouldn't ask. The last time he'd wanted an answer was half an hour before, when something dark had

469

moved in the tall rushes of the riverbank. A simple question had elicited a long lecture on the habitat of the marabou stork.

Elaborate canals had once fed the area's rich cotton fields but the narrow canals were mostly cracked open or filled with dirt, their bottoms broken and dry.

Ahead of him, when he'd first arrived, had been mud-brick ruins and beyond those foothills, backdropped by faded and cloud-covered mountains. Now the foothills were at his back and the enemy ahead.

The ruined houses behind Ka were all that remained of a town to which a handful of nineteenth-century Mamelukes had retreated, to live under the protection of Mek Nimr, Leopard King of Shendi, after their defeat by the Albanian warlord Khedive Mohammed.

But Mohammed Ali sent his son Ismail south to subdue Nubia. And in October 1822 Ismail demanded as tribute from Mek Nimr thirty thousand Maria Theresa dollars, six thousand slaves and food for his army, all to be delivered within two days.

And when Mek Nimr protested that the Sudan already faced famine, Ismail struck him in the face. The Leopard King's reply came that evening during banquet, when his followers set fire to Ismail's house, incinerating the prince, who died in the flames rather than be cut down like his fleeing bodyguard.

Word of this reached the Defterdar, Ismail's brother-in-law. First the Defterdar burned Metemma and Damer, then every village along the Nile from Sennar to Berber. Finally he reached Shendi, where his troops threw down the walls and raped and impaled its inhabitants . . . But he failed to capture Mek Nimr or his family.

Fifty thousand died.

Next the Defterdar chased Mek Nimr south along the Blue River, torturing everyone he suspected of helping the fleeing king. Men were castrated, the breasts of the women were sliced away and every wound was sealed with molten pitch . . . Ka's uncle had always insisted that things were better in the old days. But to Ka, from what the Colonel said, it just sounded like more of the same.

Ka needed to eat, only that wasn't possible. The food was gone and so was most of his water. Actually, it was all the water, if he didn't count a half litre sloshing round in Sarah's old flask, the one with the cap jammed solid. He'd tried wrenching off the top and, when that failed, had tried punching a hole in the flask with his knife, but the mesh was too hard or he was too weak, one of the two, it didn't matter much which.

'Weapons check . . .'

Whatever. Ka did a count in his head . . . twenty-one grenades, two Heckler&Koch OI/cw, an HK21e machine gun heavy enough to require a tripod, five assorted sidearms plus a dozen boxes of bullets, some of which might actually fit, plus a fat slab of ganja and a Seraphim 4 × 4, minus gas. Unfortunately, since there was only one of him, most of his riches were wasted.

The other thing he had, of course, were his spectacles and his radio. The radio and the spectacles would only work together, although it had taken Ka days to figure this out. In fact, he wasn't entirely sure he had figured it out; he had a feeling the radio might have told him. Sometimes Colonel Abad spoke through the radio and other times he showed Ka things through the spectacles.

As for the ganja, that was some good shit, as Sergeant Sarah would have said. He wore her bone cross now, along with both of Saul's amulets and that bundle of feathers Zac kept pinned to his shirt. Taking Sarah's luck had been theft but he did it to protect her. She shouldn't have been wearing a cross in the first place and Ka didn't know on which side the doctors would be. So he'd taken her luck just to be safe and borrowed her gun because it was so much better than his.

The doctors would make her well again and that was more than the Colonel could manage. Maybe it had been the river water or perhaps too much sun . . . Whatever it was, she'd taken to greeting each new day on her knees, vomiting. And she wouldn't talk to Ka or even look at him, though he gave her all the food and kept every watch himself.

Now she was in a camp and he was here, staring down on a road with ruins behind him, a jagged rock off to one side, sticking up through the earth like a broken shoulder blade, and a long line of enemy trucks directly ahead.

'Approaching,' said a voice in his ear.

'Yeah, the gun's already told me,' Ka said crossly. It wasn't exactly news: the Colonel had first warned him an hour ago that troops were due. He'd also informed Ka that he must stop the troops in their tracks. Those were the Colonel's words . . . Looking at the converted 4 × 4s and purpose-built half-tracks coming down the road towards him, Ka decided that was meant to be some kind of joke.

'You know what you have to do?'

Yeah, he knew. First he had to fit a feldlafetten to the HK21e, which was its tripod, and then fit a Zeiss scope, after that he had to lift the safety gate or whatever it was called and slot in a new belt of 7.62/51. (What Colonel Abad always called .38.)

The HK21e took either a 20-round mag, which was plain stupid, or a 110-round belt box. Only Ka wasn't planning to use either of those. He had been busy knitting together a couple of belts at a time, until he had a mountain of brass all ready for the HK21e's roller-locked bolt.

They skinned people alive, the enemy. Ate them alive too, if Bec was to be believed. Raped the youngest prisoners to ward off wasting sickness. Mind you, that happened everywhere. But eating human flesh, that was part of a fire ritual: brain for intelligence, heart for courage, liver for cunning. Bec had told them all about it, one night months back round the campfire.

'Establish . . .'

Yeah, right. Establish a position. Ka shifted the heavy gun across to a gap between two rocks, then crawled back for the long, snaking belts. To win he had to keep under the protection of the thermoflage nets, Colonel Abad was very definite about that. After the belts, Ka unwrapped an HK/cw. This was really two weapons in one and could be broken into an upper section that fired airburst munitions, colour-coded for convenience, and a lower pull-away section that functioned as a basic light machine gun.

'Distance,' Ka demanded.

Reading this off from the HK21e would have been easy enough, but Colonel Abad judged distances better. Besides, Ka liked to make the Colonel work.

'Half a klick,' said the voice in his ear. 'You should be fitting the belts now.'

With trembling fingers, Ka fed the first of the bullets into the HK21e, checking again that the belt could feed in smoothly. A single kink might jam the machine gun and bring the ambush to an early end. The Colonel would hate that.

Then Ka reached for the HK/cw and slid a mag's worth of 5.56 kinetic into a narrow slot on its underside, following this with a fat clip of bursters. Except, the fast burster he fed to the upper slot wasn't a blue meanie, it was orange with a red tip, whizbang rather than airburst.

'Take out the . . .'

He knew, God knows. The Colonel had already been over this more times than Ka could stand. 'I know. All right?' Ka said flatly.

Absence whispered down the static. A silence as impossibly distant as it was brief. And then Colonel Abad was back, sounding concerned. 'You'll be all right,' he promised. 'You'll come out of this a hero.'

Ka didn't want to be a hero and anyway. . . . For a moment Ka considered pointing out that he'd rather be alive. Instead he shrugged and raised the heavy HK/cw.

'Hold it . . .'

He held. And kept holding as ants became beetles and his spectacles adjusted for focus. There were three half-tracks and two converted Seraphim followed by a solid mass that moved across the gravel like a stain. Ka had taken a while to work out that the half-tracks growled along in second gear because the officers inside were afraid, rather than kind. Afraid to be separated from the children who followed after them.

Ka knew which truck to take out first because it was suddenly circled in green. Fat neon hairs bisecting the circle. He pulled the trigger when circle and crosshairs flipped from green to red, like they always did.

The first truck disintegrated in a crunch of fire as flame punched its way through broken windows, and every single one of the remaining trucks ignored standing orders and slammed to a halt.

Idiots.

Doors swung open and uniforms tumbled out, guns unslung. Instinct made Ka duck as bees began to spit above his head but it was not necessary. The enemy's return fire was both sporadic and random, raking into scrub, rocks and trees alike and lifting a flock of parakeets into hysterical green protest.

The officers were mostly reloading when Ka slammed off four rounds of airburst in quick succession, exploding each directly above a vehicle. Flesh shredded from bone and suddenly dying uniforms found themselves forced to their knees. The fifth and final airburst Ka expended on a lieutenant too broken to realize she couldn't swim away to safety across the pock-marked dirt.

Officers down, Ka burned out a mag's worth of kinetic on a red-circled movement off to his right, then rolled across to the waiting machine gun. All he was required to do then was pull the trigger and keep it pulled while the HK21e ate up the snake belt in three-bullet bursts.

Green.

Red.

Fire.

He kept the stutter going for as long as the coloured circles kept blossoming, which seemed forever. Maybe the enemy were just crazed by the heat, or maybe the green foothills behind him exerted too strong a pull after the bleakness through which they'd marched. There were no officers left to make anyone advance and yet, every time Ka cleared a gap it filled instantly, until the mass marching towards him grew smaller and the gaps began to grow.

Soon there was more gap than mass and finally there was only gap. Not silence, because what had become one with the ground kept quivering and moaning until Ka emptied all of his fat clips of airburst over its head . . .

CHAPTER 39

'And then?' Raf asked, glancing at a low coffee table. A small police-issue recorder sat in the middle, green light lit and numbers counting down what time was left. They were seated in an elegant club room usually reserved for senior officers. The club room was on the third floor of Champollion Precinct, next door to the general canteen. It had a fountain, leather chairs and bombproof windows.

The General, of course, would have put Hamzah in the cells. Raf had decided to do things differently.

'Then?' Hamzah thought about it. 'I walked down the slope towards the first half-track.'

'You were looking for survivors?'

'No,' Hamzah shook his head, 'I was after water. And then.'

'Then what . . . ?'

Hamzah let himself remember. 'The Red Cross came . . .' He nodded towards Hakim, who stood at Raf's shoulder. 'Any chance of someone finding a drink?'

'Check the evidence cupboards,' Raf told his bodyguard. 'Whisky if we've got any.'

What Hakim found was Spanish brandy, confiscated from an illegal club at Maritime Station, and Raf let Hamzah pour himself a drink, a heavy slug of the Carlos V mixed with Canada Dry.

Instead of drinking it straight down, Hamzah sat in his chair and stared into the glass, watching bubbles break for the surface. He looked, despite his age, exactly like Hani when she watched static on her screen. Intent on imposing meaning onto chaos. Maybe, thought Raf, everyone is trying to find a world behind the world. As if that world might somehow make more sense or, at the very least, be more real . . .

'Tell me about when the Red Cross arrived . . .'

'I was searching among the bodies for Sarah.'

474

Raf looked at him.

'We changed sides now and then,' Hamzah explained. 'We all knew soldiers who'd been raped or mutilated after a battle, but if you could get through that . . .' He picked up his glass and drank from it. 'If you could do that. If you were one of the ones left alive at the end . . . Colonel Abad said the field hospital where I left Sarah had been overrun. So I thought . . .'

'Did you find her?'

'No. Though I thought I had. You know, her skin was . . .' Hamzah opened the collar of his shirt to reveal skin the colour of old leather. 'Darker than this . . . Purple like the night. Bitter like chocolate. It shone.'

He was crying, slow tears that trickled down jowly cheeks and vanished into stubble. There was no self-pity in his eyes and precious little guilt or fear of what might come next, just grief.

'I thought I would recognize her,' said Hamzah. 'But I didn't, I couldn't. Some of the bodies were faceless and broken, but it wasn't that. In the end there were just too many for me to search. When the Red Cross landed their first helicopter I was pulling a Dinka girl from under a pile.'

'What did they say?'

'To me? They said nothing. But then, they didn't know I spoke their language. To each other . . . ? A thin woman turned to a small man and said, *At least one of them survived.*'

Hamzah finished his drink in a single gulp and banged down his glass.

'They gave me vitamins, an injection against retrovirus and water in a silver pouch with a thin straw that stopped me drinking it too fast. After that, they photographed me, took my fingerprints, swabbed my mouth for a DNA sample and airlifted me to an American aircraft carrier of Massaua. They gave me a Gap T-shirt, black Levi's and a pair of silver Nikes. All donations from a charity appeal. They offered to replace my radio and cracked dark glasses, but I said I still liked them. Maybe I should have given them up . . .'

Hamzah shrugged.

'Only, I didn't, because that wasn't what Colonel Abad wanted.'

'What the Colonel wanted?' Raf raised his eyebrows. 'What happened to Colonel Abad . . . ?'

'Koenig Pasha stole him.'

That was the point Raf turned off the police-issue recorder, thought about his options for all of thirty seconds and hit DELETE/ALL/CONFIRM.

It took another brandy and the rest of that Sunday morning for Raf to get from Hamzah a collection of facts that the drink-sodden industrialist thought obvious. Chief among them was that the Arab-speaking, Ottoman-appointed liaison officer aboard the USS *Richmond* had been a certain Major Koenig Bey.

So impressed was he by the boy's tragedy that he insisted on finding a children's home for the boy and personally escorting him to El Iskandryia, cracked radio, spectacles and all.

'And Sarah,' asked Raf, 'you ever find out what happened to her?'

'Oh yes,' said Hamzah. 'She died.'

'You eventually traced her records then?'

'No,' said Hamzah. 'But her daughter found me . . .' he added bleakly. 'Avatar's mother.'

'I thought Avatar was your son?' Raf said, sounding genuinely puzzled.

Hamzah nodded. 'That too.'

CHAPTER 40

Hamzah Effendi came down the precinct steps into a storm of flashguns. Behind him walked Raf with one hand heavy on the industrialist's shoulder. In that gesture was ownership and authority. That was what the cameras were meant to catch and that was what they reported, streaming the Monday evening press conference live to newsfeeds around the world.

Behind Raf came his bodyguards. And to one side of the front steps, watching them intently, stood Zara, her face a mask of misery.

'*Excellency* . . .'

Raf spotted the questioner in the middle of the scrum and nodded. 'In the red, blonde hair . . .'

'Claire duBois, Television 5. Is Hamzah Effendi under arrest?'

'He has put himself into police custody.'

'Yes, but . . .' The rest of her reply got drowned beneath a wave of competing questions. So Raf waited for the storm to still and pointed to a man from C3N.

'Nick Richardson, C3N. Do you expect to allow Hamzah's extradition?'

'As you unquestionably know,' said Raf, looking round at the cameras, 'PaxForce has issued a warrant for Hamzah Effendi's arrest on the charge of crimes against humanity . . .' Out of the corner of his eye, Raf spotted the limousine used by Senator Liz slide itself into a parking bay reserved for the Minister of Police.

'Excellency?'

'*Wait.*' One by one the Ishies and journalists turned to see what. His Excellency was watching. Which was why most of the newsfeeds ended up featuring the face of Senator Liz Elsing when the first bomb exploded.

It was nothing spectacular, just a rattling crump and a burst of static that drizzled snow across a dozen different camera screens.

'What was that?' The accent was English, the speaker a crookbacked little man with bad hair and worse dress sense.

Raf shrugged. 'Sword of God, I imagine.' His gaze as it took in the journalists was cool, almost amused. He smiled sourly and flicked blond hair back from the shades he wore to keep flashguns at bay. 'This is Iskandryia, bombs happen . . .'

'What about the extradition?' The man from C3N refused to let go of his question.

'What about it . . . ?'

Raf was being watched by the Senator, who was being watched by about a third of the press corps, mostly those from American channels. All of them looked anxious, torn between chasing down the distant bomb and sticking with the news happening in front of them.

'You accept the need for a trial?'

'If a Grand Jury so decides,' said Raf.

'And where would this trial be, *if the Grand Jury so decides* . . .' The speaker was Austrian, the humour heavy.

'Iskandryia,' said Raf. 'However, I will not be a judge.' He paused to let them consider that. 'And the rules of evidence will be those used by The Hague.'

'And the judges?'

'Three,' Raf said. 'French, German, and American . . .' He was selecting the nationalities as he went along. Raf wondered if any of them realized that. And if the Grand Jury did decide Hamzah had a case to answer, then they'd automatically become his judges. Though Raf didn't think he'd mention that fact just then.

'Excuse me . . .' Raf touched his earbead and took a call, nodding rapidly. 'I have to go,' he told the crowd. 'My men have found a second bomb outside a children's home in Karmous.' Pushing Hamzah slightly, Raf steered the industrialist towards the waiting Bentley and saw the man from C3N materialize beside him, persistent as a shadow.

'Will you be acting as prosecutor?'

Raf turned back and smiled in admiration. There was a lot to recommend sheer bloody-mindedness when it came to a job. 'No,' he said. 'One of the judges will be chosen as prosecuting judge. And I won't be acting for the defence either . . . She will.' Raf jerked his thumb backward and heard Zara gasp.

Which was around the point the second EMP bomb exploded, followed by a third and a fourth, so those watching newsfeeds in other

478

countries never knew if Zara's shock was at being named defender or the fact that El Iskandryia had begun to shut down around her.

'Boss.' Bodyguards closed in on both sides, obviously anxious but still functioning. 'We've got to get you back inside.'

Overhead, bright stars blossomed between clouds as the lights of the city began to flicker, its sodium halo fading from orange through palest yellow to perfect night. Somewhere far distant a dog began to bark.

CHAPTER 41

26th October

'I shouldn't be here,' said Zara, 'you know that . . .'

Here was Raf's bedroom, with its domed roof and high windows, naked babies staring down from the painted ceiling and the air rich with the scent of orchids. A newly cut bunch stood in a Lalique vase beside the bed. Where Khartoum had found tiger orchids, Raf couldn't begin to imagine. A smaller vase was thick with lilies and a silver bowl on his glass-topped dressing table contained potpourri. Neither flowers nor bowl had been there when they finally fell asleep.

But Raf's smile was at the memory of warm skin and the smell of lapsang suchong, mixed with something citrus, labelled for an American/Japanese designer and bottled in Frankfurt. The tiny scent flask was on his dressing table along with the rest of Zara's cosmetics. And, actually, that hadn't been there either . . .

'Maybe I'm the one who should be somewhere else,' said Raf and Zara smiled, rolling over with a linen sheet tucked around her. The night before she'd had darkness to hide behind and only a candle flame to let them see each other. Now the sun streamed in through high windows, turning the white marble floor to a sheet of glistening ice, and the sea breeze tasted of iodine. Outside, the whole city was silent, with Rue Riyad Pasha devoid of cars. Or at least of cars that moved.

'Let it go,' said Raf, giving the sheet a small tug.

Zara shook her head.

'Please,' he said and so she did, at least partly. Letting him unwrap her shoulders to reveal full breasts and the start of a soft stomach. Her skin was honey, her nipples dark walnut. The rest she kept hidden, one hand holding her modesty in place.

'Marry me,' Raf said.

She pulled a face and grinned, but her smile died the second she realized Raf's suggestion was serious. 'Last night you wanted to have me arrested.'

'That was last night.'

Zara nodded. 'Yeah,' she said, 'that makes sense.'

It did too, at least to him. To be honest, Raf didn't know the reason he'd shot the question. Being institutionalized did that to you. Half the time you didn't really know the reason for most things. Time was, as the fox would say . . . time was he could blame what he did on the fox. Now he had no one to blame but himself and he was, if not white-knuckle sober then, at the very least, white-knuckle sane. Sometime or other, when he was feeling braver, he'd try to explain that to Zara.

Try to explain it and fail, most probably, but he'd still try. This too was coded into that famous eight-thousand-line guarantee.

'What will happen to my father . . .'

'You'll marry me if I get him off?'

'Is that your price?'

Raf sighed. 'Is it yours?'

'No,' Zara said shakily. 'I just need to know. Will he be executed?' She would have cried, except she was all cried out. The first part of last night she'd spent wrapped tight in Raf's arms, sometimes angry and occasionally scared, but mostly just crying silently into his shoulder. The second part . . . For all that nothing really happened, that was somewhere they'd both need to go.

'Look,' said Raf, 'he may actually be innocent.'

Zara looked at him. 'I can't stand up there and defend him you know . . .'

'It's your choice,' Raf said. Meaning that it wasn't, not really.

'No,' Zara sat up, taking the sheet with her. 'You're missing the point. I refuse to defend him if he won't defend himself.'

Raf understood how she felt. Her father had killed 183 people, all but 12 of them children. What Hamzah Effendi did was, almost literally, indefensible. And yet . . . Sitting beside her, in a sunlit bedroom thick with the scent of hothouse flowers, Raf told Zara the story as Hamzah had told it to him, about Ka, Sarah and the Colonel . . .

The evening before had begun very differently. In the light of an emergency lamp, seven people had watched Zara hit Raf and only one, a female clerk from the technical section, had made any move to stop Zara from taking a second shot. Which told Raf something he didn't like about Hakim, Ahmed and the rest of his officers.

Although maybe such a reaction was inevitable in a city where crimes by or against women got dealt with by a separate force. And if any of them really thought women were incapable of being deeply dangerous, they should meet Hu San, leader of Seattle's Five Winds Society. Compared to her, Iskandryia's Dons were amateurs, which they mostly were. The only real professional among them was the man Raf had just arrested, and that was for something else.

'You poisonous . . .'

Raf had watched Zara fail to find the right word.

'Putain de merde?' he suggested.

She didn't even pause. 'How could you?'

'Arrest him? Easily, I just pulled out a card and read the words.' Which wasn't true because, for a start, Raf didn't carry a Miranda card and secondly, he had uniforms to do that shit, but he was playing to an audience and she knew it. That was one of the things making her so angry.

'You . . . I thought you liked him.'

Better than me, that was the subtext, or maybe not. Perhaps he was misreading the feeling that hung sour as ghost's breath in the air between them. Chances were, she was just scared.

Raf sighed and cleared his head of the Huntsville psychotrash that flooded it every time he tried to think about what he felt. Other people's feelings he could do. His own . . . He'd been analysed so many times by Dr Millbank that he could no longer distinguish what was emotionally real from what he'd been told were his feelings. Which was weird because, and the fox always used to agree with this, half the time Raf was pretty sure he felt nothing at all.

'Are you listening to me?' That was the point at which Zara pushed her face in close.

No, thought Raf, *not really*. And before he could stop himself, he had leant forward and kissed her, very lightly.

He apologized on the drive back to the governor's mansion. A drive so short that he and Zara could have walked it in the time it took Hakim and Ahmed to safety-check the Bentley.

Of course, before he apologized he had to get his breath back.

'Columbia,' she had told him. 'Power-punching exercises.'

She'd been reluctant to get into the Bentley until Raf explained that her alternative was to wait for a horse-drawn caleche to take her out to Villa Hamzah to be with her mother. Whatever her decision, Hamzah Effendi would remain under guard at the precinct.

Hakim and Ahmed he'd made walk back to the gubernatorial mansion. Punishment for grinning when she sucker punched him in the stomach.

'Why all the playacting?' she'd asked.

'Because that's my job,' said Raf. 'And the best way to fake something, is to pretend to be what you already are . . .' Catching Zara's appalled glance, he shrugged and yanked at the wheel, suddenly dragging the Bentley round a bend into a side street. The car had no power steering, and Raf strongly suspected the absence was intentional.

He wouldn't put it past Koenig Pasha to drive a telemetries-free vehicle precisely *because* it lacked assisted steering, voice-activated starting, electronic locks or air-conditioning, not to mention adaptive cruise control. Even the engine could be hand-cranked, though it was hard to know if that was special or had once come as standard.

The point was, while almost every other vehicle in the city had seen its electronics go belly-up in the blasts, the governor's Bentley still functioned. Which was how Raf ended up with a dusty square to himself. And it was obvious from the way pedestrians turned to watch the unlit Bentley slide slowly round Place al-Mansur, its pennant fluttering in the darkness, that they expected no less.

The city had a confidence in its new governor that Raf had never had in himself, that no one on the right side of sanity could ever have.

'Remember that lunch?' Raf asked. 'When we met officially? Your father told me you never cried.'

'That was then,' said Zara crossly. 'Things change.'

'Either that, or we change them,' Raf replied. 'Sometimes surviving is all it takes.'

'And that's what you do, is it? Survive . . .'

Raf nodded.

Sitting there beside him, her hands clasped tight between stockinged knees and her shoulders hunched forward like a frightened child, Zara took a deep breath and slowly willed herself back under control as a familiar street slipped by and the dark gateposts of the mansion came forward to meet her.

The fact Raf was right didn't make her like him any more.

'I took a detour,' Raf told Hakim, seeing him standing by the gate, and with that Raf edged the Bentley into a courtyard lit by coal-filled oil drums.

'The master arrives . . .' Khartoum was no longer dressed in his ornate livery. Instead, the old man wore a pale grey souf so long its rough edges dragged on damp cobbles. Around him stood soldiers, plus a thin clerk in a flapping suit. The old man looked amused.

'Your office is worried.' The Sufi practically had to push the clerk towards the car window. 'Tell him then.'

'Excellency . . . Ambassador Graf von Bismarck demands an immediate audience.'

Did he now?

'And the one from Paris?'

The man nodded.

'London, Washington, Vienna?'

A quick nod greeted each capital in its turn.

'And Stambul?'

'The red phone . . .' The man was embarrassed. 'It rang, Excellency, but when I finally answered it the line was dead. Perhaps the main exchange . . .'

'It's been fried,' said Raf. 'Along with the relay stations. Please tell the Graf that I'll see him for ten minutes, an hour from now, in the council chamber.'

'Your Excellency . . . The ambassador was hoping . . .'

'That I'd go there. Too bad.' Raf watched the clerk debate with himself which it would be most dangerous to offend, the Germans or Iskandryia's new governor. His decision quickly became clear when the man snapped off a smart salute and stepped back from the car.

'You scare them, don't you?' Zara's smile was thin.

'It's the aftertaste of the General.'

Zara shook her head. 'It's you,' she said. 'Take a good look at yourself in the mirror.'

'I don't do mirrors,' said Raf.

'That's what I mean.'

There didn't seem to be much to say after that so, once Khartoum had opened Raf's door, Raf walked round to the other side of the car and opened the door for Zara.

'And I wish you'd stop that,' Zara said with a scowl. 'All this heel-clicking shit.' Her scowl lasted until she reached the mansion's steps, at which point Hani came bundling out of the big front door.

'Zara!'

'Hello, honey.'

Hani grinned. 'How are you?' she added as an afterthought; visibly remembering her manners.

'Okay, I suppose. And you?'

'Terrific.' Hani suddenly opened both arms to embrace the ink-black sky. 'Someone's killed the lights. All of them. You can see what's happened better from the roof.' Hani turned to go, then swung back, remembering something, 'You and I,' said the child, looking serious. 'We need to talk . . .'

CHAPTER 42

'You know Colonel Abad stole someone else's face?'

Zara didn't.

'On the badges,' said Hani. 'It's not him. The face belongs to someone who died years and years ago. You know what that means? It means he kept himself to himself, or people would have noticed he wasn't the same as his picture . . .'

Hani nodded. 'I'm right, aren't I?' She looked at the older girl, then frowned. 'Don't you like clues?'

Zara stared round at the governor's study, her face doubtful. Official papers were piled in untidy heaps, encyclopedias, old history books, ancient maps of the Sudan. A bookcase along one wall had half the volumes pulled out and dumped on the floor. It looked like a whirlwind had hit the place. And the whirlwind was about four paces away, laying a fire and asking riddles.

'Honey, we really shouldn't be in here.'

'You *want* to save your father?'

Do I . . . ? Zara stared at the child, throat tight.

'Thought so.' Hani walked over to Zara, gave her a quick hug and went back to work, crunching old financial reports into tight balls and pushing them under kindling.

'Clues,' Hani said firmly, putting a match to a computer printout. 'Crosswords, logic puzzles, number grids, those stupid MENSA things in the papers . . . Do you like them?'

'Sometimes.'

Hani sighed. It was late. Raf was still furious about something, and Zara was so busy trying not to get upset in front of her that she wasn't really listening to a thing Hani said. Even Khartoum was useless. She'd tried to talk to him but he'd just excused himself, then come back later with matches and a jug of water from the kitchens.

Which was less than no help.

It was hard being the only one who could think properly. Especially if you were nine. Or maybe ten, there was some doubt about that.

'In a moment,' said Hani, 'I'll make you some cocoa.' She blew on the flames until the kindling caught, added a couple of wooden candle-holders from the mantelpiece and all the pencils from the General's desk tidy.

Uncle Ashraf's desk tidy, Hani corrected herself. Taking a half-eaten bar of Fry's chocolate from her pocket – it was possible for a human to last a week on a single bar, she'd read it in some magazine – Hani broke cubes off the chocolate and dropped five or six into the water jug. She should probably have heated the water first, she realized, looking at the lumps lying there at the bottom.

Still, it was a bit late to decide that now. Pushing the copper jug into the middle of the flames, Hani sucked her fingers where they'd got singed and went back to the real problem.

'Did you bring your weird picture?'

'Did I . . . ?' Zara was shocked. 'Honey, how did you know about that?'

'It must have been sent to you,' Hani said firmly. 'I've asked everyone else. The General sent you something from Dante's *Purgatorio* . . . A Doré engraving. Am I right?'

Hani pulled a yellowing page from her jeans pocket and smoothed it out on the desk. 'He sent this one to Raf. It's from *Inferno.*'

The engraving showed the man with his chest sliced open. His hands gripping the edges of the wound, not to close it but to pull it apart. From her other pocket, Hani extracted what looked like a photocopy but was actually a printout of a low-rez scan.

'I couldn't get the original,' said Hani, 'because that's locked away. But Uncle Ashraf had this copy on computer in an evidence file. When he still had a working computer,' she added thoughtfully.

'It was the General who sent this to my father?'

'That's Koenig Pasha's writing,' said Hani, turning over the printout to show Zara the handwriting script on the other side. 'So I guess so . . . In Raf's file it says Effendi asked the General for help.'

'For help!' Zara's laugh was hollow. 'How do we know that's the General's writing?'

Hani shrugged. 'I had a look at his diary,' she said, pulling a notebook from a desk drawer and handing it to Zara, who shook her head and gave it straight back.

'You read his diary?'

'No. It's in German,' said Hani. 'I don't know German . . .'

486

This was where the conversation paused, while Hani kicked off one silver Nike, pulled off the sock underneath and used it as an oven glove to lift the copper jug from the fire. The jug she put on the hearth to cool and the sock got tossed in the fire. It had started to smoulder anyway. When they drank the cocoa, it tasted more of water than chocolate, but neither Zara nor Hani mentioned the fact.

'You got a Doré engraving from the General?'

Zara shook her head, so Hani started again.

'You got an engraving?'

Zara nodded.

'Are you sure the General didn't give it to you?'

'It was sent by fax,' said Zara, 'from the SS *Jannah*.'

'*Jannah*,' said Hani. 'What does that mean?'

'It means garden,' Zara said, puzzled. Hani had to know that.

'Garden.' Hani wrote the word in pen on a clean piece of paper. 'So who do you think sent the picture?' She sounded like Raf at his most serious.

Zara blushed. 'I thought it was the Khedive . . . But it could have been Avatar. I let him go in my place.' Which, like Raf at his most serious, couldn't have been too popular with His Highness.

'Have you got the engraving?'

Zara nodded.

'Can I have a look?' Hani asked, once it became obvious that Zara intended to leave it at that. 'It would be useful . . .'

'It's . . .' Zara hunted for the right word. 'Very rude.'

'So's the angel,' said Hani, nodding to the bare-breasted woman with wings and a discreet drape of cloth across her broad, Victorian hips.

'This is ruder,' Zara said, but she went to get the picture anyway . . .

'Mmm,' said Hani. She did her best to sound grown-up, but the slight widening of her eyes and a growing grin gave away her shock. 'She's a spider.'

'That's right.'

'A woman spider, bent over backward . . .' Hani flipped to the sheet underneath, nodding to herself; it showed the back, on which the General had written a brief note, plus the word *Judecca*.

Next Hani rechecked the titles of the books from which the pictures had been ripped.

'*Paradiso, Purgatorio, Inferno* . . .' The words went down on her sheet of paper one under the other. As an afterthought, Hani numbered them. She'd already found a book called *Inferno* on the shelves by the door. Sure enough, it had the flyleaf ripped out. Hani was as certain as anything that she'd also find vandalized books called *Paradiso* and *Purgatorio*, once she bothered to check.

Only here will you find peace. That was what the General had written on the back of the first picture. Paradise. Only here will you . . . It made sense. Hani copied the words onto her bit of paper and numbered it.

Taking Zara's spider woman, she turned the weird picture over and wrote down *Welcome to limbo.* Having numbered this to match *Purgatorio*, she put *At its centre hell is not hot* directly underneath and numbered that as well.

Apollyon, Judecca and *Cocytus* came last.

She thought of drawing different-coloured lines to link the General's comments to the names of the books, but it didn't seem necessary. Instead, she drew a big exclamation mark under the list.

'Do you actually know what any of this means?' asked Zara.

'Not yet,' Hani admitted. 'But I'll let you know when I do.' Pushing the paper to one side, Hani scraped back her chair and tiptoed to the door, which she opened a fraction. Sudanese soldiers were coming and going in the hall. Mostly they seemed to be Raf's guard. 'The German's arriving,' she told Zara. 'He looks cross.'

Zara peered over Hani's shoulder at the young German ambassador. 'No,' she said, 'what he looks is nervous . . .' Just then, Khartoum came into the hall and bowed to the visitor, ushering him through an open door. 'That's not the audience chamber,' said Zara.

'No,' said Hani, 'it's a waiting room. *Now* he'll look cross.'

CHAPTER 43

'Coffee,' Raf suggested and the German youth in front of him winced; as Raf suspected he might. According to his file, the ambassador from Berlin loathed the stuff.

'In Iskandryia it's traditional,' said Raf.

'Isn't everything?' The ambassador's voice was resigned. According to Koenig Pasha's notes His Excellency Graf von Bismarck was nineteen. He looked younger, fourteen going on twelve, with the faintest trace of a blond moustache and long hair that flopped over one eye. The unflopped eye, startlingly blue, stared nervously at Raf whenever the ambassador thought Raf wasn't looking.

Iskandryia was one of the most career-destroying posts on offer, particularly for someone who hated intrigue and coffee. And from what Raf could gather, Ernst von Bismarck had taken it only because his other alternative was marriage to some Schleswig-Holstein. It seemed the Graf wasn't the marrying type.

'If not coffee,' said Raf, voice suddenly sympathetic, 'then what?'

'Orange juice . . . If that's possible.'

A clap of Raf's hands brought not Khartoum but Hani. She'd changed from jeans into a dress at least one size too big. Unfortunately, she'd retained the silver Nike trainers.

'I'm Hani al-Mansur,' Hani announced, thrusting her hand at the startled ambassador. 'He's my uncle.'

'Where's . . . ?' Raf began.

'Doing something,' said Hani firmly. 'Whatever you want – I'll get it.'

When the orange juice arrived it came on a tray complete with a silver bowl of pistachios, soft-skinned and bright green on the inside, two small brass pipes and a fingertip of sticky resin.

The German ambassador and Raf waited while Hani withdrew. Only then did Raf notice a note folded neatly on the tray under his glass.

'A sweet child,' said the Graf.

Raf reread Hani's scrawl, nodded doubtfully and pushed the note deep into his pocket. 'Endlessly surprising,' he said and changed the subject. 'You demanded a meeting . . . ?'

It seemed preposterous to call what was happening an audience, so Raf didn't.

'Berlin wants . . .'

'I'm sure it does,' said Raf. 'But first explain why your intelligence service has been waging war against Hamzah Effendi.' He stared at the boy, who put down his glass and went deep red.

Personally, Raf lacked the capacity for visible embarrassment, but then he'd had a lung deflated when he was six and a very minor blood-supply nerve to his face snipped where it ran between his second and third ribs. The surgeon went after the nerve through a tiny incision in his armpit.

'They haven't . . .'

'Are you telling me the man pulled out of Lake Mareotis wasn't *Thiergarten* . . . ?'

'You don't know that he killed the first girl,' Ernst von B said hotly. 'Whatever you've been saying.'

'What about the attack on the Casino Quitrimala?' said Raf. 'Are you telling me the *Thiergarten* didn't organize that?'

'That had nothing to do with us.'

'And I'm supposed to believe this?'

'You have my word,' Graf von Bismarck said stiffly. He looked as if he was getting ready to cry.

'But the man who died in the fire *was* German?'

The nod was slight enough to be almost invisible.

'Okay,' said Raf. 'Just suppose some of your men have been turned . . . Who corrupted them?'

Needless to say, the Graf had no idea, although he immediately suggested Paris because Berlin always blamed Paris for everything.

'And the bomb?'

'My intelligence officers suggest the mujahadeen.' Von Bismarck looked hesitant. 'But I'm not convinced the rebels have that level of sophistication.'

Raf reached behind his chair for a cardboard box and pulled out a thin tube the length of his arm, attached to a small wooden base. 'Sophisticated it's not,' he said, voice grim. 'Effective, yes. You can buy most of the components from the nearest souk.'

Circling the thin tube he held, but not touching it, was a spiral of bare copper wire, with a metal clothes hanger looped at the top, like a makeshift replacement for a vandalized car aerial.

The object looked like something from Sculpture 101 at St Mark's.

'Detonator,' said Raf, pointing to a cigarette-sized tube rammed into the underside of the weird exhibit. Copper wire, aluminium stuffed with cheap explosive, aerial loop, battery pack.

'To create a magnetic field between copper coil and tube,' Raf added, when the German ambassador looked blank. He didn't mention that he'd spent the last few minutes before the Graf arrived checking a pencil-sketched schematic for a flux generator, as e-bombs were apparently called.

'Detonate the charge,' said Raf.

'. . . and the whole thing blows up.' Graf von Bismarck finished the sentence for him.

'You got it.' Raf took a brass pipe from the tray and gave it to the young German, who absentmindedly inhaled.

'As it blows,' said Raf, 'the blast rips up the tube at six thousand metres a second or something, the exploding tube flares out to touch the wire and power gets diverted into the undamaged coil ahead . . .'

Absolute incomprehension closed down the Graf's boyish face.

'You didn't do physics, did you?'

The German shook his head. 'It wasn't an option. I took philosophy, politics and history at Heidelberg.'

Yeah, exactly as recorded in Koenig Pasha's file.

'It works like this,' said Raf patiently. 'The magnetic force gets squeezed as the tube behind it explodes. That creates a huge rise in current in the coil ahead. When the current finally hits the loop antenna it sprays out a *terawatt* of electromagnetic energy . . . From detonation to destruction takes less than . . .'

He clicked his fingers. 'A hundredth of that, probably less. There were seven of these spread across the city . . . Six went off.'

'But the worst is now over . . .'

'I wish,' said Raf, meaning it. 'The worst is only just beginning.'

'Then even more reason . . .' The Graf put down his little pipe. 'This trial . . .' He stopped and pursed his lips. 'The thing is,' he said, 'Berlin are . . .' The Graf shrugged and reached again for the pipe. 'My problem is . . .'

'Berlin are worried,' said Raf. 'Who wouldn't be?' He picked up his own pipe but didn't actually inhale, merely watched thin strands of pungent smoke spiral away into what the Graf saw as darkness and Raf knew to be a different density of light.

By now Astolphe de St Cloud, France's ambassador to El Iskandryia, would have heard that Ashraf Bey was locked in a meeting with the ambassador from Berlin and would be at the mansion's gates demanding admittance. Raf was depending on it.

'The trial . . . ?' Raf prodded gently.

'We want it in Berlin,' said the Graf.

'No.' Raf shook his head. 'Absolutely impossible.'

'You misunderstand,' the Graf said, sounding nervous. 'We demand it be held in Berlin.'

'As I said, impossible.'

Something flitted across the young man's face that looked to Raf remarkably like relief. 'We will be making an official protest . . .'

'I'm sure you will,' said Raf gently. 'But the trial will be held in Iskandryia. Not in The Hague or Paris or Berlin. And I'm relying on you to be a judge . . . The court will be calling Jean René . . .'

Ernst von Bismarck nodded knowledgeably.

'The photographer who filmed the aftermath of the massacre,' Raf explained. 'I should also inform you,' he added, pulling Hani's scribbled note from his pocket, 'that my intelligence officers tell me Hamzah Effendi may call a character witness from his own brigade.'

'Impossible,' the Graf said. 'Every one of them died except Hamzah. I've read the report.'

'If that's true,' said Raf with a smile, 'it should make for an interesting trial.'

The Graf frowned. 'I will inform Berlin of the situation.'

'How?' Raf asked and watched the Graf realize that doing so would be less simple than he'd imagined. 'How will you go about informing Berlin?'

'By letter. There's a passenger service to Syracuse . . .'

'If it runs.'

Both ferries would run, Raf already knew that, because one of the first things he'd done was send Hakim to Maritime Station to find out which of the regular boats had been caught in the blast and which, if any, had been lucky enough to be at sea.

They were currently two Soviet liners without electricity, a worthless aircraft carrier, and half a dozen expensive yachts that now needed a partial refit. The people who owned those could afford the damage. It was worse for the fishing boats. Almost all of those had lost their navigation systems and sonar. They also had engines that now wouldn't start.

'Oh,' said Raf, 'if you do write, be sure to tell Berlin that I'm closing the city. A total curfew is being imposed. Other than mine, all cars are banned, assuming any still work. No one comes in or leaves without my written permission . . . My handwritten permission,' he added grimly. 'Except for those travelling under a diplomatic passport or a *carte blanche*, obviously enough. And the accredited press. They can come in. They can even bring cameras. Leaving, of course, is another matter.'

'How long . . . ?'

'Until we catch the bombers.' Raf rose from his chair, waited until the Graf realized his meeting was over, then walked the young German to the chamber door.

'I have a city in meltdown,' he told the boy, 'a natural gas plant that can't pump natural gas, a petroleum refinery that isn't refining crude, no electricity, no telephones. The few computers that still work are dying by the minute. Most cars don't run, garages can't dispense gas . . . You know what that means? No working hospitals, no schools. Think about it.'

Raf ushered the Graf through the hall and out into the rain. Good-byes said, he went back into the darkened chamber and listened.

'You can come out now,' he said.

Very slowly, Zara appeared. 'You knew I was here.' It was half question, half statement.

'I heard you.'

'Across that distance?' She stared in disbelief from where she stood to where Raf and von Bismarck had been sitting.

'I can hear the heartbeat of a bat,' he told her simply, 'and see a hunting cat across Zaghloul Square at the dead of night. Everything that has ever happened to me I remember. Everything . . .'

I can't die, he added in his head. *I can only be killed.* But he kept those words where they belonged because her smile was already gone, shocked out of being by his honesty, her shock coloured round the edges with unease, even fright.

'You mean it, don't you?' said Zara.

Did he? Raf nodded. 'Yes,' he said. 'I'm afraid I do.' He didn't mention that he could smell expensive scent oxidizing on the inside of her wrist, an overlay of white willow extract from her shampoo and something underneath all that, much more animal.

'You remember everything?' Zara asked in disbelief.

'Exactly as it happened.' Raf stopped opposite the girl and caught the point at which her eyes widened and she remembered that night they'd spent on her father's boat. Her mouth had tasted of olives and her breasts had rested heavy in his hands, salt with the memory of a wine-dark sea and blood from where she'd bitten his lip.

There had been more, but not much, not as much as he wanted. Now things between them were broken and the memory was what he had left.

'I'd better get off to bed,' said Raf.

'What about me?'

'Choose a room, use it. Call it protective custody,' Raf suggested. 'Find Khartoum,' he added when Zara looked blank. 'Tell him to find you something or else share Hani's room. She'd like that . . .' Raf paused, took a deep breath. 'Alternatively, there's always mine . . .'

'What about seeing the French ambassador?' Zara asked. Which wasn't exactly what Raf expected her to say.

'What about him?'

'Isn't he waiting . . . ?'

'Undoubtedly.' Raf shrugged. 'I don't want to see the man,' he said. 'And besides, St Cloud hired a man to have me killed.'

Raf smiled at her surprise.

'The night I first arrived,' he said. 'Someone tried to knife me . . . I told Felix. It was one of the things he was investigating when he died . . .'

'What happened to the someone?'

'He attacked me, so I killed him.'

'And that's the scar?' Zara said when Raf had finished hanging his jacket in an old rosewood cupboard. In her hand was a wineglass, still half-full of white Rioja. It was Raf's glass. Her own was long since empty.

She pointed to a seam visible along his wrist.

'No,' said Raf, pulling off his shirt. 'This is the scar.' He traced a line across his ribs with one ringer and felt the faintest echo of hardened tissue. 'It was only a flesh wound, nothing more . . .

'What?' he asked when Zara smiled, a little sadly.

The room was lit by a single candle that sat, fat and pale in a dish turned from a single section of monkey puzzle, the ancient wood so thin that the candle's dancing flame made it translucent. The monkey-puzzle dish sat on an oak table beside a metal bed so old that its horsehair mattress rested on wire mesh. Since the room Raf had chosen was originally meant for the General's personal use, the choice of bed undoubtedly held some special significance.

Raf had selected the room because Hani had one next door. A small dark space that might once have been a dressing room to this, though the entrance between rooms had been bricked up long enough for the Persian wallpaper that covered it to have faded to faint horsemen who hunted in shadow.

'Blow out the candle.'

'I can see in the dark,' Raf warned Zara.

494

'Maybe,' she said, 'but I can't.' And so Raf blew out the single candle and the room's cool air flooded with acrid smoke.

'How?' Zara demanded suddenly. 'How do you see in the dark?'

'My eyes adjust . . .' Raf thought about it. 'No,' he said, 'I adjust my eyes. There's a difference.'

'Then don't.'

Raf looked at her.

'Stay blind.'

'If that's what you want.' The last thing Raf saw before he tuned the room into darkness was Zara unbuttoning the front of her short dress. She wore no bra and her body was as perfect as his memory of it.

He met her clumsily in space that waited between them, neither one quite certain of where the other stood in the darkness. Zara felt his hands reach up to grip her naked shoulders and he felt her fingers brush against his face. And this time their kiss was slower, much less frenzied than that time when they were drunk and tired and on her father's boat.

Zara's breath tasted of wine and her throat of salt. He got colours and memories with each kiss, though they might have been imagined. Putting both hands around her, Raf followed her spine with his fingers, pausing only when he reached the silk of her thong.

He smiled.

'No.' The command was simple, far simpler than the mix of emotions encoded in her suddenly breaking voice. Sheer nervousness Raf could have understood. His own body was almost vibrating with tension. And fear of what might come next was possible. As was worry that she'd let things get this far . . .

But this was anger.

Raf just wasn't sure it was directed at him.

He stepped back just enough to put a slight distance between them. 'You okay?'

Zara leant her head against his neck and nodded, feeling his answering smile. There was a neat scar under his jaw, the one half the city assumed was *RenSchmiss*. And another on his shoulder, so ugly that no one in their right mind could have assumed it resulted from a formal duel.

'Seattle . . . ?' Zara asked, running her fingers across ridged skin. Something else he didn't talk about, the bombing of the Consulate in Seattle.

'A fox cub,' said Raf lightly, 'when I was a child.' He touched her face and let his hands rest there before dropping them to cup breasts that were full and high, with nipples that hardened beneath his touch. They both shivered, but he did so first.

495

'You like?' Zara's voice was low, almost mocking.

In answer, Raf shifted one hand to the back of her head, feeling her lips silence and her mouth open wider.

'Of course I like.' His right hand found a pressure point between her third and fourth vertebrae and he pushed, so that her chin came up and her neck exposed itself. Her pulse beneath his lips was as loud as a bass loop.

Somewhere, in the hollow where the fox should have been, Raf knew this was merely an act of mutual empathy, the grown-up equivalent of the intimate attunement of infant to mother, mere parasympathetic arousal. Everything that wasn't the fox-shaped void didn't mind about that. It welcomed the night outside and the faint pricks of light glimpsed through a badly drawn curtain. And it bathed in the sound of gulls riding salt winds over a city struck into near darkness for the first time in centuries.

'Open the curtains and shutters,' demanded Zara suddenly.

'It'll let in the stars.'

'That much I can cope with,' she said in a voice as bitter sweet as black chocolate. 'Probably . . .'

When Raf turned round from pulling back the double shutters that usually closed off each of the room's five floor-to-ceiling windows, Zara was in bed, safely tucked under a linen sheet.

The first thing she said when he joined her there was, 'I won't have sex with you . . .'

'So how old were you when it happened?'

'Seven, maybe eight . . . At an age you don't really realize what's being done. Maybe that helps.' Zara sounded doubtful, like she was trying to convince herself.

Raf's answer was noncommittal.

'You know,' Zara added, 'I forgot all about it for years. I just thought it was normal.'

'What changed?'

She was lying beside Raf in the darkness with a late-October wind rattling the sash windows and a quilt pulled up so tight around her it almost hid her face. One of Raf's arms held her shoulder as she lay on her side, facing him, and when she spoke it was in a monotone so soft and so quiet that Raf doubted if anyone but he could have heard even half of what she said.

Sometimes she spoke and sometimes there was silence. When the silence grew too strong, Raf asked another question. Zara had been talking for hours, her voice never raised nor showing any emotion Raf could recognize. Except its very emptiness told Raf more than her answers to half a dozen of his questions.

Zara had, so far as he could tell, long since forgotten he was there. He didn't know who she thought he was . . . Maybe some part of herself.

'What changed?' Raf asked again.

'Schools changed. My mother refused but I kept insisting. And eventually Dad agreed I could go to the American High. They did a medical.'

'With a male doctor?'

'Of course not! The nurse was French. Probably not much more than five or six years older than me. She did a blood test. Asked for a sample of urine. Cut a strand of my hair and took a swab from my mouth . . . Drugs and DNA profile,' Zara added, as if Raf couldn't work that out for himself.

'She listened to my heart and lungs, took my blood pressure and did a quick CAT scan with a handheld. Then she asked about periods. Only I didn't know what those were, so she explained and I said they hadn't started. Which was when she asked me to get back on the couch.'

Zara sighed.

'I don't think she'd ever seen a female circumcision before. When she came back she had Sister Angelica, our school doctor, in tow. She was maybe thirty-five, though she seemed much older to me.' Zara spoke as if this had all happened decades earlier, rather than just five years before. 'It was the first time I heard a woman swear . . .

'Apparently, because there were now laws against female circumcision, Sister Angelica thought it didn't happen.'

'What did she do?'

Zara's laugh was a bitter bark. 'After she'd slammed the phone down on my mother, she went to see my father at his office. It's probably the only time he's stood there, utterly speechless while a woman shouted at him.'

'And then?'

Silence was Zara's answer. An absence that stretched so thin that Raf finally decided Zara must have fallen asleep, but he was wrong. She was busy remembering the bits she didn't usually allow herself to remember.

'They cut the stitches,' she announced flatly. 'Sister Angelica did it herself. There were five in total, each separate, transparent and beautifully neat, pulling together the sides of my . . .'

Zara stopped, starting up again, minutes later, as if she'd never paused.

'Sister Angelica cleaned the area where the inner labia should have been and removed an oval of surgical plastic designed to create enough

497

space for urination . . . It had been done in a hospital, you see. A good hospital with qualified doctors and a resident anaesthetist. And that was the problem. Because if it had been done by a jobbing midwife with a piece of broken glass in a back room, then I'd have struggled, which would have made it hard to cut away as much as my mother wanted.

'You know what Sister Angelica did after that? She bought me a German porn mag . . .'

'She . . .'

'I knew it was German because I'd started learning German the year before. Every spread had women naked with other women . . . I remember the Sister gave me a large cup of coffee and left me with the magazine and a mirror. By the time she came back I'd worked out the differences for myself. But Sister Angelica slipped up with the magazine because it wasn't until later, when I was sharing a shower with another girl that I discovered that some girls have this . . .'

Zara slid her hand across Raf's hip and touched the very edge of his pubic hair.

'I don't, you see. Also I don't have small labia, a clitoral hood or the very top of my clitoris. But apparently I got lucky.' Her voice was hard. 'They could have done a full Pharaonic instead of a mild Sunna. You know what that is?'

Raf knew, but he shook his head. 'Tell me,' he said.

'The first thing you'd have had to do, come our wedding night, was slice through scar tissue. But even with all Dad's money at her disposal, my mother couldn't get the hospital at El Qahirah to go that far. So, you see . . .'

Raf did. Like most things in life, luck was subjective.

CHAPTER 44

26th October

Hani dreamed of gardens. This wasn't unusual, gardens figured heavily in her stories and in most of the computer games she liked. In fact, *Rashid III* took place entirely in a nest of walled gardens, complete with fountains, djinn, houris and tiny gazelle. Only her own computer was now dead and, anyway, she'd finished all the levels of *Rashid III* months ago. All levels/all difficulties/all characters. It hadn't been a very hard game.

The software was cheap, though. And that was probably the reason Aunt Nafisa had let her have it.

When Hani woke, at the first call to prayer, she lay there under the covers, which she wasn't meant to do, and thought about gardens. Then she thought about God. After that she thought about gardens and God. And then she got up, wrapped herself tightly in her dressing gown and went to find Raf.

'Jannah means garden or heaven,' Hani told herself as she opened her door. 'And paradise also means heaven. So paradiso means Jannah. SS *Jannah*. And I've got a list of other clues.'

She was talking to herself because Ifritah wasn't there. Raf had said Hani could come to the mansion with him and Khartoum but the grey cat had to stay with Donna at the madersa. That was because Ifritah was a wild cat and no one had taught her to do her business outside.

Hani had been planning to look up on the Web how to house-train a cat that was already mostly grown-up, but now she couldn't do that either. So Ifritah had to stay where she was.

The man who stood guard outside Raf's door was called Ahmed. Hani knew this because she'd asked him earlier. He was big and dark and sometimes he looked at her and shrugged to the others when he thought she wasn't looking.

Ahmed said nothing, not even when Hani shined a torch in his face.

499

Just raised his eyebrows and turned the handle for her. Hani realized what the raised eyebrows meant when she saw a lump in the bed next to Uncle Ashraf. The lump was sleeping, safely tucked under a sheet, but Hani could see Zara's hair poking out at the top.

Hani tried very hard not to be shocked.

After a little while, she decided that she *was* shocked and went back to her room. Ahmed said nothing to Hani on her way out either. Instead of going back to bed Hani got dressed, wrote Zara a note that she left with Ahmed, then went down to the kitchens to find Khartoum.

The rest of the day, while Ashraf worked at the precinct and Zara walked, ghostlike and silent, through the formal gardens at the mansion, looking at statues without seeing them, Hani sat at a kitchen table with an Italian dictionary, three volumes of Dante and a notepad. After a while she decided it might be easier if she just concentrated on the pictures.

The volumes of the *Divina Commedia* came from the General's study, as did the notepad and fountain pen. So too did a list of all the working computers in the city that still had functioning modems/lines/firewire. The list was handwritten, distressingly brief and the original was meant for Ashraf's eyes only. 'Which was why Hani kept the copy she'd made in her pocket.

Ashraf came back as Tuesday evening began its slide into darkness, trailing his shadows behind him; although Hakim and Ahmed didn't go with Raf when he walked out into the garden to talk to Zara. Whatever he said to her, they slept in different rooms that night.

CHAPTER 45

Astolphe, Marquis de St Cloud was enjoying himself. Unfortunately for
Raf it was mostly at his expense, though the real target of the French-
man's quiet vitriol was Elizabeth Elsing, as St Cloud insisted on calling
Senator Liz.

Following yesterday's decision by the Grand Jury that Hamzah
should indeed face charges, Senator Liz seemed unusually keen that the
defendant be tried immediately, found guilty by lunchtime and executed
before tea.

Which was fine, except for the fact that Hamzah Effendi had yet to be
formally arraigned. And the reason this had been delayed was that it took
until noon for the American woman to agree that St Cloud should hold
the chair. Senator Liz also seemed slightly put out by the number of
explosions happening across the city.

'Bring in the prisoner.'

'Bring in the prisoner . . .'

The courtroom was small but it was in the nature of ushers everywhere to shout. Raf heard his demand echo down a corridor outside,
then heard an answering tramp of feet. The first argument of the day,
long before the scrap for precedence between St Cloud and Senator Liz,
had been about the suitability of the room itself.

Surprisingly, it was the young German Graf who objected most
violently to the meagreness of the room on offer. Stating that its size
was an affront to the seriousness of the case. His other complaint, that
Hamzah Quitrimala's arraignment should have been thrown open to the
press, drew a snort of laughter from St Cloud. Berlin wasn't known for
the transparency of its legal process.

El Iskandryia's law courts were in Place Orabi, almost directly
opposite the tomb of the unknown warrior and occupying what had
once been the Italian Consulate. At ground level, the central Hall of

Justice was three times the size of the courtroom Raf had chosen, and came replete with gilded chairs set out like small thrones for five judges, a seal of the Khedival arms hung behind the central chair and, above these, carved from Lebanese cedar and gilded with beaten gold, a *tugra*, the imperial monogram of the Ottoman Porte himself.

It was, Raf agreed, an altogether more imposing setting. It was also accessible from Place Orabi on one side and Rue el Tigarya on another, making it simple to attack and complex to defend.

'Defend from whom?' the Graf had demanded.

'You tell me,' had been Raf's answer and he made the Graf, Senator Liz and St Cloud, plus the ushers, the court stenographer and Zara climb three flights of marble stairs to a smaller courtroom usually used for family disputes.

At the top, just before he went into the room, Raf halted to yank open a steel fire escape. A helmeted Hakim stood on metal steps outside, clutching an old-fashioned Lee-Enfield. Next to Hakim was Ahmed, a Soviet machine gun resting heavy in the crook of his arm. The gun was chopped from sheet steel and finished on a lathe. It had the advantage of having only five moving parts, none of them involving electronics.

'If shit happens,' Raf said, 'this is the way we leave. Don't look back and don't stop to help anybody else, just move . . .'

As Raf turned to go, an explosion ruptured the city's nervous silence and flames boiled into the air from the deserted railyard at Kharmous.

'What perfect timing,' said a voice in Raf's ear. It was St Cloud, a smile on the old man's weather-beaten face as he watched smoke stain the sky. 'Almost too perfect,' he added.

Since then the Marquis had been watching Raf, his Cheshire cat smile coming and going, but never quite vanishing from the old roué's face. Now St Cloud had the defendant standing in the dock in front of him.

'Your name?'

Hamzah Quitrimala gave no answer.

'You will give the court your name.'

Eyes expressionless and mouth slack, the thickset industrialist looked as if St Cloud's order carried no weight against whatever was happening inside his head.

'Has this man been tested for mental competence?' the Marquis asked Raf.

'He has been examined by a doctor . . .'

'That wasn't quite what I asked.' St Cloud's voice was silky. 'Has he undergone the usual tests?'

'Obviously not,' said Raf. 'Since we don't have access to the usual machines.'

'All the more reason to hold the trial in Washington,' insisted the Senator and St Cloud sat back with a smile. Winding up Elizabeth Elsing and letting her go was about as subtle as winding up an old clockwork toy and twice as amusing.

'That question has already been debated and decided,' Raf said flatly. 'The trial takes place here.'

'Decided by you,' said St Cloud.

'Yes,' said Raf, 'decided by me.'

'In your capacity as governor of the city.'

Raf nodded.

'As is your right?'

Raf nodded once more.

'Remind me,' said the Frenchman politely. 'In which of your capacities are you now answering my question about the defendant's mental capacity?'

'As *magister*.'

The elderly Frenchman nodded and turned his attention back to the man in the dock. 'We need your name,' said the Marquis. 'We need to know that you understand our questions . . .'

Hamzah opened his mouth but no words came to carry his answer to the waiting court and seconds later the light went out of his eyes.

St Cloud shrugged.

'Is there any man here who speaks for the defendant?'

'Yes,' came a voice from the back. 'I do . . .'

Heads twisted but Raf didn't need to look. It was his turn to smile.

'I said any man,' St Cloud said gently.

'Whatever.' Zara walked to the front and stopped beside her father. 'Let me speak for him,' she said. 'God knows, he needs somebody.'

'The weight of a woman's word is a third of that given to the words of a man . . . Isn't that now the law in El Iskandryia? Come to think of it,' the Frenchman added softly, 'I seem to remember that being the law across most of North Africa.'

'This court operates under the rules of The Hague,' said Raf firmly. 'As you well know.'

St Cloud nodded. 'So you allow this girl to speak for her father?'

'Yes,' said Raf, without looking at Zara, 'I allow it.'

'Remind me,' said the Frenchman with a sly smile, 'in exactly which capacity did you make that decision?'

'A Grand Jury having unanimously decided that probable cause and sufficient reason exist to bring this case to trial, it is my duty as senior judge to apprise you of the formal charges . . .'

Pausing, St Cloud reached for a glass and sipped, very slowly. The tumbler was smeared and the water it held tasted stale. Chances were, the water had been brought in a jug from a standpipe hastily erected in the square outside.

It was interesting just how much the people of any city relied on electricity without really realizing that fact. At least St Cloud found it interesting; but then he found almost everything interesting, which had proved a salvation in his long and sometimes difficult life.

What interested him most, at least most for the moment, was how ready both the German boy and that irritating American were to agree that Hamzah Effendi was faking illness, when it was blindingly obvious that the defendant was crippled by despair. Not guilt, despair . . . The Marquis had been around enough of both to be able to tell the difference.

Also interesting was that the dutiful daughter who now stood beside the defendant spent more time watching Ashraf Bey than she did looking at her father or the judges. And that for his part, the young Berber princeling worked hard to do the opposite. So far he hadn't looked at her once.

'The charge,' said St Cloud as he carefully put down his glass, 'is murder in the first degree, murder in the second degree and culpable homicide. The prosecution will bring a *representative* case for each of these charges. If all three charges are found, then a fourth charge will be considered to have been brought against you . . . That of a Section 3 crime against humanity . . .

'Under The Hague Convention you have a constitutional right to be represented. But I see that no law firm has been appointed.' The Frenchman made a show of consulting documents, if handwritten scrawls on cheap, lined paper could so be called. 'Do you wish me to appoint counsel?'

St Cloud took another slow sip from his glass. He'd first learnt of the trick as a young lawyer, watching an elderly judge in Marseilles. Every few minutes, the woman would stop to sip from a small glass of iced Evian. Rumour said the glass contained vodka but rumour lied. Water was all it ever was. The sipping existed to create natural breaks that let her words trickle into the bedrock of everyone's thought. Faced with inexorable evidence and enough silence, defendants had been known to change their pleas midtrial, without consulting their lawyers and to their lawyers' considerable horror. It had taken the Marquis months of watching the judge to work out how the old woman stage-managed it.

Of course, sometimes it didn't work.

'Very well then,' St Cloud said with a sigh. 'This court orders that a public defender be appointed by the city.'

'*No.*' It was the first word Hamzah Effendi had uttered since being led into the room, the first word from the man in two days. 'No attorney, no public defender.'

St Cloud shrugged. 'If that's what you want . . . Do you wish to apply for bail?' He looked at the silent man but it was Zara who answered.

'Yes,' she said defiantly. 'We do . . . I do. And I ask that my father be released on his own recognizance.'

'Completely impossible.' Senator Liz spoke without bothering to defer to the chair. On the other side of St Cloud, the young Graf nodded frantic agreement.

'Bail, even with a bond, would be unusual in a case like this,' St Cloud said softly. 'But it might be possible, if the bond is set high enough and you, personally, give your word not to attempt to help your father leave the city.'

Her word.

The Marquis smiled at the outrage on the face of the ushers and court stenographer; even Hamzah looked momentarily shocked.

'You have my word,' said Zara. 'Now how much do you want?'

'For myself,' said the Marquis, 'I want nothing.' She had the grace to blush, though her chin came up and she refused to look away. 'The sum is a matter for the court,' he added, 'though I suggest not less than . . .'

'No bail,' announced Raf from his seat to one side of the judges. He stood up slowly and stepped into the empty area between the judges and the dock, feeling very alone. Turning to Zara, he spread his hands in apology.

'I cannot allow bail,' he said flatly. 'And that decision is taken in my capacity as governor of this city.' He stared at St Cloud. 'You know as well as I do that if bail is granted, I cannot guarantee his safety . . .'

'In that case . . . Request for bail dismissed. All that remains,' said St Cloud, 'is for the court to set a date for trial. Since it seems the case *will,* after all, be tried in Iskandryia.' He smiled sweetly at the Senator. 'And since the defendant has refused counsel I would suggest to the other judges that we begin first thing tomorrow . . .'

'Too soon,' said Raf. 'Make it Saturday . . . Iskandryian airspace will need to be opened to fly in Jean René, the photographer who took the shots already seen by the Grand Jury.'

'Saturday it is.'

'No.' This time it was Zara who objected. 'That doesn't give my father time to find a character witness.'

'For a murder charge?' St Cloud scanned his handwritten notes. There was nothing about a character witness in there.

'One only,' Zara said. 'We're also in the process of trying to organize travel arrangements.'

'You have until Sunday,' St Cloud said firmly. 'After that, the trial takes place, whether you have your witness or not.' He glanced at Raf and frowned. 'And that decision is taken in my capacity as senior judge.'

CHAPTER 46

'Hani al-Mansur . . .' The child answered her mobile at the first ring, voice extra polite. 'Can I ask who's calling . . . ?'

Her Nokia was one of only a dozen let into El Iskandryia on special licence from the governor, who turned out to be the person on the other end of the call. She had to ask who it was because these cell phones were analogue, very stupid ones without the option of vision.

For some reason, Ashraf had been most insistent about the analogue bit.

Their conversation was short. 'Yes,' said Hani, 'Ifritah's fine. She's here with me and I'm really pleased to see her.'

She listened to Uncle Ashraf's next question and sucked her teeth, but not that crossly. 'Yes . . . I've had supper and I'm ready for bed. No, you don't need to collect me in the morning. Donna's going to the market. I'll walk in with her . . .'

At the next question, Hani groaned theatrically. 'Yes,' she said. 'You are fussing. That's your job.' She listened to Uncle Ashraf's good-nights, added her own and went back to the keyboard of the *bibliotheka*'s only working Web connection.

'I'm back,' she announced quietly.

'About time,' said Avatar.

He owed Raf a life. Hani hadn't needed to remind him of that but she did anyway . . . Then apologized. Only to decide that she didn't need to apologize because it was true. After that, she asked him some weird questions about whether Zara now wanted to marry Raf.

The rest of it Avatar didn't understand and Hani had given up trying to explain. He got the bit about him forwarding on the spider fax to Zara. Things imploded at the point when Hani added the spider fax to an angel and a wounded man and came up with the fact that hell was cold, purgatory was water-bound and he knew heaven better as the SS *Jannah*.

It was only the fact that Hani swore she'd been told this by the General that made Avatar believe any of it was true. So now, at Hani's insistence, he was looking for the ninth level of hell, otherwise known as *Cocytus*.

Needless to say, it wasn't on any of the numerous wall maps dotted around the corridors and stairways of the SS *Jannah* . . .

The rucksack slung on Avatar's shoulder was heavy and awkward. What was worse, it clanked every time he brushed against a wall, which was often. Those were its bad points. On the plus side, it contained rope, pepper spray and several cans of Coke.

'Guard.' Hani's voice in his earbead was matter-of-fact, unhurried.

'Yeah, seen him.' Avatar stepped backward into a recess, out of the guard's line of sight and out of his line of fire as well. There were two men, one in a suit, the other dressed in bell bottoms and white top, a black silk folded neatly around his muscular neck. Avatar knew this was a guard, not a crewman, by the gun he carried.

Dminus4 was off-limits to civilians; guests in the parlance of the SS *Jannah*. The official reason was that Dminus4 housed the vaults of Hong Kong Suisse, the liner's official bank. *Welcome Aboard*, the induction film for the SS *Jannah*, described the vault as made from weapons-grade steel with a single time-coded, iris-specific door and reassuringly thick walls. From what Hani had said, it was a perfectly ordinary floor-to-ceiling blockhouse with a boringly ordinary lock.

But then why not? Everything except gambling chips for the casino was included in the overall and frighteningly extortionate price; the only real valuables brought on board by guests, their papers and jewellery, were kept secure in individual safes that came with each cabin. The heistproof vault was a sop to tradition, only there by repute.

'Clear now.'

'Yeah.'

Avatar stepped out of his hiding place and checked both ways along the corridor. He was in plain sight of at least three CCTV cameras but those didn't worry him, everywhere on board was in sight of cameras. Nothing obvious, mind you. At least not on the guest levels. No little robot lenses to twist their heads as one walked from room to room. Most of the guest-level cameras used little pin lenses embedded into the walls and linked to some gizmo running visual-recognition software.

Quite how Hani had spliced herself in to them Avatar had no idea. Something to do with a handshake, according to the kid. And it was a clean connection, although there was a tiny time lag between them, defined not by the miles between SS *Jannah* and El Iskandryia but by how long it took to bounce data packets off a comsat slung somewhere over Sao Tomé.

'How long we got left?'

'About thirty minutes,' said Hani.

'There wasn't another battery?'

'Dead.' The kid's voice was resigned. So resigned that Avatar had trouble working out if Hani was seriously chilled or just having trouble getting her head round how bad things actually were.

When Hani had first called Avatar, she asked if he wanted her to fix a voice connection to Zara, so he could check what Hani said. He'd thought about it for all of a second and rejected the idea. He believed what she'd told him about how bad things were looking for his old man.

'There should be a door at the end of this corridor . . .'

'Locked,' said Avatar.

'How do you know?'

'I'm guessing.'

'Try it anyway.'

Sighing, Avatar crab-walked swiftly towards the heavy door, his back to the wall and the revolver he'd stolen from the Khedive's cabin held upright, combat style.

Avatar was doing his very best not to rush things but there was an ache behind his eyes and a hollow in his gut where his stomach should be. Since he regularly went a week on two kebabs and three lines of sulphate, the hollowness had to be fear rather than hunger. Not a good feeling.

The door wasn't just locked. Someone had welded it shut with a splatter gun. Cold drops of solder beading the edge of its frame like metal tears.

'They're coming back!' Hani's warning came seconds ahead of footsteps echoing along a corridor.

'Come on,' Hani said. 'Hide . . .'

Avatar shook his head, then realized the kid wouldn't pick up his gesture on her monitor. She'd be too busy watching the guards. 'Which way are they headed?'

'Towards the lifts,' said Hani, her voice tight.

'Good.' Avatar meant the comment for himself, but the kid picked it up anyway from one of the wall mics or something equally scary. Avatar's relationship with machines was confined to his mixing decks, and he liked those dumb and pliable.

'Avatar . . .'

'Yeah, okay, I can see them now.'

They were jiving between themselves, some joke about a v' Actor on the third deck. Their laughter was not cruel, just barbed, the armour that those who lack wear against those who have. Except that in this case *lack* was relative. The crew aboard the SS *Jannah* earned more in a month than Avatar scratched together in a year.

Pulling back the hammer on his borrowed Taurus, Avatar muffled the click it made by folding his fingers over the top. Then he pressed himself back flat against the corridor wall, putting a fat downpipe between himself and the approaching pair.

They did what Avatar expected them to do, which was head straight past, still deep in conversation.

Very gently, Avatar touched his revolver to the side of the guard's hair and watched irritation turn to fear, as the hand that flicked up to brush away whatever it was met the cold ceramic of Avatar's weapon.

'Make a noise,' growled Avatar, 'and say good-bye to your head.' The threat came out exactly as he'd imagined and Avatar felt unreasonably proud. It was, he hoped, exactly the kind of thing Raf might say.

'You . . .' The suit not suffering a gun to his head spun round and found himself face-to-face with a dreadlocked stowaway wearing a *God Speeds* T-shirt. It made the suit even more unhappy. 'You won't get . . .'

'I just did.' Avatar gestured towards the lift. 'That way,' he said, herding them towards a waiting Orvis. 'Now,' said Avatar when they were both safely inside, 'how do I reach the floors below this?'

At this level the lifts didn't thank you for travelling or hope you enjoyed the rest of your day, they were blind and dumb, with buttons that needed pushing. And the lowest level on the small array of buttons in front of him was Dminus4, this one.

'There isn't a floor below this,' the suit said through gritted teeth. 'This is as low as it gets . . . And how did you get aboard anyway?' His eyes took in Avatar's black combats, the T-shirt and the strands of black glitter threaded into his dreads. Nike sneakers completed the outfit.

The SS *Jannah* had no second- or third-class cabins. Come to that, it didn't even have first-class accommodation. Everything was executive or above, running all the way up to the Imperial Suite, where Mohammed Tewfik Pasha, Khedive of what remained of El Iskandryia, currently occupied the whole seventh floor. No more than two hundred guests were ever on board at any one time. And it was the ship's proud boast that guests were outnumbered three to one by hotel staff. That was before one even considered whatever crew were actually needed to run the ship.

'The floor below this,' Avatar said crossly. 'How do I get to it?'

The two crew members looked at each other, and the suit raised his eyes to heaven. 'Look, kid,' he said, 'there isn't . . .'

Avatar shot him through the leg, just above the knee. By the time the slug exited the man's quadriceps and flattened itself against the steel wall of the lift, the suit's lungs were dragging in mountains of air.

'Don't even think about screaming,' Avatar advised him. 'Now, let's try again, how do I . . . ?'

'Okay, okay . . .' The unharmed guard had one hand out, as if to ward off bullets from the gun Avatar began to raise. 'So far as I know,' he said slowly, 'this is the ship's lowest level. Everything else below this is buoyancy tanks, turbines or ballast.'

'What about servicing the engines?'

'It's a self-functioning sealed unit. Right . . . ?' He glanced to the man on the floor for confirmation. 'It's sealed.'

'There must be hatches.'

'Yes and no,' said the guard nervously. 'They're welded shut.'

'Too bad.' Avatar looked at the puddle of red spreading itself across the lift's grey floor and pointed his gun at the injured suit's other leg.

'It's true, I promise you . . .' The man nodded like a frantic puppet, as if his frenzy alone could convince Avatar. 'There is no way down . . .'

'Find me one,' Avatar demanded, but he was talking to Hani.

CHAPTER 47

28th October

'I shouldn't . . .'

'Yeah, so you keep saying,' said Raf. 'You shouldn't be here, you shouldn't have done that . . .' He was grinning like an idiot, he couldn't help it. Beside him, Zara lay curled tight, with one of her arms thrown across his stomach and tiny beads of sweat tangled in her short dark hair, at the point where it brushed back from her forehead. Quick breaths flexed the cage of her ribs.

'You okay?'

'What do you think?' Zara untangled her legs from his and rolled away. This time round she didn't bother to pull up a sheet, merely sprawled on Raf's bed with one arm up over her grey eyes, revealing dark-tipped breasts that were high and perfect and honey-sweet in the early daylight that crept through the windows from the garden outside.

'Do you think they heard?'

Raf listened to the crunch of heels on gravel below, the unmistakable squeal of boots as a soldier executed a perfect about-turn at the end of the path, swivelling on the spot.

'I would imagine so,' he said, straight-faced, only to shake his head when Zara sat up and stared across, eyes wide.

He'd done only what she allowed. 'Which was more than Zara intended and less than he wanted. She was working to rules, though even Zara wasn't quite sure whose rules those were.

'How about you,' she asked. 'You okay?'

'Sure.' Raf shrugged. 'I'm fine.'

'Right.' Her smile was lopsided. 'Of course you are.' Zara yanked back his covers. 'Anyone can see that.'

Somewhere in the hinterland between midnight and early morning, as the stubborn darkness finally diluted, Raf had first struggled out of his shirt and then his pants, stripping himself bare. Neither of them had

512

suggested Zara might want to do the same. But his hands had caressed her beneath her nightdress and finally found answering movement from her body. Movement that built slowly until she took his hand and almost pushed it into her pants.

'Stand over there,' said Zara, and pointed to a patch of sun that lit the room's white floor. So Raf did what she asked, aware that she watched as he climbed naked out of the bed and walked across the tiles. When he stood where she wanted, he turned to face her and saw her blush.

'Now what . . . ?'

She knelt with marble tiles cold and hard against her bare knees. There were a dozen good reasons why she shouldn't be kneeling there. Some personal, some cultural, a few of them even political.

'What?' Raf asked, seeing her shoulders shrug.

'Nothing,' said Zara and then could say no more. She felt his hips tense under her grip and heard him begin to swear softly as his back arched and every muscle in his legs seemed to lock.

She was a republican and Marxist, he was an Ottoman bey. She was new money and he was wealth inherited. No, she scrubbed that, Raf had little money, either way. He was police and her father was a criminal. Iskandryia's establishment had adopted him and that too made him her enemy. Her father was on trial and he controlled the court. If it was in her power, she would overthrow everything he represented and the order to which he belonged.

And here she was on her knees before a man, something she'd promised herself would never happen. It didn't matter if it was sex, money, violence or necessity that put a woman there; once there the weight of history made it hard to get back up again.

Zara could feel Raf's fingers hard on the side of her head, so she took her right hand and wrapped it round him and moved her mouth in time to his need.

And later, with his taste still in her mouth, she led Raf back to the bed and sat beside him while he curled into a foetal ball and slept like the child she guessed he'd never been.

It was impossible that he knew how much she loved him, how much his vulnerability made her afraid.

CHAPTER 48

Avatar wasn't sure what he'd expected. Maybe a whole deck given over to the Colonel's quarters. PaxForce guards doubling as prison officers. Certainly daylight-perfect lighting tied to a season-specific twenty-four/ seven clock, some trees, birdsong and an artificial stream; even the most basic clubs had those these days. At least they did in the circadian/chill-out zones.

And if not warders, then exile in splendid isolation. Imposing state-rooms run to seed and ruin. Once fabulous tapestries grimed with dust. Avatar imagined it like something from a newsfeed novella. *Golden Youth, In Place of Trust, Forbidden Fortune* . . . Somewhere suited to murderous fathers, flirtatious mothers, drug-addled uncles and teenage schemers who usually wanted either their parents or siblings dead, if not both.

He didn't think of Hamzah like this. Hamzah was a villain, not pure but pretty simple, and his money wasn't knotted up in trusts and he had only one heir, Zara.

Avatar had no illusions about that. No real problems with it either.

All the same, he'd been expecting more from the Colonel's lair. Actually, even that wasn't accurate, he hadn't so much been expecting more as been expecting *something*. Something other than a vast hangar-like emptiness, filled with acrid dust and lit by distant portholes that lined the gloom on either side of him, like tiny holes punched out into the real world.

His feet left tracks on the carpet in dust that was undisturbed by any other sign of human passage. Just because something made no sense didn't make it untrue, however; Avatar knew that. Knew too that he needed to find a way down to the deck below, where there would be no portholes at all, unless the liner had a level designed to look out underwater. Which was possible.

'Lights . . .'

The futile command echoed back from steel walls, making him feel more alone than ever. Avatar's problem was that silence irritated him and always had done. It scared him, if he was being honest. From the grinding of gears in the narrow street outside his children's home and the jewels of music heard through other people's windows to the hammering of water pipes each night in the dorm, noise had been his comfort from the start.

'Fuck it all . . .' Avatar pulled a twist of paper from his pocket and crunched the crystals. He'd have snorted the pinch, like snuff, but his nostrils were still recovering from a batch of ice that had given him twenty-four hours' worth of paranoia and a week of nosebleeds.

The sulphate tasted sour as vomit but it did its job. Melting into his saliva and sending shivers down his neck. Life improved in a rush.

'Hani?'

There was no answer. But then there'd been no answer last time he asked either, or the time before that. No answer, no sounds . . . Put him down in any back street in the city and, chances were, he could navigate his way to a café in Shatby blindfolded, just by listening to the noise from different souks and the rattle of trams.

Here there was only the engine's slow heartbeat beneath his feet, which he felt rather than heard, like being in the belly of a whale. This was more Raf's territory than his, Avatar decided as he took another few crystals, just to be safe. That was the obvious difference between them. The only dark Avatar liked came wrapped up with neon, sound systems and strobes. For the rest, he'd take daylight and warmth every time . . .

Moving through the cold aquarium gloom, Avatar made for a distant strip of colour that turned out, minutes later, to be one long, elaborate, stained-glass window spanning the whole width of the liner's stern. On it, heroic miners swung glass pickaxes at coal seams of purple glass, fishermen pulled elaborate nets loaded with cod from dark glass waves, and a plump girl with blonde hair and impossibly blue eyes stood dead centre with a glass sun behind her, a sickle at her bare feet and a sheaf of wheat held proudly above her head. She looked as warm and happy as Avatar was cold and miserable.

Beneath the wide window, an ornate sweep of double stairs led into even deeper gloom below, looking as if it had been ripped from a New York hotel – brass stair-rods and all – and bolted between decks. A long Art Nouveau rail, verdigrised with age and missing an occasional banister, had been fixed around the edge of the drop to protect

Avatar and the ghosts of passengers long dead from falling to the deck below.

Beyond the dim pool of light at the foot of the stairs stretched icy blackness, growing colder and more inklike the further in Avatar went. He already knew, from having walked the full length of the deck overhead, that the gloom extended for more than a kilometre in front of him. Somewhere in the emptiness would be a door leading down to a level below this. All Avatar had to do was find the right door.

Whether the door Avatar found was right or not was hard to guess. True enough, it opened and had stairs leading down. Those were both plus points. Unfortunately it was also two hundred paces after where Hani had told him it should be and on the wrong side of the ship. Avatar was still worrying about these discrepancies when he came out onto the deck below and stumbled upon his first freezer pipe, promptly tripping over it.

'Oh f—' Picking himself off carpet tiles so chilled their nap was brittle with ice, Avatar let his long low variation on the theme of *fuck* segue slowly into silence.

Not his day.

Having adjusted the rucksack on his shoulder, he headed on, moving towards a point in the far distance that might as well have been hidden behind his eyes for all Avatar could really see it. And a hundred or so paces later, he tripped over his second pipe.

Fucking . . .

Echoes of swearing gave way to silence and an awareness that both shins now hurt so badly he was moving beyond the ability to curse. Tentatively, Avatar wrapped one hand around his ankle, half from gut instinct/half to check for real damage and felt warmth ooze from beneath frozen skin. Somehow, finding blood returned his ability to swear.

'You could always try turning on the lights,' said a voice behind him.

Ankle bleeding or not, Avatar spun on the spot and flipped his gun to firing position, thumb already ratcheting back its hammer. The only thing that stopped Avatar from doing what he intended, which was ram the barrel into the gut of whoever stood directly behind, was that no one stood directly behind. The darkness was empty.

'To your left,' said the voice. 'Over near the wall . . . Follow the pipe until you hit a pillar. The control is on the nearest side . . . Oh,' it sounded darkly amused, 'and try not to trip over anything else.'

The switch was where the voice said it would be. A simple square of cracked white plastic that, once clicked, lit a single bank of strips from one side of the low ceiling to the other, leaving Avatar standing in a dimly lit hold. At his feet, a frosted pipe vanished through the floor.

There was a new pipe every hundred paces or so, rising out of the deck on one side of the hangarlike space, crossing the floor and disappearing again. Most of the pipes were frosted for their entire length with ice.

'It was cheap,' said the voice. 'From a decommissioned power station outside Helsinki. You're probably wondering why the Soviets didn't use something better suited.'

Avatar wasn't. He could honestly say the question had never occurred to him.

'Inefficiency. Plus they had to take what they could get at the time. That's a good maxim for politics, you know. Take what you can. Let free what you can't . . .'

'Sounds like shit to me, man,' said Avatar.

'Oh.' The voice sounded puzzled, the puzzlement breeding a long pause that left Avatar time to look round the hold. And Avatar remained there, hung inside that pause, until he grew bored with waiting and decided to demand a few answers of his own. Get the basics, Raf had once said. Most people didn't, but then, as Raf pointed out, most people were dead.

'Where am I?'

'Where . . . ?'

'Yes,' said Avatar. 'That's what I said. Where am I, exactly . . . ?'

The voice thought about that. 'You're on Dminus7, a third of the way into krill processing. Well, what used to be processing before the partitions were bulldozed and the vats dismantled.'

'Right,' Avatar said flatly, 'and where are you?'

'Exactly?'

'Yeah, exactly.'

'I'm exactly close enough to make contact.'

Avatar smiled, despite himself and in spite of air so cold that it leached heat from his arms and dragged the questions from his mouth in wisps of smoke.

'You can do better than that.'

'And if I can't?'

'I'll leave you facedown with a bullet through the back of your head.'

'You're not Ka, are you?'

'No,' Avatar said slowly. 'You can safely assume I'm not Ka.'

'But you are armed?'

'Oh yes.' Avatar waved his borrowed Taurus in the air, so whichever camera was watching through the gloom could get a clear view. 'That's me. Always ready. Armed to the teeth.'

'Good,' said the voice. 'Though personally I'd recommend an

HK/cw, double-loaded with kinetics and 20mm fatboys, explosive and airburst.'

Silence.

'Looks like a pig and weighs like one too,' added the voice. 'Heckler & Koch, plastic and ceramic job. Kill anything. Really useful if you're an amateur.'

'If I'm an . . .' Avatar snapped off a shot in the direction of the insult, then ducked as sound waves swamped the low hold, deafening him.

'Are you sure you're not Ka?' The voice sounded amused.

'No,' said Avatar. 'I'm, um, Kamil ben-Hamzah . . . More famous as DJ Avatar,' he added quickly, refusing to compromise totally.

'Kamil . . . eh? Tell me, not-Ka, why exactly are you here?'

'To claim a debt.' That seemed to be the only way to put it.

'You mean to kill me?'

Avatar took a deep breath. Every hour since Hani first called him up he'd spent riffing this moment. He'd done what a lifetime of street smarts suggested he do, which was introduce himself. Only now Avatar couldn't remember in which order he was supposed to make his points.

'My father's on trial . . .'

No, Avatar shook his head, that wasn't where he was meant to start.

'My name is Kamil. My father's name is Hamzah Quitrimala. I've come to . . .'

'How old are you?' demanded the voice.

'Old enough,' said Avatar.

'I had tank commanders younger than that.' The voice sounded almost regretful, as if the man speaking wished Avatar was less than his fourteen years. 'Hell, by your age most of my tank commanders . . .'

'Were dead.' Relief cascaded over the boy as he realized that he'd done it right and found the Colonel; but all he said was, 'Yeah, I heard.'

If silence could have shrugged, it did.

'Everybody dies,' said the Colonel. 'Well, almost everybody.'

'You're alive . . .'

'And so, it seems, is little Ka.'

'*Ka?*'

'Kamil. The boy who hated war so much he gunned down everyone who wanted to take part, including the whole of his own platoon, if you believe the reports. And officially I always make a point of believing official reports . . .'

'He actually killed all those people?'

Avatar lowered his revolver and shook off his rucksack. He felt sick, sick and empty, like someone had ripped open his stomach and taken his guts when he wasn't looking. 'I thought you were meant to be Dad's alibi . . .'

'I think,' said Colonel Abad carefully, 'you'll find I'm meant to tell the truth.'

'You'll do it?' Avatar sounded shocked. 'You'll stand up in court?'

The way Hani explained it, the SS *Jannah* functioned as an autonomous micronation. That was, so long as the liner stayed within international waters it ran to its own laws. So why would someone like Colonel Abad put himself in danger by offering to come ashore?

'You thought you'd have to kidnap me?' The Colonel's voice was sour. 'No chance. This is my Elba. You remember Napoleon needing to be forced off that island at gunpoint?'

Avatar didn't remember anything about Napoleon at all. Zara was the one with the expensive education.

'You'll find me on Dminus9, right at the bottom of the pit. You do know that the last and deepest circle of hell is ice-cold, don't you? In the fourth round, *Judecca*. And the ninth circle, *Cocytus*. That's the problem with being captured by someone with a classical education. They want to get all clever on your arse.'

As there wasn't an answer to that, Avatar turned his attention to reaching the far end of the hangar, though now the Taurus was heavy in his combats pocket and most of his attention went on not tripping over the trip-wire pipes.

'How do I get through this?' Avatar asked, when he hit a steel wall thrown across the point of the liner. In it was a door, also steel, with three heavy, old-fashioned locks. Since this was the first door he'd seen on the entire level, apart from the one he'd used to get in, Avatar figured it had to be right.

'Try opening it . . .'

Avatar did, and the heavy door swung open in a cascade of metal dandruff as its hinges creaked and popped fat flakes of rust. A twist of riveted steps fed down to the coldness below he and then kept on going to the level below that, bypassing the turbine rooms.

Old-fashioned switches waited for Avatar at every landing but the bulkhead lights were empty of bulbs, so he felt his way through the darkness, until the fingers following the icy rail ceased to be his and vanished into a dull ache.

The deeper Avatar went, the colder it became until every inward breath froze in his throat or plated the inside of his nostrils and every outward breath condensed at his lips. The cold had a physicality that was new to him. And with the cold came a tiredness and the need for sleep.

Heat he'd lived with all his life. It arrived with late spring, sometimes earlier if a *khamsin* hit, with its fifty days of hot dry wind, and trickled away into the end of autumn. With it came catlike lassitude and pointless quarrels. But this was more than heat's opposite. Every twist of stair Avatar descended took him further inside himself, folding him into lethargy.

'What's the temperature?' Avatar demanded.

'Cold,' said the voice. 'Cold enough to shut down your core.'

'And you live in this?'

'It makes no difference to me,' the voice said. 'And Saeed Koenig wanted to discourage sightseers.'

His teeth chattered uncontrollably and his feet were a memory beyond feeling. The black T-shirt and combats he'd put on that morning now seemed less of a fashion statement and more of an absentmindedly written suicide note.

'Where now?' Avatar asked, knowing he'd been followed on camera every step of his descent.

'Straight ahead. Use the door . . .'

Still cursing the lack of a flashlight, Avatar inched through the darkness until his outstretched hand found a handle, low down and on the right. He gripped it tight with shaking fingers and everything started to go wrong. Disbelief giving way to panic as he tried to yank free his hand and heard skin rip. What panicked Avatar wasn't pain but its complete absence.

He was frozen fast to a subzero metal door handle.

'Piss on it' said the Colonel.

Avatar ignored the comment and tugged again.

'Piss on it,' Colonel Abad ordered crossly, his voice echoing from two places at once. 'Go on. Do it now.'

The man meant it, Avatar realized. Using his good hand, Avatar fumbled at the nylon zip of his combats.

'Now piss on the other hand. Get some warmth into those bones.'

Avatar did as Colonel Abad ordered, fastened his fly and stepped through to the Colonel's quarters, fingers still dripping. He didn't imagine the Colonel would want to shake hands.

The room was in darkness.

'Lights,' said the Colonel, and a strip lit overhead. What it revealed was an empty space like all the others Avatar had passed through; just smaller, narrower and less high. The walls, which curved on both sides, were blasted back to bare steel and riveted plate. Obviously enough, there were no portholes. Also no furniture, apart from a low metal table, and no cooking equipment. No sign of human habitation and no Colonel.

As jokes went, it was a bad one.

'How are your fingers?' asked a voice behind him. 'I've just checked my libraries and you may need a skin graft, when we get ashore . . . *If we get ashore*,' the voice amended, as if suddenly concerned not to push the bounds of accuracy.

Avatar looked round until he spotted a speaker, attached to the ceiling over in the corner of the room. It was so out-of-date that its grille was cloth, set into a case that looked like it might actually be wood. Soviet-made, from the look of things. 'Where are you?'

'I'm the housekeeping routine on the table.'

'You're what?' Avatar looked across to see a small radio wired into a feed socket on the wall. At first glance the radio looked to be covered with grey suede, but that was just dust fallen from the ceiling or carried in through a ventilation duct on the Arctic wind. Beside it, by themselves, stood an ugly-looking pair of spectacles.

'Yeah,' said the Colonel, 'that's me.' A CCTV camera on the wall swung slowly between Avatar and the table. It looked like nothing so much as a duck shaking its head. 'Not what you expected, huh?'

Avatar shook his head in turn. 'No, it's not.' All the same, he felt he needed to clarify the position. 'You're my dad's boss? Colonel Abad?'

' *"But in the Greek tongue hath his name Apollyon. That is, destroyer. Angel of the abyss, he that brings God's woes upon his enemies . . ."*

'Revelation,' added the voice, when Avatar looked blank. 'I'm either the true angel of God or his deadly enemy. Unfortunately, no one can decide which, though theologians once wasted a lot of time trying.' The Colonel's tone made clear what he thought of that.

Revelation? That was the *nasrani* political endgame, at least Avatar thought it was. He wasn't big on politics. 'You believe this stuff . . .'

'What do you think?'

He thought not.

'Either it was a geek joke,' explained the Colonel, 'or they needed to find a framework in a hurry . . . Lash-ups are always easier than starring from scratch, take a look at religion or computer games. My guess is the shapers fed in a couple of terabytes of world myth plus Jung. It didn't worry them if the deep background was suboptimal. I was only there for the duration of the war. And that was only meant to last a few months.'

'I'm dying of cold,' said Avatar, 'and you're talking shit . . .'

CHAPTER 49

Mohammed Tewfik Pasha, Khedive of El Iskandryia, rolled over in his huge water bed and opened one eye at the sound of knocking. The bed in which he woke was larger than king-sized, obviously enough, since this was the Imperial Suite.

It was also empty apart from him, and that choice was his. He'd seen how he was watched by the daughters of other guests, their eyes tracking him as he walked down the ornate stairs into the dining room to take his place at the captain's table. And he knew too that the Van der Bilt girl had dined alone in her cabin every night until he'd taken to eating his supper in public.

El Iskandryia was widely expected to lose its status as a free city. And the shallow end of the gene pool was preparing itself for the Khedive's new role as romantic but tragic hero (with looks, money and title).

His face was on that week's *Time*, but for all the wrong reasons. *Cosmo Girl* had even produced a poster showing him in shorts and T-shirt, standing barefoot on the deck of a yacht and staring moodily out to sea, or so he'd read. He'd never actually seen the poster and couldn't remember having been allowed to go barefoot anywhere. Just getting permission from the General to appear out of uniform usually took a tantrum.

Any one of the young mothers who promenaded their children through the upper deck's Palm Garden each morning would go to bed with him. He'd had sly smiles, batted eyelashes, even a handwritten note folded and slipped into his trouser pocket by a mother of twins. Then there was that Australian woman, her smile anything but innocent, asking him how many slaves he had in his harem . . . And would he like one more?

Yet the only girl he wanted, the one he'd actually invited, had sent her bastard half brother instead.

'*Rotate.*' Across the suite on a white ash sideboard (so retro-Cunard), a silver photo frame started to flick from picture to picture. It showed what the Khedive's guests expected it to show. The General and Tewfik Pasha standing together in the throne room. Tewfik Pasha silhouetted against the sun in the luxuriant green of the General's garden. A winter sunset over the Corniche. And, as a default setting, elegant hand-drawn calligraphy showing the name of God.

They were all an irrelevance . . . Except for the name of God, obviously. The Khedive's correction was heartfelt and instant, but all the same he felt sick at the thought of his unintended blasphemy And yet, the fact remained that the only picture that really mattered to him was a tattered clipping, tucked away in the back of his wallet.

It was taken in the early dawn outside an illegal cellar club and showed Zara naked except for a tight faux-fur coat. The grainy shadow between her half-seen breasts bothered him more than any of the pink Renoir nudes so carefully collected by his grandfather and great-grandfather.

'*Your Highness* . . .'

He'd forgotten about the earlier knock at his bedroom door.

'Yes,' said the Khedive and watched a heavy door swing open to reveal the captain, looking every inch the master of the world's largest seagoing liner. One thick and three lesser rings circled the cuffs of Captain Bruford's immaculate jacket. Her trousers had razor-sharp creases at the front and a heavy gold stripe down each outer seam. She seemed slightly embarrassed to see the Khedive, which puzzled Tewfik Pasha until he realized it might be because he was wearing nothing, at least nothing visible.

'Can I help you?'

'Yes, sir.' With an effort, Captain Bruford shook her gaze from the half-naked boy. 'You know we pride ourselves on how seriously we take the safety of our important guests. All our guests,' she corrected herself.

The Khedive nodded. It seemed unlikely that she'd come up to the Imperial Suite to make a mission statement on behalf of her company, much less discuss its core values or whatever buzzword best described the clichés he'd already heard on the induction film. All the same, the captain seemed to be having trouble coming to the point.

'*Yes?*'

'Helicopter . . .'

He looked at her in blank amazement.

'On the edge of our systems,' she said. 'Approaching the SS *Jannah.*'

'And that's a problem?' Guests came and went by helicopter all the time: that was the whole point of being aboard the SS *Jannah*; it never docked, anywhere, ever. The only time it left international waters, and that time was covered by special treaty, was when the liner passed through the Panama Canal or the Pillars of Hercules.

'They're shielded,' said Captain Bruford. 'And we can't get a handshake. Believe me, we've tried.' The Englishwoman looked something between irritated and anxious.

'I think it would be safer,' she added, 'if we were to get Your Highness off the ship. We have three high-speed VSVs available, Thornycroft-built and with submersible capacities . . .'

She just couldn't help it, the Khedive realized. Every statement she made about Utopia Lines came out sounding like an advertisement. It had to be something the company burned into their brains at training school.

'You think I'd be safer aboard the VSV?'

'No.' The captain looked at him, her mind already made up. 'I think everybody else would be safer. My chief of security has spent the last ten minutes running a risk analysis and you're the obvious target.'

Tewfik Pasha nodded. In all probability that was true.

Climbing out of bed without thinking about how that might appear to his visitor, he collected a towel from the back of a chair, only to drop it on the tiles when he reached the cubicle.

One month each year was what he got. Time off for good behaviour, that was how he thought of the SS *Jannah*. One month away from lessons, from his staff, from protocol, from the General . . .

Four weeks in which he could do what he wanted. Sleep, eat, watch old Beat Takahashi vids, if that was what took his fancy. And then it was back to the uniforms, to living in a goldfish bowl, to being immensely rich but having no money. He owned palaces and slept for eleven months of the year in a small room without either air-conditioning or heating. A room where the basin ran only cold water and his antique Chinese carpet was worn to the thinness of tapestry, its holes and stains covered by a rug, thrown down in the strategic place. Living like that was supposed to teach him humility.

Tewfik Pasha wasn't an idiot. He wasn't even a child. He knew there were whole districts of his city that had no water for drinking, washing or anything else, *arrondissements* where houses had no glass in the windows and sewage ran untreated in the gutters, alleys where raggeds slept at night, curled against walls or under benches, hiding from the police or their families, or from both – violence came in many guises.

Ten years back, when he was small, death squads had cleared the streets of raggeds and kinder whores, dumping childish bodies by the truckload into the weed-heavy waters of Lake Mareotis . . . As July had slid into August and the temperatures soared and foreign film crews began to descend on the city, the entourage around the young Khedive spoke of little else. Normal gossip ceased, as did backbiting and the daily jostle for position. A horrified fascination took hold of the palace, from which the Khedive had to be protected.

Rooms stilled when he walked into them, conversations died, no one would talk if he was there. Which made it twice as hard to work out exactly what was going on. It was weeks before he discovered that the rubbish being removed from the souks and alleys was human.

Almost everyone the Khedive overheard approved of what was being done. So much so that in the kitchens and sculleries, hardworking porters cursed each other for not having had the idea first.

The one person not impressed was Koenig Pasha.

With the arrival of autumn came the executions. An army major, two detective sergeants, a colonel in the *morales* and a uniformed police officer. After that, the street cleaning stopped and the only thing left to drive raggeds from their narrow alleys was that winter's lashing rain.

Shaking water from his long dark hair, Tewfik Pasha stepped out of his shower and blinked, surprised to find Captain Bruford waiting impatiently in the doorway to his bedroom. He hadn't actually asked the woman in, Tewfik Pasha remembered with a sigh. Unidentified helicopter or no, punctilious courtesy had kept the Utopia Line's captain where she stood.

'Come in,' he suggested and turned away to slip his arms through the sleeves of a dressing gown. 'Can I offer you coffee?'
His sudden smile dazzled Captain Bruford so much that she accepted, without stopping to remember that it was almost noon and her own breakfast had been eaten hours before. Coffee and toast, served on the bridge; which was what a few of her older officers still called the computer room.

'That helicopter . . .'

The Khedive handed her coffee in a bone-china cup with matching saucer. Both items featured a discreet Utopia Lines logo. 'Do you want me to order some croissant?'

She refused the croissant, only too aware that eyes of darkest brown watched her from a face that was perfectly symmetrical, perfectly proportioned . . . just perfect really.

Captain Bruford shook her head and glanced back to find the eyes still watching her. 'The VSV,' she said. 'You really . . .'

'I am afraid I can't.' The Khedive's shrug was apologetic. Almost as apologetic as his voice. 'You see,' he said as he spread both hands to indicate his helplessness, 'I can't be seen to run away.'

'But the other passengers . . .'

'You have an onboard defence system,' said the Khedive. He nodded to a complimentary notebook resting on his bedside table. It was that year's Toshiba, an update of the model with the lizardskin cover and silver corners. In it was everything a guest might want to know about the SS *Jannah*.

'Somewhere in the small print,' said the Khedive, 'it mentions that you carry ship-to-air defences. However, my own intelligence digests confirm that you have functioning PCB.'

'We've got what?' The captain's voice was hollow.

'Lightning throwers, three of them, LockMart-made, second-generation.' The boy wriggled the fingers of one hand. 'I've got some too. They look like black metal spiders.'

'Like . . .' Captain Bruford halted.

'If they attack you,' said the Khedive, 'attack back. If they don't, then let them land on the 'copter deck. If there's a problem, I and my bodyguards will deal with it.'

'Bodyguards?'

'Well, bodyguard,' the Khedive admitted. 'Sort of . . .'

'And where is this bodyguard?' asked the captain, still cross at being blackmailed over the particle beam weapons. It was blackmail, because PCBs were illegal under an antiproliferation treaty signed eighteen months earlier. Added to which, bodyguards were strictly forbidden aboard the SS *Jannah*. That was condition one of being accepted aboard.

'Where's Avatar?' The Khedive glanced round his suite and then at the sunlit balcony beyond. 'Now there's a question.' Dropping his silk dressing gown to the floor, Tewfik Pasha hunted for some trousers. 'To be honest, I haven't a clue . . .'

He was still looking for something to wear when Captain Bruford let herself out. In total, she'd been, in his suite for less than ten minutes. And he was, she told herself, irritating, difficult and overprivileged even by the standards of guests on the SS *Jannah*. He was also undeniably beautiful, with a charisma that made Hollywood replicas look shallow and contrived.

She considered briefly the possibility that he really was the General's lover. And then her watch chimed and she took the first available Orvis, overriding its programming so that it took her straight down to the ops room. She might be the captain, but this was a civilized ship and she didn't want to keep her chief of security waiting any longer than was necessary.

CHAPTER 50

Café Le Trianon was closed. That meant the private lift that went straight up to the floor above and the offices of the Third Circle was out of action. And that meant Hani had to use the stairs from Boulevard Saad Zaghloul. She didn't mind; in fact, things were much quieter in the HQ of Iskandryia's civil service now that the lift and the telephones had stopped working.

Unfortunately, people still kept interrupting her.

Hani hit a hot key and her list of satellites vanished. Although the subroutine that was supposed to be making contact with Avatar kept running in the background, without success.

'Hani. What are you doing here?'

Ingrid Nordstrom saw the young girl's face freeze and stepped back, forcing a smile.

Life at the Third Circle had been difficult these last few days. There was no real work for her to give the staff when they came in, but equally no one had given Ingrid permission to let them stay away.

She sighed.

None of this was the child's fault and actually Ingrid liked Hani. Much more than she usually liked children, or most other adults, come to that. The bey's young niece was the politest child Ingrid had ever met and the quietest. And if not for the child's obsession with computers, no one would have noticed she was here at all: but with just two machines working in the whole office, it was inconvenient if Lady Hani decided to monopolize one of them.

'I'm halfway through a story,' said Hani. 'I'm good at stories.'

She was too.

Raf thought she was with Khartoum, who thought she was at the madersa with Donna. And Donna thought she was shopping with Zara.

Whereas, in fact, she'd walked from Shallalat Gardens to Le Trianon by herself. Later she'd say sorry, if she got found out, but at the moment things were much too critical to explain.

'It's a fairy story,' said Hani, 'sort of . . .'

'What's it about?'

Hani's face creased in concentration, one finger hammering at the *Pg Up* key until she found the passage she wanted.

'And lo as dusk fell over the stony desert, a son of Lilith came out of the night wrapped in a mantle of darkness. Across his chest he wore a necklace of human teeth and in his hand he carried a staff carved from the wing-bone of a djinn . . .'

Out of the corner of her eye Hani could see the woman frown so she skipped down a few paragraphs.

'. . . and when the sun rose over the rose-hued walls of Al Qahirah, the son of Lilith hid in the shadow of a house and wrapped darkness tight around his thin body. And this day passed as days always pass, slowly for those who labour and more swiftly for those to whom life is joy.

'Women came with water jugs to the standpipe as did a slave leading a thirsty donkey. For though Needle Alley was too narrow for a camel to pass, the donkey was thin and the carpets it carried were loaded on its back rather than in panniers as we do now . . .'

Hani stopped. 'There's more,' she said politely. 'If you'd like me to read it.'

Ingrid Nordstrom shook her head. 'I need to go.' She seemed about to say something else but hesitated on the edge of speaking.

It would be about the son of Lilith, Hani imagined. Most of the people Hani had talked to about this, which admittedly was very few, were unsettled by the idea of djinn and vampyres. 'This vampyre's good,' explained Hani, her voice firm. 'You do get good ones . . .'

The woman looked surprised.

'It's true,' Hani insisted. 'I've checked it in a book. If a son of Lilith survives seven years undetected, he can travel to a land where a different language is spoken and become human. He can even marry and have children. Although,' Hani paused and her face grew serious, 'the children will still be sons and daughters of Lilith.'

'How fascinating.'

'And I won't be much longer,' Hani promised. 'As soon as I've finished here I'm going to the library.'

'Take your time,' said Madame Ingrid, and was surprised to discover that she meant it. Hani had become such a regular at the Third Circle it was hard to remember she was there on sufferance . . . That was what the bey had said the first time he brought her in, on sufferance. Ingrid wasn't to let Hani become a problem.

He'd been staring at Hani when he said it.

Ingrid decided to leave the child to her story. These were difficult times for everyone. And getting more difficult. She just hoped the bey wasn't being too strict with the girl.

CHAPTER 51

A window opened in the air in front of Avatar: a sleek black 'copter, blades chopping to a deep bass beat, smoked-glass windscreen and not a decal in sight to say where it came from or who might be inside.

'Floating focus,' said the Colonel. He was talking about the spectacles.

'And the 'copter . . . ?'

'Mi-24x Hind gunship, adapted for three 20mm cannon with Hellmouth, Rattlesnake and Quickdraw rockets – $189.3 million, plus $1.6m per missile. Old model.'

'No,' Avatar said crossly. 'I mean, who does it belong to?'

'No idea,' said Colonel Abad. 'It won't tell me. Didn't want to tell me its model number or price range until I told it you were in the market to buy one. Then the imprinted sales coding took over, always does . . .'

Avatar looked at the tiny machine that floated in front of his eyes. Watching as toy-sized doors blew back and even smaller figures tumbled out, guns ready. Somewhere just above his hearing, sirens wailed and a gun spat, distant as the echo of yesterday's firecrackers. The black-suited figures were firing over the heads of an unseen crowd.

'I'm in trouble, aren't I?'

The Colonel thought about this for a split second. 'As much as you want and more.' His voice was apologetic. 'It was the hidden door,' he explained. 'Not an original idea but effective. One of the Medicis did something similar at the Pitti Palace. Of course, the difference is, this one had a silent alarm.'

Even Hani had been impressed. Solder shut every normal door on level Dminus4, then leave an exit through the back wall of a strong room. The safe's entrance had featured antique defences: tear gas between inner and outer layers, tasers positioned down both sides of the frame, all the stuff that putting a gun to the wounded suit's head had miraculously disabled. But the trapdoor at the back, that had tripped an alarm satellite in low-earth orbit. And half the intelligence agencies in Europe were busy going ape-shit . . .

It looked like one of them had arrived.

Climbing the first twist of stairs was easy. More so since Colonel Abad showed Avatar how to adjust the spectacles to infrared. The cold the Colonel could do nothing about, except get Avatar back to the warmth of an upper deck as soon as possible. Although, at Colonel Abad's suggestion, Avatar did empty his rucksack of its handcuffs, pepper gas and rope, and slice a hole in the bottom and another on either side, then invert the bag to wear as a tunic.

'Protect your core temperature,' the Colonel advised him, 'if you want to stop your brain from shutting down.' Avatar was slightly surprised to learn his brain could shut down, but he did what Colonel Abad suggested, mainly because he'd been doing pretty much everything the Colonel said since it first suggested he turn on those lights.

'You're manipulating me,' Avatar said, stopping dead at the thought.

'That's my job.' The familiar bearded figure smiled sadly, having first popped into floating focus. 'Only in the specifications it's called functional motivation.' With an apologetic shrug, Colonel Abad vanished and Avatar was left staring at riveted steps lit by a dull red gloom.

His skull ached as if someone had nail-gunned a metal band around his head and the only proof Avatar had that his hands were still attached to his wrists was that he could see one of them in the half gloom, wrapped dead and pale round the handle and trigger of his Taurus.

Another endless twist of stairs, then another, and still Avatar was waiting to recognize the door that led through to the ripped-out deck with the frozen pipes. So he kept climbing, breath ragged in his throat and his jaw too numb to do more than mangle his words.

'Sweet fuck . . .'

He was swearing for the sake of it, for the company. Because every time he said something the Colonel flicked into focus at the edge of his vision. Avatar's serious, sympathetic new friend, iconic with history.

'Sweet, sweet . . .'

'Door's ahead,' said the Colonel. 'But first stop and listen to me.'

'No,' said Avatar, shivering. 'Won't be able to start again.'

'The enemy eat children.'

Avatar nodded. Quite probably. There were some weird fuckers around. One of them had left a dead body on his dad's beach.

'You need to listen. I mean it.'

Avatar tried.

'Better,' said the voice. 'Look, I don't have time to make you me . . . Tempting though it is.'

'You?' Avatar muttered. 'Why the fuck would I want to be you?'

'Then who do you want to be?'

'Me,' said Avatar. 'DJ Avatar.'

Colonel Abad sighed. 'Failing that,' he said, 'and it will fail, who else?'

It seemed an odd question. No, Avatar decided, fighting the cold for long enough to reach a conclusion, it *was* an odd question. 'Raf,' he said, not having to overthink his answer. In the past he'd always dreamed of being Hamzah, but not since that night with the kidnappers, when Raf appeared. Raf was different. Raf was . . . Everyone else thought the bey was a trained killer, one of the Sultan's best, but Avatar knew different . . .

Raf was weirder than that. Way weirder.

'You know about Lilith?'

Adam's first wife had been bounced from Eden for refusing Adam. Well, for refusing his suggestion that she spread them. When Adam got bounced in turn, Lilith fucked him against Eden's outer wall and got pregnant, while Eve was still sulking (this was before Adam repented). After Adam got Eden back, Lilith fucked the snake and gave birth to the djinn.

Like her, not having eaten of the fruit, her children never died.

Avatar had seen the vid nasty several times.

'He really is . . .' Avatar felt the need to stress that, just in case Colonel Abad thought he meant Raf was one of those kindergoths and candyravers who haunted the clubs behind Place Orabi, where the dress options were sun-sucking black or ghetto ghastly.

'Really?'

'Too right,' said Avatar. 'Raf can see in the dark and hear things better than a bat. Kills like an animal when necessary, without conscience . . .'

'You like this man?'

'Oh yeah.' Avatar nodded his head, heavy though it was. 'He was meant to marry my half sister . . . They'd have been perfect.' Realizing what he'd just said, the boy laughed but didn't quite recognize the croak that forced its painful way between his teeth.

'So what would this . . . *son of Lilith* do?'

'With the enemy? Take no prisoners.' Avatar could see it in his head, the way Raf would slide up to the door ahead, all set to kill the lot of them, never putting a foot wrong. Except, of course, Raf was some place unhelpful, trapped in El Iskandryia. A city without . . .

'Turn off the ship's lights,' Avatar demanded.

'There's a problem with that suggestion,' said the Colonel. 'I can only override components of the electrical infrastructure in an emergency . . .'

'*This is an emergency,*' Avatar said, putting a space between each word. 'Anyway, I thought you ran this ship?'

'Routine tasks only. Engine maintenance and supply systems. On-board security and oceangoing navigation. The behavioural locks are solid and the parameters tight.' The Colonel's voice was dry, almost matter-of-fact. 'Believe me,' he said, 'I looked . . .'

'The lights,' Avatar said as firmly as his shaking teeth would allow.

'To cut those,' said Colonel Abad, 'I'd have to kill the ship's entire electrical system.'

'Then do it.'

'The entire system . . .'

'Sure,' Avatar nodded. 'I understand.'

The first thing Avatar saw was a tiny dance of light in the far distance, descending from the ceiling in a ragged two-step; slide and stop, slide and stop. A second firefly joined the first, followed by a third', their dance taking them towards the deck.

Not fireflies, Avatar realized, his enemy, far off across the hangar, working their way down open steps in practiced formation. The fireflies nothing but a faint splash of warmth between the bottom of a half-face night mask and the buttoned collar of a standard-issue jumpsuit.

'How many in total?' he demanded.

All he got was silence.

'How many?' Avatar hissed.

Again silence, cold as the darkness. The Colonel was gone, along with the distant strip of lights. The cold pipes strung just above the deck no longer rattled. And the riveted plate below Avatar's feet was still, missing its heartbeat from the engine room beneath. Only the fireflies kept coming from far away across the deck.

Sliding himself through the open doorway, Avatar stepped rapidly sideways several times until he ended up behind a steel pillar. When he leant against it, the pillar felt no colder than his arm.

Cold was good if you got shot, according to the Colonel. It reduced internal bleeding. Of course, it also slowed your concentration, which made it easier to get hit in the first place.

Three in here, how many more outside?

Avatar tried to call up the picture Colonel Abad had shown him of that tiny helicopter just after it landed, doors popping open and dark-suited toys spilling out onto the deck. Six soldiers in all, maybe seven. Or was that eight . . . ?

Avatar shook his head, to free up his frozen thoughts, and knew that if he didn't act soon, the fireflies would be here and there'd be no time left to unravel that one either.

Until he knew where the rest of the enemy were positioned, silence was more or less the only real weapon he had. Silence and surprise. Silence and desperation. Or how about silence and being too cold to care?

No one was going to argue with that one.

Back hard to the pillar, Avatar flipped open the revolver he'd stolen from the Khedive. Seven fat brass circles evenly spaced in a ring, one of them already used. As he pushed the cylinder back into place, Avatar realized this was it. Whatever that actually meant.

The hammer pulled back with a muffled click, an internal lever spinning the cylinder so that a fresh brass case presented itself under the hammer's fall. Extending his shivering arm and gripping his right wrist with his left hand, Avatar sighted along the barrel at a firefly.

They were close now. Closer than he'd realized.

Time slowed and in the gap between the flash of the revolver's muzzle and its sharp bark, the vacuum of a passing slug dragged a man's voice from his ruptured throat. The man Avatar killed was at the back, the last of the three. It was luck, not skill. He'd been trying for a body shot.

Instinct made the two remaining fireflies turn in horror to stare behind them. By the time the first man glanced back, Avatar was pulling his trigger again. This time Avatar's slug took the man under his chin, deflected slightly on the inside of his jaw and ripped apart his tongue, before liquidizing the man's cerebellum. What was left of his occipital lobe splashed against the back of his helmet. For all that, the soldier still landed on his knees, then crashed forward to head-butt the steel deck.

The reek of shit mixed with the stink of cordite.

Roll, Avatar told himself, suddenly aware of the aftertaste of vomit in his mouth. That was what he should do. Avatar rolled, barely feeling the rivets that ripped into his shoulder. Then he rolled some more, stopping only when he clanged hard against a snaking pipe, the noise so loud it rang through the open area like a bell.

Instantly, a muzzle flared to his left, three quick flashes that sparked off the deck close to Avatar's leg, way too close. Rolling up and over the pipe, Avatar scrambled along its edge until he had thirty seconds of blind panic between himself and where the bullets had landed.

Adrenaline was flooding his body and for the first time in hours Avatar felt properly awake. Maybe that was what it took, what he should have done from the start; get someone to shoot at him . . . Now if he could just get them to give him their combat rations as well.

The gun the other man carried was squat, with a long magazine that curved away from him. Its barrel was the length of Avatar's thumb. Colonel Abad would have known the make, rate of fire and market price. Avatar just knew it looked dangerous.

Three shots, then another three. Each blip of the rifle's trigger registered in three fire fountains as the soldier swung his gun at random and bullets ricocheted in tight triplets from the floor. The man's big problem was that, despite the bug eyes of his official-issue combat mask, he fired blind. Avatar was just too bloody cold to show up on screen.

'So maybe I should be grateful,' thought Avatar sourly. Then he decided not to waste the energy and rolled back over the pipe. All he had to do was keep going towards the stairs. Twenty paces later, Avatar stopped to look back and again changed his mind. The soldier was still there, facing away from Avatar and staring intently at nothing much.

Avatar's options were keep crawling or else do the deed. Only he couldn't do that when the man's back was to him, though it was hard to know why turning round to die might be an improvement.

'Hey . . . behind you.'

Bursts popping through the darkness above Avatar's head. Different fireflies. When the man's clip finally hit empty, Avatar clambered to his knees and took a shot of his own.

CHAPTER 52

'I'm finishing a story . . .' Hani looked up, her head balanced on one hand and her elbow resting on her knee. 'But I can always end it now . . . ?'

She had her back to a wall and was sitting in late-afternoon sunlight, on a small balcony recessed into the sloped glass roof of the *bibliotheka*.

'No need.' The chief librarian looked momentarily flustered, as if having caught herself being unforgivably rude. Which wasn't something that usually worried Madame Syria. 'I just didn't see you come in.'

'Are you sure you don't need the machine?' insisted Hani, holding up her borrowed laptop, its solar panels still outfolded.

'Mmmm?'

Madame Syria had been going to check the status of the library's electronic texts, when she noticed the balcony door was open. Obviously she had plenty of better things to do than this. And even if the core was dead and every e-book missing, as she rather suspected, she was still responsible for 1.25 million real books, the kind people opened and held in their hands.

And anyway cultural vandalism was nothing new. Seven hundred years after the original *bibliotheka* began, Christian fanatics had destroyed all five hundred thousand of its manuscripts, including original works by Sophocles and Aristotle.

Even before that, the razing of the annexe on the orders of Theodosius had lost forever the *Alexandrian Geographica* and condemned Europe to a thousand years of the belief that Jerusalem was the centre of the world and that the world was flat.

'Madame Syria?'

The woman blinked to find Hani still patiently holding out the machine.

'No,' the woman said hastily. 'That's quite all right. I need to do something downstairs anyway.'

It was easy to forget a small girl, what with the chaos in the city as well as in the library, particularly when the child was so quiet and beautifully behaved. And Madame Syria didn't really begrudge the girl use of the computer. There were two non-Web machines working downstairs, both outdated leather-bound models. Just why only the three laptops out of seventy-five varied machines still worked was anyone's guess, though Madame Syria put it down to the fact that they'd been redundant models, stacked in a box in the lower basement, awaiting disposal. Originally there'd been five, but one had died almost immediately and one early yesterday. Fatal errors of memory, apparently, but then everyone had a few of those.

'I'm going to get a coffee,' said Hani. 'Would you like one?'

The chief librarian nodded without thinking, then frowned. 'I don't think your voice is programmed into the coffee machine,' she said apologetically, remembering too late that this was an irrelevance, the Zanussi was dead.

'There's a stall.' Hani looked round, as if about to impart a heavy secret. 'At the top of Boulevard Zaghloul. It's much better than the coffee here. When there *is* coffee here,' she added to clarify the matter.

'And His Excellency allows you to cross the road by yourself?' The librarian glanced over the edge of the balcony to the avenue below and suddenly realized just how stupid a question that was. Apart from an elderly man in a souf sitting on a bench, the road outside was completely empty of traffic. Though a makeshift donkey cart sporting wheels borrowed from a motorbike was approaching from one direction, followed by a horse-drawn calèche, its leather roof raised against the possibility of rain.

She thought it was further proof of the child's good manners that Hani didn't point out that traffic problems were unlikely. Instead, the girl just nodded.

'Oh yes,' said Hani, 'I'm allowed to cross roads. In fact the bey allows me to do what I like.'

Madame Syria smiled and decided to go with the bey's niece to buy coffee. It was true that she really needed to use the child's machine but that could wait until Lady Hani finished her story.

CHAPTER 53

28th October

The glass girl was up ahead. Avatar saw her backlit through a halo of smoke that was his own cold breath. Her blue eyes watched him stagger up out of the gloom and, as he stumbled, she tossed her head, so that long blonde strands of her hair flicked through the air.

Avatar nodded his reply, the hard band of pain across his forehead tightening its grip, still held in place by invisible screws. His fingers were so numb he couldn't tell where the dead man's rifle began and his own flesh ended. Both of his weapons seemed a part of him, or he them; it didn't matter which way round, the result was the same.

He left the girl without saying good-bye, turning his back on the stained-glass memorial to a future not on offer to those like him, whatever his half sister thought. In the Delta and along the river, the *felaheen* still used hoes rather than tractors. The only blonde girls he'd seen were rich tourists, out of their skulls on clubnite and still stuck at home in everything but actual place.

Avatar shot the next soldier without even noticing he'd seen the man. A single bullet shredding a larynx in a reflex action that saw Avatar's arm extended and the trigger pulled before Avatar's guts had time to knot with fear at what he was about to do; take his total up to four.

Another two soldiers swam into vision, radiating anxiety. They stood in the aquarium dark, arms stiff and bodies tensed. Wired into a command network as they all undoubtedly were, they'd have heard the others die.

Try mixing that . . . Avatar didn't doubt that he would, should he ever get back to his decks alive.

Stepping out from behind a pillar, Avatar raised his rifle and aimed at the nearest man. All the soldier had to rely on was equipment. Avatar had emptiness.

He pulled the trigger and felt his rifle buck. A second blip and the man behind tried to step forward on a shattered knee, only to stumble, pitching sideways as the remaining leg slid out from under him.

No prisoners.

Avatar walked forward and sighted along the barrel of his Taurus. The fallen figure shrinking into the deck, shoulders hunching as instinct kicked in and the man's body curled up to protect its vital organs from attack. Instinct based on millennia of experience. Instinct that hadn't yet adapted to guns.

Revolver in hand, Avatar crouched down and saw the figure flinch. The buckle at the side of the man's mask was a simple ceramic affair, tinted black as not to catch the light, the helmet's strap a fat strip of neoprene stitched to the lining. There were electrodes attached directly to the scalp of the person wearing the mask, though their purpose was uncertain.

Not that Avatar gave them much thought. He was much too busy staring into the pale blue eyes of a girl little older than he. Her broad face was set into something Avatar recognized instantly as acceptance. She still thought he meant to kill her.

As if he'd first bother to remove her mask. Except Avatar wasn't sure why he'd done that; unless, because it was the kind of thing Raf might have done? Certainly not because Avatar expected to find some blonde Soviet corn-daughter hidden underneath.

And she was Soviet. No other Army in Europe used women in frontline combat. A Soviet *Spetsnaz* ranger on an ex-Soviet liner come face-to-face with some Delta street bastard.

'Not even full Delta,' muttered Avatar to himself. Maybe half-Abyssinian or Danakil. It was hard to know. If a mug shot did exist of his mother, it was probably in the files of the UN or the Red Cross, along with blood type and a tissue sample.

'*What a fucking mess.*'

Some flicker of recognition in the blue eyes watching him told Avatar that the wounded girl had logged the meaning, half-recognizing his tone in what passed for consciousness amid all that endocrine stink of hope and fear.

And all the while, unanswered questions, mute but frantic, hissed from within the empty mask Avatar now held in his hand. They spilled out in a language he didn't understand, from a world he understood even less.

'Give me your rifle . . .' Avatar kept his own words simple. And though she didn't understand them, she followed his gaze until she saw what he saw and knew what he meant. But her hands remained white at the knuckle where they held her weapon tight to her body, one finger curled around the trigger and less than a shudder away from smashing her other knee, because that's where the muzzle pointed.

'Come on.'

A bullet to her head would have been Colonel Abad's solution, Avatar realized that, as he waited impatiently for the girl to process his demand and reach her decision. And in combat terms the Colonel was probably right. Of course, if she did something stupid, then that would be Avatar's solution too . . . But all the girl did was uncurl slightly and push her gun away from her, leaving it to Avatar to kick the rifle away across the metal floor. Then he smiled apologetically and stamped on her good ankle, to cripple her other leg as well.

Once, just once, Avatar thought he might have seen his mother. Standing at the gates of St Luke's and staring intently through the ancient wrought-iron bars at neatly uniformed children who kicked a plastic football across melting tarmac or tried to dunk basketballs through a single hoop screwed to a classroom wall.

She looked old to him, but was probably not. A thin face peering from the folds of her heavy *hijab*. Her eyes had scanned the playground's movement, seeking a point of silence. And the gaze she met was his. He was the one she watched, with a hunger so open it sent one of the sisters across the playground to find out who she was and what she wanted . . .

Avatar put a bullet through the head of a soldier standing guard outside the old bank vault. A single shot fired through the slightly open door. The *Spetsnaz* should have relocked the safe after sending the others through. Except she couldn't, obviously enough, not with all the ship's systems down.

In reply, Avatar took a slug through his left arm that ripped up muscle and exited at the back. Only Avatar was so cold he hardly felt the blow and was too busy killing the first guard's partner to notice the blood that stained the canvas of his makeshift jacket.

Two left, maybe one. Up on deck, where Avatar needed to be.

His mother was gone by the time Avatar brought his thoughts back to the long-forgotten and dusty playground. Gone from his memory and from the tall gates before Sister Carlotta even made it across the sticky tarmac.

Up ahead were more stairs and sunlight.

Flicking out the cylinder of his Taurus, Avatar discarded the dead brass and speed-loaded another seven rounds. His borrowed rifle already had a full clip.

CHAPTER 54

'It's paradise . . .' Hani's excitement filled the upper tier of the library, echoing off the inside of the giant pyramid to get lost among the books that lined row after row of shelves.

'Hani!'

'It is,' she insisted. 'Paradise. Jannah . . .'

Madame Syria stared up, towards the highest of the mezzanine floors where a small girl who shouldn't have been in the library in the first place, leant dangerously over a rail, while simultaneously pointing behind herself towards a dark shape on the horizon.

The SS *Jannah* had the classic profile for a great liner, a stepped ziggurat of cabins and suites rising high above the main deck along both sides, with the captain's bridge jutting from the ziggurat's front, like steel-and-glass flukes on a hammerhead shark. At the rear, a glass casino was suspended podlike between tall towers. Everything aboard the ship was white, apart from the main deck, which was planted with a long promenade of palm trees and manicured lawn.

That the huge hull had originally belonged to a Soviet factory ship was a fact remembered only by nautical fanatics, shipping enthusiasts, Koenig Pasha and Hani.

'Look!' The girl practically screamed the word.

'Hani!' Madame Syria was torn between outrage and undisguised fear that the governor's niece might tumble over the edge to the marble floor far below.

'Look,' insisted Hani.

The chief librarian did what she was told, impressed despite herself. She'd only seen the SS *Jannah* once before, as a girl, when the trimaran from Iskandryia to Syracuse had throttled back to let its passengers watch as the great liner cruised by.

542

'We've got to tell Uncle Ashraf,' Hani shouted, already halfway down the first flight of stairs. 'Really, we must . . .'

'Uncle . . .' No matter how often Madame Syria heard the child refer to the new governor of El Iskandryia by that name, it still seemed disrespectful. But then the child *was* his niece and a *mesdame* so . . .

Lady Hana bint-Abdullah al-Mansur, better known as Hani, hit the bottom of the stairs and grabbed the middle-aged woman by the hand, practically dragging her across the pink marble floor towards the exit.

'Paradise,' yelled Hani. 'It's almost here.' She'd shouted her message so often from the back of a calèche that her voice was now raw.

'What?'

'Paradise. The SS *Jannah*,' said Hani, her face split in a grin. 'It's true. Go on, tell her,' Hani insisted, turning to Madame Syria. The librarian stared at Zara, then glanced over Zara's shoulder to a study door opening beyond.

'Excellency,' she said hastily.

Ashraf Bey scowled. In the study behind him were St Cloud, the Graf and Senator Liz, representing Paris, Berlin and Washington. All three had an opinion on the final sentencing of Effendi, all firmly held, all different. None of them wanted to give way on a single point. Everything, it seemed, but absolutely everything was a matter of principle.

Execution would play badly to the world's press. So they wanted Raf to agree to life imprisonment at Ras el-Tin. And this was before a man had even been found guilty . . .

Hani slipped her hand from Madame Syria's grasp, stepped politely but firmly around Zara, who was blocking her from Raf's sight and stopped directly in front of her uncle.

'Solved it,' she told him, her voice little more than an intense whisper.

'Solved what?' Raf demanded.

'The riddle, obviously!' Hani's face exploded into a grin, then that was gone, leaving Raf looking at a quiet, satisfied smile. This too vanished as Hani noticed something on the study table behind Raf.

'Baklava!' said Hani in a tone something between outrage and admiration. 'You've got fresh baklava!' Without waiting to be invited, actually without appearing to notice Raf's other guests at all, she slipped through the door and into his seat.

'*Hani.*'

Politeness said not to answer with her mouth full, so Hani waited.

'My niece,' Raf explained and watched three faces shift their attention from him to the small girl and back again.

'There's a ship coming into harbour,' said Hani when her mouth was empty, which took a while because Hani ostentatiously chewed the mouthful thirty-two times, as her late Aunt Nafisa had instructed. 'It's the SS *Jannah*.'

Tewfik Pasha had decided in advance what he intended to say and had prepared himself to overrule any objections. The talking box that Zara's brother found in the bilges had proved invaluable on both counts. An atelier on board the SS *Jannah* had spent the previous twelve hours hand-stitching a second jacket to specifications so strict that the Khedive had rejected the first attempt as inadequate.

The coat was modelled on a jacket his father had worn when he married the Khedive's mother, as seen on endless reruns of *Lives of the Rich and Infamous*. Cut from black silk and featuring minimal embellishment, the jacket's only decoration had been a thin piping of gold around its high collar. Unfortunately, the current Khedive's replica was both narrower across the shoulders and less tailored at the hips, although the atelier had worked hard to hide that fact.

At the suggestion of Colonel Abad, the Khedive had shaved away most of his beard, removing everything except the ghost of a goatee and the faintest trace of moustache. And, helped only by Avatar, he'd showered, dried himself and climbed into the immaculately sewn costume; because that's what his new clothes were, a costume, the accretion of society's ideas on how a Khedive should look.

On Tewfik Pasha's head was a tarboosh. Over his heart was pinned a simple enamel-and-gold star. The order of the Imperial Crescent, first class. Even his choice of decoration carried a message. It was there to remind the waiting cameras that his ultimate allegiance (such as it was) went to Stambul.

And there would be cameras, dozens of them. That much was obvious from the myriad feeds he'd scanned as the SS *Jannah* steamed east towards El Iskandryia. A major city without electricity, without working computers, landlines, even cookers and cars. Its very nakedness drew the media like wasps to a honey trap. As the Khedive suspected his new governor intended it to . . .

Standing on deck with the injured Avatar slightly behind him, as protocol demanded, Mohammed Tewfik Pasha watched men the size of ants grab a stern rope and carry its giant loop to a waiting bollard. It took eight men to lift one rope and still they staggered under its weight.

When the rope was in place, a winch on the stern tightened, pulling the liner forward as a rope at the bow was loosened, removed from its bollard by another group of ants and carried forward, to be fixed around a bollard waiting up ahead. At which point the forward winch began to tighten. It was a laborious way to coax a liner along the edge of the Silsileh and perhaps there were easier ways to dock on Iskandryia's great seawall, but this was the SS *Jannah*.

Stars, starlets and actual icons, whole galaxies of famous names were aboard. At least they were according to the *Hello International*. A *panoply* was the term they used. The reality was rather different. Late October/early November was definitely out of season and the constellation was confined to three minor genome-proteone heiresses, the elderly founder of LearningCurve GmB, two balding Bollywood lotharios, the Van der Bilt girl and him . . .

Ruler of a stricken city besieged on all sides by more-powerful nations who claimed to have only Isk's best interests at heart. Nations who, according to all the newsfeeds, still demanded that he give up Iskandryia's leading industrialist. And for what? To prove Isk was fit to join their nest of vipers.

Colonel Abad was right. It was an imposition too far.

Tewfik Pasha was scowling ferociously as he let an automated gangplank carry him down to the waiting dock, a fact that registered with everyone but him. He was too busy staring out over his silent city, looking beyond the crowded Corniche and the odd-angled pyramid of the *bibliotheka* to the green of Shallalat Gardens and a distant baroque palace that had, a century back, been the winning entry to the competition to design Iskandryia's railway terminus.

His scowl had everything to do with coming home and the state of his city. Nothing at all to do with the sight of Zara bint-Hamzah standing near the bottom of the gangplank or the fact she gripped the hand of Ashraf Bey as if her life depended on it.

Or was that her father's life?

'Your Highness,' she said, dropping Raf's hand.

Tewfik Pasha nodded to the girl and let go his scowl. But even as he fumbled for something appropriate to say, Zara's attention shifted away from him to her half brother and something passed between the two as silent as thought and swift as electricity. Only then did she notice Avatar's injuries.

'I have a statement to make,' announced the Khedive loudly.

Camera crews surged. At least that was the appearance. What really happened was that the police cordon relaxed enough to let journalists flow through strategic gaps. They were getting good at that.

Cameras whirred, flashguns fired and questions were shouted.

And all the while the Khedive just stood there, counting down in his head from ten, elegant but slight in a simple black uniform. His face utterly impassive as the chaos broke around him. This was his version of courage. A refusal to engage immediately, to do from instinct what would please everyone else.

'You,' he said finally, reaching zero.

'Your Highness . . .' Having been chosen, the Englishwoman with the lacquered blonde hair appeared uncertain which question to ask first. Too many needed answering, half of them involving the huge vessel moored behind him.

'How did you . . . ?'

'I own the SS *Jannah.*'

She looked at him, the rest of her question already dead on her lips.

'It belonged to my father,' the Khedive said with a shrug. 'Utopia Lines merely lease the vessel.' He could tell them how absurd he found this idea, that such an object should be owned by one person, but now didn't seem to be the time. If possessing a ship was absurd, then how much more so to possess a city, even a broken one . . .

The journalist looked from the Khedive to the liner, then back again. A tiny camera hummed in the air a few feet above her head; one lens focused on her face, the other fixed on whatever she had in her sights. 'Electricity,' she said as understanding suddenly lifted the frown from her face.

'You're going to use the ship to power El Iskandryia.' Enough capacity to power a small city, she was pretty sure that was in the liner's specifications somewhere.

'Power the city?'

It was a good idea, the Khedive was happy to admit that. But that wasn't why the liner had made her first landfall in forty years.

'No,' he said. 'Nothing so altruistic. After yesterday's unprovoked attack on the liner, SS *Jannah* needs a refit.'

Instant anarchy. Just add . . .

Ignoring the explosion of questions, Tewfik Pasha examined the crowd, his eyes skipping bland and blind over Zara and Raf, until they finally fixed on the man for whom he'd been searching. The Soviet ambassador, Commissar Zukov.

'The attack was yesterday, at noon,' said the Khedive. 'Eight men in a Mi-24x Hind gunship . . . A Soviet-made attack helicopter,' he added. Though for most of those gathered on the Silsileh, including Commissar Zukov, no clarification was necessary.

The Commissar was an elderly diplomat, waiting out his last years in a relatively unimportant post. And the Khedive had few illusions about the fact that Iskandryia was Zukov's reward for a lifetime of doing exactly what he was told. In the man's face, the Khedive could see panic and fear, but no guilt. Which was what the Khedive had expected.

'It's possible the helicopter was stolen,' Tewfik Pasha admitted. But then pretty much anything was possible.

'They were terrorists?' The voice came from his right, a Frenchman.

'No,' said the Khedive, 'they were jewel thieves . . .' He paused to let the crowd of journalists assimilate that fact. 'At least, I assume that's what they were. They certainly broke into the safe.'

'I thought the vault aboard SS *Jannah* was unbreakable?' The Englishwoman with the lacquered hair had refound her voice. And the hunger in her blue eyes told the Khedive exactly how this story was going to play.

'Nothing is unbreakable,' he said carefully.

'Particularly not to a safecracker with a thermal lance,' Avatar grinned, his voice street smart enough to suggest he knew all about things like that.

Flashguns fired.

No thermic lance had existed, but she wasn't to know that and nor was anybody else. The helicopter had been kept. The bodies Tewfik Pasha had ordered tipped over the side. As far as the Khedive was concerned, the press could report that as burial at sea.

'Was there a battle?'

The Khedive thought about that one.

'There was a short skirmish,' he said finally, with an apologetic glance towards Avatar and his bandaged shoulder. 'As you'd expect, security aboard the SS *Jannah* is excellent.' The Khedive's lips twisted into a sour smile. Now he was beginning to sound like an advertisement for Utopia Lines.

'So the thieves were arrested?'

'No,' the Khedive said. 'They came armed and they were killed.' His gaze took in the Commissar, von Bismarck, the American Senator and that old man from Paris whose title kept changing. 'Except for two of them,' he added as an afterthought.

On cue, two burly crew members dragged the crippled Soviet girl down the walkway. Behind her staggered a small man, a revolver held to his cropped skull by a third crew member. Cameras fired, as the Khedive meant them to.

'Ashraf Bey.'

Raf stopped his whispered conversation with Zara and stepped forward. The bow he gave was slight, little more than a nod.

The Khedive raised his eyebrows. 'I'm putting these two in your charge.'

'Highness,' said Raf, and raised a finger. One of his uniforms instantly broke away from holding back the crowd. 'I'm transferring the prisoners to you,' Raf said. 'Take them both to the Imperial Free . . . And you.' Raf looked round for Hakim. 'Make sure they get full protection. And a doctor,' he added as an afterthought.

Protection from what Raf didn't say.

'Excellency . . .'

Raf turned back to the excited huddle of journalists.

'What is going to happen with Monday's trial?'

'In what way?'

'Will you continue as *magister* . . . Now that His Highness has returned?'

'No, he will not.' The Khedive's answer was clear enough to reach the back of the waiting group. And even if it hadn't been, there were enough floating cameras and mics aimed in his direction to carry his reply to the waiting world.

'From now on,' said the Khedive, 'Ashraf Bey will be acting as city prosecutor . . .'

The gaze Raf met was unbending. A decision had been made publicly and was not to be broken. 'After all,' Tewfik Pasha continued, 'combating crime is a major part of any governor's remit.'

'In that case, will you still be allowing Miss Quitrimala to represent her father?'

'What case?'

The English journalist didn't seem able to answer.

The Khedive stroked his small beard, looking for the briefest moment exactly like his grandfather as a young man. 'As *magister* I will accept anyone the defendant chooses to appoint,' he said carefully. 'Although, in the circumstances, I would strongly recommend a trained lawyer.'

'But Quitrimala refuses to appoint his own defence . . . What's more' – the Englishwoman's voice was taut with the human drama of it all – 'he categorically refuses to accept anyone appointed by the court.'

'Well,' said the Khedive, 'that is his right.' For the first time since Tewfik Pasha appeared on the jetty, he looked straight at Zara.

Hani sighed.

CHAPTER 55

30th October

The corridor was painted a drab institutional beige. Along its edges the dirty plastic floor tiles curled up to allow the floor to be sluiced clean. A relic from the bad old days when this wing had housed the insane, the incontinent and the politically inconvenient.

Three states that often went together.

At least they did under the Khedive's grandfather, after military doctors had finished their various forms of rehabilitation.

Raf moved quietly along its length, doing his best not to blink at the brightness bleeding in through windows opaque with grime. He wore no dark glasses and even five years' worth of dust and spiderwebs was not enough to soften the light.

Hakim and Ahmed he'd left hanging in the Atbinos café opposite the hospital's front steps. Not very willingly Raf had to admit, but he'd overruled them with alarming casualness before making his way unannounced into the ugly concrete building. Along with the two guards, he'd left Eduardo, who was still in shock at discovering that 'the man,' as he insisted on calling Raf, was governor of Iskandryia.

The façade of the Imperial Free had a preservation order on it, as did all the buildings that fronted the Western Harbour. The view from the sea was so famous that, years back, Koenig Pasha had decreed the skyline could not be changed.

When Raf had first arrived, the security guard inside the main door was watching Ferdie Abdullah, his eyes glued to a public screen, like somebody recently denied one of life's basic necessities. If he noticed the scowling young man with the flowers and Dynamo cap, he thought no more about it.

Raf had returned the nod of a passing porter who was vaguely aware of having seen the visitor somewhere before, probably the last time the Dynamo fan came to see whoever he came to see. His fiancée from the

549

size of that bouquet. No sane man would waste so much money on his wife.

Reaching the lifts, Raf had punched a button at random. He got out at obstetrics and took a different lift down two floors, got out again and used the emergency stairs to climb back past obstetrics to the deserted wards above. From there he walked the length of a corridor, until it ended at a large window.

Defenestration.

An ornate word for an ugly threat; but there were less messy ways to achieve what Raf wanted . . . Pulling a tiny voice recorder out of his pocket, he checked that it was fully charged and working, then slipped it back into the battered leather jacket he'd borrowed from Eduardo.

Raf didn't really need to check the machine, since the Braun was brand-new and came from a boutique on the SS *Jannah*. He was just putting off what came next. And he already had the key code for the door in front of him. He'd got that from Hakim, who'd been guarding the impromptu prison cell when he got Raf's order to meet him in the loading bay behind Athinos.

And since the consultant had already made his rounds for the day and, other than Professor Mahrouf, only Ahmed and Hakim had authority to enter the cell, it was Hakim or Ahmed that the Soviet girl expected.

'Hi,' said Raf.

Her cell was small. The walls padded with cotton waste under hard canvas. There was one slit window, high up and barred. At its edges the floor had those sluice-friendly tiles that curved up under the padding on the wall. It was, in every way, as bleak as Raf had expected.

'I said *Hi* . . .'

She made no reply, just sat there in the orthopaedic chair, her legs wrapped in lightweight casts, her right wrist handcuffed to the chairs frame. An empty bedpan rested on the floor just out of reach and Raf caught the glance that said she wanted to ask him to hand it to her and leave.

She didn't ask. Which was just as well. She'd been left like that for an hour because that was how Raf had told Hakim to play it.

'Just checking,' said Raf. He took a chart from the end of her bed and switched it on. Silk scaffolds shielded her broken, load-bearing bones. They were seeded with cells designed to deposit calcium, and produce messenger RNA for pro/C, a precursor of the collagen found in bones. Also sourced from the SS *Jannah*, undoubtedly.

'Nothing but the best,' Raf said. 'But even with all that scaffolding, it won't be hard for me to smash them again, if that's what it takes.' He sat himself down on a bed next to the girl's chair, waiting for fear to happen.

It said a lot for her training that no panic reached her pale blue eyes. Instead her broad face fell into a mask of resignation, as if she'd expected no less – and she hadn't. All Soviet *Spetsnaz* rangers were instilled with a belief so absolute that the only thing awaiting them after capture was torture and death that it was practically hardwired.

'I've been told you speak English and Arabic,' Raf said as he took a notebook from the inside of Eduardo's scuffed jacket. He'd been told nothing of the sort. A full-face search of Iskandryia's intelligence database came up with as little as his somewhat illegal DNA trawl through the records of the Red Cross. The girl in front of him had never before been captured or treated on a field of battle, come to that.

What interested Raf was that Commissar Zukov expressed so little interest in the prisoners. And the Khedive had given Zukov a chance to comment, both on and off the record. All Zukov said was, 'Not ours.'

Raf still needed to work out if that translated as *'Never ours,'* or *'Not ours now you've got them . . .'*

All the same, the girl understood some English. Enough for her brain to ignite verbal-recognition patterns during a CAT scan. The two orderlies who'd chatted indiscreetly were plainclothes. The white-coated radiologist was actually a police doctor. That, of course, had happened late last night and in a different ward.

'We could always do this the simple way,' suggested Raf.

The blonde girl just scowled, anger creating mental defences as she prepared herself to sever her mind from the pain awaiting her body. The separation never lasted, but everyone knew that occasionally people got lucky and died before their wandering mind got dragged back to hell.

'Maybe not,' Raf pulled out a snub-nosed Colt, also borrowed from Eduardo, and extracted an extra pair of old-fashioned metal cuffs from his coat pocket, flipping free one end. The Colt he put to the girl's head and the cuffs Raf flicked round the girl's free wrist, the left one, with a satisfyingly smooth flip. As manoeuvres went it was extremely professional, which was lucky. She was meant to think he did this all the time.

Snapping the cuff's other end to the bed's frame, Raf unlocked her right wrist, stood the girl up and dragged her round to the mattress, his gun still at her head.

'On you go.'

With her left hand newly secured, the only way she could do that was lie facedown. Securing her right wrist to the right side of the bed, Raf stood back. Then he yanked her ankles into position and fixed these with plastic strip cuffs.

Somehow, she still looked too comfortable.

So he took the pillows and when that didn't seem enough, pulled the sheet from under her, stripping the bed down to its striped mattress. After that, taking her hospital gown seemed obvious, so he ripped it in two from the bottom up and left himself with remnants still attached to her arms.

It was only when Raf pulled a gravity special and let drop the blade that he saw the girl tense. She was, he realized, watching him in a mirror across the room. Pretending not to notice, Raf slashed away the arms of her gown, leaving her naked except for two lightweight leg casts that looked disconcertingly like ankle warmers.

'Want to do this the easy way?'

Not a flicker of response.

With a sigh, Raf dipped into his pocket and pulled out a metal bar the size of a small torch. It was slightly pointed at one end, while at the other, a sheath of slightly sticky clear plastic formed an easy-to-grip handle.

'You know what this is?'

She did. Every combat troop in the so-called civilized world could recognize a shock baton. They were the negotiators of choice for police forces across the world, not to mention for criminal elements from Seattle to Tokyo, combining all the advantages of maximum pain with minimal tissue damage. Batons didn't leave the kind of scarring that ended up on Amnesty posters, which was one undoubted reason for their popularity.

'I'm sorry,' said Raf, folding his fingers into a half fist, 'but there's something I need you to tell me. And I need you to tell me it now.' His rabbit punch caught her in the kidney and urine darkened the bare mattress as her bladder emptied. 'It's kind of urgent.'

Walking to the head of the bed, Raf crouched down until he could see her face. Furious eyes challenged him, then he was wiping spittle from his cheek.

'Fuck it.' Raf stood up and wiped his face.

Instead of using the baton, Raf took his gravity knife and scratched a cross potent into her naked back, slicing just deep enough to draw blood. Then he stuffed a tissue into her mouth, gagged her with the cord from her gown and put the small recorder down on the windowsill. The time had come for Raf to go next door.

'Gregori,' said Raf.

Now, the small man stripped naked in the corner *had* been treated on a field of battle. At Fort Archambanlt to be precise, fifteen years before, on the Shari river in the southern wastelands of Tripoli. The name he'd given was Captain Gregori the Profligate, and a footnote still solemnly recorded a triage nurse's expert opinion that this was false.

What was much more interesting for Raf was that Gregori's DNA showed significant points of similarity to the blonde girl. Not enough points for him to be her father, but quite enough for him to be an uncle or cousin. Which fitted neatly with the Soviet habit of conscripting whole families, then keeping them together because the bonds that tied them were already imprinted.

The other interesting fact was that Gregori had surrendered voluntarily, not because he'd been wounded and unable to continue or brought to a halt by lack of ammunition. He'd taken one look at Avatar and put down his own gun seconds ahead of putting up both hands. Since *Spetsnaz* rangers didn't surrender, there was a meaning here that Raf wanted unravelled.

'You,' said Raf, 'on your feet.'

The naked man did what Raf expected him to do, which was stay slumped where he was.

'Up,' Raf insisted, producing Eduardo's gun. When Gregori still didn't move, Raf grabbed a handful of hair and yanked the man to his feet. A hood was needed and Raf had forgotten to bring one, so he stripped the case from a hospital pillow and used that instead, knotting its bottom tight round the man's throat.

Outside in the corridor, Raf spun Gregori in a circle, bounced him off a peeling wall, then spun him in the opposite direction. The man was still staggering when Raf pushed him through the door of the blonde girl's cell and untied the hood.

His partner lay naked and gagged on the bed, facedown on a urine-blackened mattress, with blood running from a cross potent cut into her back. On the floor lay a discarded shock baton. If Raf had been Gregori, he'd have tried to attack Raf too.

A kick to the knee took Gregori to the floor, his fall unbroken because his arms were cuffed. Raf kicked him again for good measure, but Raf's snarl was not matched by the severity of the kick. He wanted Gregori scared, not injured.

'Who paid you?'

The man didn't even turn his head. Just lay on the floor, curled into a tight ball, not the action of a *Spetsnaz* officer with Gregori's experience.

'Look,' said Raf, kicking him slightly, 'we already know you weren't acting on orders. So what we need is information on who instigated this attack.' He bent down and dragged the man to his knees. 'And it's information we intend to get.'

Raf walked over to the discarded baton and picked it up; Gregori's anxiety only really kicked in when Raf kept going towards the bed.

'Who,' said Raf, 'was behind the attack?'

He switched on the baton.

Gregori said nothing so Raf turned to the girl and put the live baton to her spine. The gag blocked her scream, but she still bucked in agony as muscles in her back locked solid. In the quivering aftershock, she pissed herself again. The baton had touched her spine for less than a second.

Raf breathed out, opened his eyes and turned back to the man.

'That's just a taste,' he told Gregori. 'Now we bring in the expert.' Toggling his watch to visual, Raf put a call through to Eduardo. 'Dr Lee? We're ready for you . . .'

The white coat came from a medical supply shop, as did the stethoscope Raf had given him earlier. And Eduardo extracted the coat from its carrier bag and hung the stethoscope round his neck only when he'd reached the corridor and was certain no one else could see him. He'd been assured by Raf that all CCTV cameras were still faulty, courtesy of Hakim's earlier word with the Imperial Free's security manager. Eduardo just hoped this was true. In case it wasn't, and because it looked cool, he was wearing shades. Copies of the pair usually worn by Raf.

'Excell . . .' He saw the frown on Raf's face and swallowed the rest of his word. 'I'm here,' he added, redundantly.

'Everything she knows,' said Raf. 'I want the lot.' He made to pass the shock baton to Eduardo, who shook his head.

'I always use my own.' Eduardo pulled a battered rod from his pocket, wrapped around with duct tape. 'It gives greater control.' Both Raf's and Eduardo's batons came out of stores at Champollion Precinct and Raf had made Eduardo practise this little exchange until he was word perfect, but Eduardo was still pleased with himself. Raf had explained twice that getting it right was very important.

What they had to do was trick the man.

'It won't take long,' said Eduardo, pulling a tube of lubricant from his coat pocket.

Dragging Gregori to his feet, Raf reached for his makeshift hood and began to pull it over the man's head. The last thing Gregori saw before a pillowcase closed off his world was Eduardo leaning over the facedown girl, rubbing KY between her buttocks.

The screams began before Raf even had time to spin Gregori round or bounce him off a wall. He did the spinning anyway.

554

Raf kicked Gregori's door shut with one heel, half-closing off an animal howl that began low and ran the whole register before ending in juddering sobs. Even through the tightness of a gag, it was possible to hear the utter anguish of the person being tortured.

'You can stop this,' said Raf, pulling off Gregori's hood, 'anytime you want to . . .

'Okay, your choice.'

Raf muttered into his watch and the next scream was longer, shuddering to a close in a muffled plea, spoken in no language understood by either of them, in all probability, no language that was human.

'She won't die,' said Raf, 'just wish she could.'

He pulled a sheet of paper from his borrowed jacket and skimmed it. At the top, a blue-and-yellow globe nestled within two curving sheaves of corn. Between the tips of the corn hung a red star. And beneath the globe rose a yellow sun, rising from the base of the two sheaves, which was bound round with red ribbon.

'Commissar Zukov states categorically that you were *not* involved in work for the Soviet Union, but you knew that didn't you . . .' Raf shrugged and skimmed the sheet. 'The Soviet Union disowns your actions.'

Gregori looked at him.

'You want to talk to me about that?'

The man didn't.

With a sigh, Raf muttered more words and the howls began again, animal-like and anguished, each one running into another until the very magnitude of the pain became unimaginable.

'Your choice,' Raf repeated. 'Your choice . . .'

Gregori held out for another ten minutes, during which he chewed the edge of his lip to ribbons. And then he caved, eyes blind with tears as he pushed himself to his feet and lurched towards where Raf sat on a dusty wooden chair.

'Whatever you need,' Gregori said desperately. 'Just stop your doctor.'

'Enough,' said Raf into his watch. The screams stopped dead. 'You want to go see her?'

Gregori shook his head. 'Later,' he said. 'When the shock goes. She won't be able to talk properly until then.' He looked, at that moment, as if he spoke from experience. 'What do you want to know?'

'Everything,' said Raf, except that he already did. The man and girl were there to confirm something. All the same, Raf let Gregori describe how *Spetsnaz* were hired out to the highest bidder for any currency harder than roubles. There were rules to guarantee no military action

555

was counter-revolutionary but, in practice, any job could be made to fit.

Gregori's bitterness was unmistakable.

'You recognize her?' Raf pulled a photograph from his jacket. It showed the suit he'd left on the floor of the deserted house in Moharrem Bey. The technicians had done a good job with lighting, makeup and postproduction. The woman looked only slightly dead.

'Yes . . . She died.'

'I know,' Raf said. 'I killed her . . . *Thiergarten*, right?'

Gregori nodded.

'Who both hired you and had tourists butchered to order . . . No,' Raf held up his hand when Gregori opened his mouth, 'that wasn't a question.'

The Soviet shrugged.

'So,' said Raf, 'who involved the *Thiergarten*? That *was* a question,' he added.

'I don't know.'

Raf had already figured this out for himself.

'What happens now?' the *Spetsnaz* asked. 'To me and Nadia.'

'Your cousin?'

'My niece. My brother's child'

'Sanctuary,' said Raf. 'Asylum. New identities if that's what it takes. Help us and we will help her.'

Gregori smiled grimly. 'It takes time to recover from something like that.' He jerked his head towards the silent wall. 'And sometimes people never do, but you already know this, don't you?'

'Maybe,' said Raf, 'it will take much less time than you think. Now . . .' He pulled a final photograph from his jacket. 'Tell me if you've ever seen this man.'

Eduardo looked at Raf's outstretched hand, clicked the relevant bit of his brain into gear and shook it. And kept shaking until Raf patiently prised free his own fingers.

'Excellency.' Eduardo's smile was shaky. His eyes still tearful. All he'd had to do was click on a voice recorder when Raf said turn it on and click it off when Raf said do that; but the ancient recording of a Moslem girl being tortured kept repeating in his head.

'One of the best,' Raf said to Hakim, as Eduardo turned away. 'One of the best.'

Hakim looked doubtful.

'I mean it,' said Raf, and watched Eduardo shuffle away from Café

Athinos, dodging traffic until he finally reached his ancient Vespa, which was parked up next to the Corniche wall. It took Eduardo five goes to kick-start the machine.

The man cost Champollion less than the precinct paid out each week for fresh coffee and still counted himself lucky.

'Guard the hospital,' said Raf to the two men remaining, well aware that Hakim and Ahmed were really meant to guard him. By giving them other duties he freed himself up; they both knew that and were power-less to do anything about it. And besides, governors of Iskandryia were supposed to be impossible to work for, it went with the job description. 'Find the prisoners proper clothes,' he added as an afterthought, 'and get a doctor in to see to the girl's back.'

Raf caught the look in Hakim's eye. No matter what had really happened, an enhanced version would be round the precinct within minutes. His officers could be relied on to guarantee that his reputation lived up to its reputation.

'She'll live,' said Raf as he slipped on his shades and collected his own jacket from the back of Ahmed's café chair.

There were at least fifteen other cars on the road, now that the curfew had been lifted. They were old, battered and driven by grinning men who waved to friends and sometimes complete strangers. It was an irony of the EMP blasts that those whose vehicles were oldest were those least affected.

Garages were still shut but the electricity was back in a third of the city and standpipes were already being removed from at least one *arrondissement*, which now had water. Shops were reopening. All of the newsfeeds had miraculously been restored. Foreign reporters were busy doing talking heads about how El Iskandryia was slowly getting back on its feet.

On his way out of the city, Raf halted the Bentley beside an over-flowing irrigation ditch and tossed in the tiny recorder. The woman on it had died long before he was born; and although the recording, smuggled at great risk from a cellar in Kosovo, had not been allowed as evidence at a later trial, a copy of the recording had found its way to Amnesty. Their 'democracy in action' radio advertisement was judged political and banned in twenty-four of the twenty-six countries in which it was due to run.

'What now?'

'His Excellency Ashraf al-Mansur . . .' St Cloud's major-domo was careful not to look at his master. Not seeing things he shouldn't see formed a substantial part of his duties. 'He *demands* admittance.' The small Scot spoke the word with such relish that the Marquis looked up and almost blew his carefully constructed, syncopated rhythm.

Luckily the object of his interest kept moving, eyes fixed into the far distance. Drugs, familiarity or fear had emptied the adolescent's smooth face of anything except boredom and an instinct for absolute obedience.

'Show him in.'

'Sir?'

'Show in al-Mansur.'

The majordomo bowed and withdrew, walking backward from the chamber.

'The Marquis will see you now.' He gestured politely towards a large door and the unacceptability of what lay beyond. 'You may find him . . .' The majordomo hesitated. 'A little distracted.'

Raf entered without knocking. Unlike the tiled, fountained and pillared Moorish fantasy that was Dar St Cloud, the Marquis' villa overlooking Cap Bon in Tunisia, the drawing room of his house at Aboukir could have been transported wholesale from Paris.

Gérard's *Cupid and Psyche* hung in pride of place on the far wall. An adolescent Cupid chastely kissing the brow of a blonde girl who stared wide-eyed straight at the door where Raf stood, her hands folded neatly below naked breasts. A *Vulcan Surprising Venus and Mars* hung beside it, a huge canvas edged in heavy gilt, with the frame so massive that it almost touched both ceiling and floor. And on other walls, endless young nymphs gazed innocent-eyed at lean shepherd boys, oblivious to their own seminakedness.

A Napoleon III sideboard was positioned directly beneath the Gérard, its top a single slab of horsehair marble cut from a quarry outside Milan. Along the top were ranged naked glass figures, mostly Lalique, and two decanters.

'Pour yourself a small drink.' The Marquis spoke without looking up or releasing the figure still sitting on his lap (what with the shaved skull and baggy shirt, it was impossible to tell if St Cloud's companion was male or female). 'This won't take long.'

'It might,' said Raf, 'if we're going to cover who had Kamil Quitrimala kidnapped, why three tourists were butchered to order, a casino burned and the pipeline to a refinery cut. And that's before we . . .'

'Out,' said St Cloud crossly. And the adolescent to whom he spoke disappeared in a flurry of colt like legs and a flash of thin buttocks. The oversized shirt was St Cloud's own, Raf realized; its use a badge of ownership or fondness received, perhaps both.

'Gang warfare for the casino and kidnapping . . . Psychopaths for the murders, variously dead, I believe. And I assume the Sword of God was behind the refinery, just as it was behind those outrageous EMP bombs.' The Marquis gave a smile.

'You assume wrong.'

St Cloud looked at him.

'What,' said Raf, 'do you know about the Osmanli Accord?'

'Less than nothing.' St Cloud's voice was firm. 'I never bother myself with politics.'

'So it would shock you to discover that, behind the scenes, Berlin needs French agreement to retain its spheres of influence . . . As does Moscow?'

The Marquis snorted. 'The idea that Berlin would ask anything of Paris is as unbelievable as . . .'

'The idea that someone French might demand a price of Berlin,' Raf said smoothly. 'Well, while you're at it, imagine that breaking Hamzah was the only result to matter in our little local crisis.'

'Hamzah Effendi?' St Cloud shook his head. 'Surely not . . .'

Raf nodded. 'Imagine everything else was just so much means to an end. So the question I have to ask is, Who would want to damage Hamzah?'

'Who indeed . . .' said St Cloud. 'I suspect we'll never know. Always assuming there was somebody.' He stood up from his elegant Louis XVIII chair, casually slipped himself back inside his trousers and made for the sideboard.

'Are you sure . . . ?' His hand hovered above a brandy balloon.

'Absolutely,' said Raf. 'Beyond doubt.'

'Your choice . . .'

St Cloud poured himself a generous measure of Courvoisier and swilled it round the balloon, bending close to inhale the heavy fumes. 'Of course,' he added as an apparent afterthought, 'even if this were all true . . . It doesn't change the fact that Hamzah is guilty as hell. And there's always the future ownership of that refinery to consider . . .'

'Plus the Midas oil fields in central Sudan and certain Mediterranean offshore sites.'

'Quite,' said St Cloud. 'Now, should a senior official find himself in a position to facilitate the transfer of Hamzah's part of those holdings . . . After they've been legally forfeited by Hamzah, obviously. Then any country intent on consolidating its interests would undoubtedly be very generous.'

'Generous?'

'A commission is usual in these cases.'

'Five percent?'

St Cloud looked shocked. 'One or two. Three at the absolute maximum.'

'And what would three percent come to?'

The Marquis told him.

Raf decided to take that drink after all.

CHAPTER 56

1st November

The trial proper began two days after Raf's visit to the house at Aboukir. On the morning of 5th Safar 1472, a day that Raf thought of as Monday 1st November . . .

Within the first hour, Zara reached the inescapable conclusion that the man whose bed she'd twice shared was about to destroy her father. So now she sat at a long desk at the front of the temporary court and shuffled papers, while atrocity after atrocity unravelled itself on-screen.

Atrocity was the word Raf used to describe what the judges were seeing. It wasn't a term to which Zara felt she could object.

Hani, however, sat at the back. And although the steady swing of her legs, which earlier had been flicking backward and forward to scuff the floor, had stopped completely, she resolutely watched one of the screens, her dark eyes darting from horror to horror; though whether to see more or allow herself to take in less was hard to tell.

She shouldn't have been on board the SS *Jannah* anyway, which the Khedive had declared Iskandryian soil for the duration of Hamzah's trial. But Khartoum had been strangely willing to be persuaded that he should accompany her, and the soldiers at the door had done nothing but stare at the cat on her shoulder. As a result, she now sat beside the skeletal Sufi in a makeshift public gallery, watching things she was pretty sure she didn't want to see.

The picture quality was terrible, the contrast too sharp, and the camera juddered with the reporter's every step, none of which really mattered. It was what the camera showed that counted. Oh, and spinning numbers near the bottom that gave time, date and an accurate GPS reading.

The ownership of the battleground itself was moot. So the location was translated underneath as 'Northeastern Sudan/Southern Egypt (disputed) . . .'

At first, as Raf gestured at the early images, inviting the judges, press and public to watch the evidence being presented, he'd thought the juddering was due to gyroscope malfunction in the original handheld camera, but as the lens panned across another dead boy, fist stuffed into his mouth to prevent himself from crying out, he realized the gyroscope just hadn't been able to compensate for the photographer's shock.

Raf pushed a button on his control and the picture froze.

The assignment had both made and destroyed Jean René; turning the man into a living saint and consigning him to forty years of knowing his single most significant work was already behind him.

Raf stepped back to give the judges clear sight of the elderly, shock-haired Parisian, who stood in a witness box built overnight by carpenters at the Khedive's order.

'Who took these photographs?'

The elderly man stared down his hawklike nose. 'You know who took those,' he said crossly. 'Why else would I be here . . . ?'

Raf smiled sympathetically. Nodding to show he understood the tumble of emotions through which the man must be going. 'Who took these photographs?' Raf repeated, his voice loud enough to carry to the public gallery.

'I did,' said Jean René.

'You did?' Flipping open a leather notebook, Raf pretended to check its screen. Working hardware, decent lighting and reliable power had ceased to be a problem the moment Tewfik Pasha relocated the court to the ballroom of the SS *Jannah*.

'You are a war reporter?'

'I was,' said the man bitterly.

'And you gave up when?'

The man's leonine mane of white hair rippled as he nodded towards the frozen screen, where the dead boy still lay with one fist in his open mouth. 'I gave up after that,' he said. 'How could I not?'

'And you became what?' Raf asked, glancing again at his notebook.

'I founded Sanctuary,' said Jean René, staring at the judges. His gaze bathed St Cloud, the Graf and Senator Liz in ill-hidden contempt. 'So long as countries like yours fight their wars by proxy there will always be work for people like me.'

Senator Liz opened her mouth but shut it again at a glance from St Cloud.

'Excellency . . .' St Cloud's tone made it clear Raf could continue.

Only Raf was thinking, of nothing.

Less than nothing.

'Excellency . . .'

Raf came awake with a start, glanced at the judges and realized it was still his witness, but he had no questions for Jean René. Not real ones. Hamzah had been there, DNA matching marked him out as the soldier found on the battlefield by the Red Cross. His fingerprints, taken by a teenage Jewish nurse who hoped to reunite the boy with his parents, had identified Hamzah as the person who loaded and fired the HK21e machine gun.

If that wasn't enough, the boy's inky thumbprint validated a typed confession found locked in a Chubb in Koenig Pasha's study; typed, it seemed, on an old Remington Imperial, to ensure no trace was left on any datacore. The confession had been witnessed by a certain Major Koenig Bey. A copy of this rested among the documents piling up in front of the three judges.

As for the defendant himself, guilt oozed from Hamzah's skin like sweat. Expensive and over tailored though his clothes might be, they still hung from his diminished body like a beggar's rags. Everything about the man conceded defeat.

There was very little chance that Raf could blow this case. And inside his own head, Raf was already writing his closing speech, the winning address he'd make once all the evidence, both direct and circumstantial, had been heard. Once the transcripts, old newsfeeds and actual weapons had been examined.

The press were already his, Raf could tell that just from watching them. The public gallery were glued to every unfolding moment. It was undeniably time to wind up his examination of this witness and let Zara take the floor.

Flicking his eyes from the photograph on-screen, back to where Jean René stood in the makeshift witness box, Raf opened his mouth to thank the man and did what he'd been avoiding doing all morning, somehow allowed his gaze to shift past René to where Zara sat.

Pain.

Absolute loneliness.

Enough of both to rock the courtroom around Raf.

If ever he'd needed the fox it was now. The fox would have known what to do because the fox always knew what to do. That was why it existed. To take from Raf the need to make those kind of decisions.

Ashraf al-Mansur, sometime ZeeZee, shuddered at this sudden understanding. Or else the courtroom shuddered. Whatever, something did as his eyes adjusted. And the rococo magnificence of the ballroom, with its borrowed ceiling, faux marble and fat gilded cherubs faded to a pixillated blur.

'Safety off,' said a gun.

Raf blinked at the words in his head and felt the cherubs reappear. Nothing had changed except for him and that change was so small, he wasn't even sure it was real. But then, he'd never been too sure about anything. Mostly he just accepted things. Accepted, then assimilated the accepting. Whatever he needed to become he became . . .

Some people regarded that as a psychologically adaptive advantage. Others knew it as negative capability. A few said, without quite realizing what they said, 'There but for the grace of . . .'

And then Raf found himself inside a battle.

Standing beside Ka, Zac said nothing. He'd talked little enough when he was alive and now he was dead he spoke even less . . .

Ka thought that strange.

'Distance?'

'Half a klick and closing . . .'

It was an incredibly stupid weapon and the kid with the amulets didn't know why the manufacturer had bothered. But then the kid was just that, a kid. Someone too young to make the link between action and . . .

Everything that Raf had ever read about The Hague Convention suddenly ran like water through the parched soil of his mind.

'Did you actually photograph this man?' Raf turned to point at Hamzah who, for the first time since the trial had begun, lifted his head and looked around the well of the court. Maybe it was something in Raf's voice or else he too could hear clouds growling low like thunder.

Justice. That was what a court was supposed to provide. And he was Ashraf al-Mansur, Ottoman bey and supposedly Governor of El Iskandryia, for the next few hours at least. Raf looked at Zara, then inside himself.

The living saint looked puzzled.

'It's a simple enough question,' Raf insisted. 'Did you photograph Hamzah Quitrimala?'

'Back then?'

'Yes,' said Raf heavily, 'back then . . .'

Jean René nodded.

'You photographed Hamzah Effendi as a child?' Raf said slowly, as if trying to get something straight in his head.

'I did. Yes.'

'Describe him.'

Puzzled, the elderly man glanced from Raf to the row of judges who sat watching from their raised bench. Above and behind them, alone at a higher bench sat the Khedive.

'Hamzah's over there,' said Raf. 'Not on the judicial benches. That is, if you need to take another look.'

Jean René hesitated.

'Tell us,' demanded Raf. 'How did he look?'

They stared at each other across the well of the court. And somewhere at the back of the bey's mind, thoughts continued to resonate until their growl manifested as a shiver that ran the length of his spine.

'Nothing unusual,' Jean René said finally. 'Scruffy. Wearing a man's shirt, trousers held up by a broken belt.'

'Broken?'

'The buckle was missing. The belt was tied round his waist. He had bare feet but then they all did. After a while, hot sand and gravel baked their feet to leather . . .'

'You've looked at this photograph recently?'

Raf paused, seeing Jean René look uncertain. 'It's a simple enough question,' he said. 'Did you dig out your photograph of this murderer?'

'Objection . . .' Zara was on her feet.

The Khedive shook his head, 'Objection overruled.' He turned to Raf, eyes hard. 'Presumably you have sound reasons for this line of questioning . . . ?'

Raf nodded. He had reasons all right. Half a dozen within his own head. Plus another, still standing, glaring at him. Although his main reason sat at the back of the court beside Khartoum, her eyes spilling over with tears as they flicked between him and Zara.

What was justice anyway?

Nothing most people would recognize. Nothing Hani had ever been given.

'Find the photograph,' Raf demanded. 'I want the court to take a good look at this killer.'

Finding the shot took a minute or two of skipping forward and backward, looking for the right image. And all the while, screens flickered with figures that came and went as Jean René trawled angrily through his notebook's data sphere.

A girl half-buried in a sand dune.

Camels starved to a sack of fur and protruding bone.

A burned-out Seraphim driven by something reduced by flame to the texture of bitumen. Teeth grinning from a lipless mouth.

Images enough to make the ballroom fall silent and its gilded elegance suddenly appear frivolous and out of place. And finally, when it seemed not even the judges could stand another close-up of a dead child, Jean René found the picture for which he'd been looking.

A boy shading his face against the sun as he stared into a hungry lens. The shirt he wore lacked buttons and the trousers had been hacked short in the leg. At his feet rested an open water bottle and a radio.

Half a dozen amulets hung around his neck. Most were beaten silver or brass, with one no more than a bundle of hawk feathers tied tight with a leaf. But the last one, the one that mattered because it led aid workers to get wrong which side he was on, was a small cross carved from bone. The boy's eyes were hidden by thick dark glasses and a cigarette hung from his bottom lip, tendrils of smoke vanishing into the hot-afternoon air.

Not that much older than Hani really.

'How old would you say this child was?'

'Irrelevant question.' Senator Liz Elsing was out of her chair.

'Overruled,' said the Khedive. 'The prosecutor still has the floor, as is his right . . .' Tewfik Pasha's smile was thin. 'Mind you,' he said, 'if this is the prosecution, I can't wait for the defence.'

'How old?' Raf repeated.

Jean René thought about it, looked at the screen, then back at Hamzah, an element of certainty leaving his face. Finally the man shrugged. 'I don't know,' he said. 'It's hard to tell.'

'Then perhaps we should find somebody who can tell us . . .' Raf stared at the public benches and a dozen cameras clicked. 'Presumably the SS *Jannah* has a doctor . . . ?'

There was silence while the judges tried to work out which of them Raf was asking. Finally, they realized he was talking to the Khedive.

Tewfik Pasha nodded, reluctantly.

'And may I borrow your medical officer as an expert witness?'

The boy scowled, skin darkening under immaculately applied makeup. 'Of course,' he said. 'Provided the captain also agrees.'

The court recessed while the ship's medical officer was summoned. And then everyone waited again while a tall German woman introduced herself to the court and was sworn in.

'You are Lena Schultz?'

'I am.'

'And you trained where?'

'Heidelberg . . .'

Raf couldn't resist glancing at von Bismarck. The young Graf leant forward and Raf knew he, at least, would regard her every word as absolute.

'You are the surgeon for the SS *Jannah*?'

She shook her head and dark hair flicked across to touch her cheeks. 'I am not a surgeon,' said Dr Schultz. 'I am a general practitioner.'

'I see,' said Raf, sounding as if he didn't. 'Can you tell me why Utopia Lines employ a general practitioner?'

She looked at him.

'Instead of medical software.' Raf paused, wondering how best to qualify his question. 'I thought that statistically . . .'

'Some people,' she said heavily, 'actually prefer the human touch.' *Some people* being rich. At least that was the inference.

'Really?' Raf shrugged. 'In that case, don't such people bring their own?'

'It happens, sometimes.' Her tone made it quite clear she didn't like that question or him. 'Now,' she said. 'You need me to present an opinion on a medical matter?'

'Sort of . . .' Raf pointed to where the boy still shielded his eyes from a sun that caught on the edge of his open shirt and cast its shadow across his bare chest and stomach.

'How old is that boy?'

The woman barely glanced at the image. 'Impossible to say,' she said firmly.

'Is he twenty?'

'Obviously not.'

'Six?'

She shook her head crossly.

'So you can say,' Raf told her. 'That at the very least he's older than six and younger than twenty . . .'

Sometime between my burning down a school and the killing of Micky O'Brian.

'You didn't say you wanted a rough estimate . . .'

'We can get specific later,' said Raf. 'At the moment, any kind of estimate would be good.'

One minute turned into two and still she gazed intently at the screen . . . Longer than was necessary, but Raf didn't hurry her. The cameras were hard at work catching every furrow of her brow, every tiny twitch that pulled at her mouth as she lost herself in thought.

'Was this boy well fed?'

From his place in the dock Hamzah shook his head, the movement entirely unconscious. And up on the bench St Cloud cleared a sour smile from his face so fast only Raf saw it come and go. There were other smiles, fleeting and bitter, from ordinary people on the public benches. Mostly from those, like Khartoum, who were old enough to have the memories.

Into Raf's head came thoughts of drought-twisted olive groves, crumbling irrigation channels, bushes on which apricots wizened before they were even ripe enough to be picked. Poisoned oases and fields of millet being turned to straw by a sun that hung high overhead.

'Enough,' Raf insisted to himself and the images vanished.

'Well fed . . . ?' He shook his head. 'I think that unlikely.'

'In that case . . .' The woman hesitated. 'If the child was properly nourished, then I'd put his age at nine, with a sixty percent certainty. You have to look at the wrists,' she added, as if that explained everything. 'Chest too, to check development of the rib cage . . . Badly nourished, maybe ten, even eleven. My professional opinion is that the child is unlikely to be much older.'

'Court records say thirteen,' insisted Raf, and he made a point of double-checking the UN report in his hand.

'Thirteen . . . ? Very unlikely.' Dr Schultz's stare was a challenge. 'Twelve if you must, assuming he'd been starved from birth. Except, of course,' she shrugged, 'if he'd been starved from birth, then disease would have killed him before this.'

'So definitely not thirteen?'

'Ashraf Bey.'

Raf turned round to find the Khedive watching him.

'Can you tell me where this is headed?' Tewfik Pasha's question was abrupt, but there was something unsettled in his eyes. As if the youth had only just become aware that he sat exposed in front of the world's press, acting as *magister* while the richest man in North Africa was tried for mass murder.

And there was another truth from which the Khedive could find no escape. It was widely known that Zara had taken al-Mansur as her lover. And for all that the bey wasn't a true believer, he still had *baraka*. A difficult quality to pin down, although luck, wisdom and blessing were in there somewhere. All those and an aura of strength that the poor believed clung like attar of roses to anyone who chose the stony path.

'Where is this headed?' asked Raf. 'Towards a conclusion, I hope.'

'It matters how old Hamzah was?'

Raf nodded.

'And to whom does it matter?'

To me, Raf almost said but he kept silent on that point. 'To the city,' he said instead. 'And also to you, as the city's *magister*, I presume . . .'

'Yes,' said the Khedive, 'you do.'

Raf looked puzzled.

'You presume,' Tewfik Pasha said with a tight smile. 'But then, perhaps somebody has to . . . Tell us why it matters.'

Raf picked up his notebook, tapped an icon for The Hague Convention and flicked to the relevant subsection. Ready to read . . .

'If a combatant is twelve or under at the time of a battle, s/he shall be exempt from direct responsibility and such responsibility lies with whoever issued the command . . .'

For a moment Raf thought the words were his, happening only in his head. Then he saw the fear on the face of Hamzah Effendi and realized the industrialist had also heard the gruff voice. As had Senator Liz, the young German Graf and a shocked-looking St Cloud.

Over on her bench, Zara began crying. Only Avatar looked at ease.

CHAPTER 57

There'd been tears too from Hamzah when he finally realized who was speaking. Instinctively, the thickset industrialist had straightened up, standing taller in the dock.

'*Ya Colonel,*' he said, sounding amazed.

'Lieutenant Ka.'

And then everyone in the court watched as Hamzah craned his head, looking round for his old commander. Only there was no Colonel Abad. Just a cracked radio held by Iskandryia's favourite DJ and a familiar voice that echoed from a wall speaker.

'You never did get to the source of the Nile,' said the Colonel.

Hamzah shook his head.

'But you still got me to safety . . .' The voice sounded content. 'Well, you got me to Koenig Pasha, which was almost as good. PaxForce wanted to kill me you know . . .'

'You're a radio?'

Colonel Abad chuckled. 'You might put it like that. Langley built me for counterinsurgency use in Colombia, then the Soviets patched in some ideology and relocated me to the Sudan. The CIA got me back eventually, ripped out the politics and offered me the Children of God.'

'But I was Islamic Fist, first battalion, company A.'

'No/yes . . . Well, some of the time,' conceded the Colonel. 'It wasn't always so simple . . .'

'You,' said Senator Liz to Avatar, 'bring that machine here.' Her New Jersey accent sliced through what threatened to become a conversation between old comrades.

Avatar did as he was told, placing the clockwork radio carefully on the judicial bench in front of the American woman. The radio was small, battered and scratched along the bottom. Its shattered handle suggested someone had once kicked the thing.

'You can hear me?'

'Of course I can hear you . . . Senator Elizabeth Lee Elsing.'

'And you know me how . . . ?'

'Your face matches all points on a security photograph taken when Elizabeth Lee Elsing came aboard. Your voice profile fits exactly a phrase Elizabeth Lee Elsing recorded to control the strongbox in her suite.'

'This thing is an appliance,' said von Bismarck. The expression on his face mixed revulsion with shock.

'An American appliance,' confirmed the box. 'Upgraded by Moscow and offered exile by Koenig Pasha, with the express consent of your own superiors in Berlin. A machine linked to software designed to win wars fought by children . . . Although, of course, their age was just an unexpected cost bonus. And *you* have this man on trial . . .'

'Are you saying you should be the one on trial?' St Cloud asked silkily.

'Obviously not,' said the box. 'I was thinking more that it should be all of you.'

'I suggest,' said the Khedive, when calls had been made, legal advice taken and the case reconvened later that afternoon. 'I suggest that we concentrate on one trial at a time.' He turned to Senator Liz. 'Do your friends in the CIA want to reclaim this box?'

She looked at the young Khedive as if he'd suddenly spat on her. 'Reclaim it?' the Senator said furiously. 'We don't even accept that we made it. The Soviets maybe. Although I wouldn't put it past Berlin . . .' She scowled bitterly at the young Graf, who sat carefully examining his nails.

Tewfik Pasha sighed. 'Your witness,' he said to Raf.

A hundred tiny pinhead lenses were set into the walls of the ballroom, Raf realized that well enough, but he turned to a wall-mounted CCTV camera to let the judges know he spoke direct to Colonel Abad.

'You recognize this man?' Raf asked, jerking his head towards Hamzah.

'I recognize his voice,' said the box, 'once suitable allowances have been made for vocal developments. And it doesn't matter if I say I recognize him or not. Protein pattern matching has already confirmed his identity.'

'Did he ever tell you his age?'

Colonel Abad stayed silent.

'You don't know how old he was at the time of the massacre?'

'*Massacre* . . .' The word was said thoughtfully, though whether that

571

was because Abad was thinking or because elegant programming had anchored emotions to set logic sequences was impossible to tell.

'One hundred and fifty-three people died that afternoon,' said the Colonel. 'Two weeks before, according to UN reports, 1,002 refugees were reclassified as collateral damage when a poorly targeted skySucker destroyed the oxygen over their camp. Seven days after, 503 died outside Wadi Haifa in a firefight between the Ragged Army and the Children of God. I note that neither of these incidents is down on record as a massacre . . .

'So your logic suggests,' continued the machine, 'that when 503 children kill each other it's not a massacre, but when one child kills 153, then it is. Have I got that right?'

'Answer the original question,' said Raf. 'Did he ever tell you his age?'

'Very few of them knew their age,' Abad said mildly. 'And it's unlikely that Ka was any different. But you could always try working it out. For example, your reports say Ka told the Red Cross he came from Azarat and his mother died when he was a baby . . .'

Raf waited.

'Didn't it occur to anyone to ask him from what?'

Glancing at Hamzah, Raf raised his eyebrows.

'Plague,' Hamzah said. 'That's all I was told. After the wells dried up and the crops died, she and my uncle walked north to Suakin and joined a caravan to El Makrif to get away from war.' Hamzah shrugged. 'So did everybody else.'

'Drought,' said Abad. 'War, plague and a migration of refugees . . . There were droughts in 89, 91, and 01. Beni-Amir conflicts from 87 to 91 and 98 to 03. Ebola in 91, 93 and 99 to 02.' The Colonel reeled off the figures, as if talking to itself. 'Migrations from 87 to 92, after which the UN closed the routes to stop refugees creating new vectors for the plague.'

'Which means,' Raf and Senator Liz said together, 'he was born in 91.' They'd been following the figures in their heads. The Graf was still busy writing out his sums longhand and St Cloud was doodling.

'Assume he was born in the spring,' said Raf. 'How old was he?'

'Nine on joining and eleven at the time of the *massacre*.'

Raf turned to where the SS *Jannah*'s medical officer sat near the front. 'Would you agree with that assessment?'

'It is perfectly possible,' Dr Schultz said slowly.

'Thank you.' Raf nodded to the bench. 'That finishes the case for the prosecution.' He glanced over at Zara. 'I imagine Miss Zara is impatient to make the case for the defence.'

St Cloud snorted.

'With the *magister*'s permission, this court will recess for ten minutes,' he announced, banging his gavel on its wooden pad . . .

After that, the rest was a formality. The judges decided two to one that there was no case to answer, with the dissenting vote being St Cloud. Ernst von Bismarck went out of his way to stress that Hamzah was completely exonerated. Just to make doubly sure, he explained, to the amusement of the more upscale newsfeeds, that this didn't mean Hamzah had been found not guilty. For the simple reason that Hamzah didn't need to be found not guilty. There was no case to answer.

In the seventy-five seconds it took Claire duBois's talking head to hit Television 5, Hamzah mutated from a heavily armed teen psychopath to traumatized drought victim, stranded alone in the desert, trying desperately to carry out conflicting orders.

CHAPTER 58

'If you don't move,' said the fox, *'you'll be late for Hamzah's party.'*

'Yep,' agreed Raf and reached for his cappuccino.

The power was back on at Le Trianon and the first thing the kitchens had done was whip up a fresh batch of ice cream for Hani, the kind made with vanilla pods. A glass flute of the stuff now sat, almost untouched, in front of her.

'Not hungry?'

Hani shrugged. A minute or so later, while Raf pretended not to watch, she stirred the ice cream to a pulp with her long silver spoon.

'You going to let her get away with that?' asked the voice.

'Probably.'

'You're talking to the fox,' said Hani.

Raf nodded.

'The one hidden in your head?'

He nodded again.

'Okay.' The small girl put down her spoon, then picked it up again. Le Trianon was absolutely her favourite café and vanilla supposedly her favourite flavour, but Hani obviously wasn't enjoying herself.

'Colonel Abad mended your fox?'

They'd been over this a dozen times. Raf couldn't bring himself to believe this was the real problem, but it was the point to which she kept coming back.

'That's right,' he said.

'How?'

'He took a look inside my head, then fixed a software glitch that stopped the fox from being able to feed.'

'Did it hurt?'

'Too fast,' said Raf. 'I didn't even know it had happened.'

'And Colonel Abad doesn't really exist?'

574

'He's as real as the fox.'

Hani looked doubtful. 'How real is that?'

As questions went, this one was more difficult to answer. Actually, as questions went, that one was next to impossible . . . A software program designed to mimic the cunning and charisma of a long-dead revolutionary undoubtedly existed. It had led the Ragged Army, changed sides, then changed back again. Several times, from what it said.

The view of the *Washington Post* was that it was equal in intelligence to any human and therefore as dangerous. *Le Matin* disagreed, describing it as a military chess computer, a view also held by *Pravda*.

'I think it exists,' Raf said carefully.

'But you think the fox exists,' said Hani, brushing crossly at her fringe.

They were seated at a pavement table, even though the weather was cold and the first Saturday in November had brought fewer people than normal out onto the streets. And she'd brought him there because he knew she liked it, if that made sense.

'Zara's mother says that you're insane.' Hani's voice was matter-of-fact, although Raf caught the sideways glance that checked he wasn't angry. Only he was angry and had been since the trial was aborted five days before.

And in a way he was jealous. Raf sat back in his chair and closed his eyes. He was jealous of Avatar, for retrieving the Colonel. And furious with Zara, who'd known at least some of what Hani was doing.

'Uncle Raf . . .'

Raf opened his eyes.

'I'm sorry. All right . . .' Hani picked up her spoon and ate a mouthful of runny vanilla, as if that might make a difference. 'I should have told you.'

'Yeah, you really . . .' Raf swallowed the rest of his words. 'Forget it,' he said, turning to more important matters. 'You don't like vanilla ice cream anymore, do you?'

'It's okay.' Hani shrugged.

'What happened?'

The nine-year-old thought for a second. 'I grew out of it,' she said. 'It happens.'

A butler met them at the steps. He wasn't anyone Raf had seen before. And if he seemed surprised to see a blond young man in dark glasses and drop-pearl earring holding the hand of a small black-haired child, he didn't let it show. At least not that much.

'Ashraf al-Mansur,' said Raf.

'We're here for the party,' added Hani.

'Can I ask if His Excellency is expecting you?'

His Excellency? Raf smiled. That was a new one.

'This is the Governor of El Iskandryia,' Hani said crossly. 'He doesn't need an invitation.' She squeezed Raf's hand, as if she thought the butler's question might have upset him.

'Hamzah is expecting me . . . Expecting us,' Raf corrected himself.

'Very good.' The man turned, obviously intending to leave them on the doorstep until Hani pushed her way in with a sigh.

'English,' Hani said loudly, as the butler stalked away down the corridor, back stiff with disapproval. 'Madame Rahina's price,' she added more softly.

'For what?'

'For not throwing a complete tantrum about you and about Avatar.' Hani sounded like a middle-aged woman discussing a small child rather than the other way round.

'Come on . . .' She set off towards the drawing room, without waiting for the butler to return. And Raf let himself be tugged towards a babble of voices filtering through an ornately carved door.

The Long Drawing Room at the Villa Hamzah, so called to distinguish it from the Square Drawing Room on the floor above, was decorated to Madame Rahina's taste. Which mostly involved European wallpaper in green-and-silver stripes, gold velvet sofas and faux-Persian carpets from a place called Axminster. At least that was where they came from according to the fox, who layered little bubble facts over every object until Raf ordered it to stop.

'Ashraf . . .'

Hamzah Effendi stepped forward, hand outstretched and grabbed Raf's own, wringing it hard. 'You found us then . . . ?' The barrel-chested man stopped and grinned at his own stupidity. 'Of course you found it. You've been here . . .'

'Several times,' Raf agreed.

'But not as often as me,' said Hani smugly and let go his hand to scoot away across the carpet to where Zara sat, with a cup of Earl Grey, talking stiltedly to the Khedive.

'I remember when she was never going to set foot in this house again,' said Raf. He spoke without really thinking. As the fox kept reminding him, he did a lot of that.

'She told you?'

Raf nodded. 'Months ago. After the beating. When I was patching her up.'

'I didn't know it had happened until later,' Hamzah Effendi said flatly.

'You had other things on your mind.'

The industrialist glanced at Raf, then realized the comment was no criticism. 'Yes,' he said, 'I did. And I have you to thank for . . .'

Raf stepped back and held up both hands. 'I was there to *prosecute* you,' he reminded Hamzah.

'Ah,' said St Cloud as he materialized beside them both. 'So that's what you were doing. We did wonder.' He flashed Raf a smile and, when it wasn't returned, the Marquis just shrugged and lifted a champagne flute from a passing tray.

And as the young waiter stopped dead, embarrassed not to have realized that St Cloud needed a drink, the elderly Frenchman finished his first glass, put it back and took another.

'Most kind, dear boy,' he said lightly . . .

'Don't you think,' St Cloud said to Raf, 'that our host should rescue his daughter from having to talk to that little idiot?' He jerked his head towards the sofa, where Tewfik Pasha still sat with Zara, while Hani squatted impatiently on the arm.

'Maybe she likes talking to him,' said Raf.

The industrialist raised his eyebrows and went to do as St Cloud suggested.

'What percentage?' Raf demanded, the moment Hamzah was gone.

St Cloud looked at him.

'What percentage of the Midas Refinery do you currently own?' Raf didn't bother to keep the anger out of his voice.

'Seven percent, maybe eight . . . Enough to make Hamzah respectable, not enough to make a difference. It's in all the records.'

'And you wanted more?'

'More?' St Cloud spread his hands and smiled mockingly, although Raf found it impossible to tell if he was the person being mocked or if the man was mocking himself. *'Moi?'*

'Does Hamzah know it was you?'

'Me what . . . ? Even if that were true,' said St Cloud, taking a glass from Raf's hand and finishing it, 'which I obviously deny, he can't touch me any more than you can. My advice is take his cash and leave it at that.'

'Discussing money?' said Ernst von Bismarck as he joined their small group. The German ambassador didn't know whether to look shocked or intrigued.

'Ashraf Bey's just reward,' St Cloud said smoothly. 'It's bound to be vast. Which I gather is just as well . . .'

'These Arabs.' The Graf's voice was serious. 'Debts matter to them. You must let him give you something. I'm told you didn't when you saved Miss Zara from that mad assassin.'

St Cloud laughed. 'Which mad assassin would that be?' he asked. 'The mad *Thiergarten* one?'

The Graf paid no attention. 'People tell me Hamzah Effendi was very hurt . . .'

'*Give me something?*'

Ernst von Bismarck looked surprised. 'What do you think this is about?' His gaze took in Zara, Hamzah and the Khedive, Senator Liz, Captain Bruford from the SS *Jannah* and General Koenig Pasha.

'Such a miraculous recovery,' said the Marquis. 'For which we must all be heartily grateful, no doubt.'

'And then there are those two journalists,' added von Bismarck. He ran together their names and stations, as if they were part of the same thing. 'Both of whom are desperate to interview you . . .'

'About the city's miraculous recovery, no doubt.' St Cloud shrugged. 'It's amazing how fast Iskandryia managed to get back on its feet. One's almost tempted to suggest things were not quite as bad as the world believed.'

He raised his eyebrows.

'Believe me,' said Raf. 'Those EMP bombs inflicted enormous damage.'

'Oh I'm sure that's true. I can even believe that all the cars and trams were affected and all the phone lines. But just imagine, every single electricity substation, every gas-processing plant, the entire IOL network and all of the power supplies to all of the local newsfeeds, even the pumps to the main water supply . . . Everything, suddenly dead, as if someone somewhere threw a big switch.'

'*He knows,*' said the fox.

'The e-bombs were real,' Raf reiterated.

'And as I've already said,' repeated St Cloud, 'I don't doubt that for a minute.' He twirled his empty champagne flute until it hung upside down. At which point a waiter hastily appeared, bearing a silver tray full of freshly filled glasses.

'You do realize, don't you,' said von Bismarck, 'that the reappearance of Abad leaves us with a major problem . . .'

'I rather imagined,' Raf said, 'that you'd all fight over ownership while pretending to be friends . . .' Reaching for a passing glass of champagne, he casually killed it and took another. 'Isn't that what diplomacy is about?'

'So young,' said St Cloud, 'and yet so cynical.'

The Marquis turned his attention to the German ambassador. 'And where Abad is concerned there is no *us*. Paris wasn't part of making the hideous thing, or subverting it come to that.'

'Soon,' said Raf, 'you'll be telling me you didn't know Abad still existed . . . Or where he was hidden.'

'We didn't.' St Cloud shrugged. 'At least not officially, and that's what counts. Mind you,' he added, 'we certainly intend to be part of trying the monster.'

'Assuming it can be tried,' said a voice. But the fox's comment was lost, because somewhere across the other side of the Long Drawing Room Hamzah nodded to Avatar, who hammered a whisky glass down on a wooden overmantel.

'Your Highness, gentlemen, ladies . . .' Hamzah should have got an *Excellencies* in there after *Highness*, but having had a speech carefully prepared by Olga he'd decided at the last minute to do without notes.

He knew exactly what he wanted to say.

This was payback time, in its way. He had a roomful of notables, most of whom didn't want to be there but knew better than to refuse. Twenty-seven-point-three percent of the Midas Refinery belonged to him, which was why St Cloud, its urbane public face, joked uneasily at the edge of a group that included Ashraf Bey and that young German.

St Mark's relied on Hamzah's generosity for its recent scholarships. He could see the headmaster across the room, a drab Christian Brother wrapped in dirt-coloured tweeds. The city's famous library still needed new glass, somewhat urgently after the recent bouts of rain. Madame Syria was smiling fondly at Hani, but she'd been less happy earlier, when she'd been talking to Zara about the library's need to find finance for repairs.

The two thickset men in suits, standing over by the door, headed up the Kharmous and El Anfushi crime families and were both doing their uncertain best to look happy at finding themselves in the same room as Mushin Bey, Minister of Police.

'Your Highness, Excellencies, ladies and gentlemen . . .' Hamzah draped one arm heavily around Avatar's narrow shoulders. 'I don't think any of you have been formally introduced to my son Kamil.'

'Avatar,' insisted Avatar, but his heart wasn't really in it.

On the other side of the boy stood Madame Rahina, her face dark as thunder, her arms heavy with new and unwanted gold bracelets. And it was obvious that Hamzah was as oblivious to his wife's smouldering anger as he was to the tears running down his own broad cheeks.

*

'Very clever.' Senator Liz handed Raf a fresh glass of champagne and instantly a waiter materialized to spirit away his dirty glass, depositing it on a passing silver salver. Both waiter and salver-carrier were models of professionalism, right down to the shoulder-holstered guns under their left arms. Hamzah might be everyone's favourite son but he was still taking no chances.

'What was clever?' Raf asked.

'Taking the Colonel into protective custody.' The Senator's smile was tight. 'Can a synthetic intelligence be tried for crimes against humanity?' She shrugged. 'Thanks to you, I think we're probably about to find out.'

'Only if it's first possible for software to be extradited . . .' Raf said lightly.

The woman opened her mouth and forgot to close it.

'And that's always assuming the Khedive accepts the extradition papers. Which he probably won't.'

'What?'

'Colonel Abad has asked for political asylum.'

'On what grounds?'

'That it won't get a fair trial elsewhere.'

'Then try the thing in El Iskandryia' said the Senator. 'I don't see that being a problem. If you can stand having the reptiles crawl all over you again.' She glanced at C3N's Nick Richardson, accidentally caught his eye and immediately smiled.

'I hear you're going to put Colonel Abad on trial,' St Cloud said, about five minutes later, when he tracked Raf down to a window seat overlooking the grey waters of the Mediterranean. 'If Paris can be of any help . . .'

Raf shook his head. 'It's not going to happen.'

'Are you sure?'

'Oh yes,' said Raf, taking another sip from one glass too many. 'As sure as anything.'

'Such certainty in one so youthful.' The Marquis shrugged. 'The sign of true breeding. And yet, a German recently suggested to me that you were a fake and that, for undisclosed reasons, Koenig Pasha has been colluding in this pretence.'

'Really?' said Raf. 'I'd love to meet this person.'

'That might be difficult. She died in the basement of a derelict house. After someone took out her throat.'

'Which is what happens,' said the fox, *'if you build your city on top of a graveyard. The dead forget to stay dead.'*

Raf raised his glass to his lips and wondered why St Cloud was looking at him, then realized the glass was empty, again.

People nearby looked surprised when the fox made Raf click his fingers but the fox was too tired to care. It needed more champagne and then some sleep. A long dark sleep with no dreams. But most of all it wanted this party to end before Hamzah got round to making more speeches.

It just knew Raf was going to offend the man.

'She was right,' Raf told the Marquis, once both their drinks were refreshed and a nervous young waiter had vanished. 'Your woman got it right. I'm not a bey. I don't belong in El Iskandryia. My name isn't Ashraf al-Mansur . . .'

He watched the man walk away.

'I doubt I'm even Berber,' Raf added quietly, to no one in particular. 'Hani probably isn't my niece.' He glanced across to where the small girl stood next to Zara, half-listening to someone, half-staring at Raf. 'Maybe I'm just someone who got lucky . . .'

'Uncle Ashraf.'

Everyone in the room was looking in his direction, Raf realized. Hamzah, in particular, was waiting expectantly for something.

'He wasn't listening,' said Hani. She sounded obscurely proud of this fact. 'He was probably talking to his fox.'

'His what . . . ?' Zara sounded puzzled.

'It's a long story,' Hani told her. 'Weird too.'

'Well,' said Zara. 'Are you going to take Dad's money this time?'

'Your reward.' Hamzah's grin had become slightly anxious.

'No,' said Raf. 'I really don't think . . .'

What stopped him finishing his sentence was the anguish that flooded Zara's face when she realized he was about to hurt her father's feelings again.

'The thing is . . .' Raf paused.

'Oh really!' said the fox. *'The thing is what?'*

'The thing is,' said Raf carefully, 'my niece needs a dowry. And since she can't hold property for herself . . .' He didn't make Iskandryia's laws and pretty soon he was going to stop trying to uphold them. 'I thought perhaps His Highness and Hamzah Efifendi . . . As trustees?'

Tewfik Pasha looked shocked, then resigned, Hamzah looked delighted.

'You want all the reward to go to Hani?' It was Zara who spoke.

Raf nodded and saw St Cloud shake his head in disbelief.

'It's a large sum.' Koenig Pasha sounded doubtful.

'Good,' said Raf. 'Maybe it'll be enough to keep her out of trouble.'

Hani stuck out her tongue.

Later, when everyone had gone back to talking to each other, mostly about Hani's fabulous newfound wealth, St Cloud reappeared at Raf's side. 'Well,' he said, 'you won't take my bribe and you won't take Hamzah's . . . That either makes you unbelievably stupid or even more dangerous than I imagined.'

'I'll settle for a drink,' offered Raf.

'And I'd get you one,' St Cloud said, 'but your pretty little girlfriend thinks you've had enough.'

'She's right,' a familiar voice said in his head, but Raf shushed the fox into silence. There was something about St Cloud that required absolute concentration.

'Fifty million dollars . . . That's a lot to turn down.'

Behind his dark glasses, Raf blinked. 'Money' he said flatly, 'isn't everything.'

Or was that life?

'Maybe not,' said St Cloud. 'But if ever I need to buy you, I can see it'll have to be with something other than cash.'

'I'm not for sale.'

'Everyone is for . . .' The Marquis looked at Raf, then shrugged in disgust. 'People like you,' he said, 'fuck up the bell curve.'

'I'm impressed.'

'I'm not.' Raf looked round the discreetly lit drawing room. The elegant invitations with their gilt edges, china clay surface and hand embossing had given the party's duration as 2.30–6.30 P.M. and it was now just after 10.30 P.M. Raf had sobered up somewhat, mostly with the aid of proprietary alcohol inhibitors and, as yet, no one showed much sign of leaving.

'They don't dare go,' Zara said.

Raf didn't ask how she knew what he was thinking, just accepted it as something he'd have to get used to. Like the smell of her skin or the fact she looked better in old trousers and a silk cheongsam than any other woman in the room looked in that season's Dior. And there was a surfeit of that season's Dior.

There was one other thing about her. At no time had she tried to shoo Hani away, even though Hani had glued herself to Zara's side from the moment she arrived to the point she dropped in her tracks, dead to the world. And it was Zara's Chinese silk jacket that now made do as a blanket, covering the small girl who lay curled up on a sofa.

'Marry me,' said Raf.

It was Zara's turn to blink.

'You want to get married because I gave Hani my coat?' Zara smiled. 'I saw you check to see the kid was okay,' she added, by way of explanation. 'Then I saw you notice the goose bumps on my arms. You're not the only one who can play detective.'

'That's finished,' said Raf. 'I resigned ten minutes ago as Chief of Detectives. Ibrahim Osman gets the job. The Khedive will be appointing a new governor in the morning . . .'

'Koenig Pasha?'

'The Khedive seems keen to take the job himself,' said Raf. 'Apparently there's nothing in law that says the city needs a governor.'

'There's nothing to say it needs a Khedive . . .' Zara's voice was louder than it should be. With a rawness that he'd missed earlier.

Raf looked at her. 'He proposed, didn't he?' said Raf, suddenly understanding what had been right in front of his face.

'Oh yes.' Zara's voice was bitter. 'Despite the fact I'm apparently your lover. It seems he simply couldn't help himself. . . . One way and another, it's been quite a night for proposals.'

'Then I take mine back,' Raf said hurriedly.

'No,' said Zara. 'Don't . . . If you do that, I won't have the satisfaction of turning you down as well.'

'That's your answer?'

She was about to nod when Hamzah and Madame Rahina jostled their way out of the crowd. Zara's mother had changed her outfit, but still wore head-to-toe Dior and smelled of some number Chanel that was impossibly difficult to find. She also sported a scowl and an air of barely restrained fury at the way her husband had hooked his arm through her own.

'So what are you two up to?' Hamzah asked brightly.

'Oh' – Raf glanced at Zara – 'I was just asking her to marry me.'

Hamzah's grin died as his wife yanked herself free. Unfortunately, even on tiptoe, she remained too short to spot the Khedive over the heads of her other guests.

'By the window,' said Zara, 'sulking.'

'So,' Hamzah asked, 'it's agreed? You're going to marry Raf . . .'

Zara shook her head. 'Not a chance. But Hani's busy trying to persuade me to move into the al-Mansur madersa.'

Which was the first Raf had heard of it.

FELAHEEN

PROLOGUE

'Dig,' said the fox.

So Ashraf Bey dug. Fingers bleeding and grit compacted beneath his broken nails. With only their sticky rawness to persuade him that he was still in the world of the living.

'Dig harder.'

So he did that too. Handful after handful of coarse salt tumbling into his face, blinding his eyes and filling his mouth, half-open to drag oxygen from dead, fetid air. The voice in his head had promised to help Raf reach the surface but only if he obeyed every order without argument. Foxes were good at digging their way out of traps apparently.

Raf's biggest problem before he got buried alive was that no one had told him how far his authority went as the new Chief of Police for Tunis, so he'd decided to assume it went as far as he wanted; which was how he'd ended up . . .

'Like this, really.'

Raf wasn't too worried about talking to an animal that didn't exist. For a start he had a number of hallucinogens infecting his bloodstream, from an acid/ketamine mix to a particularly virulent grade of skunk. And besides, he knew Tiri was just an illusion.

They'd been through this. It was sorted out.

According to Tiri a thousand camels once fell through the crust of Ifriqiya's great salt lake, lashed to each other in a baggage train. With the beasts went their cargo of dates, the master of the caravanserai and those who led the animals. Only one man survived, a slave who was driven into the desert for lying. His untrustworthy testimony had been that nothing existed below the ground over which they'd walked but void. What he'd thought was endlessly real was no more solid than the skin of a drum or the shell of an egg sucked dry by a snake.

'So you see,' said the fox, *'things are . . .'*

'. . . Never what they seem.' Raf punched one fist through earth to reach air, 'So you keep telling me.'

Later, when he had dry-vomited fear from his belly, wiped dirt and tears from his face and come to terms with the fact that a surprisingly small hole in the ground near his feet represented victory over death, Ashraf Bey came to a deeper realization.

He stank.

There was no doubt about it. Rancid sweat and the smell of excrement rose like heat from his body. And with it came the stink of the grave. A sour, lingering foulness that varnished his nakedness, clogging the inside of his nostrils and infesting even the shafts of his blond hair.

Maybe it was this smell that drew the ghosts or perhaps the drugs in his blood cleared Raf's eyes to let him glimpse inside the egg. Whatever, when he set out across Chott el Jerid the ghosts went with him. Strangers who looked vaguely familiar. Some man he'd seen in a queue. A Chinese boy, both too vague and strange to coalesce. Lady Jalila he recognized. Elegant in her sand-coloured silk jacket stretched across ample breasts. Eyes made up, lips perfect, neck broken . . . She started to say something, then went, her words and ghost ripped apart in a gust of night wind.

Then the fat man came.

Which was, Raf realized, probably inevitable. Of all the people he'd killed it was Felix Abrinsky who mattered the most.

'You okay, blondie?'

Raf put one step doggedly in front of the other. Shaded his eyes from the sight and tried to pretend he wasn't crying. 'What do you think?' he said.

'You know how it goes,' said Felix. 'These days I don't have much of a brain for thinking.' And with that he limped away, dragging the foot that had been shattered half a year before, along with most of his skull, in a bomb blast meant for the man he'd just been walking beside.

PART ONE

CHAPTER 1

Tuesday 1st February

'Out of my way.' Major Jalal jabbed his elbow into the kidney of one photographer and shouldered another into the gutter, watching as frozen slush filled the man's scruffy shoes. Ten paces at most separated the limo from the door of the casino but five photographers barred the way. Well, three now.

'Chill,' his boss said with a broad smile. The major wasn't sure if that was an order or if His Excellency was commenting on New York's weather. So Jalal kept his reply to a nod, which covered both bases.

'Prince . . .'

'Over here . . .'

His Excellency Kashif Pasha was used to catcalls and noise from *nasrani* paparazzi, who whistled at him like he was someone's dog. It was the only thing he hated about coming to New York.

'Look this way.'

Kashif Pasha made the mistake of doing just that and found himself staring into the smirking face of Charlie Vanhie, a WASP reporter he'd had the misfortune to meet at least three times before.

'Tell us about your plan to throw a dinner to celebrate your parents' fiftieth wedding anniversary . . .'

Having made the mistake of looking at Charlie Vanhie, the pasha then compounded his error by actually speaking to the man. 'Forty-fifth,' he corrected, 'it will be their forty-fifth.'

'What makes you think the Emir will turn up?'

Kashif Pasha stared at the man.

'Given that he won't even be in the same room as your mother. What was it he called her . . . ?'

Major Jalal began to move towards the speaker but His Excellency held up one hand. 'Leave it,' he told the major. 'Let me handle this.'

Around the time Kashif Pasha stood on a snow-covered sidewalk in Manhattan, bathed in the light of a flashgun, a small girl sat at a cheap plastic laptop. She was preparing to answer a long list of EQ questions, most of them multiple choice.

Draped around the girl's neck was a grey kitten worn like a collar. Actually, Ifritah was almost six months old but she still behaved like a kitten so that was how the girl thought of her.

Lady Hana al-Mansur, wrote the girl in a box marked name. Then she deleted it and typed *Hani* instead. There was also a box for her age but this was more problematic since no one was quite sure. She chose *10*, because either she was about to become ten, or she was ten already, in which case she'd be eleven in less than a week.

In the box marked nationality Hani wrote *Ottoman* and when the software rejected this she wrote it again. So then the computer offered her a long list of alternatives which she rejected, finally compromising on *Other*.

The room where Hani sat was in a house five thousand five hundred and seven miles from New York. In El Iskandryia. A city on the left-hand edge of the Nile Delta. Right at the top where the delta jutted out into the Mediterranean.

The madersa looked in on itself in that way many North African houses do. It was old and near decrepit in places. With a grand entrance onto Rue Sherif at the front and an unmarked door that led out to an alley at the rear.

Guarding this door was a porter named Khartoum, because the city of Khartoum was where he came from and he'd refused to reveal any other. He smoked cigars backwards, with the lit end inside his mouth and had given Hani a tiny silver hand on a thread of cotton to help her do well in the tests.

This impressed Hani greatly and it went, almost without saying, that Hani would rather have had Khartoum with her than the cat but her uncle, the bey, had forbidden it. Not crossly. Just firmly. Because the box containing the test stated that all computers were to be off-line and no other people were to be in the room when the test was taken.

First off was an easy question about being caught in a plane crash. With her plane going down would she: 1) scribble her will on the back of an envelope; 2) offer her help to the pilot; 3) continue to read a magazine?

The answer was obviously continue to read since, a) she'd never learned to fly and so offering help was pointless and, b) she was unlikely to be carrying an envelope, had she had anything to leave anybody which she didn't . . .

Next question was about her *father/stepfather/legal other*. Since Hani had never met the first, lacked the second and was uncertain if her Uncle Ashraf counted as the third, she ignored it, as she did two more questions about her family.

Then there was a section on *school friends*, which Hani didn't even bother to read. The final bit was the simplest . . . Five hundred faces on a flat screen, each expressing anger or joy, happiness, boredom, sadness or pain.

Her job was to name that emotion. The section started at a crawl and for the first twenty or so faces Hani thought this was as fast as the software could go, but as impatience set in and Hani started hammering at the keys, her screen became a blur and soon the small girl was selecting answers so fast her computer had all its fans running.

She got every expression right except for five benchmark indicators where the picture was of her. Even so, according to the EQ software, Hani's was the highest score ever recorded for that section, certainly within the time.

The IQ test that followed was infinitely more difficult. So difficult in fact that Hani ran out of time on her very first question. Which was the odd animal out – a sheep, a hen, a dog or a shark? Above each choice was the small photograph, just in case she'd forgotten what the animals looked like.

As answers went, the shark seemed much too obvious. Especially given this was an intelligence test and identifying the first three as air-breathing and the shark as a cartilaginous water dweller took no intelligence at all.

So what else could it be? Sheep were actually domesticated goats. At least Hani was pretty sure they were. Hens had also been domesticated, as had dogs, which were really domesticated wolves. So the answer could be shark but for a less obvious reason, because humanity had no history of domesticating sharks.

But what if that was still too obvious?

In the end she chose the sheep over the hen, dog and shark because it was a herbivore and all the others ate meat. Although, in the case of the hen, Hani suspected that the bird was actually omnivorous. This seemed the mostly likely of the nineteen possible answers she jotted onto a piece of scrap paper.

'So what went wrong?' her uncle asked later, when he finally tracked Hani down to the madersa's roof where the girl sat oblivious to a cold glowering sky.

'With what?'

'Your second test. You only did one question and even then . . .' His voice trailed away.

'It wasn't the sheep?'

The thin man with the shades, goatee beard and drop-pearl earring shook his head.

'Which one was it?' Hani demanded.

'The shark.'

'Because it's not domesticated?'

Ashraf al-Mansur, known also as Ashraf Bey, put his face in his hands and for a moment looked almost ill. He had a niece half the city thought was retarded. A mistress who wasn't his mistress because they'd never actually fucked. And his own life . . . Raf stopped, considering that point.

He'd recently resigned his job, the madersa cost more to run than he had coming in and yet, between them, Hani and Zara were worth millions. He was being chased for debts while living in a house with two of North Africa's wealthiest people, either of whom would give him the money, if only he'd stop refusing to consider it. As Zara said, getting that to make sense was like trying to fasten jeans with a zip one side and buttonholes the other.

Hani sat her test again next morning. This time on the flat roof of the al-Mansur madersa. And she did exactly what her uncle suggested, which was give the most obvious answer to everything. It took her less than fifteen minutes to achieve a score higher than the software could handle.

CHAPTER 2

Tuesday 1st February

Everything about Manhattan was white, from the sidewalk beneath Major Jalal's boots to the static in his Sony earbead that told the major his boss was off-line again. White streets, white cars, white noise – one way or another snow was responsible for the lot. Well, maybe not the white noise.

Five hours earlier, the windchill along Fifth Avenue had been enough to make grown men cry but now the wind was gone, snow fluttered down between the Knox building and Lane Bryant like feathers from a ruptured pillow and the avenue ahead of him was as empty as the major's crocodile-skin wallet.

While his boss sat snug in Casino 30/54 losing sums of money the major could barely imagine, Major Jalal had been down to Mount Olive trying to bribe his way into the private room of Charlie Vanhie, the Boston photographer currently being wired for a broken jaw.

The contents of his wallet had gone to the pocket of a porter who took the lot and never came back. And then, when the major gave up in disgust, six sour-faced paparazzi appeared out of nowhere to grab frantic shots of him leaving the hospital, in the mistaken belief that the quietly dressed, moustachioed *aide-de-camp* was his Armani-clad, elegantly bearded boss. The major just hoped His Excellency was having a better night of it.

Unfortunately, Kashif Pasha wasn't.

Although the casino was in New York and His Excellency came from Ifriqiya, the roulette wheel at which he played originated in Paris. This ensured it had only one nonpaying number rather than the zero *and* double zero found on US tables. It was French because Kashif Pasha placed bets so high he could dictate the choice of wheel, thus limiting the edge allowed to the house. But for all this Kashif Pasha was still losing. (A situation drearily familiar to his aged mother, the Lady Maryam, his father and his bankers.)

'Excellency . . .'

Looking up, Kashif Pasha was in time to see an apologetic croupier lean forward and rake ten scarlet chips from the grid. So busy had he been listening to the dying clatter of the ivory ball that he'd forgotten to check on which number it landed. To Kashif's ear that unmistakable, addictive clicking was pitched somewhere between an old man's death rattle and the tapping of an infestation of wood beetle.

Both of which reminded him of home.

'You there.' Kashif Pasha tried to snap his fingers and winced, making do with a quick wave of his injured hand. The effect was identical. A young black woman in a short deerskin skirt hurried forward, a box of cigars open on her silver tray. Her legs were bare, her breasts laced into a tan waistcoat that otherwise gaped down the front. A badge shaped like a feather announced her as Michelle.

'Sir . . .' The waitress waited for the well-dressed foreigner to select a Monte Cristo and take the matches she offered. Something Kashif Pasha did without appearing to notice the bitten nails of his own hands, which spoke of long nights and too little sleep.

Embossed on the matchbox was a tomahawk. The casino's designer had no idea if Mohawk Indians actually fought with hand axes or, indeed, if any Native Americans had ever used such weapons, but tomahawk sounded like Mohawk and 30 West 54th Street was Mohawk land.

Before it became such, the land on which Casino 30/54 sat belonged to Clack Associates, owners of a small hotel much loved by rich European tourists. Augustus Clack III sold the hotel for an undisclosed sum to the billionaire financier, Benjamin Agadir, who promptly swapped it with the Mohawks for seven glass necklaces and a blanket. Since federal regulations specifically allowed casinos to be opened on reservations or any Indian land held in trust, this neatly circumvented the state law that banned the establishment of casinos in New York City.

'*Faites vos jeux,*' announced the croupier, as if inviting a whole table of high rollers to place their bets rather than just the one.

Kashif Pasha ignored the man.

Striking a match, the eldest son and current heir to the Emir of Tunis lifted the match to the tip of his cigar and sucked. His mother disapproved of smoking, gambling, whores and alcohol but since cigars were not expressly mentioned in the Holy Quran, she sometimes kept her peace. Besides, Kashif Pasha was in New York City and she was not.

Quite what Lady Maryam would have made of the striking murals in the gentlemen's lavatory it was best not to imagine. Kashif Pasha's favourite by far featured Pocahontas undergoing what Americans called double entry. For what were undoubtedly good cultural reasons, her lovers both sported tails, the back legs of goats, and small horns.

At home there were no paintings in Lady Maryam's wing of the Bardo and no statues. Even his great-grandfather's famous *Neue Sachlichkeit* collection of oils had been banished, saved only by the Emir's flat refusal to have them destroyed.

Representative art was abhorrent to his mother for usurping the rights of God. But then this was a woman who found even calligraphy suspect. Which, undoubtedly went some way to explaining why she'd burned the present his father sent her at Kashif's birth. (An Osmanli miniature from the sixteenth century showing the Prophet's wet nurse Hamina breast-feeding.) And this, in turn, maybe helped explain why Emir Moncef had refused to see his wife since.

Kashif Pasha smiled darkly, his favourite expression, and pushed five ivory chips onto the number thirteen.

'Rien ne va plus,' announced the croupier, as if he hadn't been waiting. No more bets were to be made. There was a ritual to go through, even though the room was almost empty and the roulette table reserved for Kashif Pasha. The wheel spun one way and the ivory ball was sent tumbling another and when a number other than thirteen came up, Kashif Pasha just shrugged, carelessly he hoped.

Over the course of the next hour the rampart of counters in front of him became a single turret, then little more than ruined foundations and finally almost disappeared, leaving Kashif Pasha with only six ivory chips.

The casino would keep the table open for him while Kashif Pasha ordered more counters, that much was given. High rollers like His Excellency got what they wanted. Their own suites, complimentary meals, limousines to and from the airport. Even use of the casino's own plane if necessary. And what he wanted now was a break.

'Okay,' said Kashif Pasha. 'I'll be back here at . . .' He glanced at his Rolex and added two hours to the time it was. 'At seven,' he said. 'Have the table reset. New wheel, new ball, new grid, new stack of counters.' Which was what his croupier seemed to call those hundred-thousand-dollar red chips.

Sliding his six remaining counters across the table, His Excellency smiled. 'For you,' he said and watched the croupier blink. It was a good tip, more so since Kashif Pasha was sometimes known not to tip at all. The croupier would give half to the house, but that still left more than he earned in six months.

'Thank you, Excellency,' said the man, moving aside to make room for a crop-haired woman who'd been watching the game from a discreet distance.

'Your Highness.' This was a title Kashif Pasha didn't warrant but Georgian van Broglie used it anyway. So far she'd acted as facilitator on every visit Kashif Pasha made to Casino 30/54 and he had yet to complain about the social upgrade. 'Shall I have the kitchen organize some supper?'

She took his silence as assent.

'Chicken breast,' she suggested, 'on focaccia, with honey and mustard sauce. A litre of Evian and maybe some more ginger ale?' She nodded to a line of small and empty bottles of Canada Dry, the plastic screw-top kind.

Kashif Pasha's usual order. A glorified chicken sandwich washed down with three plastic flasks of champagne. Quite why a forty-four-year-old North African playboy would want to drink Veuve Clicquot from an empty Canada Dry bottle Georgian van Broglie didn't know, but then she'd never met Lady Maryam.

'Does Your Highness require anything else?'

She saw the man glance across the room to the deerskinned waitress who'd brought him his cigar. 'No possible,' she muttered apologetically. 'House rules. I'd love to make an exception but . . .'

Kashif Pasha sighed. 'Send up something similar,' he said crossly. 'After you've found me the house doctor.' He checked his knuckles, which were looking more lopsided than ever. 'And get room service to bring me a bucket of ice.'

CHAPTER 3

'Nicolai . . .' Emir Moncef's call was for his bodyguard. A small and intense Uzbek whose name was probably something completely different. The Uzbek and a Tajik called Alex took turns to protect the Emir. They were a recent birthday present from the Soviet ambassador. One Moncef had not known how to refuse.

He called again, just in case either guard was within hearing, then turned his attention back to the snake. Death was always going to come. That it chose to manifest as a slithering viper was unexpected but not impossible. Although, if the elderly Emir had been forced to bet (a vice he deplored), he'd have selected a fat-tailed scorpion as being more likely.

Scorpions got carried into camp on the flatbeds of trucks or in date baskets. Once, if he remembered correctly, a fat-tail had hitched a lift in the cuffs of an NCO's dress trousers. The man had succumbed within hours and the Emir had banned cuffs on all uniforms from then on.

He would die as he had lived his last forty years, in the simplicity of Ifriqiya's southern desert. A place where privation reduced leaves to water-protecting spikes and insects hid within thickly waxed bodies to conserve what little water they contained; where beetles survived on one meal in two years, if the habitat so demanded, and glass wort displayed a near-suicidal tolerance for salt.

Tossing back his a'aban, a heavy cloak still worn by Berber men of a certain age, Emir Moncef raised a silver-topped stick. Ready to defend himself.

'Get behind me . . .' His order was aimed at a boy in camouflage who still gripped a Nintendo game pad with frozen fingers.

The Emir's younger son shook his head.

'Murad.'

That the Emir used his real name scared the boy almost as much as

599

the viper now crawling its way across a carpet. Mostly his father called him SP, which stood for *small pasha*, a name he'd been given by his mother before she was killed. His mother had been one of the Emir's guard, an American convert from Los Angeles.

Her Jeep had gone off the side of a cliff. An accident.

'Do as I say.'

Looking from his father to the horned viper, the twelve-year-old again shook his head. Snakes were rare in the camp, dangerous or otherwise, because intricate webs of woven copper wire lay buried beneath the perimeter. The webs created an electric field that upset snakes, scorpions and spiders. That was what Eugenie de la Croix said anyway. And it was her job to know these things.

'Don't be afraid. Just back away.'

Afraid? Several options presented themselves to Murad and none involved fear or retreat. His duty was to defend his father, His Highness Moncef al-Mansur, better known as the Emir of Tunis and ruler of Ifriqiya (father of his people, loved by all). This Murad knew from reading it each morning in the cheap, Arab-language red tops the Emir insisted on having delivered by helicopter.

Kashif Pasha punches American paparazzi . . .

Today's *Es Sabah* lay on a leather and oak table, one so ancient its iron nails had gone dark as the wood and quite as shiny. Under the paper rested a photograph album almost as old. No one was allowed to look inside. Which was why Murad had never been able to ask why it contained postcard after postcard of bare-breasted women ranging from girls his own age to those as old as his mother would have been.

Berber said some, others *Taurag*. Most were simply described as *Mauresque*, sometimes *Belle Mauresque*, occasionally *Jeune Femme Arabe* . . . Once as *Tuenisch-orientalische Typen*. Almost all stared flat-eyed at the camera. As if trying to withdraw from a world where colonial officers scribbled *'c'est très intéressant'* across the back, stuck a five-centime stamp over the breast of a twelve-year-old and posted it to a cousin in Marseilles.

'Murad.'

Outside, speakers blared *male habtl madjatch*, a rai track even older than his father, whose favourite song it was. The rhythms and repetitions, drum and weird whistle as familiar to the boy as any *adhan*, the call to prayer, though Murad would never admit as much and even thinking so worried him.

So be it. His choice was made. As God wills.

Murad added *inshá allá* without even noticing. The way his mother used to say *bless you* every time he sneezed.

He was twelve, after all. Old enough for what came next.

Fires had been lit for the midday meal and someone nearby was roasting goat over branches ripped from a thornbush, both wood and goat having been brought in by truck. There was no kindling this far south. He would miss the meal and the camp and his father . . .

Their previous camp had been better, more to do and less sand. The goat-hair tents were carried on camels only when photographers were around. The rest of the time a ponytailed Texan called Pigpen bundled the tents into trucks and broke them down and set them up wherever the Emir wanted.

Few outsiders understood why the Emir allowed a *nasrani* such freedom. Those who did had seen the speed at which the Texan could break down a camp when the old man wanted it done really fast.

'*Pull yourself together . . .*' The Emir was cross now.

'I'm not frightened,' Murad shot back with all the indignation he could muster. 'I'm planning,' His father was always telling him to think ahead.

Dropping his Nintendo, Murad reached for a silver coffee jug and flipped back its lid. The jug was inlaid with copper and bronze. Even its ivory handle was hot. Out of the corner of his eye he saw the Emir shake his head but it was too late, Murad had already hurled coffee into the face of the horned viper.

Most of it missed.

'*Guards.*'

Ignoring the old man's demand and the sudden hammering of fear in his own ears, Murad threw the silver pot after the coffee, just managing to hit the viper's tail. So much for his first plan.

On a sidewall of the tent hung the sword his great-grandfather took from a dying colonel after a skirmish outside Neffatia, the year the French were driven from Tunisia, as Ifriqiya was then called.

The boy was lunging for this when Emir Moncef stepped forward, grabbed Murad by the shoulder and threw him towards the entrance with more force than the old man knew he possessed. He understood when a viper was about to attack, even if his youngest son didn't.

'*Alex, Nicolai . . .*'

Part of the Emir still hoped that fate might allow him to step back from danger; because courage was one thing and stupidity another and to grow old in this world one needed to be able to tell the difference. But the viper was ready to strike. Something the old man realized, he suspected, even before the reptilian, pea-sized brain that was his death's whole being.

601

Moncef al-Mansur looked death in the eyes, heard its hiss and felt time slow as the viper froze on the edge of movement.

The Emir was too old and too exhausted by his argument with Murad to be able to avoid a strike completely, so he made do with twisting matador style in the hope that the bite might be less than total. In this alone he was lucky. One fang buried itself deep into his calf, the other tore the cloth of a robe that time and washing had reduced to the consistency of rotten sack.

'Papa . . .'

The last thing Emir Moncef heard before he fell to the floor and found himself face-to-face with the carpet was his son begin to scream. A noise loud enough to drown out the music of Cheb Khaled and the running feet of his absent guards. The last of which, had the Emir been able to hear it, would merely have confirmed his opinion that panic and fury had no place in a well-run camp.

CHAPTER 4

Wednesday 2nd February

Kashif al-Mansur liked snow and always had done. Mostly he liked it in cities such as New York, where flakes fluttered down between canyons to bury the sidewalks and cars. Everything turning white and picture-postcard.

At home when snow fell, which was not often, white sprinkled the mountains of the High Tell and oak valleys towards the northern coast, dusting the red roofs of farmhouses built and later deserted by French settlers. He'd been impressed by that as a child, until he discovered what winter really looked like.

The snow Kashif Pasha really liked, however, fell on carefully selected ski resorts. St Mortiz in Switzerland, Geilo in Norway, America's own Aspen. Playgrounds that featured mountain lodges, black runs, and a large, interchangeable and ever-fluid collection of people who wanted to be his friend.

Thickset industrialists with salt-and-pepper hair, fake tans and astute eyes readily offered him use of their chalets, snowcats, and daughters. Not to mention unsecured loans and bribes disguised as business opportunities.

His father might be a pariah but Kashif Pasha was a different proposition, loved by those who hated every value for which Emir Moncef stood. And Kashif worked hard on his reputation. His loans were always repaid and he was politeness itself to the Western girls who, drunk or drugged, fell against him in the ritzy bars as if champagne or charlie had taken away their balance.

From time to time, there would be a flash that lit the darkness of some bar and another photograph would appear, apparently showing him snuggled up with the daughter of a German industrialist or American banker.

The inevitable result of this was a letter from his mother.

Handwritten, sealed with wax and sent through diplomatic channels. Lady Maryam's lament was always the same. At her age and in her state of health, how could he . . . The woman, needless to say, had the nerves of a trained killer and the physical constitution of a battle-hardened commando. Only her age was against her.

Kashif Pasha's replies were as ritual as his mother's complaints. The whey-faced teenager in the photograph was the daughter/niece/lover of some man he barely knew and had certainly never shared his bed. It was doubtful if Lady Maryam believed this, but then she knew far less about her son than she imagined.

His preferences had been formed early, one Saturday in early January while his mother was away, sometime between the calls to prayer at dawn and noon. That was when he'd first noticed Sophia, a barefoot Sudanese maid maybe two years older than he. He wasn't even aware of having seen her before until she came into his room to sweep up and found him still half-asleep in a *bateau lit*.

Her hurried apology got lost beneath his demand that she open his curtains, which were both long and heavy. Kashif had just been moved into a new suite of rooms, one fitted out in the English style, so that he would not disgrace himself by exhibiting unfamiliarity on arrival at his new school outside London, a city chosen largely because his father had wanted Paris.

'Open them all,' Kashif's twelve-year-old self had demanded. 'That's an order.'

With reluctance, the girl (whose name Kashif was only to ask a week later) left the safety of her doorway and yanked back the nearest curtain, though it was embarrassment not anger that made her movements so abrupt.

'And the next window and the one after that.'

Sophia went along the wall as instructed, pulling back curtains originally sewn by the venerable Paris textile house of Nobilis Fontan, until Kashif had an uninterrupted view of a courtyard outside. One so large that a regiment could have assembled there.

'Excellency . . .' Sophia's curtsy was made clumsy by her dash for the door.

'All the curtains,' Kashif demanded, nodding to the only window that mattered, a small one set high in the wall over his head. To get there Sophia would have to step onto his *bateau lit* and reach up. Kashif watched her face darken as she realized it. She had keloid scars on her cheeks, the way Berber women in the south had tattoos beneath their eyes. Scars, a face far finer than his, and huge, doubtful eyes.

'That window too please.' Kashif was suddenly polite. As for the first

604

time he understood that she might refuse. If that happened, Kashif wasn't sure he knew what to do.

'Excellency.' Sophia gave something that was half nod and half shrug, accepting the inevitable. Three steps took her to the bed and then, as Kashif watched from the corner of his eye she stepped up onto his mattress, revealing a dark flash of calf. For a moment she fought for her balance, then did what he'd only half believed she might, stepped clean over him and reached up, her fingers tugging the curtain.

He expected her to step down immediately and run from the room but she remained where she was, staring up as if at some vision. And although she wore no pants there was little for Kashif to see. A dark gash for her sex, a curve of bare buttock, more shadow than flesh. Heavy legs. An ankle showing some kind of insect bite.

He was still considering this when Sophia stepped down and gestured towards the bigger windows behind her. All of them revealing the same miracle. For the first time in Kashif's life and, for all he knew, the first time in history, fat flakes of snow had begun to fall on the city of Tunis.

Kashif Pasha smiled.

'Here you go.' He slipped a red chip into the hand of the girl who'd earlier brought him a cigar and dropped another two into the waiting fingers of the croupier. Tipping so much to Michelle was an extravagance and, from the hastily controlled expression on the face of his facilitator, Georgian van Broglie, not quite how 30/54 liked its patrons to behave.

Kashif Pasha's smile grew broader. Next time the cigar girl would come to his suite of her own accord, never realizing she'd been bought, in advance, for far less than he would have paid.

'And this belongs to you . . .'

Georgian van Broglie prepared to bristle at the indignity of being tipped, something she'd stopped needing the moment she got put on a cut of the house percentage. And found herself instead holding a business card. The card was just that, a rectangle of thick paper made from wood pulp, its china-clay surface embossed with a small logo. Below the logo, which managed to combine a torque wreath with an old-fashioned propeller was the address of a private airport, one of Long Island's finest.

'Anytime you're bored, feel free to call that number. One of my pilots will take you, plus family or friends, anywhere you want and bring you back again, when you want. Caracas, Bombay, Hong Kong . . .'

Her stunned expression was worth the gesture. Besides, Kashif gave good odds she'd never take up his offer. That card would remain in her wallet and get shown to friends, both social and business, while his jet would remain on the ground, fuel unused. So far no one had ever taken him up on a flight. Something about the very extravagance of his gesture prevented them.

Georgian van Broglie was still stuttering her thanks when someone knocked at the door. 'Excellency, I'm sorry . . .'

Outside, in the panelled expanse of lobby stood an officer from the NYPD and beside him, looking flustered, the casino's head of security, all cropped hair and diamond earstud. Accompanying them was a small man with the smell of a lawyer.

'Kashif al-Mansur?'

No sooner had the uniformed officer spoken than the small man put up a hand. 'Not in here,' he said firmly and glanced at the head of security as if expecting the man to toss the officer onto the street. 'This casino is on tribal land. You know the rules.'

'What's the problem?' Kashif's voice was calm, with an easy familiarity that didn't reach his eyes.

'There's been a complaint . . .'

'Outside,' insisted the small man, managing to look apologetic and determined at the same time. The officer got the determination, Kashif got the apology.

'A photographer alleges . . .'

Before the small lawyer had even relaunched his protest Kashif Pasha was holding up a white booklet. He put it half an inch from the officer's face. 'Do you know what this is?'

The man shook his head. They both knew that was a lie.

'It's a *carte blanche*,' said Kashif Pasha, flicking to the first page. The photograph showed a man younger by four years, a little less worn, his cheeks less full; the beard was the same though. 'Total diplomatic immunity,' Kashif explained, though this was unnecessary. The words were written in several languages across the top of each page. 'You have a problem, take it up with the embassy.'

'The embassy is in Washington.'

'So take a plane. Or even better don't bother. I'm leaving New York in about . . .' Kashif Pasha checked his Rolex, which looked silver but was actually platinum. 'Thirty minutes. Everything I need to do here I've done.' Rubbing his fist absentmindedly, Kashif rechecked the time and smiled past the officer at the snow falling onto 54th Street beyond.

CHAPTER 5

Saturday 5th February

Once in a time when animals still talked and djinn walked the earth quite openly, the Sultan of Bokhara sent for a mullah living in a distant village. His message was simple.

'Come at once. I need advice.' For the Sultan expected the arrival of an Indian ambassador and the Mullah was . . .

A rumble in her tummy made Hani suck her teeth in sudden irritation. Now someone was bound to offer her food.

'Hungry?' Ashraf Bey's question came from across the *qaa*, a reception room that occupied almost all of the first floor of the al-Mansur madersa: the mansion His Excellency shared with his young niece, his Portuguese cook, a Sufi porter and the woman Iskandryian gossip still assumed was his mistress, wrongly as it happened.

In summer the *qaa* was open to the elements along one side but now was winter and the arches overlooking the central courtyard were closed off with specially cut sheets of glass. A small fountain played in the middle of the *qaa* floor, carved, five hundred years before, from a single block of horsehair marble.

Silver balloons floated from this because today was Hani's tenth birthday. Although Khartoum, who was friends with the cook but tended to disagree with her on almost everything as a matter of principle, insisted it was Hani's eleventh. Largely, Hani suspected, because Donna insisted it wasn't.

And as no one could actually find a birth certificate for the child and Hani had been born elsewhere, the question remained open. Lady Nafisa might have been able to provide an answer but Hani's aunt was dead. Something else for Hani to feel guilty about.

'Hungry?' Raf repeated.

'No,' said Hani. 'Not really.'

The mullah's reply to the Sultan was equally simple. 'I am unable to attend, O King, as I rely for life upon the sweet air of Qasr al Arifin and have no way to bring this with me in storage jars.'

Hani paused, her small fingers hovering in midair. A matrix of fine wires across the back of her hands ended in finger thimbles. Every time her hands flicked across the invisible keys of her imaginary keyboard, words got added to a processing package installed on her laptop one floor up in the *haremlek*. Very clever but not madly practical because Hani relied on seeing a screen to write.

All the same, it was kind of Hamzah Effendi to send her a present. Hamzah Effendi was Zara's father and Zara was the girl her Uncle Ashraf should have married, the one everyone thought . . .

If only.

Hani kicked her heels against the legs of a silver chair and sighed. Another four paragraphs and she'd let herself go down to the kitchen to make coffee.

At first the Sultan was perplexed by this answer. And then, after consideration of the mullah's open disrespect, he determined to remonstrate with the man when they next met, famous sage or not. At about this time the visit from the Indian ambassador was cancelled and so the Sultan needed no advice from anyone after all.

Many months later, as fig leaves began dropping and the stars grew cold the Sultan sat down to supper and no sooner had he picked up his goblet than an assassin leapt upon him. Immediately, Mullah Bahaudin, having entered the dining room at this exact moment, jumped upon the assassin and wrestled him to the ground.

'O Mullah,' said the Sultan, 'It seems I am indebted to you in spite of your earlier rudeness.'

Mullah Bahaudin smiled. 'O Sultan,' he said sweetly. 'The courtesy of those who know is to be available when actually needed, not sit waiting for emissaries who will never arrive . . .'

Hani flicked her fingers over a nonexistent trackball to shut down her laptop and pulled of her gloves. She would write the rest of Bahaudin's story, particularly the bit where the Mullah met a miracle worker who could walk on water – but to get things right she really did need a screen.

'Okay,' Hani said, slipping down from her chair. 'I'm off to make some coffee.' She left her comment hang in the air, a fact that seemed to escape both Uncle Ashraf and Zara. 'Anyone like some?' Hani asked loudly.

'Donna can make it.' Raf replied.

It was the wrong answer.

*

608

'Just look at this,' said Donna, waving one heavy hand at her television, as she insisted on describing the kitchen newsfeed.

'Disgraceful. You could get twice the zest out of that.'

On screen a plump boy in a chef's hat was discarding half a lemon.

'Now he's adding *cream*,' Donna said, with a disgusted shake of her head. *'Cream.'* The old woman loved watching the German channels for their sheer outrage.

When Hani said nothing Donna switched her attention from the recipe for *Schwetche Kuchen* to Hani's face and jerked her head upwards, through the ceiling. 'Still arguing?'

The child nodded.

'About you?'

Hani looked at her. 'What do you think?' Everyone in the house knew what Hani thought. She refused to go to school in New York and she didn't want a tutor at home. Hani was beginning to wish she'd never taken those tests.

'Zara just wants to get rid of me,' Hani said. 'They both do.'

'That's not . . .' Donna sighed. 'Sit down,' she said in a voice that allowed for no argument.

Frying last season's almonds in a drizzle of olive oil and grating rock salt over the top, Donna tipped the result onto a single sheet of kitchen paper, which she screwed into a ball to remove most of the oil. 'Eat,' she told Hani, when the tapas was ready.

Hani did what she was told, sipping at a glass of red wine Donna had placed beside the plate of almonds.

'Now you listen to me,' said Donna. 'It's your birthday. You mustn't be upset on your birthday because it makes for bad luck. And this isn't really about you . . .'

'Yes it is.'

'No,' Donna said firmly. 'It's not . . .' She sighed and took her own gulp of Hani's wine. 'It's about something else. Something grown-up. You know what I'd like to do with those two?'

'What?' asked Hani, suddenly interested.

'Ahh,' the elderly Portuguese woman shrugged in irritation. 'No matter. You're too young to know about these things . . .'

Although if Donna's solution was anything like that of the madersa's porter, then Hani had a pretty good idea already. Khartoum's suggestion involved bricking Uncle Ashraf and Zara into a room with a bed and not letting them out until they made sheets.

Hani wasn't sure where the bricks or sheets came into it, but she got the general point.

'You want more birthday cake?'

'Not really.' Hani shook her head. 'I came to get coffee.'

'Caffeine darkens the skin,' said Donna crossly. Her own face was as brown as the inside membrane of a walnut and almost as crumpled.

'It's for His Excellency.'

The Portuguese woman looked doubtful.

'Papers.' Hani announced before she was even through the marble arch into the *qaa*. Zara and Uncle Ashraf would have had to be deaf not to hear Hani coming, she'd stamped so hard on her way up.

On Hani's tray were a collection of afternoon papers, three tiny mugs of mud-thick coffee, and the plate of baklava Donna had insisted she take. Most of the papers blamed *Thiergarten* for the attack on Emir Moncef. Only one chose Washington over Berlin. And that one was more concerned with the miracle of the Emir's survival.

'The *Enquirer*,' she told her uncle, dropping it onto his table and using it as a mat for his coffee.

Pope To Make Boy Saint?

The Emir of Tunis had been saved from death by a child's power of prayer; the *Enquirer* was quite categoric about that. An unnamed source close to Emir Moncef had confirmed how, in the absence of serum, the Emir's youngest son had prayed over the unconscious body of his father, refusing to leave Moncef's bedside until the Emir finally awoke.

Missing from the story was the obvious fact that Pope Leo VII was unlikely to beatify, never mind canonize, a minor Islamic princeling (even assuming the mufti in Stambul was willing). Also missing was the fact that, far from being a hero, Murad Pasha had found himself in deep disgrace. In fact the beating he received for not obeying an order from the Emir left the boy unable to sit for three days.

Raf skim-read the story, shifted his cup to reach the end, and tossed the lies to the floor, narrowly missing Ifritah, Hani's grey cat.

'Uncle Ashraf!'

'It was an accident,' Raf said firmly, and went back to work.

A fine-tooth comb, plus instructions on the correct way to lift potential evidence from pubic hair.

A Miranda card, one side listing *Inalienable Rights*, the other *Rules of Plain View*.

Two dozen unused postmortem fingerprint cards, both left and right.

Vacuum-packed latex gloves, eight pairs.

A booklet in Spanish on Vucetich's system of fingerprint classification, stamped *LAPD not to be removed*.

A foldout chart of poisons, arranged by the time in which they begin to react. Starting with *ammonia*, reaction time zero, and ending with *stibine*, three days to three weeks . . .

One single sheet of 80gsm A4 paper of the kind used in police stations across North Africa. On it the translation of an Ottoman wedding certificate typed on a manual typewriter, which suggested a fear of leaving electronic footprints. The names had been filled in but the dates left blank.

Polaroids, two, of a young man standing by a Jeep.

A jewellery roll made from chamois leather that turned out to contain three scalpels and a collection of surgical steel blades.

A small .22 derringer, two-shot, with an over/under configuration and mother-of-pearl grips, badly scratched. A handful of postcards . . .

Set out in front of Raf on an oval dining table, amid the debris of breakfast and the coffee Hani had just brought were fragments from two lives now gone. The Polaroids, both faded, had arrived in that morning's post; everything else belonged to Felix Abrinsky, Chief of Detectives in El Iskandryia and briefly a friend.

It was a long time since Raf had been this upset and the feeling was unfamiliar. What he felt as a tightness in the back of his throat he took to be side effects from dust thrown up by workmen in a garden beyond the courtyard outside.

Me having a good time, read a card. Flipping it over, Raf paused, eyes sweeping between two women in their early twenties, both bare-breasted and joined by a silver chain between nipple rings.

One had a bottle of beer clasped against her button-flied groin in crude imitation of an erect penis and both looked as tired and hot as the old man in the tutu behind them, the one bending bare-arsed over an open grill.

'How very American.'

Raf looked up to find Zara standing by his shoulder. Hollow-eyed, full-breasted and infinitely fragile since the night a month back she'd come unasked to his room and been sent away. She was younger by three or four years than the women in the photograph and wore significantly more clothes.

'Trudi and Barbara,' Raf said, in answer to a question not asked.

'Friends of yours?' There was enough of an edge to Zara's question to make Hani look up, though all the child did was sigh and return to her chess computer. So far she'd won seventeen games straight. She reckoned Uncle Ashraf could be persuaded to let her buy a smarter model if she managed to get the total up to fifty.

'Felix's daughter and her partner . . . That one's Trudi,' Raf added, indicating the taller woman.

It had fallen to Raf to write to Trudi with news of her father's death. A job Raf took in an attempt to assuage his own guilt. No one had suggested prosecuting Raf over the shooting of Felix because by then he'd already been offered the fat man's job. And arresting El Iskandryia's new Chief of Detectives was widely recognized as being a bad career move.

Of course, that was over too. Raf had lasted about two months as Chief, rather longer than he intended. The gun and the badge had gone back; the only thing Raf kept was the fat man's silver Cadillac and that still sat in a parking lot under the police HQ at Champollion.

'She looks that good?'

Raf blinked, realized he was still staring at Felix's daughter and put the card down, face to the table, one item among many. 'I was thinking,' he said simply. 'About what happened.'

Zara opened her mouth, then changed her mind. She was running out of fingers to count the number of times she'd screwed up in the last six months by opening her mouth before thinking. And bizarre as it seemed, probably her worst mistake was not marrying the man she was so busy insulting.

Zara had no objection to arranged marriages. She just hadn't enjoyed being a piece in her mother's game of social advancement. Other recent screwups involved finding herself seminaked in a local paper and appearing in court, supposedly defending her father.

Which one of the rest was actually the worst was a toss-up between . . . Well, that changed. If forced to choose, she'd say her current number one, her all-time recent fuck up was moving in with Raf, though that wasn't how she'd put it to her father. It was the al-Mansur madersa she was moving into, at Hani's suggestion. Raf was just coincidental.

Only he'd never been coincidental, at least not since that evening back in the summer on a boat in the Aegean, when she'd let him slip the shirt from her shoulders and watched it fall. Months later she went to his bed twice in three days; where she did more than she intended and less than he wanted. That was how she'd put it to him later or maybe that was how he put it to her.

Zara found it too cruel to remember.

'You okay?'

'Why shouldn't I be?' Zara's voice sounded mean, even to her, and from somewhere across the other side of the *qaa* came another sigh.

Raf and Zara sulking wasn't what Hani had in mind for her birthday, but it was still infinitely better than last year. That had fallen on a Friday,

612

which meant no presents. From the first call to prayer to the moment Donna put Hani to bed, her day had been spent in silence, sewing and reading. Aunt Nafisa had firm opinions on keeping Friday holy.

Now Lady Nafisa was dead and Hani had balloons, the *qaa*'s small fountain frothed with environmentally safe pink bubbles and Donna had spent yesterday baking a huge chocolate . . .

'I'm going to get some cake,' said Hani, moving her queen. 'Who wants some?' She stared at her uncle and kept staring until he finally raised his head to look at her.

'Cake?'

Raf nodded.

'Excellent,' said Hani as she recorded another win. 'You can help me get it.' Leaving her computer to shuffle through an ancient algorithm that would return every piece to its rightful place, she pushed back her chair. 'Unless you're too busy . . . ?'

'No,' he said. 'Not too busy.' Raf snapped shut the scrapbook he'd been examining as Hani reached his table. Most of the subjects were naked and all were dead, every one of them showed a wound of some kind or another. Near the beginning some of the crime shots were old enough to be in black or white and towards the end a few used the new Kodak tri-D format, which gave the wounds a disconcerting depth. Felix had annotated the lot, his handwriting hardly changing over the years.

'Not good,' said Hani.

Raf looked at her.

'Glue is much better than tape for sticking pictures. It does less damage.' Hani's smile was bright, only her dark eyes betraying her as they flicked from Raf to the album, then across the *qaa* to where Zara sat listlessly reading a novel.

CHAPTER 6

Monday 7th February

Monday morning brought clouds. Relative humidity stood at 71 percent, projected to drop ten points by early afternoon. And there was, according to Raf's watch, near certainty that it would rain – hardly shocking news for February in El Iskandryia.

Longer-term predictions featured a severe depression beginning in March. One that would, if the forecasts lived up to their current accuracy ratings, pull hot air from the Sahara and wrap parts of North Africa in a *khamsin* wind, but for now temperatures remained around 10°C and the sky was slate grey.

'*Wrong,*' said the voice inside Raf's head, '*it's molten lead.*'

He ignored this and concentrated on ripping apart his breakfast. Peeling back oily flakes to reveal sticky almond paste within.

The next voice came from the world outside.

'Excellency.' Le Trianon's very own maître d' scooped Raf's empty cup onto a silver tray and replaced it with a fresh cappuccino. 'Is something wrong with your croissant?'

'No, it's fine.'

Le Trianon was Iskandryia's most famous café. A statement both Pastroudis and Café Athineos would probably dispute. Occupying the corner site where Rue Missala met Place Saad Zaghloul, with a terrace on Rue Missala and exits on both, Le Trianon offered an aquarium darkness of spotless linen and Napoleon III chairs. Discreet wooden screens managed to combine art deco with Moorish fantasia, while a series of art deco murals displayed pert-breasted, half-naked dancing girls in jewelled slippers and diaphanous trousers.

'*You love it really,*' said the fox, who hated Orientalist kitsch. But then Tiri refused to buy into a rule that defined everything over a century as classic by default.

The table Raf used was on the terrace and he sat facing the street, because this allowed him to ignore a bank of elevators inside. There were three elevators, framed in brass, with deco moulding and coloured enamel around their doors. Only directors of the Third Circle were allowed to use these, which was fine with Raf because, as the son of a pasha, he automatically qualified for a C3 corner office with magnificent views of Iskandryia's Eastern Harbour.

Raf had his own opinion about his parentage but as no one else seemed bothered he was attempting to keep this to himself.

Between the harbour wall and Raf's office stood Place Zaghloul, so his windows also overlooked palm trees, a busy bus station and a stark plinth on which rested Zaghloul Pasha, nationalist leader and the man who drove the British from Egypt in 1916.

As befitted his rank as a bey, Raf's office featured a Bokhara rug, a white leather sofa, a filing cabinet made from mahogany and edged with brass and a large, predominantly blue-and-pink Naghi of the square outside, painted in 1943 and borrowed from the Khedival institute in Al Qahirah. What the room lacked was a computer or telephone, files to put in the elegant cabinet and any documents of real importance.

No one expected directors to work, least of all Madame Nordstrom, who in her twenty-fourth year as office manager of C3 regarded all directorships as entirely token, much like the salary. So he spent his mornings in the café downstairs, an arrangement that satisfied both Ingrid Nordstrom and Le Trianon's maître d' but was beginning to irritate Raf. Not because he disliked drinking cappuccino or reading the papers but because, every morning as Raf was shown to his table on the terrace, Tiri popped up to mutter *emotional institutionalization*. It was a phrase with which they were both far too familiar.

Most of the visitors to the famous café drank espresso or sticky, mud-thick shots of Turkish mocha; but then, what with it being February, everyone else ate their breakfast indoors.

Only Raf insisted on a pavement table.

For a while, a matter of weeks only, he'd had bodyguards to hold the tourists at bay and protect him from fundamentalists, crazies, German agents of the *Thiergarten* and anyone else who might be likely to attack the Governor of El Iskandryia; but that was before he resigned, when he had a different job.

'Wrong,' said the fox. *'That was when you had a job. Working at the Third Circle doesn't really . . .'*

'. . . count,' said someone, sitting herself down.

Raf blinked.

She was dressed entirely in grey, with a grey plait and minimal makeup. Her beauty had the fragility of old skin over fine bones, worn for so long she took it for granted. 'No magic,' she said. 'You were talking to yourself. One of the many traits you share with your father.'

There was no real reply to that so instead Raf concentrated on his visitor. And even without his acute sense of smell he'd have noticed a stink of camphor rising from her elegant skirt and jacket, spotted the dust under the buckles on her black shoes.

'Mostly I wear a uniform,' said the woman, settling back into a chair. 'These were what I could find . . . Your nostrils flared,' she added by way of explanation. 'Anyway I have a file on you. Augmented reflexes, heightened vision, hearing and smell . . . Ever since Khedive Tewfik sent me a copy I've been wanting to ask you if that also went for taste . . .'

'*Obviously,*' replied the fox.

Raf took longer to think about it, studying the woman as he did so. She wore no jewellery, not even earrings. Her blusher was so immaculate as to be invisible. Her jacket well cut, with double stitching to the buttonholes. Although the most noticeable feature was a discreet bulge to one side where she wore a small holster clipped to the back of her hip.

Something small but effective, like a .32 loaded with hollow point.

'Impossible to judge,' said Raf, returning to the question of taste. 'Because, in the end, how do I know how things taste to you?'

'How very Cartesian,' said the woman and raised a finger. 'Espresso,' she told her waiter. 'Make it a double and keep them coming.' The man actually bowed, which marked the first time Raf had ever seen one of Le Trianon's waiters do that.

'He's Ifriqiyan,' she told Raf, pulling a cigarette case from a small crocodile-skin handbag as if this explained everything. Flipping open the case, she tapped out a Gauloise, one of the old-fashioned kind without filter. 'You don't mind if I smoke.' Her question was very much an afterthought, if it was a question. It sounded much more like a statement of fact.

'Ashraf Bey,' she said. 'Colonel Ashraf al-Mansur, ex-Chief of Detectives, ex-Governor of El Iskandryia . . . You don't keep any of your jobs very long, do you?'

'I have a very low boredom threshold.' Raf's voice was deadpan.

The woman laughed. 'Good,' she said. Dragging deep, she settled back in her chair and sighed, smoke softening her thin face and making her appear suddenly younger. Her age was indeterminate, somewhere over sixty but after that difficult to say.

Expats and settlers, Raf had seen other women like her. Bodies kept lean by the heat and a diet of cigarettes and alcohol. Usually they were bottle blond with faces leathered by hard living and too much sun.

Whoever she was, this woman was different. She'd let her hair go grey for a start.

'Who are you?' Raf demanded.

She shrugged. 'Ask the waiter when he arrives.' She nodded to the man bringing her coffee, so Raf asked. And what impressed Raf most was that the waiter looked to the woman, seeking her permission before answering. It took a lot to outrank a director of the Third Circle in a café directly below C3's head office. But it was becoming rapidly obvious to Raf that this person did.

'You've heard about the attack on the Emir?'

'Only what was on the news.'

'Half-truths and guesses,' said Eugenie de la Croix. 'All of it.' She gazed at Raf, face intent. 'What do you know about the Revolt of the Naked?'

Raf's answer was honest, *less than zero.*

'They took over Baghdad,' said Eugenie. 'After the death of Harun al-Rashid. An uprising of the poor made poorer by a dispute between Harun's sons over the succession. I don't approve of chaos,' the woman said, 'but sometimes it is deserved.'

'When was this?'

'About twelve hundred years ago.'

Behind his shades Raf raised his eyebrows.

'Quite,' said Eugenie. 'So why do I have your half brother Kashif swearing that something called the NR is behind the attack on your father?'

'Because he's lying?' said Raf. 'Always assuming he is my half brother . . .'

Eugenie smiled. 'So cynical,' she said, 'and you haven't even met him.'

'Nor do I intend to,' said Raf. 'And if I were you, I'd start with the *Thiergarten*. Berlin usually seems to be behind most problems.'

Eugenie shook her head firmly. 'Not in Tunis,' she said. 'We have an agreement . . .'

'Are you sure?' Raf took a sip of lukewarm coffee. 'I thought the *Thiergarten* were a law unto themselves . . .' Popular rumour had Berlin's agents able to scale sheer walls and pass unseen through double-locked doors. A belief that sold papers and did Berlin no harm at all.

'Believe me,' said Eugenie. 'I'm sure.' She spoke like someone who had the negatives, which she probably did, or at least duplicates. Old and undoubtedly embarrassing. The fact the man in question was long dead would do nothing to make them less deadly. The Kaiser was very protective of his late father. Understandably, in the circumstances.

'Then start with Kashif's suspects,' Raf suggested. 'See if they really could mount such an assassination attempt.'

'That's why I'm here.'

Raf looked at Eugenie.

'I thought you might do it.'

'No way.' He shook his head.

'I suppose I could appeal to your sense of family duty,' Eugenie said. 'Or mention the fact your aunt's debts seem to have swallowed what little money she left, while your salary from the Third Circle is worth less than nothing. Then there's your boredom . . . Which one would work?'

'None,' Raf said.

'He *is* your father.'

'My father was a backpacker from Sweden.' Raf's voice was firm. 'I'd give you more details but my mother forgot to get his name.'

'Ah yes,' said the woman, 'Per Lindstrom. I've heard that version . . .' She looked at him. 'Some people,' she said, 'would be proud to call the Emir of Tunis their father.'

'*A lunatic,*' said the fox. '*Ruler of the only country not to sign the 2005 UN accord on biotechnology . . .*'

'Some people aren't me,' said Raf, which sounded either too smug or more bitter than he intended, but Raf let the words hang anyway.

It seemed that Eugenie was not looking for someone to guard the Emir, which had been Raf's first thought. He only understood why Eugenie was so offended by this idea when he realized she'd already taken that job for herself, along with her job as his head of security, not to mention his longest-serving aide.

'Just as well,' said Raf. 'My reputation is overrated.'

For the first time since they'd met Eugenie smiled. 'I've read your files,' she said. 'Explosives, counterintelligence, close-quarter combat . . .'

'And if I said it was all lies?'

'I wouldn't believe you. But those aren't the skills I need anyway. It's your other talents . . .'

Raf looked blank.

'You solved your aunt's murder,' said Eugenie. 'Faced down the *Thiergarten*. Got Zara's half-brother aboard the Khedive's liner and had him take a war criminal into custody, in the face of Moscow, Paris and Berlin.'

'*Yeah, right,*' said the fox, sotto voce. '*You want to tell her how it really happened?*'

Raf shook his head.

'What?' asked Eugenie.

618

'I'm not doing it,' Raf said.

And somewhere inside his skull the fox grinned and kept grinning while Eugenie told Raf what she wanted and Raf explained exactly why it wasn't going to happen.

'*Wow,*' said the fox as they both watched Eugenie stalk away, slight heels clicking on the damp sidewalk. '*That went well.*'

CHAPTER 7

Flashback

'You'll need shoes.'

Somehow that wasn't quite what Sally had expected the Chinese man to say. Of course, at first, she didn't realize he was Chinese. She had that English ignorance of Far Eastern looks and took it for granted that as he was wearing a blue-checked sarong he had to be local, probably Malay and a fisherman. The fact his Ph.D. was in X-linked mutation and he'd been fired from Bayer-Rochelle for releasing details of his research on 'GTPases and their influence on brain structure and cognitive ability,' Sally didn't find out until later.

'Why shoes?'

'Because otherwise the coral will rip your feet to shreds.' *He nodded to a point a stone's throw out from the beach where the water switched from a medium to a pale blue.* 'The reef starts there,' *he said.* 'You'll be safe as long as you swim in shoes.'

The man spoke with a California drawl, interspersed with occasional words that sounded unbelievably English, as if he'd once worked for the Home Service. His wispy white beard could be found on bamboo scrolls in hotel shops across Singapore, which was where she'd landed.

A taxi to Semberwang dropped her at the causeway, the stink of durian fruit and raw rubber thickening the air as she approached the Malay side of the straits and the jumbled buildings of Jahore Baru. A better smell altogether than the stink of hydrocarbons that had clung to her clothes in Singapore, that island of tigers where all the tigers were now dead.

As Sally wondered whether to explain she'd thrown away her shoes the better to get in touch with her instincts, she saw WuYung's eyes refocus.

'They with you?' *he asked glancing over her shoulder.*

Sally shook her head, not even bothering to turn. No one was with her and she was with no one. And that was how she intended to remain. All three of her guidebooks dealt with how to keep at bay unwelcome attention

620

from local men. Only the Rough Guide *had thought to mention that her real problem was likely to be other backpackers.*

'Hi . . .'

Rehab is for Quitters *read the blond boy's T-shirt and his shorts were the kind with long pockets and tabs with buckles. Slivers of doubt flecked his blue eyes.*

'How you doing?'

The black guy with him stared through aviator shades so cheap they had to have been given away with some magazine. His silence could have been intentional but more likely resulted from a battered iPod he wore clipped to the waistband of his cut-down Fat Boys.

'I'm Atal,' *said the blond boy and stuck out his hand.* 'Okay if we crash here too? We're out of dosh,' *he added by way of explanation.*

If the Chinese man noticed the Oyster Perpetual on Atal's skinny wrist he didn't mention it. Sally, however, made her glance obvious.

'Fake,' *said Atal quickly,* 'from a market in Bangkok.'

It wasn't.

'Pretty good copy,' *said Sally's companion and Atal blushed.*

'I suppose the trainers are fake too,' *Sally said. They were airPower, the ones with scarlet kangaroo-skin inserts down both sides.*

'This is Bozo,' *said Atal, ignoring the question.* 'He doesn't say much.'

Bozo smiled, a slow and lazy smile that revealed his teeth, which were mostly gold with a hole in one canine where a diamond had worked loose.

'Sally,' *said Sally and turned towards the old man, realizing for the first time that he hadn't given his name.*

'Wu Yung III.'

'As in . . .' *Atal stopped and did a double take, eyes widening. His next look at Sally was an attempt to work out their relationship.*

'We've just met,' *said Sally.*

Wu Yung smiled. 'And you're all welcome,' *he said smoothly.* 'Please stay for as long as you like . . . This island is mine,' *he added when Atal stared blankly.* 'I take it none of you read Chinese or Malay?' *Wu Yung nodded to a peeling sign nailed a nearby palm tree, half-buried behind a tumble of deep green.*

The three backpackers looked at each other.

It seemed not.

'You asleep?'

'Not any longer . . .' *Sally smiled to take the sting from her words and watched the elderly man duck his head under the low doorway and shut the door behind him. In one hand Wu Yung carried a bottle of white wine and in the other two glasses. A leather camera case hung from a strap about his neck, and stuck into the rolled waistband of his sarong nestled a smaller bottle, unlabelled.*

This was the point that modesty demanded Sally drag her bed's thin cotton cover up to cover her small breasts or at the very least cross her arms.

She did neither.

Instead she sat up straighter. Focusing her eyes in the darkness.

'Like the hut?'

Sally nodded. The shack was old, raised off the rough ground on wooden stilts and leaning slightly in one direction, its collapse stopped by a convenient casuarina tree. She had no doubt that the palm roof leaked and that wind entered at will in winter but none of that mattered. It was the most perfect building she'd ever seen. Simple, cheap to build and easily sustainable.

'I came to ask you a question,' said Wu Yung.

Half-naked on an old canvas bed with her tits bare to his gaze, Sally was under the impression she'd already answered it. Everything in life had a price and she had no problems with paying.

'Ask,' Sally said.

'Why are you here?' said Wu Yung. 'I mean, what exactly are you looking for?'

Sally blinked. 'I'm not looking for anything.'

The elderly Chinese man smiled, his face lit by the moon through a glassless window. 'If you're not searching,' he said, 'then why come?'

More waves broke on the beach than Sally could number. Waves, breeze and the night chatter of a troop of wak-wak, the scream of long-tailed parakeet. A busy backdrop that did nothing to hide her own silence.

'I don't believe in looking,' she said finally. 'I believe in finding. There's a difference.'

'Yes,' Wu Yung said. 'There is. So let's drink to that difference.' He held up his bottle and Sally suddenly realized there was condensation running down its sides. 'There's a fridge at the house,' Wu Yung explained, seeing her look.

'House?'

Wu Yung grinned. 'You think I sleep on the beach? I've got a fresh-water pool, air-conditioning, satellite TV . . . I come here to escape the pressures of Hong Kong, not become a monk.' He handed her the wine, waiting until Sally noticed it was already opened. 'Why don't you pour?' he suggested.

When the bottle was finally empty, Wu Yung sat back with a smile and let the minutes drift by in a symphony of insect rhythms and overlapping waves.

622

'Hear it?'

Sally nodded sleepily. Music was something else at which she wasn't very good. Her fingers never quite found the chords and her one attempt to write a song of her own had been total failure.

'What do you hear?'

'Waves,' said Sally. 'And insects,' she added when he seemed to expect more.

'Nothing else?'

Sally shook her head.

'Go to the window,' Wu Yung suggested.

Sally went. The sea breeze flowing over her bare skin.

'What do you see?' Wu Yung asked her.

'Stars,' said Sally. 'Points of light. How about you?'

Wu Yung climbed to his feet and walked to the window. Stood so close behind her that Sally could feel his breath on the back of her neck. 'I see distance,' said Wu Yung. When he turned Sally round it was to ask her something else.

'Are you worried by the thought of death?'

'No more than anybody else,' Sally said, wondering if his question was sinister. 'I'm one of life's fighters,' she added firmly. 'I work on instinct. It takes a lot to frighten me.'

'I didn't ask if you were afraid of it.' Wu Yung's voice was dry. 'I asked if death worried you . . .'

'You're saying there's a difference?'

'Oh yes.' Wu Yung smiled. 'All the difference in the world.'

CHAPTER 8

Monday 7th February

Gulls shrieked, the way gulls mostly do when circling against a wet and dirty sky. Somewhere beyond the drizzling rain the sun's last rays withdrew, unnoticed by everyone except Raf, who lifted his shades and flipped frequencies to watch that day's little death, its final flicker lost among chimney flare from the Midas Refinery.

At the back of Raf's throat was the burn of cheap speed. Crystals of methamphetamine so filthy he'd picked out the blackest of the mis-shapen lumps and discarded them into a puddle. The wrap was one of a dozen left over from his brief and glorious stint as Chief of Detectives, evidence signed out from the precinct and never returned. It was, if he recalled correctly, the second to last of those left.

There were several ways Raf could restock his supply. The most obvious was to ask Hamzah Effendi, but somehow Raf couldn't bring himself to do that. Another alternative was hit up Hakim and Ahmed, his old bodyguards, but that didn't appeal either; which left buying his own and that brought its own problems, like making contacts and the fact he'd need to find some money.

He was a notable, living if not sleeping with the daughter of North Africa's richest man. He had a title, contacts, and a reputation for ruthless efficiency entirely at odds with the facts. His niece was a certified genius. A woman he'd never met had just asked him to investigate an assassination attempt in which the only thing to die had been a snake. Short of not enough sleep and using too much speed, it was hard to work out why he was quite so depressed.

Unless it was the rain.

'Figure it out,' said the fox. *'Before we both drown.'*

As North Africa's only remaining freeport, El Iskandryia shipped tobacco, rice and oil as legal cargoes; while illegal cargoes included most

624

of the hashish destined for Northern Europe, commercial information, prostitutes, political intelligence and people in search of new identities.

At the back of Misr Station was an alley that did nothing but fake passports, identity cards, driving licences and new birth certificates; novelties all, apparently, but novelties good enough to pass the brief glance of a harried customs officer. Quality fakes came from the old Turko-Arabic district of El Anfushi, between Rue El Nokrashi and the chemical stink of the western docks.

Only, in El Anfushi there were no shop windows full of fake ID cards, no posters advertising *driving licences, any country* . . . Here you needed to be introduced, and even that took money. Zara's father ran this, the high end of identity laundering, just as he controlled the refinery, tobacco shipments and illegal runs that carried hashish to Heraklion and returned with crates of fake Intel chips and memory boards, few of them labelled accurately.

This was where Zara's fortune came from and where Hani acquired her dowry. From the trade in underage Sudanese whores, processed opium and scum on the run as much as from the vast petrochemical complex that squatted on El Iskandryia's western edge, where slums ended and just before the desert began.

Raf knew this.

His garden was being rebuilt with dirty money. It was dirty money Zara had in Hong Kong Suisse, millions of dollars worth. And it would be Zara's dirty money that sent Hani to school in New York, were he to allow that to happen.

The kind Bayer-Rochelle paid to his mother.

Of course, Raf had needed no introductions to acquire his new identity. This had been handed to him, five months back, outside Seattle's SeaTac Airport, not so much on a plate as in an Alessi briefcase, empty but for a passport, a strip of photographs and a plane ticket.

The ticket had been to El Iskandryia, the passport a white leather affair stamped with the Ottoman crest and the cheap foto-booth pictures had been of a younger Zara, happy and smiling, words Raf wouldn't associate with her now. His aunt had been responsible. The dead one.

Just after Rue L'Eglise Copte and a couple of minutes from where he would cut south across the six lanes of Boulevard Cherif Pasha, Raf tripped over what should have been a good memory while splashing through a darkened alley, so recently repaved its glistening cobbles were still unbroken.

Waves.

Opposite a new Starbucks, beside the shell of an empty shop, which was all plaster-skim walls and discarded, half-unravelled coils of wire, he came up with another memory.

Salt.

The final memory dripped from his lip as he crossed the wet expanse of Cherif Pasha and cut round a forlorn man standing in the rain selling roast quail on wooden skewers from a handcart.

Blood.

The summer before, on a smuggling VSV that operated at half stealth, giving it the radar profile of a small fishing boat, she'd bitten his lip, drawing salt. Zara's kisses tasted of olives and red wine, her breasts beneath his hands were fire. If he was honest, he'd wanted her beyond thinking.

With the harbour lights in sight she'd undone pearl buttons on her shirt, pulling his head against her until his mouth found her breasts. And later still, as the boat slid into the Western Harbour past the headland of Ras el-Tin they'd knelt together in darkness, with Hani safely asleep on the seat behind them and she'd locked both knees around Raf's leg to lose herself inside ragged breath and a spew of words that moved her lips but made no sound.

Somewhere between blood and salt and winter rain his new life had gone sour, seeding itself with ghosts and the expectation of failure. He'd like to blame the fox but it was working perfectly for the first time Raf could remember. And since his memory was eidetic, stone-cold perfect, that probably meant for the first time ever.

Blaming it on the fox had become Raf's default position. They both knew that.

Emotional institutionalization.

'Deal with it,' Raf told himself and lifted a bunch of red flowers from a bucket in front of a store near the corner of al-Atarinne and Rue Faud Premier.

'*Amaryllis,*' said the fox. '*Originally from the Andes. Discovered in 1828 by Dr Eduard Poepping from Leipzig.*'

Raf ignored the animal.

'How much?'

'For Your Excellency, fifteen dollars.' The young woman smiled from under a headscarf, mouth wide. They both knew she'd trebled the price and was daring him to argue. Just as they both knew she was in the process of closing up for the night.

Raf waved away the change from his remaining twenty-dollar bill. A stupid and empty gesture even by the standards of stupid empty gestures. 'Keep it.'

Gripping the flowers in his left hand Raf headed down al-Atarinne walking with a half twist, holding the amaryllis to his side to protect the blooms from the rain; a minute or two later and the bunch was practically hidden under his coat; by the time he finally stopped under the awning of a *suq* he was actively looking for a waste bin.

Raf was still hunting for a bin when he passed through revolving doors, planning to cross the fish market's emptying floor and use its exit onto a narrow and nameless side street that led south to Rue Cif. It was one of his less useful decisions.

'*Not your fight,*' said the fox.

But it was. All fights were his fight. Or so it sometimes seemed.

The man with a knife was shorter than Raf, fairly normal for Iskandryia, where the average height barely reached five-foot-eight. His arms were corded with muscle and his back beneath a dirty string vest was broad with years of dragging nets from the sea. Only a tangle of grey across his bare shoulders put his age at, maybe, twice Raf's own.

In his hand was a thin curve of steel, the remains of a blade honed over the years to a fraction of the original thickness. All this, the man's age and occupation, fitness, and the fact he carried a filleting knife the fox took in with a single glance. While Raf wasted time staring at the face of a small boy being dragged across the floor.

'*Forget it,*' the fox said.

'No one ever forgets,' said Raf, 'that's the problem.'

Tiri sighed.

Between Raf and the nearest wall huddled a handful of market traders and a young Japanese couple who stood openmouthed, their attention torn between what was happening to the boy and an old woman beside a stall who was slopping down its white-tiled surface, oblivious to the fuss around her.

'Do something,' the Japanese girl said.

Her partner shook his head. 'We don't know there's a problem.'

Out of the corner of his eye Raf saw both become aware that he understood them, then all Raf's attention was on the fisherman, his knife and the grip he kept on the boy's thin wrist.

'Let the kid go,' said Raf, blocking the man's path. He wasn't sure which language he used. Raf had a nasty feeling it might have been Japanese.

In reply he got a growl of dialect and a wave of the knife. And as Raf stepped sideways, easily dodging the halfhearted thrust he saw in the man's face a darkness he recognized. One that stared back at him on the days he dared face a mirror.

'The kid . . .' Raf said, in Arabic this time.

Again came a thrust of blade and again Raf twisted away.

'Increase the circle,' said a voice in his head. The fox was big on rules of combat, though having learnt the rules Raf was apparently meant to forget them.

'Let go your shoulders . . .'

'I know,' said Raf, dropping to a fighter's stance. Shoulders relaxed, knees slightly bent, ragged flowers hanging loose from one hand. Most of that stuff occurred below the level of conscious control. Now was the time for his heart rate to dip to half that of an ordinary man at rest.

Still wondering if this had yet to happen, Raf watched the blade race towards him with significantly more meaning behind it; and, as he blocked, the fisherman finally released his grip on the child, as it was the only way he could throw a punch.

Raf had time to notice an inscription on one of the rings, then he was fluid, his right hand sweeping aside the blow. And while the fisherman was still looking dazed at the speed with which his enemy moved, Raf sank two fingers into a nerve on the man's shoulder and watched pain transform his face.

Raf was showing off, he knew that; but he was doing something worse in breaking a rule so old and incorrect that humanity liked to think it had moved on: until it blinked and found this untrue, which was often.

Raf could still remember the words of an old Rasta he'd met on remand, one time in Seattle, when they were both sharing a cell. The Jamaican had murdered fourteen people, all of them strangers. It was his job.

Never kill a man in front of his wife. Don't hit a man in front of his child. Walk away if those options aren't available. Anything else is allowed.

Raf blocked the next thrust easily and stepped back to widen his circle, a quick snarl shifting the slower members of the crowd.

The small boy, his tears now dry, was hugging a young woman almost lost inside a vast *hijab* that swathed her face in anonymity but didn't quite hide a bruise below one eye. The backs of both her hands were hennaed, a cheap bracelet ringed her right wrist and the thumb on her other hand was dislocated.

It wasn't a new story.

'Enough,' said the fox. *'End it.'*

Stepping in, Raf whipped his flowers across the fisherman's face. A move guaranteed to inflame the man's fury, not finish the dance.

'Pig,' Raf hissed the insult.

'You fight like a girl,' added the fox, although the voice it used was Raf's own.

The fisherman looked as if he couldn't quite believe what he'd heard. *'You heard me,'* the fox said.

With a snarl the man hurled himself at Raf, knife ready.

'See,' said the fox smugly, *'punch the right buttons . . .'*

One second the fisherman was feinting to the left, the next his right arm was whipping up as he went for a spike shot, the blade driving for the underside of Raf's chin. And then Raf was inside the movement, no time to spare for fear or thought as he brushed the flicker aside with his left and stepped through the gap, the palm of his right hand slamming shut the fisherman's jaw, so that the man's head snapped back with an audible click.

The rest was almost too easy. A twist of the hips to put one elbow into the side of the older man's head and then, as counterbalance, a fist under the ribs, carried there on recoil. As ever, Raf punched through his target, going for that invisible point behind his enemy's spine. Four other moves promptly offered themselves to complete the sequence, but Raf didn't bother . . .'

'Knife,' Raf said.

The fisherman clambered to his knees, blood splashing onto the tiles from his torn mouth. Some of his teeth had shattered.

'Drop the knife,' ordered Raf.

Something was said to the fisherman by the girl with the headscarf and, eyes half-focused, the man glanced from Raf to the blade he still held. For a second all anyone in the market could hear was the clatter of steel on ceramic tiles, then the Japanese couple started clapping.

'Out of here,' said Raf, and stepped over his broken bunch of amaryllis.

'Ashraf Bey is leaving the building.'

'How did you know?' Hani fired off her question the moment Raf walked into the *qaa*, rain dripping from his jacket. She was very carefully not standing anywhere near the marble table, which was enough to make Raf glance at the collection of objects he'd left there that morning. At least three of Felix's possessions had been replaced incorrectly, including his notebook.

'If you're going to examine things that don't belong to you,' said Raf, 'then at least memorize the position so you can put them back in the right place.'

'I didn't . . .' Hani raised her chin.

'Yes you did,' said Raf. 'And lying's worse than touching. Anyhow, that was just a suggestion . . .'

Zara put down her book.

'What?' Raf asked.

'If you don't know,' said Zara, 'I can't tell you.' Anything else she might have said was lost when Hani yanked hard on Raf's sleeve.

'Come on,' Hani said. 'Tell me how you knew the bad man was stealing Umar . . .'

'Who's Umar?' said Raf.

Hani sighed. 'You were in the fish market . . .'

Raf nodded.

'You had a fight . . .'

It had been on Isk3N apparently, courtesy of a newsfeed supplied by a Japanese tourist. And Hani knew infinitely more about the background than Raf did. The small boy's name was Umar, his father had died two years before at Medinat al-Fayoum, ambushed by fundamentalists. Medinat al-Fayoum was known to the ancient Greeks as Crocodilopolis. This last snippet was added by Hani, who believed context was everything.

'So who was the fisherman?' Raf asked.

'You didn't stop to find out . . .' Zara's voice was icy. *'He pulled a knife on Uncle Ashraf.'*

Zara smiled sadly. 'So,' she said to Raf as she pushed back her chair, 'you want to tell me who you were really fighting out there?'

'You want to tell me what's made you so angry?'

'You,' she said. 'Nothing else.'

'Got it in one,' Raf said.

'He was her father-in-law,' Hani announced loudly. 'And kept the boy out of school to work a boat,' she added more gently, once she realized she had Raf's attention. 'But he kept hitting Umar, so Umar's mother took him away . . . You're a hero.'

Raf frowned.

'Ex-Governor stops kidnap . . . It said so on the news.'

CHAPTER 9

Was it – Sally wondered – immoral to steal a sunrise muffin before smashing up Koffe King or should she trash all the food along with the glass counter? Which was worse, wasting food in a world where hunger killed twenty-four-thousand people a day or eating corporate crap, which quite possibly contained GM flour?

Tough call.

Pressing the mute button on her Sony minidisc (an impromptu gift from Bozo, who'd liberated it from near the Exxon Building on 6th), Sally consigned New York Freeze to silence and pointed to a tray.

'One of those, please.'

'Which kind?'

There were two types, Sally realized. Both looked pretty identical to her and probably came out of the same machine, but maybe the dough mix was different.

'What's the . . .' Sally began to ask and got a mouthful of fluff from her ski mask. So she yanked up the front edge. 'Whatever,' she said. And when the boy still looked blank Sally chose one at random. 'One of those on the right . . . Your right,' she added, when the boy reached in the wrong direction.

'Would you like a drink with that?'

'Skinny latte, grande,' said Sally.

Behind the chrome counter a Hispanic kid who looked about twelve took a sneak at the baseball bat Sally held.

'Easton Z,' said Sally. 'C500 alloy, high-strain graphite core.'

The kid nodded to himself. 'You want that muffin and coffee to go?'

'Yeah,' said Sally. 'Definitely.'

They both waited while another kid made a quick espresso, slopped in milk from a plastic carton and jammed the mixture under a hissing chrome nozzle. From the metal jug to a cardboard cup took another practised slop and then the kid drizzled a streak of cocoa across the top.

'I asked for a latte, skinny.' Sally said, then shrugged. 'Doesn't matter.'

'Have a nice day . . .'

Sally nodded. 'And you.' Behind her Atal and Bozo stood in silence, waiting patiently. They were on guard duty and Sally was the person they guarded. That was because, after this, Sally had another job to do, although this was the job she had to be seen to be doing, it had all been worked out.

'Go now,' she said to the two Hispanics. 'You don't get paid enough to get hurt protecting this place.' Sally looked back, to check that Atal and Bozo felt the same and they both nodded.

'She means it,' added Bozo, his voice dark as chocolate, the 70 percent cocoa, solids kind. 'Get while you can.'

The kid who'd asked Sally which muffin she wanted looked from Sally's alloy bat to the link cutters that hung from Bozo's huge hand, then took in a neoprene-handled clawhammer stuck in Atal's woven belt. Something gluey was stuck round the claws.

Discarding their silly hats at the door, the counter staff left. Today wasn't a good day to be wandering Manhattan south of Canal Street in corporate camouflage. Anyone with a brain knew not to blame the McKids stuck behind counters, who were as fucked over by corporate capitalism as the coffee growers, beef farmers and dairymen; but not every protestor currently wandering the streets of Manhattan had a brain.

'Do the clock,' Sally ordered and Atal frowned. It was true he out-ranked Bozo, being a vidhead, in as much as anyone outranked anyone, but Sally didn't trust Bozo not to break the clock while he was trying to adjust it.

Climbing onto a chrome stool, Atal yanked the clock off the wall. It was battery-operated with hollow wood-effect surround that surprised no one. Twisting a plastic knob on the back, Atal ran the minute hand forward exactly three-quarters of an hour and wiped down the knob and casing to remove his fingerprints.

'Okay,' Atal said. 'How do you want to do this?'

'The way we agreed.' Sally lifted her baseball bat over her head and paused while Atal found the angle. There was always an angle, apparently.

'Take it from the start,' said Atal, signalling to Sally that she should put down her bat. 'Okay,' he said, 'now move in from the door and take out the countertop . . .'

She did as he instructed. Going out of the door and coming back so Atal could start running the camera at the point when the door began to shut behind her. Three steps took her to the counter, up went her chrome baseball bat and down it came, fracturing twenty feet of hardened glass.

'Now smash the front . . .'

That took two swings, because the angle of attack was awkward. Of course, the whole sequence would have been better with sound, but Atal was scared he'd pick up some interference from outside, like a passing black-and-white and the police would be able to get them from that.

'Tables . . .'

These were chrome-topped, but cheap chrome glued over fibreboard circles and edged with silvery plastic that splintered at the first blow. Ten blows, ten tables, that bit was simplicity itself.

'Now the clock . . .'

Swirling round, Atal's camera panning as Sally spun from the last of the tables to where the clock had been returned to its place high on a wall, Sally did something fiddly with her baseball bat which involved skimming it in a figure eight, then rolled it three times in a row backwards over her hand. A trick that looked more impressive than it was and the only thing of value she'd picked up from Drew, a nanchuku freak briefly her boyfriend. Since this turned out to be the only skill Drew had, Sally was loath to let it go to waste.

'Do it,' Atal said.

So Sally did.

Snapping the handle into the palm of her hand, she reached up and smashed the clock into fragments and destroyed every framed poster in the place. She didn't want New York's Finest thinking the clock had been given undue attention.

'Okay' said Sally, flipping her bat in another circle. 'Out of here. We're done.'

Koffe King wasn't the first place they trashed. At Sally's insistence they'd already hit an antique emporium on the corner of 19th and Broadway. The kind of store where narrow people bought expensive things during the week and wide people went window-shopping on Saturdays.

Only there were no tourists to gawp as Sally took her bat to the biggest window of the emporium and showered a wooden Buddha with diamonds. Everybody had decided to stay home – except the fashion crowd who were watching from roofs right across Tribeca.

Atal liked the Buddha, needless to say, and so did Sally (if she was honest). What she hated was the fact that it cost more than the person who crafted or found it made in one year, quite possibly more than that person made in one lifetime.

So she did the window and liberated the statue, leaving it on the roof of an empty black-and-white as a present for the cops when they came back.

After ditching their ski masks and cycling gloves in a bin, Sally, Bozo and Atal swapped jackets, put on shades and hailed a cab on Madison. Apparently the NYPD were waving licensed cabs through a roadblock near Grand Central. Something that made no more sense to Sally than it did to Singh, the driver with limited English and advanced negotiating skills who finally took a risk and stopped for them.

Two blocks south of 42nd Street, Sally had Singh hang a right just before the Hill Building and shoot over onto Park.

'Outside the church,' she said.

They all caught the point at which Singh flicked his gaze from Bozo's red tarboosh to the stone Messiah above the door of Our Saviour.

'Showing him the sights,' said Sally as she flicked the catch on a Balenciaga bag and overtipped horrendously. The bag came courtesy of a poorly guarded boutique next to the Thai café on Thompson, between Bleecker and West 3rd. The cash was liberated from almost everywhere.

CHAPTER 10

Wednesday 9th February

'What doesn't?' Eugenie de la Croix said, stopping opposite Raf. There were plenty of chairs vacant but she stood, slightly impatiently, until a waiter slid from the gloom of Le Trianon's interior to pull one back for her, apologizing profusely.

'What doesn't what?' Raf demanded.

'Make any sense . . . ?'

He looked at the elderly woman in front of him.

'You said, *It's impossible to work out.*'

'I did?'

Eugenie nodded. 'Then you said, *No it's not. It just doesn't make sense* . . . So my question is, What doesn't make sense?'

'To eat so many almond croissants.'

Eugenie raised her eyebrows.

'Eighty-seven,' said Raf blandly, 'since I arrived in El Iskandryia.'

'I'm surprised you can afford them,' said Eugenie, 'given how little you currently earn. Have you paid off your overdraft yet?'

They both knew the answer to that.

'So how *do* you afford to do this every day?' Eugenie indicated the table and its litter of dirty plates, a half-drunk cup of cappuccino and discarded papers, one or two of which were still running comment pieces about the ex-Governor's *heroic rescue* of Umar.

'It's on my tab.'

'Tab?'

'Credit,' said Raf. 'They keep note of what I owe.'

'Which is how much?'

Raf shrugged. 'They're the ones keeping track,' he said lightly and ignored the fox who grinned inside his head, anxious to give him the exact figure.

'You're broke . . .' Eugenie said.

'And you're repeating yourself.'

Eugenie sighed. 'I can pay you.' She opened her bag and extracted a manilla envelope. 'Very well indeed.'

When Raf raised his eyebrows it was in imitation of her earlier expression, although his shades ruined most of the effect. 'You said nothing about paying me.'

'Nothing . . . ?' For a split second Eugenie looked triumphant, but her face fell as she caught Raf's twisted smile and realized he was mocking her.

But she threw out the hook all the same.

'Your father's rich.'

'If he is my father . . .'

Eugenie sighed. 'Believe me,' she said heavily and pushed the envelope across the table. 'He is and you *are* an al-Mansur.'

'Just suppose,' said Raf, pushing it back, 'that really were true. Why would I be interested?'

'What if I told you he wants to disinherit *His Excellency* Kashif Pasha?' Eugenie said, her words curdling around the honorific. 'And that his favourite son is too young to command support of the army. And that without the support of the army Murad can't be appointed the Emir's new heir?'

Raf looked blank.

'That leaves you,' she said. 'Doesn't that make you feel like coming to his aid?'

At the shake of Raf's head, Eugenie shrugged. 'I told him this wouldn't work,' she said, but she was talking to herself.

'I've got a question for you,' said Raf. 'Ignore whether or not they were actually married. Did my mother really sleep with the Emir?'

Eugenie nodded.

'Can you prove it?'

They met again the next morning, Raf already one newspaper down with two to go by the time Eugenie stepped over the silk rope that separated the terrace of Le Trianon from Rue Missala.

The weather was warmer, almost humid, but Raf wore his black silk suit all the same and she wore the grey skirt and jacket she'd been wearing when the two of them first met, only now they no longer stank of camphor. A discreet holster still sat at the back of her hip. Her make-up remained so immaculate that Raf wasn't quite sure it was there.

As ever, Raf wore his trademark shades and nursed a headache that was three parts caffeine to one part ennui. He'd been waiting for Eugenie's arrival. Which was not to say he'd been looking forward to it.

'Cappuccino,' Raf told his waiter. 'And whatever Lady Eugenie is having.'

'Madame de la Croix,' Eugenie said firmly. 'And I'll have my usual espresso . . . I turned down your father's kind offer of an upgrade before you were born,' she added, once the waiter had gone. 'Around the time I turned down his offer of a bed to share. My chance for immortality was how he described it.' The woman's smile was so wintry that Raf looked at her then, really looked, the way the fox did when searching for stillness within life's scribble.

It was said, at least it was by Tiri, that a full-grown seal was able to sense the wake of a single fish ten minutes after that area of water had become empty. So too could people sense the ghost echo of long-gone events.

If only they knew how.

Looking at Eugenie, really looking, Raf saw a courage unusual for the world in which they lived. Not in the small holster casually clipped to her belt or in the steadiness of her gaze and her refusal to be the first to look away. Her courage showed most in the way she wore her hair, long and unashamedly grey.

The woman was old and made no pretence to be anything other.

A strength that gave her a crueller kind of beauty.

'Your mother . . .' Eugenie said once the waiter had brought the coffee.

'What about her?'

'Can you still recall what she was like?'

Raf lifted his shades, though to do so hurt because even with clouds to filter out the sun his pupils were reduced to tiny, steel-hard dots. 'Total recall,' he told Eugenie coldly. 'That's what I've got.'

'About her?'

'About everything . . .'

Eugenie nodded, like that made sense and she didn't feel it necessary to challenge what he said or have him justify the statement. 'Yeah,' she said, 'I suppose you do.'

They sat in silence after that. Raf hidden again behind his shades and Eugenie openly watching the occasional tourist couple stroll hand in hand down Rue Missala. It was too early for the Easter crowd, too late for those who'd come over New Year. The hotels were cheap, the cafés mostly empty. Out of the dozens of horse-drawn calèches that usually plied the Corniche, that great sweep of seafront stretching from Fort Qaitbey down to where the fat seawall of the Silsileh sat in the shadow of Iskandryia's *bibliotheka*, only a handful were working and those had their leather roofs up, their drivers wrapped in coats against the chance of rain.

'Do you like it here?'

'Yes,' Raf answered immediately, leaving himself wondering if he actually meant it. In many ways Seattle had been better and Huntsville had a certain charm, even though it had been a prison. 'Mostly,' he said, amending his answer.

'And you intend to stay?' Eugenie's smile was part knowing but mostly sad, as if she had reasons for doubting it, reasons she wasn't entirely sure Raf was yet ready to hear. Her attitude irritated the fuck out of him.

'What do you actually want?' Raf demanded.

'Help,' said Eugenie, 'pure and simple. Your help protecting the Emir.'

'I thought that was your job?'

For a split second Eugenie's face glazed, the way faces do when people retreat inside their head. 'I'm getting old,' was all she said. 'The Emir doesn't listen to me like he did and I know he would listen to you.'

Reaching across the table, she took Raf's hand, oblivious to the waiters hovering and German tourists on the far side of the rope that separated Le Trianon's terrace from the street. She had a surprisingly hard grip for a woman her age.

'I knew her, you know . . .' said Eugenie. 'Right back at the beginning.' She was talking about his mother.

'What was she like?' Raf's question came unbidden, sliding its way into being before Raf had time to snatch it back.

'Beautiful,' Eugenie said simply. 'Fractured even then. Wild as an animal and as dangerous. She was wanted, you know . . .'

'Wanted?'

'By the FBI and Interpol. I think even the Japanese had a warrant out. Something about a bomb in a research vessel.'

'What kind of research?'

'The kind that turned minke whales into sushi.'

Despite himself Raf smiled. 'How did the two of you meet?'

'Oh,' Eugenie's mouth twisted. 'I was there when she first arrived at the labs. Stupid bitch came trawling out of the desert in a battered Jeep, I almost shot her . . . Should have done,' she added softly. 'Might have made life a whole lot easier for the rest of us.'

Raf wasn't sure he was meant to hear that bit.

CHAPTER 11

Flashback

'What you thinking?' Atal asked, slamming the door on Singh's yellow taxi.

'About our friend Wu Yung' said Sally. 'About the islands.'

Atal blushed and they both knew why.

As light began fingering the palms that edged the beach, Sally had splashed her way onto the sand and stopped to retrieve her sarong, wrapping red-and-white dragons loosely round her narrow hips, then padded her way along a winding path between rampant bushes of sea almond and wild orchids until she reached the kampong.

At the entrance of her hut Sally stopped again to kick white sand from her heels and, glancing across the kampong saw Wu Yung leave a house on stilts that Atal had chosen. An empty wine bottle in his hand, the camera around his neck.

She ate breakfast alone that day but at lunchtime she joined the others by the jetty, sitting topless while Atal swam and Bozo chilled under a palm, spliff growing cold between his fingers as he stared in wonder at a cluster of coconuts above, any one of which could have killed him.

On the jetty itself Wu Yung worked a barbecue made from an oil drum cut open end to end and welded to the old frame of a metal table. He had two fish the length of Sally's arm crisping on its griddle, fat spitting on the glowing coals, their eyes gone opalescent with heat . . .

'You okay?' Atal asked.

'Sure,' said Sally as she watched Singh's cab roar away. 'Just remembering how we got here.'

Bozo grinned. He knew exactly how he got there, by Boeing 747 from KL to Idlewild, paid for by the weird Chinese guy and with $1,000 spending money in his pocket. 'We going to do this, or what?' he said, putting on a fresh pair of gloves.

Almost opposite the Church of Our Saviour stood the Hotel Kitano. A lovingly restored fifteen-storey redbrick hotel that majored in rollout futons and sunken hot tubs for its mainly Japanese clientele, or so Atal said, then got embarrassed when Bozo asked how he knew. And that was where Sally, Atal and Bozo went – across the four-lane, cop-car howl of Park Avenue. Although they detoured round the block to let them approach the hotel from a different direction.

Getting in meant staying confident, what with the riots and everything.

'I need to use your bathroom,' said Sally before the uniformed doorman even had time to speak. Whatever the man had been about to say got lost inside her smile.

'It's on the right, down some stairs.' He'd been about to call her lady but the kid's accent was just too upscale for that.

'Wait in the bar,' she told her companions. Shuffling the Balenciaga bag so it sat higher on her shoulder, Sally headed for a dark wood door without looking back.

The woman who exited the chrome, glass and slate bathroom wore Dior lipstick the colour of dry blood, a small pillbox hat, and a dress of tissue-thin black silk that rustled over her small breasts and made obvious her lack of a bra. The bag was gone, tossed into a chrome trash can, and with the bag her shades and Atal's jacket, all three spoof-bombed against DNA tests with crud vacuumed up from the backseat of a bus.

It looked on first glance as if she wore no knickers at all. It looked that way on second glance too.

'Champagne,' she told the barman, 'chilled not frozen.' He didn't get the reference. That was the problem with using English tag lines, few Americans ever did. 'And some olives,' Sally added. 'Preferably in brine.'

Over at his table, Atal smirked.

'You both know what to do?' Sally asked, grabbing a chair and leaning forward, so that her dress gaped at the neck. On cue, the eyes of her two companions flicked front their beers to the swell at the top of her breasts.

That worked then.

'Well?'

'We know' insisted Atal, his eyes still fixed on her front.

'Glad to hear it.' Sally sat back, picked up her drink and smiled. In ten minutes' time she'd be meeting a fiftyish WASP, probably done up in dress-down Fridays twenty years too young for him so he didn't get cashed by protestors. And the man wasn't going to listen to a word she said, which suited Sally fine since she was planning to busk that bit of the routine.

'Finish up,' she said. 'We're on.'

The Bayer-Rochelle office was two blocks from Hotel Kitano. Stuck between the Sterling Building and Doctors Mutual International. There were uniformed guards on the door, four of them, and they'd taken the mayor at his word and armed themselves with something more deadly than nightsticks.

Although their Glocks were still holstered, not drawn or combat held like guards outside one of the banks they'd driven past earlier.

'Annie Savoy,' announced Sally flicking on her smile and one of the uniforms unbent enough to check his clipboard.

'Not on the list,' he said and turned away, conversation over.

'Could you check with Charlie?' Sally's voice was saccharine sweet.

Despite himself, the guard turned back, question already forming on his lips.

Got you, thought Sally. 'Charlie Savoy, my godfather . . .'

The man looked at Sally, whose sun-bleached hair was now swept back in an Alice band, black to match her dress. Comparing and contrasting the rugged, well-known looks of billionaire Dr Charles Savoy (son of H. R. Savoia, a cheesemaker from Basilica) with the very English girl standing on the sidewalk, waiting to be invited inside.

He'd had jobs in Lower Midtown long enough to recognize expensive clothes and he knew, as you were meant to know, that only the very rich got away with wearing so little with so much elegance.

'Your name's not on today's approved list,' he said apologetically. 'But I'll call his PA.' The nod he gave the other three was perfunctory, more a reminder to stay alert than any apology for leaving them.

'Your boss?' Sally asked.

One of them nodded.

'Doesn't like doing door duty, right?'

Another nod, more emphatic this time.

'All hands to the pump I guess. What with anarchists trashing every-thing of value . . .'

Behind Sally, Bozo turned a snort of laughter into a hasty cough and swallowed his smile inside a hastily grabbed silk handkerchief. The handkerchief was blue. It matched his stolen suit.

'There's a problem . . .' The returning guard sounded more apologetic than ever. 'Your grandfather's not here at the moment.'

'Godfather,' Sally corrected. 'My godfather. What about Mike Pier-point?' That was the fiftyish WASP she actually needed to meet, the one with receding hair and a weight problem. She knew this because she'd seen a shot of him in the back of Harpers, a moon-faced academic in rimmed glasses out of his depth at some black tie do for ethical genome research . . .

'He's on the phone,' the guard recited from memory. 'He sends his apologies and asks you to wait.'

'No problem,' said Sally. Sliding past the guard, she strolled towards a bank of lifts and punched the correct button without needing to look at the list displayed in a brass frame, on the wall. A puff piece in the local business press had already revealed the right floor.

Gazing down from his twenty-second-floor office, billionaire Charlie Savoy can almost see the tiny corner shop where his father . . .

'He meant wait down here.' The guard's voice faltered as Sally turned, her face suddenly worried.

'If we must,' she said, sounding less than happy. 'Although I'd feel safer waiting in his office.'

They rode an Otis to the twenty-second floor, thanked the lift politely when it wished them a profitable day and had to wait for Atal to get over his attack of giggles. As the doors shut Atal was still grinning. The man who came out to greet them wore Gap chinos, canvas deck shoes and a striped sweatshirt with an anchor on the pocket.

'Annie . . .'

Sally shook his hand warmly, holding her grip for a second longer than strictly necessary and the man smiled politely, but only after noticing her nipples.

'Beautiful dress.' Mike Pierpoint blushed as he said this.

'Dior,' Sally agreed. 'A present from my father.' And the bald man nodded as if he knew who she meant.

'I don't think we've met?' he said, his question just the wrong side of anxious.

'We did,' said Sally. 'But you won't remember. I was much younger. More of a kid really.'

Mike Pierpoint wanted to say she was still a kid, Sally could see it in his eyes. But he resisted the urge, helped probably by the half glances he kept throwing at her tits.

'At a baseball match or company barbecue,' Sally added, busking it.

'Barbecue,' Mike said with certainty. 'It must have been a barbecue. Your godfather hates baseball with a passion.'

Sally smiled.

'I don't want to keep you,' she said. 'If you can just show me the way.'

The room was everything Wu Yung had led Sally to expect. A huge corner office full of heavy furniture and carpeted in burgundy, with blue washed-silk wallpaper between faux marble half pillars that supported a panelled ceiling probably made from embossed card, although a century's worth of paint would need to be cut away before anyone could be sure. In the six-foot drop between the ceiling's ornate coving and a slightly less ornate picture rail, bare-breasted nymphs hit stucco tambourines and flicked their hair in a static wind.

Charlie Savoy's desk was equally imposing. Solid not veneer, made from some wood so oxblood it was undoubtedly endangered.

Atal nodded. 'Meranti,' he said, 'from the shorea tree.' He looked at the wood, considering it carefully. 'Probably thought they were buying teak.'

On top of the desk stood an old-fashioned PC, a stand-alone Dell, lacking even a modern connection. Beside the PC a newish laptop slotted into a docking bay that bled wires in a waterfall to the floor. Atal switched on both machines without Sally having to say a thing.

'Too worried about being phreaked to go infrared,' said Atal, pointing to the wires, his dismissive grin that of someone who'd once read a complete stranger's dear john e-mail across a crowded railway carriage, using a basic Van Eck box.

'The fire door's out there,' Sally told Bozo as she tossed him a pack of Marlboros. 'Check it's not alarmed and go have a cigarette. Warn me if that creep comes back.'

'I don't use tobacco.'

'That's right,' said Atal, snapping on a wristband and letting its antistatic wire hang free while he struggled into new surgical gloves. 'Don't you know his body is a temple?'

'Yeah,' said Sally, 'and yours is Disney World.'

With Bozo standing guard by the fire door and Atal busy unscrewing grey boxes, Sally made a slow circuit of Charlie Savoy's office and let her instincts run free. She was big on instinct. Instinct was what steered an albatross through storm-torn skies and let salmon do feats of navigation only long-dead Polynesians could imitate; it was what let Aboriginal kids remember routes they'd travelled only once, years back. Instinct was survival hardwired and way more important than most people allowed.

In fact, Sally was pretty certain that even human belief in free will was hardwired and she didn't have a problem with that contradiction, she had a problem with what it allowed humanity to do to the rest of the planet.

So if she was Charlie Savoy, local boy made extremely good courtesy of a Ph.D. in microbiology and a couple of lucky guesses, where would she stash all those valuables she couldn't risk taking home?

Assuming she could intuit what valuables such a man might want to stash . . .

Dirty money, maybe. Negatives featuring random acts of senseless sex? Quite possibly from what she'd heard, but she doubted he'd mind having his prowess exposed to the world. It would be something technically brilliant but deeply illegal. Sally was counting on it.

643

Wu Yung was already in line for whatever Dr Savoy kept on the hard disk of his stand-alone, which, for all she knew, was kiddie porn, but Sally intended to take spoils for herself. Charlie Savoy was one of the bad guys and somewhere there'd be leverage, something to make him stop.

There always was. Look at her father.

In the corner of Savoy's office stood a filing cabinet made from mahogany with solid brass handles. When Sally opened the top drawer she half expected it to be lined with padded silk like a coffin. Instead she got bundles of yellowing papers in hanging files gone brittle with age. Accounts mostly, a few ancient tax returns. He'd been rich for longer than she'd been alive.

'Story of my life,' said Sally.

'What?' Atal glanced up, the cross-blade screwdriver in his hand a fetching shade of orange. He'd shoplifted it from The Wiz along with his antistatic band the day before. 'What's the story of your life?'

'All of this.' Sally gestured to a row of bronze figures that lined a long ebony sideboard near the filing cabinet. A Roman slave with a rope round his neck lay dying on a poorly carved patch of earth. A half-naked bronze dancer, wearing a wisp of tin over her pudendum pirouetted on one leg, both arms raised above her head.

'Collectable,' said Atal.

Sally looked at him.

'Late Victorian,' he said. And Sally realized there was a lot she didn't know about his background, but then everything he knew about hers was a lie, which probably made them even.

'Got it,' Atal said suddenly, lifting free a Southgate hard drive.

'Good. Now do the laptop . . .'

'Did most of it already,' he said, 'while you were mooning about.'

Sally sighed.

After he'd replaced the PC's casing so that everything looked normal from the outside, Atal flipped up the screen on the laptop and sat back, feeling blindly in his pockets for a disc. The antistatic wire still hung from his wrist but its crocodile clip no longer clasped anything. Atal didn't need it for what came next.

Extracting a CD from his pocket, he slipped the disc into the slot.

'Got a knife?' Sally demanded suddenly.

Atal had and he watched as Sally slid the blade between the doors of the sideboard, cracking it open. Twenty-five-year-old McClellan, VSOP Hine, two kinds of Bombay Sapphire, Armagnac XS, a bottle of Pussers Rum so dark it could have been treacle . . . The man had something for everyone, complete with matching sets of glasses.

'Okay,' asked Sally, holding up a frosted tumbler. 'What's this?'

644

'Bohemian,' Atal barely raised his head from the laptop. 'Art deco, possibly Lalique. Smashing it would be a crime.'

Atal's virus was a kiddie script, captured from a zombie and modified slightly, then signed with someone else's tag. Attached to it was what mattered, a hack he'd written from scratch.

As hacks went it wasn't bad.

A quick skim of the network showed a six-car rats' tail exiting through a router, most of those cerberus functions had been disabled, with the machines instructed to look to an IcePort X2, which doubled as a mail server and did a reasonably neat job with network address translation, meaning everyone was effectively invisible from outside.

More or less what Atal had expected. Solid but not flashy, functional rather than bleeding edge and a good eighteen months out of date. As for the network itself, well, that still used cable.

'Okay?' he asked Sally.

She nodded.

'Right we are then.' Atal switched off the laptop, counted to thirty and switched it on again. Extracting his disc, he slipped it back into his pocket.

'It's done,' he said and Sally smiled.

Come midnight when the system prepared itself to back up, a sliver of script would lock out anyone still connected, which would be nobody, and fuck over the central server. First thing tomorrow, when the network came up all the keyboards would freeze and every local disc would reformat itself, several times.

Of course, it was possible to stop this by switching off individual machines at the wall, but experience proved that few people ever did that until it was too late. And the joy of the whole hack was, what with the trashed server, failed network and general panic, it might be as much as twenty-four hours before anyone thought to check inside Charlie Savoy's stand-alone to discover exactly why its hard disk kept failing to boot.

'Shit,' Sally said.

Atal turned at the heartfelt expletive and found her staring down at the splintered front of a small drawer.

'Georgian card table,' said Atal. 'Extremely valuable . . . Well, it was.'

Only Sally wasn't listening. She was gazing at a transparent plastic folder and Atal had to agree, for that amount of damage it wasn't much of a haul.

'The drawer can be mended,' he said soothingly. 'So only an expert will be able to tell.'

'Really?' said Sally but her attention was on the folder. It showed handwritten specifications for a genetics lab recently built in North Africa

645

by Bayer-Rochelle in conjunction with the Emir of Tunis. A joint project was mentioned, provisionally named Eight Score & Ten.

'You okay?'

'Sure.' Sally nodded. 'How about you?'

'Me?' said Atal. 'I'm good.' They'd been lovers briefly at the kampong, for the week or two it took them to admit they both preferred Wu Yung. After that, their time sharing a bed was limited to those rare occasions their host summoned them both.

From his other pocket Atal produced wet wipes and started to clean down the stand-alone's grey case and keyboard, then did the same for the laptop, finishing the laptop's TFT screen for good measure.

Just to muddle forensics still further (given he'd messed over both machines wearing gloves and the wipedoum was a put-on), Atal upended a small plastic envelope of the kind banks use for loose change and dribbled the desk with crud vacuumed from a bus stop in Tribeca.

It was fair to say, Atal felt, that the obvious advantages of spoof-bombing every crime scene with a random collection of dead skin, broken hairs and artificial fibre had given a whole new lease of life to those little handheld vacuum cleaners that Radio Shack sold for extracting dust from computer vents. 'You done?' he asked Sally.

She smiled.

CHAPTER 12

'So you see,' said Eugenie, 'it went like this . . .'

Before Arabic was reintroduced as the court language of Tunis all laws were issued in Turkish, legacy code from the city having been ruled by an Ottoman *beylerley*, which translated as some kind of pasha.

The return to Arabic took place around two centuries ago, at least, it did according to Eugenie. She kept her grip on Raf's wrist while she talked.

Already prosperous, Tunis had grown fat on the rewards of slaving, piracy and trade. And when the *moriscos* were finally expelled from al Andalus in 1609, many settled in Tunis, adding their skills in cookery, ceramics, and metalwork to the city's existing richness. It was a city of pragmatic compromise, where Jewish merchants flourished alongside those princely pirates the corsairs, who built ornate *dars* to house their families and influenced Ifriqiya's foreign policy. Renegade Europeans mostly, converts to Islam from Spain and Italy, sometimes excused the requirement to undergo circumcision.

As for the wives of Ifriqiya's rulers, these were either Turkish or captured Christian, rarely indigenous. And the solid foundation of the state, those who worked the fields, led caravans or bartered in the markets were often Berber, a people given to mixing magic and mysticism with their Islam.

Quite why Eugenie felt it necessary to tell him all this Raf wasn't sure; until she got to the bit about captured foreigners giving birth to ruling beys. And then the grip on his wrist was as sharp as the steel in her grey eyes.

'Think about it,' she said.

Bizarrely, Eugenie stood to say her good-byes, first shaking Raf by the hand and then dipping forward to kiss him on the cheek.

'I'm sorry,' she said.

'For what?'

Eugenie paused, briefly considering her answer. 'I could say,' she said, 'that I'm sorry I couldn't convince you. That I failed to persuade you to help the Emir. But it's more than that . . .'

'If you can fake sincerity,' said the fox and got shushed into silence. If Eugenie was counterfeiting, then she was a better actor than he. Raf could almost feel her regret punctuate each word.

'I'm not faking anything,' Eugenie said flatly. 'You're not doing yourself any good behaving like this and you're not helping Zara or Hani. I've read your file,' she said. 'I know when someone's got *issues.*'

'I . . . don't . . . have . . . issues . . .' Raf said.

'No,' said Eugenie. 'Of course you don't. You have the fox instead.'

Breakfast slid into elevenses, a very English meal that seemed to exist nowhere but in Raf's memory, the way elevenses would eventually slide into lunch. At which point, he'd have read the *Alexandrian* at least twice, and be sick of the sight of the waiter who hovered on the edge of his vision, anxious to provide anything His Excellency might need.

'Which would be what?'

Raf thought about it.

'Well?'

To give the fox its due, Tiri waited ten minutes for Raf's answer and only reentered Raf's mind when it realized the man had no intention of replying.

'How can I reply,' thought Raf, 'when I have no idea of what the right answer is?'

'Can I ask a question?'

Raf nodded to himself.

'Why didn't you just fuck her?' said the fox.

'Because I didn't.'

'You want to tell me why?'

'The time wasn't right.'

'And is it right now?'

'No,' Raf shook his head. 'Now it's too late.'

Whether that was strictly true Raf had no idea but it was becoming, almost by default, an article of faith for him. What might have been with Zara was fractured, smashed into fragments too many to identify, never mind glue back together again . . .

*

'Excellency . . .'

Glossy and elegant, wrapped round an old photograph and placed in an envelope from El Iskandryia's most famous hotel, the snakeskin was soft enough to be finest leather. The only flaw Raf could see was a ragged hole where the reptile's head should have been.

The envelope was delivered at lunchtime by a man on a scooter. A Vespa with a Sterling engine conversion. The man wore a black biker jacket, one that looked scuffed until you got close enough to see that the damage was imprinted on the surface.

The lining was spider silk impregnated with steel and could stop a blade, no matter how narrow. It also spiralled around a slug (should anyone fire one), enabling paramedics to extract most handgun bullets with the minimum of tissue damage. High-velocity bullets, of course, were a different matter. They did their own extracting, mostly of soft tissue that got caught in the vacuum on pass-through.

Eduardo was very proud of his jacket. And in the list of his prized possessions it came a close second to his scooter, which was Italian and nearly original, apart from its engine and the new seat.

'Sorry to trouble you . . .'

The man at the table looked up and frowned.

Once, several months before, Eduardo had made another delivery. That time the envelope had been much bigger, the contents more obviously dangerous.

In the first package had been a chocolate box from Charbonel & Walker, empty apart from a slab of high-brisance explosive. The man now at the table had been the target, Felix Abrinsky took the blast and the *plastique* had been stolen from the offices of the Minister of Police.

Now Eduardo worked for Raf. Although Eduardo used the term loosely. He didn't exactly work *for* His Excellency, more helped him out occasionally in return for a small monthly retainer and the use of office space behind the tram station at Place Arabi.

Both the office and retainer came out of El Iskandryia's police budget, from an account reserved for high-level informers. Raf had never thought to mention this to Eduardo. Nor had he thought to cancel the arrangement when he resigned.

'This was delivered to my office.' *My office,* Eduardo still liked the sound of that.

'When?' asked Raf.

Eduardo examined his rather impressive silver Seiko. 'Twenty-eight minutes ago,' he said firmly, then watched the big hand click forward and amended his answer to twenty-nine.

'Who delivered it?'

'A woman,' said Eduardo, 'very neat. Looked old, behaved young . . .' He paused, shuffling his thoughts into a logical order, the way he imagined an ex-detective like His Excellency might do. 'She had a grey jacket, neat skirt, dark shoes. A watch . . .' Eduardo smiled at his own powers of observation. 'Which was silver like this one.'

It had been platinum and matched Eugenie's cigarette case. Made long enough ago that the metal was grey and slightly matte, having been manufactured in the early 1920s before jewellers discovered how platinum might be polished as brightly as white gold. A fact Raf didn't bother to mention.

'And her hair?' he asked, already knowing the answer.

'Long,' said Eduardo, 'and grey.' He stopped to look at the bey. 'You recognize her?'

Taking the envelope, Raf noticed that its flap was folded inside, the way his mother insisted he do. The snakeskin he wasn't expecting; the photograph Raf was. He shook the skin from its envelope the way Felix once taught him, dropping it onto an open napkin without once touching it, so that he left no DNA traces of his own. To handle it this way was ridiculous, because Raf knew who'd sent it, as one simple call to her hotel would confirm.

In fact, one simple call was what he would make. Toggling his watch, Raf chose *voice only* and told his Omega to connect him to the Hotel Cavafy.

'I'd like to speak to Madame de la Croix.'

'When?'

'You're certain?'

'What flight?'

Madame de la Croix had checked out. Her limousine had been booked the previous night. And the clerk on the desk didn't know which flight she'd been catching. Not one to Tunis, certainly. A UN resolution, bolstered by edicts from the IMF, had closed down commercial flights to Ifriqiya more than forty years before. To get the ban lifted, all the Emir had to do was sign the UN Biodiversity (Germ Line Limitation) Treaty and allow entry to an international team of inspectors, the make-up of which was to be chosen by Washington, Paris and Berlin.

Until then, flights to Tunis remained banned.

All this meant, of course, was that she'd catch a flight to Tripoli and join the bullet train for Tangiers, changing at the border before the *turbani de luxe* was sealed for its journey through Ifriqiya. A variety of local diesels ran from just over the border to Tunis itself.

Raf knew this because in the week following his arrival in El

Iskandryia he'd checked the trans-Megreb timetable and in so doing had memorized it.

'Is Your Excellency all right?'

Raf looked up to find Eduardo standing rather too close. 'Sit,' Raf said and Eduardo did, suddenly self-conscious to find himself on view in the city's most famous café.

'Have you had lunch?'

Eduardo shook his head. In the top pocket of his coat he had a pair of Armani sunglasses, like the ones Raf wore. Only Eduardo didn't quite dare wear his, what with the grey sky and Place Zaghloul being a patchwork of slowly drying puddles.

His Excellency on the other hand always wore shades, even after dark.

'Omelette,' Raf told the waiter. 'And for you?'

'The same',' said Eduardo. 'And a Coke with ice,' he added, keen to show his independence. 'Make it Diet.'

'As Your Excellency wishes.'

Eduardo grinned.

While Eduardo ate most of the bread basket, Raf extracted the brittle photograph from its wrapping and flipped it over. Then spent the rest of lunch trying to make sense of the picture. He'd expected to find himself in the face of his father as he'd done once before. And in that, at least, Raf was right. A young man with a goatee beard and drop-pearl earring did stare into the camera, shading his eyes from sunlight. It was the two people with him who were wrong.

Behind the Emir stood a huge patchwork tent sewn from strips of striped carpet, old prayer rugs and squares of black felt, its flap held open with ropes. And in the entrance, smiling and topless was a blond girl wearing a smile and baggy shorts. A leather choker with a fat amber bead was around her neck and her breasts had been made prominent by a trick of the sun. She was unquestionably beautiful.

She was also, Raf realized, undoubtedly his mother.

A bare-chested boy in ripped jeans and open-toed sandals sat at her feet, his blond hair pulled up into a samurai topknot and tied with red ribbon. One of his legs was in plaster, his arm firmly around Sally Welham's legs. He was glowering.

On the back, in one corner, Raf found two dates in black ink, one under the other and beneath these a question mark. The second of those dates Raf knew. It was the death of his mother. While the first, presumably the death of Per, was long before Raf had even been born. Which made no sense at all.

651

'Suppose the Emir dies,' Eugenie had written, 'who will you ask then . . . ?'

'Yeah right,' said the fox.

'What?' Eduardo glanced up from his omelette, realized he might have been rude and amended his question. 'Did Your Excellency say something?'

CHAPTER 13

Flashback

Four nuns sat by one window, two pairs facing each other across the carriage like sour-faced crows. They had black habits and whatever those white hats were that went straight down, giving them cheekbones they didn't deserve.

They all wore sensible shoes for the journey, flat soles and laces. And they carried sandwiches wrapped in grease-proof paper and a salami in its own cotton case, like a fat cloth condom. Sally was pretty sure she'd seen sisters in New York wearing pale blue jumpsuits, God Loves Baseball caps and trainers; but maybe convents were tougher in North Africa or perhaps this kind were just a different genus – or should that be species?

Whatever, they didn't approve of Sally's bare legs and T-shirt and that struck her as unfair. Particularly as she'd been on her best behaviour ever since tumbling into the carriage at Banghazi in a clatter of rucksack and carrier bags, with her ancient Leica still safe in its pigskin case. And it wasn't her fault the boy opposite her had decided to practise his English, which was adequate, or his seduction techniques, which stank . . .

Sally, however, had to admit that whipping up his white shirt to show her a stab wound was a new one. Clever too, since it let the boy show off his six-pack and slim hips without being obvious. Unless, of course, it really was his wound she was meant to be admiring.

The scar was bigger than Sally expected. An ugly strip speckled with pigment-dark dots where both edges had been stitched. A nightclub was involved somewhere and a Danish girl, blond like her but not as beautiful, the last said hastily as if Sally, might suddenly take offence . . .

'Seven litres,' he told her proudly, 'that's what I lost.'

Sally considered pointing out that the human body couldn't hold seven litres of blood but restrained herself. Maybe the red stuff had been pouring out one-side while being pumped in the other.

He'd told Sally his name, she was sure of that. And unfortunately they were several hours too far into a conversation for her to ask it again. Particularly since her name peppered his every sentence, Sally this and Sally that . . .

If every compartment hadn't already been full and the corridor outside locked solid with people standing, she could have moved; but the very thought of pushing her way from carriage to carriage past hundreds of grinning men was enough to make Sally stay where she was.

So what if the nuns stank of garlic sausage cut in fat slices from that salami? She didn't smell so hot herself. A stink was on her own fingers from using a station loo at Tripoli, and she needed a bath. It was five days since she'd stayed at a tiny pensione outside Catania airport, where a fat Sicilian customs inspector had stopped midsearch when he reached the box containing her contraceptive cap.

'What's in here?' he'd demanded.

Dropping to a squat, Sally had spread her knees and mimed shoving a finger into her vagina. He'd let her go after that although his scowl followed her all the way through the air-conditioned hell of Arrivals and out into the sweet heat that told her she was back in Sicily.

The pensione was the first one she'd come across. A drab little house with peeling yellow paint that turned out to be immaculate once she stepped through the door. Clean sheets in her attic room, a double bed charged as a single as there was only one of her and the little hotel was hardly overbusy. A dining room that they opened especially, so that the English student didn't have to eat alone in her room.

And then a bath to wash away the dirt of New York. The pensione had plenty of hot water the owner told her proudly, little knowing that Sally would take hers shallow and almost cold. A habit she traced back to school.

She was tired from the flight and a twelve-hour stopover in London. Most of her spare money had gone towards a ticket that agreeing to the stopover made just about affordable. Although breaking at London meant she spent one night camped at Heathrow fighting off bad pickup lines and assuring the security staff that yes, she did have a valid ticket for onward travel. Of course, Sally could have afforded to fly more or less direct, with a simple change of planes in Frankfurt but then she wouldn't have had enough money left for what she needed to do.

Later, as she dried, staring in the looking glass of the pensione's attic, Sally tried to see herself as Atal had seen her, as Wu Yung and the boy before the man that Wu Yung was. Wondering what had they seen, the three men she'd bedded in the two years since she first let herself seduce Drew, the nanchuku nut, from boredom . . . She'd told Wu Yung fifteen

lovers, to stop him thinking she might take him seriously; which Sally had,
though common sense made her keep that private.

A thin face. Good bones, her grandmother would have said. Pale blue
eyes. Narrow shoulders and small breasts. A flat stomach and no hips.
That was her most obvious flaw. She had, an early gym mistress once told
her, the figure of a natural athlete. That was shortly before the woman
tried to massage knots from the cramped muscles of Sally's inner thigh.

Examined coldly in the flecked mirror of a cheap pensione within
spitting distance of the airport's razor wire, Sally still looked good; a fact
that made life easier but did nothing to make her proud. She kept herself
fit, she didn't take drugs, not even the pharmaceutical kind, and she
avoided meat. All the same, her looks and intelligence were the product of
good genes which were, whether she liked it or not, the result of careful
breeding on the part of her grandparents and parents. Though her
grandmother referred to it, rather sweetly, as making a good marriage.

Something Sally had no intention of doing.

After rough bread and rougher wine for which she was not charged,
Sally relinquished her room, the bed unused, and took a bus south to
Siracusa. She'd been planning to hitch but the owner's wife told Sally that
good girls didn't do that in Sicily and when Sally discovered how little a
ticket would cost, she decided to be good after all. She stayed with the bus
until it reached its destination, the port.

So white in the sunlight that it almost burned Sally's eyes, the SS
Gattopardo *was anything but inside. Stairs scabbed with chewing gum,*
heat-mottled lifeboats, walkways and rusting steps painted an institution-
al green and rough unshaded benches bolted in rows on the upper deck.
Made worse by a stink of oil from the engine room and a sour tang of
static that clung to every surface.

To top it all the Gattopardo *broke down six hours out from Malta, its*
first stop, and, having sat out a blazing afternoon, decided to limp back at
dusk, arriving just as Valletta's cathedral rang midnight. Invited to go
ashore and return at daybreak, Sally refused and ended up sleeping on a
floor in a women's loo, having first made safe the door by tying a short
length of climbing rope between its handle and the nearest tap. Just one of
the survival tips she'd picked up on her travels.

Noon next day found Sally arguing with a steward who refused to
accept she'd been aboard the previous day and was thus entitled to the
complimentary lunch recently announced over the ship's tannoy. Eventu-
ally the man gave up and watched in disgust as Sally stuffed her rucksack
with oranges and figs, pocketed a fat shard of hard cheese that wanted to
be Parmesan but wasn't and took a dozen slices of prosciutto just because

she was pissed at him. *The fruit and cheese she kept, the meat went Frisbee style over the side to feed the gulls.*

All that remained after that was to negotiate customs at Banghazi and she was running for a carriage, filthy clothes, rucksack and all.

'Sally . . .'

The Arab boy with the scar was tapping her bare knee, which was a new one, except that it seemed he really did want to get her attention.

'What?'

Looking round, Sally realized their train had halted in the middle of nowhere. At least nowhere that looked like anywhere. All she could see from her dusty window was a wide expanse of red earth dotted with bushes of some kind.

'We've stopped,' she said.

The boy nodded and one of the nuns suddenly started to fire short, frightened sentences at her in a language Sally definitely didn't understand. When Sally shrugged, the woman repeated herself louder.

'Any idea what she's saying?'

He nodded.

'Well,' said Sally. 'Are you going to tell me?'

'Sure,' shrugged the boy. 'Why not . . . ? She says this train's been hijacked by bandits who will kill her because of her faith and rape you because you're not wearing enough clothes.'

'Is that true?'

He shrugged. 'Anything's possible,' he told her. 'Not likely, but possible.' The boy looked from Sally to the nuns and back again. 'Do you have anything with longer sleeves?'

She did, in her rucksack.

'And anything other than shorts?'

Jeans, if those were any good.

'It's probably unnecessary,' said the boy, sounding apologetic, 'but you might want to change just in case.'

Peeling off her top while simultaneously popping the plastic buckle on her rucksack to extract Atal's favourite shirt, Sally shook out a Paul Smith she'd borrowed on the Islands and never returned.

Needless to say, Atal had insisted it was a fake.

The shirt was white with thin stripes, made from cotton and had tails old-fashioned enough to cover her modesty as she wriggled out of her shorts and slid into jeans. At school, most Friday nights she used to change back into her uniform in the rear seat of a taxi that would drop her fifty yards from the small gate.

With her rucksack safely shut and back in an overhead rack, Sally

656

turned to find the entire contingent of nuns glaring, not at her this time but at the boy who'd been watching with obvious interest.

'Thank you,' Sally told him.

'My pleasure.' His smile revealed the kind of teeth that travelled third class on a slow train between Tripoli and Tangiers. As ruined as Sally's own were perfect.

And although her father, ever the unthinking traditionalist, openly admitted to choosing Sally's mother on looks alone (just as Sally's mother admitted marrying for security), her mouth's perfection was down to more than genes. It was the product of three years of night braces, nylon train tracks and restrainers. Every kiss had tasted synthetic. Which maybe explained why there'd been so few.

'You think it's bandits?' she asked the boy.

'Probably not,' he said, 'but better to be safe.' For a moment he looked serious. 'Your clothes . . . Long sleeves are better. And only small girls have bare legs here. Very small,' he added in case she hadn't understood.

CHAPTER 14

Friday 11th February

'He'll be back from his mission soon,' said the note. *'Look after yourself, Tiri.'*

That was it, nothing more.

And Uncle Ashraf hadn't even bothered to disguise his handwriting. As for its being a real mission . . . that seemed unlikely because then he'd have left a better note under her pillow, one that bothered to lie properly. He was running away, from her crossness and Zara's anger, the noise of the builders and breakfast at Le Trianon and Hani wasn't at all sure he'd ever come back.

Keying the note into her diary, Hani recorded the time – 19:58 – and shut down her screen. She was trying fairly hard not to cry and even harder not to mind that Zara was still sitting in the *qaa* with some stupid book while Hani was banished upstairs and Donna had rattled round the kitchen all day, so put out by His Excellency's unexplained absence that she'd shouted at Hani for bothering her.

Pushing open a box of matches, the long kitchen ones, Hani put flame to her uncle's message and watched curls of ash crumble into her basin.

Hani kept her diary inside a lion. When the words got too tangled she hacked off whole threads and hid those in other animals. Uncle Ashraf's arrival in Iskandryia occupied a hippopotamus. Anything to do with Zara got a gazelle, which was being generous. The murder of Hani's Aunt Nafisa filled a vulture, Egyptian obviously. And since *Neophron percnopterus* had a scrawny neck and nasty little eyes, this was entirely appropriate.

What had happened to her other aunt occupied no space at all, since the General had decreed Lady Jalila's death a secret, back when General Koenig Pasha was still Governor and Hani wasn't confident her idea of scrambling text inside picture code was entirely original.

The day-to-day details of life at the al-Mansur madersa got a Barbary lion, one that stared myopically from her screen with an awareness in its pale blue eyes of approaching extinction.

I knew you before you knew me.

I knew you before you lived . . .

The words were Uncle Ashraf's own. Well, Hani strongly suspected they weren't, but he'd been the one to say them on first seeing her lion and no amount of Web searching had pulled up their real owner. Hani wasn't too sure what they meant but the sentiment sounded sad. And sometimes Hani liked sad but at the moment she was just plain furious. That was why she'd refused to go to noon prayers. She'd have gone with Khartoum to his little mosque, only she was a girl and he was a Sufi, wasn't he?

So she'd been sent to her room by Zara, which was novel. A waterfall of raw emotion tumbling across the older girl's face, as sudden fear that Hani might refuse turned to shock that she'd just scolded someone else's child and ended with anger at being put in that position. Hani was good at reading faces. Growing up with Aunt Nafisa one had to be . . .

And Hani had been tempted to refuse and probably would have done if it had been her uncle, but that was silly because if Uncle Ashraf had been there Hani wouldn't have refused to go to prayers and Zara wouldn't have been upset. So Hani went to keep Zara happy, if that made sense.

The problem with being eleven or ten (or whatever she was actually meant to be) and having a dead mother and two dead aunts was that Zara now felt the need to look after her. Hani had a dead father too, of course, but since she'd never met him that was different.

'Weird . . .' She tossed the comment over her shoulder. Ifritah glanced up just long enough to make certain that nothing important had been said.

On her way out of the *qaa*, Hani had stopped at the lift, turning back. 'He loves you,' she'd shouted louder than she intended. 'Even if you don't love him.' And as she slammed the grille she knew absolutely/for certain that tears already blinded Zara's eyes.

Highlighting the code for some sad-eyed bush baby, Hani opened the picture with a word-processing package so cheap it failed to correct her grammar. Page after page of scribble filled the buffer and right towards the end, round about where anyone normal would begin hitting page down out of sheer boredom, Hani found her list of clues.

1) Suits still in cupboard.

Ascertaining this was less hard than it sounded given that her uncle's total collection came to three suits, two pairs of shoes, five shirts and a red tie.

2) Missing jellaba. One of Hamzah's men working on the garden had complained his jellaba was gone.

That was it . . .

CHAPTER 15

Monday 14th February

'Isaac and Sons?' The street sweeper repeated Raf's question slowly, unsure of its exact meaning. The Isaac he got, this was a foreign version of Isacq which was a common enough name, the rest of it.

He shrugged.

'Máa Saláma.' Raf said a polite good-bye to the man with the broom and stepped back from the pavement, running his eyes along a row of shop fronts. He was looking for a sign. Something hand-painted onto board to judge from the other signs that hung above darkened windows. Actually he was looking for far more than that.

Ali bin Malik watched the beggar limp away. The stranger's shoes were those of the very poor. A slab of rubber cut from a tractor tyre and punctured with two loops of twine to fit the whole foot and the largest toe. But even these shoes were better than the striped jellaba he wore. This was torn beneath one arm and stained around the ankles with mud or dried concrete.

'Wait,' Ali called after the beggar and the man stopped. 'Ask Ahmed, my uncle.' Pointing along the street he indicated a shadow crouched by a dustcart . . .

'Es-salám aláykum.'

Ahmed looked up from his spoils.

'Ahmed?'

A brief nod. And then the man remembered his manners and returned the peace. *'Waláykum es-salám.'*

'Máhaba,' Raf said. Hello.

That earned him another nod, less abrupt this time.

'I'm looking for an office,' said Raf, 'that's meant to be on Rue Ali bel Houane.' With a shrug he glanced both ways along the almost deserted street. As if the office might be hiding somewhere in the half dawn. It was maybe six in the morning and Raf could see everything as clearly as if it had been high noon with the sun direct overhead; a lot clearer than most people in Kairouan could have seen even then.

Raf's eyes liked early morning. When the world came into complete focus. There were times when Raf felt sure his circadian rhythms were reversed. That what his body expected from him was to sleep in the day and wake at night.

Baudelairian delusions of Bohemia, Zara had called it in one of her crosser moments. Maybe the only moment he'd ever really seen her cross. After she'd come to his room in the haremlek at night and found him dressed, sitting by an open window in the dressing gown of a dead man. He'd tried to explain to her then who he thought he really was. It was an unwise move. After she'd gone, he looked up Baudelaire and Bohemia to confirm what she'd been saying. A verdict he would dispute but understood how she got to where she got. But then that was negative capability all over, an overdeveloped talent for seeing both sides of everything and agreeing with neither.

Putting the time at six was a guess as Raf had left his watch in El Iskandryia. The *fajr* call to prayer had been twenty minutes before, however, and the sun was somewhere on the horizon, although buildings prevented Raf from knowing exactly where.

'This office . . . You know the number?' Ahmed had a smoker's voice and nicotine stains on the sides of his fingers to match.

'Its number . . . ?' Casually Raf pulled a packet of *bidi* from the ripped pocket of his jellaba and lit one, dragging deep. As an after-thought he passed the packet to Ahmed and offered Ahmed his cigarette so the street cleaner could light his own.

'Afraid not.' Raf shook his head.

It was a lie, of course. That number became fixed in Raf's head the first moment he stood in the *qaa*, with steps leading from the courtyard to the madersa's first floor behind him and Lady Nafisa ahead, angrily pushing a letter in front of his face only to withdraw it and read him extracts, her tone furious and disdainful.

On the 30th April, Pashazade Zari Moncef al-Mansur, only son of the Emir of Tunis, married Sally Welham at a private ceremony in an annexe of the Great al-Zaytuna Mosque. She was his third wife. He divorced her five days later.

He'd had to take her word on that because the only bit he'd been able to read was the letterhead. Isaac & Sons: Commissioner for Oaths, 132 Rue Ali bel Houane, Kairouan, Ifriqiya. The rest was in Arabic, a language he now spoke but was still unable to write or read.

(A fact Raf justified by telling himself that Arabic script had a minimum of six styles, codified in Baghdad by Vizir Ibn Muqla at the beginning of the tenth century. Three used for the Holy Quran and three for official work, administration and correspondence. And out of these had developed other styles, at least one, *shikaste*, decipherable only to a practised reader. Added to which, letters changed shape according to their position in a word.)

'But you know the owner's name?'

Raf nodded. 'Its a law firm,' he said. 'With offices in Kairouan. Isaac and Sons.'

The old man thought about it, shook his head and sat back down on the pavement where a pile of rubbish waited to be sorted into heaps. There were cola cans, empty and sticky, discarded paper, mainly oiled wrappers from the pastry shops lining Rue Ali bel Houane, empty packets of cigarettes, local mostly but one of them, the one with a broken cigarette still inside, an Italian brand of which Raf had never heard.

Ahmed tucked the foreign cigarette behind his ear and went back to sorting out rubbish. All the cans went in one bag, the paper in another. Rags got tied to each other until they looked like a string of drab bunting. 'It doesn't bring much,' Ahmed said, 'but it brings a little.'

'*Inshá allá,*' Raf said.

'*Inshá,*' the street cleaner agreed.

Around them Kairouan was beginning to stir. A small woman with arms as thin as twigs and a birdlike strut bustled onto the pavement from a nearby shop and scowled as soon as she saw Raf. Then she noticed Ahmed sitting on the other side and promptly relaxed. Everyone offered the peace, then said good morning and finally said hello. By the time that was done another shop had begun to open, the metal grille being pulled back from the doorway and an awning being wound down in a screech of rusty metal.

'Ishaq and Sons?' Ahmed said to the woman who twisted her thin neck to one side, making her seem more birdlike than ever.

'Ishaq?'

'This man's looking for their office.'

And not finding it, Raf thought to himself. Most of the shops did without numbers but even counting forward from some that did and back from others he'd failed to work out where number 132 should be.

With one hand on a tarnished metal pole she'd been about to use to wind down her own awning and her other on a bony hip, the woman considered Ahmed's question, head still cocked to one side in thought. 'Ishaq and Son . . .' Slowly she straightened up, small eyes turning to gaze at Raf.

'Perhaps this was a notario?' she suggested.

Raf nodded.

'Ibrahim ibn Ishaq,' she told the street cleaner, jerking her head backwards to signify somewhere behind her. 'He used to be above the French bookseller.'

'Used to be?' Raf said.

'He died,' said the birdlike woman. 'Years ago. Pneumonia. After that really bad spring.'

'His son took over?'

'Ibrahim was the son. That was it. The place is empty.'

Surprise should have been the first thing Raf felt. Or maybe shock, disbelief and blind refusal to accept the impossible. All of those would have been normal. But what Raf actually felt was sick. A cold nausea at the centre of his gut spreading out through his veins, his skin growing pale as blood withdrew from his capillaries and shivers syncopated the length of his spine. It felt like static playing across his body, twitching muscles and burning like ice along the branching pathways of his nerves.

The fox coughed, its bark close to laughter.

Just because something is chaotic doesn't make it random. Raf remembered a man in a white coat telling him that. Years before. The term *phase space* kept cropping up but the surgeon had been talking about his brain.

'Are you all right?'

'Ibrahim was family?'

Two questions asked together, voices male and female but both worried, though the man at least glanced away from the tears that had sprung into Raf's eyes. Wiping them clumsily with the back of his hand, Raf laughed. The small embarrassed laugh of a man who has let emotion get the better of him.

'My mother's cousin,' he said with a small shrug. 'I'm fine but I know she will be upset.'

To make up for Raf's disappointment the woman insisted on showing him where the office had been, walking slowly so that he could keep up with her in his crude shoes. Kairouan was Ifriqiya's most important city, she told him on the way. A place of real learning, unlike Tunis, with its crowds of *nasrani* and unsavoury way of life. If he was lucky he might find a job at the market.

From Kairouan to Tunis was maybe 150 kilometres by road, perhaps less; although, as no railway reached the city and Raf had been forced to leave at M'aaken to catch a bus, the distance would be more than this by the time he returned to M'aaken and rejoined one of the local services for Gare de Tunis.

'There you go,' she said, pointing to a window above a dusty shop front. 'That was where your cousin used to work. We had to reach his office from the back . . .'

Raf thanked her, then did so again, leaving her standing on the pavement a hundred paces from her own shop as the first customers of the day came out to buy pastries and fruit for breakfast.

On his way to catch the return bus to M'aaken, Raf detoured into an alley that ran parallel to that side of Rue Ali bel Houane and walked slowly along the narrow street, counting openings and looking at signs painted directly onto the peeling length of wall. He found the one he wanted halfway down, faded and partly lost under a smear of concrete that someone had used to patch a hole in the plaster.

Isaac & Sons: Commissioners for Oaths. The only words he'd been able to read from the letter in Lady Nafisa's hand. The door to the office was bolted from the inside and had an extra padlock hooked through a rusting clasp at waist height, as if locking an empty office from within might not be enough. Next to the door was an odd cast-iron blade set into a small arch at ground level, which Raf eventually worked out was for scraping mud from boots during the winter months.

'Talk to me,' said the fox.

All Raf gave him was an angry shake of the head. He knew how absurdly easy it always was to give in. To welcome Tiri back and make it speak to him or, rather, make Tiri speak *for* him, because that's what the fox did, they both understood that now.

And Raf wanted the cold deep in his bones to go away and the memories that flooded his veins like iced water to vanish. Most of all he wanted to spend the rest of his life, however long that was, knowing that when he woke each morning the room in which he slept would not have changed colour, that no hedges would have grown to maturity from seedlings outside his window, that the season when he awoke would be the same as when he shut his eyes.

If banishing the fox from his head was the price Raf had to pay to achieve this, then the fox would have to go. And it had been a stupid idea of Tiri's anyway to go ask advice of a lawyer who was already dead.

CHAPTER 16

Flashback

Sometime around noon, with the sun burning down on the outside of Sally's airless carriage, three men wearing combat trousers, khaki T-shirts and checked kufiyyeh *came by to throw passengers off the stalled train. At least that's what Sally assumed was happening given that the nuns suddenly stood up and began to collect together their baskets, wrapping what was left of the salami inside its white cloth and burying the package at the bottom of the biggest basket, as if bandits might have stopped the train to steal their food.*

'I find out what's happening,' said the boy and nodded to Sally, pointedly ignoring the nuns as he jumped down onto the track. Sally watched him walk away, dodging between exiting passengers until he disappeared from sight. After a while she realized he probably wasn't coming back.

Everyone waited in the sun for two hours beside the train. And then its diesel engine fired up and the abandoned carriages began to reverse slowly away from where the passengers still sat, picking up speed as they went. True to type, the nuns immediately formed a small circle with their baskets in the middle, as if they were the wagons and their luggage the settlers waiting for an Indian attack. Occasionally one or another would glance over to where Sally stood, too nervous to sit, but that was all.

As dusk arrived so did the soldiers. Teenage conscripts with hard haircuts and soft eyes, the clash between appearance and their friendliness not yet kicked out of them. They carried stubby submachine guns stamped out of cheap metal which they played with endlessly, flicking the safety catches and snapping out quarter-curve magazines only to snap them back again. The conscripts seemed to have no more idea of why they were there than Sally did.

Night never really came. The moon was too bright and, though air convected and a warm wind blew from the distant sea and a whole

666

orchestra of insects finally fell silent, darkness stayed away. Sometime after midnight a new train rolled up. It looked much like the old train but dirtier, with carriages that were separate, unlinked by any corridor. The man driving wore combat fatigues, with an AK49 slung across his back.

'Great,' said Sally. No corridor meant no loos. And that meant six hours locked in a carriage with an uncertain stomach.

'Need help?'

Sally turned to find a barefoot boy wearing a samurai topknot, the baggiest Fat Boys she'd ever seen and a leather choker with a plum-sized amber bead tied round his neck. The orange lettering across his T-shirt proclaimed Rock and Ruin. *And underneath in much smaller letters was a line that read* archaeologists do it in spades.

Sally sighed. 'Help with what?'

'Getting on the train. 'The blond boy pointed at her rucksack, then nodded to the nearest carriage which stood empty with its door still shut. It was, Sally suddenly realized, going to be hard enough clambering up without having to drag her luggage after her.

'Yeah,' she said, 'that would be good.'

Still smiling, the boy pushed out his hand and announced, 'I'm Per.'

'Sally,' said Sally without thinking about it and remembered too late that she'd meant to travel as someone else.

Together they clambered up into a dusty-smelling carriage and Per yanked down the blinds on the side where everyone stood, blocking out moonlight and the shuffling crowd beyond. For about five minutes it looked like this might work, as compartments either side filled with noise but no one tried their door.

And then, with the train shuddering as its diesel fired up, the door was jerked open and a close-cropped skull gazed up at them. Whatever doubts the conscript felt about being faced with two nasrani *lost out to his need for a seat. Pulling himself up, he was about to shut the door when someone shouted his name.*

Five conscripts tumbled in after him, pushing and swearing until they saw Sally by the far window with Per opposite.

'Hi,' said Sally and six faces blinked as one. They were kids she realized, only a few years younger in age but a dozen in experience, uncertain how to react to some foreign girl in men's clothes. Their problem, Sally decided, not mine, and nodded to one of them to shut the door.

'Sleep tight,' said Per, settling into his seat.

Sally wasn't sure if that was the Swedish boy's idea of a joke.

Along with everyone else in the carriage Sally found herself slipping down in her seat as the minutes turned into hours, until her head rested on her arm and her legs were supported by the seat opposite. She had Per's bare toes almost in her face, clean but dirty (if that made sense). And her own sandalled feet were being used by Per as a cushion. Without even thinking about it he'd wrapped his arms round her knees, pulled her feet in close and fallen asleep, so that now his breath came slow and regular as waves against a summer beach.

'Sleep tight,' she said but he was already.

Headed for sleep herself, Sally hardly noticed Per shift onto his side and brush one hand along her calf. For a second she imagined it an accident but then the touch came again, so softly she could have been dreaming if not for the rattle of rails and dark sky scudding past outside.

Shutting her eyes, Sally decided to be asleep; remaining asleep as Per's fingers crept up from her ankle to knee before smoothing down towards her ankle again. He moved his fingers in time to the lurch of the wheels. As if that somehow made it coincidental, merely part of the journey. And she kept feigning sleep as Per's stroking became heavier and his hand moved higher, until the top of every stroke almost reached her buttocks.

Part of Sally, the part to which she usually refused to listen, regretted changing out of her shorts, because those were baggy and, well, short really.

'You awake?' His voice was soft, concerned.

Sally almost shook her head.

Shifting in her seat, she moved lower so she was almost balanced between the seats. At the same time she kept her eyes shut and her breathing regular, even when his fingers found the backs of her thighs and slipped between them, smoothing along a seam.

That was where Per's fingers stayed, their movement so slight Sally could barely sense it though the effect was like water rising behind a flood wall. The warmth between her legs more than mere body heat, the dampness not just sweat.

'Per . . .'

The Swedish boy stopped. One bare arm still hooked round her leg and his hand crushed between her thighs. A barrier was formed by his half-turned body, screening them from the others, those sleeping children with their cruel haircuts and faces made soft by rest and dreams.

'Too much?'

Sally wondered what he'd do if she said yes. Not that she would.

'Wait,' she told him and sat up in her seat. Switching sides quickly, Sally snuggled down facing Per. Only this time round she was the barrier between the woken world and the snoring conscripts.

'Better,' she said.

'Much,' Per agreed.

668

They kissed or rather Sally kissed Per. And when his hand reached for her, Sally didn't move away but put her own fingers over his and snuggled closer, holding it there.

Per skipped several of the stages she'd come to expect from boys her own age, stages that Wu Yung had also ignored. And when Per removed his hand it was to reach between the buttons of Atal's shirt and expose one breast.

'Small,' she told him.

'Perfect,' he replied, dipping his head.

When Sally eventually opened her eyes, it was to see one of the conscripts watching her in the window, his distance doubled by reflection. The boy said nothing but neither did he look away.

'Okay?' Per asked, his head still buried between her small breasts, licking salt and a distant echo of cheap soap from a bath she'd taken in Catania; so distant as to be almost lost under the dirt of five days' travelling without a break.

'Sure,' said Sally, 'everything's fine.'

Per's back was to the window and his head was bent, his arms tight around Sally and little doubt could exist as to what his reflection tasted. On the other hand, for two strangers making out in a railway carriage they were being unusually discreet. So Sally shrugged and shut her eyes again.

Somewhere between barest dawn and reaching the Italianate Gothic monstrosity Tarabulus station Per dropped his fingers to the waist of Sally's jeans and discovered she'd already freed the top button. As she wouldn't let him ease the jeans past her hips, he made do with sliding his hand inside.

She bit his shoulder so hard when she came that Per was the one who cried out. A muffled yelp, hastily swallowed. Although had Per turned round he'd have discovered how redundant that was. Every conscript in the carriage was already awake, wide-eyed and envious.

Discreetly, so that her move wasn't too obvious Sally put her hand down and held Per, watching him tense. She waited until he shut his eyes at the intensity of her grip, then let go.

'Your turn after Tarabulus,' she said. 'That is, if you're not getting off at this stop.'

Per hesitated.

'I'm going on to Gabes,' Sally added.

'Take a break,' he suggested. 'Spend a few days in Tripoli.'

'No time.' Sally shook her head. 'I've got stuff to do.'

'What stuff?'

Sally dropped her hand into his lap, making it look casual. 'I'm on a quest,' she said.

669

'For what?'

'The Libyan striped weasel,' said Sally, and gave his trousers a squeeze.

As they pulled out of Tarabulus less than an hour later, sat in a carriage that was once again theirs alone, Per asked what had been troubling him from the first moment they met beside the stopped train.

'How old are you?'

Without even stopping to think Sally lopped three years off her age. And tried not to grin when the Swedish boy looked suddenly appalled.

CHAPTER 17

Monday 14th February

'Yeah,' said Raf, 'I already know . . .'

A life of brain-rotting boredom awaited Tunisia's last bey, who took with him into exile his wife, his German mistress (standard *Thiergarten*-issue, one), a dozen, French-educated ministers, most of his children and a 392-piece set of china made in the Husseinite colours by Noritake.

And while the brave speech made from the door of his departing train was enough to make some doubt the probity of supporting Colonel al-Mansur's plot to overthrow the government, the convenient discovery two days later of an empty beyical treasury was enough to make those same people realize how right Colonel al-Mansur had been to propose himself for the new position of Emir.

'You done now?' Raf asked.

Inside his head, Tiri nodded and smiled, glad to be back. Raf's refusal to talk had lasted a whole bus trip and half a train journey. So now the fox was sticking to easy thoughts and simple facts. Which was why it didn't mention what was happening up ahead.

The secret police were waiting for Raf on platform three of Gare de Tunis. It was nothing personal. They were waiting for everyone. Although, to be honest, Raf didn't care. He was being someone else for the day, maybe longer.

Maybe forever.

Slung under the arms of each *mubahith* was a new-model HK7, the complete works right down to Zeiss laser scope and double-length magazine. Since Ifriqiya was on the UN embargo list for weapons sales and the ministry in Berlin responsible for overseeing HK shipments obeyed the ruling when it suited them, shipping must have been via false end-user certificates. Presumably the same applied to the military-issue BMW bikes parked on the concourse behind.

Their black uniform wasn't one Raf recognized but whatever force they represented it seemed to require them to wear steel-capped eighteen-rivet boots cut from shiny leather. Always a bad sign. For his part, Raf still wore sandals cut from an old tractor tyre and a filthy jellaba. His skull was hidden under a cheap Dynamo's cap and three-day stubble accentuated rather than hid the scar on his jaw; he looked rough, made worse by the fact that seventy-six hours of not eating had hollowed his cheeks and put dark circles round his naked eyes.

The smile on his face was that of an idiot savant. Or maybe just an idiot.

That the *mubahith* wore aviator shades went without saying, since mirror shades and big boots went together across most of North Africa like midsummer riots and tear gas. Raf's own dark glasses were missing and in their place he wore cheap contacts that turned his eyes brown and overlaid the world with a haze of ghostly smoke.

'You.' A hand clipped his shoulder, sending him stumbling. 'Can't you read?' A soldier with corporal's stripes was pointing to a sign. A dozen soldiers and an officer in khaki were there to do the actual work. The *mubahith* just stood around in black uniforms looking bored.

Raf shook his head mutely and the corporal sucked his teeth.

'Into line,' he ordered and indicated a row of barriers set up to funnel passengers through one of two metal arches. Men, who made up the bulk of the crowd, jostled and pushed their way towards one arch, where a bored soldier sat off to the side, chain-smoking in front of a bank of screens.

The few women alighting from Raf's train had their own arch with no screens visible. All results of their strip scans were hidden within the walls of a tall black tent and seen only by trained nurses. *Sécurité's* gesture to common decency.

'Come on.'

Most of those who passed through the arches raised little interest. Although a few of the men were pulled out of line and made to turn out their pockets just for show.

'*Your turn,*' said the fox and Raf nodded, dropping his *bidi* to the platform and grinding it under heel. Raf had no real idea why he did that. Unless it was meant to be polite.

Shuffling forward with the *felaheen* gait of those too poor to own correctly sized shoes, Raf passed under the arch. And all might have been well if he hadn't looked up and stared straight into the eyes of Sergeant Belhaouane, recently promoted, to the *mubahith*.

'You,' the man jerked his heavy chin. 'Come here.'

Raf did what he was told.

'Look at me.'

Reluctantly Raf raised his head then looked away. He stank of sweat and his jellaba was rotten beneath the arms from lack of washing.

'Your papers.' The order was barked out. It didn't take the fox to tell Raf that the security man was enjoying himself, which didn't stop the fox from telling him anyway.

'What did you say?'

'Nothing.' Raf shook his head. 'Nothing, Captain.'

Sergeant Belhaouane looked almost mollified by his sudden promotion. Although that didn't stop him from clicking his fingers loudly to hurry Raf along.

'Come on . . .'

Raf hurried. Scrabbling in his jellaba pocket, then in all the pockets of the tattered trousers he wore beneath. Finally, when the sergeant's patience was almost gone he found his wallet.

'Your Excellency,' said Raf, producing it.

The *mubahith* flipped open the battered square of leather and looked inside. Then he checked the pocket behind the empty slots where credit cards would have been were this *felah* the kind of man to have credit cards.

A hundred US dollars hid there, in tatty green ten-dollar notes. One month's wages to the sergeant, three months' wages to someone like Raf. About as much as a family might scrabble together to send one of them to the city to find work.

'These your identity papers?'

Raf shuffled his feet.

'Thought so.' The man pocketed the notes with a twist of the wrist as deft as any magician making cards disappear. 'Right,' he said when that was done. 'What's your business in Tunis?'

'Work,' said Raf. 'I came to find a job.'

'Doing what?'

'Unloading ships . . . There's a strike.'

Sergeant Belhaouane snorted. Work at the docks passed from father to son, strike or no strike. The only way an outsider like Raf could ever get dock work was to marry the daughter of a stevedore and hope that, when the time came, the jetty bosses were open to bribes and the man about to retire didn't already have a son.

'What's your village?'

Raf named a place so small it didn't occur on most maps.

'Where?'

In reply he named a town nearby not much larger. Although the sergeant appeared to have heard of it this time, probably because Segui was known as a place of annual pilgrimage for Soviet *nasrani* who spurned UN sanctions and raced the salt lakes with sail boards on wheels.

It was obvious from the sergeant's dismissive gaze that he held out little hope of Raf finding work enough to send money back to his village. The concrete-stained sandals and filthy jellaba identified Raf as a man mostly used to casual graft. And construction in Tunis was run by one family. If you didn't pay for an introduction, you didn't work. Life was that simple. And since the last thing Tunis needed was another itinerant from the south Sergeant Belhaouane decided his best course of action would be send the idiot back to Segui on the next train.

Unfortunately the fox disagreed.

'*Run,*' suggested the fox. But Raf was already running through a crowd that didn't so much move out of his way as trip over their own feet in their haste to let him get to the exit on Rue Ibn Kozman. A woman screamed, Raf noticed, freezing an image of the chaos around him. An old man burst into tears and a boy put a hand to his mouth like he was about to vomit.

'*Ditch that gun.*'

'What gun?'

'*Heckler & Koch, fifty-two-shot magazine. Laser targeting. Night sights . . .*'

The one with blood on its stock.

'Fuck.'

'*Yeah,*' said the fox. '*Something like that.*'

Jinking round a fat man wearing white robes that marked him out as from the Trucial States, Raf sprinted for the black Zil from which the man had just alighted, only to have it pull away in a squeal of tyres, back door flapping.

The driver behind took one look at the gun in Raf's hand and reversed hard, straight into a taxi. Headlights shattered, fenders tore and then it too was gone, followed by the cab trailing diesel fumes and fear.

When Raf next bothered to look he was running down a slip road with a shunting yard to his right and overlooked on his left by redbrick tenements. Dark windows, mostly shuttered. A car without wheels raised on cinder blocks. It could have the wrong side of the tracks anywhere. Although the air smelled different to that of El Iskandryia. Fresher somehow, owing less of its taste to the sea. Fewer cars. Not so heavy on the hydrocarbons.

'*This way . . .*'

Raf ignored the voice. Only to freeze when a hand grabbed his sleeve and swung him round, pushing him towards a metal fence.

'Through here,' insisted the voice. It wore an old uniform with a peaked cap and fat leather belt, black tie and pale blue shirt. The belt was new and the uniform slate grey, with silver-piped epaulettes on a narrow jacket and a cheap metal monogram adorning each lapel, letters intertwined so tightly that it took Raf a second to make out SBCF.

'Société Beyical des Chemins de Fer,' said the fox.

Raf shrugged. 'Whatever.'

'Come on,' hissed the small man, still gripping Raf by the sleeve. 'Do you want them to catch you?'

'Who?'

'Kashif Pasha's *sécurité*, of course . . . He's taking control,' added the man as he bustled Raf through a mesh door in an inner fence and simultaneously pulled a key from his pocket to lock it behind them. 'Everyone knows his father is dying.'

Raf froze.

'You must know,' said the man. 'A week ago in Tozeur the Emir was bitten by a poisonous snake. They're keeping the seriousness a secret.'

Raf knew all about *them* and *they*. Most of his childhood had been spent in *their* hospitals and special schools. Suits, smoked-glass windows, pretty little mobile phones. And endless lies, half of them his.

'I thought the Emir was unharmed?'

'That's what they want you to believe.'

'What proof do you have?' Raf demanded, regretting it immediately.

'What proof . . . ?' Key still in the lock the man halted then started to scrape the key in the opposite direction, infinitely slowly. This time round the man was worrying about his own escape route. Raf's tone had been wrong. Not just his question but the position from which that question was asked . . . One that posited a right to make such demands and an expectation that these would be met; assumptions totally at odds with Raf's ragged jellaba and homemade sandals.

Of course the small man didn't think of it like that, he just felt tricked, his closing down into sullen imbecility the defence of the weak against someone who might represent those who were strong.

Raf took a deep breath. 'Forgive me,' he said and shrugged, then shrugged again and switched into Arabic. 'My French is not good. Only what I learnt as houseboy at a hotel when I was young. I was just asking if the illness of the Emir was true . . .'

Between being a houseboy at a hotel and an itinerant labourer lay a whole life's worth of wrong choice that the old railway worker was much too polite to investigate. So he smiled instead and shrugged in his turn. 'That explains your accent,' he said. 'It's very elegant. And yes, it's true about the Emir.'

675

He hustled a silent Raf towards a shed that stood dark and near derelict at the foot of an abandoned signal box, pushing his new friend inside.

'Wear this,' he ordered as he ripped an orange boiler suit from a locker. 'And carry that.' The bag he offered was long and made from oiled canvas. On both ends the SBCF logo could just be seen inside a faded circle. 'It's for the gun,' he said with a sigh when Raf just stared at the thing.

'Sorry.' Raf ripped the magazine from the HK, wiped it with a rag taken from the floor, then did the same for the weapon, dropping both into the bag before zipping it shut. The rag he returned to the floor.

'Who are you?' he asked the man.

'Someone whose eyes are open,' the man replied and grinned, exposing a row of crooked teeth. 'You can call me Sajjad. I work the Gare de Tunis. How about you?'

'Me?' Raf glanced round the tiny hut and spotted a two-ring Belling in the corner, plates thick with grease. A stack of take-out trays next to it said the old-fashioned cooker didn't get much use. 'I'm a chef,' said Raf. 'One who's looking for a job. Name's Ashraf. My mother was Berber.'

Which wasn't exactly true. It was his father who'd been Berber according to everyone from Eugenie de la Croix and the Khedive to Raf's Aunt Nafisa, but she was dead and most of what she'd told Raf had turned out to be lies anyway.

'And your father?'

'I never knew my father,' Raf said and was shocked to realize that he probably never would. And even more shocked by how much he minded.

Sajjad shrugged. 'These things,' he said as he clicked on a kettle and reached for a tin, 'they happen.' Such unhappy beginnings went altogether better with the torn jellaba than did Raf's earlier question, abrupt and barked as it had been.

'Lose the jellaba in a locker,' said Sajjad a minute or two later, pouring water onto coffee grounds. 'We'll find you another,' he added when Raf looked doubtful.

Any residual doubt Sajjad had about Raf got forgotten the moment he saw the scar tissue mapped onto the young man's back. A veritable landscape of pain, with ridges of scarring that fed between a star-shaped city on Raf's shoulder to ribbon developments of raised tissue around his ribs and abdomen.

To Raf the only thing remarkable about it all was how little of the pain he'd actually felt, mostly that had been the fox's job.

Sajjad whistled.

'They did this to you?'

'They certainly did,' said Raf.

CHAPTER 18

Friday 18th February

The lift in the al-Mansur madersa was an old-fashioned Otis that worked on counterweights, great slabs of lead that rose between two greased poles as the Otis descended and went down when the lift rose. Apparently the lift was now so ancient it was valuable.

For the bulk of her short life Hani would no more have dared visit the men's floor than she'd expect a man to visit the haremlek, where her own room was situated. Uncle Ashraf's arrival from America had changed all that. Along with other things such as eating breakfast in the kitchen, to the intense disapproval of Aunt Nafisa's elderly Portuguese cook.

Uncle Ashraf's cook now, she supposed.

Donna was afraid of Hani's uncle. That much was obvious from the way she always tapped her forehead, tummy and one breast after another every morning when Uncle Ashraf first came into the kitchen. For herself, Hani relied for safety on a silver hand of Fatima worn under her vest on a length of black cotton. Not that Hani believed her uncle possessed the evil eye.

His power was *baraka*, the sanctity that clung to those who walked the difficult path. Hani had discussed with Khartoum her idea that *baraka* might have required her uncle to vanish and the fact the old Sudanese porter hadn't dismissed her idea out of hand was beginning to convince Hani that she was right.

Easing open the brass grille, Hani slipped into the Otis and pushed herself into a corner; all of which was unnecesary because Hani had only just seen Zara cross the darkened courtyard below the *qaa* and disappear under a marble arch that led to the covered garden. Gone to see how far her father's workmen had got, probably . . .

Hani checked her watch. Four hours since lunch. Well, if the tray of pastries Donna had left discreetly outside Hani's door passed for lunch. And two hours before their visitor was due to arrive.

His Highness Mohammed Tewfik Pasha, Khedive of El Iskandryia and ruler of all Egypt . . . One time puppy prince to Koenig Pasha's mastiff. Hani reeled off her cousin's titles, adding a few choice ones of her own.

These days of course the General was fighting US attempts to extradite him for kidnapping a psychotic battle computer that answered to the name of Colonel Abad. Since Washington simultaneously insisted that Abad was merely a machine, Hani was puzzled as to how General Koenig Pasha could be charged with kidnapping, particularly in an American court; always assuming Washington managed to extradite him, which was unlikely because the General was many things (including her godfather), but what he wasn't was without friends.

The day before the day before yesterday, which was a Tuesday. (Hani checked that fact in her head and discovered she'd got it right.) The day before, etc. an invitation had arrived for her uncle and in his absence Hani had felt obliged to open it, watched unfortunately by Donna who'd also heard the knock at the door onto Rue Sherif. And Donna had been less than happy when, having skim-read the Khedive's note, Hani promptly vanished up to her room to feed it through a pink plastic scanner.

Having saved the file, Hani typed an answer on her uncle's behalf, folded it neatly and took it down to the kitchen for Donna to post. The reply, brief to the point of rudeness, regretted that Ashraf Bey was unable to attend the Khedive as invited and suggested that instead the Khedive might visit the al-Mansur madersa at 7:00 P.M. on Friday 18th Jumaada al-awal, AH 1472 . . .

'Stay there,' Hani told her cat and lost Ifritah's reply in a crunch of lift wheels. Until Zara took Hani shopping at Marshall & Snellgrove, Hani had assumed that all lifts were like this one; but then, until eight months back when Uncle Ashraf first arrived, Hani hadn't been outside the madersa, ever . . . So what did she know?

Hani shrugged.

She had work to do.

Two facts were insufficient. Hani had stopped calling them *clues*, because they revealed so little. Her uncle was gone. A workman's jellaba was missing. *Not clues*, Hani told herself crossly, *isolated facts*. A situation she was about to change by finding others.

The room her uncle used was dark, silent and damp so Hani folded back his shutters to let in air and with it sodium haze from the surrounding city. Directly below was the courtyard, its fountain silent, and beyond the courtyard a flat-roofed store used by Hamzah's builders. In the old days the open-sided store had been a room for entertaining visitors not quite grand enough to be invited up to the *qaa*. Now it was full of sacks of cement, endless sheets of glass sorted into piles and machines for sandblasting metal.

On the far side of the store began the garden. Only most of its roof was gone, each glass pane carefully removed so that the supporting framework of Victorian girders could be stripped back to metal, treated against rust and repainted. In the middle of the garden, staring blindly into a muddy pit that would become a carp pond stood Zara, unaware of being watched. Unaware, it seemed to Hani, of anything very much since Uncle Ashraf's disappearance.

In one corner of her uncle's room was a *bateau lit*, sheets folded down neatly. A silver chair, made from walnut overlaid with beaten metal, stood next to it. Apart from that there was only a double-fronted wardrobe against one wall, doors inset with matching oval mirrors that reflected Hani back to herself, a silhouette watching a silhouette, and a bow-fronted walnut chest against another wall. A tatty rug occupied the floor in between.

Having confirmed that there were no loose tiles beneath the rug, Hani debated her next move and decided on the wardrobe. In a shoe box underneath it she found a revolver and picked this up by the handle, only then remembering to consult the notebook she'd borrowed, her tiny Maglite playing over the fat man's spidery writing. It took Hani longer than she liked to find the right page.

Never touch evidence with bare hands . . .

Well, that was a good start.

Doing something clever like hook her torch through the revolver's trigger guard was out because Hani needed that to see what she was doing. And while it was true there were wire clothes hangers, any one of which would have done, dozens of the things on an otherwise empty rack in the wardrobe, just looking at those stung the back of Hani's legs. So instead Hani transferred her grip from handle to trigger guard and brought the barrel up to her nose. It stank of old fireworks.

Other than this the wardrobe was bare. Nothing on top or in either drawer beneath.

Search systematically, said the notebook.

For all its dusty elegance and probable value, Raf's chest of drawers was equally devoid of clues, lined with crinkled white paper and filled mostly with dust and dead spiders. Just to be thorough Hani yanked out one drawer after another to check that no one had taped anything important to the back.

She knew for a fact Donna had tidied no clues away because the old woman was far too terrified of her uncle to enter his room. It was

Khartoum who cleaned this floor and Khartoum had been nowhere near the main house for . . .

Now that was interesting.

Hani thought about it and grinned.

Once she was done here, she'd wander over to the porter's room next to the back entrance of the madersa and have a serious talk with Khartoum, assuming she still had time. The arrival of her cousin the Khedive obviously took precedence.

Make notes, the book said somewhere. So Hani wrote *bedroom* in pencil on a blank page towards the end and put a tick next to it. On the line below she wrote *bathroom*.

Her uncle's cast-iron bath was full of dust, its enamel yellow with age. One of the claws at the tap end showed black metal where an old accident had chipped the surface away. Maybe his shower cubicle would hold more clues.

Make that any clues, Hani thought to herself.

Coal tar soap. A dry flannel. Camomile shampoo. The shampoo was half-full and the flannel as stiff as peeled skin. It was the soap that was interesting. Tiny splinters of hair porcupined its surface. Not washed-out strands as one might expect but clippings. Dropping to a crouch, Hani ran one finger across the bottom of the shower tray and came up with a whole crisscross of clues.

He'd cut his hair then. No, Hani crossed that out and pencilled in *cropped* instead. Uncle Ashraf had cropped his hair. And that meant he *was* in disguise. Something she should have known from the missing jellaba. Disguise meant Uncle Ashraf *was* on a mission. Hani nodded to herself, heading for the lift. There was work to do. Khartoum would have to wait.

'His Highness the Khedive . . .' A lifetime of cigars gave the old Sufi's words gravitas to go with their edge.

The slim boy in the dark suit nodded to Khartoum, then glared around the almost deserted *qaa*. Etiquette demanded he be met at the door to the al-Mansur madersa but the only person to be found at the entrance on Boulevard Sherif had been polishing its door knocker.

And it didn't help Tewfik Pasha's self-esteem that Khartoum still had his cleaning cloth dangling from one hand like a dead hare. In fact, thinking about it, Tewfik Pasha decided he should have insisted on bringing his bodyguards with him rather than leaving them on the sidewalk by the Bentley.

'*Your Highness.*'

*

681

Very slowly Zara put down her needlepoint and climbed to her feet. She was working on a circle of canvas stretched over a large hoop, onto which she'd sketched a map of the world. Zara hoped the Khedive appreciated her artistry. Particularly the fact she'd chosen to edge his domains in the exact blue used to outline Prussia.

'This is a pleasure,' said Zara, her tone indicating that it was anything but . . .

If Tewfik Pasha noticed the cheap silver band on Zara's finger he didn't let it show. Wedding rings were gold and what Zara wore signified, as it was intended to signify, that whatever she had it wasn't a marriage.

Actually it wasn't anything at all. A quick grope on a boat and two nights heavy petting at the gubernatorial palace—while Raf stood in as Governor and her father was on trial.

'Are you all right?'

'Why shouldn't I be?'

'No reason . . .' The faltering in the Khedive's voice revealed him for what he was. An anxious seventeen-year-old standing in front of a girl both older and out of his reach.

'Well, I'm here,' Tewfik Pasha said.

'So you are,' said Zara.

Glancing round anxiously, the Khedive almost flinched when he met Khartoum's sardonic gaze. 'Perhaps Your Highness would like coffee?' The old Sufi's voice was slightly gentler than before.

'Coffee . . . ?' Tewfik Pasha wanted to be peremptory. To have grown men falter at his gaze and women wait on his slightest word – or was it the other way round? Whichever, the General could manage both without even noticing. While the most Tewfik could manage was to hold a room for a few tense minutes, provided one of his audience didn't answer to the name of Zara Quitrimala.

'That would be good,' he told Khartoum. 'And perhaps some cookies . . . ?'

'At the very least Ashraf Bey should have been here as well,' said Tewfik Pasha as he put down his tiny brass cup to suck mudlike coffee grounds from between his teeth. He sounded peeved and not at all princely. Somehow the thought of Zara with Ashraf Bey always had that effect on him.

'Yes,' said Zara. 'Then the three of us could have had a cozy chat.'

Hani snorted. She couldn't help herself. And having given away her position, she jumped down from the top of the lift, which was an

682

excellent place for seeing everything without being seen, and landed in an untidy jumble of arms and legs.

The Otis had been unused for the last half an hour; which was twice as long as Zara had been sitting in the *qaa* wondering exactly why His Highness the Khedive of El Iskandryia might suddenly decide to pay an impromptu visit. Now she knew.

'*Hani . . .*'

'Your Highness.' If the child's greeting skirted the edge of mockery, her curtsy on standing was right over the edge, its flamboyance made even more absurd by the oil blackening her palms and streaking one leg of her jeans with a dark tiger stripe.

'That's . . .'

'Risky?' Hani grinned at her cousin. 'Everything interesting always is,' she said, adding. 'Someone once told me that.'

Zara blushed.

Switching her attention back to the Khedive, Hani's small face became serious. 'This is for you,' she said and untucked her T-shirt to pull a long white envelope from her waistband. 'Well, not for you exactly, but you'll see . . .'

The envelope she gave the Khedive came complete with oily thumbprint. It was only when Tewfik Pasha held the envelope that he realized it was made from bleached chamois.

He looked at Hani.

'It arrived a week ago,' she lied. 'Special messenger. At night.' She had intended to say that the messenger came disguised as a motorcycle courier but decided this might be too much. 'Uncle Ashraf didn't say who brought it.'

The Khedive lifted the flap carefully and extracted a sheet of foolscap that was surprisingly ordinary given its sublime wrapping. He skimmed the letter. 'You've seen this?'

The small girl nodded apologetically.

Without a word, Tewfik Pasha handed the letter to Zara.

Raf was to undertake a mission of the utmost danger and secrecy. No good-byes were to be said. No one was to be told. At the top of the page were the Sublime Porte's personal arms. At the foot a scribble in purple ink.

'Raf showed you this letter?' Zara asked, her voice flat.

'Yes, he did.' Hani blinked at the misery on the face of the woman opposite. 'The Sultan's my cousin,' she said lamely. 'Ashraf Bey is my uncle. It's just family stuff . . . Everyone's my cousin,' Hani added. 'Even him.' She jerked her chin at the Khedive, who stood shuffling from foot to foot, embarrassed to see tears threatening to brim from Zara's eyes.

'I'm not,' Zara said and stalked from the room, slamming the *qaa* door behind her.

CHAPTER 19

'In here.'

The bar was narrow and smoky. Little more than a low vault hidden behind bead curtains at the rear of a café in one of the poorer suqs. The brick walls were windowless and the effect was to make those inside feel they were below ground. A sensation heightened by the fact that the street outside was also roofed over.

'Sit,' someone said.

Raf sat.

From above, the roof of this part of the medina looked like sand dunes frozen solid and painted white, or giant worm casts under which hidden streets ran into each other or branched off only to meet again. Scrawny weeds forced their way between cracked plaster, scrabbling an existence amid bird droppings, feral cats and rubbish that shop owners had carried up three flights of stairs to dump onto this bizarrely beautiful moonscape.

Mostly the rubbish included bicycles and broken electric heaters, rusting cans of Celtica (a cheap beer allowed on sale by the Emir because it upset the mullahs) and cardboard boxes gone soggy in the rain and dried into improbable angles.

There were other things. Stranger things.

None of this Raf yet knew.

'Why bring him here?' The boy speaking wore a charcoal-striped suit cut from Italian silk, the only person in the whole café not wearing a jellaba. His upper lip hid behind a new moustache while a Balkan Sobranie dragged at his lower lip. Raf disliked Hassan on sight.

Sajjad shuffled his feet. 'It seemed like . . .'

'It was,' said a dark man sat by the far wall. 'In fact, in the circumstances, this is the ideal place.' And it seemed to Raf that levels of significance resonated within the words; but then Raf was tired and filthy, unshaven and ravenous from surviving on what little food Sajjad had been able to bring to the hut by the signal box, so stripping meaning from obscurity was probably low on his list of talents.

There were no tables in the narrow room, only stone benches that ran down both sides and a shorter bench against the far wall, where the dark man was sitting.

He was bald and muscle-bound, with the face of a street brawler and five gold hoops in one ear. Someone had smashed his nose years back and although it had mended well there was a telltale scar at the top of the bridge where flesh had ripped. He wore a rough woollen robe.

'How long have you had him?'

'Five days,' Sajjad shrugged. 'Maybe a week.'

'And no one saw you leave?'

Sajjad shook his head.

'Good,' said the man. Pushing himself up off the bench he threaded his way between people's feet and stopped in front of Raf, dropping to a crouch so he could look straight into the newcomer's eyes.

It was all Raf could do to stare back.

'We live, we die, we live again,' said the man. 'Always remember this.'

There didn't seem to be much of an answer.

'And you are welcome,' the man added, bowing slightly. 'My name is Shibli. I've been looking forward to meeting you.'

'*Right,*' said the fox.

Shibli nodded. 'Right,' he agreed and went back to his seat.

When a boy tapped Raf's shoulder, Raf thought he was being offered a plastic mouthpiece for the glass-and-silver *sheesa* currently doing a circuit; but what the boy in the check shirt actually held was a spliff, plump as a cockroach and already sticky with tar.

'I don't . . .'

'Then start,' said the boy, 'you look like you need it.'

Watched by Sajjad, the kid with the check shirt and the fat boy in the Italian suit, Raf slotted the spliff between his first and second finger, cupped his hand and sucked at the gap between first finger and thumb. Paper flared and transmuted to ash as half the roach vanished in one massive hit. He had their attention now, Raf knew that.

All it ever took was simple and childish tricks.

He held the smoke in his lungs as he counted himself into darkness. On remand in Seattle where everything was freely available and widely used, most of the dopeheads held down their swirl for a minute or so but Raf could double that, which had to do with possessing more red blood cells or maybe just better ones.

686

Three minutes after he'd taken the toke, with all eyes on him, he tossed out the dregs of his breath in one whalelike blow . . .

(There was little Raf didn't know about *cetacea*. Not that he ever got to travel on the observation ships with his mother. Although she never forgot to mention in interviews that she always took with her a photograph of her young son, or that the picture was by some photographer better known for naked models and ageing rock stars.)

(The other thing she never forgot to mention was the time Norwegian commandos boarded SS *Valhalla* outside Spitzbergen and she'd had to hide two rolls of Kodachrome in her vagina and follow it with a tampon. This, she reminded everyone, was the point she converted to digital photography.)

'You done with that?'

Raf looked at the olive-skinned woman sat opposite. Given that every single café he'd seen on his short walk through Souk El Katcherine had been filled only with men, her sex made her a rarity.

'It's obvious,' she said, plucking the roach from his fingers. 'I'm allowed in because Jean-Marie, my uncle, owns the café. Besides, I'm half-French so I don't know any better.'

Isabeau Boulart had one of those ambiguous faces, angelically innocent from the front but slightly dissolute in profile. A gap separated her front teeth and she had a gold nose stud. Her chin was strong, her lower lip narrower than the upper as if top and bottom didn't quite meet or match. Her figure looked good, though, neat breasts pushing at a cotton top slightly too short to cover the soft curve of her tummy.

'Finished staring?'

Raf smiled blissfully and across the room Sajjad laughed. 'Prime kif,' he said. 'Idries imports it himself. Guaranteed to take away your senses . . .'

'Yeah,' said the woman, 'if you have any to start with.'

Idries was the boy in check shirt and jeans who'd handed Raf the roach. Somehow, in a way Raf hadn't yet worked out, Sajjad was waiting for Idries' agreement on something. And Raf was still just about awake enough to know it concerned him.

'Where are you originally from?' Idries' voice was casual, unthreatening. Which was enough to make Raf try to clear his thoughts.

'I'm, well . . .'

'You can tell us,' said Isabeau. It was hard to work out whether or not she was being sarcastic.

'I don't know,' Raf admitted finally. 'I've never known the answer to that question,' he added, when Isabeau raised her eyebrows. 'People ask and my mind goes empty.' It would have been easier to give them the

687

name of the village he'd told the soldier but that had gone out of his head.

'What was your father's name?' Idries demanded.

'He doesn't know his father,' said Sajjad flatly. 'And I saw him half kill a member of the *mubahith*. He's one of us.'

The fat boy in the Italian suit kept hogging the *sheesa* and Shibli went on quietly sipping his hot mint tea from a small glass, but the others were listening and watching, weighing up his words.

Waiting.

The kif had done its job if that was to flood Raf's brain with delta-9-tetrhydrocannabinol and make him reveal the truth. Something he'd be happy to do if only he could recognize it.

'Where did your train come from?' asked Isabeau.

This Raf could handle.

'Ben Guerdane.' He named a two-horse town on the Jeffara plain in the shadow of Jebel Dahar, maybe twenty klicks from the border with Tripolitana. Originally the fox's plan, such as it was, had been to bus the distance from Ben Guerdane to Kairouan, then take another to Tunis, but the night bus had already gone so Raf caught a local train instead, buying his ticket at one window, booking his cracked wooden seat at a second and confirming the ticket he'd just bought at a third. The entire cost of his ticket and seat reservation was less than a cappuccino at Le Trianon.

'That's true,' Sajjad nodded. 'I saw it come in.'

'Where were you standing?' Hassan demanded.

'In the café overlooking the concourse. The one with the balcony.'

A place with a façade that could have been lifted straight from the Marais in Paris and probably was. All green tiles and glass. As well as a whole sprawl of red-roofed suburbs, the French had managed to build a cathedral, an Art Nouveau theatre, an opera house and the Gare de Tunis by the time the Emir's great-grandfather threw them out of his city.

Raf was glad he could remember that.

'No other way onto the platform?' Shibli asked.

Sajjad shook his head firmly.

'Okay,' said Shibli, 'so we assume he got off that train. Let's deal with the next point.' He nodded to Idries and told the boy to pass Raf the leather bag Sajjad had lent to him.

'Open it,' he said. So Raf did and pulled out the submachine gun. Someone, probably Sajjad, had slotted the magazine back into place and without thinking Raf broke it down again. Separating clip from chassis.

'How did you get this?'

Raf told his story for a third time. Sajjad having been both the first and the second time.

'Didn't you realize there would be *mubahith* and soldiers?' Shibli looked more puzzled than anything else.

No, Raf could honestly say the thought never occurred to him. Police yes, in North Africa the police were everywhere, but soldiers questioning every *felah, khamme* and Berber clansman to climb from a local train . . . ? That was something else again.

'Okay,' said Shibli, putting down his tea glass. 'Let's take this from the top . . .' He smiled and for a split second it was possible to see the man he'd been. Someone whose hunger for meaning had taken him through all life had to offer and out into a stark stillness beyond.

'Do you want to keep the gun?'

Raf shook his head.

'Good . . .' The Shibli held out his hand, looking puzzled when Raf made no attempt to hand over the HK.

'Fingerprints,' Raf explained apologetically. Without really thinking about it, Raf freed a catch on the side and dropped to his knees, field-stripping the HK on the dirty floor in front of him. When the weapon was reduced to barrel, breech, stock and chassis, Raf reached behind him and took a tiny bowl of olive oil from Isabeau's plate without even asking.

Ripping a strip from the leg of his borrowed SBCF jumpsuit he soaked it in oil and wiped over the parts in front of him. As an after-thought Raf flipped the bullets from their magazine and reloaded them, having first made sure each was clean.

Thirty seconds later the gun was whole and the room was in silence. Most of the expressions when Raf looked up were unreadable.

'You originally travelled from Egypt?'

Raf looked surprised.

'The jellaba you wore,' said Shibli, 'Sajjad said the pattern was Egyptian.'

'Not mine,' Raf said.

'Meaning what?'

'I needed some clothes so I stole them.'

'And what were you wearing when you stole someone else's jellaba?'

Raf thought back to his black Italian suit, white cotton shirt and red tie, the shades, his black shoes and the gold cuff links Hamzah Effendi gave him for something he once did.

'Uniform,' said Raf finally. 'I was wearing uniform.'

*

In Tunis, as in many cities along the North African littoral, *salafi*, those who followed al-Salaf al-Salih, the venerable forefathers talked about war as if it were always within or between religions, but those with eyes open knew it was between poverty and wealth. Yet Shibli found it hard to blame them. Soviet kids in particular came to the city on holiday, UN sanctions or not, bringing their currency and worse behaviour. Object lessons in the fact that despite the words of the saints, humility and virtue did not automatically bring material reward.

And it was hard to explain to those with nothing, that compared to the rest of Europe the 'packers and Soviet kids with their jeans and weird jackets were as poor as most Ifriqiyans were in relation to the Soviets.

Only those whose eyes were open could see these things.

'Who has *marc*?' Shibli's question was so blunt that Idries mistimed his draw on the *sheesha* and collapsed into a fit of coughing; one that lasted longer than strictly necessary as he tried to work out the right answer. In the end, Idries did what he usually did when faced with one of the Sufi's questions. Told the truth without knowing if that was the right thing to do or not.

'I have a small flask . . .'

Shibli held out his hand.

Spirits were prohibited in Tunis by tradition not law. Those who wanted to drink *marc* or armagnac could go to a café or visit the bar of a big hotel. The Emir's reasoning was simple. Those who wanted to drink could while those who knew spirits to be evil didn't need his law to tell them this. Besides, the Soviets all drank heavily. In his own way the Emir was a very pragmatic man.

This was the cause of his wife's discontent. Or so it was said. Shibli didn't know if her son, Kashif Pasha, also believed what the old mullahs told his mother or if His Excellency was just using them as they used him. It was, as he'd once heard Isabeau say, a bitch of a call. What was unquestionably true was that most of the army believed, but then uniforms and absolutes seemed to go together, whether God willed or not.

Flipping open Idries' flask, Shibli took a long swallow and felt cheap brandy burn his throat on its way down. Seconds later it ignited his stomach, which served him right for forgetting, once again, to eat before leaving his madersa.

He drank to make a point. Whether any of the others had eyes open enough to understand his point was their business. Offering the flask to Raf, he watched the man drain what was left and wipe his mouth with the back of his hand. He did it without hesitation. Without the slightest thought of refusal.

An officer, Shibli decided, noticing soft fingers and unbroken nails. An officer who broke down a gun like any grunt. One who drank. An officer on the run. Or an infiltrator, an *agent provocateur* willing to break sharia law in the course of his job? A man who would need to be watched while he watched them . . .

'Who are you really?' Shibli's question was aimed at Raf but Sajjad got in his reply first.

'A conscript, he said so.'

Which wasn't what the soldier had said at all, though Shibli let that pass. Taking another glance at the drunken man in the orange jumpsuit, Shibli tried again. 'What are you running from?' he asked.

'What have you got,' said Raf.

And fell sideways off his stool.

CHAPTER 20

Per gutted supper with a swift cut, turning his knife sideways to hook out the rat's intestines, which tumbled onto the coals at his feet. Without pause, he sliced a ring around the neck of his catch and tossed the blade aside to ease his fingers beneath the animal's skin, peeling it back like a man turning a glove inside out. Only then did he answer the blond girl sitting in the dusk opposite.

'Sure I'm sure . . .'

'It's safe to eat?'

Per nodded. 'You'd be surprised what's safe if you cook it properly. You certain this isn't a rare species?'

Sally was.

When Per first returned with supper wriggling in his hand he'd asked Sally if his catch was rare. Since the rat was obviously still alive at this point Sally had assumed Per was trying to avoid killing something endangered. Now she was beginning to wonder. The small stuff she knew, his hatred of shoes, the fact the first thing he did each morning was retie his hair, and the raw scratch marks across his back were definitely hers: but she still had little idea as yet of what was inside his head. But then it was fair to say that Per had less than no idea of what was in her own.

'Rosemary,' Per said, crumbling leaves under her nose. 'And this one's fresh thyme.'

Sally had watched the snake-hipped Swede build a fire from brush-wood, doing everything the way Sally felt it should be done. First he dug a small pit and ringed it with stones collected from the outcrop under which they camped. Raked a wide area around the pit with his fingers as a second move, brushing aside anything that might flare like tinder. And filled the pit with twigs, arranged by thickness as his third move.

Spaghetti-thin in the middle, pencil-fat around that and fatter still around the outside and over the top.

The flame came from an old lighter; so old she hadn't seen that kind before.

'Just petrol,' said Per, noticing her interest. 'Works even in a high wind.' He did something vaguely obscene with the chrome circle at the top of the lighter and Sally realized he was jacking it up and down like a metal foreskin. 'Belonged to my grandfather,' he said proudly.

'And you still use it?'

'Why not?' said Per. 'It still works.'

Sally smiled. He was an odd mix. A carnivorous technopagan who thought modern war inherently immoral but happily believed killing to be a hardwired human reaction, if only on a personal level. As for global politics, genetics and the other stuff that really interested Sally, they hadn't even begun to go there. The only thing that really fired Per was history and old ruins.

'What are you thinking?' His voice studiedly casual, borderline curious. Something about her obviously fascinated him and Sally had yet to work out what. Leaving aside the obvious.

'That you're a good fuck . . .'

Per grinned. 'And you're a good judge of these things?'

'You're not?'

Still grinning the boy put his lighter to the kindling and they both watched flame catch. An immediate helix of twisted vision ruptured the air between them. There was no smoke to disturb the summer sky, only a spiral of heat haze. Sally was impressed by that.

They could have got off at Gabes but Sally wanted a bank and knew, because she'd already checked, that Coutts & Co. (Tunis) kept a branch where Avenue de Carthage intersected with Avenue de Paris.

So she made Per look after her luggage in a café across the road while she sauntered into one of those grey-stoned colonial mansions with sash windows, bay trees at the door and industrial-strength air-conditioning and banged her chequebook on the counter, which was Italian horsehair marble, obviously enough.

The florid young man who glanced up looked first at Sally's tatty chequebook and only then at the blond foreigner and Sally was glad it was that way round. The five minutes she'd spent cleaning up in the thin trickle of water extracted from an ablutions hose in the café loo had done little but smear dust across her sunburned face. Dirt still grimed her arms and Sally's hair was a mess under her scarf. Although Sally had to admit that tying back her hair helped make her look local.

'Madame?'

693

'Mademoiselle,' Sally corrected without thinking. Mademoiselle it was and mademoiselle was the way it was going to stay. She'd seen the price her mother had to pay for security and that was just too high.

'I'd like to check my account.'

Sally pushed her book to Kaysar Aziz and watched him flick back its cover and discreetly check the laser-stamped photograph embossed on the inside. Equally discreetly, Aziz fanned a dozen of the most recent stubs. The amounts scrawled in a variety of cheap pens got smaller each time.

'If you could just wait here.' He vanished through an oak door to check her balance, something he could have done quicker by flicking alive a flatscreen angled into the countertop. This was discretion apparently.

She knew the answer the moment Kaysar reappeared, long before he had time or need to frame his reply.

'Empty?'

'I'm sorry . . .'

Sally shrugged. 'Not your problem if my father's a prick.'

His blink was lightning-fast.

'Cancelled,' Sally explained. 'Until I come home. He's been threatening it for months. Now he has . . . You got a loo round here?'

Aziz looked blank.

'Toilet,' Sally said. 'Which way?'

Rinsing her hands to wash off the soap, Sally started on her face and realized, too late, that she was splashing water down her front. The decision made itself. Unwrapping her scarf she shoved it into the pocket of her jeans and pulled her damp T-shirt over her head, revealing bite marks below one breast and a barbed-wire tattoo round her upper left arm. The tattoo was a mistake, an old one. The jury was still out on the navel stud and the gold dumbbell through her left nipple.

The body of an animal, Wu Yung had said, and that was when Sally knew she'd finally outgrown him. The old man meant lean and muscled like a predator but he'd missed the essential truth. What he thought was a compliment was merely a statement of the obvious. And the fact Wu Yung never realized this disappointed her. She was an animal as was he, as were Bozo and Atal, that overprivileged, underchallenged little idiot with his kangaroo-skin shoes.

Homo sapiens. One point three percent off being a chimpanzee. A species outside evolution and seriously in need of an overhaul.

Sally sighed.

When she'd wrung out as much water from her hair as she could Sally wrapped it still damp in her scarf, splashed cologne onto her breasts from

694

a bottle on a glass shelf above the basin, struggled back into her T-shirt and turned to go. That was when she noticed an elderly Arab woman sitting in an alcove.

Gazes met and held, pale blue and darkest brown and Sally nodded, shrugging off the lack of a nod in return.

To make a point she left her last US dollar in the saucer by the door.

'Well, that went perfectly,' Sally announced as she slumped into the chair opposite Per and reached for her Leica.

'You got your money?'

'Yeah.' Sally picked up the dregs of Per's espresso and downed it in a single gulp. 'Every last penny in my account.'

'What now?' Per asked.

'We go our separate ways I guess.'

'And your way is where?'

'Into the desert.'

Per smiled. 'You've been practising that,' he said.

'Practising what?' Sally demanded, her puzzlement real.

'That line,' said Per, brushing aside his floppy hair. He put one hand to his pale eyes to shade out a sun already kept at bay by a café umbrella and pretended to peer into the far distance. 'Searching for your famous weasel?'

Sally nodded and Per laughed.

'I don't believe you,' he said. 'Not even an Englishwoman chases into the desert after a weasel.'

'I do,' said Sally. 'Chasing things is how you find them.'

'But they're not even rare,' Per protested. 'I know, I looked them up.' He pulled a battered Nokia from his rucksack and flipped up the number pad to reveal a foldout keyboard and pop-up screen. 'So what are you really after?'

'Really?'

Per nodded.

'Lions,' said Sally, smiling at his expression. 'Barbary lions. The kind that ate Christians in the Roman circus.'

'What do they look like?'

'Much like this,' Sally said and she pulled a tatty newspaper clipping from the back of her wallet. It showed a lion cub so pale it almost looked grey. 'The last known Barbary lion was shot in Morocco eighty years ago.'

'So how are you going to find one?'

'By looking,' Sally said flatly. 'There've been rumours for years that a pair exist in captivity at a private zoo.'

'Whose?'

Sally smiled. 'The Emir's own,' she said. 'Apparently he sees nobody, but I think he might see me. He's partial to single blondes . . .' She tapped quote marks either side of the words, stressing the irony.

'You want company?'

Sally was about to point out the contradiction between what she'd just said and his question when she noticed the local newspaper tucked into the side pocket of Per's rucksack. It was folded open towards the back and she could just about see the small-ad headings from where she sat, not that she needed to. The boxed-out advertisement for Hertz told her all she needed to know.

'You're going to hire a car?'

'Too expensive,' said Per. 'I'll buy one.'

'This works out cheaper?'

'Depends what I buy. Get a Mahari and it'll run like clockwork, Soviet clockwork . . . Four-cylinder, two-stroke, made in Portugal,' he added, seeing Sally's blank look.

'And that runs like . . .'

'It was a joke,' he said patiently. 'Maharis break down daily but even a child can mend them. What I actually want is a Jeep.' Tossing the paper across, Per said, 'Take a look.' He'd ringed three possibles and put lines through two of those. 'Too old,' he said, jerking his head towards the first one. 'And the other's too expensive. The last one looks okay though.'

As she expected the price was substantially more than Sally had. 'You off to see it now?' she asked hopefully.

'I wish.' Per shook his head. 'I called and the first time they can do is ten o'clock tomorrow. Which means finding somewhere for the night.'

'Not a problem,' said Sally. 'There were a dozen guesthouses near Gare de Tunis. We can try there.' And so they did, although they ended up with separate rooms because the woman behind the desk refused to rent them a double. She did this through the simple expedient of refusing to understand what Sally and Per were asking for.

One room was under the roof of a narrow four-storey guesthouse that advertised itself as L'Hôtel Carthage, the other on the second floor, up a flight of stairs from the reception area. Both looked onto a narrow side street parked with cars but only the lower one had a shower and loo. Sally chose the roof because her window had a better view. That was what she told Per anyway, in fact the main thing her room had going for it was being a third cheaper than the room Per took.

'You want to go eat?'

'Not really hungry,' said Sally. 'Although you could always pick up a *bottle of red if you go out.' She watched Per nod and smiled to herself. Now she had a reason to drop by his room later if that was the route she decided to take; it would be, but Sally was planning to spend an hour or two fooling herself first.*

CHAPTER 21

Empirical evidence proved that sitting quietly in front of a half-eaten croissant could keep a waiter from Le Trianon at bay for half an hour. The secret was not to run over thirty minutes. Doing so resulted in someone coming to ask if there was a problem with the food.

Opening her laptop, Hani called up a photograph and stripped off yesterday's additions, starting again. The foreigner's strange shirt was replaced with a new scoop-neck top, her hair made presentable courtesy of digiGloss, which billed itself as the software make-up experts used. Hani had downloaded a fourteen-day trial version of this and a freeware version of Wardrobe v3.1 from a teen site in Kansas City.

Her uncle was missing, check.

Khartoum knew why but wouldn't say, check.

And check Zara moping about in the *qaa* like some consumptive. *Merde* and *merde* again, as Zara herself would say. Hani took a large bite from her croissant and chewed hard. Yesterday she'd come across the woman sitting by the small fountain in the *qaa* reading Rumi. If this was a side effect of love then . . .

Hani sucked her teeth.

'Is everything all right?' The waiter who materialized beside her table looked worried, his eyes flicking from the child's face to her plate.

'The croissant is delicious,' Hani said firmly, 'and I don't need another coffee. But actually I do need to see the maître d' . . . to borrow a pen,' Hani added, when the man looked worried. Slipping down from her chair, she strolled through the terrace door into Le Trianon and headed for the elderly person standing at a small lectern, leafing through a reservations book.

'Problems?' Hani asked politely.

'Nothing serious.' The thin Italian smiled at her. 'A double booking for the same cover . . .' He nodded to a table for six beneath a mural, the one decorated with a dancing girl in jewelled slippers and a wisp of cloth. 'Sometimes I just think it would be easier to do everything myself.'

'It is,' said Hani, raising the lip on her notebook and hitting a hot key. It would have been obvious even to someone less versed in the ways of Lady Hana al-Mansur that the child was hovering on the edge of a question.

'What is it?' the maître d' said and kept his smile in place to stop the girl from being anxious. 'You can ask . . .'

Hani held up her pink plastic notebook. 'My uncle's on a mission,' she said seriously. A flick of her eyes around the almost empty café found it safe to talk. Her look swift, instinctive and enough to convince the man that Hani believed what she said. And why not . . . ? Everyone had heard the rumours that her uncle Ashraf Bey was in the direct employ of the sultan in Stambul.

'A mission?'

'Secret,' said Hani. 'Very secret.'

Not being too sure how else to proceed, Hani thrust the screen at the man. 'I have to find this woman,' she said and watched his eyes. Glad that he didn't like the look of her either. 'To deliver a message.'

'This message is from His Excellency?'

Hani shook her head and left it at that.

'I see,' said the thin Italian, visions of the Khedive using his young cousin to pass secret messages to unsuitable foreigners flicking through his head. Or maybe it was Hamzah Effendi, because rumours had the industrialist quietly financing a return to power for Saiid Koenig Pasha.

'The thing is,' Hani began. 'I was wondering if she'd ever eaten here?'

'I forgot to give you this . . .' Hani held out the pen.

'Thank you.' The maître d' smiled. It was only after she'd slipped away the previous afternoon that he realized Lady Hana had taken his silver Mont Blanc with her. He should have known she'd return it just as soon as she realized.

'A parcel came for your uncle.'

'I know,' said Hani, 'I'm here to collect it.'

The maître d' looked doubtful.

'It's wrapped in brown paper,' said Hani. 'Madame Ingrid brought it down this morning. Gave it to you herself.'

At least Hani imagined that was what had happened. She'd been very specific in her instructions to the bank. His Excellency needed the money wrapped in paper and delivered to his office. The parcel was to be given only to Madame Ingrid. The note Hani sent to Madame Ingrid on her uncle's behalf was actually a postcard taken from a box in her dead aunt's old room. The card's surface was waxy, ivory rather than white. Across one side, at the top, ran the words, *al-Mansur Madersa, Rue Sherif, El Iskandryia*. That alone must be enough to make the card an antique, since the door onto Rue Sherif had been walled up for . . .

Hani wasn't sure, but ages anyway. And it had only been un-bricked after Aunt Nafisa died. She'd risked using her printer to fake Uncle Asraf's signature on this, because she was pretty certain Madame Ingrid wouldn't be feeding the card through any machine. All the woman would do was what she was told, which was deliver any parcel left at C3 straight to the maître d' at Le Trianon.

It was a smooth-flowing, perfect circle of transferred responsibility.

Hani held out her hand.

'The parcel's in my office,' said the maître d' and Ham nodded wisely, although she hadn't even known the Italian had an office. 'Why don't I have someone bring you a cappuccino while I fetch it?'

Hani did her best not to sigh.

CHAPTER 22

Wednesday 23rd February

Mubahith came looking for Raf. At least they did according to Isabeau. But this Raf only found out later, and first there was another shift to get through. His seventh in three days. Two scraping dishes, one suds diving, three prepping vegetables and now this.

'*More fire* . . .' Chef Antonio skimmed the hot chicken breasts across his kitchen, one after the other and a commis chef ducked.

It was inevitable the new broiler man should fumble the catch. If only because he had two hands and there were five flying breasts of chicken. But he caught three and won $20 for Idries who'd bet Raf would catch more than he dropped.

'Owe you,' Idries told him.

The kitchens at Café Antonio were thick with steam. The floor slippery. A radio spat raiPunk and the only thing louder than the fury of Cheb Dread was the chef's voice.

'Burn it,' Antonio snarled. 'Blackened chicken needs to be fucking *blackened*.' With a scowl he swung round, gearing up to persecute somebody else.

Out of the fat chef's sight Raf grabbed a hand towel and began to wipe off his fumbled catches.

'Run them under a tap ,' Idries said over his shoulder.

So Raf did, then tossed the five chicken breasts back into oil and smoking butter. Sixty seconds later, having seared both sides to charcoal against the pan's heavy bottom he scooped them out, rolled them on cheap kitchen paper and dumped them back on a plate.

'Ready,' he shouted and discovered the plate was already gone.

'Swordfish two,' came the cry from a teller, 'and let's hustle, tagine three.'

The tagine would be lamb because that was the only kind Café Antonio served. Lamb tagine, blackened chicken and pan-seared

701

swordfish, those were Antonio's bows to ethnic cookery; and if the Soviet kids with their rucksacks and cheap condoms didn't know that tagine came via Morocco, the chicken courtesy of the Caribbean and the swordfish recipe from Malta then Antonio wasn't about to tell them. His ingredients were local, mostly . . . The fish caught by boats from Odessa and frozen on-site. When the Soviet crews docked at Tunis, which was rarely, Antonio would be waiting, ready to come to an agreement.

The captain would eat free for his entire stay, much vodka would be drunk and one or maybe two sides of frozen swordfish would go missing.

Other than these dishes Café Antonio served pizza and that was all. Antonio pushed the pizza because he was from Naples after all, and his staff also pushed pizza, whatever their nationality, because that's what they were told to do. Pizza was good to eat, quick to cook and the markup was excellent; the other dishes took more time, cost more to make and irritated Antonio with their inauthenticity.

'So why serve them?'

Idries shrugged. 'Have you seen the real thing?'

Apparently Antonio needed the ethnic dishes for the kind of tourists who thought they wanted to eat local food but never did when actually presented with lumps of goat heart, fatty lamb still on the bone or fish that scowled back from the plate.

'Swordfish three.'

'Got it,' said Raf and reached for a dish, realizing suddenly that it was empty. 'I'm . . .'

'Fucking amateur,' said a dark boy, dumping a pile of swordfish by Raf's station. He was wearing check trousers and clogs, a white jacket and a scarf to keep curling hair out of his eyes; only his grin removed sting from the words. 'Next time, call me before you get eighty-six.' They both knew the boy should have got there first.

A quick flick with a blade to free a steak from the frozen stack and Raf rattled it, still hard, onto the griddle, following it with a second and a third. Ninety seconds later the fish was seared.

'Chicken, fire five.' Antonio grabbed a ticket from a teller he felt was working too slowly and shouted out the orders, hanging each yellow slip from a peg when the list was done.

'Come on,' he howled at Raf. 'What are you waiting for?'

Fallout from the oil that hissed in his pan worried Raf not at all. He'd assigned the pain to colours, running the rainbow according to intensity and length. Most of his double shifts sped by in a low-level intensity of blue with the occasional flashes of purple.

Already his wrists were freckled with tiny burns and his first finger raw from pressing down on a knife. There would be real calluses later,

Isabeau had explained to Raf the day before, turning over her own hands. Somehow he'd felt the need to check and then, holding her hands, had not known how to give them back.

Which, obviously enough, was the point Hassan slammed into the cold locker. And the sudden snatch of her fingers had looked like guilt to all of them.

'Chicken,' Raf shouted and scooped blackened breasts onto kitchen paper, rolled them over, then dumped them into a heated dish. Someone else would dress the plates. Glancing over to the hatch to see what other orders were headed his way Raf found the teller leaning against the wall, a cigarette ready for lighting.

A redheaded Australian waitress with a flour handprint on her behind was scowling as she dusted the ghostly fingers from black jeans. Raf looked round for anybody with an answering print on their face but all he got was Hassan looking smug.

The last order had just been served. Wind-down could begin.

Café Antonio had a shower room in the basement. This saved the staff from having to climb five flights to their dorm in the attic. Unfortunately there was only one shower and both sexes worked the kitchen, so it alternated as to who got to use it first.

But today that didn't matter because Isabeau was doing a morning shift at Maison Hafsid, the Australian waitress refused to wash at all, something about natural oils and the Bosnian dishwasher and the one who wore tights but no knickers had resigned yesterday, shortly after Raf was promoted to work the broiler instead of her.

'Call for you,' said a pearl diver, soap suds still gloved down both wrists. He held the dripping phone in one hand, a plate in the other and was looking at Idries.

'Tell them to fuck off,' Antonio ordered. 'We're going drinking.'

'I think you should take it,' the boy said to Idries, very carefully not looking at the chef.

'It won't take a minute,' Idries promised as Antonio scowled.

Afternoon sessions were banned unless the chef suggested them. In the three days he'd been working double shifts Raf had discovered a dozen such rules. Spoken and unspoken. Along with a web of loyalties, pragmatic friendships and alliances, feuds that simmered below the surface and a few that didn't. All institutions were the same and few places came more institutional than a restaurant kitchen.

Small wonder Raf felt at home.

Over at the vidphone Idries was talking intently. His body hunched around the phone in his hand.

'Time's up,' said Antonio. His voice hard. A tumbler of cooking brandy away from developing a dangerous edge.

'It's Isabeau,' Idries said over his shoulder. 'She needs to talk to Raf.'

'You like snakes?' Isabeau's voice was neutral. All the same Raf knew it was a loaded question because he'd sensed her distance grow as he went from one dirty window to the next, matching labels to the reptiles inside. By the time they'd reached the third row she barely bothered to glance into the cases at all.

She was lost somewhere inside herself. Arms folded across her front. Shoulders hunched as she walked beside him. Dressed in what looked like new jeans and a pink T-shirt with three-quarter-length sleeves. A blue scarf hid her face.

If Raf hadn't known better he'd have said she was afraid.

Maybe he was meant to have reacted more to her news. That strange men were searching for him. At least, they were searching for someone. A soldier on the run. Only, Raf knew there was no soldier, was there . . .

Or if there was it wasn't him.

'Put it this way,' said Raf. 'Snakes remind me of my childhood.' Absentmindedly sliding his hand into the pocket of his own jeans to touch the memento Eugenie had given him, Raf added, 'You could call it a family interest.'

His mother had once shot a series in the Amazon with the working title *Good Snakes Gone Bad*, probably for the Discovery Channel. It became *Renegade Reptiles* and paid less than zilch and took eight months out of her life. She came back with dysentery, ringworm, different colour hair and a brooding Brazilian boy who lasted two months in New York before demanding a ticket home.

Before this was footage for Channel5 involving a python and a naked baby, taken using a table-mounted Sanyo with remote control, so she could also be in shot. A thin woman in her early twenties, bare-breasted and with hennaed toes on a Berber rug beside the snake and child. Because she showed no fear of the reptile, the infant showed no fear and because the infant lacked fear it yanked happily at the sleepy python, digging small fingers into snake flesh and pushing the python around like a toy.

When this didn't elicit a response, the child dragged a heavy coil to its mouth and tried to chew its leatherlike skin. Finally the infant got bored and crawled out of shot, leaving the woman smiling into the camera.

A fifteen-second snip later got used for a campaign selling life insurance.

It was years before Raf realized the child was him.

'But do you like them?' Isabeau insisted.

Raf shook his head.

'Then why suggest we meet here?'

'You wanted to talk . . .'

She would age, Raf realized as he watched her frown. Her compact body would fill out and her face acquire lines. That residual puppy fat on her arms would become less puppyish, more obvious, her looks would go and breasts lose their battle with gravity. She would put on weight and grow old, something the fox once promised would never happen to him.

'Sometimes,' said Raf. 'I get voices that tell me what to do . . .'

Or maybe that was *invent*? Raf was uncertain. For as long as he could remember there had been a fracture between mind and body, observed and observer. A rupture of identity that kept him distanced from himself, often thinking of himself as *he*. What if the fox was right and it didn't exist . . . If his memory wasn't as perfect as he pretended?

What if he was just running away?

Isabeau stared back. Worried but not frightened, not yet.

'And these voices told you to look at snakes?'

'Actually,' Raf's smile was rueful, 'I think that was my idea.'

'Your . . .' And after a second Isabeau almost smiled back. It was a nervous smile but it lifted her face and bled some of the anxiety from her eyes.

'These voices?'

'Once there was a fox,' said Raf, staring into a darkened case. 'A dangerous and deadly ghost. Always waiting, always there.' On the other side of the filthy glass a bootlace tasted the air with a sullen tongue. Around its nostrils splashed colours that no human eye could see. Knowledge Raf could tell Isabeau or keep to himself. 'And then it wasn't.'

'What happened?'

Raf looked at her. There were no colours hidden in her face. Nothing Isabeau couldn't see in her own reflection.

'To the fox?'

She nodded.

'Someone repaired the bloody thing . . .'

Hammered into a grassy bank between the ring road and the main fence surrounding the zoo were enamel signs every hundred paces or so, to warn visitors not to climb over. A crude silhouette of a wolf reinforced that message.

At the bottom of the track stood metal gates and on the far side of those, just before a main road, was a neat ornamental lake crowded with wading birds and waterfowl. Around the edge strolled what looked like smart Tunis. Girls walking hand in hand and young men with their arms around each other's shoulders in expressions of friendship that could only have been political back in Seattle.

A small wading bird with clockwork legs and a blue bottom raced across damp concrete and plopped into the lake, bobbing beneath the spray of a fountain on its way towards a tiny island in the middle. The concrete was damp because the fountain plumed straight out of the water and every gust of wind carried fine droplets towards the shore.

The scene was sickeningly normal.

'Let me buy you a coffee.' Raf nodded to a low café across the lake, its tables almost as crowded as the paths. 'Then you can tell me about Maison Hafsid and who these men were who came looking for me . . .'

In reply, Isabeau glanced at her wrist.

'You need to be somewhere else?'

Isabeau looked suddenly embarrassed, even slightly panicked; a blush suffusing her face. 'No,' she said hastily, 'being here is good.' They finished the stroll in silence. Only this time it was a quieter, less strained silence and could almost pass for friendship if not for the anxious glances she kept throwing in Raf's direction.

All that changed when Raf saw a child feeding bread to a duck. No one he'd ever seen before. Just a girl of about nine wearing a headscarf and feeding crusts to a duck so full it could barely waddle. She had long hair, tied back, white sneakers and cheap dark glasses that kept sliding down her nose. So wrapped up was she in watching the duck that the rest of the world might as well have not existed . . .

'Raf,' said Isabeau. She was pulling at his arm.

'What?'

'What are the voices saying?' Worried eyes watched him. 'And why are you staring at that child?'

'No reason,' said Raf. And was shocked to discover he was crying.

'You miss your kid?' Isabeau demanded when the waiter had gone.

Raf put down his coffee, thought about it . . . 'Yes,' he admitted finally.

'Because he lives with his mother?'

'She,' Raf corrected, 'and I think her mother's dead.'

'You think . . .' Isabeau tried hard not to be shocked. Divorce was more common in Ifriqiya than in other North African countries. But not in the way it was in the West. All the same, Isabeau obviously figured she'd know if a person she'd married was alive or not.

'You *were* married to her mother?'

'I've never been married,' Raf said. 'Although I was engaged once but that was to someone else.' He caught Isabeau's expression and smiled. 'It's a messy story,' he said.

'They usually are.' Glancing round the café terrace with its noisy children and couples relaxing after a stroll in Jardin Belvedere, she shrugged. 'You don't have to tell me that.' When Isabeau spoke again it was to ask a question that appeared to have been troubling her. Her voice was hesitant, as if Isabeau was uncertain of the wisdom of asking.

'You're not really who you say you are, are you? If you know what I mean . . .'

Inside Raf's head the other Raf grinned, all teeth and no smile. *'Okay,'* it said smoothly, *'answer that and stay human.'*

Raf couldn't. Which he guessed was Tiri's point.

The *capuchin* was milky, came in glass mugs and had a scum of thin froth across the top. Raf promptly embarrassed himself by mishearing the price and blithely handing the waiter a note roughly equivalent to U$5, a good portion of Raf's wages for that week.

'Does Your Excellency have anything smaller?' It was obvious the old man thought Raf was trying to impress Isabeau.

Raf shook his head. 'Wednesday's payday,' he said. 'That's how I was given it.'

'Must be a good job.'

'Kitchen work, seven shifts in a row,' Raf said wryly and saw rather than heard the old man suck his teeth.

'No so good . . . I'll get you change.'

A dozen grubby notes and a fistful of change, some of it old enough to be real, arrived on a chipped saucer, while Raf and Isabeau sat at their table and watched two toddlers, an old man wearing a red felt *chechia* and a young woman cross the wooden bridge leading from the gates of Jardin Belvedere over a narrow strip of lake to where Isabeau and Raf sat nursing warm coffees.

At Raf's end stood a camera crew trying to film two laughing girls in red headscarves, arms tight around each other's waists as they strolled across the same bridge, but every time the girls got halfway some toddler would run into the shot or a passing family would halt and stare. Once, an old woman halted the two girls just as they reached the café end of the bridge. She wanted to ask them the time.

'Who are they?'

Isabeau snorted. 'Now I *know* you don't come from around here,' she said and named a famous Tunisian soap that had been running for eighteen years. 'They've been friends since before kindergarten,' Isabeau explained. 'But their fathers have hated each other ever since Jasmine's father had Natasha's mother's kiosk at Gare de Tunis torn down because she hadn't applied for a tobacco-sellers' permit. So now they have to meet in secret.'

'Are they lovers?'

Isabeau's eyes went wide. 'Such things don't happen in Ifriqiya. Especially on television.'

'Don't happen or aren't talked about?'

'Both,' said Isabeau. And for a moment Raf was looking through a broken window into the darkened basement of her soul.

'So why the fear?' Raf asked.

Part of Isabeau obviously wanted to ask *what fear?* And for a second, Raf was afraid she might just get up and walk away. Instead she sipped at cold coffee and watched two twenty-three-year-old actresses pretend to be fifteen.

'In America,' Raf said, 'they'd close this café, hire extras to drink coloured water and have police tape off the road both sides of the gate. Everything would be done in one shot . . . The only people allowed near that bridge would be the actresses and the crew. And if the actresses decided to fuck each other it would be out of boredom.'

'You've been to America?' Isabeau sounded disbelieving.

'Once,' said Raf. 'Years back. When I thought I was somebody else.'

'Why tell me this?'

'Because I can?'

'And I can't tell anybody.' Isabeau nodded, as if that was obvious. 'Without you telling them about me . . .' Her voice was thoughtful.

'So Hassan doesn't know?'

'Hassan!' Raf could almost taste her irritation. 'Oh, Hassan wants to marry me, all right. So he can get his hands on my quarter of the café.' It took a second for Raf to work out that Isabeau meant the smoky tunnel in Souk El Katcherine where he'd first met Idries. 'That won't be happening . . .'

'You already have a lover?'

The broken window was instantly back. The room inside darker than ever. As black as those places where the fox hid. In the days before Raf finally accepted that the fox was him.

'Okay,' Raf said. 'No lover.'

'No,' Isabeau agreed. On the far side of the bridge the camera crew began packing equipment into a white van, faces relieved; and both the actresses now sat in an old green Lincoln that waited to pull out into traffic, watched by a crowd of schoolchildren.

'What about you?' Isabeau asked, her eyes never leaving the car.

What indeed. Any answer Raf might be prepared to give was aborted by a sudden buzz from Isabeau's bag.

'It's me,' she said, having reached for a cheap cell phone. 'What?'

The answer froze Isabeau's expression. One second, she was watching a distant schoolgirl with bare legs and checked dress; the next blood drained from Isabeau's cheeks and her mouth went slack. Spiralling adrenergic hormones. Textbook shock.

She turned off the Nokia without saying another word.

'I have to go.' Eyes unfocused.

'Go where?' said Raf. And when Isabeau didn't answer he reached forward to take the cell phone from unresisting fingers and put it back in her bag. Without thinking he also wiped a fingertip of sweat from her forehead and absentmindedly licked it. *Shocked and scared*, the Raf inside Raf decided, *been there/done that/probably about, to do it again.*

'You in trouble?' Stupid question really.

'I have to go.' Metal scraped on concrete as Isabeau pushed back her chair and three tables away people winced. 'My brother, Pascal . . .'

'I'll come with you,' said Raf.

She shook her head.

Raf sighed. 'Whatever it is,' he said. 'I can help. And if you're really in trouble, then a couple is less easy to spot than a single girl in a city like this.' His nod took in the café crowd and the busy sidewalk on the other side of the bridge.

'How can I trust you?' Isabeau demanded. 'And how do I know you are who you say you are?'

'You don't,' said Raf. 'And I'm not.' He tossed some change onto their table for the waiter and gripped Isabeau's hand, refusing to let her pull free. 'Smile as you walk away,' Raf ordered, and Isabeau's face twisted in misery.

Halfway across the little bridge he made her stop to watch a waterbird swim beneath their feet, take a last look round the lake and then stroll arm in arm with him towards the gates. On the way out, Raf bought a loose bag of cookies from a stall. They were sweet to the point of sickness and warm from being on display.

CHAPTER 23

'I wonder if you could help . . .' Hani's voice was polite but firm. As if she regularly wandered alone as evening fell, trawling expensive Italian boutiques on Rue Faransa, a street once famous for its Victorian brothels and opium dens.

'A dress?' Returning Hani's demand with a question was all the sticklike owner could manage. Backed up inside Madame Fitmah's head were certainly a dozen other, infinitely more important questions, starting with how was this child planning to pay and ending with what should she, Madame Fitmah, call the small girl since *madame* was obviously out of the question?

'I've got cash,' said Hani, yanking a roll of dollars from her fleece pocket. 'And you can call me *mademoiselle.*' She grinned at Madame Fitmah's blossoming shock and nodded towards an antique brass till inlaid with silver and bronze, although the mechanism was strictly electronic. 'You glanced at that,' Hani explained, 'then you looked at me and seemed puzzled.'

'*Mademoiselle?*'

Hani nodded. 'And I've got cash,' she stressed, holding out the roll of US dollars, but still the woman looked doubtful.

El Isk was, by the standards of North Africa, surprisingly liberal in its approach to life. In part this was due to its status as a freeport and, in part, to the fact that liberalism had been General Koenig Pasha's only defence against creeping fundamentalism. True, a woman still couldn't inherit property, hold a job without the consent of her father or husband, drive alone on Fridays or initiate a divorce; but she could own a credit card and was liable for any debt she incurred. Unlike, say, Riyadh or Algiers, where all a man had to do was repudiate his wife's right to incur debt and no court would enforce an order.

Children were different, obviously enough. In Iskandryia, boys were considered responsible from the age of fourteen; for girls the age was twenty-one. Although where marriage was concerned the differential reversed. Then the legal age was fourteen for the girl and sixteen for a boy.

Even if Hani had possessed a credit card, Madame Fitmah would have been unwilling to sell her anything without an adult present to countersign the slip. Cash on the other hand . . .

'What kind of dress?'

'Gold,' said Hani. 'Thin as the wings of a Great Admiral butterfly, with pearls around the neck and sleeves seeded with emeralds.'

'I'm not sure we've . . .' The Italian woman looked round at steel shelves lining her *haut minimaliste* boutique. A shop space taller than it was wide. And when she shrugged apologetically her scarlet Versace dress creased at the shoulders. 'I doubt if anyone's ever . . .'

Hani sighed and the gown that Scheherazade wore on the last of her one thousand and one nights crumbled in her imagination and was gone.

'Show me what you've got,' said Hani and sounded so like Zara that she tagged on a hurried *please*, before climbing onto a chrome-and-glass chair to position herself so that she stared at a red flower painted on the far wall, her spine rigid and legs bent at the knee. A move that would do more than cash could to convince Madame Fitmah the child belonged in her boutique.

'You've been measured before.'

'Oh,' Hani smiled sweetly. 'I'm always being measured.' And so she was, against the edge of a door in the kitchen by Donna, who took a fresh measurement every month and wrote the date against it. Although obviously this wasn't what the woman meant.

'But you don't have your card . . . ?'

'I've grown,' Hani told the woman. She sounded ridiculously smug about this, as if the growth spurt had been down to her and not to nature. That wasn't the real reason Hani had left her card behind, of course. The one she'd had done with Zara featured Hani's name and address encoded on the chip.

The scanner was silent as it passed through the small girl's fleece, T-shirt and jeans to map the skin beneath, then looked through skin to the bones and measured those as well. Any clothes cut to measure would fit perfectly but Hani was too impatient to wait so Madame Fitmah matched her measurements to an inventory of stock.

'I'm sorry,' the owner began to say and stopped as the face of the child in front of her immediately dissolved into tears. Half a second later and the grief was gone, pulled back into glistening eyes and a trembling mouth. A second after that and Hani's face was neatly composed.

711

'I'm sorry to have troubled you,' Hani said as she slipped from the chair. Pushing her bundle of dollars back into a fleece pocket, she headed for the door.

'Wait.' Madame Fitmah stood beside a screen, scrolling down the list. 'I'm sure we can adapt something. Is this for a special occasion?'

'Oh yes,' said Hani. 'One of my cousins is having a party for his parents.'

CHAPTER 24

Wednesday 23rd February

'Next time,' Chef Antonio's voice was flat, 'I sell your ass to my nephew Hassan, who likes that kind of thing.' He took back his high-carbon Wusthof and threw the recipient of his scorn a cheap Sabatier kept for casual labour.

The Australian boy in question looked from Antonio to the blade that quivered in the door beside him and his shock, outrage and (let's be honest) unconcealed admiration went a tiny way towards restoring the chef's good humour. There were basic rules in life and first up was touch someone else's knife at your peril.

Antonio pointed to a half-full bucket of tomatoes. 'You don't stop until you've skinned the lot. You understand?'

The Australian did.

With a sigh the chef turned back to his radio. 'Sources close to the police say the man just arrested has known links to fundamentalist terror groups.' The newsreader spoke with an accent so impossibly Parisian it had to be fake.

Antonio twisted the dial and watched a needle judder its way across a thin strip of glass inscribed with stations that, like as not, no longer existed. The radio was Soviet, the size of a cinder block, only three times as heavy. Someone, probably a prisoner in a gulag workshop, had painted individual swirls of grain across its metal casing.

'. . . more news for you on the hour.'

'Try another station,' demanded Hassan.

Antonio took time out to stare at his wife's nephew but he still did what the fat boy suggested, stopping as the hiss of static thinned into Arabic.

'No further news on the murder at Maison Hafsid . . .'

Running the length of the dial twice, Antonio checked out as many of the local stations as he could find. It was easy to tell an approved station because those were the ones carrying identical versions of the same story. The pirates were more interesting but nothing they suggested sounded remotely like the truth.

'Any news on Isabeau?' Chef Antonio demanded.

'She hasn't phoned back.'

'Okay,' Antonio told Idries. 'Let me know if she does . . .' But when a call finally came it wasn't from Isabeau.

'For you,' Hassan said.

'Who?'

Hassan returned the stare he'd been given earlier. 'For you,' he said and dropped the receiver to let it spin, vinelike, tipped by a matte grey plastic fruit.

Sometime or other Antonio was going to have to talk to his wife. It was all very well having her nephew on board, but the deal was that the boy was here to learn, not behave like he was already part owner.

'Yes,' Antonio barked, voice harsher than he intended. 'What?' Whoever answered had presence enough to fill the chef's voice with something very close to respect. 'I'll be there.' The chef listened again. 'We'll be there,' he agreed, amending his words.

'Scrap the tomatoes,' he told the Australian boy. 'We're closing for tonight.' He nodded at Idries. 'Turn off the ovens and put everything back in the cooler . . .'

'You know,' said Raf, the nouvelle ville rattling by behind his head in a succession of dusty shops and pavement tables. 'There's something I still don't quite get.' Tapping his last Cleopatra from its packet the way Hamzah's builders did, Raf crumpled the empty box and dropped it. A flick of a cheap lighter and he passed the cigarette to Isabeau, who dug deep and handed it back.

'What's to get?' Isabeau asked flatly.

'Who are you running from?'

Jagged glass/broken bulbs, Raf was going to have to get over matching images to emotions, his own and other people's. Shock of some kind had finally swallowed Isabeau; shaking her hands and dragging her thumb repetitively across her fingertips, grinding her heels into the floor.

One 30c ticket each had bought them an hour in which Isabeau shipped her growing panic out towards Tunis Maritime, back towards Place de Barcelone and up to Place Halfaouine. Parc du Belvedere. Place Bardo. Crossing the rails for a different line, switching directions. Two stops this way, one stop that, change lines every third move. Regular as clockwork and about as useful. It was like watching chess played by a child who lacked the rules but had one set of winning moves written on the back of someone else's envelope.

'Welcome,' said Shibli as he climbed to his feet and touched his hand to his heart. Chef Antonio made do with returning a slight bow, not quite confident enough to return formal greetings to a Sufi master; particularly as the man still looked more like a bouncer than a mystic, what with his freshly shaved head, bare arms and pirate earrings. Although, admittedly, this time round Shibli wore a pale kaftan rather than his usual striped jellaba.

'Discard your knife.' Shibli pointed to a brass tray by the café door. It contained a handful of cheap switchblades and one ancient revolver.

'My knives remain in the kitchen.'

Shibli smiled. 'Then find a space,' he said, 'and make yourself comfortable.'

Antonio and his staff had reached Bab Souika in two taxis, passing through the gate into the medina on foot with a five-minute gap between each taxi. Partly this was caution, but mostly it was because the majority of taxis stuck to nouvelle ville, leaving the suburbs to buses and illegal cabs. And Idries said calling cabs out to Café Antonio would be a risk.

By the time the chef ducked under the low doorway to greet Shibli, his sous-chef was already settled on a bench at the far end of the room, apple-scented smoke filling the crowded vault from a *sheesha* on the floor in front of him. Chef and sous-chef looked at each other and Idries stood.

'Take my seat,' he suggested.

Antonio shook his head and pointed to a space on one of the longer benches. 'I'll be fine there,' he said. The embarrassment between them was palpable, made more obvious by this very public reversal of roles. In his kitchen Antonio was god, though he'd never claim so in the presence of his staff, most of whom were believers. Here it was Shibli and, to a far lesser extent, Idries who commanded the room. A dozen races and twice that many languages survived within the walls of the medina and there were very few penalties to being born *nasrani*.

Except now, except here. In the presence of those whose eyes were open, the wool wearers and Those Who Went Naked.

Every café, shop, restaurant and brothel in the city paid protection to Kashif Pasha's police. A few, no one knew how many, chose to pay again, a different kind of insurance. Chef Antonio was one of those. How much he paid was up to him and depended on how good a week he'd had. Sometimes, at the height of the 'packer season, a week could be very good indeed and Antonio would stuff an envelope with enough notes to make it fat and give this to Idries, who passed the envelope to Shibli. Where the money went after that neither Antonio nor Idries asked.

'Drink and eat,' ordered Shibli, nodding to a trayful of painted glasses filled with sweet mint tea and half a dozen yellow bowls rimmed around the top with white metal that wanted to be silver. The tray hung on a strap from around the neck of a small, one-armed man wearing *shalwar kameez* and a three-fist beard so wispy it hung like unspooled cotton. He was the only person in the room to whom Shibli was unfailingly polite and rumour had it that he was one whose eyes had been so completely opened that he was now near blind.

When everyone had eaten baklava and drunk tea Shibli clapped his hands once and the room fell silent. 'Where's Isabeau?' he demanded.

'With the soldier.'

'And where's the soldier?'

'Here,' said a voice from the curtained doorway. Pushing his way through dangling beads, Raf blinked at the thickness of smoke. Behind him, wearing a new coat, minus her scarf and with her hair tied back, came Isabeau. She was still shaking.

'We've been hiding,' Raf said.

'Who from?' Shibli looked interested.

Raf shrugged. 'Ask her,' he suggested, but his voice was gentle and his hand on Isabeau's arm was light as he guided her towards a space at one end of a bench.

'Take a seat,' Shibli told Raf. 'I'll ask when the time comes.' And with that, he reached into his kaftan and extracted a book-sized block of hashish, stamped on both sides with Arabic lettering. Pulling a clasp knife from his pocket, the Sufi prised it open and shaved a dark sliver from one corner.

'A fresh *sheesha*,' Shibli demanded and Idries disappeared through the bead curtain, returning with a waterpipe into which the Sufi crumbled both honey tobacco and fragments from the block. He took the first puff himself and passed the water pipe to Isabeau.

'I'm sorry about Pascal,' he said gently and Isabeau nodded. 'Such things happen,' he added. 'Sometimes they're unavoidable.' Shibli sighed. 'If you know who might have wanted him dead, then you must tell me . . .'

'I don't.' Isabeau's voice was small. Already distant.

'Then who were you running from?' The question was Hassan's, from the far corner of the room.

Isabeau glanced from Shibli to Raf, then back at Hassan. 'From myself,' she said and both Raf and Shibli nodded.

The story was complicated the way such stories usually are. But it seemed Isabeau's brother had been found murdered in an alley behind Maison Hafsid, a restaurant at which some of Café Antonio's staff regularly worked and where her brother was pastry chef.

Ahmed, a cousin to Idries, had been arrested for the crime. Shock mixed with outrage in Idries' voice as he admitted this, but his predominant tone was worry. Despite their apparent closeness Idries admitted his cousin was not eminently likable. Ahmed's habit of using his fists was mentioned. His inability to walk away from a brawl. His use of alcohol.

'But Pascal was stabbed?' Raf asked.

'Yes,' said Idries, 'that was what it said on the news.'

'Did Ahmed carry a knife?'

Raf's question earned him an amused glance from Shibli.

'We all carry knives,' Idries said gently.

'But Ahmed was the kind of man to use his fists?'

'That's true,' Shibli admitted, eyes suddenly shrewd.

'So, what about witnesses?' Raf asked gently. It was a dangerous game he was playing. Giving them more of himself than was safe to give. But one that was worth the risk. Maison Hafsid was a step closer than Café Antonio. And Shibli had Isabeau under his wing. A wing Raf imagined to be vast and black, batlike, spreading its spines across the city and hiding wonders in its shadow.

'Did anyone see what happened?'

'God . . .' Hassan's voice was harsh. 'You talk like a policeman.'

'That's because I was a policeman,' said Raf flatly. 'I've been many things. Not all of them good.' He stared round the windowless room and when his gaze stopped it was on Idries. 'So, were there any witnesses?'

'We don't know,' admitted Idries. His voice tired. 'And we can't ask Ahmed,' he added, 'because the police won't let anyone see him until he's pleaded guilty.'

Raf nodded, as if this was to be expected. 'Okay,' he said, 'you'll need to show me the site.'

CHAPTER 25

Thursday 24th February

'You be good,' Hani told Ifritah, placing the cat firmly on her bed. No sooner done than Ifritah jumped for the suitcase Hani was trying to buckle, claws ripping into old leather as she scrabbled for a hold.

Hani sucked her teeth. 'Try,' she told Ifritah. 'At the very least, try . . .'

Hong Kong Suisse had delivered her cash. Late, admittedly, but Hani was no longer cross about that. She had a party dress made from red silk, green velvet and real gold embroidery. It was designed for someone several years older than Hani and on Zara would have been indecently short. On Hani it fell to her ankles like a ball gown. Added to which Madame Fitmah had even given her a discount on a pair of matching shoes.

Mortgaging her uncle's madersa to finance the trip had been wrong, Hani realized that. And if she'd been allowed access to her own money it wouldn't have been necessary. But to get that would involve asking Hamzah or the Khedive, and they'd want to know why she needed money. Hani shook her head. Sometimes simplicity was everything.

So she'd written to Uncle Ashraf's bank instead, using headed paper and quoting his account number, which had been ridiculously easy to find since it featured on various statements kept in a desk outside his bedroom. Marked *confidential*, her letter inquired delicately about the opportunities for mortgaging a famous seventeenth-century madersa in a prime position. An equally circumspect (Hani liked that word) reply from HKS suggested that, unless His Excellency really wanted a mortgage of the kind that needed repaying over a number of years, the best option might be a straight loan, at no interest, since usury was obviously forbidden. A settlement fee to be paid as the final part of the reckoning, please see sample contract enclosed.

The bank had used longer words than that – because banks always use complicated words – but that was what Hong Kong Suisse meant.

Hani's reply ended with a flamboyant impression of her uncle's initials and the only thing that stopped her from scanning an original into her laptop and using that was a slight worry that HKS might use some kind of fluorescing system to distinguish fountain pen from printer ink.

As a final touch, Hani found her uncle's spare comb, removed a single hair and dropped it into the envelope, which might be one touch too many but by then she'd stuck the envelope and used her only stamp.

Next morning and the morning after found Hani waiting for the postman, cat in hand. Swapping Ifritah for his fat bundle of letters she chatted about the weather while sorting through the pile. The letter she wanted was one of five. Four of these were bills, three of them red reminders . . .

The loan was agreed and the fact Ashraf Bey had initialled rather than signed his contract as requested was nowhere mentioned: but then Hani remembered reading that the Empire State Building had once been mortgaged against an unsigned deed and she was no longer surprised. All that remained, those were the words HKS used, all that remained was for His Excellency to nominate a receiving account.

Hani took this to mean she should tell the bank where to send the money. So she wrote again on a sheet of the paper taken three days earlier from her uncle's office at the Third Circle.

Stealing it was easy. All Hani had to do was buy a chocolate sundae at Le Trianon, leave most of it and use the café's internal lift to go straight to C3's reception on the floor above. The story she'd prepared about wanting to collect a toy dog from her uncle's office went unused. Madame Ingrid was giving evidence to a tribunal investigating the crimes of Colonel Abad and with their office manager gone, most of her junior staff had left for lunch early, while the rest just nodded at Hani or ignored her.

Taking a single sheet of headed paper from its holder on Uncle Ashraf's desk, Hani promptly changed her mind and slipped a thick wad of the stuff into her rucksack. One never knew when it might become useful. As an afterthought, she added a rubber stamp that sat on the desk beside the wooden box holding the paper. It was a very ornate rubber stamp with brass claws to hold the block of rubber and an ivory handle, but it was still a rubber stamp.

From the desk of Colonel Pashazade Ashraf al-Mansur, Ashraf Bey.

Looking at the faint script left by the stamp on the inside of her wrist Hani raised her eyebrows. She hadn't realized her uncle was a colonel; at least, she didn't remember knowing that, but the fact didn't surprise her. Secret agents and assassins were bound to have military ranks, it was obvious really. Everyone in North Africa had a rank of some kind or other.

Hani was just letting herself out of the office when she finally realized what she'd missed. A briefcase, with a gunmetal grey combination lock, below a black coat hanging from a rack topped by an Astrakhan hat she'd never seen Uncle Ashraf wear, tight curls of baby fur soft enough to make Hani cringe.

Hat, coat, briefcase.

Hide in plain sight.

Since Madame Ingrid might notice if the case disappeared, Hani resolved to examine it in situ. Would it be very conceited . . . ? Assuming she really was eleven, not ten, Hani fed her own birthdate into the combination lock and Uncle Ashraf's case opened first try. Which was just as well, because there was serious potential for stalemate if it had been his own birthday and it was bound to be the birthday of someone or other.

Statistically most combination locks used a birth date within the owner's immediate family, 73 percent of them in fact. And Hani knew just how hard her uncle worked at appearing normal. Being a son of Lilith required one to hide in plain sight, normal being interchangeable with invisible. Hani knew all about it. And if she ever forgot, all she had to do was stare in a mirror.

Hani paused to think that last thought through, which was slightly recursive but necessary. She had no doubt she could become exactly like her uncle if she tried. Actually, Hani suspected she'd become like him whatever. Flipping open his case, she spread her catch on the tiles. Another gun. No, she corrected herself, a Colt *revolver*. Specifics were always important. A *carte blanche* which was – Hani flipped it open – less than a month out of date. And inside it something else.

Folded within the *carte blanche* was a letter from a lawyer in Tunis adressed to her aunt Nafisa. Skimming the script as it flowed, elegant and fluid, from right to left across a perfectly ordinary piece of office paper, Hani began to memorize the contents word for word. It seemed that Zari Moncef al-Mansur, eldest son of the old Emir of Tunis had married Sally Welham, an English photographer on the . . .

The date was so wrong that Hani brushed it aside, stumbling over the fact that he'd divorced her five days later and halting altogether when she got to the date of her uncle's birth. Had the letter been printed out on some computer she'd have dismissed the year as a simple typing error but the note was handwritten, which made the date either beyond careless or very odd indeed.

Pocketing the letter, Hani turned to a strip of Zaras, the photo-booth kind. Younger, somewhat fatter, her eyes less troubled than now, despite the scowl with which she faced the camera. And then a photograph of Uncle Raf, staring into the sun with the *Jammaa ez Zitouna* in the background.

Okay, so whatever he'd told Aunt Nafisa before she died, Uncle Raf *had* been to Tunis because la Grande Mosquée, built by the Emir Ibrahim Ibn Ahmed in 856 c.e. was not only the second largest mosque in Ifriqiya (the largest was in Kairouan) but also one of North Africa's most instantly recognizable heritage sites.

In the photograph he looked older. That was, Uncle Ashraf looked as he did now, not as he should have done back when this was obviously taken. There was one final photograph.

'Oh . . .' Hani placed it facedown on the tiles and carefully packed the Zaras and Uncle Ashraf outside la Grande Mosquée into her rucksack, sliding them between sheets of headed paper. The Colt she put back into her uncle's case. That left his final photograph.

The girl didn't look poor – on her wrist was an Omega and an empty camera case hung around her neck. But the Fat Boys were definitely frayed and her feet were both bare and dirty. Her hair also looked like it needed a wash, being matted into rat tails around her thin face.

What shocked Hani was not the dirty hair or bare feet. Not even the half-open shirt she wore, washed so fine that what couldn't be seen of the woman's breasts through the gap was revealed by the translucence of the cloth. It was the way she leered into the lens, her mouth half-open, her eyes obviously fixed on the person holding her camera.

This Hani hadn't considered and she doubted if Zara had either. Men went to brothels and, if they were sensible, women ignored this fact. So Hani had learnt from listening at the door to her late aunts, Nafisa and Jalila. As for mistresses, if a man could afford to run more than one house, this too was acceptable. Not least, Aunt Nafisa had sighed, because it did so help to lighten the load.

But a *nasrani* girlfriend . . . One who was thin, dirty and badly dressed?

Hani took another squint at the photograph. What with her rat's nest of fair hair and narrow face, washed-out eyes and tight lips the barefoot woman was unlikely to be anything but *nasrani* . . . If this was the real reason her uncle refused to marry Zara, then that changed everything. For the first time since he'd stamped up the stairs into the *qaa* all those months ago, Hani came close to deciding that maybe she didn't like her uncle after all.

CHAPTER 26

Flashback

'Too fucking hot.' Even at 30 mph, which was way too fast for the ruts in the track, the wind roared in Sally's ears and swept words from her mouth. So she said it again, just in case Per hadn't heard her the first time.

'Yeah,' said Per tightly, 'I know.' Swinging the wheel of his black Jeep to avoid a missing bit of road, he bounced Sally hard into her door, setting off a new round of swearing. The Jeep was eighteen years old, cigarette burns pocked the top of its plastic dash and he'd been forced to buy a petrol rather than diesel version. Black was also, in Sally's opinion, just about as stupid a colour as it was possible to find for skirting a desert; since it positively lapped up direct sunlight and made the interior too hot to touch.

The Jeep's air-conditioning – and there'd been air-conditioning when they started – had lasted for all of three days. Per blamed Sally's habit of hanging out of her side window for burning out the unit. Sally's view was that if he'd bought an open top model as she originally suggested, he wouldn't have needed air-conditioning and she wouldn't have had to keep opening the window to take photographs.

She now knew about his interest in mythology, bush meat and oral sex. His plans to open a restaurant and the age he first smoked blow. He knew she liked cameras.

Having first dwindled into tight-lipped sentences, their conversation had since shrunk into near silence. They still fucked like animals but no longer had anything to say to each other afterwards. There were a lot of relationships like that, Sally realized. And she did enjoy fucking Per far more than talking to him. And they were animals. So . . .

Opening the Leica with one hand, Sally removed a completed roll of film and dropped it into the foil packet she'd already ripped from its replacement.

'What the fuck is there to photograph?'

The whole absurd and cruel beauty of Ifriqiya's Chott el Jerid. Shrubs so hardy they came back from the dead, Lazarus-like; grasses able to tolerate saline levels that killed other plants; the distant pinks and yellows of minerals blooming across a flatbed of salt.

'Nothing,' Sally said, snapping shut her camera. 'Absolutely nothing.' Beside the road stretched the largest salt lake in North Africa. Rock-hard in summer and partly flooded in winter, drying in early spring to brine pooh and a treacherous skim of crust. Mysterious and wonderful. Utterly at odds with the olive groves and ubiquitous hedges of prickly pear that had made up yesterday's trip south. Those could have been found in southern Spain, Sicily or Greece.

This was different.

How different the Swede could not even begin to realize. Here life was leaner, sharper and better able to deal with exotic levels of deprivation. At the edges of existence, life was forced to make a compromise. One that the world would soon find itself forced to make if the canker of global interests could not be cured.

In that at least Wu Yung was right. Although his way was not her way. Something the old Chinese man had still to realize. Any more than her way was Atal's way or even Per's . . .

Sally Welham shook her head. Per had the soft liberal reflexes of his class, race and age. He would no more understand what she wanted from the chott than accept how she intended to achieve it. He was a mindless fuck and a zipless one at that; defined by overprivilege, education, a simplistic rejection of Calvinism and a carpetbag of beliefs strip-mined from other cultures.

Whereas she . . .

At least Sally had the grace to grin. Grin, shrug and discard the comparison. She was the same, the difference was that she knew it.

'Ruin,' said Per, seconds ahead of slamming on his brakes. Sand slid down a bank like snow and when the Jeep stopped it was half on the track and half off, one rear wheel hanging over the side of a ditch.

'How about giving me some warning?' Sally snapped.

'I just did,' Per said and, pushing open his door, he was gone, all stiff-backed and straight-shouldered.

Sally sighed.

Once out of the jeep, she casually dropped her jeans then stayed to watch the warm stream run mercury-like over the sand's crust, hardly touching its surface. That was the problem, rainfall raced across the desert's surface like piss, filling oueds and flooding chotts and wadis. Grasses grew, flowers happened, insects bred; life blossomed and died in the time it took the sky to squat.

Still grinning ruefully, Sally stepped out of her jeans, yanked her T-shirt inside out and went to find Per. He'd be looking for mosaics in the ruins of some hovel he'd insist was Roman.

'Don't walk on it,' Per said, not looking round. He was on his hands and knees sweeping rubbish from a floor with his fingers. Sally was willing to bet it was made from stamped-down dirt and that she had a better chance of becoming pope than Per did of finding a priceless mosaic beneath the crap that carpeted his goat hut.

Still, she let him brush away ring pulls and screw caps, plastic bottles and disposable nappies until his enthusiasm faded and he looked round to see Sally behind him, naked and with filthy feet. An equally dirty grin written across her face.

'Lie flat,' she told him, so Per did and Sally stepped forward and squatted again. His face was hot between her thighs, his tongue frantic. He licked and (later) fucked with the hunger of someone still drunk on her body. And Sally might have found such innocence endearing if she wasn't already waving Per good-bye in her head.

She found the Swedish kroner at the bottom of his sleeping bag, along with a passport that revealed Per to be three years older than he'd admitted. For a second Sally was tempted to take the money but Ottoman banks liked dollars, marks and francs; even sterling gave them trouble, so God alone knew what they'd have made of kroner.

Besides, her quest was almost over. And what Sally already had, sewn into the lining of her rucksack, was worth more than Per's cash or passport could ever be. Still smiling, she put his money back.

Sally woke Per with a hand job, something of a speciality for her, then rolled him onto his back and unzipped his bag before Per had time to notice its bottom end had been slashed open. He fucked with his eyes closed, even in daylight, spasming beneath her.

Little death they used to call it. They being almost every culture at some time or other. And so it was, in its way. Sex was the point at which individuality became unimportant. Life's purpose over in everything but name the first time one fucked and was fertile; or would have been, but for contraception, medical advances and falling levels of fertility introducing design flaws into Darwin.

When the deed was done the torch was passed, to flame or die, except that now science kept even the weakest flames alight. Mutations happened for a reason, Sally accepted that utterly. And benevolent or not, Galton was right. This was not a statement Sally would have dared say in front of anyone she knew. Only to herself did she dare say it and only recently,

725

once she realized that if the planet could not be saved, then humanity itself would have to be changed.

What the world needed was fewer farmers and more hunter-gatherers. Fewer cities and more wilderness . . .

'Sally?'

'What?'

'I need a pee,' Per said suddenly. He looked apologetic.

Sally stopped trying to rock the Swede back into action. 'No problem,' she said, shrugging as she clambered off him, watching Per watch the darkness between her legs.

'I'll see you in a second,' he said, blushing.

The moment he was gone, she rolled up his sleeping bag with the money and passport still in the foot, and stashed the roll in his Jeep alongside her own. And by the time Per came back Sally was dressed and in the passenger seat, ready to go.

'What about . . . ?'

'Later' said Sally. 'First let's get breakfast.' Glancing at their map, she pointed to a gap between two red hills. 'There's a town on the other side with a government hostel. It's got showers.'

For the first time in days Per looked almost happy.

The hills turned out to be sand dunes and the road which had been worn when they set out quickly became little more than a path. Per's fleeting happiness vanishing with the blacktop. Tyre marks were few and mostly softened to shadow with a drifting sand somewhere between grit and dust. The only fresh tracks were donkey or camel.

'It's an oasis town,' Sally promised. 'Probably ancient.'

Per kept his doubts hidden behind a pair of shades.

'Another mile,' said Per, when ten minutes had turned into half an hour and the hills were behind them, 'then we turn back.'

'Sure thing.' Sally lifted the Leica off her lap and tucked it inside its leather case, stuffing the case under her seat. The rolls of film she pushed through a crease between the upright of her seat and the seat itself, casually reaching behind her to do so. If another mile came and went without incident, then she was in the wrong place and several months of her life had been wasted.

Only Sally was in the right place and it took less than five minutes to run over a screamer. At least Sally assumed that was what alerted Moncef Pasha's guards as Per's Jeep crested a ridge and stopped.

'Shit,' said Per and Sally could only agree.

Spread out below them was a complex of squat buildings, painted a dirty red-yellow to blend in with the earth. A handful of antique-looking trucks was parked in the middle, hidden beneath a hangar's worth of

726

camouflage netting that looked like it had been there forever. Under the cover of another awning two antlike figures were working on the blades of a helicopter.

Sunlight heliographed from a roof as an officer swung his binoculars and finally caught sight of the Jeep.

'That doesn't look like an oasis town,' Per said, slamming his gears into reverse. Somewhere below a siren was sounding.

'Soldiers,' said Sally but her warning was unnecessary. No one, not even Per at his most stoned could miss five teenagers strung across the track, squat rifles pointing directly at his windscreen.

'Bad idea,' she said.

In reply Per stamped on his throttle and hung a left, stalling when he hit the base of a dune. Which was how Per, rather than Sally, got shot through the leg by a fourteen-year-old in designer combats, Armani shades, a silk kufiyyah. Every thing from tyres to doors got raked in one long burst and all the shots stayed low. Combat training had conditioned the soldier to take her opponents alive if possible.

Opening her door, Sally tossed out her rucksack and stepped out of the Jeep, her hands already clasped behind her head. She'd been in enough trouble to know the drill. Unasked, Sally assumed the position, face so close to the hood that she could feel heat shimmer from its surface.

Per meanwhile had a white T-shirt at arm's length and, between sobs, was waving it frantically through his window. Sally almost pointed out that in the desert white wasn't necessarily the colour of surrender (the Mahdi's battle flag had been pure white, until dust, blood and machine-gun bullets rendered it into sullied rags), but she decided not to bother. The Emir's guard looked competent enough to recognize an idiot when they met one.

'Prince Moncef?' said Sally, pointing to the complex below. Although no one replied, she got the feeling that at least one of them understood. Unless it was just that the word Moncef was familiar.

'He's famous,' Sally added. 'For making plants grow where most plants die.'

The soldier with the highest cheekbones stared at Sally with interest. Since the entire troop was female and any vibes, conscious or otherwise, came in under Sally's school-tuned gaydar, she figured the soldier's look was entirely professional.

'He improves on nature,' said Sally and promptly wondered if what she'd just said counted in North Africa as blasphemy. 'Takes the potential God has given it,' she amended, 'and develops that.'

'You think this is good?' Although she obviously understood English, the

727

lieutenant asked her question in French, in an abrupt and very Parisian way that made Sally glance at her, wondering.

'The man's a genius.'

'Whatever that means . . .'

'It means,' said Sally, 'that you leave an area of art or science changed from how you found it . . . I learnt that at university,' she added.

'What did you study?'

'Genetics at Selwyn College, Cambridge.' She named a college at random. Although, when she thought about it, that wasn't entirely true. Selwyn was where Drew, the nanchuku nut, went, which was random enough.

The woman nodded and loosened the kufiyyeh that was half-obstructing her mouth. She was not, Sally realized, Arab in origin; her face was European. And now, when she spoke, her amusement came through clear and unobstructed.

'I suppose you want to see Moncef Pasha?'

'Yes,' said Sally, 'if that's possible . . .'

Blond hair, small breasts, skin like milk . . . Once the questioning was done, then yes. 'Chances are that might prove possible,' said Eugenie de la Croix. The smile on her face turned sour.

Halfway down the track, with the Jeep temporarily abandoned somewhere behind them and the Emir's complex up ahead, Sally clutched at her gut and begged, practically in tears to be untied. She needed to use a nearby thornbush and she needed to use it now if she wasn't to soil herself.

'You leave your bag with me.'

Sally nodded meekly and dumped her rucksack at the feet of the officer, running towards the bush with indecent haste. Only, once there, what Sally actually did was kneel, hook out her contraceptive cap and kick sand over it. Then she counted to sixty and pulled up her shorts.

'Feeling better?'

Sally smiled at the woman. 'Much,' she said. 'Thank you.'

CHAPTER 27

Monday 28th February–1st March.

Goats grazed in three rooms at the back, wandering in from a darkened courtyard through a hole in the rear wall. They were white with black faces and stunted horns, too fat, overfed and pampered to be convincing scavengers. Besides, their leather collars betrayed them. Most goats kept within the medina made do with string, if they had collars at all.

Chef Edvard kept the goats to amuse. And amuse his dinner guests they did. But then Maison Hafsid's evening crowd were usually friends of Kashif Pasha, those with money and those who had actually travelled outside Ifriqiya, the kind of customers cosmopolitan enough to pay for the privilege of eating elegantly prepared retrofusion in the dining room of a draughty, half-wrecked Ifriqiyan palace opposite a mosque still called *new* because it was constructed during a trade boom in the mid-eighteenth century.

Maison Hafsid was owned by a tall and elderly Madagascan called Abdur Rahman, so labelled because this was one of the names specified by the Prophet as beloved by God. And, as his mother had reminded him often, 'Names matter. So will you be called on the day of judgment . . .'

On his arrival in Tunis ten years earlier Abdur Rahman changed his name to Edvard. And under this name he was known to most, even Kashif Pasha and his mother Lady Maryam. But it was as Abdur Rahman he owned Maison Hafsid, because this was the name that mattered. And it was as Abdur Rahman that he had shares in Café Antonio and three other restuarants.

'You done yet?' Chef Edvard shouted.

'Nearly,' said Raf and raised his chopper. Steel bit into flesh, then wood. Slicing the lamb into rough chunks, Raf slid them off his chopping board and into a glass bowl. Some kitchens kept specialist butchers.

At Maison Hafsid the work was done by whomever Chef Edvard designated. It kept the cuts from getting too neat.

'I'll take it,' said Isabeau and the bowl was gone.

'Well,' Raf said, entirely to himself, 'we're here.' His voice echoed the fox's growl. That was their compromise. The fox still spoke but now Raf realized the fox was him. So far it seemed to work for both of them.

'Yeah,' said Raf. He tried not to mind that the fox sounded impossibly smug. As if it, rather than chance or Raf, had been responsible for getting Raf to the kitchens of Maison Hafsid, site of one murder and supplier of culinary staff to the notables of Tunis. 'Right where we need to be . . .'

Had the fox been someone else, Raf could have reminded it that its plan of sneaking off to hunt down Ibrihim Ishaq of Isaac & Sons, Kairouan, had not been an unmitigated success. As well as mentioning that Those Who Went Naked had not turned out to be the revolutionary masterminds Eugenie seemed to suggest. He could even have admitted that he missed Hani and Zara and was adrift in a city with only an instinct that here was where he was meant to be to keep him from going home.

But he'd only be telling himself. And they both knew that.

There were Turkish baths less hot than the cellar kitchens at Maison Hafsid, so everyone kept telling Raf, who was beginning to believe them. Idries had already taken him to one of the city's poorer public baths, a place of cracked tiles and broken mosaic situated just behind the central market, where he'd sat surrounded by a dozen strangers, sweat dripping from every pore as a robed attendant ladled water onto heated stones.

The cleansing room had stunk of physical effort and butchers who killed most days but sweated themselves clean once or twice a week because that was all they could afford. They were polite to the stranger in their midst. Not friendly but polite. And once, when talk touched on Carthage Dynamo vs. Sophia Crescent, the conversation widened to include him. Other than that, the atmosphere had been restrained, almost elegant in a peeling, impoverished sort of way.

Maison Hafsid was something else. No one was polite. At least not down in the kitchens. And what constituted conversation was a hard-edged banter likely to get you knifed in most bars in Seattle. Ear-bleeding nu/Rai ripped from a corner-mounted wall speaker. In the kitchen Raf didn't speak at all. He screamed into the steaming chaos. And others shouted back. Mostly about his parentage, race, sexual orientation and short life expectancy.

Anyone who took offense at Chef Edvard worked elsewhere. Actually, anyone who took offense, full-stop, left for some other industry: one not driven by impossible hours, heavy attitude and dirt-cheap drugs.

'You,' he said to Raf, next time Raf staggered by under the weight of a lamb carcass. 'I want to know where to file you.'

Three kinds of scum ended up in kitchens apparently. Those on the run too stupid to do anything else, brilliant and spoilt artists, and finally mercenaries, those in it for the money, mostly solid and reliable line cooks. Some American years back had given his name to this law, but Chef Edvard didn't mention that, he merely wanted to know which label fitted Raf.

'All of them,' said Raf.

'All?' The elderly Madagascan eyeballed his newest recruit for a long second, then slapped Raf on the shoulder. 'Misfits are good,' he said, his Arabic thicker than coffee grounds, 'they stay longer.'

Everything Raf had learnt at Café Antonio was unlearnt at Maison Hafsid. At Hafsid no one ever served swordfish or blackened chicken, even if customers asked politely. Right now Raf's job was to braise those chunks of lamb (bone and fat and skin and all). The ironically crude chunks reached the table drizzled with a custard-yellow sauce made from cloudberries flown in from Table Mountain. Given the price Maison Hafsid charged for its speciality dishes, Raf could only imagine the berries travelled first class.

'Faster,' Edvard barked.

Raf nodded, but the chef was shouting at someone else.

On a marble slab to Raf's left were a series of bowls filled with herbs and spices, which a kid of about eleven kept topped on a regular basis by ripping handfuls of wilting oregano from fat twigs or grating nutmeg against a tiny grid hung on a string around his neck. Raf used a lot of oregano and nutmeg; also olive oil, anchovies, dried juniper berries and small pods for which Raf didn't yet have a name. The chef seemed to use those in almost every dish.

A great aluminium pot roiled on the edge of a hundred degrees at a station behind Raf, creating its own microclimate, waiting to soften whatever pasta was required. Linguine mostly, with a weird locally made thread noodle that came semiopaque and ended up near invisible; not that much of either got eaten to judge from the quantity scraped from dirty plates into a metal trough that ran the edge of one wall. The noodles and pasta seemed to be something between a base and a garnish.

'A hand to six . . .'

The chef's eyes found Raf, who held up five fingers and nodded. Five minutes to braise the lamb for table six and pass it across for plating. That was the difference between home cooking and doing it for real.

731

Restaurant food got dressed, just like the customers. And an artistic sprig or a near-odourless tasteless swirl of sauce could hide culinary sins as easily as discreet makeup and good clothes could hide sins of the flesh. Warm plates, flamboyant furnishings, elegant garnishes and adequate food, the demands of haute cuisine at Maison Hafsid were less than its devoted clientele imagined.

'Three,' shouted the chef and Raf swirled his pan, smelling oil, seared flesh and oregano. Across the other side of the cellar was a wood oven for which Raf sometimes seared lamb or beef to be roasted, so that no steam from raw meat might dampen the oven's desertlike dryness. It wasn't really Raf's job but Raf was racking up favours, taking shifts he didn't want, helping to hump crates too heavy for one person alone. He'd even rescued a cucumber sauce for wild greyling with a nylon sieve, a splash of Chablis and nerves of steel, decanting it onto a warm plate seconds ahead of the plate heading for the hatch.

Mind you, Raf probably wouldn't be forgiven that one. The sauce came from an Algerian sous-chef and the deputy was less than happy. Particularly now Chef Edvard had decided Isabeau's earlier boast about Raf's having been a sous-chef himself in Seattle was true.

To test the claim, Raf had been handed a red fish of a species he'd never seen and been told, in front of a watchful kitchen, to find a knife and fillet the thing.

Pulling a Sabatier from the back of his belt, Raf oiled up a sharpening block and set about giving himself an edge. All the while checking the fish, noticing its every curve and the geometric relationship between anus, eyes and upper fin, the way the scales changed near the tail.

When Raf cut, it was swift, taking his stance and the looseness of his wrist from a Sushi master who ran a dockside café his old boss Hu San often frequented. Raf spent one memorable evening there near the beginning of his time with the Five Winds, as Seattle's most influential triad was named. And for a while, with tiny dish after dish reaching their table and Hu San chewing in silence, her eyes closing at particularly impressive slivers of raw fugu, Raf thought he was in disgrace. And then, when she looked up and smiled almost without thinking, he realized she intended to sleep with him.

He still hadn't started to shave and she was in her late thirties, maybe more, but her tastes were for the raw and the fresh. Whatever, the moment never arose and as her Lincoln pulled up outside his flat Hu San dismissed him with a polite good-bye and left him standing on a sidewalk in the rain.

Raf cut three times in all; Once to gut the fish and discard its entrails. Once to fillet one side of the fish and once to fillet the other. The skin he'd already removed in a single scoop of his thumb, not using his knife and not damaging the flesh.

'Done?' Chef Edvard had asked, his face impassive.

Raf nodded and waited while the chef told a boy to fetch a set of scales. First Edvard weighed the entrails, then both fillets and finally bones and skin.

'Not as bad as I expected.'

Behind his eyes Raf scowled but he kept silent, eyeing a strip of skin so clean it could have been sent for tanning. Not a flake of flesh clung to the spine or ribs, the cut at tail and gills was near perfect.

'I'm out of practice,' Raf announced finally and the skeletal chef almost smiled.

Then came three questions.

Where had he cooked before?

Raf named Antonio's pizza place and a five-star hotel in Seattle so famous that even the silent and anxious Isabeau recognized its name.

'This true?'

That question was for Isabeau. Asked almost politely. No one had said anything to Raf but he'd caught the glances. There wasn't a single person in the kitchens unaware of her brother's murder. Even Chef Edvard was making allowances.

'He's been working for Antonio,' she said. 'I can't guarantee the other.'

'Why do you want to change jobs?'

'Debts,' said Raf. 'Waiting to be paid.'

'I work my staff harder,' Chef Edvard told Raf flatly. 'Believe me I make you sweat for every extra cent.'

And so the slot became his, at least until Idries' cousin got released from prison, if he did. Two points went unspoken. One, should Raf turn out okay then Edvard might keep him on anyway, and two, if Idries' cousin was not released, then Raf had the job until someone better came along.

But first Raf had to do a day's suds diving to show he was serious. And do it for nothing. Those were the rules. So he scraped plates, hosed them down and loaded them into a washer the size of a small truck for as long as it took for some elderly Philippine to fry his own fingers in a red-hot wok – which was about four hours. The man wanted to work on but Edvard insisted on wrapping his hand in a towel filled with ice and ordered him home. Only the promise of a full day's pay got the crying man out of the kitchen and into a corridor that ended in steps leading up to an alley at the back. Even then someone had to walk the man up the stairs and shoo him out into the alley.

'Want me to handle his station?'

'Screw up and you're out.'

Raf took that as a *yes* and stripped to the loose cotton trousers he'd borrowed from Antonio's and would one day return, with luck. He took a coat someone handed him.

'Nice scars.'

The chef's smile was mildly mocking, as if his own might prove far more impressive if only he could be persuaded to discard his white jacket with the word *Edvard* embroidered over the pocket in red silk. And to judge by the jagged seams up both wrists and a yellow callus thick as tortoiseshell at the base of one thumb anything was possible.

So Raf cut lamb and braised goat, spatchcocked quail and generally kept the meals coming, on time and done as ordered.

'It's not a skill, you know . . .'

'What isn't?'

'This shit. Being able to do everything. That's just a design function. You telling me you can't recognize an adaptive mechanism when you see one?'

'Hey, white boy . . . You okay?' Raf looked up from wiping out his iron skillet to find the tall Madagascan standing next to him, frowning. A couple of the others were staring across as well.

'Sure,' Raf said. 'Just talking to myself.'

'Well,' said Chef Edvard, 'when you've got a moment.'

They went to the table, an old black thing that looked as if it came from a French farmhouse that had burned down. Fire damage chewed along one edge but someone, probably years before, had scraped most of it away with the flat of a knife and put that edge to the wall.

'Drink,' Chef Edvard said, pouring Raf a glass of *marc*. 'And then listen . . . I've got a job if you're interested. You know about Kashif Pasha's party?'

The whole of Tunis knew. At his mother's suggestion, the Emir's eldest son was holding a dinner to celebrate his parents' forty-fifth wedding anniversary. If both of them turned up, it would be the first time they'd met in slightly over forty-four years. The meal was Kashif Pasha's attempt to heal the rift, a peace offering to his father and a sign of the pasha's developing maturity where the Emir was concerned. That was the official version anyway.

'You want me to cook?'

Amusement tinged the old man's eyes. 'You're not that good,' he said. 'You wait tables . . . Still interested?'

'Oh yes,' said Raf, 'it's exactly the kind of opportunity I've been waiting for.'

Juggling a fat cowpat of harissa in her hands, Isabeau tried to stop it from dripping oil onto her jeans. Chef Edvard preferred dry mix that needed added oil but none Isabeau and Raf had seen in Marché Central looked good enough, so she'd bought freshly made paste.

That was a difference between them, Raf decided. If the old Madagascan had sent him to buy dried harissa, then that's what Raf would have bought. The best he could find from the range available. However, he was there to buy lamb. And talk to Isabeau.

Raf sighed.

'What?' Isabeau asked.

'Chef Edvard's worried about you . . .' He shrugged. 'Everyone's worried. So if you need to take time off, maybe go back to Tarbarka?' Raf named a town on the northern coast. The only town in Ifriqiya where descendents of French colonists still outnumbered residents of Arab and Berber stock.

'That's why we were sent out together? So you can suggest I go home to my grandmother?'

'In a way.'

'Yeah' said Isabeau, 'I can see everyone liking that. Solves the problem doesn't it? Isabeau's gone off the rails so let's send her some-where else . . .' Isabeau's voice was loud enough to make a man standing by the shellfish stall stop shovelling cracked ice onto a marble tray and watch them instead, iron trowel poised in his hand.

'I don't think chef meant it like that,' Raf said.

'Really?' said Isabeau. 'How did he mean it?'

'He's trying to help.'

'No one can help,' Isabeau said fiercely. 'What's happened has happened. Pascal is dead. Nothing anyone can do will bring him back. I have to live with that fact.' Tears were rolling down her face, glittering trails of misery. 'Nothing can make it better.'

Carrying a cape of lamb over one shoulder, Raf watched the crowds part to let him through rather than risk having blood dragged across their clothes. The floor of the indoor market beneath his boots was wet with melted ice and slick with tomatoes dropped and trodden to pulp, the green walls sticky with handprints and streaked with condensation. He walked ahead at Isabeau's insistence. She needed space. Time enough to get a grip on her tears.

They exited near Bab el Bahar, the city's sea gate in the days before the ground between the medina and the Gulf of Tunis was mapped by

French engineers for ersatz Parisian boulevards now old enough to be heritage sites in their own right.

The bab still functioned as the main gate into the walled heart of Tunis. By law, no buildings within the medina could be changed from one use to another. Shops remained shops and cafés remained cafés but little money existed to pay for their upkeep so even the famous suq roofs that cast whole alleys into half gloom were pitted and peeling, cracked across their roofs like lightning, sometimes actually dangerous.

There were also alleys where people lived rather than just made or sold things. And the houses that lined these looked in on courtyards just as the walled city looked in on the suqs and the surrounding ville looked in on the walled city. Within the medina were small squares, the result not of planning but of enough narrow alleys meeting to make a passing space necessary. Maison Hafsid looked onto one of these.

The entrance doors to Chef Edvard's restaurant were studded with nails, as was usual, and with hammered strips of black iron that formed crescents, six-pointed stars and spirals, this last being reserved for the medina's grander houses. Both doors were mirror images of the other. Crescent for crescent, spiral for spiral.

These Raf avoided, heaving the lamb carcass around to the rear, where his struggle to lift it off his shoulder without covering himself in slime was observed by Isabeau and a boy sitting in a door opposite. Aged about seven, the boy was sorting straw hats into those damaged by winter rains and those still good enough to sell.

Every city was like this. Interlocking circles, poverty and plenty. As was every life. The only difference being that no one bothered to write guides about the picturesque poverty of London or New York, Seattle or Zurich. Or if they did, it was in no language Raf read.

'Has anyone asked him if he saw anything?'

'What?' Isabeau sounded puzzled.

'That boy,' Raf said, nodding to the child who was now watching them. 'Has anyone asked if he saw what . . .' He stopped as soon as he realized Isabeau was no longer listening. She had leaned against the wall, near the top of the stairs that led down to Maison Hafsid's cellar kitchens, hands over her face.

'It's okay,' said Raf, which was about as dumb a thing as anyone could say.

'No, it's not,' Isabeau said.

Raf took the lamb and the large lump of harissa Isabeau held, neatly wrapped in its grease-proof paper, and carried them down the steps, along a short corridor and into the kitchens. He spoke to Chef Edvard, got the man's agreement for letting him have time off to take Isabeau back to her flat, then went back to the alley. Isabeau was standing exactly where she'd been when Raf left. The boy with the hats was gone.

Salt on his tongue. Raf woke with Isabeau naked in his arms. Worrying enough. What made it worse was a blinding headache and the packet of condoms by her bed. They were unused, unlike the brandy bottle beside them.

Taking one out, Raf squinted at the small print. American, which he could have guessed from its gold coin wrapper. A quality mark, a use-by date and a warning from the Surgeon General about retrovirus.

'Belonged to my brother . . .' Isabeau said, opening one eye.

Nodding hurt, so Raf just watched her go back to sleep.

The use-by date was two years ahead.

Very slowly, Raf shifted one arm from under Isabeau's shoulders, twisted until his legs hung over the edge of the cast-iron bed and sat up, regretting it immediately. For the time it took him to stop feeling sick, he played that game where the room spun when he looked at it but stopped if he shut his eyes again. Between spinning and darkness Raf played a second game of remembering what was in the room and wondering, why?

Once expensive but lately fallen into disrepair, its sash window glazed with only a single pane of glass, the room was soulless, almost sullen. A small music system sat on a metal table, both chrome. Although the sides of the music system were ersatz, coated plastic. There were no pictures on the walls. No looking glass or dressing table.

'This isn't her room, is it?'

'No,' said Raf, agreeing with himself. 'It's not.'

The room was emotionally cold and Raf imagined Isabeau's real room to be littered with mementoes from a recently discarded childhood. A Cheb Rai poster. A row of those kitsch blue Chinese foals, piebald with dust as they rolled across some glass shelf. A vase, bad cut glass. An anorexically thin marble Madonna. The kind sold in St Vincent de Paul . . .

Raf reined in his headache. Ran that thought back.

Someone like him, or rather someone like the *him* he'd become back in El Isk, might wear jade wrist beads while carrying a silver-and-coral Fatima key ring but neither Hani nor Zara would ever own something forbidden just because they liked the way it looked. Even a rust-eaten antique Buddha that Raf had found in a suq and placed in an alcove in the *qaa* drew odd looks from both of them. Mind you, it drew scowls from Donna and she was Catholic.

Which meant . . .

737

'Let me get this right,' said Raf. 'You're sitting in a dead man's room beside a naked woman and you're internalizing some seminar on comparative religion?'

Yeah, Raf nodded to himself. That was it exactly.

He'd fucked Isabeau. No matter that his memory of the exact act was bricked off with rising doubts, alcohol poisoning and emotional shutdown. The very fact he was having this conversation with himself was proof enough.

Pulling back Isabeau's covers, Raf swallowed what he saw. Flash-freezing her high breasts, soft stomach and hips permanently into memory. Comparing her figure, despite himself, with his memory of Zara. They were alike enough to make Raf feel ashamed. The only real difference, apart from the fact he'd fucked one and not the other (and the one he'd fucked was not the one he loved) was that a small crucifix on a gold chain twisted sideways in the crease between Isabeau's breasts.

'Okay,' agreed Raf. That did explain the marble Madonna of his imagining.

There were plane trees beyond the window. Chrome blinds. A crack that ran across the floor where grouting between tiles had snapped along a stress line, then opened up, until the crack changed direction and broke tiles instead.

But the tiles were clean and recently scrubbed. Come to that the whole room was spotless.

'Which says what?'

That Pascal was too poor to afford repairs on the flat he shared with his sister but still liked it kept clean?

'Or wasn't anal enough to worry about interior decoration.'

That too, except the tiny music system, sandblasted metal bed and chrome table had anal-retentive written through them like rock. Walking to the bedroom door, Raf glanced at the area beyond. A living space with Toshiba screen. Black leather sofa. Another chrome-and-glass table. Doors led to a small kitchen. A bathroom with shower stall. And finally, a second bedroom, half the size of the one in which he awoke. The other difference was a lock recently fixed to the inside of that door. Ceramic foals sat on a glass shelf but there were no posters or pictures and no slim marble Madonna. Nothing of real interest in the small bedside cabinet.

'Well,' said a voice behind him, 'find what you were looking for?' The question came from Isabeau. She was leaning against the doorframe of what he now knew was her own room, wearing a towel, which only made Raf more aware of his own nakedness.

'What I was looking for?'

'You were going to find out who Pascal was, remember? Get inside his head and work out who might have really killed him. Since everyone believes Idries, who's convinced it wasn't his cousin. And apparently I'm meant to believe Idries too . . .'

Raf put a hand to his aching head. 'I told you I wanted to come here so I could *empathize*?'

Isabeau nodded.

'And the other stuff,' he looked at her towel, 'that just happened?'

'Sure,' said Isabeau, turning away. 'If you must put it like that.' Raf heard her feet on the tiles all the way back to the room they'd shared. There was a slam of the door. Two minutes of muted shuffling, then the noise of the door being opened again. He listened to her shoes slap the tiles, then she was gone with a slam of a different door.

Having dressed, Raf let himself out.

CHAPTER 28

A neatly bearded man in a tarboosh stared out from a creased page. Below him a caption informed the scruffy girl in black headscarf, jeans and silver trainers that the Emir's eldest son would be dining at the Domus Aurea and, in a return to best Ottoman tradition, his mother had asked that all attendants at the celebratory meal be both deaf and dumb.

Unfortunately, finding staff who fitted this profile while possessing sufficient experience had proved impossible. They had, however, all been carefully screened for suitability.

The rest of the page was equally bland, its headlines subdued and reverential; which was probably why someone had dumped that day's *El Pays* under a chair in the buffet car.

Putting down the paper, the girl swallowed the last of her coffee and returned her plastic cup to the attendant, even though she had to stand on a cat basket to reach his counter. Then, just to be tidy, she collected up half a dozen other discarded cups and returned those too.

'Thank you.' The man at the counter smiled. 'Are you this tidy at home?'

Hani nodded, even though it wasn't strictly true. Donna did all of the kitchen cleaning at the madersa and got cross if Hani tried to help. And although Khartoum had explained that Donna was the kind of person who preferred others not to interfere, this wasn't much help because Hani's aunt Nafisa had spent her life telling Hani to pick things up, tidy away her toys and generally be busy and industrious, preferably somewhere else.

So now Hani tidied on instinct. It was a hard habit to break.

'Problems?'

'Not really,' said Hani, putting down the last of the cups and nodding towards the next carriage. 'Unless you count blocked loos and messy basins.' She shrugged. 'You know soldiers . . .'

The man looked at her. 'Ifriqiya needs conscripts,' he said, more serious than before.

Hani looked like she wanted to disagree but all she did was shrug her thin shoulders and wrap her *hijab* more tightly around her face. 'You're probably right,' she said, 'but I'm not entirely sure it needs them to vomit in the basins . . .'

Despite himself the man smiled. 'Luckily,' he said. 'I have my own loo.'

Hani looked at him.

'For attendants only,' he explained carefully.

The girl kept looking and it was the man's turn to sigh.

'Through there,' he said and pointed to a blank door. 'Don't take long. I'm closing up in a minute.'

The girl who entered the first-class carriage wore dark glasses with drop-pearl earrings; and the only thing that detracted from the look, besides the fact Hani's glasses were too big and blood smudged one ear (where an earring had been forced through flesh), was a tatty rattan cat basket so large it scraped against her leg as she walked.

Catching sight of herself in a window Hani wiped away the blood with her finger and thumb and adjusted her shades.

'Is that seat taken?'

The foreigner in the stripy jacket looked so bemused that Hani switched to French and, as she thought, the seat by the door was free. Hani hadn't really expected him to understand Arabic, but Zara insisted its use was politically essential so Hani tried to remember to use it first. Quite why Arabic should be the natural language of North Africa when almost everyone she met spoke French, Hani wasn't sure.

'Okay,' said Hani as she scratched a fingernail against rattan. 'We're here.'

Inside Hani's basket, Ifritah scratched back, meowed noisily and then hurled herself against the grille with a thud, leaving the foreigner looking more bemused than ever.

'Wild cat,' Hani said, reaching for its handle. And it was almost true. The one thing Ifritah wasn't was house-trained . . .

Even before she stepped onto the platform Hani knew she was going to like Tunis. It had as much history as El Isk plus pirates, corsairs and freebooters. She really didn't understand why the Germans, in particular, and the Americans hated it so.

'Ready?' Hani asked her basket. Without waiting for Ifritah's answer, Hani pushed herself out of her seat, slammed down the window of her

741

still-moving carriage and swung open the door to a shout of outrage from a porter on the platform.

Jumping down Hani almost tripped over her new shoes. Really she'd wanted to keep her trainers, but dumped them in a bin along with her jeans, T-shirt and *hijab*. In their place Hani wore a skirt made from red silk with an embroidered green waistcoat over a white shirt. Since the silk, velvet and white cotton were sewn together, the outfit probably counted as a dress even if it didn't look like one.

On the breast of her green waistcoat Hani had pinned a spray of diamond feathers so impossibly extravagant they had to be fake. As the white shirt left more of her neck bare than Hani really liked, she'd borrowed a fat row of amber beads from Aunt Nafisa's old leather jewellery box. She knew the beads weren't of good quality. If they had been, her aunt would have sold them.

Stalking past the scowling porter, Hani worked hard on looking like someone who knew exactly where she was going. Grown-ups tended only to notice anxiety. So the secret to being invisible was to be seen. Hani smiled at that, pleased to realize she was finally beginning to think like her Uncle Ashraf.

'Okay,' she told Ifritah, 'first we send Zara a postcard, then we find a taxi . . .'

The postcard bit was easy. Hani had taken a free card from a rack in the transAtlas express and also a free pen; one of those cheap blue ones too short to write with neatly. It was currently pushed under half a dozen rattan strands on Ifritah's basket.

'Table,' Hani told herself, looking round the crowded platform. There were a lot of soldiers at one end, plus a dozen men in black uniforms with guns who might have been police. Whoever they were, they were so busy watching the soldiers separate people by sex and herd them into a tent or under a metal arch that they forgot to glance at Hani as she slid under a barrier and strode towards a café near the entrance to the station's marble concourse.

'Is this seat taken?' This time the man Hani asked understood Arabic and smiled an old man's smile as he told her it was free. He left Hani in peace to scribble her message and no one appeared from inside to take her order, both of which were a blessing. Message written, Hani thanked the old man for partial use of his table and headed for a nearby postbox.

Zara was going to be cross, that much was obvious. She'd been coldly furious when she first realized Raf was gone without a word and now she'd be more furious still. And not just with Uncle Ashraf.

'Tough.' By the time her card got delivered Hani intended to have found her uncle, delivered the diamond *chelengk*, and given him back his dark glasses. So if Zara did turn up in Tunis, she'd never know that Raf wasn't really on a secret mission. Mind you, that would probably just make her more furious still.

In the end Hani decided against trying to get a taxi. All her notes were too big anyway and she wasn't really sure where she needed to go . . .

Lieutenant Aziz liked station duty. It was undemanding, he got to drink endless cups of hot sweet cocoa given free by grateful cafés, and there was a long list of brother officers only too happy to share the work. This meant the lieutenant got to go home on time. He wasn't a real lieutenant, of course, just some math student from Bizerte unable to graduate until he'd done national service. That was the deal. Between passing his finals, which he already had, and actually graduating came a year in the army.

That he'd been commissioned into the National Guard the same month that he got married was his own bad luck. Or bad planning on the part of his mother. Either way, he'd been taking weeks' worth of grief from his colonel about his eagerness to sneak off early.

Of course, some of that eagerness really was about getting back to his new bride. The rest of it, well, politics weren't his thing but somehow everyone else in the regiment seemed to feel different.

'Excuse me . . .'

Lieutenant Aziz looked down to see a girl in ludicrously large dark glasses holding a rattan basket. She wore a dress that might have belonged to a gypsy princess in some German operetta.

'I'm trying to find my cousin.'

The girl looked so serious that Aziz almost laughed. Luckily he had a young sister and enough imagination to know that his sister hated people laughing at her. So instead he dropped to a crouch, aware that his men were watching.

'Are you lost?'

'Not yet.' The girl looked around her. 'But I will be soon if you don't help.'

Aziz smiled. 'When did you lose him?' He took it for granted that her cousin was male.

Hani looked blank.

'Your cousin,' said the lieutenant.

'He's not lost,' Hani said. 'I just haven't found him yet.'

Lieutenant Aziz paused. 'Okay,' he said. 'Your cousin was meeting you from the train . . .'

Hani shook her head.

'He didn't expect you to find your own way home?' Aziz looked so shocked that Hani reached out and patted his shoulder without thinking.

'Of course not,' she said. 'He doesn't know I'm coming yet.'

'He doesn't?' Runaways were the responsibility of the Ministry of Public Order, which meant he'd be perfectly justified in handing over the child and walking away. Something the lieutenant knew he wouldn't be doing.

Aziz started again.

'Where does your cousin live?'

'In the Bardo Palace. But he's going to be at Domus Aurea tonight.'

Hani wasn't quite certain how to put what happened next but whoever had been smiling out of those eyes was now hidden. All she got was perfect blankness.

'Domus Aurea . . .' Lieutenant Aziz dragged the address out as if uncertain where it should stop.

'That's right,' Hani twirled round to show off her outfit. 'I've come for the party.'

'And your cousin . . .'

'Kashif Pasha,' Hani said. 'Or the Emir, he's also a cousin.' She put her head to one side as she thought about that some more. 'Actually,' she said, 'everyone's a cousin, except Zara . . .'

The lieutenant commandeered a parked taxi by the simple expedient of telling its driver that his passenger was Emir Moncef's cousin. And having handed the child to a flustered officer at the gates of the Golden House, Lieutenant Aziz told the taxi to take him home.

CHAPTER 29

Flashback

'So, tell me . . .' Accompanying the demand came a mild slap. An aide-memoire, little more. A warning of what might become real. 'Why are you really here?'

'To see Prince Moncef.' Sally chewed the inside of her lip, hard enough to tear flesh, then spat the salt taste from her mouth, allowing it to dribble slowly down her chin. 'As I already told you. So why not just fuck off and . . .'

The second slap splashed blood across her cheek, as Sally had known it would. She spat more of the salt onto her chin, readying herself for another blow.

There were rules to this game. Hell, there were whole Web sites devoted to handling how to be questioned. Not that Sally needed Web sites for instruction. She'd been through the mill for real in London, Vienna and Florence. She'd got away without questioning in Madrid and never even been picked up in New York.

In Zurich the police had skipped on questioning and tossed her over the border with a warning that to return would result in a long prison sentence or worse. A leer from a fat uniform as he told her this was intended to indicate what might be worse than several years' incarceration in Europe's most boring country.

'Enough,' said a new voice. The light in Sally's face went out. A moment later fingers grabbed her bottom lip and yanked it down.

'Quite the little professional.'

They'd met before on the ridge overlooking the complex. Only this time Eugenie de la Croix wore black trousers and a white shirt, Jimmy Choo slingbacks and a scarf that did little to hide a waterfall of dark hair. Her beauty was such that Sally almost forgave the fingers pulling at her bleeding lip.

'Where did you learn that little trick . . . Seattle?'

745

'I wasn't in Seattle,' Sally replied from instinct and saw Eugenie grin.

'How about New York?' Although her eyes were amused, Eugenie's hold on Sally's lip tightened and there was a realness to her questions lacking until then. Eugenie was not the baby-faced guard she'd replaced. She could, and would, rip apart Sally's mouth. 'Well?'

Sally's answer was just about comprehensible.

'Really' said Eugenie, suddenly letting go the lip. 'You weren't in New York either?' She dropped a handful of papers onto a table and stood back so Sally could see. Photocopies of NYPD reports, mostly. Plus a fat file from a detective agency in Kuala Lumpur. There were also a handful of flimsies but what Sally noticed first was a P10, request for arrest, issued by MediPol, the terrorism-clearing group for Southern Europe, the Levant and North Africa.

'Cut off her clothes,' Eugenie ordered the puppy-faced recruit, who blinked. 'What?' said Eugenie. 'You have a problem with that?'

The recruit shook her head. 'No, ma'am.' She glanced between Eugenie and the English girl tied to a camp chair. 'Which end do you want me to start?'

The only remotely painful thing to happen after this involved a caustic lip salve and Eugenie's demand that Sally rinse her mouth out several times with Listerine. What remained of her shorts and the T-shirt she'd been wearing on arrival were removed, along with the contents of her pockets, never to reappear.

Having been washed and shampooed in a canvas bath, Sally was handed a cotton towel and told to dry herself and dress. The robe the young recruit offered Sally was white. The shawl was red, with tassels and geometric patterns. It took Sally a second to realize that she was meant to put it on her head.

'This is what you wanted, isn't it?' Eugenie said, stepping through a curtain that separated the bath from a room beyond. She was holding a gun, but loosely, like some expensive fashion accessory.

'What is?'

'To have Moncef Pasha's babies . . .'

The two women looked at each other. Their hard stares holding until it seemed that neither would break the gaze binding them tight. And then Sally nodded.

'He's been working on . . .'

'Quite probably,' said Eugenie. 'He's always working on some plan.' Her voice was studiedly dismissive. 'Most of them come to nothing. Does your friend know what you intend?'

The woman meant Per, Sally realized. 'I doubt it,' she said. Driving straight at the soldiers had been Per's choice. And if the Swede wanted to be that stupid then, once again, that was also his choice. All Sally wanted to do was meet the pasha and make her offer. Although, looking down at her gown, Sally realized this wish might be redundant. The man was already one giant step ahead of her.

Berlin always insisted the al-Mansurs controlled a network of spies that threaded the cities of the world, corrupting and turning good to bad. Offshore oil provided the means and dogma the driving force. Camps deep in the desert hid training facilities; shown only as occasional smudges against sand in satellite photographs released on Heute in Berlin, usually in the run-up to an oil summit.

Sally had always dismissed it as so much propaganda. Now she was no longer sure.

'What will happen to Per?'

Eugenie stopped twirling her Colt. 'He'll be shot,' she said lightly. 'Unless Moncef Pasha has a better idea.' Sally found it hard to work out whether or not the woman was joking.

'Why should humanity change?' Sitting next to Sally in the rear seat of a small Soviet attack helicopter, Eugenie was having trouble making herself heard. 'Especially given we're the ones winning . . .'

'What!'

Eugenie smiled at Sally's outrage and nodded towards the ground. 'Kairouan,' she shouted at the English girl. 'Almost there.' They were on their way to Tunis, to an annexe of the great mosque where Moncef Pasha had an iman waiting.

If the Emir's eldest son wanted this woman, then fine. Equally fine if he wanted access to those precious papers she'd found in New York. But it was as well he'd lacked the time to research her properly. Eugenie had read Sally Welham's files, copies of the originals. Had her boss understood that Sally was a card-carrying atheist, he'd never have proposed what was to come next.

Static crackled in Eugenie's headphones. 'I have a message.'

'From Moncef?'

For a second Eugenie was irritated. 'Who else?' she said. 'His message is this, The smaller the lizard the greater its hopes of becoming a crocodile . . . I hope that means something to you because I doubt it means anything to anyone else.'

Eugenie took a sideways glance at the English girl. Thinner, taller, a little younger than Eugenie had been expecting from the photographs snatched along the way. Trailing Sally had been Eugenie's idea from the moment she came to Moncef Pasha's attention. An intrusive foreigner scouring the Net for awkward information.

A blackbird had followed the woman for much of the most recent trip before fading into the background with a change of clothes towards the end.

For a while, early on, Moncef himself had decided that flying a blackbird might work, but even without having met the target Eugenie could have told him otherwise. No one that desperate to become Moncef's lover would risk being foolish. Which was why Eugenie steadfastly refused to believe a single word of Per's story about passionate nights spent with this girl.

'You ready?'

Sally adjusted her headscarf and nodded.

'Wait for the blades to stop,' said Eugenie, 'then follow me.' Ducking under the doorway, she dropped to a crouch, eyes already scanning La Kasbah for the Zil that would drive them to meet Moncef Pasha.

'I'll be your interpreter,' Eugenie added. 'But for the actual marriage you have to make the responses yourself, in Arabic. They're very simple and I've written them out phonetically on a piece of card.'

CHAPTER 30

'Quiet,' hissed a black-haired boy sitting next to Hani. He stared down at his plate, on which a tiny bird sat in the centre of an elaborate matrix of sauce dribbled into the shape of recurring arabesques. So far he had yet to touch his meal.

'Why should I?' Hani demanded, still not bothering to lower her voice. She wanted to know why her Uncle Ashraf was not at Domus Aurea and no one seemed able to tell her. Hani found it hard to believe he hadn't already achieved what he set out to do. Whatever that was.

It also hadn't occurred to Hani that her uncle might miss Kashif's party.

Dressed in a silk kaftan with gold embroidery around the neck and wearing a Rolex several sizes too big, Murad Pasha glanced nervously across to where his half brother sat watching them. 'My brother doesn't approve of noise.'

'And I don't approve of the pasha,' Hani announced rather too loudly. A grey-haired woman standing with two Soviet guards behind the Emir glanced across to smile. Hani got the feeling she didn't like Kashif either. 'Anyway,' Hani said, 'if he prefers silence, why are *they* here?'

A jerk of her chin took in a white-robed group who stood slap-bang in the middle of the cruciform dining room, below an impossibly huge chandelier. Five of them were chanting while a sixth beat time on a goatskin drum.

'These are the Emir's choice,' Murad Pasha said, as if that should be obvious. 'Those are the artists selected by Kashif.' He pointed behind him to a group of *nasrani* over by a far wall, all dressed in black suits and white shirts with black bow ties, like Kashif, in fact. One of them carried a Perspex violin, which he swung loosely by its neck.

'Great,' said Hani. 'I can't wait.'

749

The boy seemed roughly her age but still half a head shorter, which made him rather small for eleven. He had narrow shoulders and girl's wrists and might have been good at running, except he looked far too sensible to run anywhere. Everybody else at the top table was talking, but the only time the boy opened his mouth was to answer one of Hani's questions. The rest of the time his eyes slid past her to watch Kashif, the Emir and Lady Maryam.

'Don't you want that?' Hani pointed at his quail.

Murad shook his head without bothering to look at her.

'Why not?'

Murad Pasha sighed. 'I'm vegetarian,' he said. 'I don't approve of killing animals. And I'm only here under protest.'

'So you don't mind if my cat has it?'

The area in which they sat had once been a *biat bel kabu*, the living quarters for a corsair and his family. Shaped like a fat, crudely drawn cross, with a long downstroke leading to a courtyard, now glassed over, and the shorter upstroke opening onto a smaller, still-uncovered court-yard where Chef Edvard had set up his kitchens, the cruciform room had sidebars that led nowhere.

In total there were six archways into the dining room. And in the centre, below the chandelier, three tables had been positioned, one high table at which sat Murad Pasha and Hani, Kashif, the Emir and Lady Maryam and two lesser tables, at right angles to the top table.

The Berber musicians occupied the open space between the three and because they always faced the Emir, everyone on the side tables saw the singers only in profile. Behind the Emir stood Eugenie de la Croix, flanked by two guards in jellabas, their striped robes in contrast to the drab uniform of a single major who stood behind Kashif Pasha.

Hani didn't recognize Eugenie or anyone else and was happily unaware that at least one of the men sitting at a side table had recognized her.

'So who's the girl?' Senator Malakoff demanded of his elderly neigh-bour, a Frenchman famous for knowing everything about everyone. His enemies, who were legion, would say this was because St Cloud traded in souls. His friends, of whom there were fewer, limited themselves to describing the Marquis as the kind of man who never let go a favour or forgave a good deed.

'The al-Mansur brat.'

'But I thought . . .' His American neighbour looked puzzled. 'Aren't they all al-Mansur?'

'After a fashion,' St Cloud said heavily, helping himself to oysters flown in from Normandy. Without thought, he held up a glass and felt its weight change as a waiter hurriedly filled it with Krug. St Cloud made a point of not noticing servants unless they were both young and beautiful, and then, man or woman, his charm hit them like prey caught in a hunting light. The sex of his conquests mattered little: as St Cloud readily admitted, he was strictly equal opportunity.

'That's Lady Hana al-Mansur,' he explained, returning to the question. 'She recently came into a rather large sum of money. Courtesy of Hamzah Quitrimala . . .' Having mentioned North Africa's richest man, St Cloud watched understanding finally reach the American's face.

'Ahh, yes,' said the Senator. 'Her uncle is Governor of El Iskandryia. Wasn't he implicated in that dreadful . . .'

'Ex-Governor,' St Cloud said firmly. 'He *resigned*.' The way the Marquis said this suggested that Ashraf Bey's resignation had been anything but voluntary.

'Wasn't there also something last year about his niece being kidnapped?'

'Apparently,' said the Marquis, draining his glass. 'Something like that. And I have to admit to being rather surprised to see Lady Hana.' *Not to mention furious*, St Cloud thought to himself. Quite apart from the fact he was now unable to gossip loudly about Ashraf al-Mansur, and the Marquis had been counting on doing precisely that, St Cloud had paid hard currency for a *complete* list of guests, then paid out again to swap his chair for one two down, less prestigious, obviously, but infinitely more useful.

Five thousand dollars had been the cost of getting to sit on Senator Malakoff's left rather than his right. US dollars well spent because Malakoff's right ear was perforated, a fact known only to its owner, his doctor and the Marquis de St Cloud who'd made a point of acquiring his medical records. Apparently the Senator's partial deafness was the result of a recent diving accident in Baja, California. And since the Senator was forbidden to dive by his wife, who believed he'd been revisiting his misspent youth with a prostitute in Tijuana, well . . .

So now the Soviet first secretary was juggling the upside of finding himself in a better seat than expected with wondering exactly why America's latest roving fact finder consistently ignored every comment the ambassador made.

'I'm having a little party afterwards,' St Cloud said quietly. 'Very select. I was wondering if you'd be interested?'

'A party?'

'Out at Cap Bon. At my house.'

The building in question was actually a palace erected for an exiled prince of Savoy and St Cloud's parties were anything but small. The Marquis was relying on the American to know that. 'You, me, some friends, a few girls . . .'

He'd have mentioned boys but the Senator had voted against repealing legislation outlawing homosexuality and St Cloud was not someone to come between a man and his prejudice. At least not when that someone was retained by some of the biggest oil shippers in the world.

'Mostly Japanese girls,' St Cloud admitted. 'Although I have borrowed a rather lovely Mexican, a bit inexperienced but very beautiful.' The girl in question, who was actually Spanish, had been told to keep that fact to herself.

'Mexican?'

St Cloud nodded. 'Lovely girl,' he said, 'you'll adore her.'

After oysters and champagne, Kashif Pasha's nod to the two terms he'd spent studying at the Sorbonne, came wood pigeon stuffed with dates and wrapped in layers of fine filo pastry, so that each mouthful became an adventure in archaeology.

With the smoked pigeon came a wine St Cloud didn't recognize, tannat and auxerrios, almost prune-flavoured, made from grapes grown in an iron-rich subsoil beneath a sun slightly too hot for real subtlety. One of the Emir's own vineyards probably. Although, if this was the case, then St Cloud wasn't sure why each bottle was carefully wrapped in a linen tablecloth to hide its label.

The very fact Emir Moncef served wine outraged half his visitors, while the fact he justified this by quoting Jalaluddin Rumi, rather than relying on timeworn arguments of modernization and rationality, worried the other half.

St Cloud looked to where the old man sat silent at the top table, trapped between his son and the wife he hadn't seen for decades. This was, everybody understood, an important moment of reconciliation. Getting father, son and wife into the same room had taken high-level negotiation and no one quite understood why the Emir had finally agreed.

'God he looks miserable,' Senator Malakoff said, noticing St Cloud's gaze.

'Wouldn't you?' said St Cloud. He glanced pointedly at Lady Maryam whose moon face was almost hidden beneath a silk *hijab*. There was no doubting that she was almost as wide as she was tall.

Senator Malakoff nodded. Yes, he could honestly say he'd be miserable if that was his wife. 'How much more of this do we have to endure?' he asked the Frenchman.

'Hours,' said the Marquis. 'We've only just begun.'

Which wasn't strictly true. As well as the guest list, St Cloud had seen the menu and, provided one discounted the palate-cleaning offering of sorbet and the snails, goat's cheese and fresh figs which were to be served last, the number of courses was limited to five, since wild trout and rabbit were due to arrive simultaneously as were baklava and baked Alaska.

'Hours?' The Senator looked so sick that St Cloud smiled. As well as partial deafness the man suffered from a notoriously weak bladder; a serious flaw in someone charged with establishing contact with the party of Kashif Pasha.

St Cloud knew about that too . . .

Clicking his fingers for a waiter, the Marquis whispered something in the boy's ear, leaning rather closer than was necessary and watched the waiter scurry off, reappearing seconds later with an empty Jeroboam of champagne.

'Piss in this,' St Cloud said, placing the bottle beside the Senator's chair. 'That's what most of us do.'

Pigeon was replaced by lamb roasted in charcoal, testicles still hanging from each gutted carcass like fat purses. Each table got two of the animals. Enough to enable every guest to reach forward and pinch fingers of hot meat without having to stretch. Unnoticed by most guests, the Sufi dancers gave way to a shaven-headed young man backed by a trio of *nasrani* jazz musicians dressed in black. Each note that ululated through the dining room had a haunting quality that filled St Cloud with feelings of loss and regret. The Marquis hated it as a matter of principle.

'He's good,' said Hani.

'Who is?' Murad Pasha spoke though a mouthful of roast peppers. He was fastidiously picking slivers of vegetable from the dish on which the lamb sat, his fingers getting so soiled and greasy that he'd abandoned his napkin and taken to using the edge of the tablecloth instead.

'The Sufi.'

'Is he?'

Hani looked at her cousin, who shrugged.

'How would I know?' Murad demanded. And there was a sadness to his words at odds with the wry smile that lit his face. No boy should have eyelashes that long, Hani decided before considering his question.

Knowing such things came naturally to Hani and so she'd never stopped to wonder how she knew. Reading was part of the answer. She did a lot of that. And questions. Aunt Nafisa always told her she asked too many of those. But mostly she just made connections. Adding one fact to another to arrive at a third that was obvious in retrospect.

'Our porter,' she said carefully, 'he's a Sufi and this is his kind of music. Also my Uncle Ashraf . . .'

Murad Pasha raised dark eyebrows. He'd heard all about Lady Hana's uncle. 'He's a Sufi too?'

'Possibly,' said Hani with a shrug. 'They like the same music. I was going to say that really he's . . .' She lowered her voice and the boy bent closer, head tilting so that Hani could whisper; but the truth about the sons of Lilith went unspoken as one of the guards behind the Emir suddenly yelled.

And grabbed for his automatic.

'Emir.'

Time slowed and within its slowness Hani watched the Sufi raise a revolver, thumb back the hammer and let go, the trigger being already depressed. His first shot drilled the bodyguard through his still-open mouth. Blood and splinters of vertebrae exiting in a vivid splash from the back of Nicolai Dobrynin's neck.

'No . . .'

Murad's scream broke time's crawl and in the acceleration that followed Hani saw the grey woman try to throw herself across Moncef just as his other bodyguard decided to do the same. Flame flared again from the Sufi's muzzle, there was a crack of gunfire and, in the utter silence, Eugenie and the second Soviet guard tumbled together. As for the man with the gun, a shot from behind dropped the Sufi where he stood.

All this took maybe a second. Perhaps fractionally less.

Murad Pasha was still rising from his chair when Hani grabbed him and tipped hers back, their chairs hitting the floor with an impact that knocked what little was left of the boy's shout from his body.

'Stay down,' said Hani.

Murad shook his head.

'You'll be killed.'

'Look,' Murad said, as he snatched free his wrist, 'No one's shooting at you or me. It's my father they want to murder. Okay?' The boy's scramble to stand upright ended abruptly, when Hani grabbed one ankle and yanked hard.

She didn't mean to let go, but the moment Murad's other foot raked across her knuckles instinct cut in, and by the time she'd taken her hand from her mouth Murad was on his feet, looking for his father, who appeared to be missing.

Hani swore. Bad swearing. The kind Zara used when she thought no one was there. But Hani clambered to her own feet all the same, trying to stay low so bullets went over her head, if there were any more bullets.

Which was how she came to see a distant waiter, thin and white jacketed with a staff tag that read *Hassan* wrestle a Browning hiPower from a tuxedoed musician.

'Shoot him,' barked the officer who'd stood behind Kashif Pasha. Hani wasn't sure which one he was talking about either. 'Do it,' Major Jalal insisted. When no one moved the major drew his own automatic. Only Major Jalal never got to pull the trigger because one second the waiter and musician were struggling and then they weren't.

For a moment the waiter just stood, watching the other man crumple and then he retreated towards the outside kitchens, Browning hiPower still in his hand and muzzle pointing firmly at Major Jalal's head.

A parting shot over the head of the crowd kept Kashif's guests from rushing after him. The metallic clunk that followed was the waiter ramming a spit between handles on the other side of the courtyard door.

'Shoot out the hinges,' Kashif Pasha ordered.

'No,' said an older voice. 'Not before securing the room.'

Hani knew without looking that she'd just heard the first words Emir Moncef had uttered all evening. It was a grey-haired, steel-eyed kind of voice. One that allowed for little compromise. Although that didn't stop Kashif Pasha from pushing Major Jalal towards the blocked door.

'Do it . . .'

'We said no.' Moncef's words were firm. Far firmer than the steps that carried him back into the room. 'That exit could be booby-trapped. Either wait for a bomb squad or send someone round to check from the other side.' The Emir addressed his remarks to everybody but most guests understood, as did Kashif Pasha, that the rebuke was aimed at him alone.

'But . . .'

'Do what His Highness says.' Flat as a line showing cardiac arrest, the voice came from behind Moncef. The woman to whom it belonged was neat, compact and had skin the colour of ripe aubergine. A single pip on her shoulder gave Fleur Gide's rank as lieutenant. The gun she carried was a Heckler & Koch, capable of 850 rounds a minute. She carried it low so it raked across everyone in sight, even her commander.

'I thought we agreed . . .' Kashif's voice was harsh.

'And we thought you promised to provide adequate security,' said the Emir, his face hollow with grief. 'Nicolai and Alex are dead. And our oldest companion.' He stared down at the grey-haired woman killed with a .45, one that had drilled through her ribs and still held enough velocity to kill the guard who had been standing behind her. She lay in a cloak of blood on a white floor, eyes still open.

Leaning heavily on his cane, the Emir knelt to close the woman's eyes himself, muttering a prayer for the dead.

Kashif Pasha was shocked to realize his father was crying, in public and openly. Over two Soviet guards and a *nasrani* mercenary. In the circumstances the only thing he could do was ignore the fact. 'Where's my mother gone?' he demanded.

'I took her to safety,' said Lieutenant Gide. 'As I did your father when the shooting started. Those were *madame*'s orders, should the need arise.' Her gaze made it clear that the madame to whom she referred was the elderly woman dead on the floor. Kashif Pasha ignored her. 'Arrest everyone in the kitchens,' he told Major Jalal. 'Before they run away.'

'And just why would they do that?' the Emir asked.

'Because they're *nasrani*,' Kashif Pasha said through gritted teeth. 'Because one of them just shot an undercover member of military intelligence.'

'Undercover? *I thought we'd agreed . . .*'

Kashif Pasha scowled at his father's mimicry and the Emir smiled. 'Arrest them if you must,' he said, 'but release them afterwards.' He held up one hand to stop his son from interrupting. 'Understand me. None of them are to disappear.'

CHAPTER 31

Wednesday 2nd March

Hani, three seats away from where Eugenie got shot, eyes locking on his, too frightened to be puzzled at not recognizing a face so familiar.

Raf reran that sequence in his head, letting Alex, Nicolai and Eugenie tumble endlessly in time to his own, real-world punches. To turn back like this, to attack an enemy was probably the last thing anyone hopelessly outnumbered was meant to do . . . But then, as he'd spent a lifetime telling himself, Raf wasn't anyone.

He was the guy with an eight-thousand-line guarantee and weird-shit eyes, batlike hearing and a sense of smell acute enough to revolt a dog. A man with pixel-perfect memory for every last one of those bits of his life he was able to remember. And ice-cold gaps where the rest should be.

Slamming the soldier's head against a wall, Raf lowered a limp body to the ground and began stripping it. The tunic was too tight across Raf's shoulders and the trousers short. The boots were good, though, and the cap fitted. After dressing the conscript in his discarded trousers, shoes and shirt (the waiter's tunic having already been dumped), Raf dragged the unconscious man into position against an alley wall.

'Drunk,' said Raf as he stood over the body. He sounded disgusted but not quite disgusted enough. Pushing his fingers down his own throat, he retched across the other man's chest and down into his lap. Alcohol and scraps of food stolen from serving plates being taken back into the kitchens.

'Who's that?' demanded a voice. An NCO stood behind him in the entrance to the alley. Ahead of them both was a side door into the Domus Aurea.

'Some filthy drunk,' Raf said and kicked the body.

Originally, way back, the *dar* had been built for some half-Alicantean *taifa*. Isabeau had told Raf its history as they both helped Chef Edvard set up his makeshift kitchen in a small yard off the *bait bel kebu*. The red-and-white horseshoe arches that provided access to the dining room, the carved capitals in Mudejar style, gilded stucco *muqarnas* work across the ceiling, the intricate, impossibly complex tiling. All had been purchased with the spoils of piracy. It was like discovering that Dick Turpin held up stagecoaches because he had a passion for snuffboxes and French enamel . . .

'Keep looking,' ordered the NCO.

'Yes, sir,' Raf said.

There were days now – whole days, sometimes days that ran into each other – when Ashraf Bey understood that he'd created the fox. What had happened when he was seven was his responsibility alone. He had chosen to walk out across that girder, the soles of his school slippers melting with every step. Just as he'd chosen to steal a fox cub from its cage and hide in the attic. Not knowing that the fire he'd set would reach his hiding place. And certainly not knowing it would burn down his whole school.

He'd wanted to destroy the biology building. An ugly block of cheap polycrete faced with pine slats like some tatty ski lodge. That was where the animal experiments were done. Where frogs were dissected and roadkill skinned to reveal underlying muscle structure. Where he'd been made to peg out the pelt of a badger and rub salt into stinking leather, having first scraped it so thin that in places it looked almost translucent. 'What's done is done,' Raf told himself and headed into another alley, stopping at a door to kick it open. 'So why cry?' The question was rhetorical, Raf accepted that. But he answered it all the same.

'No reason.'

He was beginning to see how it worked. Every question he'd ever asked the fox he answered for himself. Pulling information from memory to provide those clinically precise, unhelpful answers. Sweating the small stuff to make the big stuff go away. His life had been one long refusal to take the real facts and make them add up.

Raf searched the house swiftly, five rooms on three floors, saying nothing to the frightened inhabitants. On his way out he shook his head at a couple of conscripts on their way in. 'Empty,' Raf told them. 'No one hiding.'

Why was he upset? Good question.

Tiri had been kept in a wire cage at the rear of the biology block. Most of the smaller animals lived inside. Hamsters and rats, mice bred for so many generations that generations of biology masters had lost count. A black widow spider permanently catatonic with cold. Sickly stick insects. Guppies in water thicker than fog. And a single, magnificent Siamese fighting fish, all broken fins and ragged tail.

Raf freed the rats and shook the stick insects onto grass at the front of the block. This had seemed like a good idea at the time. Although later, looking down from his burning attic at fire trucks lining up on the lawn he realized he hadn't given them a better life at all. He hadn't known what to do with the fish so he removed most of the water from the guppies because their tank was dirtier than that of the Siamese fighting fish, then tipped one tank into the other. If Raf couldn't free the fighting fish he could at least give it a decent meal.

He'd never liked guppies anyway.

Some soldier had lit the spotlights around Domus Aurea but these only did what they were meant to do, threw walls into relief or picked out aspects of architectural interest.

There were trucks on the road beyond the medina, circling the old city walls with soldiers hanging from their open doors. Kashif Pasha's men. All of them searching for him. A grinding of gears came from a square ahead, more trucks arriving for the hunt. From Raf's left came shouted orders. Farther away, to his right, beyond a low line of workshops, more orders, more shouting. Engines racing and truck doors that slammed.

This was no way to track a fugitive. Even without the fox Raf knew that. Or rather he knew that without needing the fox, because he *was* the fox. One and the same. Separated not at birth but standing on that burning girder. What Raf knew (such as it was), he knew for himself and in himself. Just as Raf knew that he needed to get out there. To become himself. A man with responsibilities and a life.

And if not a man, then whatever he was.

759

CHAPTER 32

On the dirt track a group of hunters struggled with a dead boar. They had its carcass lashed to a pole and slung between two of their party. A third man had a Ruger across his back and carried the rifles of the first two, one slung under each arm. Behind those three walked two more men, rifles ported across their broad chests.

Gravel crunched beneath their boots and each wore a loden coat with broad belt, tweed plus fours and long woollen socks.

Every last one of them watched the Bugatti Royale grind past. All their guns had telescopic sights and featured extended magazines that came only as an (expensive) optional extra. The man at the back had two dead rabbits hanging from his belt.

'Season ends in about three weeks,' said Hani. She waved to the hunters, who stared back, eyes hard. The Bugatti, one of only seven ever made, had been climbing for the last five minutes towards a distant farmhouse that kept vanishing behind the hill. The track over which it rattled was rough, edged with thorn and a few bare oaks unwilling to accept that spring was due.

'There it is . . .'

Thick walls washed white under a roof of red pantiles. Windows kept small to protect the inside from winter winds. Protecting the glass were oak shutters, their wood stripped bare by winter frost and summer heat. A hunting lodge really, built by a wine shipper from Cahors. It could have been lifted wholesale from the Lot valley and set down amid the pines and oaks of Ifriqiya's rugged north coast.

Its original owner was long dead. His marble tomb was decaying in a colonial churchyard where a pubescent angel stood guard over his final resting place, her downcast eyes at odds with the plumpness of her body and the thinness of her robes. Now she waited, rendered wingless by vandals, an atrocity victim waiting for eternity.

Claude Bouteloup began his life as a peasant farmer and ended it a baron, gold having dug deep enough to discover a previously overlooked family title. The walls of his old home remained lined with heads taken from the boar he'd shot in the Northern Tell. An implausible spread of horns over the main door stood memory to his plan to reintroduce aurochs, a few of which still roamed the hills, but fewer by the year.

All this Hani read out to Murad and Raf as her uncle yanked the Bugatti's fourteen-foot wheelbase round a tight bend in the dirt road while trying to ignore a drop that fell away to a white, storm-fed river far below.

'Put the book down,' Raf told her. 'Before you make yourself feel sick.'

'Too late,' said Hani. She flicked backwards for a few pages, then flicked forward. 'This guide doesn't say who owns it now,' she complained, skim-reading the entry again.

'It wouldn't,' said Raf.

The first clue that this wasn't just another hunting lodge came at the gates. These looked normal until Raf got close enough to see otherwise. Tiny cameras tracked his arrival, watching from stone gateposts where they were bolted discreetly between the open claws of granite eagles.

Micromesh, fine enough to be virtually invisible, lined the far side of the gate's flowing wrought iron. Its heavy, old-fashioned lock was electronic. Cracking paint covered hinges that Raf was willing to bet conformed to some exacting military standard he didn't even know existed.

'You step out of the car,' said Murad. 'And then someone opens the gates if they like the look of you . . . I've been here before,' he added, without glancing up from his toy Ninja Nizam. Hani and he had spent from Tunis to Bizerte arguing about whether or not action figures were childish.

Hani kept on saying they were. Until finally Murad announced that as Hani did nothing but play with a stupid cat, her opinion didn't count.

'Ifritah's not a toy.'

'Did I say she was?'

After that came blessed silence, from Bizerte to just past Cap Serrat, where Raf turned the Bugatti off the crumbling blacktop onto something that barely qualified as track. The Ettore-Bugatti-built coupé Napoleon had been a present from the Prince Imperial in Paris to the Emir's grandfather and, until Raf claimed it, had been garaged in a mews at the back of the Bardo Palace.

No one had dared to stop Raf from commandeering the 275bhp, 12.8-litre monster. But then, from the chamberlain who ran the nearly empty palace to the uniformed sailor who first saw a blond notable in shades and black Armani suit striding towards its main door, no one had known how to treat Ashraf al-Mansur at all.

Finding a new suit had been as easy as kicking in the window of a boutique opposite Ibn Khaldoun's statue in Place de la Victoire, about three hundred paces from Bab el Bahar. By then, dawn's call to prayer had come and gone and only isolated trucks still circled the medina like flies disappointed by the quality of their meal. The boutique was very elegant, with a wide range of supposedly embargoed Western goods, but it should have spent more on security.

On his way out Raf met a handful of other looters on their way in. They liked his suit too. In fact they liked it so much he went back to point out the appropriate rack. And it was only after he left the second time that he put on the shades he'd taken to match, casually ditching his cheap contacts into a storm drain.

An hour's walk from Ibn Khaldoun's statue had taken him to the edge of the Bardo. A complex of original buildings with rambling faux al Andalus additions, the Bardo featured palaces built on palaces, the bedrooms of one situated over the reception rooms of another until the different parts ran together into one impossible mess.

No one had ever cataloged its contents. Records even differed as to the number of rooms. And each attempt at rationalization made matters worse. Although it was widely agreed among architectural historians that the rebuilding of 1882, during which medieval mashrabiyas were replaced with sash windows along one whole side, was undoubtedly a low point.

All the same, the Bardo complex still counted as the most recognized façade in North Africa. One result of an old etching featuring in the opening credits of *A Thousand Flowers*, a long-running, widely syndicated Turkish soap based in the nineteenth-century harem of Ahmed Bey, where a thousand concubines languished under the guard of five eunuchs, played by bald Sudanese women.

No men were ever seen. And although some flower would occasionally be plucked from her languid divan and sent through *the Door*, she would return an episode later, usually in a state of unspecified bliss, distraught or just more worldly-wise.

Gossip, treachery and friendship, the plot ran regular as celestial tram lines. Its avid following the by-product of the originator's desire to draw her cast from a dozen nationalities, as Ifriqiya's beys had filled their harems with a variety of Egyptians, Turks and Southern Europeans, mostly captured slaves.

Various bearded Jesuits were sent, both in reality and in the soap. And indeed, in reality one such missionary spent three years camped in a wing of the Bardo Palace waiting for an audience that never actually came; despite an invitation from a bey devoted to the memory of his *nasrani* mother.

Now the Bardo was home to the world's largest collection of Carthaginian mosaics, an unquantifiable number of bad Victorian paintings and Kashif Pasha, his retinue and his mother. (With only Kashif's direct appeal to the Emir ensuring that Lady Maryam and he were allocated different sections of the crumbling complex.)

No flag flew from the mast over the main gate when Raf arrived, which meant no adult member of the al-Mansur family was currently at home.

'We're closed.' The young sailor guarding the gate held his rifle slung across his chest, the way those on guard always did. His face was set. And only his eyes revealed uncertainty.

Raf halted, smiled . . . Made a minute adjustment to his maroon Versace tie. 'Good morning,' he said. 'I'd like to see your commander.'

Sailor and notable stared at one another. Although all the sailor saw was himself reflected in the blankness of Raf's new shades.

'Now,' Raf added, his voice polite but firm. He'd once watched his school doctor use just that mixture of courtesy and menace on Raf's Swiss headmaster.

'I don't have a commander.'

Raf sighed. 'Then get whoever you do have,' he suggested.

Leaving his post, the boy vanished through a small door cut into one of two double doors behind him. Endless heavy nails had been hammered into both to form repetitive patterns which, to Raf's eye, looked out of place against the delicacy of the pink marble columns supporting the arch into which the doors were set.

With a shrug, Raf stepped through the arch after him and found himself in a courtyard.

'You left the door open,' Raf pointed out, when the returning guard opened his mouth to complain. Behind the boy Raf saw a grey-haired man in blue uniform raise his eyes to heaven.

'Morning, Chief' Raf said.

The elderly Petty Officer nodded. And in that nod was everything he felt about using untrained conscripts as guards and about notables who turned up at dawn, expecting to be shown round the Bardo.

'The palace is shut, Excellency.'

'I know.' Raf knew nothing of the sort, but that wasn't really the point. Straightening up, he adjusted his cuffs almost without thinking.

'I'm Ashraf al-Mansur,' he said, 'the Emir's middle son. I've been asked to investigate last night's attack on my father.'

'Attack?'

Raf didn't bother to reply.

'So it was . . .' The NCO's voice faltered.

'I think you'd better introduce me to your commander,' Raf said and stepped farther into a courtyard overlooked by fifty sashed windows and a dozen balconies. The European kind.

He looked around him. 'My father here?'

The old man shook his head.

'Lady Maryam?'

Another shake and a quick suck of yellowing teeth.

'Okay,' said Raf. 'How about Kashif Pasha?'

The NCO opened his mouth, then shut it again. Had the pasha been in residence then, as well as having the al-Mansur flag flying, that gate would have been guarded by Kashif's own soldiers instead of raw recruits. As it was, Kashif's men were rumoured to be busy, making wide-ranging arrests.

The one person Raf did find was Hani, although he found Ifritah first, scooping the grey kitten up from a tiled floor and tossing it over his shoulders like a stole.

'Hey,' shouted a young girl who slid through a door and kick stopped, leaving a smear of burned leather on the marble under her heel. 'That's my . . .'

She took a look at the man facing her.

'Oh,' she said crossly, 'you're back.'

'No,' said Raf, 'I've been here for days. You're the one who's just arrived.'

'I was here yesterday,' Hani said. 'You can ask him.' She pointed to a door through which a young boy appeared. He was dressed in a blazer and had a striped tie quite as smart as the one Raf wore.

'Murad al-Mansur?' said Raf and watched the boy glance round before nodding. They both knew what was missing from the picture. 'Where's your bodyguard?' Raf asked.

'Kashif Pasha doesn't think I need one.'

'Because no assassin would want to kill a child?' Raf's voice made it obvious what he thought of that.

'That wasn't what I said.' Shrewd eyes watched the newcomer. 'Or what he meant.'

'Murad's my cousin,' Hani announced.

'And this is my niece,' said Raf, nodding to Hani. 'I do apologize.'

764

The boy looked between them. 'Then you're . . . ?'

'Ashraf Bey,' said Raf. 'Your half brother, her uncle and the new Chief of Police.'

At the bey's side the NCO froze, his reflex reptilian. Almost as if stillness could put a wall up around his thoughts. All it did was draw Raf's attention.

'You,' Raf said to the man. 'Tell me what you've heard . . .'

'Heard, Your Excellency?'

'Outside, you said, *So it was* . . . The question is, *so it was what?*'

'The Army of the Naked,' said the man, his voice hesitant. 'My chief said they'd carried out an attack.'

'That's a lie,' Murad Pasha said. And blushed when the NCO gazed at him in surprise. 'I've got a radio,' he explained hurriedly. 'A *Radiotechnika Atlas*. The kind that gets all the stations . . . A birthday present from the Soviet ambassador,' Murad added, as if owning a radio needed explanation. 'The AN absolutely deny having anything to do with the attack.'

'They have a radio station?' Hani asked.

'A pirate station,' Murad stressed. 'Which changes frequency every night. You have to look for it.'

Hani nodded. 'Zara's brother has a pirate station,' she said. 'But Avatar only has to change every week.'

'Who's Zara?'

'My uncle's mistress,' said Hani, then stared in bewilderment at the elderly NCO who suddenly broke into a coughing fit.

'The AN want to overthrow the government,' Murad said. 'But they didn't try to kill my father.' A tremble in his voice was the first sign Raf had sensed that the boy was not nearly as composed as he wanted to appear.

'I thought you said you were in the government?' Hani sounded puzzled.

'Minister for Education,' Murad agreed. 'Also for archaeology. Kashif's everything else apart from bioscience and technology. The Emir kept those for himself.'

'Did you see the attack?' Raf demanded.

Murad nodded. 'We were there,' he said. 'I was invited and Hani invited herself. We sat next to Kashif Pasha as it happened.'

'When *what* happened?' Raf asked.

'Someone tried to shoot the Emir,' said Hani. 'Eugenie died saving him. And two guards, a Sufi and a musician. Now everyone's arguing about . . .'

'Who tried?'

Hani paused. She'd got older without him noticing, Raf realized. More confident. A little bit taller. He tried to remember back to that age and couldn't.

'Well,' said Murad, 'there was this waiter.'

'You can't go in there.' The birdlike woman was out of her seat before Raf got halfway to the door of Kashif Pasha's inner office.

'Tell me about it,' Raf said tiredly. People telling him where he couldn't go was getting to be something of a refrain. He kept walking and the woman dropped her hand, as if she'd somehow just scalded her fingers on the cloth of his sleeve.

Used to wielding power but resigned to it always belonging to someone else, the woman fell back on formality. 'Can I ask if you have an appointment?'

'I don't need one,' said Raf. 'Police business.' He pulled a leather cardholder from his pocket and flipped it open, flashing an identity card he'd taken off Kashif's unconscious soldier. It was shut again before her eyes even had time to focus.

'Well, he's not here.' The woman's hair beneath her scarf was thinning and deep lines slashed down both sides of a thin mouth. The world had not been kind to her. 'So you'll still have to come back.'

'Even better,' said Raf, hand already turning an enamel door knob. 'That gives me a chance to search his office.'

'You can't . . .'

'What's your name?' Raf asked her.

'Leila el-Hasan. I'm the pasha's private secretary.'

'Get yourself another job then,' Raf told her, not unkindly, and shut Kashif's door behind him, shooting its bolt.

The décor could go either way. High Arabesque, which got called Moorish in guidebooks, or ersatz European, which usually meant oak panels, dark furniture and oil paintings. Those were the default options when it came to North African government buildings. There was a third alternative, of course. Seattle Blond was what you got if you fed old Scandinavian through late-period Edo, but pale kelims and steam-shaped ash was never going to be Kashif Pasha's thing.

What Raf found was High Arabesque. An office centred around an alabaster fountain so massive that this bit of the Bardo had to be last century despite the obvious antiquity of the horseshoe arch surrounding its door. No floor underpinned with anything but steel could have supported that weight. Beyond the fountain began carpets, large and probably priceless; obscured by a faded leather ottoman and a couple of wing chairs. And against the farthest wall, beneath a window so vast it

766

needed sandstone pillars down the middle to support it, stood an office desk, notable only for its ordinariness.

Raf read the subtext in a single glance. Look at the magnificence imposed upon me by birth. Notice how modest my own expectations. Contrast the two and be aware of my modernity. And it must work, because half of Europe regarded Kashif Pasha as Ifriqiya's up-and-coming saviour.

The only thing missing from the room was a portrait of the Emir and it didn't take a man of Raf's talents to read that. Although he read the subtext below the subtext, that suggested that while Kashif was ambitious he lacked advisers to help him plan his moves with subtlety.

But then lack of subtlety was never a problem when dealing with Paris, Washington or Berlin. Particularly Berlin.

None of Kashif's desk drawers were locked. Which either said look how open I am, or else, so great is my power no locks are needed to protect my privacy. Alternatively it might have been because there was nothing in the desk of the slightest significance.

No state papers or smoking gun. Not even a bottle of Jim Beam or a *Hustler* imported under diplomatic seal. Mind you, Raf had expected little less. He'd visited Kashif's office for one reason only: to rattle a few bars and see what tried to bite.

And to judge from the hammering at the door he was about to find out.

Opening the door was one option; letting whoever was on the other side smash apart original ninth-century panels was another.

'Wait,' Raf ordered, voice hard.

On the other side of the antique door the hammering ceased.

Raf took his time to walk across the office, but then, given the size of Kashif Pasha's room, this was not unreasonable.

'Right,' said Raf, slipping back the bolt. 'It's open.'

Two men in bottle-green uniforms came tumbling into the room. They had heavy moustaches, light stubble and hard glares. One glance at the glowering pasha behind them showed where that look originated.

'Up against the wall,' the thinner of the two barked. 'Now.'

Raf shook his head. 'You can go,' he told the man. 'Take your fat friend and shut the door. I want to talk to my brother.' That got their attention. Got the attention of Kashif Pasha as well.

Ashraf Bey stepped forward and held out his hand. 'This won't take long,' he told Kashif Pasha. 'I need to ask a few questions about last night's shooting.'

'You need . . .' Despite himself, Kashif Pasha's eyes slid to the *chelengk* recently pinned to Raf's lapel. Such exalted signs of Stambul's favour were rare. Given only to victors in battle and those who had rendered personal service to the Ottoman throne.

'Who are you?'

'Ashraf al-Mansur,' said Raf, letting his hand drop. 'Acting on behalf of the Emir.' Which was almost true. He'd been asked to act by Eugenie, who'd led him to believe that this was the Emir's suggestion. Close enough to count. He shrugged. 'I thought you'd like to be first,' said Raf. 'Before I track down your guests.'

'That won't be necessary,' said Kashif Pasha crossly. 'Everyone who should be has already been pulled in for questioning. My men were arresting people all last night.'

'Everyone who should be . . . ?' Raf raised his eyebrows.

Kashif Pasha's nod was abrupt. Furious.

'So you've questioned the Marquis de St Cloud?'

'Don't be ridiculous.' Kashif's fingers were knotted into fists. Although Raf doubted if the man even realized that. 'The Marquis is a personal friend.'

'How about Senator Malakoff? Ambassador Radek?' Raf was enjoying himself. 'Or are you carefully ignoring anyone important . . .'

A crowd had gathered in the outer office and through the door he could see Kashif Pasha's secretary, her face twisting with anxiety as a man in a grey suit attempted to comfort her. Behind them hovered a handful of clerks.

This was exactly what Raf had needed most, an audience.

'So,' said Raf, 'why haven't you questioned the Marquis?'

'What are you suggesting?' Kashif Pasha stepped in close, like someone facing down an enemy but Raf knew different. Once, longer ago than he remembered, a Rasta on remand in the same jail as him had explained about clinches. They were where weak fighters hid when seeking protection, nothing more.

'I don't know,' said Raf. 'Why don't you tell me.'

CHAPTER 33

'Why did Kashif's soldiers walk you to the car?' There was something in Murad's voice that said he'd been mulling over this question for most of the trip. Which he had. He'd been trying to decide if asking it would be rude.

'No idea,' said Raf and pulled the borrowed Bugatti into a parking space in front of the farmhouse and cut the engine.

Behind him Hani snorted but Raf ignored her. He was too busy watching Murad in the rearview mirror. Everything from eye colour to skin hue was different. The boy had narrower shoulders than Raf. A softer face. And thick dark hair instead of the fine ash blond that made Raf so visible. But there was something lost in his face, the same closed-down expression and the boy even chewed his lip in the same way.

Only Raf's squint was missing. His habitual reaction to trying to see without shades. Those had come later, after the second round of operations in Zurich. Besides, the dark glasses were meant to be a temporary fix, Raf could remember being told that.

'You okay?' he asked the boy.

'Sure.' Murad shrugged. 'Why not?' And in a way Murad was telling the truth. For a twelve-year-old who'd recently seen four people murdered he was doing fine, especially as one of them was a woman he'd known all his life. Opening the Bugatti door, Murad stepped out onto gravel. It was the only way he could avoid more questions . . .

'You know,' Raf told Fleur Gide, stepping through the front door, 'my brother thinks Berlin turned that Sufi.'

'Berlin, Your Highness?' Major Gide looked genuinely shocked. 'I assumed it was Washington or Paris.'

She'd been the one to take the decision to let the Bugatti through the gate. A responsibility that fell to her as Eugenie's temporary replacement.

769

Fleur Gide was as ambitious as the next special forces officer but this was one promotion she would happily have done without.

'Someone turned him, you agree?' said Raf. 'And you don't have to call me Highness. I'm an Excellency at the most. If that . . .'

The newly promoted officer nodded doubtfully.

'Word on the street has the Sufi working for Kashif Pasha,' Raf said. 'Only that's wrong. Well, it is according to my brother.'

Mentioning that the nearest he'd got to checking the word on the street was listening in while Murad Pasha scanned a dozen pirate stations seemed inappropriate. A twelve-year-old princeling lacked something as an information source when dealing with Ifriqiya's new head of intelligence, temporary or not.

Rough flagstones covered a hall that made do without carpets. On the walls, sporting prints showed stags at bay and scenes from a duck shoot. There was a fireplace, carved from granite and featuring an ornate coat of arms with two of the quarterings themselves showing quarterings. Above the mantel hung a simple mirror while flames danced in the hearth below, filling the ground floor of Eugenie's old house with the scent of burning pinecones.

A thickset, bejewelled woman stood in front of Raf and refused even to glance at the prints on the walls. Only a boar's head mounted onto a mahogany shield with the date 1908 engraved onto an ornate silver label below drew any reaction. Lady Maryam shuddered every time she accidentally turned in that direction.

'I came because duty demanded it,' Lady Maryam said heavily. And Raf knew he was being warned not to judge her by the objects to be found in the house.

'Sometimes,' said Raf, 'that's all you can do.'

He'd heard the other version. The one where Major Gide bundled the Emir into a car to get him to safety. Only to have Lady Maryam clamber in the other side and refuse to budge. What upset Major Gide most was her certain knowledge that Eugenie would have had no hesitation about dragging the sullen overweight princess from the car and leaving her in the courtyard. And that was before factoring in the Emir's fury that she'd allowed Lady Maryam to travel with them while leaving Murad, his favourite son, behind.

'Wait here,' said Lady Maryam, 'while I see if my husband is awake.'

Tracking her footsteps across flagstones, Raf followed them up a flight of stairs and across bare boards. The knock at a distant door was surprisingly gentle.

A creak of hinges died when the door shut, leaving Raf with a waterfall of near silences, none of them significant because they were not what Raf listened for. Below the clatter of dishes on a work surface and the small-arms pop of water pipes stretching, he heard the rustle of wind through a pine tree beyond the window. The wings of an owl. Slow and methodical. And under this the claws of a rat scurrying across the gravel at the front of the farmhouse where Major Gide's guards patrolled creaking gates. Falling through silences, one at a time. Hyperreal . . .

'Uncle Ashraf!'

Ashraf Bey came awake to find himself watched by Hani, Murad and Lady Maryam. There was one other person present. A thin man with swept-back grey hair and blue eyes above a hawk nose that had once been broken. A day's worth of white stubble only heightened the hollowness of his cheeks. And he leant heavily on a stick. All the same, there was a ferocious intensity to his gaze; as if he burned with fever or was some celestial body in its final stage of immolation.

'So you're Sally's child . . .' The Emir's smile was sad. 'You know,' he said, 'she told me you died. And then you turn up all those years later in El Iskandryia. I wouldn't have believed it without seeing you.'

The hand that shook Raf's own was hot, dry like paper, the bones beneath the age-bruised skin weak as twigs. Even the slight grip Raf gave was enough to make the old man wince. There'd been a dozen things Raf had always wanted to say to his father and none of them seemed appropriate.

What the man opposite felt, Raf found hard to tell.

'Don't you *want* to talk to each other?' Hani demanded.

'It can wait,' said the Emir. 'What are a few minutes after this long?'

When the old man walked, it was slowly, leaning heavily on his stick. And at every change of level Murad Pasha positioned himself at the Emir's side so the old man could reach out and steady himself. A fact Lady Maryam obviously hated, to judge from the sourness of her expression.

Although that could also have been down to the Emir's refusal to admit she even existed. She might as well have been a trophy mounted on the wall since she obviously created in him the disquiet that the boar's head seemed to inspire in her.

The farmhouse had been built into the hill, with its back only slightly higher than the front. This meant that the room into which they finally passed had earth reaching two-thirds of the way up its outside walls; good for warmth in winter and useful in other ways too.

'Don't tell me,' Raf said, 'the place was like this when Eugenie found it.'

Emir Moncef smiled.

'She made a few adjustments,' he admitted. 'Mostly involving chicken wire and concrete. Well, loosely . . .' Which was true. If chicken wire included military-grade titanium mesh and reinforced polyfoam walls could be described as concrete.

'How much of the farmhouse is actually left?'

'Ask Major Gide,' he said and clapped his hands.

It seemed the answer was virtually nothing. Apart, that was, from the original eagle gateposts, the granite fireplace and the flagstones in the hall. All walls, internal and external, conformed to Moscow's best standards for blast resistance. Steel-cored doors hid beneath veneers of oak. Screamer wire looped the immediate forest at ankle height. A Molniya spysat hovered high overhead, streaming live data to combat software stashed in the cellar. The fat pantiles on the roof featured thermal feedback to keep the surface at ground ambient, day and night. Even the glass in the windows, double-glazed and shatterproof, vibrated at a random pitch to confuse anyone hidden outside with a parabolic mic.

All of it was black tek. All of it shipped in contravention of numerous UN resolutions banning the sales to Ifriqiya of weapons-grade technology.

'Those hunters,' said Raf.

'Georgian *Spetsnaz*.'

'What about the boar?' Hani demanded.

'Fake,' interrupted the Emir. 'Eugenie de la Croix's idea.' He nodded to Hani and smiled at Murad, who just looked at him, eyes wide, then glanced between the Emir and Raf and scowled.

'You think we look alike,' Moncef said. It wasn't a question.

The small, dark-eyed boy nodded but Hani just shook her head.

'No,' she told the Emir, 'you look way older.'

'It's flu,' Lady Maryam said when Raf finally asked.

'You're sure?'

'Of course, I'm sure.' Lady Maryam's voice was sharp.

'How do you know?' Raf demanded. He'd already seen the whole farmhouse and apart from two large rooms upstairs, one used by the Emir, with another on the ground floor now claimed by Lady Maryam, meaning Major Gide had to share the dorm with her troops, that was it. Apart from the hall, kitchen and cellar. The *Spetsnaz* slept at a house in the village. One of the major's jumpsuited teenagers did the cooking. There was no one else and nothing that looked like a surgery. As it was, Raf and the others were going to have to make their way back to Tunis that night because anything else presented too much of a risk.

'Major Gide is also his doctor,' Lady Maryam said shortly. 'I'm surprised you didn't know that.'

They were back in the hall by the fire. The darkness outside was such that stars bled diamonds across black velvet through the one window left uncurtained. The longer he stayed, the jumpier Lady Maryam became, her politeness becoming ever more brittle by the minute. She'd already added Murad to the list of things at which she was unable to look, banishing Hani and her cousin to the kitchen.

'I should go,' Raf said.

'Yes,' agreed Lady Maryam and as she clapped her hands a wattle of flesh on her wrist quivered. She was old, Raf realized. The way the Emir was old. Made older by bitterness and four decades of marital exile. All she had on her side was that her son had been born first.

'I'll have someone fetch the children,' Lady Maryam said.

Raf nodded. 'That would be kind,' he replied, knowing that kindness had nothing to do with it. 'But first I need to ask the Emir some questions . . . That's why I'm here,' Raf said, when the woman looked at him blankly. Turning for the stairs, he was irritated to hear Lady Maryam's heavy steps following behind.

'I need to see him alone.'

'He's my husband,' said Lady Maryam.

And my father, apparently, Raf said. But he said it under his breath.

The huge room was hot and dark. The smell of vomit obvious. A glass of water stood on a table beside a hardly touched bowl of couscous. Most of what had been eaten splattered the floorboards beside the bed.

Within the round belly of a wood-burning stove flames flickered. On a mattress, leaning back against his pillows lay the old man, his pillowcases tallowed with sweat. A window that shouldn't have been open was. So it was just as well that Lady Maryam remained outside, kept from entering by a shout that reduced her husband to a coughing fit.

'She keeps cooking me food,' the Emir said tiredly when his breath was back. He smiled at Raf's surprise. 'Don't worry,' he added. 'I make her eat a spoonful of everything first. She's only here to look after me because she knows how much I hate it.'

It was Raf's turn to smile.

'So tell me,' said the Emir, 'before we talk about things that matter. What did you do to get her wretched son so upset? I've had Kashif on the line swearing undying loyalty and warning me not to trust you.' The Emir sounded amused. 'What did you do, besides tell him you were now Chief of Police? Which, I have to say, was news to me . . .'

'I didn't say that at all,' said Raf. 'Merely that I was investigating the attack. And I suggested, obliquely, that he might have hired the Sufi.'

'Do you think he did?'

'That depends,' said Raf, glancing round the room until his gaze reached an angular chair made from pine and painted in a brown so deep it looked black, 'on who else would like to see you dead.'

'Paris, Washington, Berlin. Half the mullahs in Kairouan. That woman outside. And then there's you . . . Feel free to sit,' he added as if he thought Raf was angling for permission rather than working out exactly what worried him about the Emir's room.

'Why would I want you dead?'

Moncef's only answer was to glance at a ring resting between a revolver and a copy of the Quran. The ring was gold, set with blood-stone and a swirl of script; the *tughra* engraved into its surface was that found on every fifty-dinar coin for more than forty years.

The gun was a Colt .38 with pearl grips.

'There's more to ruling than owning a ring,' Raf said.

'Not much,' said the Emir, his laugh a foxlike bark, carrying more pain than amusement. 'Especially if you have the other two as well. You don't really like me, do you?'

'Probably more than your wife does,' Raf said sourly. 'She tells me this is the first time she's ever visited . . .'

'First and last,' said the Emir. 'This house was bought for Eugenie. Government money but her name on the deeds. She was many things, that woman. Only one of them my chief of intelligence.' Unashamed tears were in his eyes. Or maybe just unnoticed.

'You were lovers?' Raf said. It was barely half a question.

'That's one way of describing it.'

'She said you weren't.'

He smiled sadly. 'Eugenie kept her life in compartments,' he said. 'Jobs that people knew about. Those they didn't. Her personal life was one of the smallest. Maybe the least visited. Sometimes Gene needed to forget what she kept there . . . You see,' he explained, 'sleeping with me was probably the only unprofessional thing Gene ever did in her life. And all I did was get her killed . . .'

The Emir gestured to the table beside his bed where the ring lay between the book and the gun. 'Make your choice,' he said, 'and learn to live with it. That's all any of us can do.'

A glow from the wood-burning stove gave the Emir's face the look of a fallen angel, broken and beautiful; haunting in its promise and cruel beyond imagining. Behind the words was a desolation so deep it went beyond Raf's ability to understand. And in that moment he finally believed something his mother once said, which in itself was unusual.

His father was certifiably insane. She'd been holding a vodka when she said this. Her anger filtered through a freebase crash and the bottom of a Bohemian shot glass. Somehow they'd moved from filming Arabian wildcats as they learned to hunt, her latest project, to Raf's father, the man she refused to talk about. Of course, back then Raf thought she'd been talking about the Swedish hitchhiker.

'Why come now?' the Emir said into Raf's silence. 'When you wouldn't come before?'

'I was busy.'

'Having your garden rebuilt with someone else's money . . . Going to a job you didn't do . . . What changed?' asked the Emir, his eyes watching from within the red shadows of the stove. The very feet he hadn't asked why Raf wore shades in a room that sweltered in near darkness told Raf that Eugenie's original suggestion was right and he had been wrong. Whatever had been done to Raf, his mother had not made those choices alone.

'What changed . . .' The answer died on Raf's lips. The snide, the furious and the easy comebacks all wiped by the obvious. 'I did,' said Raf.

CHAPTER 34

Dr Pierre smirked from the side of a barn, his mouth supercilious above the fading remains of a silk cravat. A lifetime of rain had worn his luxurious sideburns to a ghost of their former glory. A jagged scar split his chin where a builder had repaired cracked brickwork with no thought for the advertising mural beneath.

He was advertising *pâté dentifrice*. As used in Paris.

'Where are we going now?'

'Cap Bon,' said Raf. 'To question the Marquis de St Cloud.'

It said much for Murad's cool that he didn't ask why his half brother had the Bugatti's headlights switched off. Recalibrating his eyes, Raf glanced in the mirror and saw Murad lit by screen glare from Hani's pink plastic laptop.

'Can you turn the screen down . . . ?'

'Why?' Her voice was petulant. As if she still hadn't quite forgiven him for one or more of the many things for which he still needed her forgiveness.

'Because too much light makes driving difficult.'

'If I must,' said Hani and flicked off her laptop. Adjusting the screen was much too easy an option.

Raf didn't tell Hani his other reason. That somewhere above them would be a UN spysat capable of tracking their journey from the farmhouse to Cap Bon. If they were lucky, that was. If they were unlucky, then the satellite had probably just captured every one of Hani's keystrokes.

He drove in silence. Letting darkened walls and hedgerows flow around him until the dirt track became a minor road, then something that actually had central lines. Shortly after that came the *périphérique* around Tunis, the city flickering by in a smudge of suburbs as the huge

Bugatti burned up the outside lane, lights out and its three passengers shadows held in darkness, like ghosts going on holiday.

One of the cardinal points of the Emir's work creation programme was that everyone in Ifriqiya should have a job. And if that meant more road sweepers, line painters or ditchdiggers than there were roads then so be it.

What Ifriqiya needed, of course, at least in the opinion of every visiting dignitary, was fewer donkeys and wider roads. Only the land lost to build the roads would, when added together, shave hectare after hectare off the country's reserve of perfectly good smallholdings. On the Emir's orders, a survey had been carried out after some commissar with mining interests in Gafsa had complained that trucking phosphate was becoming increasingly uneconomic.

In response to a hint from Moscow that the CCCP might help Tunis fund a programme to build new motorways, the Emir sent them the address of every family who'd lose land and invited Moscow to write to each, explaining why it was necessary.

To the reply that this would be pointless, since most of those would undoubtedly be unable to read, he pointed out that the literacy rate in Ifriqiya was slightly higher than western Russia as a whole, and at least 25 percent above that of Georgia, which was where both the commissar and the Soviet president originated.

The roads remained unwidened, still lined with prickly pear except in the far south, where the ground was too barren to grow even that.

'What are you thinking?' Hani asked, her voice no longer sullen. On her lap the computer balanced on top of Ifritah's cat basket. Now forgotten.

'About prickly pears,' said Raf.

Hani nodded, as if that was to be expected. 'The roads,' she said, 'and Moscow's plan to widen them. It's mentioned in the official guidebook.'

'Probably,' said Raf. From what he'd just seen, Emir Moncef was quite capable of having it included just to signal his independence from the only country still willing to trade openly with Ifriqiya.

'How do you two do that?' Murad demanded, his tone more interested than aggrieved.

'Do what?' Hani and Raf asked together.

And the answer was he didn't know. Raf accepted that he'd no more understood what his own mother was thinking than she'd known what hid inside his head. They had remained, from his birth until her death, two strangers separated by common blood and long silences: every glance between them was embarrassed, each hug brief and gratefully cut short. If ever he took her hand she flinched. Every time she touched him he froze.

It was a relationship safe only when conducted at a distance by e-mail or letter. So maybe Zara was right and he really was the last person to be looking after a troubled, hyperintelligent, unquestionably lonely small child.

Alternatively, he was ideal.

'You okay?'

Raf glanced in the mirror and saw Hani watching intently.

'Thought not,' she said. One thin hand came up and gripped his neck, small fingers digging into muscle knots on both sides. 'Twist your head,' said Hani.

Raf did and heard bones crunch as something slid back into place. 'Donna does it,' she said, 'every time I get a headache.'

'You get many headaches?' Murad asked. And Raf realized he had no idea of the answer either.

She looked at Murad. 'Since my uncle arrived,' said Hani, 'life's been one long headache.' She smiled as she said it and neither of the other two quite noticed she'd avoided answering Murad's question.

'Almost there.' Hani's announcement came just before Raf turned right between two houses and edged his way through a tiny village, headlights still unlit. She'd been collecting old advertising murals and so far she had a *Dr Pierre*, two *Fernet-Branca (la digestif miraculeux)*, a faded blue *dubo, dubon, dubonnet* and one for underwear by *Rhouyl*, which, if she understood the faded French correctly, was guaranteed to induce health-giving static.

Staring from his window of the still-moving car, Murad tried to focus on the world outside. Just enough moon was filtering through the clouds to bathe the soft slopes of Cap Bon in a ghostly fuzz which was almost, but not quite, light. 'How do you know that?' he asked.

Hani shrugged. 'I just do.'

Around them were orange groves in blossom, wizened pine trees, the occasional villa set back from the coast and even a wrought-iron bandstand. The spindly confection set down on a promenade over-looked blue-painted fishing boats that bobbed at anchor.

On the wall opposite, another notice, paper this time, reminding everyone that falcons could not be captured for training until the second week of March. The warning was pasted next to an older poster advertising the *festival de l'épervier*, dated from June the previous year. Light from a bakery window lit both and through its glass could be seen an old man in vest and floppy trousers kneading dough . . .

They ate their brioche from the bag, the pastry still warm enough to make the paper turn translucent down one side. The old man had been polite. Totally unsurprised to be disturbed at 3:00 A.M. by a man and two children wanting food. And he threw in two tiny tarte tatin for Hani and Murad, smiling and nodding as he shooed the three of them towards the door.

'Work to do,' he explained.

Raf nodded.

What passed for a plan in Raf's mind the fox would undoubtedly have dismissed as cage circling, the dysfunctional repetition of a narrow range of gestures. Have an idea, repeat it endlessly until all value is wrung from the original . . . With a sigh, Raf straightened his shoulders and pulled a bell handle.

Welcome to the Andy Warhol school of detective work.

Somewhere inside Dar St Cloud a Victorian bell tipped sideways far enough to hit a silver clapper and the faintest tremor of that blow whispered back through the wire to reach Raf's fingers. The bell was an affectation. One made worthless by two small Zeiss cameras that swivelled, cranelike to catch Raf and his companions in their gaze.

Returning his eyes, Raf shifted through the spectrum. Checking out what he already knew, the three of them were blanket-lit by infrared and targeted at waist height by pinhead lasers. He could see tiny lenses set into the portico walls. Then the door opened and Raf forgot about armaments. Only panic could make the Marquis do something that stupid and this was not a character trait associated with Astophe de St Cloud, recognized *bâtard* of the French Emperor and a man who'd once offered Raf more money than he could even begin to imagine.

Three percent of the price of North Africa's biggest oil refinery, plus the same cut on oil fields in the Sudan and various offshore sites. All Raf had needed to do in return was betray Zara's father. Hamzah Effendi would fall. His share of a refinery that flickered ghosts of flame across the night sky on the edge of El Iskandryia would go up for sale. Enabling St Cloud to significantly increase his prestige and personal wealth.

Raf had not forgotten that offer any more, he imagined, than St Cloud had forgiven Raf's refusal to oblige.

'Tell St Cloud that Ashraf Bey needs to ask him some questions.'

'Is His Excellency expecting you?' The man who showed them into the hall was Scottish – though he spoke in an Edinburgh accent so clipped it could have come from an English film, the kind where butlers wore frock coats, which, actually, was what he seemed to be wearing.

'What do you think?' Raf replied.

'I'll see if His Excellency is in.' And with that St Cloud's majordomo shuffled off towards an arch outlined in two shades of rose marble, leaving the three of them alone in a hall lit by gas-fired sconces designed to look like candle flame.

'Well, what a pleasant surprise.' The voice was higher than one might have expected given the undoubted gravitas of the man limping his way toward them in gold dressing gown and leather slippers.

'You know why this room is so high?'

'No,' said Raf. 'But no doubt you'll tell me.'

The Marquis laughed. 'I had to make a trip,' he said and something in those words raised hairs on the back of Hani's neck. 'So I left my butler in charge . . . This was years ago,' he added, as if the age of the house wasn't obvious. 'And I told him to tell the *felaheen* when to stop and gave him a height to which to work.'

The old man raised a silver-topped cane and gestured at the nearest wall, where tiny alternating blue and white tiles filled the spaces between evenly spaced double pillars, each of which was topped by a broad capital. The pillars were pink marble, the capitals sandstone.

'You based it on Cordoba,' Hani said.

St Cloud nodded. 'Only my man got so drunk that when I got back, this had happened.' He pointed to a second tier of double pillars above the first. 'Not those pillars, obviously, just the height of the wall behind. The workmen expected to be told to stop so they kept on building.' The Marquis shrugged. 'Fair enough,' he added, in a tone of voice that made Hani decide on the spot that, where St Cloud was concerned, fairness was unlikely to come into it.

'What happened to your butler?' asked Murad Pasha, his voice thoughtful.

A smile broke across the face of the Marquis and in it Raf saw pure emptiness. 'There was a building accident,' said the Marquis. 'Such things happen. Well, they do in North Africa.' Glancing from Hani to Murad, St Cloud raised his eyebrows. 'You should know,' he told Raf, 'I've been very cross with you – so it was sensible to bring me presents.'

Hani merely blinked, but Murad's eyes widened and he might have stepped backwards if the girl at his side hadn't taken his hand, then hastily let it go. Both Hani and Murad suddenly blushing.

'This isn't a social visit,' Raf said flatly. 'And the children stay with me. We're here so Murad Pasha can meet the man who tried to murder his grandfather.' He turned to the still-flustered boy, almost as if intending to introduce him formally to St Cloud.

'I did no such . . .' Outrage froze words in the old man's throat.

'You are not to leave this house,' announced Raf. 'And you will surrender your *carte blanche* to me and the keys to all the cars in your garage.'

'And the helicopter,' Hani whispered. Catching Murad's eye, she shrugged and explained, surprisingly gently for her, 'there's a helipad on the lawn.'

'Out of the question.' St Cloud had found his voice. One that Raf could only describe as oozing bile. 'I have total diplomatic immunity. God . . .' The old man shook so hard with fury that for the first time since his visitors had entered Dar St Cloud he actually need his silver-topped stick. 'You can't just march in here.'

'Actually,' said Raf, 'I think you'll find I can. Because the alternative is that I place you under arrest and call police HQ in Tunis to have a van come out to collect you.' Raf shrugged. 'Who knows,' he added, 'given your tastes you might enjoy a week in the cells with a child molester. I'm sure you'd have lots to talk about . . .'

'And if I refuse?'

'Refuse what?' Raf asked. 'To be arrested?'

St Cloud's nod was stiff. His scowl that of a man who'd faced worse things than two nervous children and the black-suited son of an Emir. 'What will your officers do,' said St Cloud coldly, 'manhandle me into a car? They wouldn't . . .'

'Dare?' One second Raf was watching St Cloud, the next he had a pearl-handled Colt pressed hard into the side of the old man's neck, at an angle guaranteed to remove most of his skull.

No one could remember seeing him move.

'Other people might be afraid of you,' said Raf. 'I don't have that problem.' Pulling back the hammer the way the Sufi had done, he squeezed the trigger so that only his thumb kept the hammer from falling. 'You really think you can resist arrest?'

Around the Marquis the hall began to darken as the face in front of him changed unexpectedly/impossibly from human to something positively other.

The old man could taste smoke and feel a flat wall of heat that threatened to sear his papery skin. Every tile beneath his feet was burning. Except that there were no tiles because he was walking over a glowing chasm of red ember and flickering flame, while some unseen thing ripped mouthfuls of flesh from his shoulder.

He knew, without needing to be told, that he was standing over the entrance to hell.

'Well?'

St Cloud blinked.

The tearing in his flesh dissolved as the pressure against his throat lessened, then almost disappeared.

'Well what?' he asked in a voice little more than a whisper.

'Still feel like resisting arrest?'

Merely blinking was enough to spill tears down cheeks no amount of laser peel had been able to give back their beautiful youth. 'No.' St Cloud shook his head, the slightest movement. All he wanted to do was check his shoulder for scars and look in a glass to see if that unforgiving heat had seared his face, but he didn't quite dare.

'I had nothing to do with that attempt,' he said. 'Nothing at all to do with the death of Eugenie de la Croix. You have my word.'

'And you have mine,' said Raf, 'that I *will* find who tried to kill my father. And when I do that person will be arrested, no matter what.' The very flatness of Raf's words threatened more clearly than any anger could do. 'Feel free to pass that on to anyone you think should know . . .'

CHAPTER 35

Thursday 3rd March

As dawn's white thread became visible over the Golfe de Hammamet a call quavered onto the wind from the minaret of Nebeul mosque, *Allahu Akbar* intoned four times, followed by *Ashhadu anna la ilah ill'-Allah*, I testify there is no God besides God. And finally, towards the end, a phrase to distinguish this call from those that came later. *Al-salatu khayr min al-nawn.* Prayer is better than sleep.

Though both of those were a rarity for Raf.

Only now was he beginning to understand, as opposed to know, the difference between various types of Islamic building. A *mosque* was a church, well, it was to Raf. A *marbarat* the tomb of a saint at which believers might pray (a habit discouraged in the Middle East, but popular in North Africa where Berber instincts lightened the stark purity of their conqueror's interpretation).

A *ribat* was a fortified monastery, *medressa* were schools, somewhere between a tiny university and a religious college, *zaouia* were shrines, often Sufi . . .

What Raf didn't understand, or even know, was what value this knowledge had for a man who lacked all belief in God; for whom mosques were works of intricate beauty and calls to prayer haunting echoes of antiquity; but who saw nothing at the centre. Who saw, in fact, no centre at all.

'Can I ask you something?' said Hani, when she'd finished her prayers.

'Of course.' Raf dropped the Bugatti down a gear to overtake an elderly truck loaded with soldiers.

'Who's Tiri?' She hesitated for a second. 'When you left that note. You signed it "Tiri." '

'My fox,' Raf said and Hani nodded.

'What fox?' Murad demanded crossly. He was leaning on Ifritah's

783

basket, which rested between Hani and him on the fat leather backseat of the Bugatti. Raf wasn't sure where he'd put his action figure but Ninja Nizam hadn't appeared once since Hani accused Murad of being childish.

'The fox . . .' Raf thought about it. 'The fox is an identity.'

'Ashraf Bey's an assassin,' said Hani. 'So he needs to be lots of different people . . . I didn't know the fox was called Tiri,' she added.

'It's called lots of things,' said Raf. 'And I'm not an assassin.'

'No,' Hani said. 'Of course not.'

Beyond Hammamet was a turning for the Al, south towards Sousse and Kairouan. Glancing in his mirror before overtaking the next truck, Raf saw Murad still staring at him. The moment the boy met Raf's gaze he dropped his own.

They'd had a brief quarrel on the road back from Dar St Cloud. Anger exploded from the boy as he demanded to know why Raf had failed to arrested the Marquis. In that shouted fury had been everything the twelve-year-old felt for his father; mostly love and fear, plus a primal, night-waking panic at the thought of life without certainty or comfort.

'You should have arrested him.'

'St Cloud didn't do it,' Hani had said softly, resting one hand on the boy's arm. Murad shook her off.

'But Ashraf Bey said . . .'

'He was bluffing,' explained Hani as she climbed into the car. Her smile faded the moment new fury twisted Murad's face. This time it was at being excluded from what Raf had known and Hani only suspected. Their visit to Dar St Cloud had been cage rattling, little more. The Marquis paid no taxes, had tastes that were highly dubious and based himself in a country without a single extradition treaty. He had more to lose from Emir Moncef's death than almost anyone.

Since learning this, Murad had been almost translucent with silence. Pointedly ignoring Hani and her endless spray of facts about Khayr el Din, better known as the Barbary pirate Barbarossa, and the sack of Tunis by Charles V of Spain, in which seventy thousand men, women and children were slaughtered.

That he'd asked about the fox at all was significant.

'I'm sorry,' Raf said. 'One problem is I don't always know what I'm going to do or how things are about to work out.' He yanked the Bugatti's thin steering wheel and managed to avoid a cartload of goatskins, untreated ones to judge from the smell. 'That makes it difficult to warn people in advance.'

'It's a children of Lilith thing,' Hani added. Although it was obvious from Murad's blank stare that this didn't make it any clearer.

The boy shrugged with all the weight of coming adolescence on his shoulders. 'I just was wondering,' said Murad. 'You know, back there, what exactly happened?'

Raf opened his mouth to answer but Hani got in first.

'What happened,' she told Murad, 'was that Uncle Ashraf put a curse on the Marquis. Children of Lilith can do that.'

Murad's eyes widened and, without even realizing, he made a sign against the evil eye. And then flicked his glance fearfully from the face of his cousin to the dark-suited stranger in the front. The elder brother no one had bothered to tell him he had.

'Do you believe in magic?' Raf asked.

Murad nodded, fiercely.

'You shouldn't,' Raf told him, 'it doesn't exist. There are no djinn. If you hear something go creep in the night and it's not a burglar then it's a cat . . . Everything can be explained,' he added, before Hani had time to protest. 'Even those things that can't.'

'How do you explain things that can't be explained?' Murad demanded doubtfully.

'By admitting we don't yet have an explanation.'

The boy thought about that for as long as it took Raf to drop back a gear and overtake three trucks, leaving soldiers radiating outrage as he roared by in the half dark, lights still off.

'So what happened with the Marquis?' said Murad. He spoke slowly, listening to his own words as he said them. Raf could remember another boy like that. A boy who tasted each word as it was said. Who survived in dark places because his words, wielded viciously, could do more damage than the fists of other boys.

Which left Raf wondering whose fists Murad had been avoiding. Or if he'd learnt to think before he spoke for other reasons.

'I put a gun to his throat,' said Raf. 'That's usually enough to make anyone afraid.'

The boy nodded uncertainly. 'But he's St Cloud,' Murad said, obviously unable to think of another way to put it. 'Even my brother Kashif Pasha is scared of him.'

'Kashif is scared of Uncle Ashraf,' Hani pointed out. 'Anyone with any sense is. He works for the Sublime Porte.'

'No, I don't . . .'

'Then why wear the *chelengk*?' Hani asked triumphantly.

He thought about what she'd said before that. 'Are you?' he asked.

'Afraid of you? Of course I am,' Hani said. 'Every time you do whatever you did back there.'

785

Raf sighed. 'Did you notice a mark left on his neck afterwards from the muzzle of the gun? And my hand on the back of his neck?'

Hani nodded.

'I cut off his blood supply. Oxygen starvation combined with panic. It made an ancient part of St Cloud's brain kick in, nothing else.'

'That was it?' said Murad.

'Sure,' Raf said. 'Simple oxygen starvation.' He avoided mentioning the flames still dancing djinnlike across the inside of his eyes or the rawness that tightened his face like the aftereffects of searing heat.

CHAPTER 36

'Wait in the car,' Raf told them when they finally reached Kairouan. 'I'll get some breakfast.'

'Crêpe,' suggested Murad, 'with jam and cream cheese.'

'I don't think so,' Hani said. 'Does it look like that kind of place?' She wound down her window and sniffed, inhaling the cafés, street stalls and rotisseries. 'Get some *briek*,' she told Raf. 'And Coke, if you can find any.'

A dozen signs for local colas swung in the breeze. All variations on a theme of red and blue. None had names Hani recognized. This whole country was less like El Iskandryia than she'd first imagined.

'I'll see what I can do,' Raf promised.

Watching her uncle stride away, Hani waited until he was lost in the crowd. His black coat swallowed by the burnous and jellabas of those around him. 'Okay,' she said, turning to Murad, 'I'm going shopping. You wait in the car.'

Murad Pasha stared at her.

Hani eased open her door and checked that the road was clear before beginning to slide herself out.

'I'm coming with you.'

'No,' Hani said hastily. 'Someone has to stay with the car,' she insisted, 'and you're the boy . . .'

'So?'

Wide eyes watched him, apparently shocked. 'I'm a girl,' said Hani. 'Surely you don't expect me to stand guard over the car all by myself in a strange city?'

Murad settled back. His eyes already scanning the shop fronts. 'Don't be long,' he said.

The first chemist Hani entered was full of old men who stared as if she'd walked in from another planet. So, muttering an apology, she gave an elegant bow, which she hoped would muddle them even further. The second catered to Soviet tourists. Hani knew this because a poster in the window had pack shots of painkillers and cough mixture above simple descriptions written in five languages, three of which Hani could read.

Catering to Soviet tourists was entirely different to there being any. Hani realized this as soon as she pushed her way through the shop's bead curtain and found the place empty, apart, that was, from an old man with what looked like the inward stare of a mystic or kif smoker. Although, it turned out to be neither because when Hani got closer, she realized his eyes were milky with cataracts.

'*Saháh de-kháyr*,' she said politely.

'*Saháh de-kháyr*,' he replied, then added, '*Es-salám aláykum.*'

So Hani had to start all over, replying *and to you peace*, before rewishing him good day. Formalities complete, she stopped, unsure how to continue. She could see what she thought she needed on a shelf behind the counter, low down and almost out of sight.

The man waited while Hani opened and shut her mouth so often she was in danger of turning into one of Zara's promised carp.

'*Telephone?*' she muttered finally.

Absolute silence greeted this request.

Pulling a note from her pocket, Hani held it out to the old man. The note was American, a five-dollar bill.

The man called something over his shoulder and a young woman appeared, hastily wrapping her scarf around her head. Only to relax slightly when she discovered her customer was a child.

'Telephone?' Hani repeated.

Taking the bill from the man's hands she held it up to the light and slipped it quickly into her dress pocket. Man and woman had a hasty conversation, so fast and so low that overhearing was impossible. Whatever the content, they seemed to reach a conclusion.

'No telephone,' said the woman. 'Not here. But I take you . . .' She gestured towards the rear and Hani realized that she was meant to follow. For about fifty paces she fought her way down a busy back alley, then the woman steered her towards a small door set in a crumbling wall.

'Through here,' she said, as she pushed Hani ahead of her, shouting '*Hamid!*' as they came out into a small courtyard.

A second yell produced a head peering from an upstairs window. Another burst of conversation followed in what Hani finally realized was *chelha*, the original dialect of Kairouan's Berber inhabitants.

'Where do you want to call?' asked the woman, tossing Hani's answer up to the boy, then stopping for his reply.

'El Iskandryia we can do,' she agreed, 'but it will cost more than five dollars . . .'

Reluctantly Hani peeled another note from the roll in her dress pocket and palmed it into a small square before making a pretence of searching her remaining pockets, muttering crossly all the while.

'My last one,' she said.

The cell phone was a Siemens. Unquestionably illegal in a country where all cell phones had to be registered with the police.

'Two minutes,' said the woman, 'call me when you're done.' And she vanished into the house to give the foreign girl some privacy. The boy remained sitting on a stone bench next to the courtyard entrance just to make sure Hani didn't suddenly disappear with his phone.

Hani could just imagine it. Donna stood in the kitchen surrounded by pans, trying to ignore the buzz of the coms screen, Zara out shopping and Khartoum lost in thought or rereading tales of the Ineffable Mullah Nasrudin, all of which he already knew by heart.

She sighed.

The message Hani left was simple. She was in Kairouan with her uncle. On her way to Tozeur. There was nothing to worry about.

'Where have you been?' Murad demanded when Hani finally got back.

'Getting these,' said Hani, handing him a cardboard dish of *makrouth*, lozenge-shaped sweetmeats filled with date paste. She dropped a cheap paper napkin next to his knee and clambered up into the huge Bugatti. The rest of the napkins she stuffed into a side pocket. She let Murad eat the sweetmeats because, unfortunately, even after her walk her tummy still had cramps.

CHAPTER 37

Second coffee. That was how Eduardo counted his days. First coffee, second coffee, third coffee . . .

The first always found Eduardo listening to IskTV. While others watched the newsfeed avid for every close-up, Eduardo listened carefully as he doodled hats and moustaches onto pictures in *Iskandryia Today* or filled in the Os in every headline.

The Emir of Tunis had been taken into protective custody following the declaration of martial law in Ifriqiya. The story was in his paper as well as on-screen. *Iskandryia Today* treated this as news while IskTV assumed it was background, leading with a different story. One that had His Excellency Kashif Pasha, the Emir's eldest son, swearing that his father was alive, safe and would remain that way. Apparently Kashif Pasha swore this on his life.

What IskTV found interesting was the fact that this promise was relayed on Kashif's behalf by a half brother, Ashraf al-Mansur, who personally visited the *Mosque de trois ports* in Kairouan to pass the message to the head of the Assiou Brotherhood.

The head of the brotherhood had, as requested, released Kashif Pasha's promise to the world.

So Eduardo wasn't surprised to receive a scrambled call just after second coffee. Although it took him a moment to remember that he needed to connect an optic from the silver Seiko he wore to the computer on his desk. That was what the man had told him to do, plug in as soon as Eduardo heard the hiss and never try to make a connection using infrared. Which was fine, because Eduardo wouldn't have known where to start.

A doctor at the Imperial Free once suggested Eduardo reduce his coffee intake to one cup a day but Eduardo had barely paused to consider this. The man was a foreigner, newly arrived in the city, and would learn. No one who actually lived in El Isk for longer than a week could have made that suggestion.

Instead, Eduardo had agreed with himself to cut his intake to eight cups a day. This wasn't always possible, given the nature of his job; but his success or failure gave Eduardo something to talk about to Rose, a mild-natured whore he'd met a few months earlier, when the man sent him to do a job at Maison 52, Pascal Coste.

Rose claimed to be English and, although she had the hips and buttocks of an Egyptian, the smallness of her breasts convinced Eduardo that this might be the truth. As did the half-smoked Ziganov forever hanging from her fingers, its gold band stained with lipstick. In Iskandryia, even licensed whores didn't smoke in public.

But then women tended not to visit cafés either. Unless it was one of those expensive places around Place Saad Zaghloul like Le Trianon, where ordinary rules seemed not to apply. Money did that, Eduardo had decided. It rewrote the rules. Or perhaps it just remade them into something so complex and discreet that ordinary people like him no longer understood what they were. The man was like that, governed by rules Eduardo took on trust.

Eduardo's office was above a haberdasher's at the back of a bus station on Place Zaghloul. The place was a walk-up with winding stairs and a toilet on the half landing, which Eduardo had to share with the shop below. It had a melamine desk, a cheap chair in black plastic that looked almost like leather and a grey metal filing cabinet. Plus a state-of-the-art computer, quite out of keeping with the rest of the furniture.

The computer lived on a side table. Well, it would have been a side table if it hadn't actually been an old door supported at either end by plinths of crudely mortared bricks. Eduardo, whose work it was, had tried to apologize for its ugliness but the man had waved away Eduardo's explanation. It seemed Ashraf Bey liked the door/table combination more than he liked anything else in the office.

Sharing Eduardo's office space were two cockroaches and a colony of ants who dwindled come autumn and, Eduardo imagined, would be back with the spring. He wasn't sure, not having had the place long enough to find out. The cockroaches remained, however, sharing his desk and living off a diet of sugar that fell from Eduardo's morning doughnut.

With his first coffee, which he drank just after dawn, Eduardo ordered an almond croissant. He'd adopted the habit after having breakfast one morning with the bey because this was what the bey ate.

'Eduardo?' The voice came hollow with static and thin from being bounced off a satellite too far above El Iskandryia for Eduardo to really comprehend. All the same, he would have known it anywhere.

'Excellency . . .'

The voice sighed.

Eduardo was meant to call him *boss* on the phone. Even when answering his watch in the office out of sight of everyone else.

'I'm here, boss,' the small man said hurriedly.

'You listening?' The voice on the other end wasn't cross, just careful.

'Sure, boss. Always . . . No, I mean it.' Eduardo tried to sound hurt but the man was right, Eduardo hardly ever listened. And when Eduardo did he always had to concentrate extra hard to make sense of what the other person said.

'Yeah, I got it,' Eduardo said finally, when the voice had finished explaining what Eduardo was expected to do. 'Well, except for that bit about becoming a policeman . . .'

Life was a series of comings and goings . . .

Some philosopher said that, or it might have been Cheb Rai; every time the thought popped into Eduardo's head he got a tune just out of reach. Three chords leading to a fourth that Eduardo knew would, should he ever remember it, give him the whole.

All the same, whoever said or sang them, the words rang true. People came and went. They walked into one's life and walked out again with no reason that Eduardo could see, but then he wasn't very clever. Lots of people had told him that. Smarter people could see the threads that tied together events. And none were smarter than the bey. Eduardo really believed that.

In the cafés people talked of how the trial of the warlord Colonel Abad was tied to a dock strike rolling out across the North African littoral. And how Ashraf al-Mansur, now in Tunis, had gone there to kill the father who'd abandoned him. Others insisted he was there to save the old man's life. And a few, mostly Bolsheviks, were of the opinion that the Emir was already dead and all al-Mansur wanted was to make sure he got his share of the inheritance.

Eduardo knew different.

Ashraf Bey was trying to find his mother's original wedding certificate . . . Sometimes politics were way more complicated than Eduardo could understand.

CHAPTER 38

Friday 4th March.

An elegant young woman outside Arrivals was waving for a taxi. Something Eduardo didn't need to do since he had a car already waiting. At least, he had a uniformed driver clutching a board with Eduardo's name on it so Eduardo assumed he had a car as well.

Eduardo almost offered the woman a lift into the centre but when he nodded to her she just scowled. So Eduardo went back to helping Rose navigate her way through a crowd of C3N cameramen waiting for taxis at the front of Tunis Arrivals.

This was what happened if one suddenly lifted the embargo on flights to facilitate the departure of nonessential diplomatic staff. More people turned up than left. He was pretty sure that wasn't what the UN had in mind.

'We're here, sir.'

Eduardo liked that last word. It suggested that the driver thought he and Rose looked properly Western, which they were more or less. Soviet tourists would have got *commissar*, not meant obviously but always good for increasing *baksheesh* as tourists called tips, getting wrong both country and language. Anyone local wearing a suit like Eduardo's would have merited *effendi*, just to be on the safe side.

So that *sir* meant the young driver realized Eduardo was not local and not a Soviet tourist. Unless, of course, the boy called everybody that.

Originally Eduardo had been planning to fly alone and travel first class, the man having said buy any ticket he liked as long as the flight left that afternoon. But when Eduardo realized that premium cost half the price of first he decided Rose should come with him.

So that was what they did. And though Eduardo got the feeling Rose had never flown before, she insisted she'd flown dozens of times to numerous destinations. But then he'd told her exactly the same.

What's more, she'd enjoyed the flight. Eduardo knew, because he'd been careful to ask. And she looked great. He'd been careful to tell her that too.

The Benz waiting outside Tunis Arrivals was big and black, smarter than Eduardo could ever have expected, with metal pipes coming out of the engine and running down either side of the hood. The pipes had been silver to start with but now they were grey with wide bands of kingfisher blue, like petrol floating on top of a fresh puddle.

Alexandre, who was young and wore the uniform of a Tunis detective (something he suspected his visitors might not yet have realized), walked round to the back door of the Emir's second-favourite car and held it open.

At a nod from the small man, the woman clambered in and smoothed a black dress covered with red roses down over her pink knees. Leaving her partner still anxiously eyeing their luggage, such as it was.

'My case . . .'

Ashraf Bey's original call had told Eduardo to buy a new suit, new shoes, several shirts and a tie. The man had even specified the colour of each: dark blue for the suit, white for the shirts and red for the tie (no stripes). He'd said nothing about buying a case in which to put these things.

'Of course, sir.' Alexandre was apologetic. 'I should have realized you'd need your case with you.' He picked up the cardboard box with its cheap handle, wondering at its lightness, and waited for Eduardo to join the woman. Only then did Alexandre put the case in the well of the borrowed car, beside Eduardo's feet.

'Where to, sir?'

Eduardo thought about it. 'What are my options?'

Alexandre tried not to sigh.

Accelerated entry to officer level and descent from an ex-*colon* family that had owned dairy farms in the High Tell guaranteed he got given the shitty jobs by sergeants who grew up in the medina or the nouvelle ville, people he'd outrank within the year and who knew that fact but could never forgive it.

All the same, the fact Alexandre had been warned to handle this job with discretion meant the anxious-looking man in the rear seat had to be somebody important. Exactly why that might be became clear when Alexandre opened his mouth to answer, only to discover that the man sat behind him was already talking, mostly to himself.

'We could start with the Police HQ, I suppose.'

Alexandre nodded.

'Or we could go find the boss . . .'

To Alexandre that meant his colonel. He got the feeling this man had someone else in mind. 'The boss?' Alexandre asked, in a tone he hoped was politely casual.

'Ashraf al-Mansur . . .'

'You know the bey?'

'He's my boss.' Eduardo sounded as proud of the fact as he felt, which was very proud indeed.

'And my boss too,' Alexandre said. 'Apparently Ashraf Bey is the new Chief of Police.' That was what he'd been told anyway. It was all change at HQ.

'Actually . . .' Eduardo glanced at Rose and looked embarrassed. 'The thing is, you see . . . I'm the new Chief.' Eduardo tasted the words as he said them and sat up a little straighter in his seat.

And, like a good detective, he noticed the way Alexandre immediately did the same, straightening his shoulders and quickly adjusting his cap. That was when he realized Alexandre was one of his men.

'I'm sorry, Your Excellency. I didn't know.'

'Why should you?' Eduardo said, feeling expansive. 'And you don't need to call me Excellency, sir is fine . . . All the same, I have a question for you. An important question.'

Alexandre froze.

'What do you know . . . ?' Eduardo whipped out a leather notebook he'd bought at Iskandryia airport, flipped it open, and watched the opening page come alight. 'Let me see, what do you know about a pâtissier called Pascal Boulart? Other than the fact he was stabbed in an alley behind Maison Hafsid and a sous-chef was arrested . . .'

It turned out Alexandre knew even less than that. He knew the killing all right, he just had no memory of anyone having been arrested by the police. As Alexandre tried to point out, as circumspectly as possible, this might just mean the murderer had been picked up by Kashif Pasha's men.

Although the military wing of the police was meant to liaise with the civilian branches, this sometimes failed to happen, very occasionally, obviously.

'Find out if they did,' said Eduardo. 'And get me files on everyone killed in the massacre at the Domus Aurea.'

'There were only four.' Alexandre regretted the remark as soon as he made it. 'I mean, the fifth one got away.'

'Four is enough,' Eduardo said firmly. 'Now take me to the hotel.' He needed a shower, as did Rose. And with luck, if the shower was big enough, they could share.

'Hotel . . . ?'

Eduardo nodded.

'You are not staying at a hotel, sir. My orders were to take you wherever you wanted and deliver your luggage to the Dar Ben Abdallah.'

'*Dar, maison, hôtel,*' said Eduardo, 'it's all the same, you know.' He turned to Rose. 'In French,' he explained, '*hôtel* means big house, like in *Hôtel de Ville*. Isn't that right?'

Alexandre nodded, not taking his eyes off the road.

On their way into the city all the other traffic moved out of the way. Eduardo was wondering about this until he remembered the flag. He wasn't sure what the flag on the hood stood for but it looked very official.

CHAPTER 39

Sunday 6th March

Palms shaded yellow earth, so that sunlight sketched patterns across the banks of a narrow stream, highlighting twigs and dead fronds. The water in the *seguia* was dirty, the grass edging the ditch and the undersides of the palms less bright than Zara expected. Only ungrown dates, tiny and green and still vulnerable to the sand winds, seemed created from a brighter scheme altogether. This was a world of ochres and earth hues. An Impressionist umbrella restricted to the palette of a Klee.

Farther along, half-in/half-out of the stream lay a fallen palm with its trunk ringed like an endlessly extruded pinecone. The crown was gone but, since fronds extended fingerlike from beneath the sand that covered a newly repaired footbridge, the reason was not hard to find.

The coolness of the gardens was in welcome contrast to the last fifty miles across the chott, when the air had been salt and hot, unseasonably so the taxi driver had told her, several times.

'I'm here to collect Lady Hana al-Mansur.'

Zara stood on the edge of Tozeur's famous grove, home of the translucent *deglet nur* and site of a quarter of a million palms fed by two hundred springs that carried water to the date trees. The only thing to stop her reaching a small palace on the other side of the stream was a single soldier guarding a narrow bridge. The palace had been built by one of the old beys or emirs. It must have been, because only a notable could get away with building a palace on land historically reserved for growing dates.

Over the centuries, gold and slaves had passed through this area, carpets and priceless manuscripts, swords and spices. None of them creating the wealth of the date palms. At its height, a millennium before, a thousand dromedaries a day were said to have left Tozeur, laden with dates and even now many of the towns inhabitants were *khammes*,

797

sharecroppers who maintained the groves and in return took one-fifth of the harvest as their pay.

Behind Zara in an airport taxi sat a driver, looking in disbelief at a pile of notes on his lap. She'd paid him what was on the meter, Tunis to Tozeur, having brushed away his offer to negotiate.

In fact, the man could honestly say she'd hardly glanced at the meter their entire trip, most of which she'd spent watching distant green fields turn to sahal before becoming moonlike around the phosphate town of Gafsa. A place of which a wise man once said, 'Its water is blood, its air poison, you may live there a hundred years without making one true friend . . .'

'She is here?' Zara said, frowning at the guard. 'Hani al-Mansur?'

The soldier to whom Zara spoke was thickset, with cropped hair more salt than pepper. He'd been having one of those weeks.

'I'm not sure, my lady . . .' The man made a show of unclipping a radio from his belt, wondering as he did so, why the young woman's face suddenly tightened. 'I'll make a call.'

'Zara Quitrimala,' Zara said, *'Ms* Zara Quitrimala.' The way she said it made her name begin with a hiss. 'And you don't use honorifics when talking to me. I'm perfectly ordinary.'

The look the guard gave her begged leave to differ.

Moncef Hauara was unmarried which was rare for a middle-aged man in Tozeur, unmarried and about to retire from active duty. Living with his mother, a woman who'd spent her life repairing clothes for notables, he recognized both shot silk and the French way of cutting on the bias. Although, if asked, he'd have said the jet buttons were what he noticed. Most manufacturers used black plastic while a few of the flashier labels chose machine-cut obsidian. Only Dior and Chanel still used buttons hand-carved from Italian jet, the way they'd always done.

He knew, the way he knew a storm was brewing, exactly how long it would have taken someone to sew that jacket. How long it took to double-stitch the hems and edge each buttonhole. There were a dozen differing grades of silk, variable in their wear and lasting qualities as well as their ease of cutting and ability to hold dye.

There was nothing ordinary about that dress or the cut. And Corporal Hauara doubted strongly that there was anything remotely ordinary about the woman who wore it. At least not in any sense that a soon-to-retire soldier who still lived with his mother would understand.

'Yes, sir. I'll do that.'

The corporal clicked off his radio and promptly dialled a fresh number. Sweat was beginning to show beneath his arms. A short conversation followed, of which Zara heard only one half.

'A young lady.'

'Zara Quitrimala.'

'Quitrimala.'

'Yes, sir. Quite possibly.'

'Yes, sir. I'll ask.'

'Forgive me,' said the guard, 'but Major Jalal would like to know if Hana al-Mansur is expecting you? Also, why you think she is here . . .'

For someone so determined Zara did a good imitation of not having foreseen that question. 'My father's . . .'

Corporal Hauara knew who her father was. At least he did now.

'He's guardian to . . .' Stumbling over the sense as much as the words, Zara tried to work out exactly what her father was to Hani, other than extremely fond. A fact replete with problems for someone whose own childhood memories were of a loud, occasionally threatening figure; a version of himself Hamzah Effendi seemed to have left behind.

'She told me she'd be here,' said Zara finally, waving a piece of headed paper, signed by her father and the Khedive of El Iskandryia. This announced that they were the child's trustees and Zara acted with full authority. It slid over the fact they were trustees only where the child's money was concerned. Zara's furious request to her father that he let her go save Hani from imminent civil war had seen to that.

As for the Khedive, Zara had no doubts that he countersigned Hamzah's letter because she had tears in her eyes when she asked.

'What time does curfew begin?' Zara demanded.

Corporal Hauara looked at her. 'Curfew?'

'It was on C3N. What time do Kashif Pasha's troops lock down the streets at night . . .'

'There is no curfew,' the guard said carefully. 'At least not in Tozeur. Perhaps in Tunis.' He wanted to add something else, but the years had taught him to swallow such thoughts. That was the secret of surviving. To stay silent while seeming to do nothing but talk.

The small anteroom into which Zara was shown looked vast, largely because all four walls were mirror. Each mirror was framed within an elaborate double arch, each arch supported on stick-thin pillars topped by gilded capitals that displayed endless repetitions of a simplified, stylized acanthus.

It was in the worst possible taste.

The left-hand arch of one wall hid a door. Zara thought she knew which mirror it was but had a feeling that, if she so wished, it would be easy to forget. Forgetting about her reflection was more difficult.

An intense, neatly dressed Arab woman with scraped-back hair, still not yet out of her teens and with perfect, almost American teeth. Thinner than she used to be if not as slim as she wanted. Unmarriageable, way richer than could be justified and very much alone. Zara swept tears out of her eyes with a furious hand, only to wince as a thousand doubles made the identical movement.

First Raf had gone, then Hani. So she was here to take Hani back, while there was still time. As for Raf . . .

'My lady.'

'I'm not . . .' She turned to where a man in major's uniform stood by the open door, his sudden appearance and the opening of the door having rendered the room small again.

'His Highness is busy welcoming his mother, Lady Maryam. So he sends his apologies. When this is done, His Highness requires a word.'

'About what?' Zara demanded. Only too aware that her eyes were red.

Major Jalal shrugged. 'I'm only Kashif Pasha's *aide-de-camp*' he said modestly. 'But these are difficult times so I imagine His Highness is worried for your safety.'

CHAPTER 40

'Okay, let's try that again.'

Eduardo spun the knife in his hand and tossed it at a door scarred by more cuts than it was possible to count. At least, impossible to count without taking the offending object off its hinges, having the thing carried to Police HQ and getting someone to shoot it, resize the photographs and cross off the cuts one at a time.

A lifetime's worth of staff at Maison Hafsid had stood in a short corridor outside the cellar kitchens and honed their throwing skills or taken out their frustration on that cupboard door.

'You know what's really interesting?' Eduardo said.

No one answered, but then that wasn't surprising. He'd recognized them all. Not the names and not even the faces, but the types. Loners and misfits. The usual scum found working in kitchens. And they'd recognized him. As one of them.

Besides, the knife he threw was the one found plunged into the heart of Pascal Boulart. In the alley behind Maison Hafsid.

'What's really interesting is that the killer left no fingerprints on his blade . . .' There were, in fact, dozens of fingerprints on the blade, but all of them belonged to the coroner, his assistant or members of the police who'd processed the knife later, when it was being bagged for evidence.

'Why do you think that is?' Eduardo asked.

A boy shrugged.

'Because he wore gloves?' The man who spoke was tall and dark-faced, his hair grey with age. A heavy bruise ripened over one high cheek and his mouth was split. According to a report recently filed by Kashif Pasha's *mubahith*, Chef Edvard could be a difficult and sometimes violent man. So far there had been nothing to suggest that either of those statements was true.

801

'Gloves? Possibly,' Eduardo admitted. 'But then there are none of the victim's fingerprints on the blade either. Which is very odd, because Pascal was stabbed five times . . .' He paused and was disappointed to realize they didn't all immediately see the implication. 'Have you ever been stabbed?'

Only Chef Edvard nodded.

'Show me your hands,' Eduardo demanded.

There were faded slash marks across one palm and a long cicatrix that vanished beneath his sleeve. In return Eduardo showed the chef his own hands with their wounds from days Eduardo did his best not to remember.

'There were no defensive cuts on the hands of Pascal Boulart. His fingerprints were missing from both blade and handle. Do you know what this suggests to me?'

Ripping the knife from battered wood, Eduardo walked ten paces to the far end of the corridor and threw again. Another bull's-eye. Straight into the middle of the door, where it joined a hundred other cuts.

Behind him, where the corridor gave way to the kitchens, someone clapped, probably mockingly but maybe for real. That was Eduardo's tenth throw and the tenth time he'd put the knife in the door exactly where he wanted it.

A misspent childhood had its uses.

'You try.' He pointed to the boy who'd been clapping. A thin youth with a rash on his chin hidden beneath what looked like blusher. 'Come on . . .'

Reluctantly Idries stepped forward. Well aware that he had no choice.

The first thing Eduardo had done on entering the cellar was flash his shield. This was gold, maybe real gold, in a crocodile-skin case with a top that flipped up, like one of those little vid-phones. It had been left for him at Police HQ, in his office, along with a matte black .45 para-Ordnance and a scribble pad of notes covered with Ashraf Bey's writing.

Eduardo hadn't even known he had an office until a fat man with sweat stains under his arms, a man who wouldn't meet his eye, silently offered him the key. Concerned with trying to make sense of His Excellency's terrible writing, it took Eduardo until the next morning to realize his scowling deputy with the striped shirts and perspiration problem was the old Chief.

In the end, unable to translate Ashraf Bey's notes into any language he understood, Eduardo stored them for safety in the top drawer of his new desk and turned to the files he'd asked Alexandre to bring him. Sometimes in life it was just easier to start over.

And he was right; the files were much more interesting.

'Find me the man with stripy shirts,' Eduardo demanded. He had a box on his desk that let him talk to a serious-looking woman in the office outside without having to get up and open the door.

'You wanted me?'

Eduardo indicated a seat without looking up from his files. 'You used to run this place?'

The man's nod was sullen. Although he added, 'Yes, sir,' when Eduardo raised his head from a folder.

'You can have it back once I'm done,' Eduardo said. 'I don't imagine I'll be staying. In fact' – he stared at the unhappy man – 'assume you have total autonomy in everything except the Maison Hafsid case, but first find me . . .' Eduardo glanced down at a crime report. 'Ahmed, cousin of Idries, who worked at the Maison Hafsid.'

At first Chef Edvard felt sure Eduardo was there to shut down his restaurant. Given the disaster at Domus Aurea and the fact he'd put an Egyptian deserter on the staff list as Hassan, because that was the only way to get the man through security clearance, Chef Edvard could hardly have been surprised if this was true.

Mind you, if the *mubahith* had even suspected that second fact he'd already be dead. Chef Edvard's position, held to under questioning, was that he'd assumed the thin-faced blond waiter was just another under-cover police officer providing protection.

Neither he nor his staff had ever seen the man before.

'Throw it,' Eduardo told the boy.

'What about prints?' Idries glanced back at the others, looking for support. At least that's what Eduardo assumed he was looking for.

'I don't want to trick you,' Eduardo said. 'I just want to see you throw the knife.' Pulling a pair of cheap evidence gloves from his suit pocket, he tossed them across. 'Wear these.'

The boy threw as expertly as Eduardo had expected. Without even bothering to heft the knife to find its balance.

'Now you,' he told a girl hovering silently near the back.

She struggled with the gloves, finally throwing with the latex fingers only half over her own so they flopped like a coxcomb. The knife bounced off the door.

'Try again,' said Eduardo as he handed Isabeau the knife and a clean tissue, something Rose insisted he carry. 'Get rid of the gloves,' he said, 'then wipe down blade and handle when you've finished. I don't mind.'

She stared at him.

'Throw,' said Eduardo.

Without the gloves to hamper her, Isabeau put the blade straight into the door.

'I don't understand,' Chef Edvard said into the silence that followed the thud of the blade. 'Are you saying Ahmed flung this knife at my pastry cook? That was how Pascal was killed?'

'Of course not,' said Eduardo. His tone of voice made it clear he'd never heard anything quite so ridiculous. 'Wipe the blade,' Eduardo told the girl, 'and give it to someone else.'

They all threw after that. Taking the handkerchief and carefully wiping clean the knife before passing it to the next person. Even Chef Edvard, his throw little more than a dismissive flick of the wrist that buried the blade in the door at throat height.

'Right,' said Eduardo. 'Only two more questions and we're done.' Plucking the blade from the door one final time, he wiped it on his own shirt and dropped it back into its evidence bag. The stain on its steel blade was rust not blood and its edge was blunt. The only thing this knife had ever been good for was throwing at a door.

'Where's the fat boy?'

Eduardo had read the files, seen the photographs and memorized the names. But just to be safe he'd had the serious-faced assistant at his office type out a list of everyone working at Maison Hafsid and then he'd read them of fat the beginning, like doing a roll call at school. He knew who was missing. Ahmed, obviously. Also Hassan.

'Gone,' Chef Edvard said flatly.

'Where?' Eduardo demanded.

'We don't know. He just didn't show up today. And he missed his shift at Café Antonio last Friday.'

'Let me know if he appears,' said Eduardo. 'Okay, final question. Where *exactly* in the alley was Pascal Boulart's body found? I want each of you to show me in turn.'

Back at his office desk, a plate of *droits de Fatima* lifted from Maison Hafsid already reduced to a blizzard of pastry flakes, the new Chief of Police drew up his own list of clues, using a fountain pen he'd found in the drawer.

Blunt knife, broken handle, rusty blade; no fingerprints; damaged door; empty corridor; clean steps. A body that changed position. And finally, most bizarrely, one misplaced murderer.

Eduardo drew circles around each and joined them together as he'd once seen Ashraf Bey do, but because his clues were written in a list one under the other, the links just sank, like lead weights on a fishing line. So Eduardo wrote his clues out again, arranging them in a circle and joining them with new lines. And then, because it looked so good, he wrote it out a third time, folding one copy to put in his pocket and leaving the other on his desk for everyone else to see.

It was only when Eduardo reached the end of the street, still surreptitiously brushing flakes from his pastry-stained fingers that he realized his detective work would go unappreciated. He was the boss. The only person remotely likely to go near his desk was Marie, who stood up every time he came into her outer office. She seemed far too nervous to take such liberties.

He'd just have to show his clues to Rose instead. Then he'd tell her the answer, maybe. Licking his fingers, Eduardo wiped them afresh on his trousers and went to buy Rose some chocolates. Somehow eating always made him hungry.

CHAPTER 41

'Your Excellency.'

Given that someone had stolen all three door knockers, the barefoot Nubian in the white silk robe had little option but to hammer ever louder on the door of Dar Welham. As a method of attracting Ashraf Bey's attention it proved surprisingly unsuccessful, all but the final knocks being drowned out by the thud of ancient and unserviced fans inside.

Until he made his stop at Kairouan the previous week, Raf hadn't even realized he owned a house in Tozeur, let alone one in the oldest district; but the tall dar with its ochre, geometrically laid brickwork and dark interior had been a wedding present from the Emir to his mother, apparently.

Un présent de mariage.

Isaac & Sons' files were dust-buried on the shelves of their deserted walk-up when Raf and three uniformed officers cut the padlock on the rear and kicked in a door at the top of the stairs.

All it took was Raf presenting himself at Kairouan's Police HQ and demanding the loan of three good officers, bolt cutters and a hydraulic battering ram, one of the small handheld versions. His name alone had been enough to turn his wish list into reality. The officers were uniformed, respectful and obviously experienced. And the really terrifying thing, at least the thing that Raf found really terrifying was that at no point did anyone ask him for any form of identity.

He went looking for a wedding certificate and came back with copies of a deed of ownership, which did just as well. The date he wanted was at the top. While his mother's signature and that of Moncef were at the bottom. Fifty years earlier, on the day after they were married, Moncef had presented his mother with a house in Tozeur and another in Tunis. Fifty years . . .

Lady Nafisa, his aunt, had known this because it was for her that the copies were made by notario Ibrahim ibn Ishaq. Thanking the police officers, Raf had taken one copy of the deed and ordered the men to remove all other documents from the office and have them shredded, then burned. He made the most senior officer repeat that order, all documents, all shredded, all burned.

When Raf left to find Hani, Murad and the Bugatti, the officer was already radioing for backup while the other two had begun to arrange the files into dusty piles on the floor.

Dar Welham, his new house, stood behind the main road from the Palm Groves to Zaouia Ishmailia, on the right, halfway down an alley too old and narrow to merit a name. One side of his street had already been partly rebuilt using traditional yellow brick. Raf's side remained a mess of crumbling façades and locked doorways, with most of the houses obviously empty. Almost all of the triple door knockers, which allowed long-gone inhabitants to know if the person calling was a man, woman or child, had been stolen. As had a number of the old iron locks and the door handles themselves.

The private courtyard of Dar Welham still stank of cat's piss and sewage, although Raf had slopped it down at least three times and tipped buckets of rusty water through the open grilles of the drains. Hani and Murad had concentrated on the inside of the dar, sweeping floors and scrubbing at mineral deposits that had leached up through the floor tiles.

That the dar had electricity to drive its fans at all was a miracle. One involved twisted flex glued direct to rough walls and fed through a large hole into next door's cellar, where Raf jammed open the trip switch of a junction box with half a clothespin. Air-conditioning would obviously have helped. Although being somewhere other than Tozeur at the start of a *khamsin* wind might have been better.

Sand fall was expected. And Murad kept referring to a *chili*, alternating that word with *khamsin*. It had to do with a depression moving into the Gulf of Gebes. One that had kicked the afternoon temperature up to 98°F and threatened to drop sand as far north as Madrid. The local radio station talked about little else.

'Door,' Hani said, looking up from a game of chess. She was winning five games to zero. The only way Murad had been persuaded to play again was her promise that this would be his last for the day and her assurance that he'd soon be good enough to beat her. But then, as Murad pointed out, she'd said that the day before as well.

At Hani's feet stretched Ifritah. Panting in the heat.

'What?' Raf put down the deeds to Dar Welham.

'Someone's at the door,' said Hani. 'I'd go but it's probably for you.'

And it was. Apparently Kashif Pasha's messenger saw nothing odd in presenting an envelope featuring an ersatz version of a European coat of arms, one bearing a Western interpretation of an Othman turban, on a silver salver in the style of Napoleon III, overlaid around the edge with Quranic script in beaten gold, bronze and copper.

'Will there be a reply?'

Having read Kashif's message, Raf put it carefully in his pocket.

'No,' he said, 'I think not.'

The Nubian might have come to the door of Dar Welham barefooted and dressed in a white robe but he drove off in a black four-by-four with smoked windows and roo bars big enough to knock down a buffalo.

'Who was that?' said Hani. She stood on the stairs with Murad behind her. A windup radio was in the boy's hand.

'Just one of Kashif Pasha's friends.'

'My brother Kashif doesn't have friends,' Murad said firmly, then paused, worried that he might have sounded rude. 'I mean,' he said more politely, 'he has only allies or enemies.' The boy's voice made no secret of which camp he'd found himself in. 'What does the message say?'

'That's private.'

Two heads turned to face Raf. Hani's frown now a full-on scowl. 'No secrets,' she reminded Raf. 'Remember? That's what you told me when Aunt Nafisa died. Anything I asked you would answer.'

It had been a simple enough promise, made to a crying child who wanted to know why life was so unfair. One that Raf would have liked an adult, any adult, to have made to him. And it was proving impossibly difficult to keep.

'Hani, I'm really sorry . . .'

'You promised.'

So he had. 'It's from Kashif Pasha,' Raf said.

'But that's the Emir's coat of arms,' Murad insisted.

'I know,' said Raf, 'but it's not his message. Kashif and I need to meet.'

'You're not going to go . . .' Murad sounded appalled that Raf might even consider it. 'Have you listened to the latest news?'

Raf hadn't.

Apparently C3N had been told by St Cloud that Ashraf Bey was behind the attack on Emir Moncef. Colonel Abad, that well-known war criminal, was mentioned. As was Raf's part in helping Abad avoid being brought to justice. The Marquis even managed to suggest that the bey might be behind last autumn's attacks on the Midas Refinery, jointly owned by St Cloud and Hamzah Effendi.

'If you go, Kashif will hurt you,' Murad said flatly. 'I know him.'

'All the same,' said Raf, 'I think I must.' Skimming the note, he ran through words he already knew by heart. The message was short. 'It seems Kashif's captured the missing waiter,' Raf told them both. 'He'd like me to be present at the questioning.'

Hani opened her mouth and shut it again. 'Something else,' she said finally. 'What else?'

'Because of the *current danger*,' said Raf, failing to extract the bleakness from his voice, 'my brother has extended his offer of protective custody to include Zara.'

'She's here?'

'Apparently . . .'

'So what do you want Murad and me to do?' Hani asked.

'Stay here,' said Raf. 'And keep out of trouble. If that's remotely possible.'

Hani's look was doubtful.

CHAPTER 42

Three hours after Raf left, men in black jellabas locked off the unnamed alley using Jeeps they swung across both ends, isolating the stretch in between.

Once again the Jeeps had smoked glass, fat roo bars and whip aerials. The man who seemed in charge had dyed hair combed forward like a Roman emperor, a heavy moustache and a black *mubahith* blouse on without insignia of any kind. Only a slight bald patch and the fact his choice of top accentuated his paunch took the edge off an effect that was, Hani had to admit, still quietly threatening.

'You take a look,' she said, handing Murad an old pair of opera glasses. The boy did what she suggested, staring down at the alley entrance.

'Soldiers,' he said.

Hani nodded.

'In disguise,' she said. 'Who's the man?'

Murad took a second look at the *mubahith* with the weird hair. 'No one I recognize,' he said, like he wasn't sure if that was good or bad.

'Are they from the Emir's guard?'

'Of course not.' Murad shook his head. 'All Eugenie's troops are women.' He spoke as if Eugenie were still alive. 'Those are not women . . .'

Only fear let Hani restrain herself. Some people shouted when they got afraid, others closed down, went silent. That was her. 'Look,' Hani said, 'you think they support Kashif Pasha?'

'You heard the radio,' said Murad. 'All the soldiers support my brother Kashif.'

'Now there's a surprise.' Hani sounded like Zara at her most cross. The way the older girl had been those last few days at the madersa before Raf vanished, sharp and snotty but nothing like as cruel as Raf had been with his dark silences and exile inside his own head.

'Kashif,' Murad said. 'He won't hurt you.'

'Yes, he will. And he'll hurt you. And it won't be the first time, will it?'

'He's still my brother.' Murad's voice was quiet.

'And the Emir is his father,' said Hani flatly. 'But he still ordered that attack.' She didn't know this, of course, but she knew her uncle and it was obvious he thought so.

'I don't believe it.'

'You don't want to,' Hani told him. They were sitting together on the flat roof of Dar Welham, peering over the parapet. Behind them, sheets dried on a line and drifting sand wrote patterns across cracked tiles and gathered into tiny dunes.

Picking herself up, Hani stepped back from the edge. And four floors below, now unseen by Hani or Murad, the man without insignia ordered one of the jellaba-clad men to knock on the door. After that, the soldier tried the door without being told and found it locked. So he hammered again, harder.

Faces appeared from the roofs of houses opposite and disappeared just as rapidly when their owners realized what was happening.

'Open in the name of the NR.'

When this unnaturally loud cry went unanswered, the man tried the handle himself. Finding it still securely locked, Poul Fischer nodded to a young Berber. 'Plastique,' he ordered.

The flexible breaching charge the corporal pulled from under his disguise wasn't strictly plastique. At least not in any sense he understood. It was a short length of three-hundred-grain-an-inch cutting charge with a soft rubber body that could be bent into any shape needed and a sticky foam that glued it to the door and helped reduce the danger of back fragmentation. Correcting a *mubahith* officer, however, was not in the corporal's career plan.

Fixing one length around the lock, the corporal positioned two more around the hinges, then did top and bottom where bolts might be, just to play safe. The FBC series also came in six-hundred-grain and twelve-hundred-grain densities but for hinges of this age three-hundred-grain was probably already overkill.

'It might be best, sir, if everyone stood back.' Quickly, so he didn't have to see Poul Fischer's answering expression, the corporal fixed an electronic match to each charge and began to enter his identity code into a firing box.

'Ready when you are, sir.'

Raf had never explained to Hani how he'd managed to break Zara's brother out of the basement of a locked house in Kharmous and she'd been careful never to ask. But with her screen, a satellite shot of El Isk and some serious intuition she'd been able to work it out.

Intuition was part inherent and part learnt. The percentages were open to debate. As they always were with anything involving socialization versus heredity. Hani, however, was pretty sure she'd been born with heightened levels.

Hypersensitivity was one description. Hani knew this because she'd done a quiz on a medical Web site. It suggested childhood stress might have made changes to an area of her brain called the *cingulated gyrus*. Or rather, her time with Aunt Nafisa had ensured changes were *not* made: reducing Hani's ability to filter out life's raw mixture of competing noise and demands.

Persistent stress-response state was a term she got fed by the site in Santa Fe. And Hani had all the symptoms; stomach ache and sleepless nights, a tendency to focus on nonverbal clues rather than speech. A preference for animals over humans.

'Ifritah,' Hani said suddenly.

'What about Ifritah?'

'I've got to find her . . .' Hani was heading towards the stairs down into the house before Murad had time to move.

'Wait,' he said, louder than he intended. 'Let me see what's going on.' Putting his head above the parapet Murad watched a man far below glue something to the front door. 'I don't think it's safe,' he said.

'We can't leave her behind.' Tears had started in Hani's eyes and her face was set. Her cheeks pulled back as if battling through a wind tunnel of misery. 'She'll be in danger.'

Murad sighed. 'I'll go,' he said.

The cat wasn't on the top floor or the floor below. Just to be sure, Murad looked under beds and inside cupboards, fighting with the rickety shutter of a mashrabiya to check that Hani's kitten hadn't some how got inside, even though the mashrabiya's bolts were rusted almost solid and there was no way this was possible.

She wasn't on the floor below that either, where Raf, Hani and Murad had made camp in a huge room containing two sofas woven from rattan and a drinks cabinet still full of half-empty bottles of liqueur. Old copies of *New Scientist* and *The Ecologist* sat in a magazine rack. Someone had left a paperback facedown and open under a stool so long ago that most of the pages had rotted away or been eaten by beetles, but there was no Ifritah.

'Any sign?' The question came from above.

'No. Not yet.'

Murad was halfway down the last flight of stairs when the door blew in. A pressure wave threw him back so he landed in a ragged heap. One of the steps caught his spine as he landed and it hurt.

The first soldier through the door shot the cat.

Get up, Murad told himself and was relieved to discover that he could. Taking the steps two at a time, he raced away from the black shadows tumbling through smoke, their weapons at the ready. At the very top of the house, at the foot of the stairs leading to the roof, Murad removed the key from the bottom door and used it to double click the lock from the other side. Then he did the same for the top door, the one that led out onto the roof and took that key as well.

'Ifritah . . .'

'Not there,' he told Hani. 'I'm sorry.'

'You're bleeding.' It sounded as if she'd only just noticed the fact.

'What?'

Hani touched her nose and Murad touched his own, fingers coming away sticky. 'And your ear,' she said. That turned out to be sticky too.

'We'll be in worse trouble,' Murad said, 'if we don't hide.' Which proved to be easier to say than do, as there was only one exit to the flat roof of the dar and it was already locked.

'Down there,' suggested Hani, pointing over the rear parapet to a dusty garden which obviously belonged to a neighbour. 'We can use that.'

Below them, built so that its nearest end joined the back wall of Dar Welham was the tiled roof of a fourth-floor balcony. The drop from where they stood to the tiles was maybe twice Hani's height.

'Unless you're afraid?'

Instinctively Murad's chin went up. 'Of course I'm not,' he started to say, then met Hani's dark eyes and stopped. 'Okay,' he said, 'I admit it. I've been scared ever since we left Tunis.'

'Me too.' Hani reached out to wipe dirt from his face, as if that was just a natural thing to do. Maybe it was, Hani didn't know and probably wasn't the person to ask about stuff like that. Until six months ago she'd believed that keeping a toy dog in her room deserved the slaps it invariably earned her, because Ali Din was male and her Aunt Nafisa had rules about such things.

Only now Hani lived with Raf, whose rules were less strict. Which made life easier but doing the right thing more difficult, because most of the time Hani just had to guess what that was . . .

'Like now.' Hani said to herself.

'Like now what?' demanded Murad.

'We need to move.'

She nodded to the sloping roof of next door's mashrabiya. 'You first,' she said.

'Wait . . .'

'No time.'

'But I'm not ready,' Murad protested. And that was when Hani realized that both his ears must be damaged. Someone was trying the handle of the door at the bottom of the roof stairs. A fact that seemed to escaped Murad.

'Do you want Kashif's men to catch us?'

Sliding over the edge, the boy twisted round until he hung by his fingers, then she heard a clatter below as Murad flailed for a grip to stop himself tumbling over the edge.

Hani's landing was rather better, although less catlike than she'd have liked; her knees coming up to hit her chest as she met the tiles. Something else to add to the list of bits that hurt.

'This way,' Hani said, dropping to her belly so she could peer over the edge of the mashrabiya. Its original carved screen was stolen and whoever had ripped it out had tacked a rotted tarpaulin in place to hide what they'd done. There was a market for architectural salvage, particularly at the top end. Back in El Isk, Hamzah Effendi had a houseful of the stuff. Hani was about to explain this to Murad but decided to save her words. He looked a bit preoccupied.

'I'll go,' Hani said. 'You went first last time.'

The difficult bit turned out to be lowering herself over the edge, what with tiles scraping against knees, legs and tummy until the pull of gravity left her hanging. And that was before Hani edged rapidly along the drop looking for a tear she'd seen in the tarpaulin. Swinging once for luck, Hani flipped through the gap to land inside the mashrabiya.

It was all she could do not to miaow.

'Now you,' Hani hissed, ripping aside some of the rotted canvas. 'That should make it easier.'

She saw his shoes first, scuffed oxfords followed rapidly by socks, turn-ups from his flannel trousers and then the length of his body up to the waist. She thought for a second Murad was about to freeze but he kept coming until he hung, eyes shut high above the courtyard.

'Do it,' Hani said.

So Murad swung once, jackknifing like a gymnast and when he landed it was on his toes.

'That was okay,' Hani admitted and Murad almost smiled. Together they refixed the rotten canvas as best they could. Hanging the tarpaulin from the holes that Hani had made when she ripped some of it down.

The empty house had two exits, a main one onto an alley and a small door, cupboardlike, that opened into a cul-de-sac so tight it was little more than the gap between two barely separate walls, one obviously much newer than the other. They chose the narrow way and finally exited on a street called Rue des Jardins, walking quickly with their heads down until they passed through a car park behind a hotel.

Walking slowly would have made more sense. Only neither one quite had the nerve so they hurried instead, trying hard not to run. And when they finally reached the market on Rue Ibn Chabbat, Hani made Murad stop in the shadow of a lorry.

'Let me,' she said. Her handkerchief was unused and still held creases from where it had been ironed by Donna. Just looking at it made Hani want to cry. Licking a corner, she steadied Murad's chin with one hand and wiped crusted blood from the side of his mouth with the other. When she tried to wash blood from his left ear Murad began to cry as well.

'We *are* running away, right?' Murad asked, once his face was clean again.

'Not exactly,' said Hani. She smiled at the boy's exasperated expression. 'We're staying out of trouble . . .'

It was Murad who first saw the bus. And Hani who pointed out that the vehicle was actually a coach. A brief argument about the difference then followed before Murad eventually bowed to Hani's insistence that coaches had smoked-glass windows, air-conditioning and their own loos.

This one even had onboard newsfeed, computer games and four private cabins. A fact advertised in large gold letters along both sides. Right below a line that read *Haute Travel: Tripoli* and above the URL for a site few locals could get, because Web connections without licence were banned by law in Ifriqiya. Not to mention most other parts of North Africa.

'We need a disguise,' said Hani.

Murad stared at her.

'Think about it,' said Hani. 'Those soldiers were after Murad Pasha and Lady Hana al-Mansur.' That Hani admitted her own first name was unusual in itself.

'If they *are* actually after us,' Murad said. He'd been thinking about that.

'Who else would they be after?'

'Ashraf Bey?'

'They waited until he was gone,' Hani said firmly. She turned to Murad, face serious. 'You're certain they were Kashif's men?'

'I'm sure,' said Murad.

'Even though they said they were the Army of the Naked?'

'Yes,' Murad said 'That's why I'm sure.'

'Okay,' said Hani. Peeling $5 from her roll she gave it to Murad. 'You got this as a tip from an American journalist,' she told the boy.

'Why?'

Hani sighed. 'It doesn't matter . . . For showing her the way. For fetching her a glass of water. Make it up.'

'What do you want me to get?' Murad demanded.

He bought a white T-shirt, made in Morocco, size XXL and a pair of plastic sandals with *sputnik* in red across the strap. Murad also bought a Dynamo's hat, which he wrecked by ripping off the brim so that from the front it looked like a skullcap.

'What did you buy that for?' Hani asked.

'The cap?'

'No silly, that . . .' She pointed at the T-shirt still draped over his arm.

'Watch,' said Murad and stripped off his soiled Aertex shirt and scrunched it into a ball. Slipping the new shirt over his head, Murad turned his back on Hani and unbuttoned his trousers, stepping out of those as well. With a T-shirt down around his knees, his socks gone and cheap sandals Murad looked like most other kids in the market, his new shirt making do for a robe.

When he turned back Hani was pointedly staring into the distance.

'Your turn,' said Murad.

CHAPTER 43

Friday 11th March

'You came,' said Major Jalal, as if he'd been waiting hours for Raf to appear. Hawk eyes glittered above a sharp nose and heavy moustache. And the smile that accompanied his comment hovered on the edge of contempt.

'How could I refuse my brother?' Raf said lightly. A single glance was enough to swallow the scene: Major Jalal in full uniform, a lieutenant and, standing behind him, the inevitable black Jeep.

Two soldiers stood by the Jeep trying to look casual.

'Well, now you're here,' said Major Jalal, 'where would Your Excellency like to sit, front or the back . . . ?'

'Zara?' Raf asked, not moving.

'Your mistress is safe,' Major Jalal assured him. 'And you can see her soon. But, before that, I've got orders to take you to Kashif Pasha. He would like a word.'

Raf smiled. 'You know how it is,' he said. 'Family comes first.'

'I understand that's one of the things His Highness wants to talk about.' Major Jalal's voice was dry. 'The fact you seem to believe he's your brother.'

Kashif hadn't always been manipulative. So people said. Mostly those who'd never met him. As a small boy he'd been loved and loving, open and happy to consider the feelings of others. That was how Kashif Pasha's official biography reported it anyway.

One day, maybe thirty years ago when he was first made a general, so sometime around seventeen, Kashif had demanded sight of his early school reports. Harrying some minor archivist into finding the file and doing whatever was necessary to get it released.

This was during one of Emir Moncef's periodic bouts of madness. With the man camped out under a summer sky somewhere south of

817

Wadi al B'ir, speaking to no one and sleeping between two of Eugenie's troop for warmth. Wearing nothing, apparently. Although the girls were allowed to retain their pants. It was all extremely adolescent.

Of course, only Lady Maryam dared call it madness. Everybody else spoke of the Emir's retreats and his need to remain in touch with the land. But it was madness all the same. A howling depression that had Moncef claiming (literally) to be someone else. At these times only Eugenie could help. Wherever she was and whatever she might be doing, Eugenie stopped doing it and came, elegant and stern-faced. He was quieter after her visits. Sometimes for months and once for the period of a whole year.

The school Kashif attended was at the rear of the Bardo Palace next to a mosque. School and mosque were not connected. It was, however, reasonable to assume they were and many people did, both in Tunis and abroad. There were eighteen and a half pupils in Kashif's class, this being the national average. And his year was taught the national syllabus, which included French, gymnastics, mathematics and poetry. The half pupil was achieved by allowing one boy to attend every other lesson.

If one left out the fact the other seventeen and a half pupils in Kashif's class were either his cousins or chosen from the sons of government ministers, then Bardo High was a typical local school of the kind found all over Ifriqiya. What most news reports forgot to mention was that Kashif's school had only one class, his own. The school opened when he reached five and shut when he reached fifteen; there never was a year below Kashif or a year above. The pupil to staff ratio was two to one.

His reports had been as exemplary as his marks. Each master describing a warm and outgoing child. A boy who'd unquestionably have had a great future ahead of him irrespective of birth.

Having reread these, Kashif Pasha demanded the real reports – on the basis that these must exist. A request which sent the already nervous archivist into near-terminal decline. Faced with arranging the forbidden, the archivist tried to explain to Kashif about *secret bags*, inadvertently offering the seventeen-year-old boy a whole new source of information and income.

Secret bags were kept in a vault below the Bardo, that much the archivist knew. Once sealed they could only be opened in the presence of a witness, provided . . . There'd followed a long list of stipulations to which the young Kashif hadn't bothered to listen.

Practically dragging the archivist to where the man believed the secret bags were stored, Kashif demanded they both be given entry. With the Emir gone and that wing otherwise empty, the chamberlain had done the obvious; opened the front door and saluted smartly. It had taken Kashif ten minutes to identify the vault and another five to bully someone into unlocking the door. A problem never to arise again after Kashif relieved the porter of his key.

Goatskin, Kashif decided, maybe sheep, nothing too fancy. Cured in a way that was almost intentionally perfunctory and stitched crudely with gut. Impressive signatures covered each bag, mostly from his father and occasionally Eugenie. One from the Soviet ambassador and even one from the Marquis de St Cloud. Any person wanting to open a bag to examine its contents had to sign the outside before the seal was cut. Some of the newer seals were almost silver, others oxidized down to a dull black.

Kashif was inordinately proud to discover that he had a whole rack to himself. Seven leather bags in total. Starting with the first, Kashif cut its seal and began to read an account of his life that he recognized.

He was surly, bad at games and prone to violence. His unbroken run of goals, his easy knockdowns in boxing and rapid fencing victories owed more to who he was than to any innate physical talent.

His marks suffered an automatic 25 percent inflation. The French mistress he liked most had been paid off after complaining that he'd molested her in a corridor.

The summer Kashif turned seventeen was the year he got his reputation for working hard. He'd appear every morning at the relevant wing of the Bardo, notebook in hand and a nervous young archivist two steps behind. And each evening he'd make his way back to his mother's dar with another courtier's life pinned to the board of his memory.

He made friends fast that summer and was given three cars, including his first Porsche and a speedboat he used to take Russian girls water-skiing, until he hit a sunken rock and an attaché's daughter ended up a casualty. The high point was when he acquired his own villa on Iles de Kirkeah, from an elderly general whose devotion to his childless, long-suffering wife was apparently exceeded only by his devotion to a long string of pretty Moroccan houseboys.

Every bag he chose Kashif dutifully signed, leaving it to the archivist to repack the contents and affix a new seal. The one for his mother was especially interesting. Particularly in relation to a visit made to Gerda Schulte three weeks before she married his father. A surgeon briefly famous for patenting the only medically undetectable, biologically foolproof method of restoring virginity. A technique surprisingly popular among the middle classes of North Africa and the source of her heir's considerable wealth.

It was a snippet of information Kashif parlayed with his mother into a new apartment in the Bardo, one with its own entrance. His other knowledge Kashif kept close as an enemy, deadly as a friend; using it only as necessary once that first flush of power was gone. Murad wasn't even born when Kashif discovered the bags and, by the time he was, the bags had gone. Exactly when they vanished Kashif never discovered. He'd gone to Monte Carlo one Monday and come back two years later to find the room empty and repainted, awaiting delivery of an apparently valuable collection of late-nineteenth-century tax returns.

One thing Kashif knew for certain though. No bag had made reference to his father having married again. At least not until that American girl to whom Eugenie introduced him, Murad's mother. The one who went off a cliff. And the bag that dealt with Moncef's bastards made no reference to an Ashraf al-Mansur or Ashraf anything else, come to that . . . Whatever the late Eugenie de la Croix or his father might claim.

'Afternoon,' Raf said to a guard by the side of the path. The man looked at Major Jalal, trying to work out if he was meant to salute Ashraf Bey or not. Just to be safe, he saluted anyway.

Up ahead stood Kashif Pasha, with no one else in sight. At least not obviously; one sniper hid in a clump of palms to Raf's left. *Phoenix dactylifera*, tree of the Phoenicians with finger-resembling fruit. Raf had Hani to thank for that snippet of information.

Another sniper was behind him. The smell of tobacco as Raf entered the amphitheatre had been too strong not to whisper its warning. That Kashif Pasha felt such protection was necessary almost made Raf feel better.

'Brother.' Raf drawled the word. No greeting and no title, zero hostility either. Let the other man make the running on this. Kashif Pasha was supposed to be a poker player, famous for it apparently . . .

Raf smiled.

'Feeling happy about something?' asked Kashif.

'Always glad to see you,' Raf said. 'You know how it is.'

'No,' said Kashif, 'I can't say I do.'

Raf's grin was bleak as he adjusted his Armani shades and smelled the hot wind. Sweat, fear, anger and triumph. Beneath the distant tobacco and Kashif's cologne there was a veritable symphony of olfactory molecules being ripped apart by a breeze that filtered between salt-stunted thorns.

'Oh well,' he said.

They stood in the ruins of a small Roman amphitheatre with fifteen circles of seating cut direct into crumbling pink rock. The central circle was half-buried in dust and a cheap kiosk near the entrance had signs that read *Closed* in seven languages. Its filthy window and padlocked door suggested the site had been shut since autumn.

There was undoubtedly a lesson there if only Raf had the mind for it, because according to Khartoum there was a lesson in everything; in appearance and the reality behind appearance and in the reality behind the first appearance of reality. In Khartoum's opinion to hunt knowledge was to lose it.

'You seem amused . . .' Kashif's voice was cold. 'Am I missing something?'

'We all are,' said Raf. 'That's the very essence of being human.'

Two of Major Jalal's soldiers looked at each other. One of them mouthing to the other and Raf caught the silent word. *Moncef* . . . His father, that was what they were saying. He was like his father.

Mad.

Even Kashif Pasha nodded. As if willing, for the moment, to admit that the one might be son of the other.

'This missing waiter . . .' said Raf. And got no further.

'He's confessed.'

Behind his shades, Raf blinked. 'To what?'

'Disguising himself to infiltrate the Domus Aurea with the express intent of killing the Emir.' Kashif's face burned with anger. Or maybe triumph. 'He was working for the French. As an *agent provocateur* in a revolutionary cell that also included the dead Sufi. He's admitted everything.'

'And you know his confession is true, how?' A reasonable enough comment one would have thought.

'Because he wrote it himself.' So close to Raf was Kashif Pasha that Raf could identify at least three of the things Kashif had eaten for lunch. 'Ask the criminal if you don't believe me . . . And then we can shoot him.' A minor tic at the edge of Kashif's mouth pulled it out of shape. His pupils were large and his gaze direct.

Kashif Pasha meant it.

This was when Raf realized the pasha was serious. He'd summoned Raf to watch the execution of a man Kashif Pasha genuinely believed had tried to kill his father. All because of a throwaway line from Raf about suspecting Kashif. A barb that had dug deep into the pasha's flesh, dragging him to a point of intensity that owed far more to indignation than fear or guilt. That worried Raf.

Bluster, threats, fake fury, those Raf could handle. But a demand for approval, this expectation that he would immediately withdraw all accusations when faced with evidence . . . There was a sour note to this that rang like a cracked bell.

If not Kashif, then who . . . Berlin/the *Thiergarten*? It seemed unlikely.

'Your waiter,' said Raf. 'Where is he?'

In reply, Kashif jerked his head towards yet another black Jeep, parked beside the ticket kiosk. Smoked windows, roo bars and a radiator grille like the baleen of a loose-lipped whale. One could only assume the *mubahith* imported them in job lots.

'Get him,' Kashif demanded.

Major Jalal nodded and seconds later, as two guards tossed a naked figure at Raf's feet his heart sank. He should never, ever have let Chef Edvard register him with Domus Aurea security using someone else's name.

Hassan stank of fear and bled from a split mouth. His nose was broken, three front teeth were gone and his face was a veritable rainbow of pain. Whip marks scored his heavy shoulders. A dozen cigarette burns speckled his soft belly. There had been nothing subtle about the questioning.

'This is your waiter?'

Major Jalal nodded.

'According to my niece,' said Raf, 'the missing waiter was tallish and thin. This man is short and fat.'

'Lady Hana is mistaken.' Major Jalal's voice was firm. 'But then the dining room was lit by chandeliers and somewhat dark so it would be an easy error for a frightened child to make. Besides, Your Excellency has his brother's word that this is the man.'

'Let me guess,' said Raf. 'He protested his innocence for a couple of days, then decided to tell you the truth . . .'

'Is there a point to this?' Kashif's voice was hard.

'Of course there's a point,' said Raf with a sigh.

The three-day rule had been explained to him by two people he admired. One of them, as mother of Seattle's famous Five Winds Friendship Society had inherited an administration that kept *surgeons* on its payroll. And it had taken using their undoubted skills on two soon-to-retire elder brothers to get that anomaly changed, or so Hu San had said. The other person was Felix.

The rule of three was simple. And in a list of five it came just before the one that said blustering men broke faster than quiet women . . . No matter how brave or well trained, even a saint was ready to confess to devil worship by the third day; there were no exceptions. Keep death away and rack up the pain and by day three all anybody wanted to know was where to sign.

Chef Edvard's sous-chef had been no different. Poor sod.

'Hassan,' said Raf and watched as the fat boy raised his head, eyes widening as he saw the man in front of him.

'You're . . .'

'Ashraf Bey,' said Raf, kicking Hassan in the stomach. 'Well done.' He kicked again and when Hassan finally looked up with imploring eyes, Raf went for the kidneys. It was this blow that knocked Hassan unconscious.

'You know the man?' Kashif's voice was thoughtful.

'Of course I know him,' Raf said. 'I'm Chief of Police. He's the main witness to the Maison Hafsid killing and on the precinct payroll as an informer. One of my lieutenants was wondering what had happened.'

You recognized by sight a man who tried to shoot my father.' Kashif seemed to be trying the sentence for size, considering its usefulness.

On either side of the pasha his guards had gone very still. Maybe it was Kashif's tone of voice or perhaps he had some signal like a finger tapping against his nose, a shift of his weight or a certain nod of his head. Most people in his position had special signs and ways of giving instructions.

One of them must have said club this impostor to the ground.

'Well done,' said the voice. Raf ignored it. He had more important things to do than talk to the fox.

Twisting steadily, Raf pulled against his shackles until he felt one arm dislocate. It hurt no more than many other things in his life and far less than waking after the operation that replaced his kidneys as a child. About as much as a beating he once took in Seattle from a street punk called Wild Boy, back when they both worked for Hu San.

Raf hadn't seen the blow coming. Hadn't even felt the pistol butt that brought oblivion, the state to which his life seemed eternally drawn. One minute Raf was standing facing Kashif Pasha, then darkness came.

When Raf woke the first time he was in a waiter's uniform. The white blindness in his eyes the afterglow of a camera flash; and for a moment, floating on pain and watching the camera burn on the inside of his eyelids, Raf believed he was young again.

And then he knew he wasn't and hadn't been for a very long time.

CHAPTER 44

Opening the door was easy. Hani just pushed a button that read *emergency release* and a swirl of blissfully cool air exploded onto Ibn Chabbat Square. To close the door behind her she hit a button marked *shut*. This button was on the inside, obviously enough. And then they were in the coach, examining its hydraulic seats and checking the spiral stairs that led to a glass observation bubble.

'Too obvious,' said Hani.

At the very rear of the coach was a wall of showers and toilets (two of each, divided into male and female). Between these and the seating area farther forward was a short corridor featuring a couple of sliding doors on each side. So the bus went seats/narrow corridor/wall of loos where a back window should be. The sliding doors were marked *stateroom 1, 2, 3 and 4 . . .*

'I don't get it,' Murad complained, not for the first time.

'Good,' Hani told him. 'Stick with that.'

She pushed him through one of the sliding doors, having first flipped up its lock with a penknife, an act of breaking and entering made much easier than she expected by the coachmakers' fear of litigation, which guaranteed that every door was simplicity itself to open from the outside should the need arise. Which, in Hani's opinion, it had.

A man's room, Russian to judge from the phrase book and an open magazine left on the side. 'Try the next one,' said Hani and bundled Murad back through the sliding door, relocking it behind her.

A woman, travelling alone. The upper bunk unmade, blankets still folded, the lower one exhibiting neatly turned-back covers and a perfectly straight pillow. Also Soviet. Too neat by half. 'We'll try the other side,' Hani said.

Both bunks in the next cabin had been used. The cover on the bottom one hung neatly, the cover to the top bunk was still crumpled. A

Bible in English, translated by someone called St James. Hani didn't want to be prejudiced, but . . .

Actually that could be good.

On a bedside locker, open and facedown, lay a Discovery Channel guide to Ifriqiya, its spine cracked in half a dozen places. A handful of foreign change filled a saucer.

'*E pluribus unum* . . .' From one, many. Or was it, from many, one? Hani's Latin was too rusty for her to be certain which it was if either. So she put down the coin and picked up a flowery dressing gown draped over a peg on the door.

'Nylon,' she told Murad.

The garment was surprisingly short, albeit still long enough to drag on the carpet when Hani tried it on without sandals. It was the gown's width that impressed her. She and Murad could have hidden inside the thing three times over.

'This'll do,' Hani said with the certainty of someone who distrusted thin people even if she was one. Years of living with Aunt Nafisa had seen to that. 'We hide here.'

'Hide?'

'Okay, then,' said Hani, settling herself on the floor. 'We wait.'

Around dusk, Hani heard the tourists finally clamber aboard and felt the coach settle on its dampers. Or maybe it was springs? Mechanical things weren't really her area. Computers now . . . But hard as it was to believe, the *e pluribus unum* couple making this trip were doing so without a single computer, PDA or screen. Unless they'd taken the lot with them and Hani found that hard to believe.

'We're moving,' said Murad, his expression worried.

'That's what we want to happen,' Hani told him. She indicated a spot next to her on the carpet and Murad looked doubtful. He was still slightly afraid of her, Hani realized. And of everything else. Beneath that buttoned-down manner her cousin was as raw to the world as she was, maybe more so, because she knew how to adapt while Murad was still learning.

Meanwhile he just looked bemused.

'Uncle Ashraf will be fine,' Hani promised, realizing as soon as she spoke that this was not what worried the boy. She might worry about her uncle but Murad had his own problems, ones unknown to her.

'Do you think getting older makes you weaker?' Murad demanded suddenly.

Hani thought about it. 'I thought it made you stronger.'

'That's what they tell you,' said Murad, 'but is it true? I feel like I know less every day. Everything always used to be clear but now . . .'

'What was clear?' Hani asked.

'Knowing what to do . . .'

'And were you allowed to do it?'

They sat together until Murad was so desperate for a pee that he could sit still no longer. Hani didn't tell him she also needed the loo. Some things were still private for girls.

'Use the basin,' Hani said . . . 'Now rinse it out,' she suggested afterwards.

Murad and Hani then had a brief discussion about whether or not to bolt their door from inside. Hani won and the bolt was left open. Darkness arrived long before someone finally slid a key into the lock.

'We have to get them in here,' Hani said.

'What? We're not going to . . .'

'No,' said Hani. 'I've already told you, I just need them to myself for a few minutes. We . . .' she amended. 'We need them.'

'Why?'

'Because we do,' Hani announced firmly and together they crawled into a narrow space previously occupied by a suitcase.

'Who moved that?' The voice was Midwestern American and female, puzzled rather than angry. Hani didn't care who the voice belonged to, she liked them already. 'Carl, Carl . . .' The admonition was addressed to thin air. It had to be, because only one pair of legs could be seen in the room.

White plastic sandals shuffled over to the wall, the case rose from the floor and then it was being tipped on its side and pushed towards Murad.

He grunted.

That was what they'd agreed on, a simple grunt. Now came the dangerous bit when the cabin's owner might shout or rush out into the coach and demand help. They'd decided how to handle this too.

Hani whimpered.

'Who's there?'

The case pulled back, tipped upright.

'Come out,' the woman demanded. 'Come out right now.'

Murad crawled from under the bunk and scrambled to his feet. His eyes were lowered and his shoulders slumped. Inside his head he was trying to remember how Hani had suggested he should shuffle his shoes.

'Oh great. A thief.' The woman sounded exasperated. 'I suppose you've already pocketed all our stuff.' Her glance took in the whole cabin, all five paces of it and found nothing missing. 'Maybe not,' she

admitted, 'but then what are you doing here? And what happened to
your face?' She took Murad's chin in her fingers and turned his head to
the light, tutting as she did so. 'Someone hit you?'

When the boy stayed silent, Micki Vanhoffer sighed. She was a large,
home-loving woman very far from Ohio. Doing what her husband
thought she should be doing, taking a break from comfortable cruises
around the Caribbean. A month in North Africa was his idea. Well, and
her eldest son's, Carl Junior. An anniversary present supposedly. So
here she was on a glorified bus in the middle of a heat wave, in March for
heaven's sakes.

'I'd better tell the driver,' Micki said mostly to herself, reaching for
the door handle. 'And then we can call your parents.'

'He doesn't have any,' said Hani, rolling out from under the bunk in a
tumble of arms and legs. After scrambling upright, she took Murad's
hand and gripped hard when he tried to pull away. 'We're orphans,' she
added quickly. 'From an orphanage. A cruel place.'

Huge black eyes looked up at Micki Vanhoffer from beneath a rather
dirty scarf. Eyes that swam so deep with tears they appeared larger than
was humanly possible. Below those eyes jutted a nose too prominent to
fit any Western idea of beauty and under this a mouth that positively
quivered with anguish.

'You speak English . . .' Micki meant it as a statement rather than a
question, but her words were inflected, rising towards the end so Hani
found herself answering.

'Yes,' Hani said. 'I learnt it from tourists. When I was working in a
café with my mother.'

Micki looked puzzled. 'I thought you said you lived in an orphanage?'

'This was before my mother died,' Hani said firmly. 'When I was
little.'

'When you were . . .' The large woman looked at the small girl and
sighed. 'Things like this never happen on cruises,' she said. 'I'll get Carl
Senior down from the bubble. You wait here.'

'You say he's your brother . . .'

Hani looked at Murad, then nodded. 'My brother,' she agreed.
'Unfortunately he's not very bright.'

The man asking Hani questions was big in a different way. His
shoulders so broad that they seemed to stretch against his very skin. On
his T-shirt was a simple fish made from a single line that curled back
over itself at the tail; Hani had a feeling she'd seen the sign before.

'You have the fish.'

The man nodded. 'You know what it means?'

Hani nodded. 'Of course I know,' she said. 'Everyone knows.'

'*Carl* . . .' The word was a warning. 'I know you want to do good in this heathen place but remember what our brochure said about preaching.'

'I'm not preaching,' said the man. 'She mentioned it first.' He dropped to a crouch in front of Hani. 'What's this about an orphanage?' The words were soft, unlike his eyes, which were pale, watchful and just a touch angry. Mentioning his shirt had obviously been a bad move.

'We're running away,' said Hani.

'I can see that.'

'From an orphanage.'

'What's its name? Come on,' he said when Hani hesitated. 'Spit it out.'

Hani looked puzzled. 'Spit what out?' she said.

'*Carl!*'

'It's a fair question,' Carl Vanhoffer said to his wife. 'If she can't instantly name the orphanage, then it probably doesn't exist. And that boy isn't her brother. Not full brother anyway. The skin colours are way different.'

'You'll have to excuse Carl Senior,' said the woman with a tight smile. 'He used to be a police officer. He gets like this sometimes. You should have seen him with Carl Junior when he was growing up . . .'

'That's okay,' said Hani. 'My uncle used to be a policeman. He gets like that too and your husband's right. We're not really running away from an orphanage.'

'Told you,' Carl Vanhoffer said. 'What are you running away from?'

'Marriage,' said Hani and slowly pulled the shawl tight round her face, shrinking inside it. With her hunched shoulders and narrow back she looked frighteningly young. 'And you're right about the other thing too, Muri's not my brother, he's my cousin.'

'How old are you?' That was the woman.

Hani thought about it.

'Well?' The man's eyes were less hard than they had been. Slightly mistrustful to be true enough but not out-and-out disbelieving.

'Twelve,' said Hani, adding a year to her age. Assuming Khartoum was right and she really had just turned eleven.

'You don't look it.'

'*Carl!*' Again that outrage, almost maternal. Like there were things men couldn't be relied on to understand. Hani glanced at the both of them, the American man and woman. Most husbands and wives she'd met had harder edges to their lives and stricter boundaries. However, Hani had to admit to not having met many.

828

Hamzah Effendi and Madame Rahina were not a good model. Aunt Jalila and Uncle Mushin even worse. One now dead, the other apparently in a sanatorium. Uncle Ashraf and Zara? They weren't even a couple, not properly.

'It's all to do with food,' Hani told the woman. 'The less you get to eat the smaller you look . . . A doctor told me,' she added, before Carl Senior had a chance to ask her how she knew.

'And the poor get married younger,' said the woman.

Hani wasn't convinced this was true because, the way Zara told it, the really poor people in Iskandryia couldn't afford to get married until their twenties, which might be why they got so cross. And that fact probably applied to Ifriqiya as well.

But Hani kept her silence.

Despite what Uncle Ashraf, Zara and everyone else thought, she always had known when to keep her opinions to herself.

'Have you met the boy you're meant to marry?'

'Oh yes.' Hani nodded.

'What's he like?' The woman sounded interested. Appalled, but still interested.

'Okay, I guess,' said Hani, jerking her narrow chin towards Murad, 'As boys go . . .'

'This is him?'

Hani nodded again.

'And he's running away with you?' Carl Senior sounded doubtful.

'Of course,' said Hani, 'Muri doesn't mind getting married but he doesn't want to leave school.'

'Why would he leave school?' It was Micki's turn to look muddled.

'Because he'll need a job for when I have a baby . . .'

'*When you* . . .' Their voices were so loud that Hani was afraid the Russian in the next cabin might start to wonder what was wrong.

'What exactly are you telling them?' Murad hissed, his Arabic so flawless he could have been reciting poetry at the court of a long-dead caliph. Needless to say Micki and Carl Senior understood not a word.

'That we're running away,' said Hani. 'Because our parents want us to get married.'

'*Married?*' Murad stood openmouthed in outrage. 'You're eleven,' he said. 'I'm twelve. Fourteen is the earliest a girl can get married in Ifriqiya. Sixteen for boys.'

'But they don't know that, do they?' said Hani.

'What are you telling him?' Carl Senior demanded.

'That Muri shouldn't be afraid of you,' said Hani. 'That you won't hand us over.' She was glancing at the man but she was talking to Micki.

CHAPTER 45

He stank and there was little doubt that he'd just pissed himself again. Liquid his body could ill afford to lose. Raf had also started to think of himself as *he* and that was never a good sign.

Maybe it was this that allowed the fox to return. Alternatively, Raf had just got bored with trying to hold himself together.

'Now dislocate your other shoulder,' ordered the fox.

Raf shook his head. His teeth gritted not from bravery or pain but because he was trying to stop his upper left canine from falling out and keeping his mouth closed was all he could come up with, given both his hands were shackled behind his back and fixed to a wall.

Impossible.

'Not impossible,' said the fox, *'just painful. Work on the difference.'* And then Raf stopped letting the different bits of himself talk to each other and started to listen to the sound of a sea that had vanished millions of years before, after the Chott el Jerid finally separated from the Mediterranean to become first an inland sea, then a lake and ultimately the flood-prone salt flats it finally became.

Except that the waves like the voices, came from within him and there was nothing supernatural about them.

What Raf could hear was the sound of his own blood echoing off the stone walls of an azib, a domed shelter built for goats and now his prison. At first the noise had been slight as meltwater over pebbles, growing louder, until now it splashed like a fosse falling into a cool meltwater pool far below. He was listening to what was left of his own life.

'Do it,' Raf told himself. 'Dislocate.'

His first idea after Major Jalal had bolted the heavy azib door was to somersault out of his predicament by rolling forward to hang upside down from his shackled wrists, then twist sideways to land on his feet, facing the wall, with the shackles now in front of him. All he needed to do then was free his wrists and dig himself out.

Two failed attempts had convinced Raf this was impossible. So now he was going with the fox's suggestion, that Raf begin by convincing himself he was really merely testing the strength of the chains shackling him to the wall.

As ever, when facing something unpleasant, the trick was to remove oneself from the pain. A trick he'd previously spent many months unlearning. Although back then he'd been somebody else. Or rather, Bayer-Rochelle had made him somebody else and done a good job of it too; much better than any of his schools had managed.

Removing oneself from pain wasn't a trick everybody could master. For a start, it required a certain working knowledge of the subject, preferably one built up over many years. Unless, of course, it was possible to go for a single cataclysmic-thunderburst that shocked the flesh into learning something it never forgot.

Raf didn't know, that wasn't the route he'd taken.

The secret was to be somewhere else. Answering questions other than those asked. While hunting for the fracture behind reality.

Breathe through nose or mouth . . .

Saturday or Sunday . . .

Live or die . . .

'Just one collection of questions after the next, isn't it?' said the fox. *'Life I mean. Or what passes for it . . .'*

How long he'd been in the azib Raf wasn't sure. Being knocked unconscious did that to you. At least it always did to him. And his back history was punctuated, at significant points, by such bouts of darkness, although often differently induced.

Actually, it was probably more accurate to say his life, back history, call it what one would, was a string of cold darkness punctuated by sharp, occasionally contradictory memories of being awake. What Raf had taken to calling the *sickroom conundrum* and what the fox insisted on calling Schrödinger's paint pot.

If he went to sleep in a ward that was green and woke in the same room but it was grey, what had changed? Reality, the room or Raf? There was something very primitive about that question. Almost classic. A puzzle replete with a dozen resonances Raf undoubtedly failed to appreciate.

There was, of course, an even more primitive conundrum slumped against the wall opposite, quietly decomposing in note after note of sweet decay. At what point did Hassan cease to be human? And what exactly did death remove from that original mix of 65 percent oxygen, 18 percent carbon, 9.5 percent hydrogen and all those other elements neither Raf nor the fox could be bothered to remember?

Dying seemed simple, decomposing less so, if Hassan was representative. A veritable matrix of influences constraining or facilitating the metamorphosis: beginning with attack by insects, originally flies, then beetles, finally millipedes; amount of clothing intact, in this case none; level of physical trauma, considerable; ambient heat, sweltering . . .

The fox and Raf also agreed on the probability that soil type made some impact.

Felix would have known. Having wiped his finger on the floor of the azib he'd have announced a high saline content was hindering decomposition or saltpetre was causing mummification. Of course, the fat man was quite capable of wiping his finger straight on the body.

When Raf first woke, Hassan had been coming out of rigor, locked muscles slowly relaxing, starting with his eyelids, lower jaw and the soft jowls of his neck. And Raf didn't need voices in his head to tell him this was decomposition of muscle fibre.

By evening the boy's face had turned a weird greenish red, with a veritable tie-dye of corruption brightening his flabby chest and blotching his naked thighs. It was around this time that Hassan began to smell. At least that was what Raf thought then. Now, reassessing, he understood that corruption had barely started.

After the face began to melt, millipedes arrived to eat mites busy feeding on flesh, the blowflies having already gone. And gas-filled blisters began to appear under the skin as liquid leached from anus, nostrils, mouth and ears. In all probability, Raf realized, he was taking more interest than was wise in the intricacies of what was happening. But it was hard to avoid when shackled in a stone azib, five paces from one's very own *memento mori*.

'*Enough with the thinking,*' said the fox, its voice completely present for the first time in weeks. '*You can dislocate your way out of this or stay here and die. Make a choice.*'

It looked out through Raf's eyes. The bit of him that had never been entirely human.

'*You want this to end,*' it said, '*then end it. But ask yourself this . . . How many more times can you afford to die?*'

CHAPTER 46

Saturday 12th March

Sometime after the lights went down in the main part of the coach, and
those who had couchettes let back their seats, and the loos and showers
occupied by tourists preparing for sleep finally emptied, Micki took Hani
to the loo, using the width of her hips to shield the child from anyone
who might glance round.

Micki was pretty sure everyone was safely dozing. She'd already made
three visits, earning herself pitying glances from a middle-aged, pudding-
faced Soviet woman in the back row who'd finally fallen asleep with a
crumpled copy of the previous day's *Pravda* on her lap.

'I'll keep guard,' Micki told the child, ushering Hani through a door.
'Don't worry,' she added, when Hani looked anxious, 'I'll be here when
you come out.'

'Micki,' Hani's voice was little more than a whisper.

'What now?'

'Um . . .'

The child had the face of an angel. A foreign angel obviously but an
angel all the same. Men were going to fall into those dark eyes and never
find their way back. Not for years though, Micki told herself hastily.
When the girl was properly grown-up.

'What is it?' asked Micki and when Hani still didn't answer, she
dropped to her knees the way she used to do when something was
worrying Carl Junior. Carl Senior never got the importance of this,
although she'd tried to explain it more than once. He always towered
over the boy, then wondered why he got frightened.

'You can tell me, honey . . .'

Something fleeting and sad passed over the face of the child as she
bent close and whispered in Micki's ear.

'You know,' Micki hissed to her husband, when Hani and Murad
were safely dozing on the floor, wrapped in separate blankets that they

both managed to kick off in their sleep. 'She hadn't even heard about Kotex. It was a miracle the child even knew what was happening to her . . . Can you imagine it?'

Carl had less than no interest in imagining any such thing but had long since learnt not to say as much, so he muttered something he hoped sounded suitably shocked and had another go at drifting off to sleep.

'That must be how their parents decide they're ready to marry,' Micki announced. 'The first time they . . . You know.'

That was one *you know* and a couple more *theys* than Carl could follow but he didn't mention this either. 'Could be,' he said and drifted off to sleep, leaving his wife to the comfort of outrage.

'We've got problems,' Carl Senior said.

'Nothing we can't fix,' Micki insisted hastily, when she saw the anguish in Hani's face. The roadblock was waiting at Dehiba, thirty klicks after the blacktop shrank from two lanes to one. Right before Ifriqiya's border with Tripolitana.

Jebel Dahar's stark red spine with its low fringe of thorn and scrub was mostly behind them and ahead was a sixteen-hour trip to take in the hilltop town of Yafran. A double-page, spread in Micki's *Insight Guide* revealed an area of olive groves and good red soil; while a box-out of traditional Yafrani architecture revealed squat buildings with heavy doors, intricate wrought iron and what looked like plaster helicopters, jets and butterflies fixed to the side of Berber houses.

'Stay in here,' Micki told the children. 'They'll probably just count us.'

Carl Senior stayed silent.

'We could hide under the bed,' Hani suggested.

'Good idea,' said Carl. 'No one would ever think of looking for you there.' He grabbed his passport and camera. 'I might as well get a shot of the frontier. If they'll allow me,' he added crossly, sliding back the door.

'Ignore him,' Micki said. 'He's nervous.'

'About what?'

Micki smiled. 'Some people don't like breaking the law. Carl Senior's one of them.'

'But you don't mind?' While watching the large woman from the corner of her eye, Hani thought about that. The American was very pink and very big, with wavy blond hair made fat by too much brushing.

'Honey,' said Micki, 'how do you think Carl Senior and I first met? It was in a lineup. I was standing there and he was the one walking an elderly man down the line.'

'What happened?'

Micki shrugged. 'Old Amos had bad eyesight. So after the civilians had gone I told Carl Senior he owed me a coffee for my inconvenience. We went on from there.'

'You're not Carl Junior's mother, are you?' Hani was surprised she hadn't realized that before. 'Not really . . .'

'Honey,' Micki looked at her. 'You can be one weird kid.'

'But I'm telling the truth?'

'Yeah, you are that. He needed looking after and Carl Senior was useless. So he got me.' Micki shrugged. 'Whatever good that was. Now, you stay here and we'll soon be safely across that border.'

'If only,' said Hani. She could feel a decision coming on. The kind Uncle Ashraf might make. *When in doubt, change the rules.* She was pretty sure he'd said that to her sometime or other and if he hadn't then he'd probably meant to . . . Unless it was Hamzah Effendi.

'We're going to hide, all right,' said Hani, 'right in front of the cameras.'

'You're . . .' For the first time since Hani had met her, Micki was lost.

'In front of the cameras.' Pulling back the cabin's curtain, Hani nodded to sand-filled barrels blocking off one-half of the narrow road. 'That isn't a border post,' she told the large woman. 'That's a roadblock and those men with guns belong to Kashif Pasha. His half brother,' Hani added, taking Murad's hand.

Micki Vanhoffer looked as bemused as she felt.

'This is His Excellency Murad Pasha,' said Hani. She took off her scarf and tried to comb out her hair with her fingers. Then she straightened her shoulders and raised her chin. 'And I'm Lady Hana al-Mansur. Those soldiers out there have orders to find us.'

'To make you marry?'

'No,' said Hani. 'So Kashif Pasha can have us killed. Although he'll try to blame it on terrorists or my uncle Ashraf . . .' She shrugged away the thought. 'You do have a cell phone?' Hani said, pointing to Micki's handbag.

The American woman nodded.

'Good.' Hani upended the bag and began to sort through tissues, tampons, a shop load of loose makeup and what Hamzah would called a boasting book, a plastic wallet full of family photographs. The cell phone was near the bottom, switched off.

'What's your code?' asked Hani.

Micki gave her a six-digit number.

'Don't tell me,' said Hani, 'that's your date of birth . . .' She sighed at

Micki's embarrassed nod. 'Think about changing it,' Hani suggested, fingers flicking through menus. When she reached the option she wanted, Hani punched in a number, remembering to make allowances for international dialling.

Then she took a deep breath.

'This is the truth,' Hani said. 'I promise you . . . I'm not an orphan,' she stopped dead. 'Well actually I am,' she said, 'but I'm not running away from an orphanage. And we're not engaged. But someone is trying to kill me. Well,' Hani thought about that one too. 'I guess they're really trying to kill Murad.'

'It was a lie about the marriage too?' Micki seemed to be one twist behind Hani, understandable really . . . Most of the adults Hani had met hadn't been too bright.

'No one is forcing us to get married,' Hani said.

'So you're not going to marry your cousin?'

Hani smiled. 'That wasn't what I said at all.'

'*Micki.*' The voice came from Carl Senior and, by the sound of things, he was either yelling from outside or standing in the doorway. 'They got guns,' he said. 'And they want everyone out because they intend to search the coach.'

'God give me strength,' said Micki loud enough to be heard. 'Tell them I'm coming.' She banged her hip against the door and slammed a tiny drawer. 'Just as soon as I get this damn skirt on.'

'Take this,' Hani said, shovelling everything back into Micki's bag. 'As soon as you get across the border turn on the cell phone and it'll remind you that you need to make a call.'

'I do?'

'Yes,' said Hani, 'definitely. Call the number that appears and demand to speak to Effendi.'

'What if Mr Effendi doesn't want to speak to me?'

'He will,' promised Hani, wondering if the American realized she'd just agreed to make the call. 'And if he doesn't, tell whoever answers that Hani says, *If Effendi doesn't come to the phone she'll stop letting him play with her money* . . . He keeps investing it in his own companies,' Hani added, as if that explained everything.

The words were Hamzah Effendi's guarantee that the message was real. What he did would have nothing to do with money. It would be done for Raf. A debt repaid.

'What do I tell him?' Micki asked anxiously. 'When Effendi does come to the phone?'

'Tell him that Murad and Hani have been murdered by Kashif

Pasha . . . Tell him to tell everyone he knows.' Catching the American woman's appalled expression, Hani held up one hand as the first tears started to trickle down Micki's face, cutting tracks in her heavy makeup.

'It might not happen,' Hani said.

CHAPTER 47

The call from the minaret came harsh as a crow. Only there was no minaret and when Raf kicked at a shadow it squawked into life and sliced the night in a spread of serrated black blades.

'Very pretty,' said Felix, nodding at Raf's shackles. So Raf swung them at him and missed, earning himself a smile. A real fat man grin.

'Ignore him,' the fox said. *'He's just like all the others.'*

Tiri was talking about the ghosts who walked out of the salt wilderness towards Raf, their carcasses destroyed, their faces twisted in the final moments of death or smoothed free of all memory.

'I know,' said Raf and forced one foot in front of the other, extracting another step from his shaking body. They were dead and so was he. At least that was what it felt like. This razor state between existences, flash-filled with waterfalls of exaltation that appeared one minute to run down his spine, then vanished the next, leaving him spent as an hourglass.

Behind Raf stretched footprints speckled with blood from where he'd slashed his feet on rose petals. *Rose de sable*, crystallized gypsum. He'd come across a field of the things, stone flowers sharp as knife blades, and had walked through, being too tired to walk around.

Raf thought they grew there naturally. But the fox insisted they'd been dumped as second-grade goods, unsuitable even for tourists like him. It claimed to have been there when the dumping was done.

'I'm not a tourist,' said Raf, but the fox had to disagree, informing Raf that he was a tourist in his own life. A hit-and-run recidivist who fixed himself on occasional moments of clarity. Their argument lasted so long that Raf forgot to feel pain and when he next looked around, he'd walked two, maybe three miles without ever seeing anyone he'd killed.

Felix came round twice and looked happier the next time he appeared, face shredded and egg yolk running from one eye but definitely more smiley. 'You're fragmenting,' he told Raf.

'You can talk.' The retort just came and Raf was still wondering how to apologize for his tactlessness when the fat man gave a shrug like he agreed and blew apart in the night wind. Without shades, minus clothes, his hands chained. And now rudeness. The fox was right. Raf was excelling himself.

Sharp edges cut his ankles every time Raf's feet broke through salt to hit one of the many puddles of brine beneath. Smears of what looked like rust threaded the chott's drying surface, marbling its saline whiteness. Blood on snow, his mother's favourite shot. Only the saline sting to tell Raf that what he walked on wasn't ice or snow.

Somewhere up ahead should be a road. A strip of tarmac floating on treated polystyrene blocks, linked together and slung across the chott, Raf seemed to remember that was how it went. Polystyrene blocks so the weight of the road didn't sink it into the chott's soft surface.

Raf couldn't have used the road even if it had been heading north towards Camp Moncef rather than west towards Tozeur. But Raf needed to cross it and until he did, he was, by definition, more than half a day away from killing Kashif Pasha.

'You know what?' said a voice.

Raf didn't.

'You look shit.' The drawl was skin-crawlingly familiar, the lips from which it issued tinted with a shade of Shu Uemura too deep to class as ironic. A turned-up collar framed a face sharp enough to break hearts. 'Life not treating you too well?'

'I'm fine,' snapped Raf.

'Of course you are,' said Wild Boy. 'Anyone can see that.' He touched pale fingers to his brow in a mocking salute, swept dark hair back from his eyes and vanished.

'I don't remember killing Wild Boy,' Raf muttered.

'You don't remember much at all, do you?' said the fox. *'And what you do remember changes each day. I've never met anyone like it for avoiding the obvious.'* The animal paused, took a look through Raf's eyes at the night wilderness of the chott and sighed. *'What do you think happened to him after you went missing?'*

'He came looking for me?'

'And did he find you?' asked the fox.

Raf shook his head.

'Did anyone?'

There wasn't an answer to that. At least not one that made real sense. Although maybe that wasn't surprising given his mind was full of ghosts and memories and things that might have happened but probably didn't or were about to happen, but only . . .

'Only what?' the fox demanded.

But Raf was already asleep. When he woke the walls had changed colour again. His bed was the same but the windows were different, wood not rusting metal. The oak outside was bare where it had been green. Only the firs on the far slopes looked the same. Like lazy smoke frozen in the act of rolling uphill.

'You can sleep again now,' someone said.

He'd had days like that at Roslyn. Dozens of them. And before Roslyn, days in a white room with flowered curtains across the window. Steel bars painted in childish reds and greens and blues because some expert decided bright colours made window bars look less intentional. As if the security measures had been put up by accident and no one could be bothered to take them down again.

For maybe a year Raf had believed the bars were there to keep him in. Only towards the end did he realize they existed to keep others out. Evil people, one nurse told him. Misguided protestors. She was Swiss, much younger than he realized and she vanished the morning after he took a bar of chocolate from her. Neither had realized they planned to do double blood tests that day.

One morning, shortly after that, Raf woke feeling stiff and cold with an ache in his ribs and new scars on his wrists. And his mother was sitting in a chair in the far corner of his room. She was crying, which wasn't unusual and carrying primroses, which was . . .

'You look older.' He said it without thinking.

When she'd finished drying her eyes she came over and stood by his bed, her fingers reaching out to touch his face. 'You don't,' she said. The coat she wore was new and her shoes were different, shiny at the toes and unscuffed on the heels. She'd also changed the colour of her hair.

As always, Raf forgot how angry he was about everything and agreed to come home. Although it was difficult to remember where home was at that point. Not New York for the second time, that came later.

He'd been . . . Raf found it impossible to remember how old. Somehow birthdays and candles and parties with presents had always seemed to pass him by.

'That's what this is about?' said the fox. *'Massive sulks that Mummy never gave you a proper birthday party?'* The voice was sardonic, darker than Raf remembered it having been for years. *'You're going to die in the wilderness because no one let you blow candles?'*

'I'm not going to die,' said Raf.

CHAPTER 48

Tuesday 15th March

'Count them,' said the fox. So Raf did. A handful of *mubahith*, teenage girls in khaki jumpsuits, jellaba-clad orderlies and two visiting Berber elders wrapped respectively in lengths of blue and black. Awaiting a day that threatened to be as impossibly hot as the day before.

Eleven in all.

And then there was Raf watching from the chott, flayed by UV that already filtered through scummy cloud to tighten his skin.

Sweat shivering down his spine in anticipation.

He stank of shit and piss and blood, the smell assailing him every time he halted long enough for his own body heat to reach his nostrils. Evidence of his own humanity.

St John the Baptist. Minus the loincloth.

Now that a road existed between Kibili and El Hamma du Jerid, carefully skirting the edge of the wilderness before slanting off from the chott's edge to cross at the narrowest point, few people except packers and Soviet tourists in fat-tyred UAZ four-by-fours tried to cross the salt lake any other way.

The camel trains were gone, along with the slave markets and spice routes. And while it was true that an annual Sand Yacht Championship was held on the chott, this was only ever attended by Soviets and, in any case, was not due for another three months.

So the khaki-clad teenager sweating out her early shift on the southern perimeter of Camp Moncef watched the arrival of a naked apparition with disbelief. At first she assumed the tiny speck was an animal either lost or abandoned. Dogs escaped from cars, half-dead donkeys were cast loose when the amount they could carry stopped being worth what they cost in feed.

Not yet worried enough to find herself a pair of binoculars, Corporal Habib kept an eye on the approaching animal. But sometime between tucking a cigarette inside her hand because one of Kashif Pasha's men had suddenly roared up in his open Jeep and saluting the departing sergeant without getting caught, the speck vanished.

'Shit.'

Corporal Habib blinked into the chott's acid glare, ground the butt of her cigarette underfoot and reached into her pocket for a pair of shades; circumstances demanded it even if wearing them on duty was almost as bad as smoking, being the preserve of officers.

Her shades cut down haze and cancelled out most refraction but the figure was still gone, leaving only early-morning shimmer and diminishing slivers of what had to be surface water left over from the winter rains.

Fifteen minutes later, Corporal Habib was still squinting into the distance when the emptiness beside her suddenly took her feet from under her and followed the corporal down, slamming itself into her rib cage. Bone splintered, on the wrong side; Corporal Habib's heart kept pounding and by the time she realized her aorta wasn't pierced and both lungs still drew breath the emptiness sat back on its heels, waiting, with the corporal's own machine gun to her throat.

Only the camouflage of her jumpsuit had kept Corporal Habib alive. Had her uniform been bottle green, the colour of Kashif's own guard, or the black of the *mubahith*, she would have been dead. Something that might still happen to judge from the blue eyes that stared down at her, pale as cracked ice.

'Single shot,' said a crow's voice, raw and bitter. 'All you'll get at this distance is a gas star and no chance to cry for help. You ever seen a gas star?'

The corporal nodded. A *gas star* happened when muzzle flash entered flesh, from guns almost touching you got *burn rings*, and then *powder tattoos*: part of the corporal was certain gas stars only occurred on upper limbs or torso but she kept that to herself. Something about the apparition staring down at her suggested he might have a more intimate knowledge of the phenomenon.

'You want my clothes?' The corporal's strangled question did exactly what she meant it to, told the apparition she wasn't about to put up a fight.

'Water,' Raf demanded. Watching as the corporal silently unclipped her flask and held it out. She did a very impressive job of not looking at his nakedness or chains.

He drank.

'And those,' said Raf, 'I want these, too.' Lifting the shades off her nose, he nodded to the two spare magazines on her belt. 'And those.' The weapon he held in shaking fingers was an old-model MP5i 9mm Heckler & Koch, the one issued with a thirty-round mag.

'Now get up.'

Corporal Habib did what she was told.

Conditioning, Raf told himself, worked every time. He should know.

'Is Kashif Pasha here?'

The corporal nodded, only to freeze when she saw Raf's scowl. Very slowly, probably unconsciously, she began to shake her head, as if that might change the answer.

'And the Emir?'

A frightened nod. And with it a look that suggested she wanted to say more but wasn't sure whether to risk it.

'What?' Raf demanded.

'He's dying. So if you've come to kill him, there's no point.'

'I haven't,' said Raf. 'I wouldn't . . . One last question. What's that over there?'

Corporal Habib never saw the blow that dropped her into a heap. Or realized, until long afterwards, that when Raf went through her ammo pouch he took only her bar of chocolate. Everything else he left . . .

'Fuck, no.'

Not that.

Jammed into a pocket on the passenger side of an open-top Jeep, Raf found a copy of the previous evening's *La Presse*, final edition.

He found it shortly after swinging his shackles into the face of the NCO driving, wrapping them around the man's fat throat, bringing his screams to an abrupt halt. The NCO was still alive but his jaw hung crooked, his moustache was thick with blood and his face sported bruises which would last for a month. His arm was also broken. But some of that was self-inflicted. The NCO had run his Jeep straight into a rock.

Having read the headlines Raf wished he'd just killed him.

'You're crying,' said the fox.

'Of course I'm fucking crying.' Talking to the fox avoided thinking and thought was the last thing Raf wanted. He wanted emptiness. The dislocation of mind from body and body from action; not so much cognitive as psychic dissonance, blood music. The sound of glass spheres as they ground against each other.

Behind reality emptiness. Behind emptiness . . .

This.

'You want me to take it from here?' asked the fox. If Raf hadn't known otherwise, he'd have said Tiri was worried. Smart move. Raf watched himself watching the fox, standing naked on a dirt track below Jebel Morra, scanning a headline he already knew.

Kashif Pasha accused of killing half brother and cousin.

A photograph of Murad showed him staring into the lens with childish seriousness. The picture of Hani was an old papp shot, grabbed outside Le Trianon. A fact made obvious by a section of café canopy and writing on the ice-cream glass on the table in front of her. *Lady Hana al-Mansur.*

All the picture did for Raf was reinforce how fast Hani had changed in those last few months. In the picture she looked as he still thought of her. Would always think of her. Small and thin, with a wry smile and more imagination than was good for any child.

Rolling the NCO over with his foot, Raf bent to take his pistol and found it attached by lanyard to a leather holster, along with three spare magazines.

'You plan to do this for yourself, don't you?' said the fox.

Raf nodded.

Unbuckling the sergeant's broad belt, Raf ripped it through a handful of trouser loops to free the holster. And once he'd got the belt off, Raf decided to keep it anyway. His only problem being that, even on its tightest setting, the belt threatened to slide over his hips, so he slung it across his right shoulder instead. An action made difficult by the fact his hands were still linked by their length of rusting shackle.

One H&K with 3×30 rounds. One Browning, plus a total of four magazines. That made . . . Raf ran his eye down the edge of a black metal clip, counting rounds, two at a time. Twelve to each, made forty-eight, add ninety from the submachine gun . . . How many guards could Kashif Pasha have?

There was only one track into Moncef's latest camp and at its entrance stood a temporary barrier; one of those striped aluminium poles, counterbalanced by a square weight at the pivot end. A single soldier stood guard, shaded by an open-fronted hut.

Possibly she should have been watching the track but most of her time was taken up wiping perspiration from her face or pulling at the armpits of her uniform where sweat had stained the camouflage almost black.

When she did look up the djinn was almost upon her.

'I've got a question,' it said.

Staring in disbelief, uncertain whether to be most shocked by the shackles, the brandished weapons or the apparition's sheer nakedness, Leila de Loria broke every rule she'd ever been taught and took two steps backwards, ending up against the wall of her hut.

844

'Eugenie still dead?' the apparition demanded. It stank of battlefields and corpses, words as hot as any *khamsin* flowing across her face.

A shocked nod.

'Major Gide?' Raf dragged Eugenie's replacement from his memory. Her face and voice, even her weapons becoming visible to the fragment of his mind still interested in those things. 'Well?'

'She's been arrested.'

A bark of laughter greeted these words.

'By Moncef?'

Sergeant de Loria, who at twenty-seven had killed five men (all but the first in battle), dared a glance at this djinn who used the Emir's name so freely. He was too emaciated, too feral to be human. And yet his elemental fury was hidden behind cheap shades of a kind found in the local market and the sores around his wrists bled lymph.

'Who . . .'

'Lilith, son of,' said Raf. 'Busy failing to make the seven years' anonymity necessary to become like you.' His words were clear and stark, the meaning behind them less so; but then Sergeant de Loria had never met Hani or had her life told as a fairy tale.

'Who arrested Major Gide?' said the figure. 'Answer me . . .'

A kiss of warm steel convinced the sergeant that this really was happening. She stood helpless in front of an apparition that held an automatic to her head. The apparition was naked, shackled and stank of rotting flesh but the gun was a standard-issue Browning and its knuckle was turning white on the trigger.

'Kashif Pasha or the Emir?'

'Kashif Pasha,' the sergeant said, voice sticking in her throat. 'Kashif Pasha arrested Major Gide . . . The Emir is dying. They say he was poisoned.'

'Who by?' Raf demanded.

'It happened at a feast Kashif Pasha gave in Tunis. There was a waiter . . .'

Raf stepped around her sentry box and swung up the road barrier as he went through. Allowance for the faint possibility he might have to exit in a hurry.

'Leave it like that,' he told the sergeant over his shoulder.

Leila de Loria looked from the raised barrier to the Browning she'd just wrenched from her own holster. Then she stared at the buttocks of the naked djinn as it stamped its way up the path, a gun in either hand and rusted chain swinging noisily.

Returning her revolver to its holster, the sergeant shrugged. Her mother was from the Nefzaoua and followed the Ibadite branch of the

One True Faith. She knew better than to interfere with the games of princes, madmen and djinn. All the same, she thought she'd better see if she could find Major Gide, arrested or not. This was something the major would want to know about.

Arrested or not? Leila de Loria thought through that bit again and unbuckled her gun for the second time.

'Not,' she decided. 'Make that not . . .'

On his way through the outskirts of Camp Moncef, Raf saw three more of the Emir's bodyguard. Although not one of the girls seemed to notice him. Serving boys stopped to gape, old women made fists against the evil eye or clutched pendants but the guard kept doing whatever it was they did while Raf stamped passed.

It was Moncef's camp and they were Moncef's bodyguard but Eugenie was dead, Major Gide was currently under arrest and their Emir was dying. They all knew the opinion of Kashif Pasha's mother, Lady Maryam, where Eugenie's guard were concerned.

Once Raf passed so close that he saw a jumpsuited girl hold her breath against the stink that clung instead of clothing to his body. All the same, her eyes slid over him and when he was gone she tapped a button transmitter attached to her lapel, muttering what sounded like an evocation.

Up ahead two other jumpsuited guards stopped moving towards Raf and turned to walk away.

'You.' Raf grabbed an elderly falconer by the sleeve and let go when hard eyes turned to face him. The man was old, with small tattoos like crude tears on both cheeks, a neat beard gone completely white and teeth so perfect they had to be false. 'Show me the Emir's tent.'

'No,' said the elderly Berber. 'That I will not.' Reaching for a curved knife in his belt, the man held it in front of him in fingers that shook with more than age. All the same, he dropped into a fighting crouch. 'No one can escape death,' he said. 'But I refuse to help you take the Emir.'

'The Emir?'

Raf's sour smile trickled blood from lips so cracked they'd begun to peel and when he whispered there were no words, just breath. Removing his shades for a moment, Raf tried again, pale eyes locking on the man's face; the curved blade that shook in front of his naked belly already forgotten.

'I haven't come for the Emir,' he said. 'I want Kashif Pasha.'

'This could be a trick.'

'It isn't,' said Raf, knowing that really the old man had addressed the question to himself.

Raf would have found Moncef's tent anyway even without help. It was huge, stood right in the centre of the camp and its ropes were made from palm fibre, something ancient and traditional anyway, unlike the nylon guys holding up the military tents in the distance. The tent was old, rotten in places and heavily patched with black goats' hair; rugs were spread round its edge to enable the Emir to circumnavigate his tent without once touching sand or gravel.

'Wait,' said the old man and Raf waited in the shadow of a generator truck. 'Don't move from here.' When the falconer returned it was with rusty bolt cutters he struggled to use, further lacerating Raf's wrist as he snipped the padlocks fastening the shackles.

'The entrance is round the other side,' said the Berber.

Raf nodded.

'There are soldiers,' the old man added. And when Raf made no reply he sighed. As if he'd always suspected death was stupid. 'Kashif Pasha's soldiers. Two on the door, an officer inside, the small one . . .'

'Major Jalal . . .'

The man shrugged.

'Who else?' demanded Raf and held the old man's gaze. 'The more I know,' he said, 'the fewer I kill. That makes sense, surely . . . ? Lady Maryam?'

The man spat.

'Lady Maryam,' Raf told him firmly, 'was not responsible for the attack at the Domus Aurea.'

'She is Kashif Pasha's mother,' said the old man. As if that was crime enough.

'No one else?'

'Not really,' said the old man, bending to pick up the discarded chain. 'Apart from a *nasrani* television crew . . .'

CHAPTER 49

Tuesday 15th March

'So we now know that the kids are unharmed. The reports of their death undoubtedly NR black propaganda. This is Clair duBois for Television5 . . .'

Flanked by Hani and Murad, TV5's most famous reporter was talking direct to camera when Raf spun into the huge tent, leaving two dying soldiers in the dust behind him, windpipes crushed.

One was the corporal who killed Hassan, the other had just gone for a gun.

'Yeah,' said Raf, eyes locked on Major Jalal, 'it's us.' Behind him stood an impossibly beautiful Japanese boy and a fat man with half his head missing. Although when Clair blinked, looked again, those two were gone.

'I've brought you a present.'

Over by the door, Major Jalal continued scrambling for his own weapon. A pearl-handled Colt that had belonged to his father. It was elegant and valuable, came with the original buckle-down holster and was an incredibly stupid choice.

Clair duBois's backup camera was still trying to pull focus when the major finally freed his Colt and the feed went live on a naked man in shades, framed by the tent's doorway, an old-fashioned H&K in one hand and a Browning automatic in the other. Backlit by daylight/filmed without lights from shade. One of the world's worst options.

'Drop your toy.' The words were in French, the whisper dry as dust. A change of angle caught the apparitions gun come up. 'One chance,' it said. 'More than you ever gave Hassan.'

Despite herself, or maybe because Clair duBois was who she was, she glanced at her notebook and made two minor adjustments for sound. One for volume, the other an echo on the apparition's voice, too slight to be noticed by anyone not in the business.

'Do as he says . . .' The command was soft, sickly sibilant, the words not much louder than those Raf had used; but it carried total authority, a complete awareness of the futility of the situation. 'That's an order.'

And there it might have finished, with Raf turning to the Emir, and Major Jalal returning his Colt to its holster if only Kashif Pasha hadn't stepped forward. 'This is the assassin,' he told his father, voice furious. To his *aide-de-camp*, he said nothing, just nodded.

Major Jalal raised his gun, a young girl who was meant to be dead howled out a warning and Raf's head flicked sideways.

The major died on camera. Wounds pixilated in some countries, not shown at all in England, Sweden and Korea and featured widely every-where else. Looped, in one case, into ultraslow motion that let the major's brains crawl like sticky rice after Raf's casually fired slug, flowering into a fat cherry blossom that tumbled apart in a mass of bone, jelly and blood. So close to chaos in appearance and so utterly removed in reality.

Clair duBois screamed.

As genuine a response as she'd ever made and one, her unkinder critics later claimed, that went a long way towards explaining the clean sweep she made of most of the coming year's press awards.

As Clair watched, the naked apparition's searching eyes finally found the two children who stood behind her.

'You,' it said to the boy, 'are not me.' Then it turned to the girl who gripped Murad's hand, her knuckles white with tension.

'I thought you were dead.'

Picking up a mic, Clair duBois thrust it towards Raf.

'Who are you?' The mic was totally unnecessary, given the TV5 camera was already wired for sound but it made for a great image. Elegant reporter in lightweight silk suit (black obviously, with Clair duBois it was always black), interviewing a naked, stinking man in shades, carrying a still-smoking gun. 'Tell me,' she insisted. 'The world wants to know.'

'Ashraf al-Mansur,' said Raf. 'Guardian to Lady Hana and half brother to Murad.' He stared at Kashif. 'Also to him.'

'I refuse to believe it,' said the pasha, 'without proof.'

Raf shrugged. 'What you believe is unimportant,' he said, adjusting the H&K so its first burst would take out several lengths of Kashif's intestines. 'I'm arresting you for murder.'

'I don't think so.' Kashif's voice was silky. 'Given they're obviously still here.' He nodded dismissively towards Hani and Murad. 'Their death was a lie. I wouldn't be surprised if you spread the rumour yourself.'

Nothing happened. It's a lie.

Away, to one side of the huge tent, Zara shivered and stepped back until she was pressed against an outer wall, which was still too close.

Really, nothing happened.

Shortly after Zara mentioned her uncle to her nanny, the man disappeared. There'd been more shouting, twenty-four hours of plate throwing by her mother. Zara had gone into Al Qahirah hospital for her *operation* a few days later, delivered personally by Madame Rahina while her father was on business in Sicily. The Monday following, when Zara got home was the only time she ever saw her mother with a black eye.

'I'm not talking about Murad or Hani,' said Raf. 'If you'd hurt either in any way, you'd already be dead . . .' So intent was Raf on Kashif Pasha that he missed Hani's wide-eyed shock; missed too a softening in Zara's expression.

'You had a sixteen-year-old boy tortured,' Raf said flatly. 'And then gave the order for his death.'

'He was an NR terrorist,' Kashif Pasha announced to the camera. Neither of them wanted TV5 there. Neither could afford to be the one to tell Clair duBois to get out. 'Who tried to assassinate my father.'

'Crap,' said Raf. 'By the time your *aide-de-camp* had finished Hassan would have signed anything.' He scowled at the body on the tent floor for as long as it took for the camera to follow his gaze. 'How do I know? Because *I* was the waiter. Acting for Eugenie de la Croix.'

Clair duBois turned so fast that the tiny Aeriospecialle camsat locked on her face went out of focus, something the manufacturers claimed was impossible.

'The missing waiter I can understand,' said Clair duBois, 'but how can Your Excellency talk of charging Kashif Pasha with murdering the Emir, when His Highness is not dead?' Even to Clair, her voice sounded childish.

'If not dead,' said Raf, 'then dying.' Wrapped in his borrowed kaftan and with his face sticky from analgesic barrier cream, Raf looked more ghoul-like than ever. 'Ask him.'

'That depends,' said Moncef, 'on your definition of *dead* and *emir*.'

Clair duBois sighed. Kashif was under guard courtesy of one very angry Major Gide, Murad was introducing Hani to the racing camels and Clair had just been handed the opportunity of a lifetime.

Since this was, so far as Clair knew, the only interview Emir Moncef had ever given she was sure TV5 would forgive her for agreeing to record the interview rather than have it go out live. As for handing over copy approval, they gave that to two-bit actors with only a fraction of the charisma.

'I'm not sure I understand,' she said to Raf. 'His Highness has Asiatic flu. I've talked to his doctor.' This last was only half-true. She'd talked, briefly, to a Soviet nurse who'd pocketed a 1000F note with rather too much ease before confirming that a long-lasting flu variant was indeed the most likely possibility.

'Ask,' Raf told her.

She swallowed. 'Your Highness . . .'

The only way Clair duBois could force herself to ask was to pretend someone outside her did the asking. The same way that many years before, as a sixteen-year-old, she'd turned up on the doorstep of a haunted-looking soap actress and forced herself to ask the woman about a miscarriage, vomiting in a flower bed the moment the actress slammed the door in her face, having first called Clair every name under the sun. All the confirmation her editor had needed.

'You have a question for me?' Moncef's voice dragged Clair back from her memories and shrivelled the snakes knotting inside her stomach. The very fact Emir Moncef prompted her meant he intended to answer.

Briefly the woman toyed with asking whether he had flu. What Major Gide, as his doctor, had diagnosed. How he was feeling . . . But then she asked the single best question of her career.

'Are you dying?'

'It's probably safe to say,' said the man, his voice amused, 'that we're all dying . . .' He sat up straighter in his bed, rug still tight around him and spoke direct to his interviewer rather than the camera, his hooded eyes never leaving her face. 'Except, of course, those already dead. And those who are immortal.'

And then he smiled that smile seen in stills around the world. The one that was either ineffably wise or completely insane. Verdicts differed, with Berlin willing to consider the first and Paris and Washington definite that it was the last.

'Is that your only question?'

If the Emir found it odd to be answering questions while blood glazed like sugar icing on a carpet he'd refused to remove, then Moncef didn't let it show, but then . . .

Clair duBois shrugged, mostly inside her head. Who knew what the Emir found odd?

'Ask if he's immortal . . .'

Jumping, Clair looked round. It took her a moment to realize that

Antoine, her backup cameraman had activated his throat mic and was hissing the suggestion through her Sony earbead.

She asked it.

'No,' said the Emir, 'not since I ate the mushrooms.'

CHAPTER 50

Thursday 17th March

Bells rang from the twin towers of St Vincent de Paul, that Gothic monstrosity with all its pews removed and a Persian carpet covering the altar. Flags hung from office windows or whipped in the slipstream of car aerials. Drifting on the wind came the stink of cordite, bastard cousin to the endless firecrackers let off all morning, too close to gunfire for the peace of everyone.

Martial law had been lifted, the act signed by Ashraf Pasha, newly created heir to the Emir. He'd signed the edict on behalf of his father, a man now too weak to hold a pen, even to write his own signature.

The return to normal law came the day after Raf had questioned his half brother in the presence of their father. This took place in the al Andalus-inspired HQ of Dar el Bey, overlooking Place du Gouvernement.

Raf sat at a desk with Kashif on the other side; the Emir had a motorized wheelchair and only Major Gide stood.

It was a very polite questioning. There wasn't a blowtorch in sight and no one in the room, from the Emir to the major, even suggested tying anyone else to a table.

'The snake,' Raf said to Kashif. 'That was your first mistake. A simple enquiry could have revealed that all venomous snakes at Tunis Zoo have their poison sacs removed. Only Major Jalal couldn't risk asking that question, could he? So you made an assumption, the Emir got bitten and Ifriqiya got its very own miracle . . .'

'I know nothing about a snake.'

'Of course you don't. How about the death of two guards, bribed or blackmailed into releasing the snake in the Emir's tent . . . ?'

'I know nothing about any guards.'

'They got shot,' said Raf, 'at the banquet you threw for your father. Remember? The one where Eugenie died.'

Kashif was blaming it all on his dead *aide-de-camp*. In fact, he was horrified to discover some of the things Major Jalal had done in his name.

'I take it,' said the Emir, 'that you have proof for this accusation against your brother?' His words were thin and took longer to say than they should, but there was amusement in them and something close to admiration lit his lined and leathery face.

'If Kashif is my brother . . .'

Moncef looked at him then. 'Meaning?'

'I just wondered.'

'You are Ashraf al-Mansur,' said Moncef, almost firmly. 'And I am Emir of Tunis. Your mother was the love of my life.' Sad eyes swept the small office, barely noticing Kashif as they passed over Raf, a selection of police files in front of him. One of which contained the results on DNA testing that Raf had yet to mention to anyone.

When the Emir's gaze finally alighted, it was on the young girl half-perched on an office chair and the boy who gripped her hand, rather tightly. 'You have your responsibilities and I have mine.'

'Obviously,' said Raf. And when the Emir smiled, Raf was waiting with the only question that really mattered. 'What do you want done with Kashif Pasha?'

'And if I say kill him . . .'

'Then he dies,' said Raf and took a gun from, its holster under his arm. Placing it on the desk at which he sat.

'If I say let him go . . . Which is what I'm minded to say?'

Raf paused, all too aware that Hani was watching him, just as Murad watched the Emir, both holding their breath.

'If you say let him go,' said Raf, 'then that's what happens. But it places this family above the law. And gives victory to everyone who thinks Ifriqiya is corrupt beyond redemption.' He added the second consequence as an afterthought. Not quite realizing how much weight it would carry with the Emir.

'So what would you suggest?'

'Let him stand trial . . .'

The Emir nodded and struggled with the control pad of his wheelchair. Waving Murad away, Emir Moncef rolled slowly towards the door and stopped, one hand reaching for the doorknob, his other edging the chair into reverse. 'You're right about everything,' he told Raf in a voice little more than a whisper, 'except for Alex and Nicolai. The decision to have them shot was mine. My only regret is not warning Eugenie, but then' – Moncef shrugged – 'she'd only have tried to stop me.'

CHAPTER 51

Thursday 17th March

Eduardo sat on the edge of a metal table swinging his feet. Every time his shoe scuffed the floor it produced that unmistakable mouselike squeak of leather against ceramic.

A noise that was driving everybody else in the room insane. And the really great part was that none of them could do a thing about it. He was the most senior officer present at the briefing, a thought so bizarre that Eduardo shut his eyes just to savour it.

'I'm sorry, Boss.' Alexandre looked worried. Under the mis-apprehension his question had been stupid enough to drive the Chief to anger.

'No,' said Eduardo, 'it's a good point. Just not one I can answer.'

This truth elicited a frown from a thickset sergeant at the back. A man with a bald patch, common enough, and a Kashif-like moustache, which now made him something of a rarity in the Tunis PD. It was truly staggering the number of officers who'd decided in the last twenty-four hours to shave off their moustaches, reshape them or else begin to grow a beard.

'Got a problem?' Eduardo asked the man.

'Yeah,' a bull neck raised an even heavier chin. 'With all due respect, sir, I don't see how a case involving a dead pastry chef can be so secret that the master file has to be shredded in front of two witnesses.'

It was obvious from his tone that respect was the last thing the sergeant felt for the small *morisco* in the leather coat sitting on the old Chief's table.

'I can understand that,' said Eduardo, 'to you it looks like a simple open-and-shut murder, hardly worth bothering about. To me it had all the marks of a *cause célèbre* from which Ifriqiya needs to be protected. Maybe that's why I'm kicking my heels up here and you're kicking yours at the back.'

855

Several officers smiled and Eduardo resisted the temptation to take a brief bow. He was in the operations room; a large space of cheap desks and dirty grey chairs, wall charts, holiday rotas and a small kitchen, which might have been slightly too grand a name to describe a corner partitioned off with hessian boards and containing a sink, two ancient kettles and a cheap microwave.

Eduardo had called his officers together to make an announcement and the announcement was simple, the Maison Hafsid case was closed and, for internal security reasons, the files would be shredded and all evidence sealed in sterile bags and remain so for the next hundred years. The reason was actually very simple but Eduardo had explained this only to Rose.

She'd been lying there on a big double bed in their room at the Dar Ben Abdallah. And as she'd rolled over, a frown on her face, Eduardo had smiled as a breast popped out of her dressing gown. He'd almost forgotten what he intended to say, the way he did some mornings when he looked over the foot of the bed and saw Rose, with her back to him in the early dawn, wearing nothing but a G-string and black tights.

'So what happened to Cousin Ahmed?' She'd read the files and knew the names.

'There was no cousin.'

'So who did the *mubahith* arrest?'

'No one,' said Eduardo with a satisfied smile. 'That's the whole point. No one vanished in police custody. I've had every file checked. Even the ones that don't exist.'

'So who killed Isabeau's brother?'

'I think that's got to remain a secret,' said Eduardo. It seemed odd to be making those kind of decisions but no one else was available and someone had to . . . Well, Eduardo assumed that was true. His Excellency couldn't have dragged him from El Isk just to unravel who did what, that would be far too simple.

There was unquestionably more to the equation than could at first be seen.

It had taken Eduardo a while to work out the unseen integer but he'd got it the moment he saw the knife supposedly used for the murder. Once, long before, Eduardo had worked in a kitchen, although there was nothing very special about this, everyone worked a kitchen at some time in their lives. At least, everyone Eduardo ever knew.

The first rule of kitchen culture was that no one, repeat no one, touched anyone else's knives. Spit in their face, mock them and, if you must, insult their football team, that was fine, but no one messed with another person's steel.

Knives were sacred. *Touch my arse before you touch my knife. Mess with my arse and die* . . . Eduardo knew the sayings. Three months grilling *merguez* in a workingmen's café in Karmous had been enough to guarantee that.

So what was anyone meant to think when presented with a blade that was blunt, bent at the tip and stained? Well, Eduardo couldn't actually say what anyone else might think. To him, however, it suggested no one really owned that knife. And if no one owned it . . .

The more Eduardo thought about it the more he was convinced he was right.

Notes said the mysteriously arrested Ahmed owned the knife when it was obvious that no one owned it or it wouldn't have been such a mess. Someone was lying. Actually, he told Rose, several people were lying.

She'd been dressing when he said this. After she'd undressed at his insistence and gone to take a shower while he lay in bed getting back his breath, Eduardo had returned to his thoughts.

They ate breakfast in a café. Rose choosing coffee and a croissant and Eduardo eating rough flatbread cooked on a clay griddle by a middle-aged woman who sat on a stool by the door. With the unleavened bread he ate slivers of some meat that obviously wasn't pork, with a helping of menakher dates, as befitted a man making the most of being in a different country.

Then he left Rose to her shopping and jumped a cab to the Police HQ without bothering to wait for his official car. A decision made easier by his discovery, right at the start, that naming the Police HQ as his destination was enough to ensure that no driver ever asked him to pay the fare. Their surprise on the few occasions he did offer payment was worth double the handful of change his journey actually cost.

So now he was on a table in the operations room, trying to explain without really doing so that there was no murderer; at least not one who could be arrested by the police. Eduardo knew exactly who killed Pascal Boulart and he was certain (as certain as he ever was about anything), that His Excellency knew too. Why else would he have brought in Eduardo but to tidy up such loose ends?

CHAPTER 52

Saturday 19th March

Isabeau checked her rail ticket and re-counted the notes. No writing appeared anywhere on the envelope and she was willing to bet there'd be no fingerprints either. In her memory, she had it that the small man with the black coat kept his gloves on throughout his entire visit.

She was bathed and dressed, standing on the platform of Gare de Tunis beside a cardboard suitcase that looked like leather until one got close. She wore new shoes and black Levi's, a shirt and a shawl as befitted the cooler weather. Her hair was covered in a waterfall of blue silk; not quite a *hijab*, not exactly a scarf; something elegantly in between. And though Gare de Tunis was less than a klick south of St Vincent de Paul and the air was clear enough for sound to travel, Isabeau ignored the bells. Despite the small cross she wore, politics not religion had been her life. All seventeen years of it.

The *MediTerre* ticket in her pocket was an open one. A month's rail travel anywhere in North Africa and Southern Europe. With the ticket came a student ID, an Ifriqiyan passport and glowing references from Café Antonio. So far as Isabeau could see all of these looked real; except they couldn't be, for a start she'd never passed her baccalaureate and no university would take her.

Isabeau had no illusions about what was happening. She was being bought off, which was, she realized, preferable to being jailed or killed. The small man who'd limped into her life with a simple telephone call had more or less said as much.

All he wanted was a meeting. It seemed not to have occurred to him that Isabeau might refuse and it was only afterwards, once she'd meekly agreed, that Isabeau realized it had never occurred to her either. And no, he didn't need an address.

He seemed scarily knowledgeable on most aspects of her life.

Four o'clock would do. He expected her to meet him in the hallway and to let him in. She would recognize him by . . . His voice had paused at that point. She would recognize him by a copy of that afternoon's *Il Giornale di Tunisi*, which he would carry under his left arm, folded in three.

And so a small man limped up the tired steps to her apartment block, his black leather coat bigger than it should be, a fedora pushed down over his eyes. The paper he held had a black border round the whole of the front page and was folded to reveal a headline:

L'emiro morto . . .

And below the news a picture of someone Isabeau had been telling herself for at least a day she didn't recognize. Only half of his face was showing because of the way Eduardo had the paper folded, but it was that double worry line like a knife flick that gave him away, where the top of his nose met his eyebrows. They'd thought Ashraf Pasha was *mubahith*. An infiltrator. And then Domus Aurea happened.

'Mademoiselle Isabeau Boulart?'

Respectably dressed in a blue jersey and denim skirt, sneakers without socks. Her lack of makeup made her seem younger than he expected, but then she was younger. All the same, Eduardo wondered if that look was intentional.

'I'm . . .' Eduardo paused, thought about it. 'You don't really need to know my name,' he said and glanced round the entrance hall. 'Where's the lift?'

Isabeau smiled. 'We have stairs,' she said. Whoever the man was, he lived somewhere other than Tunis. The only places Isabeau knew with their own lifts were big hotels and those huge stores in nouvelle ville, the ones with canvas awnings over street-front windows and French names.

'Show the way then.'

She looked at him and he stared back, indicating the stairs with a slight wave of his hand; nothing impolite, just impatient like a man unused to being kept waiting.

'After you,' he said.

Isabeau walked ahead, all five flights, and at the second she stopped worrying about him staring at her bottom and concentrated on climbing, each turn of the stairs widening the gap between them. By the time she reached the third floor's half landing, Isabeau was a whole quarter turn ahead and he'd lost sight of her anyway.

'Can I get you anything?' Isabeau asked when Eduardo reached the door she'd left open.

'Water,' he said. And then said nothing for a whole five minutes.

On the street below, workmen were busy stringing green-and-red bunting from one lamppost to another and adjusting crowd barriers under the bored gaze of traffic policemen. One of the many street parties would be held there. Enthusiasm fuelled by Ashraf Pasha's announcement that all the food would be free. *Bread and circuses*. Eduardo was still trying to work out exactly when His Excellency meant.

'You own this?'

'I rent it from the city,' Isabeau said. 'My brother also used to live here.'

'You have a bedroom?'

'Obviously.'

'Show me,' Eduardo said.

The sex was perfunctory, almost matter-of-fact. And Eduardo thanked her when it was done. Not daring to show her contempt, Isabeau shrugged, sat up from where she'd been tipped backwards onto her bed and adjusted her denim skirt, smoothing it down over her legs and his smell. She'd known what was coming. Expected it.

For his part, he hadn't bothered to use a condom or remove her shoes.

'Now what?' Isabeau asked.

'We talk . . .' Zipping his fly, Eduardo reached for his notebook and tapped it to make it open. 'I know you killed Pascal. That's not the issue.'

Eduardo paused, giving the girl an opportunity to deny it but she just looked at him.

'You want to tell me why it happened?'

Isabeau shook her head. 'You don't want to know.'

'But the others knew? The rest of your group . . . ?'

She spread her hands, neither denying nor agreeing.

'And so when you killed Pascal they covered for you,' Eduardo said. 'In itself, that is significant. The way I see it.' He was proud of that phrase. 'You stabbed your brother in the kitchen and had someone help you drag his body up to the alley . . . All those clean stairs,' Eduardo explained. 'But first you swapped knives. Probably put your own through the industrial washer.'

Isabeau smiled.

'So what did you do with the real one?'

'There was no real knife,' said Isabeau. 'And he died in the corridor outside the chill room. The stab wounds came later. Someone else did those.'

'So how did you kill him?'

860

'With a leg of lamb,' she said flatly.

Eduardo looked at her.

'It was frozen.'

'Ah . . .' Eduardo thought about the coroner's report. A perfunctory half page with a throwaway line noting the victim had obviously smashed his skull on the cobbles of the alley when falling. 'And what happened to the leg of lamb?' asked Eduardo.

'We ate it. One night when a shift was finished. Me, the others, even that Egyptian waiter, the one who looked so very much like . . .'

Eduardo held up his hand, consulted his notebook. 'I believe the waiter's dead,' he said.

Isabeau nodded. 'A bit like my brother.'

As she waited for her *turbani* at Gare de Tunis, the first Fez – Iskandryia express to stop there in thirty years and a sign of the West's sudden faith in the new regime, Isabeau told herself to be realistic. Everything in life had a price, including freedom. And if two perfunctory bouts of unwilling sex with a stranger were it, then there were worse ways to stay out of jail. As well as worse people to have such sex with, much worse.

When he was done questioning, Eduardo had tipped Isabeau onto her back again, pushed up her skirt until it reached her hips and, almost apologetically, grabbed the sides of her new knickers and pulled those down. Unzipping, he'd given himself a few jerks to strengthen his resolve and pushed into her, the toes of his shoes sliding on the tiles . . .

'I'm pregnant,' Isabeau said, her words enough to startle Eduardo into stopping midstroke. 'Did you know that?'

For a second he almost shook his head but the temptation to be seen to know everything was too great, so he nodded instead. All the same, he retreated to the edge of her bed and tucked himself inside his trousers. A manoeuvre made simple by the fact he never wore underwear. Too much extra washing.

'What do you intend to do about it?'

'About what?'

'The baby?'

'I don't know,' Isabeau said, bending forward to retrieve her knickers. 'What do you suggest?'

'I suggest a holiday.' Dipping his hand inside his coat, Eduardo produced an envelope. 'I was going to give you this when I went,' he said, looking shamefaced. It contained a fat and tattered wad of Ottoman dollars. Almost no one used Ottoman dollars anymore, except in the suqs and most of those could manage credit cards. Only the very old still insisted on keeping their lives in boxes under the bed.

861

'Call it severance pay from Maison Hafsid.'

At least they were high-denomination notes. Higher than Isabeau had seen before and in one case higher than she knew existed. To this man though, used as he must be to such things, they were probably small change.

'And this,' said Eduardo, 'is also for you.' As the exchange rate stood, the second, far smaller wad of US dollars was worth about twice all the other notes put together. On the black market the dollars were worth maybe five times that.

'You want me to leave,' said Isabeau. Although it wasn't until later that she realized she was only putting into words what she already knew.

'Wait, Madame DuPuis . . . You have to wait.'

A railway porter glanced round and saw a young police lieutenant in brand-new uniform stride towards a woman about to clamber through the door of a second-class carriage. Alexandre scowled at the porter and the elderly man decided he had business elsewhere.

'Madame Isabeau?'

Isabeau nodded. No one had ever called her *madame* before. And DuPuis definitely wasn't her surname.

'These are for you,' Alexandre said as he handed her an envelope. 'The Chief told me to deliver them.' Jagged as a tidal pull between rocks, an undercurrent to the young man's politeness suggested he was less than happy to be hand-delivering notes on the morning the old Emir was buried.

'Thank you.' Isabeau flashed her sweetest smile and watched Alexandre melt. It wasn't their surliness or even the fact they often seemed to smell that put Isabeau off men, it was the fact they could be so childish, so unbelievably easily led.

'Oh,' said Alexandre, 'and I'm sorry . . .'

Isabeau raised her eyebrows.

'About . . .' He shuffled his feet, apparently unable to get beyond that word. 'About your husband. It was a messy campaign. A just one, obviously, but messy and I'm glad it's over.' He clicked his heels and gave her a salute, the smartness of which was utterly at odds with the state of his fingernails, which were bitten to the quick.

Once sitting, with her case pushed into the space behind her seat and a *capuchin* from a cart that had passed by on the platform outside, Isabeau ripped the flap on her new envelope, then glanced round. The carriage was almost empty despite this being the first *turbani de luxe* to run for years. Outside, the concourse was crowded, but with people arriving, not departing. *Nasrani* tourists, Nefzaoua up from Kibili to visit recently remembered family, farmers from the High Tell, pickpockets. Few wanted to leave a city when so much was about to happen.

Twenty-four hours of mourning for the old Emir, then seven days of celebration for the new. Isabeau supposed that made sense if she didn't think about it too hard.

Shaking out her envelope's contents, she saw two rings slide out and clatter across the table, along with something on a dull-metal chain. The small, official-looking booklet which followed landed without a sound and Isabeau wouldn't have known the envelope contained a letter of condolence if habit hadn't made her check inside.

It seemed her husband had died in a police operation, somewhere unspecified, south of Garaa Tebourt while rescuing his superior officer. Isabeau liked that touch. As if any man she married wouldn't frag all the officers and NCOs first opportunity he got, then head off down some wadi for Tripolitana. As if she'd marry any man . . .

They were returning his ring, his police tags and a photograph they'd found in his wallet of her wedding day. The face was Isabeau's although the body belonged to someone else; someone marginally thinner than she'd ever been with less full breasts. The man could have been anyone.

Isabeau was impressed to see they'd had a modern ceremony. She wore white and her husband was in uniform, their priest had a simple jellaba, his beard recently barbered and not at all wild. The room in which they stood was panelled in dark oak and had a photograph of the old Emir on the wall behind. It might have been more useful if someone had thought to write the exact location on the back.

The official-looking leaflet was a pension book made out to Madame DuPuis. At the bottom of the first page a space had been left blank for her signature. A footnote told her she could collect money monthly from any branch of the Imperial Ottoman Bank or arrange to have her widow's pension paid direct by filling in a form on the last page.

As for the letter, this offered Isabeau the condolences of the state, commiserated with her over all she'd lost and hoped that her future from henceforth would be happier. It was signed with an illegible scribble, although the first letter looked like an A . . .

CHAPTER 53

'Well,' said Raf, breath jagged and a grin on his face.

'Well what?'

Outside Zara's bedroom window, crowds were already gathering beyond the gates of the Bardo and Raf could hear the growl of early traffic and clattering as impromptu market stalls were erected.

The police would be along later to take them down but trade would continue all day, stalls going up as soon as the old ones were broken down. Food sellers, hawkers of rice-paper rose petals and purveyors of cheap plastic flags, Raf had even, seen his face on the side of a balloon.

The woman lying beside him had already made her opinion plain on all of that. As indeed she had on many other things. It had been the kind of discussion that, in later years, would raise smiles and get described, only half-ironically, as full and frank. At the moment they both still felt slightly vulnerable.

'Come on then,' Zara demanded. *'Well what?'*

'Oh, I don't know . . .' Raf wrapped one arm round Zara's shoulders and pulled her on top of him. 'How about, *Well, what do you plan to do with your day?'*

She laughed, kissed him back.

So Raf slid down slightly on the bed and took Zara's nipple in his mouth, sucking comfort from her breast. She watched him as he did so, seeing only the top of his head and feeling his uncertainty.

'Are you all right?'

When Raf didn't answer, Zara stayed where she was and closed her eyes. They had another hour before they needed to leave and if that wasn't long enough then the wretched ceremony could wait.

Last night had been difficult. Difficult and different. Zara so nervous her whole body shook. And Raf . . . ? She took him to her room, something she'd done with no other man and stripped to her thong in

864

front of him, only losing her nerve at the last minute. Having sent him to the bathroom, she killed the light and hid under the covers.

Except that when he came back, all Raf seemed to want to do was lie in the darkness and let the moment wash over him. Something impossible for Zara.

'This is not fair,' she'd said suddenly.

And thinking he knew what Zara meant, Raf nodded agreement and in that second's movement shut down his night vision until everything in her room became outlines and shadow.

'It is now.'

'No, I mean *this*.'

And he knew then that Zara meant their lying in the dark, so much unspoken between them.

'There's something I need to tell you . . .' Raf said tentatively.

'Let me guess,' she said. 'I'm not the first. In fact you've fucked your way through an entire phone book of my friends. You have three children, well, that you know about . . . You're only after my millions . . .'

'This is serious,' said Raf.

'So was I,' Zara answered. And pulled Raf to her and kissed him as her hand slid under his rib cage and then both her hands locked behind his back, so that Raf's full weight rested on her trapped arm.

She felt him go hard.

'You're naked,' said Raf, the fingers of his right hand tracing the crease of her buttocks, just to make sure he hadn't got that wrong.

He hadn't known, Zara realized. She'd been safely tucked under a quilt by the time he returned to the room.

There'd been one night, months before, when she'd talked and he'd listened, although she couldn't remember it and he could; but then, if Raf was to be believed, he remembered everything, which was maybe not a good place to be.

'It's important,' said Raf, holding her face between his hands. 'And it concerns who I am. What I am . . .'

'You're you,' said Zara. 'That's enough.'

'No,' said Raf sadly, 'it isn't. It's not anything like enough.'

Zara wanted to know why, so Raf told her. Or rather he didn't. He told her a fairy story instead. 'Once,' said Raf, his fingers caressing the side of her face, 'there was a son of Lilith . . .'

Raf took it as read that Zara knew Lilith's story. Adam's first wife, mother to vampyres and djinn. A woman expelled from Eden for fucking the snake.

'He was older than he looked because, although his days were as your days, his nights were often longer, one of them so long that fir trees grew and houses were built while he slept. Someone who loved him grew old and stopped loving him, seeing her own life and increasing age reflected in the puzzlement in his eyes every time he woke from the cold sleep . . .'

If Zara thought it was odd that Raf told her a folktale she kept this thought to herself. Remembering stories Hani had told her. Small girl's stories. Of the kind easily dismissed.

'He slept the cold sleep because that was the easiest way not to die. Until one day he awoke and Lilith had died and her friends had forgotten him or no longer cared if he escaped. So he did what sons of Lilith do, moved to a strange country to live undetected as a human for seven years. For if a vampyre or djinn can live undetected for seven years he will become as human.'

'So Hani told me,' said Zara.

'She did?'

'She's told everybody,' Zara said. 'It's in a book, the original story. About how a son of Lilith can become as human. But the children will be born sons of Lilith.'

'Sons of Lilith, daughters of Lilith,' said Raf. 'In my case it's called germ line manipulation. Whatever I am my children will become.'

'And what are you?'

Raf thought about it. 'I'm not sure,' he said finally. 'I get voices. I see in the dark. There are three extra ribs on either side of my rib cage. My eyes hurt in the daylight. My memory is too distressingly perfect for my mind to manage . . .'

'All of this is your mother's responsibility?'

'Or Emir Moncef's,' said Raf, 'but it gets messier.' He felt the girl go still and shifted gently away from her, giving Zara space. 'I've opened the bags . . . Secret files,' he added, when he realized she didn't quite understand. 'It's like reading the technical specifications for a new type of car. One that might not work.'

'What's the worst?'

'Immortality. Or if not immortality, then longevity. How long I don't know but longer than is now normal.'

'You knew this when you refused to marry me?'

'Some of it,' said Raf. He stopped himself. 'More than some,' he said but the anger was directed at himself. 'What I wasn't told as a child I overheard. It's relatively easy to code for heightened hearing. Less easy to understand the implications if one's own hearing is normal and the subject is three rooms away.'

'I'm sorry,' Zara said. Her hand moved up to touch his face and came away wet. She believed him implicitly.

'So am I,' said Raf.

Later, when he hung over her in the darkness, both of them drunk with longing, Raf bent forward and kissed Zara lightly on the forehead. There was something else he hadn't mentioned. If he understood it right, then immortality was sexually transmitted; the act of being pregnant infected both mother and embryo.

The second time they made love began slow and ended up hard and fast. It started with Zara swinging herself on top of Raf and straddling his hips, her face only inches from his. Outside their window, the city was expectant for what would come the next day. Guards stood at the gates of the Bardo and patrolled the streets around the palace complex. Major Gide and Raf having agreed this as a matter of protocol only. Done because it was expected.

'Remember the boat?' Zara said.

As if he could forget. Water so blue it was almost purple. The scent of rosemary and thyme carried on a warm wind across a bay. And then the return trip. Hani safely asleep and Zara bringing him a beer as he sulked outside and time and the ocean slid past.

'What boat?' Raf demanded.

Leaning forward, Zara put her mouth over his and bit, hard enough to draw blood. 'That boat,' she said.

They kissed and, slowly and rather clumsily, Zara reached down to position Raf against her. To Zara he was a shadow against white sheets, a watchful silent silhouette; for Raf she was lit clear as daylight . . . He could see her mouth twisting, eyes open and fixed on nothing, her breasts swaying forward with each rock of her hips, impossibly beautiful.

Reaching up with open hands, Raf felt warm flesh overflow his fingers and tried not to be offended when Zara absent-mindedly lifted his hands away and went back to her rocking. After she'd ridden him in silence long enough for Raf to fade out his vision and lose himself in the rhythm, Zara took his hand and positioned it on her abdomen so that Raf's thumb reached between swollen lips.

'There,' she said, 'keep it there.' And went back to her darkness and a burst of half cries and swallowed words. There was no sharing this time. And angry was the only way to describe the abruptness with which Zara shuddered to a halt, her hand still holding his own hard against her smooth mons.

Smooth, because she lacked all body hair.

Zara had given him the list once. One night in another palace; the time she'd cried herself to sleep and woken to swallow him as she knelt on white marble tiles in the middle of a sunlit floor, three days before he prosecuted her father for murder. A fact neither one had ever mentioned.

The list was relatively short and went no body hair, no labia minor or hood or tip to her clitoris . . . But, as she'd pointed out, a full Pharaonic would have been infinitely worse.

According to a doctor in New York (the one Zara saw at seventeen, the week after she arrived at Columbia), a rewarding sex life was perfectly possible. It might just take more effort than for some other women. And she stood, the doctor said, a better chance than many of those whose scar tissue was mental rather than physical.

The tiny vibrator the woman gave Zara went unused. Ditto a collection of glass dilators from small to medium. Zara found one article on female genital mutilation, attended one meeting at which she said nothing, then went back to writing law essays. And lying in the darkness as she said this, that time in El Iskandryia, Raf had been unable to work out from the flatness of Zara's voice if she regarded this as common sense or cowardice . . .

'My turn.' Raf rolled the two of them over, so Zara lay underneath and he was between her legs. Widening her knees, Raf withdrew until the tightness at the entrance to her sex was about to release him, only to slam back, watching Zara's chin go up in shock or surrender.

Her hands rose and fell, arms crooked at the elbow as fingers fluttered batlike in darkness. Tied to some plea forever unsaid. On her breath were white wine, hashish and the faintest trace of capers. Tastes that Raf took from her lips. And then her legs locked over his and her hips began to grind against him.

They came together with that blinding luck those new to each other sometimes get and slept, still locked in each other's arms.

CHAPTER 54

Saturday 26th March

'Take a guess,' said Hani, nudging Murad Pasha and nodding to where Zara and Raf stood beside a wall, holding hands. A half dozen of Major Gide's handpicked guards stood impassive against the opposite wall of the decorated alcove, carefully not noticing. 'Go on, guess what they've been doing . . .'

Murad blushed.

'How do I look?' said Hani. She twirled on marble tiles, her silk dress spinning out like the cloak of a dervish. The dress was meant to go with knee-length socks but Hani had refused. Not just refused but refused totally. Sitting naked and dripping on the edge of her bath, unwilling even to let Donna dry her until the old woman agreed that white socks were out.

And Donna, still furious at being dragged from El Iskandryia to Tunis, had threatened to fetch Khartoum but even that failed to move Hani. In the end they settled on short white socks rather than the black tights Hani had wanted.

'How do you look?' Murad considered the question. She was dressed in white silk. Around her neck was a single row of black pearls, fastened at the back with a clasp made from jade and gold. Her ears were now properly pierced and a tiny drop-pearl hung from each lobe. On her feet were silver pumps.

'Anachronistic,' he said finally.

Hani punched him.

Not hard. Just enough to deaden his arm.

'The correct answer,' she said, 'is like a princess.'

They were waiting near the entrance to a *salon de cameras*, hidden from the crowd by an elegant carved screen. Admission to the ceremony was by order of precedence and some people, mostly *nasrani* lucky to

869

be there at all, had been sitting for over an hour as more upscale arrivals filed in to be shown their places.

It had given the new Emir great pleasure to make sure that the Marquis de St Cloud was one of those forced to wait in the cheap seats. Sitting much closer to the front, looking slightly bemused, were Micki Vanhoffer and Carl Senior, dressed for what could only be a night in Las Vegas.

Outside, Rue Jardin Bardo was lined ten deep with people waiting for the Emir's Bugatti coupé Napoleon to sweep past, only to be hidden on arrival by veils of silk as it disgorged its occupants, a colonel from the engineers, his young wife and their two children. Decoys insisted upon by Major Gide, who'd gratefully accepted the new Emir's suggestion that she remain his head of security.

The actual players in the spectacle about to unfold in front of TV5, C3N and one other, randomly selected, camera crew had been the first to arrive, spirited into the salon via a back route.

'You ready?' Raf asked Zara.

She nodded. Not entirely convincingly.

Outside in the audience were Hamzah Effendi, Madame Rahina and the brother Zara had tracked down to a squat on the edge of Kharmous, half brother really. Hamzah's bastard. Once a factory and later an illegal club, he'd soundproofed his squat with cardboard and spray painted it gunmetal grey. The floor had been earth, friable and damp but he'd doped it with liquid plastic, tipping the can straight onto the ground.

'What are you thinking?' Raf asked.

'About Avatar. You know, back when he was a kid, was it right to take him home with me – or was I just being a spoilt brat . . . ?'

'Ah,' Raf smiled. 'The *what-if* factor.'

Zara stared.

'For every action we take,' said Raf, 'there's probably a better one.'

'Does that apply to this?'

'Which this?' Raf demanded. *'Us this or this this?'* The sweep of his hand took in the coughing and restless shuffle of feet beyond the screen.

'Both,' said Zara.

In a different world Raf might have answered that there was nothing he'd do differently where Zara was concerned, not even his jilting her which put Zara across the front of *Iskandryia Today* and nearly cost him his life. He loved her and had no certainty that any other course of action would have led him to where he stood; but Murad turned and caught Raf's eye and the words went unsaid.

Checking his watch, Raf listened to something in his earbead and nodded.

Three, two, one . . .

On cue, an unaccompanied voice rose in the salon outside. *Maaloof al andalusi*, the music Ifriqiya made famous. Frail and strong, haunted and ancient. The words a lament for those who had gone before and a greeting for those who were to come after.

Near the far end of the suddenly silenced room, Khartoum raised his head and hung a note on the air so unearthly that Hani shivered. The poem that echoed off the salon's high roof came from Rumi, the great Sufi sage but the intonation was Khartoum's own.

Slowly, one note at a time an *'aoued* filled the spaces around the words. Then an instrument that Raf thought might be a *nai*, only deeper than any flute he'd ever heard.

'Time to move,' Hani whispered.

'Yep. Everybody's waiting.' This was, Zara knew, a stupid thing for her to say. Unfortunately it was also true: five hundred carefully chosen people were waiting on the far side of that screen to see the proclamation of the new Emir. A ritual intentionally designed to mix Western with North African traditions.

For religious reasons the proclamation needed to happen in the salon de cameras, the hall of ambassadors, rather than the Zitouna mosque, because women and men could not be allowed to mix in the mosque and, anyway, letting *nasrani* into the prayer hall would outrage the mullahs.

Officially the beards were no longer a problem, Kashif's arrest and subsequent suicide had seen to that. Major Gide's interim report suggested reality was different. The fundamentalist tendency would remain quiet only for as long as their embarrassment lasted at having backed a man given to treachery and wicked living.

'*Come on . . .*' Zara was shaking Raf's arm.

And as Khartoum's voice rose to a note as ethereal as waves against rock, then ended abruptly, leaving only silence, Murad said, 'We can't do this.'

'What?'

'We just can't.' There was a sadness in Murad's voice, a maturity at odds with the anxious smile on his thin face. This was a boy who'd sat holding his father's hand while the old man died. A boy who'd insisted on attending not just the funeral of his father, as was expected but also of his brother, after Kashif shot himself through the head. Three times. The funeral of Lady Maryam, who succumbed to the same flu that killed the Emir, he refused outright to attend. And that took a different kind of strength.

'Look at us,' Murad said.

Age was more than a simple sum of years. Into the load went experience and modes of survival. Strength could be learnt and adopted or developed through necessity and nothing tempered it faster than learning to stay alive.

Murad nodded towards the hidden crowd. Then swept his gaze across Hani, Zara and Raf, finally ending with a glance at a mirror which showed a twelve-year-old boy in a tight uniform, stars of gold and enamel across his narrow chest.

'Look at what I'm wearing . . .'

Murad's new uniform, identical to one worn by Raf, was based around an Egyptian version of the old British cavalry tunic, borrowed by an earlier Emir and introduced as court dress. No North African or Ottoman regiment had ever gone into battle wearing such clothes. Its use was strictly ceremonial. The only difference was Murad's lack of shades.

'I don't support this,' said Murad. 'I didn't think you did.' He looked sadly at Hani reflected in the mirror. 'And I don't want to be part of it. I refuse to become Emir.' Lifting a felt tarboosh from his head, the boy nodded to a guard. The hat Murad held was inlaid with gold thread and seeded around its base with tiny freshwater pearls. Pinned to the front was a priceless diamond spray of feathers. The *chelengk* a recent sign of favour from the Sultan in Stambul.

The guard who reached out to take it retreated at a scowl from Raf.

'You have it then,' Murad said and Raf shook his head.

'Wrong size,' said Raf. 'And anyway, it belongs to you.'

'Why?' Murad asked, and everyone looked at Raf.

That was the real question. All of Raf's life had been leading up to this, it seemed to him. Standing in an alcove off a crowded *salon de cameras*, off-loading his responsibilities onto a child. Which was one way to look at it. The other was that Raf was trying desperately to do the right thing in a situation where there was no right thing to do.

'This is difficult,' he said.

'Really,' said Hani. And when Raf nodded she sighed. 'That was irony,' she said.

Beyond the screen, Khartoum's voice edged into the silence and soared away, stilling the crowd again. *'Ya bay.'* Raf caught the word in a refrain and lost the meaning as he looked down and saw Murad still waiting for his answer.

'You think it should be me,' Raf said, not bothering to make it a question. They'd been through this. None of them believed there should be an Emir to start with, but that wasn't really the point. A coup had been averted.

A new era had arrived.

The last of the UN sanctions had been lifted that morning.

Five hundred people were waiting within the salon for sight of Ifriqiya's child ruler. A hundred thousand filled the streets. Camera crews wandered the Medina recording anything and everything for worldwide syndication. There were two members of the German Imperial Family, a first cousin to the Sublime Porte, the president of the United States, both presidents of Russia and the Prince Imperial of France, despite his recent disgrace. All gathered to welcome Ifriqiya back into the family of nations.

As squabbling, incestuous and venal a group as ever existed.

In thirty years the country hadn't seen half that number of VIPs. Hell, even one VIP would have been more than Ifriqiya had seen in thirty years. The ice age was over and the state's political and diplomatic purdah had been quietly brought to an end.

At a high cost, a fact not doubted by any of those who stood in the alcove; although they differed in their understanding as to how high. What they now discussed was, if one were honest, who should be the first to pay.

'The problem,' said Raf, crouching until his face was level with Murad's own, 'is that your father was not my father.'

That got their attention.

'Yes he was,' Murad insisted.

'No.' Raf shook his head. 'I've known this for days. One of us had Emir Moncef as a father. The other didn't.' From his pocket, Raf pulled a sheet of paper folded into three and Hani, being Hani, recognized it for what it was. A sanguinity report.

'This is your father's DNA,' Raf said to Murad as he pointed to a column down one side of the slip. 'And this is your own,' he pointed to the next. 'And this third one is mine. You can see there is no relationship between the first two and the third. My mother was not your mother and my father was not your father; we are not even cousins.'

'I don't understand,' said Murad, face crumpling. 'Who are you then?'

'My mother once told me my father was a Swedish hiker. That's probably as true as anything else she ever told me.'

The boy nodded, a movement so small as to be almost imperceptible. And then, meeting Raf's eyes, he nodded again, his second nod firmer, more confident.

'Give me that printout,' he ordered.

Without a word Raf handed Murad the DNA results. Instead of looking at them, the boy ripped them in two, did it again and then one more time, struggling in his final attempt.

'You're my cousin,' he said in a voice that allowed no room for argument. Only Murad's eyes, made larger than ever by sadness, betrayed him.

'And your bodyguard,' added Raf. 'Should you need one.'

Hani raised her eyebrows.

'I thought you might enjoy living in Tunis,' Raf told her. He didn't quite glance at Murad as he said this but Hani scowled anyway. And he got the feeling she might have stuck out her tongue, if Murad hadn't been watching. 'Or we could commute between here and El Isk,' added Raf, 'if that works better for everyone . . .'

Zara's face was unreadable.

Beyond the screen, Khartoum fell into expectant silence and the guards around the edges of the alcove strained forward as if they might toss Murad's group into the waiting hall themselves, so worried was Major Gide's expression.

Hani, Zara and Raf began to move. Only to stop when Murad held up his hand.

'I go up there alone,' he announced. That wasn't how it had been planned or practised in dry run after dry run, but Murad's voice was firm as he stepped through a gap between wall and marble screen. 'It's my responsibility.'

'And us?' Hani asked. 'What are we expected to do?' There was hurt in her eyes and her chin was up. Had Murad not been on the point of walking out in front of the world, he'd have had a serious fight on his hands. One look at the boy's face showed he understood that.

They were children, Raf reminded himself, balanced on the cliff edge of puberty, behaving as adults because that was what politics required of them. In a different world there might be other answers and other systems that worked better. But they were here, in the salon de comeras in Tunis. And it was all the world they had.

'Well?' said Hani.

'You come with me,' Murad said, compromising. 'When we get to the two steps you stop and I'll stand at the top.'

Hani considered this.

'No,' she said, 'you walk ahead when we go out but I climb the steps and stand just behind you.'

Murad sighed.

'And us?' Zara asked.

Hani and Murad looked at each other.

Raf and Zara went first. Walking through the silence beneath infinitely repeating *muqarnas* vaulting, inset with imported roundels of flying

874

babies. Although the cherubim had the wooden rounds to themselves, an elegant script edged the space where ceiling and tiled wall joined. It said what the *Fatiha* always said, words that had echoed across the sands of North Africa for centuries.

Bringing war, civilization, coffee and the veil. Poetry and bloodshed. Algebra, an understanding of the physical working of the human body and civil war. No worse or better, in Raf's opinion, than the beliefs it replaced or competed against. Although maybe the words were more beautiful.

'In the name of God, the merciful, the compassionate . . .'

They walked in silence, Zara staring straight ahead.

Her parents were sitting near the front but by a sidewall. A position chosen to reflect Hamzah Effendi's vast fortune whilst not ignoring the occasionally dubious nature of its gathering.

Hamzah smiled, proud and slightly disbelieving.

Zara stalked by without noticing.

Two rows ahead, Koenig Pasha, whom Raf still thought of as the General, sat beside Tewfik Pasha, whose ghost of a beard and moustache were now almost manifest. The Khedive and the General had been busy ignoring each other ever since His Highness decided to dispense with the General's position as Iskandryia's governor. Suggesting they sit side by side had been Raf's way of breaking the ice. Just ahead of them, assorted *uber*VIPs squatted the front two rows, except for three seats left blank on the right; one should have been Hani's, but obviously she wouldn't be needing it.

Raf stood back to let Zara go first and the look she gave him was hurt and slightly disbelieving. There were tears in her eyes. Although once she realized he'd noticed, she started to scowl.

'What have I done now?' Raf whispered.

'How could you say that to Murad?' she said. 'And how long before Hani realizes that if you're not Murad's half brother, then you can't be . . .'

'Her uncle?' Raf asked.

Zara's nod was abrupt.

'What will you tell her?' she demanded.

A smile just wide enough to create laughter lines lit Raf's face. 'I'll tell her the truth,' he said, leaning close. 'And then swear her to secrecy.' Behind him Raf could hear a double shuffle of footsteps where the aisle started at huge double doors neither Murad or Hani had actually passed through.

'The truth being what?'

'That I *am* her uncle,' whispered Raf, 'but Murad is not her cousin.'

He took Zara's hand and though it lay slightly unwilling in his own, she didn't try to remove it.

Who had gone to whom with what, Raf had found impossible to discover from the secret files. Somewhere in the mix was the Emir, his mother and Bayer-Rochelle, who'd been working on cerebral transplants, the operation that killed Emir Moncef and left Eugenie de la Croix with a dead commander, international pressure to open labs that could not possibly be revealed to the world and a frightened Swedish hitchhiker as his replacement.

Obvious really, when one thought about it.

And Lady Maryam hadn't been the only woman Eugenie had refused to let see the ersatz Emir. Raf's mother had been the other.

He spoke quickly and very quietly, always aware of the footsteps getting closer. Khartoum, who still stood at the front, both silent and watchful in a simple woollen robe, watched Raf and Zara with interest; when he saw Raf had noticed, the old man nicked one hand in quick greeting and smiled.

'Eugenie knew this?'

'Of course.'

As Murad and Hani reached Micki Vanhoffer, the large American burst into tears and wrung Carl Senior's fingers until he almost joined in. 'They're going to get married,' she told the Japanese ambassador sitting next to her, who only stopped looking appalled when Carl Senior leaned over his wife's ample lap to explain that this wasn't likely to happen for some years yet, if at all.

'Okay?' Hani demanded.

Murad nodded.

She could hear her cousin humming softly as he climbed first one marble step, then another, stopping at the point where his proclamation would begin. It took Hani a second or two to recognize the tune.

Emir Murad al-Mansur, Ifriqiya's ruler and bey of Tunis was humming the chant from 'Revolt into Nakedness,' street song of North Africa's disposed. The new Cheb Rai/Ragged Republic version obviously.

He'd heard it that morning on his radio.

ACKNOWLEDGEMENTS

Thanks to

Pathology guy Ed Friedlander MD for answering idiot questions on exactly what happens if someone sticks a spike in your heart. Hassan in Tunis for taking me up onto the roof of the souk to look at the Great Mosque of Zitouna. Aziza and Mafida, cooks from the Maison Arabe (Marrakech) for not laughing too much at my attempt to make chicken tagine. Anthony Bourdain for writing the best insider book on kitchens ever written (plus some seriously sick/slick crime novels). The Yugoslav girl with no knickers in the kitchens at Oslo airport for giving me the idea of the knife. And the soldier on the train outside Palermo who insisted on showing the backpacker opposite his scars. Everyone at rec.arts.sf.science for endless tolerance in the face of questions about genetic manipulation, gravity and the nasty side-effects of vacuum (ok, we're going back some years here). *New Scientist*, just for existing. Dick Jude, ex head-honcho of Forbidden Planet, New Oxford Street, for taking a punt on *neoAddix* and declaring that 'Weird Shit' was a perfectly good publishing category. And finally, Peter Sherwen, a good friend much missed, who froze on Bergen bandstand and crashed my mother's bike in Morocco, then decided to ride it back to London because the forks 'weren't that bent'.